STOLEN FIRE

Dominic Fairchild is a man haunted by his past, and the cruel terms of his grandfather's will which, thirty years ago, bequeathed him the Fairchild empire – in exchange for his most precious possession . . .

Rhiannon Grantham is beautiful, clever and mega-rich – and has come to Honolulu to buy Fairchild Enterprises and ruin its Chairman . . .

Set against the lush tropical mountains and valleys of Hawaii, *Stolen Fire* uncovers a nightmare of loss and betrayal, of white man's wealth and Polynesian mystique, and of a low- community and its enemy, the police.

Maxine Barry lives in Oxfordshire with her parents. She worked at Somerville College in Oxford as the Assistant College Secretary for five years before turning to full-time writing. *Stolen Fire* is her first novel.

STOLEN FIRE

Maxine Barry

ORION

An Orion paperback
First published in Great Britain by Orion in 1993
This paperback edition published in 1993 by Orion Books Ltd,
Orion House, 5 Upper St Martin's Lane, London WC2H 9EA

A CIP catalogue record for this book is available from the
British Library.

ISBN: 1 85797 997 4

Typeset by Deltatype Ltd, Ellesmere Port, South Wirral
Printed and bound in Great Britain by
Clays Limited, St. Ives plc

To Mum and Dad,
for enduring

Prologue

The young man running down Broad Street turned every female head in sight. It was not his impressive height, nor the fluid grace with which he moved that caused the sensation. Nor was it his head of thick jet-black hair, unusually golden tan or the startling flash of his green eyes. And if the companion sprinting along by his side had happened to call him by the name to which he was entitled, it would not have been the reference to royalty, either, that set female pulse-rates rocketing.

Dominic Fairchild, quite simply, had 'it'. The 'it' that clung to a man like an invisible cloak, raising the hackles on other men's backs and a quite different set of hackles on the backs of their women. The 'it' that warned you to run whilst at the same time enticing you to stay. The 'it' that was tantalizing, intoxicating, annoying, intriguing and above all, dangerous.

And he knew it. Women had been making it clear ever since he'd reached his fourteenth birthday. The first had been his grandfather's private secretary who had willingly introduced him to experiences even more interesting than those of corporate wheeling and dealing. Like a duck taking to water, he had taken to sex and soon his prowess on the track and field at school were more than mirrored by his performances in the bedroom, and from his first fumbling beginnings he'd graduated quickly into a knowledgeable athlete. But it had not taken him long to understand that sex and affection were two totally different animals. And at nineteen he'd matured enough to realize which was the gold and which the bronze.

At Oxford he'd begun to discover the diverse delights of a woman's brain, and long debates in the JCR had given him an even deeper insight into the thoughts, philosophies and aspirations of the emerging modern young woman. So much so that Amanda, the highly-bred daughter of an ambitious

Scottish bank manager, had been taken by surprise by his lack of smug masculine arrogance. Bowled over (and into his bed) by his self-effacing good humour, her conservative soul thrilled and admired his intense hatred for racial prejudice of any kind and his deep commitment to what he always called 'my people'. His wealth hadn't hurt, either.

'There's the car,' Graham Grantham, puffing from their short run, pointed suddenly to a dark blue Jaguar that had just turned from St Giles into the Broad, and within moments they were both seated in the back.

The car lost no time speeding up the tree-lined Woodstock Road, resplendent now with cherry-blossom and lilac. Oblivious to the natural beauty around him, Dominic tapped long fingers against his knees. But it was not so much a gesture of impatience as a device to mask the boilerhouse of his emotions. That his grandfather had interrupted his escape to Oxford to go and die on him was enough to make him want to scream out loud. It was as if he couldn't tolerate even Dominic's minor victory in avoiding going to Harvard, as Frederick Fairchild had tried to insist. But the old man was too damned mean to die. He had to be. He'd always been too mean to listen to him when he'd talked about employing more native Hawaiians – too mean even to pay the Hawaiians he did employ the same wage as the white Americans he favoured. Too mean and stubborn to diversify and much too mean to understand that Hawaii, glorious Hawaii, was more, much more than just a super-resort for mainlanders.

Dominic leaned back against the plush leather upholstery, deliberately relaxing his tense muscles. Now, just when he was beginning to fight free of the despotic and manipulative control his grandfather had always exerted over him, Fred Fairchild had to carry on living – if only to see that his grandson had been right all along, and admit, damn it, actually *admit* that he had earned the right to Fairchild Enterprises; that he had worked damned hard, as he had, to take over the multi-million dollar corporation; that he had the brains, the vision, the ambition and yes, the necessary compassion, to sit at the head of the Fairchild board table. The latter had more power than some governments, as well as the potential to create more work than several trades put together and to become responsible for more prosperity amongst working-class people than State hand-outs and charities combined.

Aware that his hands were clenched into hard, white-knuckled fists, he swallowed hard and absently rubbed his fingers over his eyes, sighing deeply. Damn it all to hell, it would be so ironic if his grandfather died now, when he was at last about to become his own man. And he would be so alone . . . Free, but alone. No longer having to fight for his own identity, no longer having endlessly to defend his own principles, but alone. 'God, Gramps,' he murmured, and shook his head.

Graham glanced at him, his jaw tensing, then deliberately turned his head to stare out of the window. His own fists were clenched tight, but unlike Dominic he didn't have the inner strength to dare relax them. If he did he might try to strangle the man beside him, the man who still had the gall to call himself a friend. He felt sweat trickle down his back with the effort to appear as if nothing had changed but a deep shudder of pleasure at the thought of Dominic's death rippled through him. Graham had never felt such hatred before. He'd never felt much of anything before, until he'd been introduced to Jess – and love. Then his life had become perfect. In Jess' arms he didn't have to prove himself to be a man, as he'd always struggled to prove himself in his father's eyes. And when she'd written to him from Hawaii, telling him she was pregnant, he'd been over the moon, planning on dropping out of Oxford, going home and joining his father's law firm as Arnold Grantham had always wanted . . . He cut off his thoughts viciously. So much for all his plans, plans that had been turned to ashes after the results of a routine medical check-up had been broken to him by a sympathetic doctor. Plans that now lay in ruins *thanks to Dominic Fairchild*, who'd always had everything he'd ever wanted – and whose money, power, respect and everything else he, Graham, had always coveted.

'Has the plane arrived at Kidlington, Jackson?'

'Yes, Your Highness. Five minutes ago. They'll have refuelled by the time we arrive.'

Dominic nodded and leaned back, only then noticing that he was still wearing subfusc. Impatiently he tugged the black undergraduate gown over his head and let it fall to the floor. Graham wiped the hate from his face and said mildly, 'How do you think the prelims have gone?'

Dominic shook his head, too tense to answer. What the hell did he care about exams? His grandfather was dying. Perhaps, even now, he was dead . . .

The car turned into Kidlington Airport ten minutes later; a jet bearing the Fairchild insignia awaited them. Inside, Smith Flanaghan, Frederick Fairchild's right-hand man, poured himself his second drink.

Dominic wasted no time and as soon as he'd climbed aboard he barked sharply: 'How is he?'

Smith, a heavy-set and normally hearty man, shrugged eloquently, his red and smiling face now pale and grim. Even his rich voice was old and tired as he said flatly, 'You know him as well as I do. He's refusing to die until you get home.'

Graham, meanwhile, was looking around awkwardly. He always felt inadequate when confronted by Dominic's mind-boggling wealth. Smith, surprised by his presence, glanced quickly at Dominic who shook his head wearily. 'One of life's little jokes. Graham heard that Jess had gone into labour just before you called about Gramps. I offered him a lift home.'

As the jet took to the air Smith surreptitiously watched Dominic, wondering if he really knew what he was doing. Recent events in Honolulu made him doubt it, and the boy was still so young. Too young to have the full weight of Fairchild Enterprises dumped on his shoulders. The richest hotel business on the islands, it was a greedy and demanding mistress. And with Fred calling in his lawyers at the last minute, Smith suddenly began to feel deeply nervous. Things were happening too fast.

Damn cancer, he thought with sudden viciousness, chucking a measure of bourbon to the back of his throat and swallowing quickly. Damn it to hell for choosing to eat away at Frederick Fairchild, a man too strong to take the easy way out when the pain had begun to bite deep, less than six months ago. A man who'd stared a slow and ugly death straight in the face as only those of almost superhuman strength and courage can do. A man who'd left him, Smith, in charge of his grandson and the Fairchild millions, trusting him to look after both, God help him. He fixed himself another drink and thought, 'God help us all.' Catching Dominic's eye, he gave him a silent toast. He'd known the kid since birth and loved him like a surrogate son. Very aware that the youngster both hated and loved his grandparent, he wondered nervously which emotion was predominant at the moment. Or was he just secretly relieved? Smith wouldn't have blamed him. Life with Fred had been like living in a constant battlefield; both of them were too much alike to get along peacefully.

Graham wondered only how he could make Dominic, who had once been his friend, suffer. In the sunlight filtering through the jet's reinforced glass, his eyes glittered.

As the jet headed inexorably towards a dying old man, Dominic's mind jumped from one thought to the next like a cat with scalded paws, putting him through an emotional wringer that left him feeling alternately elated then depressed, and even frightened, an emotion almost totally new to him. He could be sure of only one thing: Fairchild Enterprises was at last going to be all his. But at what cost? And could he really afford it?

Chapter 1

'I don't understand you,' Carol Birkhead said to her friend as the last of the few mourners disappeared down the drive in their hired black saloon cars. 'Not one of those people actually knew your father. They only wanted to come back to the house to satisfy their damned curiosity. If it had been me, I'd have told them where to get off.'

Rhiannon Grantham sighed heavily and sank into an overlarge armchair in front of a roaring log fire. It was the end of May and blazing hot outside but she still felt cold and in no mood to explain to her friend that she simply didn't care what others thought. Leaning forward to rub her hands in front of the flames, her raven hair fell forward, hiding her expression from Carol who continued to watch her nervously. She looked so pale and vulnerable, the very antithesis of her usually healthy and determined state. Of course losing your father was a terrible blow to anyone, but Carol was sure there was more to it than that. And since that visit from her father's solicitor, her friend had been acting very peculiarly indeed.

She looked up as the door opened and smiled in relief when Ben Fielding walked in carrying a tray of tea which he placed on a small Chippendale table set beneath the large bay windows. At fifty-two, Ben was still by far the most desirable man Carol had ever seen. Five feet ten, he had the chunky but fit body of a man ten years his junior. His sandy hair was just running into a distinguished grey, and his blue eyes with their attractive crow's-feet at the corners still had the power to make her toenails curl. And as the owner of one of the biggest privately-owned business empires in Britain, Carol had always secretly thought that her friend was mad not to snap him up.

And that Ben was more than willing to be snapped up, everyone knew only too well. The moment the late Graham

1

Grantham had introduced his business partner to his then sixteen-year-old daughter, the tycoon had been enthralled. Widowed with a teenage son, he was ripe for a second marriage. And over the years, as Rhiannon grew up and began to learn the ropes, and then to take on more corporate responsibility, consequently coming into contact more regularly with the industrial billionaire, Ben had only fallen deeper under her spell. An engagement had been expected for years.

Now, as Ben handed her a cup, Carol took it with a smile then frowned as Rhiannon made no response to his murmured words asking if she wanted milk or lemon.

'Rhia? A cup of tea.'

Rhiannon jumped as her friend's voice loudly cut across her train of thought then smiled automatically at Ben as she took the delicate china cup and saucer from him. But both Ben and Carol noticed she didn't even attempt to drink from it.

Ben took his favourite place on the sofa, perfectly at ease in the Granthams' Oxfordshire country home and sipped desultorily at his own brew. Carol, feeling awkwardly second-fiddle, wandered to the windows and looked out over the traditional cottage garden, beautiful at this time of year. Lupins competed in borders with hollyhocks and foxgloves; delphiniums were in bud, along with sweet williams, love-in-a-mist and several varieties of iris. With the sun shining and birds singing, Carol reflected sadly that it was hardly the day for a funeral and briefly wondered why her friend's father hadn't wanted to be buried in the Hawaiian islands that were his birthplace. Then she shrugged the thought aside. Moving to Britain when his daughter hadn't yet reached her first birthday, he'd no doubt considered himself to be as English as the next man.

Rhiannon was thinking much the same thing. She still felt numb – as if she couldn't quite believe her father was dead and gone. Her last relative – the last link with her own flesh and blood. And she had loved him so much.

As a little girl she had loved him as fiercely as she was able, to make it up to him for not having a wife. She'd learned to cook at the age of eight, pestering their cook-cum-housekeeper to teach her all of her father's favourite recipes. She couldn't wait for him to come home from 'the office', that horrible place that always took him away from her. It was the office that had kept him from her eleventh birthday party, and not even the pony he'd bought her had made up for it. It had been the office that kept him in his study, instead of reading her a bedtime story. And it was the office that Mrs Cavendish, their housekeeper, said was so important because it kept the roof over their heads.

And so she'd taken to doing everything she could to make their home all the more appealing, to make her father want to come home and escape the dreaded claws of 'the office'. She'd bake his favourite scones then walk the half-mile to the farm to buy the cream so that it would be extra-fresh. She got books from the library on flower-arranging so that she could brighten the house with the gladioli and chrysanthemums that Mr Cavendish grew in the garden. She bought ornaments with her pocket money, instead of the sweets and toys her playmates favoured until Mrs Cavendish put her foot down and said she couldn't dust them all.

And then she'd grown up, and her love for her father had matured into a more adult version of her childish devotion. She no longer saw him as an all-magnificent, do-no-wrong figure but as a man like other men, with all the strengths and weaknesses of a human being. For the first time she became aware that some of the villagers mocked her father, calling him 'Sir Graham' behind his back. She knew it was unfair, and that he only felt a compulsive need to fit in with their neighbours' idea of what a 'country gentleman' should be.

It was around this time that she'd also began to wonder exactly *why* they had left Hawaii. Was it really because he couldn't stand to live in the same place that he had lived in with Jessamine, her mother, who had died when she was still a baby? Rhiannon began to secretly doubt, and to question. Why had he never remarried – was it truly because he'd loved Jessamine so much? And although he denied it fiercely when Rhiannon asked him, had Jessamine died because of her? Had complications set in during the birth that had eventually resulted in her mother's death?

Despite constant reassurances that she was not the reason

3

Graham had been deprived of his beloved wife, Rhiannon was driven by the need to please him. At school she took all the subjects he recommended, mainly to do with commerce and economics, and found them surprisingly satisfactory. Studying hard she came home regularly with 'A's. Playing chess in the evenings, she had finally beaten him one night and he had sulked for hours before finally laughing with her over her first, landmark victory. To regain his honour he'd taught her how to play poker, secure in his superiority once more.

In those days, the only cloud on the horizon had been the worry over the firm. Graham's advertising company wasn't doing quite so well as it should and at one point it even looked as if the company might fold. But then, like a miracle, Fielding Co. had come into their lives with the offer of a merger, and she'd met Ben. Ben, who was popular and well-liked and respected, who was kind and understanding – and more than willing to help train her to take over the business reins that would one day be handed on to her.

With their financial future once more secure, and with Ben Fielding monopolizing most of Rhiannon's time and attention, Graham had returned to practising law and, over the years, began to drink. He was soon drinking quite heavily, and the more he drank the more he talked about the bitter feud between himself and an old rival called Dominic Fairchild.

Rhiannon knew all about it, of course. Throughout her childhood her father had made passing references to a Dominic Fairchild and all the wrongs Fairchild had done him. As a child, Rhiannon had hated the mysterious Dominic Fairchild too, but as she grew older Graham talked of him less, and she almost forgot about him. But recently, within just a few short weeks of his death, Graham had suddenly become like a man possessed, insisting that Fairchild was 'out to get him'. And to her everlasting shame and guilt, Rhiannon had tried to reassure him that it was not so.

She groaned aloud now at how wrong she had been. 'Oh, Daddy,' she whispered, and felt the cup in her hand shake precariously.

Carol made a small sound of distress and moved toward

4

her, then caught Ben's eye as he jerked his head at the door. Muttering some excuse about cutting herself some flowers she left them alone, her heart heavy. She'd never much cared for her friend's father, but at a time like this, it hardly seemed to matter. Carol knew she was not an ideal best friend. She often spoke first and thought later, and had an annoying habit of being suspicious of everyone and everything. But Rhiannon was nothing if not loyal, and they had been as close as sisters for almost eight years. It cut her up to see her friend so devastated and acting so out of character.

Rhiannon didn't hear or notice her leave. Staring into the flames she could hardly bring himself to think of all that must now be done. It was strange to think how her life could be so normal and happy one moment, then shattered and broken the next. And all because of one man. One inhuman bastard of a man called Dominic Fairchild.

'Rhia, why don't you come back to London with me? Stay at the house. Mrs Wilkins will make it her life's mission to fatten you up once she sees how much weight you've lost. A bit of tlc will do you the world of good.' Although he smiled, Ben was perfectly serious. In just under two weeks she had shed so many pounds that she now looked almost distressingly slender.

'What?' She looked around vaguely, then shook her head. 'No. No, I'm all right.' But she spoke automatically, already staring back into the flames.

'Darling, I know how hard this is for you.' He leaned forward on the settee and with a gentle hand rubbed her back through its thin suit of black chiffon. He could distinctly feel her vertebrae and frowned, inwardly cursing Graham Grantham for dying and leaving his daughter so heartbroken.

He had never felt particularly close to the man. They had met years ago when Fielding Co. had taken over Graham's small advertising firm. Although moderately successful, the firm had hardly been more than a footnote to his giant company, and if it hadn't been for Rhiannon, who had quite simply taken his breath away, Ben doubted that he would have let Graham stay on and continue to run the outfit. The fact that during the last ten years the firm had tripled in size and profitability was due solely to Rhiannon, who, after university, had served a much more useful apprenticeship by his side.

Looking back, Ben wondered now what had surprised him most about his business partner's daughter – her stunning beauty or her equally acute business brain. Both had delighted him to such an extent that he had all but taken over her business education, lock, stock and barrel. After studying in college rooms, Rhiannon had flown around the world at his side, studying corporate law and finance, working at all levels of management as and when he decided she was ready. He would have liked to become more than her mentor but was sadly coming to recognize that that would never be. Recognize it – but not accept it. Not yet. Not while there was still a chance. Not while there was no other man in her life.

He had become so used to her quick wit, laughter and singlemindedness when dealing with high finance, that her vague expression now came as a distinctly nasty shock. She was obviously shattered by the loss of her father, and he wondered whether he should tell her what Graham had told him one night not long before his death. Graham had been roaring drunk and confessed in a moment of intense self-pity that he was not her biological father. The next morning he had been unable to remember a word of his confession and Ben had never referred to it. Now he wondered if he should, but quickly decided against it. What did it really matter anyway? Graham had loved and raised her as his own, and Rhiannon had certainly loved him as much as any true daughter could love her father.

'I know it's a cliché, Rhia,' he said softly, wishing there was something more he could do, 'but work really is the best cure for all that ails you. And time really will heal the pain you're feeling right now. It'll dull, pipsqueak, I promise you.'

Rhiannon smiled at the use of his pet name for her, and began to listen to what he was saying. Not the actual words so much as their meaning. She knew time would have nothing to do with healing her – perhaps only revenge could do that. And it was to achieving this aim that she at last turned her mind, fighting free from the all-consuming waves of guilt, anger and frustration that had been threatening to drown her these past few weeks. Ever since the phone call that had changed her life.

SUMMER had come early, and already the May sunshine was hot and appealing. Outside Rhiannon's flat, delicate, silver-birch trees swayed in a gentle breeze. The window by her desk was open where she sat catching up on a report Ben wanted the following day. The Mayfair street outside gently hummed with traffic and the gracious antique carriage clock on the mantelpiece had just chimed four. And then the telephone rang and a stranger's voice shattered her peaceful existence for ever.

'I'm sorry to tell you this, Miss Grantham, but your father was admitted to our hospital fifteen minutes ago with a suspected heart attack.'

'Heart attack,' she heard herself echo stupidly. 'Is he all right?' Strange how her brain seemed to have stopped working.

'The doctors are with him now, so I'm afraid I have no more information at this point.' Strange too, how alien a professionally sympathetic voice can sound.

Roaring up the motorway way above the speed limit in her E-type Jaguar, the same words kept hammering in her brain: *Hold on, Daddy. I'm coming. Daddy's girl is coming. Hold on.*

In his hospital bed, Graham Grantham was in pain. Every breath he took hurt him, lancing jabs of agony down his ribs. He was dying and he knew it and the knowledge terrified him. He tried to swallow but couldn't, and felt the tubes in his nose tug whenever he moved his head. The ceiling above him was white and featureless and he closed his eyes, trying to breathe as little as possible.

'Your daughter is on her way, Mr Grantham,' a nurse whispered in his ear but he did not open his eyes and did not try to respond. Rhiannon was coming. He could hold on till then, couldn't he? He had to. But there was something missing. Something important he had to remember. He opened his eyes and looked around at all the frightening medical equipment that filled the room, his eyes straying to a nurse who looked to him like a mannequin in a shop window – lifeless and meaningless. And it was then that he understood what was missing. Dominic wasn't there. And somehow he'd always thought that he would be, staring down at him as he died with a mixture of pity and anger and hate.

The nurse noticed that his vital signs were slowly disintegrating and pressed a buzzer. Graham licked his painfully dry lips and tried to clear his head, but it was hard. Dominic Fairchild was nothing but a ruthless predator, a man who had ruined his life and that of many others. Graham had spent so much of his time and energy trying to be the one who finally made him realize he couldn't destroy people without expecting to pay the price, and as a reward for all his efforts had succeeded only once in teaching Dominic Fairchild the lesson he so richly deserved. One victory out of a lifetime of failures.

He thought back to the last time he'd seen Dominic, many years ago, when he, Graham, had at last dealt a winning blow. He might have suffered years of humiliation because of the Hawaiian Prince, but in the end he had succeeded in robbing Dominic of his most treasured possession.

But just what good had it really done him? For years Dominic had waited with that diabolical patience of his before finally striking, and at a time when Graham had least expected it. As he felt his heart twinge and the world go horrifyingly dark then light again, Graham moaned softly. Dominic had won after all. Not only had he exiled him to England but, within the last month, had stretched his vengeful fingers all the way across the Pacific to finally destroy him once and for all. And destroy him he had. He was dying, wasn't he?

But Graham was determined that Dominic would not win this final battle. Once Rhiannon, his lovely daughter came – his face twisted – once *Jess'* lovely daughter came, he would make Dominic Fairchild really pay. Pay and pay and *pay*.

LEANING back in her chair, Rhiannon pushed the memory of her mad dash to the hospital away, at the same time brushing the hair from her face; she looked at Ben properly for the first time that day. Dear Ben – so familiar. Even now the scent of his French aftershave and the faint aroma of the Turkish cheroots he smoked made her feel better – more on an even keel in a world turned suddenly crazy. She owed him everything she had, she knew that – all her experience, her values, her code of ethics, her small fortune.

Suddenly she frowned. Yes, while it was true that she would have a small fortune if she decided to sell her shares in Grantham Advertising, under the circumstances a small fortune was as useless to her as none at all. And she must fulfil her father's deathbed wish. She must, or she truly was the most unloving, ungrateful daughter ever to have been born.

Slowly she turned to him. 'Ben,' she said softly. 'I need your help.'

'You have it. You know that.' He reached forward and gently placed his hand over hers, surprised at how cold it felt. As he looked into her troubled emerald eyes he felt a sudden overwhelming urge to kiss her. More than ever he wanted to take her to his bed and love away her grief for a man who didn't deserve it, to be so much more to her than just a friend. Even if, as she so often said, he was the greatest friend she'd ever known.

But she was already shaking her head, as usual oblivious to his real desires. 'No, Ben. I mean I *really* need your help. I need a huge, huge favour.'

Surprised by the sudden intensity of her voice he frowned, but didn't hesitate. 'Of course. You know I'd do anything . . . What exactly do you need?'

Rhiannon looked deeply into his blue eyes, searching for something she was not sure she would find, but something that she needed badly if she was ever to keep her promise and grant her father's dying wish.

'I need money, Ben – hard sterling. Millions and millions of it. And I need power. Your kind of power.'

'You already have that, Rhia. You know . . .'

'No, Ben. You don't understand.' Slowly she curled her fingers around his and took a deep breath. 'Ben, I need you to trust me with *all* of Fielding Co.'

Chapter 2

OAHU – HAWAIIAN ISLANDS

The sunshine was bright and strong between the blinds and cast a striped pattern on the beige linoleum floor of the hospital ward. Three of the four beds were occupied by old women, but in the corner bed a young girl lay sleeping.

'I wish I had hair that colour,' a young nurse said to her companion, envious of the silvery cap of hair that framed a piquant heart-shaped face.

'She should be conscious soon. Dr Jago's diagnosis is a mild concussion.' The older nurse checked her watch. 'Which reminds me – he's due to begin his round soon.' She cast critical hazel eyes over the small ward, checking that everything was spotless.

Bright flowers cascaded from simple vases, there being no shortage of blooms on the one hundred and thirty-two islands that stretched sixteen hundred miles across the Pacific Ocean and are collectively called Hawaii, the fiftieth State of America. Sisters of Mercy from the local convent came daily with huge baskets of flowers gathered from the wild, or donated by local residents such as Dominic Fairchild, whose gardens were famous throughout the islands.

'Have the sheets been changed, nurse?'

'Yes, sister.'

'And is that policeman still outside?'

The junior nurse quickly tiptoed to the open end of the room and glanced to her left where a uniformed man sat yawning in a too-small plastic chair. 'Yes, sister. I don't expect he'll go until he's had a chance to talk to our mystery patient.' Both women glanced at the girl who had been found in an alley after an anonymous tip-off, no doubt a mugging victim since both her handbag and the contents of her pockets were missing.

The sister frowned and rechecked her watch. Dr Jago was

one of the best doctors the hospital could boast, and was certainly the most skilled, if not the most popular, of their surgeons. 'Doctor Jago's late.'

'Doctor Jago apologizes.' A surprisingly deep voice made both women jump as a man moved briskly into the room. Richard Jago was a big man in every way, and as he moved his six-feet-four-inch frame past the women, they took a hasty step back. His body was large but compactly so, and no one could truthfully call him fat. His hair was neither blond nor brown but resembled overripe corn and his eyes were a contrastingly dark grey. He was rumoured to be forty-one, though he looked much younger.

'Sister. Anything special I should know about?'

'No, Doctor. Mrs Alworthy had a restless night, but she's sleeping peacefully now.'

'Good.' The grey eyes barely flicked in the direction of the old woman with tuberculosis and the sister suddenly recognized the real reason his colleagues held him in such little esteem: he was not a compassionate man. As his large figure stooped to take the pulse of another elderly patient who'd had a hip replacement, she witnessed the methodical unemotional manner of the man. A doctor without a true vocation for healing was, in the sister's view, almost useless, no matter how highly impressive his qualifications. Just then a slight movement caught her practised eye and she turned to glance at the young girl, who began to moan softly.

'Doctor.'

'I heard,' he said crisply, and moved quickly to his newest patient. When she'd been admitted in the early hours, casualty had been particularly busy, and the patient's preliminary tests which he'd read that morning confirmed the obvious mild concussion he'd diagnosed. As he watched her, a small pink tongue flickered from between her pale rose lips to relieve their dryness and something stirred within him. Something alien, something . . . tender.

Her wrist looked fragile between his fingers as he routinely checked her pulse. Slowly she opened eyes of a pale shade of blue and winced in the bright light, instantly becoming aware of two things at once – the overpowering presence of the man now seating himself on the edge of her bed and a vague, nameless fear that made her shiver deep down inside of herself.

'Hello.' The deep but smooth voice was pleasant and she responded weakly. 'I know this is going to sound foolish, but how do you feel?'

The girl thought about it for a moment, then said, 'I have a headache.'

'You will have. You were brought in yesterday with concussion. How many fingers?' He held up three fingers in front of her and she gave the correct answer, then he fished in his voluminous pocket for a tiny torch, clicked it on and leant closer to her. The girl cringed back, feeling dwarfed by his bulk. 'Follow my finger with your eyes.' He moved his finger to the left. 'No, keep your head still.' The hand he put on her chin was strong but gentle and she felt her heart thump in a mixture of fear and something else less familiar. 'Just with your eyes, follow my finger.' The torchbeam made her wince but she did as she was told, aware of a cold sensation of loneliness seeping over her. She felt strangely lost. There was something wrong – something horribly wrong, but she couldn't seem to catch what it was.

'Good.' Richard took his hand away from her reluctantly but the sensation of her soft skin remained on his fingertips, and he surreptitiously rubbed them against his thigh. 'You must have a very thick skull.'

'Thanks!' She responded to the teasing automatically, aware that she was only postponing something that she didn't want to deal with, not when it felt so safe in the tidy room with the sleeping old women and the big doctor.

'I'm in a hospital,' she said, then felt silly. Of course she was. But . . . 'What am I doing here?' She put a hand to her head, relieved to find no bandages and no bumps. Concussion, he'd said. That meant being knocked out, didn't it?

'Don't you remember what happened yesterday evening?'

Yesterday? The girl's frown deepened. Yesterday was just a gaping void, an expanse of frightening nothingness. 'No – no, I can't!' she said, her voice panicked and unnaturally high. Shadows suddenly swooped down on her, blocking out all light and warmth: *she couldn't remember anything!*

12

Richard reacted to the panic in her eyes immediately and pushed her back against the mattress. She was shaking so hard that he felt an unexpected but overwhelmingly strong desire to cradle her in his arms, an impulse that he fiercely resisted. 'Just try to keep calm. Can you tell me your name?'

The girl began to cry, helplessly fighting the hysteria that engulfed her. 'No. No!'

'All right. Do you know where you are?'

'A hospital.'

'Yes. Where?'

'I d-don't know,' she whispered after a short painful silence, stiffening as he took a tissue from the shelf by her bedside and carefully wiped her cheeks.

'You're in Honolulu. Do you know where that is?'

This time she knew the answer, the word coming to her automatically, bringing with it a blessed surety. 'Hawaii.' Her trembling mouth lifted in a smile. 'It's in Hawaii.'

Richard nodded. Hysterical amnesia, brought on by some kind of trauma – the mugging, probably. 'OK. Let's see what else you know.'

'Don't you know my name?' she demanded, her hand reaching out and desperately clutching his forearm. He felt the touch as if he'd been electrified. Slowly he raised her arm and nodded at a simple silver bracelet on her wrist. 'This was the only thing the police found on you.'

The girl took the bracelet off, her hand trembling as she held up the only slender link to her past and read the single word inscribed there. '*Vienna.*' She repeated the name over and over in her mind but it meant nothing to her. Not even the sound of her own voice was familiar, and a yawning chasm of fear opened inside her.

'It's not as bad as you think. Most forms of amnesia aren't permanent.'

She looked at him, noting the firm jaw that housed a narrow mouth. His nose was just a little too fleshy perhaps, but it did little to detract from the overall picture of a handsome, mature man. And he was her only link to . . . to what? She didn't even know what was out there! Her eyes flew to the window where sunlight shone on carelessly.

Who was out there? A mother, a husband? How old was she?

'I don't even know what I look like,' she said in an appalled whisper.

'Fetch me a mirror, sister.'

As the sister moved swiftly away Richard noticed the younger nurse. 'You can carry on, nurse.' The voice was a curt dismissal and the girl flinched even as she moved quickly away. He turned back to his patient and smiled gently, picking up her hand and squeezing it. 'Don't look so terrified. You're very pretty – I promise.' She managed to smile but did not look convinced, and her nerves stretched as she waited. 'You're young too – twenty-three, twenty-four at the most.'

She had to talk, to do something normal or go mad. 'What's your name?'

'Nothing special. Nothing mysterious or original like Vienna.'

'Please tell me. I n-need to know.' Her nails bit into his palms and he felt a fierce pleasure wash over him. Never could he remember a patient affecting him like this before. And never had any woman aroused such strong desire in him.

'My name's Richard Jago.'

'Richard . . . I like it.'

With his forefinger he gently stroked her wrist, stopping when the sister came back and handed over the little oval mirror. Vienna froze for a second, too terrified to look, then slowly lifted it to her face, meeting her reflection head-on.

'Didn't I tell you you had nothing to worry about?'

Vienna reluctantly lowered the mirror. What had she expected – to instantly recognize herself? 'I . . .' She took a deep breath and shook her head, the bitter disappointment almost choking her. Looking up at Richard she felt a little better. Already he was familiar to her in a world where everything was strange.

'Now let's see what you do know. What's two and two?'

Vienna caught her breath nervously but the answer came easily. 'Four.'

'Who was the first President of the United States?'

'George Washington.'

'OK. What other countries can you think of?'

'Countries? England, France, Spain, Sweden ...' She waved a hand in the air in a gesture of frustration. 'I don't know ... lots.'

'Good. And you thought you couldn't remember anything,' he teased.

'But I can't!' she cried, disappointed that a doctor of all people should fail to understand her predicament. 'I can't remember anything worth knowing. Don't you understand?' And then she heard her own voice screaming: '*I don't know who I am!*'

'Calm down!' Richard said sharply, standing as she began to cry in earnest.

'Calm down? How can I? I don't know who I am, for God's sake. I don't know anything!' She lashed out desperately, needing to hold on to something – anything – and her flailing arm knocked over a vase of flowers, the noise of its crashing to the floor echoing like an explosion in her head.

'Hold her, sister,' Richard commanded grimly.

Vienna hit out in panic as a strange woman tried to push her down even further amongst the cloying dark caverns and with a terrifying helplessness she watched Richard's large hands efficiently preparing a hypodermic needle, knowing exactly what he was going to do.

'It's all right, Vienna. I'm just going to make you sleep.' The voice was soft, almost regretful, but the words only terrified her more.

'No, I don't want to sleep,' she moaned, as Richard's deft hands slid the needle into her arm. He's so big, she thought, muzzy and light-headed. He's so powerful – too powerful ... 'I don't want to sleep,' she repeated, her eyelids drooping. 'He'll get me if I go to sleep.'

The sister straightened up, checking that her cap was still in place after the brief struggle. But whilst one part of her mind admired Dr Jago's cool professionalism, another part was trying desperately to tell her something quite different. But what? She couldn't quite put her finger on it. Certainly he was being more human than usual, but why did she have the feeling that something unhealthy was happening?

'Delayed shock,' he said now, in a matter-of-fact voice.

'Yes, Doctor. What do you suppose she meant by "He'll get me?"'

Richard disposed of the needle carefully and glanced at Vienna's peacefully sleeping face. 'I imagine it was a reference to the mugger. She's obviously buried the memory deep, but it's still there.'

'The policeman is still outside waiting to speak to her.'

'I'll see him. You'd better put her through the scanner. I don't think there's any brain damage but there's no point in taking any chances.'

He dealt brusquely with the policeman then made his way to the canteen, pausing to check the society noticeboard outside. He knew that joining the Kaneohe Yacht Club had caused much covert snickering from a lot of his fellow doctors, but the jealousy of others had never worried him, and his eyes lingered thoughtfully on the date of the annual hospital dinner – one event he had no intention of missing since the hospital administrator's guest-list read like an Hawaiian version of *Who's Who*. Which reminded him – he had a round of golf lined up on Sunday afternoon with Farleigh McIver, the chairman of the hospital board.

Richard's move to Hawaii had been no mere whim. His first visit had been on vacation but it hadn't taken him long to realize that the fiftieth State was unique in the United States of America. In Hawaii, history stretched back thousands of years, not merely the few paltry centuries that it did in the rest of the US. Richard had been soothed by the mixture of white man's wealth and Polynesian mystique. He had been charmed by the compact integration of the islands and dazzled by the colours, the sights, the smells. Now he couldn't envisage living anywhere else. Nor would he ever want to.

Several women looked up as he passed by and one, Bridget Farley, watched him with frankly hot and hospitable eyes. 'Careful,' her friend Clare said. 'On the medical side of things, he's the golden boy around here. And as for the ladies, the queue stretches around the block.'

'I'll bet.'

'I'd keep away from him if I were you. He cuts up more than just his patients. That model he moved here with, for instance.

16

He soon left her in the lurch after she'd paid for the move and the flat and everything.'

Bridget shuddered deliciously. 'He's a right bastard, isn't he? I wonder why he doesn't date nurses? For a chance with him I'd even think about chucking this all in. I wonder if . . . everything else . . . is big on him?'

Clare laughed. 'Bridget! Someone might hear. Matron's looking at us in a funny way.'

'Screw Matron. I bet she wouldn't say no to our Randy Richard if he asked!'

'Why do you think he never married?' Clare whispered and Bridget grunted.

'Why should he? He gets enough variety as it is. Why ruin a good thing?'

As he approached Vienna's bed Richard hoped that he'd feel nothing, but when she looked so pitifully pleased to see him he experienced again that stab in his abdomen that was halfway between pain and pleasure. He wanted her, this beautiful little waif who was so dazed and alone and who looked at him with such desperate need. He wanted her badly. 'Hello. Feel better now?'

Vienna nodded. 'Yes. I'm sorry about before. I didn't mean to get so . . .'

'Forget it.' He ignored the chair, opting instead to sit by her side on the bed. His eyes dipped to where he could see her small but perfectly shaped breasts outlined beneath the plain white hospital gown and quickly looked away, a reaction stirring in his groin. Why did he want her so badly? So much so that he was tempted to lean forward and kiss her small lovely mouth right there and then. 'You'll be pleased to hear that there's no brain damage. Your amnesia is only hysterical.'

'But my head?'

'Oh, you've had a knock all right, but that has nothing to do with the amnesia. It's common in people who've suffered a trauma. They don't want to remember, so the brain acts as a safety valve, carefully locking away all memory of it. And in the process all previous personal memory gets lost too. We call it retrograde amnesia.'

'Are you saying I'm faking it?'

'No. Your memory loss is real but categorical – and non-medical. I'll arrange for you to see a therapist while you're here, a specialist in this kind of thing. He'll be able to tell you more about it.'

Vienna watched him stand, her eyes pensive and nervous. 'You're leaving?'

'Yup. I've just got out of surgery – an eight-hour kidney-transplant is no picnic.' He yawned, stretched, then laughed. 'Normally I'd head straight for the sack, but for my special patient I thought I'd bring the good news myself.'

Vienna felt a small warm glow begin in the pit of her stomach and she took a shaky breath. 'I can't believe that I used to be like everyone else. That I had a life, perhaps even a husband . . .' She trailed off as Richard's face tightened and he let her hand fall away. 'Isn't there anything you can tell me about myself? Something I can cling on to?'

'I can run a few tests. Perhaps you should have a complete medical anyway. It might come in handy later.'

'Thank you. I will see you tomorrow, won't I?'

'You bet. Nothing could keep me away.' He left, stopping by the desk to give orders for a series of gynaecological and other tests to be carried out on the amnesiac case in C4. Once outside he drove his Mercedes home. The car was a birthday present from Cynthia, an attractive thirty-five-year-old advertising executive he'd dated for over a year before she'd moved back Stateside.

His apartment was in an exclusive block off Kalakaua Avenue. Inserting a key in the lock he opened the door and walked into a long lounge where a single massive window overlooked the city lights, Waikiki Beach and the Pacific Ocean. He flicked on the light switch and yanked off his tie whilst walking to a dark mahogany drinks cabinet where he poured himself a small quantity of Napoleon brandy.

Sipping his drink, his eyes narrowed as he came abruptly to a decision. Crossing to a white marble pedestal where a telephone rested, he punched out the numbers of his apart-ment manager's home residence. 'Hello, Mr Risely? This is Richard Jago, the tenant in eight hundred and two. Is that flat

18

on the seventh floor still free? I'd like to rent it. No, not instead of this one, but as well as. Yes, that's right, I'm expecting a . . . friend to move in.' He paused to listen to the response and took another small sip of brandy. 'I'll pay cash. Good, I thought you might. I'll pop into the offices tomorrow.' He slowly hung up, his eyes doubtful. Then he shrugged and tossed back the rest of the brandy, carefully placing the empty glass beside the telephone.

VIENNA'S strange new world was taking shape. Some things she knew she'd done thousands of times before, like drinking coffee, watching a portable black and white TV, reading a magazine and even recognizing some of the celebrities featured inside. It was only matters of a personal nature that were missing. So when Richard walked into the ward the next morning with a man in uniform, she knew at once that he was a policeman—but what she wasn't prepared for was the sudden chaos to her emotions caused by his presence. As he introduced himself, she knew that she was afraid of him. *Very much so*. But why?

'Are you all right?' Richard asked sharply, noting her sudden pallor.

She nodded, looking at him with a desperation that was plain for all to see. 'Yes. I was just taken by surprise, that's all. I mean, a policeman . . .'

'Perhaps they've found out who you are.' Sister Ho, a very pretty Japanese nurse who had supervised her treatment all morning, smiled hopefully.

'I'm afraid not,' the cop said, genuinely regretful. 'Is there nothing you can tell me about the mugging? Anything you might have remembered since yesterday?'

'No. Sorry. It was definitely a mugging, then?'

'Yes, ma'am. An anonymous caller saw you being attacked and called us. You should be grateful for that at least. Most people don't want to get involved.'

'And nobody knew anything about me where you found me? Where was that, exactly?'

'Wright Alley, not far from Chinatown. There's nothing around there but bars and strip . . . nightclubs. Er, have you decided on a name yet, ma'am?'

Vienna wished he'd go away. She couldn't pinpoint it but something about him – or more accurately his uniform – upset her. Silent bells of alarm rang deep in her head and she couldn't shake the feeling of – oh, it was impossible! Trying to remember was like trying to catch smoke with her hand.

Richard told him of the bracelet and he checked it briefly. 'Hm. No hallmark, nothing to tell us where it might have been made.'

'How about using Wright as a surname?' Sister Ho asked. 'If that's where you were found?'

'Why not?' Vienna agreed listlessly. 'Until I find out or remember my own name, it's as good as any.'

The policeman took his leave, promising to send over a police photographer to take her picture. Running it in the island's three main newspapers, along with a caption asking if anyone knew her or had seen her recently might bring some results, but he hadn't sounded particularly hopeful.

Matron said quietly, 'Doctor, Mr Kingslade has been on the telephone about Miss Wright. There's a problem with medical insurance. Since we don't know who she is we can't claim from her cover.'

Vienna stiffened, made rudely aware that there was a whole world outside this small room, a world where many things were needed, like money, papers, a place to live . . . Richard saw her distress and said quickly: 'Tell Kingslade not to worry. I'll get on to Welfare personally.'

'Yes, Doctor,' Matron said, her face deadpan.

'What if they find out that I'm married? Or divorced?' Vienna asked.

'I don't think they'll find out either. Look,' he held up her left hand, 'no ring-mark.'

'I might be divorced – I could have stopped wearing the ring.'

'I don't think so. Anyone who married you would be a fool to let you go,' he said softly, then noticed that Sister Ho was beckoning for his attention. He moved impatiently out of Vienna's earshot. 'Yes, sister?'

'I've got the preliminary results of the tests you ordered, Doctor.' She handed over the clipboard, her oriental face impassive as she said quietly, 'The gynaecological results are especially interesting.' The hesitation was barely perceptible but Richard picked up on it immediately. It was not like the very competent Sister Ho to be surprised about anything.

Quickly turning over the pages of the cardiac graphs, he scanned the appropriate test-sheets thoroughly. Sister Ho saw him absorb the startling information recorded there, his eyes widening briefly before he slowly and very carefully restored the papers to order. When he looked at her again his face was as expressionless as hers, but the knuckles that gripped the clipboard were white.

'Thank you, sister,' he said emptily.

Sister Ho inclined her head graciously. 'Doctor.'

Chapter 3

Many heads turned to watch the silver-blue convertible Ferrari growl down Kalakaua Avenue, as much to admire the man driving it as the car itself. In many ways the passing years had been kind to Dominic Fairchild. The wind whipped through hair as black as it had ever been, and his face was still virtually unlined and bronzed from the constant Hawaiian sun. All of his hotels possessed a fully equipped gym, as did his penthouse at the Blue Hawaiian Hotel and his offices downtown. Years of a daily hour-long exercise routine and careful diet had paid off. On the wrong side of forty, his body was still that of a man in his thirties. He pulled the car into the underground parking lot of the Blue Hawaiian Hotel, parking in the spot marked *Owner*. The garage was spotlessly clean with good overhead lighting. Strategically placed wrought-iron lifts were all carpeted, air-conditioned and played clear Hawaiian music.

'Another nice day, Mr Fairchild,' the garage attendant called out with the easy familiarity that all of his staff used, and Dominic detoured to the orange and black booth.

'Looks like it, Kalani,' he agreed. Kalani, with grizzled hair and skin like leather, looked positively ancient but there was nothing about cars that he didn't know. Dominic always hired the best, and expected to get the best in return. 'Everything OK?'

'Yes, sir. The Count Orlendi's Lamborghini is running well now. I know a man in Waipahu who deals in foreign parts.'

Kalani turned as a Rolls Royce Corniche belonging to the British Earl in the Royal Suite pulled in, and he felt a ripple of pleasure shoot through him. Without this job, Kalani knew that he and his family would have been in serious difficulties; when he'd gone to his Prince he had been prepared to take any work at all. However, it had only taken one hour for Dominic to see that Kalani's talents lay in the garage, and within a few months, he had been able to implement his latest community service programme whereby Kalani trained young Hawaiian men and women in auto-mechanics. To his accountant's delight, the Fairchild grant scheme he set up for them was tax deductible, of course, so everyone won. And to Dominic Fairchild, winning was everything.

Nodding briskly, Dominic left him to it and made his way to the hotel's large and busy lobby with its hand-painted ceiling depicting scenes of sea, palm trees, and blush-red sunsets. The walls of the circular room were white and hung with tapestries embroidered by local women in which colourful flower gardens, ancient Hawaiian gods and towering volcanoes lush with verdant forest were displayed in all their glory. In the centre of the breeze-swept room was a fountain, its centrepiece a single maiden swathed in cloth carrying a lotus blossom that sprayed a delicate arch of slightly scented water. Lilies flowered in the round marble basin, the species mixed so that during every month of the year, flowers bloomed pink, white, buttercup-yellow and delicate dotted orchid-like creations in cream and rose. The floor was of cool cream and green dappled marble, and attractive greenery in giant wicker baskets stood in every corner. Wide French windows opened out to the balcony that overlooked Waikiki Beach and the blue ocean, whilst the scent of frangipani and jasmine wafted in from the extensive hotel gardens on the January breeze.

Dominic looked around with pleasure, never tiring of the elegance and simple beauty of this, his first hotel. Under his astute and innovative guidance, the three hotels left to him by his grandfather had been rebuilt, renamed and redirected, and now the Blue Hawaiian rivalled the famous Pink Palace amongst the rich jet-set circles for which it catered. He also had hotels on all the other major beaches, but the Princess Liliha Hotel, which looked out over the less commercial, peaceful Waimea Bay was his favourite. He had named it after his mother, working to imbue it with a native Hawaiian flavour, that had made it 'The' place for those discriminating holidaymakers who were after the 'real' Hawaii. Yet Dominic catered for all classes of tourists. The Waikiki Sand and Surf further down the strip was a big, cheerful hotel destined for the younger element who partied on a strict budget; it boasted an all night disco in a sound-proofed basement, a games room the size of a baseball pitch and a swimming pool that would comfortably house a killer whale.

At first, when all this empire-building had been in its infancy, it had been enough for Dominic. Working flat out for years had kept the yawning ache of his grandfather's treachery at bay, allowing him to disguise his loneliness and deny the futility of his vast wealth and influence without a child of his own to inherit it all. Only now, with the mountain climbed, was Dominic slowly coming to realize how cold was the air at the top, how spectacular but oh how empty, the view.

At the entrance he could see that Julie Sui was on *lei* duty and as he watched, a middle-aged couple alighted from a taxi. Two bellboys were swiftly on the scene, taking competent charge of their luggage as Julie stepped forward and placed a *lei* of plumeria and orange blossom carefully over their heads, flashing them the pretty smile for which she had been hired.

It was nearly one o'clock, so he moved across to an arched entranceway and down four wide steps to the east wing or Silver Sky Restaurant, where the carpet underneath his feet was a smoky blue, the walls pearly grey, and the ceiling hand-painted with a silver, white and dusty-pink design. The twenty tables in the room were pentagonal in shape, an idea that had occurred to him when noticing how awkward it was to accommodate families who were not the regulation four in number, or groups of guests who wanted to dine together. The pentagonal tables could be joined together to make easy clusters, their flat sides forming all manner of unusual possibilities that aided interesting dinner conversation. Already he'd noticed several other hotels and restaurants in Honolulu and elsewhere following his lead. It was not an uncommon occurrence, but he felt no thrill of triumph as he might once have done.

Now the tables were covered in the finest blood-red linen. The colours changed with every meal – white at breakfast and burgundy at dinner; along with the lunch-time red, all three coordinated beautifully with the elegant carved chairs of imported teak. The support of local craftsmen had always been one Dominic's priorities and their skills were visible throughout his hotels, from the elegant furniture down to the *hua* fruit bowls that were in every room. The woven mats scattering the cool tiled floors were made from the leaves of the ubiquitous Pandanus trees by local women, and their handiwork made each room in every hotel just that little bit different – a quirk that his regular guests greatly appreciated.

'Prince' was not a title Dominic himself used; nevertheless he was aware of the responsibilities inherent in his title, which was still observed by many natives of the islands. He'd kept the promise he'd made to himself, one that had sustained him throughout those stormy early years with Fred, and had continued to live his life as an Hawaiian, first and foremost.

The head waiter Ling, a Chinese of impeccable manners and appearance, spotted him quickly and made a rapid check of the tables. They were full, but not too full, and as Dominic approached him Ling took in his casual but expensive appearance with deeply-felt approval. The head waiter had started work at the Blue Hawaiian as a kitchen assistant, hardly expecting to become anything else, but his quick efficiency, cool head and perfect manners had attracted Dominic's eye and his well-earned rise to head waiter had eventually followed. Yet he never took his position for granted. Dominic was not the kind of man you should disappoint.

'Ling.' Dominic nodded at him now, his green eyes as always startling the Chinaman, who always expected to encounter the doe-soft brown eyes of an Hawaiian native.

'Sir. You wish for a table?'

'If there's one free.'

'I believe so, sir. This way.' Dominic followed the black-and-white figure to a chair near the stage at the far end, a polished expanse of deep red-dyed wood. Behind this, French windows opened out on to the gardens, so that the people strolling there or sipping drinks on the terraces were also serenaded by whichever band was performing. Unlike most hotels, all of Dominic's entertainers sang and played genuine native music as well as middle-of-the-road pop, their instruments fashioned from native rosewood by a spectacularly ugly but perpetually cheerful Malay craftsman whom Dominic had discovered in the 1970s. He had immediately seen the potential for a small stall in all of his hotels, selling genuine Hawaiian instruments such as *ulivli*'s – a feather-topped gourd filled with seed, to be rattled – Ipu drums and other items that were also, under Quan's dextrous hands, things of considerable beauty. And they were still selling well, the ideal momento for every moneyed holidaymaker.

As he took the seat Ling held out for him, Dominic's eyes wandered to the stage where Farron Manikuuna was singing *Sweet Leilani* in a soft, and evocative voice.

Farron was not tall – at five feet ten his height was slightly above average for that of a native Polynesian – but he had that indefinable something that people in the know refer to as 'stage presence'. His powerful, compact body held an exciting energy that an audience reacted to quite subconsciously. His dark eyes made many feminine hearts flutter and he had a face that was a mixture of boyish charm and a smouldering meanness that Dominic knew was totally misleading and very much at odds with his relaxed, friendly nature.

It had been a pleasure for Dominic to build up the boy's reputation with careful publicity and now, at the age of twenty-nine, Farron was almost as famous as Don Ho and enjoyed a professional status equal to that of Danny Kalekini. It only irked him that Farron would not have been able to enjoy such status, had he not been born in Honolulu. Only in Hawaii could Farron be the success he was.

Dominic took the menu from Ling and waved him away, his eyes fixed on the stage. When he'd finished the song, people put down their silver-plated cutlery to clap and Dominic felt a fierce stab of pride and satisfaction as he joined in the applause. Farron bowed briefly, spotted him, and his smile stretched a little further. 'Thank you, ladies and gentlemen. We hope you're enjoying your meal . . .'

There was a contented murmur of general consent as the singer paused and Dominic cast a critical eye around the room. His guests had a sheen that only money could produce; the women had hair that had been cut and arranged for hours, their gowned bodies swathed in designer-label creations, their jewellery glinting in muted overhead lighting, their perfectly made-up faces as glossy as a magazine cover.

'We'd like to perform for you now *Treasure Island* and hope you feel that in Oahu you've found just that.'

The band struck up the gentle chords and Dominic nodded. Just right – not too loud to be intrusive, but not too soft to be drowned out by the clinking of cutlery. As he half-turned he noticed that one of the huge old-fashioned propeller-type fans that hung attractively from the ceiling was not working, and he beckoned the head waiter over with a sharp snap of his fingers. 'One of the fans is out, Ling,' he said impatiently. 'Get it fixed when the lunch-shift is over, will you?'

'Yes, sir,' Ling said, smarting under the cool tone of his employer, spotting the fan in question and hiding his anger carefully. Any and every tiny imperfection in the dining room was something that Ling took personally. 'Are you ready to order?'

Dominic looked down at the beautiful handwritten menu of gold and black, making a mental note to congratulate the art student who earned money by writing them out every evening. The dishes were listed in French, but underneath there was a discreet English translation of the Cordon Bleu dishes. 'I'll have the Nutted Veal Steak with the Cordini side salad, and Lilikoni for dessert. No wine.'

Ling bowed and retrieved the menu. 'And Ling,' Dominic detained him quietly with a slight movement of his hand. 'Don't tell the chef who it's for.'

Barely five minutes later, Ling carried his lunch to him on a silver tray and hovered unobtrusively as Dominic judged its presentation. The golden-brown steak steamed slightly and by its side on the Wedgwood green and gold dinner plate attractive wedges of lemon and macadamia nuts mixed with tomato added a colourful garnish. The nut-encrusted steak crunched pleasingly under the sharp blade of his knife, the meat inside succulent and tasty in his mouth. The side salad, served in a wooden handcrafted bowl with equally attractive salad fork and spoon, consisted of crisp white lettuce and Chinese chestnuts, sprinkled with walnuts, freshly grown watercress and parsley mixed with chives. The whole concoction was given a pleasant tang by the chef's own salad dressing.

Dominic nodded. 'Tell the chef that if he keeps this standard up, I'll renew his contract next fall.'

'I will, sir. He'll be pleased.'

His meal finished, Dominic rose and left as Farron began to sing *Moon of Manakoora*. Back in the lobby his gaze rested thoughtfully on the boutique, which was positioned discreetly yet strategically by the exit to the pool, where its eye-catching window display of swimwear, casuals and elegant evening wear would catch the attention of every guest passing that way. Opposite the Princess Liliha Boutique (Blue Hawaiian Branch) was a men's tailoring outfitters, but the real money-spinner was the boutique, attracting like moths to a flame the wealthy female clientele. Dominic walked through the open entrance and was assailed immediately by the pleasant fragrance of the freesias that were replenished daily from the greenhouses at the rear of the garden. Unlike most boutiques, the Princess Liliha shops did not have racks of clothes, but mannequins scattered at a comfortable distance displaying Parisian evening dresses with feline grace. On each of the three walls, items of clothing were displayed in attractive settings – the beachwear on a backdrop of beach and blue ocean, rife with palm trees. At the counter beach accessories were sold – suntan creams, beach balls, bags and the usual paraphernalia, all quality merchandise that did away with the cheap, throwaway atmosphere usually present at such displays.

Dominic smiled with a curious mixture of pain and pleasure. He'd put so much effort into the Fairchild business empire, all his creativity and all that attention which should have gone on a woman or a child – on the family he'd never had. Suddenly the very success of his efforts seemed pathetic and meaningless and he had to fight off a serious wave of despair. Just recently he'd found himself confronting that particular demon more and more. Perhaps, he thought wryly, he was getting old.

Jenni Akino, the boutique's manageress, was talking

quietly with a woman who was almost-dressed in a fuchsia-pink bikini that was no more than two daring straps of material. Dominic let his eyes run over the svelte suntanned figure from the upper and lower orbs of her breasts, clearly revealed by the pink swathe that barely covered her nipples, down over the slightly concave stomach and lower, to where pubic hair had surely been shaved to accommodate the tiny downward thrusting V-shaped straps that almost left her crutch completely bare. As Dominic looked back up at the cascading mane of sun-streaked blonde hair he smiled ruefully, almost regretting the no-sex-with-hotel-guests rule that he'd made fifteen years ago.

'It's quite something, this place. I expected to find the usual tourist-trap trinkets and stuff,' the blonde was saying.

'Oh no, madam. Princess Liliha has a reputation equal to that of the best fashion houses. We have branches in all the local shopping centres, and most of our designs are either Parisian or from Rome and London.'

'Yes, so I see. With a price-tag to match.'

'Well, madam, it is true that you get what you pay for.'

The lipsticked mouth of the blonde curved into a wry smile. 'Isn't that the truth?' she drawled, and at that moment Dominic placed her. She was the 'travelling companion' of the toothpaste king in the Presidential Suite. Dominic pursed his lips and smiled deeply, hoping she didn't give the seventy-two-year-old multimillionaire a heart attack whilst he was staying at the hotel.

He moved in smoothly. 'Hello, Jenni. Everything all right?'

Jenni tensed nervously. 'Oh yes, Your High ... Mr Fairchild.' Jenni was the great-granddaughter of one of Oahu's oldest inhabitants, and during her childhood Dominic Fairchild had always been referred to as 'His Highness' by her grandparents. She'd started work at the boutique five years ago as a salesgirl, rising through the ranks to become the manageress, quickly learning how to dress, apply make-up properly and even walk with model-like grace. Now, like all other girls in Dominic's employ, she was as good to look at as she was knowledgeable about fashion and pleasantly helpful to talk to. Turning his attention to Maria Whiting, who had perked up at the sound of his name, Dominic smiled. No doubt she was pricing his clothes to the last cent, and he smiled charmingly as he introduced himself.

She responded instantly. 'Hi. I'm Maria Whiting.'

'Yes, I know,' Dominic murmured softly, watching her blue eyes narrow. He could almost hear her mind clicking over, wondering if he'd make a better proposition than the toothpaste king. Physically speaking, of course, there was no comparison and Maria knew it. This man oozed sex, and those eyes! They seemed to be searing a hole right into her, making her breath catch in her throat. He was worth a packet too, but that only meant the competition was harder. And a man who'd managed to remain a bachelor was a hard fish to catch. At least with Heinz she was convinced, and confident, that she could persuade him to marry her and put his snotty-nosed kids in a lather. So it was that she regretfully passed him over.

'It's a very nice place you have here,' she said sweetly, and Dominic bit back a grin at her condescending dismissal.

'Thank you – I try. But I mustn't detain such a . . . lovely lady as yourself any longer.' He let his voice drop an octave and moved a scant inch nearer, holding her eyes with a level but smouldering green gaze as he reached for her hand, letting his fingers curve around the wrist provocatively before placing a kiss square in the palm of her hand, feeling her reaction instantly. He smiled wolfishly; something about dishing out some of Maria's own medicine appealed to him. Then he wondered why: was he really so warped that such a petty thing could actually please him?

Maria paled slightly. Shee-it, he was potent. She could feel the warm spot between her legs melting into hot warm honey and parted her lips slightly.

'I wish you an enjoyable stay, Maria,' he added, his voice cooler now as he turned and walked away. Maria watched him until he was out of sight and then heaved a sigh. She'd actually found a man who not only lived up to, but actually excelled, his reputation! She could hardly believe it. She turned back to the assistant, her eyes falling on a sequined gown in black velvet, and she smiled in self-satisfaction. An

Alaia Azzeddine original – easily ten thousand dollars and just what she needed as a compensation prize.

In the lift, Dominic pushed his hands into his trouser pockets and leaned back against the wooden panelling, ignoring the soothing music. What he really wanted to do was forget caution and have a wild affair. Damn the old man for hogtying him so effectively. Too strong to fall prey to self-pity for long, he smiled ruefully as the elevator came to a smooth halt. No, he couldn't damn the old man – wherever he was. Though if he knew Frederick Fairchild he was probably telling the Devil how to run Hell by now! Nodding to his secretary, he walked past her into his office where Philip Pearce rose from a chair. 'Hi Phil! When did you get back?'

'Just.'

'How's the big island?'

Philip Pearce grimaced. 'Hawaii hasn't changed that much. Still all volcanoes, cattle ranches and black beaches.'

'I'd better not let you write the travel brochures for the new hotel, then,' Dominic grinned then added sharply, 'There *is* going to be a new hotel?'

Philip grinned back. 'You don't think I'd dare say anything else, do you?'

'Not if you want to keep your job, MD,' Dominic threatened, but Philip knew better than to think he meant it. He'd joined Dominic's all-new fledgling company straight from Harvard, working under Smith Flanaghan until Dom had finished his own business schooling. He often wondered what old man Fairchild would have made of the modern Fairchild Enterprises Corporation. He'd be as proud as Punch of course, but he'd be sure to have something to say about the diversification. 'Bloody women's clothes is a nancy boy's job,' would have dispensed with the Princess Liliha boutique chain, whether or not it brought in a yearly profit of four million dollars. The Fairchild Real Estate Company was a goldmine, and Dominic Tours, with its three luxury tourboats doing regular trips around the island and to Maui, a less commercially-orientated island, was growing nicely. The Candida Coffee Company and the second biggest fruit

31

company on the islands, Lanai Fruit, would all have received the thumbs-down from Fred Fairchild, too. To him a single hotel was worth any amount of canning factories. It had been a hard slog for Dominic, and like all successful men, he'd made his share of enemies, but not as many as Fred Fairchild.

'So, just how do things stand?' Dominic asked, sitting down in a black leather swing chair behind a huge desk. They discussed the new hotel project that was set to rival Volcano House, the famous luxury hotel built on the mouth of a volcano, for some time, Dominic determinedly steering the course of least resistance through the usual time-wasting red tape with a brisk humour and resolution that was typical of him. Finally, towards tea-time, when all the details were ironed out, he poured them both a drink and relaxed back in his swivel chair with a satisfied grunt. 'So how are the kids?' he asked, and Philip gave a longsuffering laugh.

'Monica's threatening to send them packing to a Stateside summer school. You should hear them howl.'

'I'll bet. What on earth made you have so many?'

Phil grinned. 'Seven's my lucky number.'

Dominic laughed, then tossed his drink down, his face suddenly grim as he said softly, 'You're a lucky son of a bitch.'

Philip looked away from his friend's tight face. 'Yes, I know.' Philip didn't know the story behind Dominic's continuing bachelorhood but he was damned sure it was not through choice. Dominic was like a second father to his own kids, and Philip had seen for himself the look of bleak longing on his face when Phil and Monica exchanged glances or words of affection and closeness. At Christmas especially, Dominic plunged headlong into the rough and tumble of domesticity in the Pearce household with such obvious happiness that Phil hated the thought of him going home alone to the great mausoleum of a place where he lived in such cold and isolated spendour. But he knew better than to say so.

'I don't like this sudden rise in Princess Liliha stock, Phil, even if the companies involved *are* all respectable bastions of English commerce.' Dominic quickly changed the subject, aware as he spoke that the feeling of unease was back with a vengeance. He'd been worried about the unusual stock activity ever since it had first started over a month ago. And since Fairchild Enterprises was all he had, he guarded it with a fierceness that he knew deep in his heart was unhealthy.

'You think there's going to be a takeover bid?'

'I'm not sure. Just run a check, will you?' Dominic rose and walked restlessly to the window. 'I don't like its smell. Hell, I need another drink. Let's go downstairs.'

EACH of the two dining rooms had a bar, and it was the Sunset Sky Restaurant in the west wing that they entered a few minutes later. The afternoon-tea trade was over, and only Farron and the band were left, rehearsing on stage. The Sunset Sky Restaurant was an exact replica of its twin, differing only in its colour scheme. Here the walls were that pale mauve of twilight, the carpet the navy blue of deepest night, and on the ceiling was a glorious painting of a tropical sunset.

'Hello, Mr Fairchild.' The barman on duty was George, a man who'd been with the hotel since its opening.

'Scotch — double,' Dominic ordered crisply, and George paused momentarily from wiping the bar. In all the years he'd worked for Dominic, he'd never ordered a double scotch during the working day.

On stage, Farron broke off their number. 'OK, that's it. Everyone happy?' There was general consent and the musicians began to pack away their gear. It was the sex siren's turn to sing tonight, and none of them were sorry.

'How's the windsurfing going, Farron?' the question came from Danny, his oldest friend and lead guitarist.

'OK. I haven't been practising as much as I'd like to, though, and Perry's looking good.'

'No problems, champ,' Kim the drummer said. 'The Islanders' Cup is in the bag.' Farron smiled as he thought about the amateur, strictly local freestyle windsurfing competition at Sunset Beach in three weeks' time. He'd won the cup twice in a row but Jimmy Kwan was runner-up both times and was hungry for the title. 'Hey, is that whisky the boss is drinking?' Kim added.

Farron looked swiftly towards the bar, his face clouding over. 'Looks like it.'

Kim shrugged. 'I heard he's in trouble over somethin' or other. You know, somebody out to take over one of his companies. At least, that's the word.' Kim's father was a stockbroker who'd long since disowned his youngest son.

A shaft of sympathy rippled through Farron. He felt as close to Dominic Fairchild as he did to anyone, save for his *tutu*, the old woman who'd raised him from childhood. It was Dominic who'd given him his first break, Dominic who'd seen his potential and helped him build his career. It was also Dominic who had loaned him the money to get his first flat, and buy his first car.

The man lived for his work, even at the cost of everything else, and Farron knew just what his companies meant to him. Hell, they were all he had.

'Damn,' he said softly to no one in particular. 'Why is there always someone willing to take it all away?'

Chapter 4

LONDON

The corporate office block of Fielding Co. stood in the heart of the City, towering twenty storeys high. Stepping out of the lift at the penthouse offices, Rhiannon nervously brushed down her already creasefree dark green pencil skirt and matching velvet jacket and smiled bravely at Linda, who had been Ben's private secretary for over twenty years.

'Hello, Miss Grantham. Go on in.'

Ben's office was an expanse of white and chrome that looked out over a spectacular River Thames view. As she walked in Ben, who was seated behind a huge desk, looked over the telephone at her and silently gestured to show that he wouldn't be long. As he continued his transatlantic call she wandered over to the wide windows and gazed out past Tower Bridge to the Houses of Parliament, but the view did little to distract her. Her throat felt dry; today Ben had promised her an answer.

The day was cloudy and grey, and Rhiannon sighed as a brief shaft of sunlight struggled from behind a cloud. Beautiful though it was, London looked grey and grim, and she wondered what the islands must look like now. Were they truly as colourful, warm and tropical as people claimed? As she heard Ben hang up she knew that she was about to find out whether his answer was yes or no. Although what she'd do if it was no, she wasn't totally sure. She only knew that she would not give up – she could *never* give up.

Slowly she moved around to face him and placed her black briefcase on the desk top. Ben looked at her closely. The dark rings under her eyes were less pronounced now, and she had mercifully filled out a little since her father's funeral.

'You're looking better,' he said softly.

'Thanks. I feel better.'

'That wouldn't have anything to do with all those

purchases you made of Princess Liliha stock, by any chance?'

Rhiannon sighed, not really having expected to keep it a secret from Ben for long. 'You don't approve?'

Ben rose from behind his desk, an elegant figure in his navy-blue pinstriped Savile Row suit, and lifted the silver top of his cigar box. Extracting a cheroot he lit it thoughtfully. 'It might help if you told me why you're so determined to bring this man down.'

Rhiannon watched him light the cheroot and blow out a thin stream of grey-blue smoke as he retook his seat, looking the epitome of a successful man. 'I can't. I've already told you that. It's . . . personal.'

'Personal,' Ben repeated flatly. 'Like my company is personal to me?'

Rhiannon closed her eyes briefly, then rubbed them tiredly. 'I understand, Ben. Really I do. It was too much to ask.' She picked up her bag and headed to the door wondering what she could do now. She'd already spent all of her considerable savings on the Liliha stock, and trying to take on Fairchild Enterprises with a half-partnership in a single company, namely Grantham Advertising, would be tantamount to financial suicide.

'Wait, Rhia! I never said . . .'

She spun around quickly, hope lighting up her lovely green eyes and Ben bit back the groan that rose to his lips.

'Come and sit down. I've been . . . busy these last few months. You do realise I can't hand everything over just like that?'

Rhiannon sank into the black chair opposite his desk, her heart pounding with both exultation and fear. 'Of course not, Ben. I never expected you to.'

'However, I've been looking through the books.'

Rhiannon laughed. She couldn't help it. Fielding Co. was so vast that their 'books' probably housed enough papers to sink the *Titanic*. Ben, interpreting her amusement, grinned and sucked on his cheroot.

'As you know, you hold controlling stock of Grantham Advertising, as set out in the merger documents. And although your father's will was, well, a bit of a disappointment, it hardly matters. Over the years you've gradually bought stock in over fifteen of Fielding Company's more rapidly expanding enterprises. Not only was that astute buying on your part,' Ben leaned over his desk, stabbing a pen in the air, 'but it also makes you, besides myself of course, one of our major board members.'

Rhiannon smiled gently at him. 'You own Fielding Company, Ben, and we both know it. I bought stock only because you allowed me to. You even had to release the stock in the first place. As for being a board member, again, that's only with your blessing. True, I have a lot of money invested in Fieldings, and a lot of power, backed by stock, in some areas. But . . .'

Ben leaned back in his chair. 'You need a bit more clout than you've got at present, hm?'

'In a nutshell,' Rhiannon said quietly. 'And, of course, I don't expect you to just hand it over. Whatever business decisions I make will be based on two factors, one of which will most definitely be to improve Fielding's assets. And hotels, which are the linchpins of Fairchild Enterprises, are definitely assets worth acquiring. But there are other areas I think we should concentrate on first . . .'

For the next hour, Rhiannon expounded her plans for the assault on Fairchild Enterprises, detailing, to almost the last penny, capital expenditure and intitial outlay, plus the projected earnings and every possible benefit and gain to Fielding's. Ben watched and listened in silence, asking the odd question here and there, but satisfied, as always, that Rhiannon had done everything possible to minimize the risk to his company. And that was no minor detail, as Ben knew only too well.

When she'd finished, she waited as Ben settled back in his chair, his hands steepled under his chin as was his habit when he was deep in thought. 'You know why it's taken me so long to come up with an answer, don't you? Apart from finding the least disruptive way of transferring power and stock to you, I've been having a complete and if I may say so, extremely thorough check made on this Fairchild character.'

Rhiannon nodded. 'I know. Why do you think I haven't been on the phone, breathing down your neck night and day?'

Ben grinned. 'You always did have trouble learning patience,' he admonished gently, then suddenly became very serious. 'Fairchild is rather more than an Island bigwig. For a start he's a financial whiz kid. And I'm not just talking about mathematics. He's an innovator – a pioneer. And his empire isn't by any means a piffling little island dynasty. He's a shaker – a mover. We won't be able to take him on without causing tidal waves on the monetary market. Like all giants, he'll have his own network of spies and tame officials.'

Rhiannon felt dismayed. 'I see. I had no idea. I thought, well, I suppose I thought he was just another millionaire despot, ruling the roost in his little kingdom like a puffed-up peacock.'

Ben grinned, then frowned. 'It's not funny, is it?'

Rhiannon shook her head grimly. 'No. It's not funny.'

'This has something to do with Graham, yes? He was born on Oahu, wasn't he?'

'Yes. Me too.'

'Rhia.' Ben moved slowly around the front of the desk and leant against it, looking down at her with a mixture of concern, want and sadness. 'Don't let yourself get dragged into something that's probably best left dead and buried. I don't know what passed between this Dominic Fairchild and your father but think twice before getting involved.'

Rhiannon slowly leaned back in her chair, her beautiful face pale and tired. 'You think that I'm looking forward to this? Do you really think that I wouldn't rather stay here, where I know what's what and who's who? Ben,' she sat forward and looked him straight in the eye. 'Would you be able to ignore your own father's dying wish? Could you?'

Ben sighed and looked away. 'No,' he said eventually. 'I suppose not. But that's not to say that I wouldn't have to clear it with my conscience first. What you're planning ... Rhiannon, I don't think you quite understand what you're taking on. A man like Dominic Fairchild isn't just going to stand idly by whilst you take pot shots at him and his empire. This is a man who lives for his work – he's never married, never had children. His Company is his whole life. I don't think you realize how great an enemy he's going to be.'

38

Rhiannon smiled grimly. 'You're wrong, Ben. I know exactly what he's capable of. He persecuted my father into the grave.'

Ben blinked, shocked by the cold certainty in her voice. 'Graham said that? Darling, I don't mean to be heartless, but he was dying. He may have been confused. Who knows how his emotions might have been twisted by the pain? Oh, I'm sorry. That was thoughtless of me.'

Rhiannon shook her head even though the memory of her final moments with her father made her blanch. 'No. You're right to warn me. I know you've only got my own best interests at heart. But I have proof, Ben. Solid proof. The kind that won't go away, no matter how hard I wish it would.' Rhiannon thought back to the visit from her father's solicitor, and the documents he'd brought with him. Documents that showed Dominic Fairchild's vindictiveness in all its stark detail, and her eyes darkened ominously.

For a long while Ben stared at her helplessly. His instincts told him that if he let her go now he'd never get her back. Having lived in the shark-infested waters of high finances so much longer than she had he knew a dangerous man when he saw one. And everything he'd learned of Dominic Fairchild told him that he was definitely not someone to be trifled with. The man had built an empire from a few hotels, and that in itself showed strength and determination way beyond Rhiannon's experience. He had broken monopolies, forged new directions, diversified and multiplied as only a truly tough man can do. He was ruthless, and almost breath-takingly clever.

'Rhia, if I ask you, as a favour to me, will you forget all this? Stay here and . . . just stay here?'

'Oh, Ben! Don't, please. I have to go. You don't understand. I have to know why he did it. And,' she paused, taking a deep breath before murmuring grimly, 'I have to be the one to make him pay.'

Slowly Ben took her hand, unclenching her long, slender fingers. 'Revenge never did anyone any good,' he warned softly.

She shook her head. 'I know that, and I'm not talking of

revenge. What I want is justice, Ben. He destroyed and eventually all but killed my father – what might he have done to others?'

'You really believe this?'

'Yes, Ben. I do.'

He nodded, reluctantly let go of her hand and walked to his wall safe where he extracted a huge folder. 'In that case, I'd better explain what I have in mind and exactly what power and capital you have to play with . . .'

THREE hours later Rhiannon's head was spinning with a welter of new knowledge and an even greater respect for Ben Fielding. What he had done had been tantamount to a business miracle. Put at its simplest, Ben had agreed to 'sell' several companies to her in exchange for every share she owned. Of course, once it was all over, she would 'sell' the companies back in exchange for her stock, and everything would be exactly as it was before. Naturally there were legally-binding clauses and conditions which prevented her from re-selling any of the companies to anyone but Ben, and other assorted safeguards, all of which were designed to protect Fielding's. But in a move that pleased both his own accountants, the Inland Revenue and Rhiannon, Ben had managed to give her a firm and independent power base from which to operate, thus allowing her to act without being bogged down by miles of red tape. It also meant that, should she lose the up-coming financial battle with Dominic Fairchild, it would ultimately be she, and not Fielding's, who would take the fall.

'So, let's recap,' Ben said, yawning around a cup of coffee that Linda had brought in a few minutes before. 'Jack Gunster is going to meet you in Honolulu. He's been my right-hand man in the trouble-shooting division for ten years now, which is probably why you've never met him before. Everything you've suggested has turned to gold. But if it hadn't, Jack would have been the one called in to see where things were going wrong.'

Rhiannon grimaced. 'He sounds ominous.'

'He is. Aren't you glad he's on your side?' Ben laughed and

took a large gulp of nearly-cold coffee. 'Don't worry about Jack. He'll steer you right. These are the lists of all the companies that you and he can jointly call upon when the time comes.'

Rhiannon took the list of eight companies, all of them in some way related to the areas of operation that Fairchild Enterprises had an interest in, and nodded slowly.

'And banking?'

Ben smiled and handed over a list of account numbers. Some were in Switzerland, others in Honolulu, London and New York. 'Don't forget. It's going to be Jack's job to see that any transactions you make are (a) legal, and so can't rebound on you or us, and (b) potentially profitable. I warn you now Rhia, I don't mind helping you but I'll be damned if I'll allow you to put any of those companies in jeopardy. Don't forget —when all this is over, I want them back. In one piece, and hopefully in better shape than when I gave them to you.'

Rhiannon looked up, surprised at the strange intensity in his voice. She knew he was warning her, but was a little uneasy that he thought she needed it. 'I know that, Ben. I wouldn't have it any other way. I love you too much.'

Ben went hot, then cold. He coughed into his coffee and raised a shaking hand to his mouth.

'You must know you and Dad have had more influence on my life than any other men,' she carried on, hurt that he could think so badly of her. 'You're the older brother I never had. The rich uncle who made all my dreams come true. I owe you so much, Ben – I owe you a lot.'

Ben looked away quickly, his eyes falling on a print of his favourite early Dali hanging on his office wall. But the sight of melting clocks reminded him that fifty-three was fast approaching and he looked away again.

Rhiannon was checking through the pile of documents, a strange excitement lighting up her face. Reminded of a tigress on the hunt, Ben shook his head. This merciless vendetta was not like her at all. Just what the hell was she getting herself into? And why? He took a deep breath. 'Rhiannon. Be careful.'

She looked up, so young and so beautiful that he felt his heart turn in his chest. 'I will, Ben.'

'I mean it. Jack will take care of you as much as he can but this Fairchild . . .'

'Ben! I don't need taking care of. You seem to forget – I've had a very good teacher. It'll be Dominic Fairchild who needs to look out.'

'You're good, Pipsqueak, but you're not yet thirty and you've been restricted to Fielding's where it's nice and safe. Remember, the man you're taking on has been fighting since the day he was born, first with his grandfather, then with the sharks who tried to muscle in when the old man died. And ever since he's been taking on the world and winning. He's not used to losing, Rhia.'

Rhiannon leant back in her chair, a tight hard smile on her face. 'Then it's time he learnt, Ben,' she said softly. 'It's time he learnt.'

Chapter 5

OAHU

The Falling Pearls Palace, Princess Liliha's ancestral home, had been a poor, dilapidated place when Dominic had visited it just two days after his grandfather's funeral. Determined to alienate him from his Hawaiian ancestry, Fred had refused to spend any money on it. Dominic had been just as determined to restore it to its former and rightful glory and now it was a spectacular residence boasting thirty-two bedrooms with en suite bathrooms, a library, seven lounges, huge indoor and outdoor pools, a modern study, a famous ballroom, a hall that housed a marble semicircular staircase, a vast kitchen complex, five dining rooms and a conservatory. It was open to the public once a week, and Dominic provided free buses for any and all Hawaiian natives who wished to see the royal palace and walk in its famous gardens.

Now, as Dominic drove his car into one of six garages, he was oblivious to the beauty of his grounds where a stream cut through twenty acres of gardens and woods, and where several ponds had been dug out to accommodate koi carp, black long-barbelled catfish and a subtropical outdoor aquarium. Hand-carved wooden bridges trailed colourful vines into the water. Carefully tended lawns were mown into diamond patterns and everywhere bushes and shrubs exploded in the perfumed colour for which the islands were famous. Waterfalls, flowerbeds, fountains and gazebos were liberally scattered throughout. An army of local Hawaiians, mostly the old and young whom no one else would employ, kept the Fairchild gardens in perfect condition.

As he walked to the front entrance the sun bounced brightly off the white plasterwork of the three-storeyed exterior. Once inside the cool hall he collected the mail his butler stacked on an antique Georgian bureau every night and took it through to his favourite lounge. Pouring himself an iced tea with a splash of bourbon he collapsed into a chair. He was expecting Ralph Dorrington, MD of the Liliha boutique chain who'd just caught him leaving his office and by the harassed tone of his voice on the phone Dominic knew it wasn't good.

He walked across the hall into his study and extracted the boutique folder, his eyes going to the portrait of his mother on the wall. As he looked up into the lovely face of the woman he had never known, he wondered if the artist had captured on canvas the true spirit of the ebony-eyed, ebony-haired Hawaiian Princess. Her skin was creamy coffee in colour and the hands that rested on her lap were small and dainty. She was relaxing on a chaise longue, wearing a Japanese-style loose kimono of scarlet flowers on a pale blue background. Her nose was long and slightly uptilted but her small mouth curved in good humour. A lovely and regal woman, she looked as if she might have smiled a lot. No wonder his father, who was also no more than a name to him, had fallen in love and married outside his own family's race, religion and class. Not that the old man had ever liked to think of her as royalty.

Dominic took the folder into the lounge and studied it thoroughly. On paper it all looked inviolate and lucrative, a monument not only to American enterprise but also to good taste. 'Mr Dorrington, Your Highness.' Koana, butler to his family for more than fifty years, introduced his visitor then backed out of the room.

Ralph Dorrington was in his mid-fifties with two divorces behind him and his present marriage on the rocks. He was fat around the middle and thinning on top, with sharp grey eyes behind which lurked a meticulous brain. He also had that seemingly effortless ability to get through huge volumes of work which had made him one of Dominic's favourite directors. Now he looked tired and harassed, and he fidgeted with his tie, a habit that Dominic knew was a sure sign of trouble. 'More stocks have been bought?' he hazarded, sitting down and motioning Ralph to do the same.

'It's worse than that. Oh hell, here.' Ralph handed him a paper, wanting the explosion to be over. Dominic read, his face tightening and paling.

'*Takeover* notification? Are they mad? Who is this . . .' he checked the form '. . . Grant Corporation? I've never heard of them. When did it arrive?' His staccato questions shot out like bullets, but Ralph was ready for them.

'An hour ago. Since then I've had our people on it and so far all they've come up with is more questions. The main company holders were all English, owned by one Ben Fielding. But our men in London tell me there's a rumour going around that all three companies were recently sold but nobody knows to whom. The deal, if there is a deal, is buried deep.'

Dominic paced up and down, panther-like. 'These companies only have thirty-five per cent,' he said, reading the document's specifics as he paced. 'They can't possibly mount a successful takeover campaign with that.'

'That's what I thought,' Ralph said, 'so I had our brokers in Wall Street and the London Stock Exchange do a little checking on the individual shareholders. As well as five per cent of them looking very suspiciously like front men, I've had several reports of our so-called "friendlies" selling out, some at a very exaggerated profit.'

Dominic's tone was misleadingly mild as he enquired, 'Who?'

'Carson, Moore, Romanski and Cow-Tek for sure. But I got a call as I was on my way out, and I think you can add Van Styker and the Frenchman to it.'

'So, it looks as though Grants, whoever they are, have got the other eleven per cent they need?'

'They may be bluffing, or even overextended.'

Dominic poured them both a drink and then turned his own squat crystal tumbler in his hand, the fiery liquid shining in the light. 'I doubt it. The whole thing has been too carefully planned, timing it so soon after the annual audit. No, even if we get every lawyer in the state on it I doubt they'd find a loophole. Besides, I've done enough air-tight deals of my own to know when I've been stitched up by a professional.'

Ralph licked his dry lips. 'If you want my resignation . . .'

'It came in an hour ago, you say?' Dominic asked, ignoring the quiet offering.

'Yes.'

'You've been busy.'

'Yes. But I should have seen it coming.'

Dominic tossed back the last of his drink and then threw the glass with vicious force and precision into the fireplace, where it exploded into splinters. Ralph nearly jumped out of his skin but when Dominic turned, his face was as blank as Ralph had ever seen it – which, during some heated and dangerous board meetings, schemes and takeover bids of their own, had been pretty blank. 'Your resignation wouldn't do me a damned bit of good, Ralph. What I need now is your help.'

'You have it, you know that.'

'Right. I want to know who and exactly how.'

'The how is being worked on right now. The who . . .'

'You have the phone number of this Fielding man?'

Ralph smiled. It had been good thinking on his part to second-guess the request. At least he didn't come out looking like a total idiot. 'Right here.'

Dominic took the paper from him and got through to the overseas operator. Within minutes he was connected. 'Hello? I'd like to speak to Ben Fielding, please. No, it's important I speak to him personally.' As Ralph listened to his bland and pleasant voice cajoling his way through barriers of secretaries, he could only admire Dominic's ability to hide his real feelings. He didn't doubt that the loss of the Princess Liliha chain meant more to him than just a business loss. It must have cut deep – very deep.

'Hello, Mr Fielding?'

In his office, Ben held the phone in one hand whilst he looked thoughtfully at a small black Turkish cheroot in the other. 'Who is this, please?'

'Dominic Fairchild. I'm calling from Honolulu.'

Ben blew out grey smoke slowly. 'Ah, yes. Dominic Fairchild – of Fairchild Enterprises, I believe? We have heard of you.'

Dominic felt his teeth grate and walked to a chair, slowly sitting down. 'I'm so thrilled. I'm calling in connection with three companies that are, I believe, part of the Fielding stable?'

46

Ben's teeth bit into his cigar at the insolence, almost chomping it in two, and then he forced himself to relax, taking another long drag of smoke as he listened to Dominic listing them. 'I'm sorry, Mr Fairchild, but those companies are no longer my property. They were sold not long ago.'

'To which company?'

'Oh, not to a company. An individual – a close personal friend of mine.'

'Who is?'

'I'm afraid I can't tell you that. It's protected information, as I'm sure you understand.'

'Oh yes. And you must understand that I have my own sources of information. It'll only take a phone call from me to discover his identity.'

Ben smiled, suddenly enjoying himself enormously. Over the years he'd become so successful that he'd forgotten the thrill of battle. 'You seem to be under some misapprehension, Mr Childish. The new owner of the Princess Liliha boutiques is not in hiding. In fact, I have it on the best of authority that the owner of the Grant Corporation will shortly be arriving in Honolulu to take personal care of your few little shops.'

Very slowly, and with extreme care, Dominic hung up.

'Well?' Rhiannon asked, looking at Ben's smiling face. 'How did he sound?'

'Extremely miffed.'

'Ben!'

'I think he was contemplating murder. Mine, but yours first, I think.'

Her smile faltered as a small shiver of fear slid down her spine. Was she strong enough to cope with all this? Her father hadn't been ... Abruptly she sat up, eyes glinting with renewed determination. 'Can I borrow your secretary for a while?' she asked grimly. 'There's a cable I have to send.'

VIENNA looked around the apartment in amazement. The bedroom had a large double bed, plain cream walls, a built-in wardrobe and a brown-speckled beige carpet. There was a spacious living room and a small, functional kitchen and a bathroom. Richard Jago watched her as she walked around the rooms like a cat, cautiously examining a new home. He smiled as she turned to him, her blue eyes wide and delighted. 'It's lovely, Richard. Thank you. And I'll pay you back as soon . . .'

'I keep telling you. There's no need.'

'But it wouldn't feel right.' She walked to sit beside him, feeling tiny and very feminine beside his large frame which was dressed casually in white cotton trousers and a loose navy-blue shirt. 'It's hard to explain but I feel the need to pay my own way. You do understand, don't you?'

Richard nodded. He'd have to play it very carefully. She was a skittish creature. So far he was the only person she really knew or trusted, and her natural fear of the outside world would keep her close, but underneath that lovely exterior he'd already begun to see signs of a toughness, an independence of nature that would soon start to rally. 'OK. You can start by cooking me lunch. I'm starving.'

His apartment was even more luxurious than hers. On the next floor up, it faced the beach and the kitchen partly divided into a dining room. She'd noticed two bedroom doors and she was grateful and strangely touched that he had not suggested she move in with him. Not that she might not want to, but she couldn't remember ever having been with a man before. Was she prepared to live with someone, to be lover as well as friend?

As she watched him collect perishables from the fridge to make a salad she admitted to herself that he was certainly handsome enough. And kind and generous and helpful. She literally didn't know what she would have done without him over the past few weeks. And yet something warned her to be cautious, overriding her vague sexual needs and her thirsting desire to anchor herself firmly into the role of a woman who was loved and needed. That was the worst part of not knowing yourself or your past. You didn't feel complete. And Richard was offering her that. He wanted her – she could tell by the expression in his eyes whenever he looked down at her from that great height of his. And she was tempted. The city had frightened her – its size, its hungry bustle, its cruel impersonality . . .

48

Turning, Richard saw her expression and walked quickly over to her. Taking her small pointed chin in his hand he stared down solemnly into her wide, frightened blue eyes. 'You'll always have me,' he murmured softly, then bent his head quickly and kissed her before she could react.

Vienna found herself humming a tune as she prepared shoulder of boned lamb and mixed a stuffing of grapefruit, breadcrumbs, chopped parsley, sultanas and beaten egg. Simply to be out of a sterile environment and in a man's flat cooking him dinner was like a salve to a gaping wound, and as he set the table, his face absorbed with the task of uncorking some red wine, she felt a stab of tenderness grip her. 'Richard, I ...' She hesitated as he looked up, then smiled into his watchful eyes. 'I'm glad you're here.'

An hour or so later they sat back, stomachs replete. 'Well,' Richard sighed, sipping the last of his wine. 'Now we know you can cook.'

Vienna paled, the innocent words sparking off a sudden fear inside her. 'I never thought, until you just said ... Richard, are you married?' she blurted out.

'Do you think I'd bring you here if I were?'

'No,' she blushed, wondering if she'd offended him. 'I mean it's just that you're such a catch ...'

'I'm flattered. But I've never been married. To begin with I was just too busy. My family wasn't rich by any means and during Med. School I had to work. Then, after I'd qualified ...' He shrugged. 'I've never met the right woman, I suppose,' his voice lowered an octave, 'until now, maybe.'

She caught her breath at the obvious hint, then sighed. If he could be so honest and brave about it then she could do nothing less and this time she ignored the warning signals that clanged like far away alarm bells in her head. 'Now I'm flattered.'

Richard knew better than to rush it. 'Well, I think it's time we did something about filling that empty wardrobe of yours. You can't go about in those all day – in this hot climate you'll soon begin to attract flies.'

Vienna threw the wet dishcloth at him but he ducked expertly. Even so, the thought of shopping was a little daunting and she told herself not to be such a rabbit. But why did she feel so vulnerable out there? As if . . . as if somebody was out to get her? Even on the drive from the hospital she'd been nervous, wondering who was watching her, waiting. Still, the therapist had warned her to expect some paranoia.

'OK. But only a few dresses and some underwear.'

They took the car back down the strip, Vienna looking out on to the crowded beach as they passed. Waikiki – yes, she'd heard of it, she was sure. But had she ever been here before? Did she live here or was she a tourist? A tourist of little means, apparently, if her disappearance could go so unnoticed. Richard parked the car and she walked nervously around the bonnet to his side, afraid of being separated from him and getting lost in the crowd.

'It's OK,' he said softly, taking her small hand in his. 'I won't let you out of my sight.'

It was meant to reassure her, she knew, so why did she interpret it as a threat? She was getting silly. She needed Richard, didn't she? He was her anchor in the stormy, unknown seas. If she began to doubt him she might as well just give in. Abruptly she stretched on tiptoe and kissed him. His hands tightened fractionally on her small waist, then, as she drew back, he let her go. Only his eyes continued to glitter, steel-grey in the sunlight.

He took her past the Liberty House stores that dotted the island liberally and on to a Princess Liliha boutique where she fell in love with two dresses – one a dusty-rose wrapover dress that fastened at the waist with a cleverly designed butterfly of a lightweight silver metal, the second a simple navy-blue silk that was sleeveless and deeply V-necked. Richard insisted she choose several skirts and blouses and, although the things were all lovely and oozed that understated pedigree of class, the discreet price tags worried her. The bikini she chose was a modest one in stripes of red, gold and white; this was the only item she did not model for him. Shopping finished, they walked to the car and then made their way to a table on the terrace of a small, beachside café.

'What would you like?'

The simple question made her world darken again. 'I don't

know. I don't know what I like or don't like.' And she would do something about that soon. The moment that she got her bearings and at least a semblance of equilibrium.

Richard smiled and squeezed her hand. 'Try a piña colada.' He ordered the two drinks, watching her as she scrutinized a small portion of the most famous beach in the world. Richard was used to playing the courting game – knew how to seduce the most uninterested of women. He also knew how to excite and please bored women, those who thought they'd seen it all. He knew himself to be a man of great sexual appetite, a man who liked women who knew how to please him and knew what *they* wanted – and so far his life had been full of them. But the more time he spent with Vienna, the more sure he was: she was THE one. And that knowledge both thrilled and terrified him.

Vienna's eyes widened as the drink was put in front of her. Served in a half-coconut with the fruit still inside lending a delicious fresh flavour to the alcohol, it was a complete surprise, and floating on top of the rum, pineapple juice and coconut cream, was a bright scarlet flower.

'It's supposed to make it Hawaiian,' he said drolly. She laughed, feeling, quite literally for the first time that she could remember, happy to be alive, and Richard caught his breath. In spite of what her gynaecological tests had revealed, he wanted her badly.

When he reached for her hand she did not pull away, and Richard hid his triumph behind a gentle gaze. 'You must start learning to live for the here and now, you know. Your memory might be gone, but everything else is still there, Vienna. Your personality, your talents, your quirks, even your bad points.'

And although Vienna laughed, his words stayed in her mind.

'IT'S still early,' he said, after they'd driven home and she'd put away her packages. 'Why don't we cruise around for a bit of sightseeing?'

'Lovely. I'll have a shower and change and then come up in half an hour. I can hardly believe I've only been out of the hospital for a day. It seems longer, but I'm still hungry for more!'

True to his word, Richard gave her a knowledgeable tour of Honolulu and the nearby sights, keeping up a running commentary on such landmarks as the Iolani Palace and the Aloha Tower which had at one time been the tallest building in Honolulu. With the city finally left behind, he drove along Route 61, showing her the Punchbowl, an area that had once been used as the site of human sacrifice.

As the sun gradually began to redden he turned north, driving along the east coast past Kaneohe Bay where his yacht was moored. Ten minutes later the road petered out to a dirt track and he parked on a grassy knoll overlooking the ocean. The sun was still fairly high in the sky, but thick, ominous clouds were gathering as they looked out over a small cliff towards the sea. Vienna felt the soft breeze on her face and breathed deeply of air smelling of clean sea and flowers. 'What a lovely smell.'

'It's the orange blossom. Some eccentric in the 1930s went out and planted all kinds of flowers out here in the wilds. The orange blossom survived.'

'That's lovely!'

'There are villages all around here – it's not so commercial once you get past Kaneohe. Do you want to walk on the beach?'

'Can we get down there?'

'Easily – there's a sandy trail over there. Take off your shoes and leave them here – they'll only fill with sand if you don't,' he advised as he slipped off his own leather loafers. She sighed blissfully as they walked on the beach, the gentle outgoing tide lapping under their feet and tugging away the sand. The sun was obliterated by black clouds now but the night stayed balmy. 'Look, there's a boat on the beach,' she said, pointing further along the sand.

Richard corrected her. 'Canoe – see how it's raised upwards to a point at both ends? It's a big one – a six-seater at least. It probably belongs to a local fisherman. They just pull them up the beach above the tidemark and leave them. Uh-oh,' he added, as a rumble rolled out from across the sea. 'I think we're going to get wet!' The first huge drops splattered on to their heads. 'Quick – let's run for the boat. You can help me turn it over. We'll shelter beneath it.'

'You're a regular Boy Scout, I can tell,' Vienna yelled as she took one end and helped him roll the boat so that its bottom faced the sky.

'Come on, in you get.' Richard helped her scramble under the side, the pointed bow and stern raising the boat just enough for them to squeeze beneath it. Inside, the sand was warm on their backs and the sound of the rain splattering on the roof made Vienna feel snugly sheltered. For a few moments they lay close together without talking but then Richard moved to a more comfortable position and his fingers brushed her ribs. Vienna caught her breath, wondering how such a simple and innocent touch could send her pulse-rate rising. Richard turned on his side and looked down at her.

'I want you.'

'I know.' Her voice was little more than a whisper. His words sent a deep thrill shooting through her, a thrill that felt somehow . . . alien.

'Do you want me?'

'Yes,' she whispered, her eyes closing as his head lowered to hers, her lips parting as he kissed her. His free hand cupped her jaw and then slid down her throat, and his fingers were the nimble fingers of a surgeon as he undid the tiny buttons of her blouse and slipped his hand through the parted material to gently glide across her breasts. Vienna gasped and arched as he gently placed his palm over her nipple and stroked in a circular motion. 'Richard,' she moaned, awe in her voice. It felt so new, so . . . wonderful.

'Ssh . . . I know.' He kissed her again, his hand straying to give the same treatment to her other breast before he awkwardly disposed of his shirt in the cramped confines of the upside down boat. Outside, thunder growled and they could both feel lightning crackle all about them as Richard moved to kneel over her, his legs straddling her hips as he leaned forward and slowly pushed aside her blouse and lowered his mouth to her breast, licking its contours in a slow, teasing exploration until she moaned, running her fingers through his hair and forcing his mouth on to her nipple. The sensation made her cry out, her arms stretching wide either side of her head, fingers digging into the sand. Richard clumsily unzipped his trousers and wriggled out of them, at the same time sliding down her body, his tongue dipping into her navel, smiling with satisfaction as her legs jerked in instant reaction. She raised her hips in silent cooperation as he tugged down her skirt and panties, making her tremble with the sensation of being wide open and vulnerable. She felt his warm hands caressing her calves whilst his lips moved to the inside of her thighs. She moaned, opening her eyes to look at him looming over her.

Her fingers dug into his back as he carefully parted her thighs and probed into the hot and ready place he found there. Suddenly he remembered the results of her gynaecological tests, and he hesitated. Then she gasped and arched her back, and he forgot everything but the passion of the moment. His expertise was so great that although his shaft filled her, the pain as her inner muscles stretched to accommodate his huge size was soon overtaken and forgotten in the overriding sensationalism of his lovemaking.

Richard closed his eyes as her warm tightness slowly sucked him in, and began to stroke inside her, a fierce surge of elation gripping him when her legs locked around him, holding him willing captive between her thighs. Vienna moaned as their rhythm quickened, pushing her higher and further, and began to buck beneath him as the climax was suddenly upon her, exploding in her womb, stretching upwards and outwards. Her scream of satiation was loud in his ears, making his own climax spill from him in a hot rush. Afterwards, as their bodies cooled, she became aware of his weight upon her and smiled in satisfaction. She felt whole now, for she knew if nothing else that she was a woman. Richard stirred and moved away, leaving her suddenly cold. And with the cold came back the doubts. 'Richard, what we've just done . . .'

'Was wonderful, wasn't it?'

'Yes. But you don't even know who I am.'

Richard rolled on to his side and ran an idle finger over her breast, his eyes following the movement in the fast-fading light. 'I may not know who you are,' he admitted softly. 'But I know what you are.'

Vienna tensed, the thunder outside suddenly sounding frightening rather than exciting. 'What?'

'*Mine.*'

TEN days later, Farron paused in the act of lifting the microphone from the stand, totally forgetting the words of the song as he saw the new waitress for the first time, weaving in and out of the empty tables with a grace that took his breath away. Luckily it was only a rehearsal. 'Sorry, you guys. I lost concentration there. What say we take a break?' Even before he'd finished speaking he was leaving the stage, landing with a light thump on the restaurant floor and nearly overbalancing. Windmilling his arms to keep his balance he felt his wrist connect with a tray and heard a dismayed gasp, followed by an ominous crash.

Vienna stared down at the empty but broken coffee cups on the floor, then looked up at the figure that had fallen out of the sky in front of her like a clumsy angel. Farron groaned, then grinned.

'Sorry about that. I'm not usually such a klutz. Well, actually I am,' he laughed, then thrust out a hand. 'Farron Manikuuna.'

Kim looked down from the stage, shaking his head at his friend's recklessness then noticed a large man moving quickly across the floor, his eyes fixed on Farron and looking ready to kill.

Still dazed by the onslaught of his laughing chocolate-brown eyes, Vienna felt a bit flustered. She found herself offering her hand, which was quickly swamped by his strong brown fingers. 'Don't worry about these.' Farron knelt at her feet and began to gather together the broken shards. 'I'll tell the Oriental Wonder it was all my fault. He'll believe it. I'm always breaking things.'

Not knowing whether to laugh at his irreverent reference to Ling or blush at his position at her feet, Vienna did neither, and as Farron, last piece of crockery in his hand, looked up,

55

their eyes locked. She felt the firm ground beneath her feet change into quicksand, and took a hasty step backwards, colliding with solid muscle.

'Hello, darling.' Richard slipped a hand around her waist and Vienna almost screamed in surprise. Half-turning, she met his hard grey eyes and felt strangely guilty, as if she'd somehow betrayed him. She smiled shakily.

'Richard! I didn't know you were coming to meet me.' She saw him lower his head and knew he meant to kiss her, and for one awful second she wanted to turn away. She quelled the reaction at once, but was very much aware of Farron Manikuuna watching him, his melting chocolate eyes darkening and dulling to black.

Raising his head, Richard stared at Farron coolly. 'You're the boy who sings for his supper, aren't you?' He smiled his most charming smile, intending it to confuse the younger man.

It didn't. Farron met the grey gaze without flinching. 'Actually I sing for more than a hundred bucks an hour.'

UPSTAIRS, Dominic nodded to his secretary and walked through his office and into the lounge of his living quarters. It was very much a traditional room, with colourful local tapestries on two of the walls and several Gaugin paintings on the others. The wood furniture was solid and comfortable, and huge windows looked out over the beach. Long velvet curtains of the darkest green matched the carpet and cushions thrown on to chairs and sofas.

Dominic sighed as he drew from a Hepplewhite writing desk the final document that had been delivered yesterday, confirming that the Liliha Boutique chain now officially belonged to the Grant Corporation. He hesitated as he looked down into the open drawer, his eyes falling on to the cable. He didn't need to read it to know what it said since every word was now ingrained in his memory.

WILL BE SELLING ALL CURRENT LILIHA STOCK, STOP. HAVING NO DESIRE TO USE BOUTIQUE SITES IN YOUR HOTELS, WILL BE SENDING REMOVAL MEN TO ALL HOTELS TO COLLECT SAID STOCK, STOP. WILL BE CHANGING NAME, BUT RETAINING

OWNERSHIP RIGHTS TO PRINCESS LILIHA NAME. STOP. END OF MESSAGE. It was unsigned.

At first Dominic's anger over the last sentence in particular had made him overlook the glaringly unprofessional tone of the missive. It had taken a less emotionally involved Philip Pearce to cut through the red fog of fury and point to the strangely personal nature of the message, which indicated that it was not at all the cold-blooded business deal they had all assumed it to be.

'So, who hates you to this extent, Dom?' Phil asked, and there Dominic was stumped. He had his fair share of disgruntled business rivals, of course – but none who hated him personally. He had never gone out of his way to boast in public of his triumphs over others, knowing that sooner or later he'd have to deal with them again.

'Whoever it is knows how much the name means to me,' Dominic stated, looking at that last sentence again. 'They don't want to use it themselves, but are making damned sure I can't restart and use the name again.'

'Makes sense financially,' Phil commented. 'After all, the name is famous throughout the islands.'

'No, I don't think that's it,' Dominic disagreed. 'Why are they selling the stock? It doesn't make sense. Whoever it is wants to change the whole character of the boutique, wipe out all it stands for, wipe out all traces of me from the way it's run, or looks. And financially, that's suicide. Left alone, the boutiques would continue to rake it in.'

'So I repeat,' Phil had said. 'Who hates you that much?'

Now Dominic crumpled up the offending telegram and threw it back into the desk along with the document whose dry legal wording had confirmed that next to his hotels he'd lost that which was most precious to him. Walking to the window he shoved his hands in his pockets and stared blindly out. According to the English ass on the telephone last week he'd soon be finding out who it was who hated him so much.

Dominic smiled wrily and slowly shook his head. Whoever it was had caught him napping once, but would never do so again. He'd spent years acquiring a bag of tricks to foil the most persistent of business rivals, and he hadn't lived this long without learning how to spring a surprise or two of his own. From now on the fight wasn't going to be so one-sided – as the mysterious owner of the Grant Corporation was about to discover!

Chapter 6

The grey Persian cat yawned, orange eyes watching the hall for signs of activity and, as a young girl dressed only in cami knickers and a seethrough slip collected the papers and mail from the floor, it padded down the scarlet-carpeted stairs and followed her through a narrow hallway into a large lounge where five other girls sat on mock French Regency-style furniture. Leaping lithely on to the warm and comfortable lap, the cat purred contentedly.

'Not this time, Madam Meow. Go on – go and say hello to someone else.' Chi-Chi, a tall Japanese art student with a burning ambition to paint a twentieth-century masterpiece, used gentle hands to evict the cat, which landed lightly on the carpet, grey tail flickering angrily at the undignified treatment. But Jo-Jo, a small redhead with large pansy-blue eyes called invitingly to the animal, making a sucking squeak with her lips.

The lounge was a curious mixture of homey atmosphere and suggestive allure, decorated throughout with a theatrical hand. Walls lined with red and gold flocked velvet were adorned with prints of chic-looking women from the 1920s era. Over an ornate fireplace hung a reclining nude with enormous thighs and breasts, and a smug come-hither-and-be-pulverized look. The ceiling was low, and cheap but effective chandeliers hung in both the hallway and lounge. On the table were magazines covering a whole range of subjects, none of them pornographic. Gloria Gaines, the owner of the 'The Glorious Motel' did not believe in cheap smut, a fact that her clients found both unusual and oddly comforting. Just then Gloria herself walked through a concealed door and looked around. 'Hi, girls.'

'Ouch!' Jo-Jo winced as the cat dug claws into her thigh and pumped gently. 'Madam Meow, cut that out,' she scolded, scowling into the cat's innocent eyes.

'Madam Meow!' the new girl echoed nervously. 'What sort of a name is that for a cat?'

Pammy, a tall and quiet brunette suddenly looked up from the papers. 'That's a long story. Right, Gloria?'

'Damned right it is,' Gloria agreed, snitching the last paper from the coffee table and rattling it into position, her blue eyes scanning the headlines quickly and efficiently. The new girl watched her cautiously. She might only be five feet four but her reputation was enormous. Although in her mid-forties, Gloria's face, framed by naturally blonde hair, was made up perfectly, wrinkles and sags kept at bay with facial exercises. She wore a simple but flattering lilac skirt and jacket with a toning pinky-cream blouse. A strand of pearls that could have been either fake or real hung discreetly around her neck and the scent of Opium wafted gently from her as she moved. She didn't look like a particularly tough cookie, but the new girl was too wise to be fooled by appearances any more. Gloria was THE madam on the islands, the woman the pimps on the streets never messed with. Frank Gillespie, her closest friend and one-time lover, was a powerful and persuasive ally and everyone knew that he and Gloria went way, way back.

'Yeah. Er . . . do we get afternoons off?' the new girl asked gingerly.

'Sure,' Pammy said, pilfering a pen from Gloria's handbag and beginning the crossword puzzle. 'Be back at six, though.'

The new girl nodded – she'd had only five johns last night but the pay was good. It sure beat working the streets. She counted herself lucky that she'd run into one of Gloria's scouts on Hotel Street where she'd been checking out the lie of the land before finding herself a pimp. 'I'll be off, then.' Having just got in three days ago she was eager to do some exploring. She'd already seen for herself the varieties of nationalities the islands supported – Portuguese, Chinese, Puerto Ricans, Japanese and Koreans. And last night, two of her johns had been Filipinos. It made her anxious to see how their influences mixed and merged with the typical American society of Macdonalds and baseball.

'Where's Ann?' Gloria asked, knowing which girls had no one to go home to and usually hung around in the afternoons, and which ones took off first thing in the morning to get their kids off to school and prepare a husband's breakfast.

'She's upstairs with Rambo,' Chi-Chi said, yawning and checking her watch. She had an art class at twelve-thirty.

'He still here?' Gloria asked, checking her slender silver watch. 'Trust a bloody cop – hasn't he got anything better to do? No wonder the crime rate's going sky high.' Gloria, like most businesswomen, knew that her livelihood depended on bribes and backhanders. Hawaii was run, politically, just like any other big state – and local politicians had to be kept sweet at all times, especially the mayor and the Chief of Police. Only Dominic Fairchild, a member of three of the most important committees – Health, Tourism and Environment – was exempt from Gloria's 'Backhander' file. His title, unique in an American citizen, gave him a certain amount of political power by right, and over the years his work on charities especially had made him a man to be watched. If he ever ran for Governor, Gloria knew, there would be more than a few sweaty palms in City Hall. But he was also a good friend of hers, and friends didn't need to be paid. At least, Gloria's friends didn't.

A doorbell began to peal the first line of *Big Spender*, and Gloria quickly walked down the narrow hall and looked through the spyhole. 'Frank!' she cried, opening the door, her smile wide and sweet as she ushered him in and gave him a quick peck on the cheek. Frank Gillespie, casino owner and unofficial moneylender, gave her hair an affectionate ruffle then followed her through the lounge and on into her office.

'Afternoon, ladies.' He waved a jaunty hand to them as they walked through, and the girls responded with varying degrees of interest. Gloria's office was as different from the rest of the fussy, larger-than-life motel as it was possible to get. The walls were painted a clear matt white and were totally devoid of any ornamentation. The carpet was black, as were the business-like chairs. The single window was spotlessly clean and open, allowing a cooling breeze to infiltrate the room. A dark green filing cabinet inhabited one corner beside her desk whilst a giant prayer plant stood in the other. There was no computer because she didn't trust them. Besides, with a business brain worthy of many an international executive, she didn't need one. Every aspect of her business was firmly recorded in her memory.

'Coffee, Frank?'

'Not just now, thanks,' Frank declined, sitting his five-feet-ten-inch frame easily into the swivel chair in front of her desk, sweating slightly. In summer the temperature on the islands soared to the ninety degree mark during the day, then dropped to around seventy at night. Women could add or take off clothes much more easily than men, but Frank, as ever, looked immaculate, At fifty-two, his hair was that iron-grey that was most attractive in men, his face lean and tanned from years spent in the tropical sun. His eyes were halfway between blue and grey, his cleancut face pleasant and yet with that hint of predatory power in it that belied his benign businesslike image.

Gloria unlocked the drawer of her desk and withdrew an envelope which contained five hundred dollars and handed it over. She had come to this arrangment with him many years ago when she had 'inherited' the business from Madam Bernice when they still conducted their business from a sleazy hotel a couple of blocks away. It was a bargain that Gloria was glad to honour. For a small percentage of her profits not only did Frank recommend to his gambling customers the merits of The Glorious Motel, but he also kept foraging pimps and troublemaking johns away. To begin with Frank had done the service for free, as a favour to his lady, but since the 1960s had given way to the commercial 1970s, and they had slowly drifted into becoming mere friends and no longer even occasional lovers, Gloria had insisted things be put on a firm business footing. She was too fond of Frank and too much aware of his importance to her business to let the want of a firm financial understanding get in their way and cause any friction. Frank took the envelope from her and slipped it into his pocket, not bothering to count it.

'You OK?' he asked, lighting a cigarette and narrowing his eyes to look at her through the haze. 'Last time I was here you were still as jumpy and nervous as hell.'

Gloria shrugged, but her heart began to thud uncomfortably in her chest. 'I'm fine. I just don't like my girls getting attacked by psychos in back alleys, that's all.'

Frank grunted. He knew by now that Gloria was very protective of her girls and sometimes wondered if she wasn't indulging her frustrated maternal instincts. 'Look – relax, will you,' he told her. 'You know damned well you won't be having any trouble from that madman again.'

Gloria smiled wanly and leaned back in her chair. 'I don't believe I ever did properly thank you for helping me out of that mess, Frank.'

He waved the cigarette in a dismissive gesture. 'Forget it. Any time you need a favour you know who to call. How is the girl, by the way?'

Gloria's eyes flickered but it was so slight a betrayal that Frank didn't notice. 'She's going to live,' she said abruptly.

'Never doubted it. Stop worrying, will you? It's been weeks and there's no sign of trouble – not from the law or the girl. I'd better get going. I heard rumours from one of my regulars yesterday about a crap game operating at the strip joint on the corner. Heard anything?'

Gloria shook her head. 'No, but I'll tell the girls to keep their ears open.'

'Thanks. I've got a feeling that Brian Chin is behind it. I can see that reasonable persuasion isn't going to work.'

Gloria smiled. Frank might fool the others with his mean mask, but he and she had grown up together back in the Bronx, and she knew him too well to be fooled. He might get rough when he had to but he didn't like it. He didn't enjoy it – not like some of the sadistic bastards she'd known. 'Frank,' she said softly. 'Don't forget your anniversary tomorrow.'

'Oh shit! Sheena will kill me if I don't get her anything.'

Sheena, his wife of the last twelve years and the apple of his eye, was one of those women whom everybody liked. A wife, mother, housekeeper, local charity worker, babysitter and handyperson, she was a little dynamo with short brown hair, laughing brown eyes and the body of a teenager that not even giving birth to a son had changed. She was also, with very good reason, totally confident of Frank's love and loyalty which had allowed her and Gloria to become the best of friends over the years.

'Thanks for reminding me, Glory.' Frank blew her a kiss and left.

Gloria stood at the window feeling strangely depressed. She knew why, and knew she had to snap out of it. Even the girls were beginning to notice a change in her. They knew about the trouble a few weeks ago, of course, but it was more than that. Much more. Still, as Frank had said, so far it was all quiet. Gloria could only hope that it stayed that way – for all their sakes . . .

THE new girl was gone when she returned to the lounge. Ann was back down, snoozing on the sofa, her long legs draped over the end.

'How's the new girl seem to you?' Gloria asked them, having made it her policy a long time ago to consult her regulars in certain areas of the business. Girls who were listened to made for happy workers. It was many years since she had worked as one of Madam Bernice's girls herself, but she had not forgotten the fear of getting stuck with a pervert, nor had she ever forgotten the times when she had been slapped around by a drunken john.

'I think she's all right. She's still a little cautious, you know? I don't know about the others but I get the feeling that she hasn't had much luck lately. You know, in her personal life?' Chi-Chi commented, already feeling depressed. She supposed it was her artistic temperament that made her so sensitive to other people's moods.

'Yeah,' Tani agreed, looking away from the TV as the commercials came on, interrupting yet another cliff-hanging scene from a daytime soap. 'I get the feeling she's so used to life dumping on her that she can't quite believe the setup here. It's like she's looking around for the catch.'

'Can't blame her for that,' Pammy said, struggling with the last three clues of the crossword. 'When I first came here I couldn't believe it was all so straight and above board, either. I kept wondering who it was I should be paying off.'

'It was the medical plan that Gloria had set up for us that really threw me,' Jo-Jo said sleepily, and then blinked as the cat on her lap snored loudly.

Gloria picked up the paper again and settled into a chair. Her eyes strayed vacantly to the TV where a woman was holding on to a baby and crying prettily into the camera. 'No – you can't have him, Tony. He's my baby.' The actor was a dark Italian type, the girl a candy-floss creation who would normally have made Gloria laugh with scorn. But the scene, unrealistic Hollywood soap though it was, nevertheless cut deep and Gloria felt her muscles tighten as the actor reached for what was obviously a lifeless doll and pulled it from her arms. 'You know I can give him a better life, Marilou. I can give him all the good things in life – status, money . . .'

'You can't give him a mother's love, Tony.'

'I can't marry you, Marilou, you know that. But Pa will let me keep him – after all, he is his grandson . . .'

Gloria wanted to get up and turn it off, but now all four girls were watching so she left them to it, going to the kitchen where Nancy was busy preparing tea.

Nancy was sixty-nine. She had been Madam Bernice's oldest and least profitable girl and was on the verge of being thrown on to the streets when the old madam had suffered her heart attack. Now she worked quite happily as Gloria's private housekeeper, cook, maid and masseuse. It had been Nancy who had tended her cuts and grazes when a john had left her bloody and bruised, and it was Nancy who had told her where the deceased Bernice had kept her 'insurance' – books with names and dates and even black-and-white photos of the most distinguished, powerful and rich of their johns. This had enabled Gloria to hold on to the business that she had built up into what it was today.

'What's for tea, Nance?' she asked, business demanding that they eat their main meal on or around five o'clock in the afternoon.

'Beef stew,' Nancy said shortly, kneeling awkwardly on the kitchen formica surface near the sink to give the windows a hearty clean. 'What's the matter with you?'

Gloria, used to her uncanny ability to read people, shrugged. 'Just some stupid soap on telly.'

'Some actress in twelve-inch heels and false eyelashes doing an imitation of a mother giving up her kid, was it?' Nancy guessed with cruel accuracy.

Gloria plugged in the kettle and spooned instant decaff into a cup. 'Yeah.'

'You should have been over that long ago,' Nancy said without sympathy. 'The kid must be grown now. You're probably a grandma.'

'I know. But you can't forget a thing like that, Nance. Be it twenty-five years ago or twenty-five days, it still hurts just as much.'

Nancy harrumphed and gave the window a final swipe then wriggled off the counter, a hand on her aching back. 'You did the right thing though, girl,' she said, having called Gloria nothing but 'girl' since the day she'd first come to work for Madam Bernice. 'A brothel is no place to bring up a kid.'

The kettle whistled and Gloria made a cup of the mint tea that Nancy favoured and handed it over. 'The crèche stays, Nance,' Gloria said firmly, knowing that the old woman was going to badmouth the new crèche on the top floor yet again. 'More and more of my girls are mothers who need extra cash to help with the household expenses. The crèche is always full. Besides . . .'

'You don't want none of your gals to have to give up their kid like you did. Right?' Nancy shook her head, picking up her cup and leaving the room muttering, 'Soft as shit on a hot day. Always knew she was as soft as shit . . .'

Passing her in the hall, Jo-Jo grinned widely as the old woman walked up the first flight of stairs and she was still shaking her head and grinning as she found Gloria in the kitchen. 'What's eating her now? Another war story? According to her you'd think she serviced the whole bloody Navy at Pearl Harbor singlehanded! Hm, something smells good,' she added, nose twitching.

'Nancy's beef stew. Want to eat here?'

'Do you think she'll mind?'

'Undoubtedly,' Gloria said drily, and Jo-Jo grinned, not falling for Nancy's dour attitude, either, though it might take the new girl a while to figure out that Nancy was really just a big softy wearing a careful disguise.

'OK. Johnny was supposed to be taking me out to dinner, but . . .' Jo-Jo shrugged. 'Oh well, I suppose it's for the best. I mean, let's face it – with a name like John, and me in my line of work, it's hardly a match made in heaven, eh?'

Gloria was still smiling over that as she returned to her office. Glancing down at the brass-handled drawer to her left she slowly pulled it open. Lifting up a framed photograph she turned it over slowly, looking at the face behind the heavy, old-fashioned glass. She'd been easy pickings for Bernice – alone, depressed, poor. And she'd been so hellbent on self-destruction, that not even Frank had been able to talk her out of it. Her eyes shimmered with unshed tears as she looked down at the rompersuited baby, no more than four weeks old, lying on the rug. It had been January when they had taken her away – January, the coldest month of the year. So cold . . . And it had rained and rained . . .

'Oh, Pauline,' she said, her finger tracing the tiny outline of the blonde-haired blue-eyed baby with a tenderness that would have surprised some of her customers. 'I'm sorry, baby, but Nance was right – this was no place to bring up a little angel like you. Oh baby, if only you knew how much it hurt me to give you up. I thought I'd die – for a long time I wanted to. If only I'd known how it would turn out.' She took a deep breath and put the photo away, reaching for a tissue in the dispenser on her desk and drying her eyes with a fierce determination that had saved her from sinking all those years ago. Taking out a make-up mirror from her handbag, she checked that her mascara really was water and run-proof, and began writing cheques for the bills.

GLORIA was back in the lounge when Tani came down with George F. Benton, the owner of one of the island's largest chain of launderettes, and she put her paper down, her smiling face polite but bland.

'George – I'm surprised to see you here at this time of the day.'

'Gloria, you look as lovely as ever. Er, what do I owe you for the . . . rent?'

Gloria named the sum, from which she would take fifty per cent. 'Would you like tea, George?'

'No thanks, Gloria. I have work waiting back at the office. Oh, you've heard the latest, I presume? About Dominic Fairchild?'

'No. Tell me.'

'He's lost the Princess Liliha boutique chain.'

'What?' Gloria said sharply. 'You mean it's been taken over?'

'Lock, stock, and evening gown apparently. By some English company – nobody seems to know which.'

'I'll bet he didn't think much of that,' Gloria said softly, genuine sympathy clouding her normally clear blue eyes.

'Absolutely enraged, apparently. Not that you can tell to look at him, of course. Played poker with him once – never again, I can tell you.'

'He's quite an operator,' she admitted diplomatically.

'Yeah. Well, I must go. I have letters to dictate, premises to inspect, and all that.' Gloria doubted that George Benton had ever set foot in one of his launderettes in all his life, but nodded to Tani to show him to the door.

Poor Dominic. It seemed like only yesterday that he had been a lean and hungry eighteen year old, draped over a chair like a gangly but thoroughbred stallion, looking like a handsome, misplaced creature amidst the dirty squalor of Bernice's old place. He'd been waiting for Akaki then, of course. Akaki . . . the Hawaiian prostitute so heartily disliked by all the other girls. But she had been beautiful, with sultry brown eyes, sunkissed warm and perpetually perfumed skin and thick, ripe lips; Dominic had been smitten.

Gloria could remember the first time she'd seen him when he and a few of his friends had come to the sleazy hotel, laughing and drunk and definitely out for female company. Graham Grantham had been the only one reluctant to indulge, but everyone knew that he was obsessed with Jessamine Potana, a pretty girl who was too good for a nonentity like Graham.

Dominic had been the least drunk and the most interested of them all, scanning the place with those expressionless green eyes that had taken Gloria by surprise. She hadn't been surprised though when all the girls had tried to attract his attention. A boy as handsome as he, in a business dominated by fat, middle-aged and unattractive men, was instant material for a cat-fight. Even more so as he was rich. And as for a title!

Akaki had been upstairs with a john, but as Dominic's pals chose their women she appeared on the landing. Her speculative, lovely lying eyes had zeroed in on Dominic like guided missiles. Even now Gloria could remember how her avaricious face had lit up and could still silently applaud the way she'd sashayed down the stairs like an undulating cobra. Dominic visited her regularly after that, but Akaki had not been satisfied with so little. Yet although she soon moved out of the brothel and into a small bungalow Dominic rented for her, he was not blind to her nature nor as hopelessly entangled in her silken but dangerous web as she would have liked.

Gloria shook her head as she heard the telephone ring in her office and hurried to answer it. Picking up the receiver and leaving the past behind her she said 'Hello? Glorious Motel.' It had been Nancy who had jokingly suggested the outlandish, pun-on-words name for the new motel.

'Oh, it's you. Yes, what is it?' she asked bluntly, listening to the voice on the other end, occasionally jotting down the odd piece of information. 'Good. Keep on it. Bye.' She hung up and sighed, running her fingers over her temples and closing her eyes briefly. She could feel a headache coming on and walked through the office and into the kitchen, taking two aspirin and sipping some cool mineral water which she kept stocked in the fridge.

Thinking of Dominic, she couldn't help but wonder what Graham Grantham was doing now. Now there was a man with a lot to answer for. But then the old man, Fred Fairchild, had been equally to blame. Making up her mind, she looked at her watch and wrote a quick note to Nancy, saying she was going to have tea at the Blue Hawaiian and that Jo-Jo was eating in, and propped it against the jar of jasmine resting on the kitchen table.

GLORIA did not often go to the hotel, mindful as she was of Dominic's need for discretion, but as she walked into the cool, breeze-swept loggia she knew that she did not look out of place amongst the Blue Hawaiian's wealthy guests. For a moment she hesitated and then turned left, standing in the doorway of the room, her eyes scanning the waitresses as they catered to the tea trade. After a few minutes, unable to spot her daughter, Gloria turned to the other dining room, her heartbeat accelerating as she once again thought of the risks she was so foolishly taking. Murder was not something to treat cavalierly, and if Frank knew she was here he'd have her strung up. But she knew she would not sleep at nights until she'd seen for herself that Pauline was all right. Besides, she was safe surely? Both the newspapers and the doctors at the hospital said she had amnesia. And as long as she didn't remember, they were all safe.

She took a seat at the back and listened with pleasure to the pianist up on stage gently playing the old classic *Spanish Eyes*. Telling herself she had nothing to worry about or reproach herself with, she cast a quick eye over the menu which stood in the centre of the table.

'Can I help you?'

Gloria jumped, a momentary shudder of shock hitting her as she looked up. Now that they were face to face for only the second time in their adult lives, Gloria felt her blood run cold. Hell, what if she remembered her?

Vienna waited patiently, a little puzzled by the woman's nervous behaviour. 'Are you all right, madam?'

'Yes, yes I'm fine. Never could make up my mind,' Gloria joked, taking a deep and relieved breath that overrode a sharp and savage bite of disappointment. 'I'll have, er, iced tea and oh, let me see – a fresh pineapple sundae.'

At the kitchen door, Vienna stopped and looked back at Gloria, a small frown tugging at her brow. She couldn't be sure, but there was something about that woman . . .

Gloria slumped back in her chair. She had been a fool to come – a fool to give in to that dangerous and totally pointless desire to come and see for herself that the girl was all right. What if the amnesia was only temporary? If she should suddenly remember . . . She flinched then sat up straighter as Vienna returned carrying her order on a silver-plated tray. 'Thank you.' She placed several bills on to the tray. 'Keep the change.'

'Thank you, madam,' Vienna said, a generous tip always a welcome sight even with the decent wages Dominic Fairchild paid. She was determined to repay Richard every cent as soon as she could, especially after what had happened yesterday.

Richard had come down to her flat for breakfast as he always did, letting himself in with the key he'd had duplicated on the day she'd moved in. Handing him almost thirty dollars, she'd smiled and said shyly, 'It's the first repayment. For all that I owe you.' Expecting him to make some light comment, she'd been unprepared for the way his face had darkened, and even less prepared for the quiet savagery of his words.

'*Money?*' he'd hissed, crumpling the bills in his hand. 'You can't repay me with cash! When I was younger and living in 'Frisco, I used to hate the people on Nob Hill with all their millions. Now I've made it . . . me.' He'd thumped his chest with one rigid thumb and opened his mouth to say more, but suddenly he'd seen how shocked she was and the frighteningly intense expression on his face changed into a shaky smile as he ran a hand through his hair and shrugged. 'I'm sorry. Of course you want to be . . . independent.' He stuffed the money into his pocket, but Vienna could tell it was done only reluctantly, and with a sudden flash of insight, knew that he desperately wanted to keep her in his debt.

She cooked breakfast then, but the atmosphere remained tense. This minor incident seemed to crystallize all the misgivings that had been growing in Vienna's mind for some time now. Since their first coming together inside the boat, she had never experienced another orgasm. Not that that worried her, for she knew there was more to any relationship than just sex.

But it was the unhealthy — or what felt like unhealthy — aspects of their relationship that worried her the most. With no memory of past affairs she was not confident of how men and women *should* be together — but surely they should be equals? A healthy partnership should surely leave room for both people to grow, to learn, to develop?

It seemed that Richard wanted to keep Vienna in a golden cage of his making. He hated her talking to other people, even their fellow tenants in the apartment block. He insisted on collecting her mail from the lobby and, although she had no proof, she suspected that he read it. And he made sure he knew her working timetable and phoned her at the flat regularly from work. At first she had been touched, thinking only that he was worried about her being on her own: now, she suspected, he merely wanted to reassure himself of where she was and what she was doing. And that she was alone.

And lately she was beginning to feel the pull of her shackles. Every time Farron Manikuuna looked at her, she could feel the weight of them and she was both annoyed and frightened.

Aware that she was still hovering at the table, Vienna smiled and quickly turned away.

Gloria took in how well the black-and-white uniform suited her daughter's silvery-blonde hair and wide blue eyes. There was no getting away from it – she'd be much better off if she was left alone. Why blight her life when she had the perfect chance to start anew? Squashing the pain her thoughts inflicted, Gloria sipped her tea, outwardly composed.

Vienna pushed all thoughts of Richard from her mind with a feeling treacherously akin to relief. Concentrating instead on her latest customer, she frowned. There was something familiar about the way the woman talked. Something . . .

DOMINIC paused in the restaurant doorway, his eyes spotting the woman at the back. A lazy smile stretched over his lips as he joined her. 'Hello, Gloria. It's been too long.'

'It has,' she agreed. 'I miss our long chats. Why don't you come over one night – the back door is always open to you.'

'I might just do that. It'd be nice to talk about old times.'

'You haven't changed! I heard about the boutiques. It's true?'

'Yeah,' Dominic said, his voice suddenly as cold as ice. 'It's true. So, to what do I and my humble establishment owe the honour of this visit?'

'Humble in a pig's eye,' Gloria said bluntly. 'I just fancied a bit of luxury that's all. And to remind myself what the beach looks like. You stripdwellers take Waikiki for granted. My God, that sand's white and that sea's blue!'

'Come on,' he said, his eyes twinkling. 'I heard tell you've got the most spectacular scenery around.'

Gloria laughed and then noticed how Vienna turned to look at her as she took a neighbouring table's order, and sobered quickly. Sensing her mood, Dominic chatted for a few minutes longer then excused himself.

Farron and the rest of the band walked into the rapidly clearing restaurant and made their way to the bar, waiting to set up for the evening's performance.

'How are the kids down at Gino's coming along?' Kim asked, sipping a beer with thirsty relief.

'They're fine. One or two of them have real talent but the main thing is for them to have fun,' Farron replied vaguely, his eyes instantly finding Vienna and following her movements. Gino's was an unofficial youth club in the poorest area of the city. Gino himself was a local priest who turned his church hall over to several worthy clubs during the week, rent-free. When he'd approached Farron and asked without much hope if he'd like to come down for one day a week and sing for the kids, maybe even give a few guitar lessons, Farron had been glad to do it. It hadn't taken long for the kids to find a special place in his heart, either. Farron's fame, humble beginnings and Hawaiian blood gave him instant street-cred. It was no secret that his mother died a junkie prostitute.

Vienna collected Gloria's dirty crockery. 'Would you like anything else?'

'No, no I don't think so.' Gloria's myriad number of sources told her that Vienna was living with the same doctor who had treated her at the hospital, and she knew she should be glad she was doing so well.

The nagging feeling that said this woman was important to her in some way made Vienna say tentatively, 'Don't I know you from somewhere?'

Gloria felt herself go pale and her heart began to thud in her chest. She shook her head and got to her feet so quickly that she almost knocked over the table. 'NO! No, I don't think so. I would have remembered, I'm sure. Well, I must be going.' She managed to walk quietly across the room, even though every instinct she had urged her to run.

Farron took his chance and lithely slipped across the room whilst Vienna's back was turned. He sat down in Gloria's empty chair and smiled. 'Hi. I saw you talking to the madam and my curiosity got the better of me.'

'Hi. The madam?'

'Sure. She owns the best brothel in town.'

'And how would you know that?' she asked, hands on hips, her eyes dancing with teasing gaiety. It felt so good to be talking at last like normal human beings and not treading warily around one another like nervous cats. Then she went cold. If Gloria was a madam, and Vienna really had recognized her from somewhere, then did that mean that she could be a prostitute? No, surely not. Gloria had denied any past association, and why should she lie?

Farron's jaw fell open at her smart rejoinder and then he too was laughing. 'Rumours – strictly rumours, I swear.' He held out his hands helplessly.

'Oh yes? A likely story.' She turned slightly as she said it and saw Dominic Fairchild looking at them from the bar and her stomach churned in yet another uncomfortable lurch. Vienna smiled grimly to herself. First she suspected herself of prostitution, then the very next minute she'd convinced herself that the boss was about to fire her. Talk about being paranoid!

Farron, following her line of vision, read her thoughts accurately. 'You shouldn't let Dominic's reputation put you off. It's only the people who've tried to stab him in the back and ended up wishing they hadn't that like to talk about him as if he's next in line to Don Corleone! If you're straight with him, then he's straight with you.'

'If you say so,' she said quietly.

'I do,' Farron said firmly, then decided to take the plunge. 'Can I walk you home tonight? My show ends roughly the same time as your shift, and I can see you haven't learned to carry an umbrella yet.'

'Umbrella?'

'Sure. This is Oahu! Sunshine, rain, sunshine, rain. That's how it goes over here. You wouldn't want to get wet now, would you?' he teased.

'No. I . . . my boyfriend is coming to pick me up.'

'Oh yes – the doctor. He picks you up most nights, doesn't he?'

Vienna felt a satisfied and feminine thrill as he cleverly told her he'd been watching and noticing, but at the same time there was an ugly sense of guilt. 'Yes, he's been very good to me. You know who I am?'

'Of course,' he said chidingly, as if she could ever have doubted it.

'Well, he's been taking care of me,' she finished lamely. 'You have no idea of the amount of forms there were to fill in, the hassles, the worries. Dr Jago took care of everything for me. Even a place to live – on my own,' she added hastily, and then wondered why she had wanted to make that so clear. But deep inside she knew why, and she was angry at herself for being too weak and so fickle.

Farron did not contradict her; he didn't have to. She was trying too hard to convince herself. Instead he said quietly, 'Does that make him your keeper?'

Vienna flushed angrily. 'Of course not!' She was not sure why, but the idea of somebody owning her made her break out in a cold sweat.

'Then there's no reason why I can't walk you home tonight, is there?'

Vienna looked helplessly into his gentle brown eyes and surrendered to the inevitable. 'No,' she agreed softly. 'No reason at all.'

Chapter 7

The lobby of the Blue Hawaiian Hotel was lit with soft pink and lavender lights at night and Vienna felt as if she had wandered into a fairy-tale setting. The fountain bubbled attractively, the lilies floating on top had their petals closed against the night and outside she could see the moon above and its reflection on the ocean. She was even waiting for her Prince Charming, a dark-eyed dark-haired man with eyes that melted her and a voice that shivered under her skin, making her heart do wild and wonderful things. And it was all wrong. It was Richard who was her real Prince Charming. He was the doctor who'd healed her body, a friend who'd helped her take her first stumbling steps into the world, and finally a lover who had reintroduced her to the pleasures of physical love.

Farron paused in the doorway, his breath knocked out of him by the sight of her, her hair turned silver by the moonlight as she stood at the window. He was mad – he had to be. Wonderfully, idiotically, determinedly mad.

Vienna tensed and slowly turned around. He was dressed now in simple white cotton slacks and pale green shirt. 'Hi,' she said shyly. 'The show seemed to go well.'

'Thanks. How did you like the new number?'

'I'm sorry, I didn't notice.' She was lying, of course. She noticed everything about him, and only wished that she could stop. She was beginning to feel as if, between them, Richard and Farron would pull her in two.

Farron nodded, not fooled and not hurt. 'So, whereabouts do you live?' She told him and he gave a low whistle. 'Not bad. Not bad at all.'

'Richard has been very generous,' she agreed firmly, then added for good measure, 'I owe him a lot.'

He took her arm and led her through the doors and on to the wide porchway, trying to hide his jealousy. He could understand her feelings of loyalty to the man who must have seemed like a saviour to her, but at the same time a nasty little voice wouldn't stop asking him if she'd still feel the same way if the good doctor weren't quite so wealthy, or quite so good-looking.

Over recent years, and especially since his career had begun to take off and interviews for magazines had become almost commonplace, Farron had had his fair share of lovers. But his first, a girl he'd been at school with, still lived on the island with her husband and two kids and they remained friends. It was only the 'groupies' that he remembered with something akin to shame. At twenty-two it had seemed like a dream come true to have his pick of lovely girls. A night here, a week there, revelling in sun, sea and sex. It had taken him a while to understand that the girls didn't care for the man, only the image. And it had taken slightly longer for him to understand that he didn't have to accept all the invitations that came his way to prove that he was a man. Over the last three years there had only been two women in his life – his *tutu* and a courier with a travel agency. The courier had left for a permanent job Stateside just over a year ago, and since then there had been no one. Thinking back, Farron knew that he'd never been 'in love' in his life. Never before had he felt this instant, deep-core feeling of something being so right. Of one woman fitting into his life and personality like the second half of a whole that he hadn't even suspected had been incomplete before. Of one woman fulfilling every dream, every want, every need. And never before had he taken a woman away from another man . . .

Aware that the silence was stretching both her nerves and his, he smiled and shrugged. 'Well, it's too far to walk, that's for sure. At least it is after you've spent four hours on stage! Hang about and I'll fetch my car.'

'OK.' She watched him go, telling herself she was crazy to complicate her life even more. Taking a deep breath she walked down the wide white marble steps and on to the path that meandered through gardens redolent of wild ginger and fragrant orchids. The large leaves of an Australian import, the umbrella tree, looked like waxy expanses of silver-tipped greenery in the moonlight and she could hear the burbling of water. A stream trickled through the garden and cascaded into a rockpool where large clusters of orchids grew in colourful profusion and tiny goldfish darted in and out of succulent trailing roots. She wanted to be free of guilt. Right now Richard needed to be at the hospital doing vital humanitarian work, or else he would have been waiting to take her home. And here she was loitering, hoping Farron Manikuuna would come after her, find her, kiss her, tell her . . . She left the pool and quickly walked through the gates on to the sidewalk. Looking left and then right, exasperated that there was no taxi in sight, she turned in the direction of her flat and began to walk briskly.

The man in the red Beetle Volkswagen lit a cigarette and watched her. He was a heavyset man who packed his five-feet-ten-inch frame with a lot of power. His hair was a muddy brown and the eyes that observed her were small and brown and deeply-set. He squinted through the smoke from his cigarette as he leaned forward and started the engine which spluttered into noisy life. The girl was a pretty little thing who got prettier every time he saw her. He sneered, a snake-like expression that barely altered his features, and slipped the car into gear, his foot hovering over the accelerator just as another car pulled out of the hotel driveway. It was a convertible sports car and the Beetle driver recognized the driver.

The man nodded knowingly. Now wasn't that interesting?

Farron told himself to be cool and careful as he slowed down to drive alongside her. 'I didn't think it took me that long to get the car,' he admonished, and Vienna felt herself yearning for him with a dangerous potency. It was one thing to be sexually attracted, but a totally different thing to find herself admiring him, the strength of his personality and character.

'I'm looking for a taxi,' she said shortly.

'Why? Are you afraid of me, Vienna? Or is it something else you're afraid of?'

Vienna stopped dead and looked at him and Farron rammed on the brakes, causing a car coming up behind him to honk on the horn in anger. He leaned across and opened the door, meeting her eyes with a level expression that flipped her heart in her breast. For just a moment she hesitated, telling herself she could resist the pull between them if she really needed to, then slipped onto the passenger seat. He glanced in the mirror but only a decrepit red Beetle chugged up the centre lane, and with a powerful surge the car pulled away, the wind cool and pleasant on their faces.

'It's a lovely night,' she said nervously, suddenly afraid of the silence.

'Moonlight becomes you,' he crooned softly. 'It goes with your hair . . .'

'Cut it out,' she laughed, knowing when she was being teased but nevertheless feeling totally unnerved by his charm. 'I don't need to be serenaded, thank you.'

'Serenade . . . My love is a serenade . . .' He crooned the golden oldie with a perfectly straight face but chanced a quick look across at her.

'Are you going to keep this up all the way there? If so you can just stop!'

'In the name of love, before you break my heart,' he sang, but the last few notes wavered as they both chortled. 'There, that's better. It's not hard to laugh, is it?' he asked softly, and reached across for her hand, lifting it from her lap and squeezing her fingers gently.

'No, not hard,' she agreed and swallowed, tugging gently on her hand.

'So why don't you do more of it?' Instead of letting go, he drew her hand to his face and kissed her knuckles, keeping his eyes on the road.

'That's easier said than done,' she responded, her voice quavering as a vague depression settled over her like a fine mist as she thought of Richard. Richard with the kind face and gentle hands. Abruptly she yanked her hand from Farron's and buried it protectively under her folded arms.

'Perhaps you're not going about it the right way.' He looked across at her, the headlights from on-coming cars illuminating his face briefly before it fell once more into darkness and shadow. She shivered, even though the expression in his eyes sent hot tingles screaming through her bloodstream.

'Oh well. Look, speaking of fun, there's a freestyle surfing competition the day after tomorrow. Just us local lads mucking about on sailboards, you know, doing tricks and generally showing off. Ever watched the sport?'

She shook her head. 'I don't know if I have or not. I'm still rediscovering a lot of things. And one of them is that the police are no nearer to finding out my identity than I am. I phone them every day, but . . .' She shrugged. 'No luck. And I've done everything I can think of. I even tried to check with the airport to see if any woman of my age hasn't gone back Stateside when she was supposed to, but they won't give out that kind of information. Besides, I suppose the police have already done all that.'

Farron nodded but didn't offer meaningless platitudes. 'Why don't I pick you up and take you to the meet? It is your day off then, isn't it?'

'Been doing some checking, have you?' she asked sharply.

A passing headlight illuminated his handsome profile. At that instant he turned and burned her with his eyes. 'Of course I have,' he said, sounding almost disappointed in her.

She dragged in a large, shaky breath and shook her head. 'I can't. Thanks anyway.'

Farron shrugged. 'OK. If you prefer to stay cooped up in the flat or wandering around the shops with a bunch of tourists from Arkansas instead of watching the best local talent perform death-defying feats, then so be it.'

Vienna paled. 'Is it dangerous? I mean, you won't get hurt, will you?'

Farron smiled in the darkness. 'Hell, no. The worst that can happen is we capsize and get even wetter than I think we already must be to do it in the first place! Only pride can get hurt – I promise. But afterwards we have a *launa* – the real thing, mind.'

She smiled slightly and looked away. 'I hope you have a good time,' she said pointedly in a small, cold voice.

Farron smiled again, enigmatically this time. 'Oh, we will. We will.'

She looked at him sharply but his face was innocent. 'There

it is,' she said with some relief as they finally pulled up in front of the apartment block.

'I'll walk you to the door.'

'That's not necessary,' she said, suddenly nervous.

'Let's not take any risks, hm? You've already been coshed and robbed once. It's not going to happen again, at least not while you're with me.'

'My hero,' she drawled sardonically. 'I may not have much of a memory, but even I know a line when I hear it.'

In the shadow of the building he curled his hand around her waist and felt her stiffen in fear and anger as she swung to face him, her mouth already opening to spit venom. Slowly he shook his head and Vienna felt her resentment cringe away like a whipped dog. 'You don't have to give out all these signals, Vienna,' he said softly, one long finger reaching out to brush a strand of hair from her cheek as he looked deep into her eyes. 'I'm not going to hurt you.' He took the pass key from her and inserted it into the lock.

Inside the lift Farron leant against the wall feeling content. She was lovely, inside and out. And she was born to laugh, of that he was sure. Laugh and love, and he wanted both for her. But are you ready for this, he asked himself. You've never been down this road before – never even been close. What if one day a man with three little girls looking just like her turns up and introduces himself as her husband? What then?

At the door Vienna felt her hands begin to shake and to cover it she straightened her shoulders abruptly and said as aggressively as she could manage, 'I suppose you want coffee? I don't have a machine so you'll get a spoonful of instant and hot water – take it or leave it.'

Farron smiled lazily and folded his arms across his chest. His eyes were like melting chocolate as he said softly, 'Oh, I think I'll take it.'

Vienna blushed and looked away, turning the key without success before realizing it was the wrong one. Feeling like a fool, she nearly jumped out of her skin as the door opened from the inside and Richard's tall frame filled the doorway. It shouldn't have surprised her – Richard spent more and more of his time in her flat. 'Richard! I thought you must have had the night-shift.'

'I did, but one of the interns asked me to swap so he could have tomorrow off. I didn't mind, but I thought I was too late to pick you up. I assumed you'd already be here when I got back.'

Vienna blushed guiltily. 'Er, no. Farron here offered me a lift home so I hung around to catch the end of his show.'

'That was kind of you.' Richard looked directly at Farron with a friendly smile and opened the door wider. 'Why don't you come in.'

Farron looked quickly at Vienna, noticing the lines of strain around her eyes and felt a rush of protective rage assail him. But picking a fight now was not a good idea. And he had to know a lot more about the set-up between them before feeling comfortable about butting in. After all, he might have misread the signs, and the last thing he wanted to do was to jeopardise Vienna's relationship with this man, if she loved him. 'No; thanks anyway. I just wanted to make sure she got home safely.'

'You're the singer – I couldn't place you for a moment,' Richard said, holding out his hand. 'I'm Richard Jago.'

'Hi,' Farron said. His eyes did not flicker as Richard's fingers painfully crushed his hand. Richard smiled with his lips as his eyes narrowed.

'You must come over to dinner one day – mustn't he, Vienna?'

'If he wants to,' she said, her cautious answer sounding flat and ungracious as she walked a little further into the flat.

'I'll see you tomorrow,' Farron said, waiting until Vienna looked at him before smiling briefly and then nodding to Richard. 'Goodnight.'

'Goodnight.' Richard closed the door behind him with extreme gentleness. He paused for a thoughtful second then turned to look at Vienna who, in turn, glanced swiftly away.

'Want some coffee?' she asked, going into the kitchen. He stood in the doorway watching her, his relaxed stance totally belying the fear and rage simmering in his brain.

'By the way,' he said casually. 'I've arranged with the bank for them to issue you with some credit cards. Normally they'd need referees and a credit check but I put my name forward as a guarantor.'

Vienna switched off the kettle and poured the boiling water into the cups. 'Thanks, but I don't suppose I'll use them much.' She had insisted on opening her own account just two days ago and found herself wishing he'd kept out of it. Then she told herself not to be so damned ungrateful as they walked into the small lounge where the radio was playing softly. 'I've also got you a provisional driving licence. You'll have to pass a test before you can get a full one, though. Shall I arrange for some lessons for you?'

Vienna put down her coffee and swallowed hard against helpless tears. 'You're so good to me, Richard,' she said softly. 'And I'm not at all sure I deserve it.'

Richard put down his own coffee and walked over to her. Lifting her easily from the chair, he cradled her in his arms. Looking down into her shadowed blue eyes he said quietly, 'I love you. So it's easy.'

'I know you do,' she admitted, her voice little more than a whisper and she closed her eyes and he carried her through to the bedroom and laid her on the bed. His hands were artful and experienced as he stripped the black and white uniform from her unresisting body and he watched her closely as he ran a hand over her slender waist and upwards to cup her right breast.

She closed her eyes and sighed, but behind her closed lids the man she saw had melting brown eyes and when Richard said, 'You're so beautiful, so lovely,' it was not his voice that she heard. She opened her eyes with a snap, feeling dirty and guilty and lifted her lips to kiss him passionately, desperately, pushing her small tongue into his mouth. He placed her against the pillows and lowered his head to suck on her breast, a small triumphant smile on his lips.

Vienna stared at the ceiling with blank, despairing eyes.

THOUSANDS of miles away in the City of London, another woman lay staring at another ceiling, her eyes equally blank and full of pain as dawn came stealing into her room through a chink in the curtains. It was always worst first thing in the morning when the memories came flooding back.

The nurse at the desk in the Intensive Care Unit reception

83

had told Rhiannon to wait, but when the doctor approached his expression said it all. She did not need to hear the words that were now scattered and fragmented in her memory. '*Severe cardiac arrest . . . infection . . . deterioration . . . only for a few minutes . . . prepare yourself for the worst.*'

She pushed open the door, feeling strangely guilty as she saw him on the bed looking pale and fragile amongst tubes and the paraphernalia of machines. She should have loved him more . . . She approached the elevated bed very gingerly, as if just breathing on him might hurt him. 'Oh, Daddy!'

The voice was a last taste of life and Graham forced his eyes open, taking in the beauty of her – the black hair, so like her mother's, lush and thick, the dark creamy skin, the green eyes . . . green eyes . . . How had Dominic ever thought to deceive him? Even if he hadn't found out all those years ago at Oxford about the attack of mumps that had left him sterile. But he would pay. Oh yes, Dominic Fairchild would pay.

'H-hello, my darling g-girl.' His voice was cracked and warped and so weak that Rhiannon felt tears trickling down her cheeks as she tried to smile.

'Yes, Daddy. I'm here.' He felt his fingers being taken in a soft but strong hand, and he closed his eyes briefly, gathering together the last vestiges of the strength and spite that had sustained him all his adult life.

She was strong, this daughter of Fairchild's, strong and capable. But could he send her to Hawaii to avenge him? Could he risk sending her into Dominic Fairchild's orbit?

The nurse frowned as the heartbeat on the monitor tripped and wavered.

'He d-did this to me,' Graham said, his voice little more than a croak.

Rhiannon frowned, lost. 'Who?'

'Dominic Fairchild.' His voice was stronger now and Rhiannon felt fresh tears run down her cheeks. Dominic Fairchild – of course. How often had she listened as a child to Graham telling her about the evil man who lived in the beautiful islands? At six, she'd imagined Dominic Fairchild to be the serpent in the Garden of Eden. At ten, she'd hated him as passionately as Graham did, resentful of the way he'd forced her father into exile. At fifteen, she'd begun to wonder how her father's hated nemesis had been able to force him to leave and at twenty she'd begun to suspect that the vendetta between her father and the Hawaiian Prince had been all in his imagination.

'You m-mustn't let him g-get away with it, Rhia.'

'Daddy?'

'He k-killed me, Rhia. He loved your mother . . . but she loved me.'

This was something new — something she'd never heard before. She frowned fiercely, her eyes straying over and over again to the wavering monitor at his bedside. 'I don't understand, Daddy,' she whispered, holding his hand tighter.

'I only w-wish he'd done it to my f-face. Had the k-kindness to stick an honest knife into my h-heart instead of th-this way.' The gnarled and weak hand in her own suddenly curled and clenched and she looked back over her shoulder at the nurse.

'Is he delirious?'

'N-no. R-Rhia . . .' he whispered urgently, the room darkening frighteningly, the air suddenly cold in his nostrils. '*Rhia!*' he screamed in panic.

Her own heart felt as if it, too, were going to stop as she saw him slipping away.

'R-revenge, Rhia. I w-want r-reven . . .' The face in front of him shimmered, wavered and turned into the face of his lying, cheating wife.

Graham Grantham said quite clearly: 'I've always loved you.' And died.

THE alarm sounded and Rhiannon padded to the bathroom. In the shower she washed away all traces of her tears. She'd done enough crying — the time for tears was now past.

Three days after she'd stumbled out of the hospital, numb with shock and grief, she drove to her father's country home where she'd been visited by Marcus Fletcher, Graham's solicitor. Dressed in a sombre black suit, he delivered his commiserations in his normal toneless voice as she showed him apathetically into the library. 'You've come about the will, I take it?' she said dully. 'Isn't it usual to read it after the funeral?'

'Er, yes. But in this case . . . Rhiannon, how much did you know about your father's affairs?'

'Practically nothing. He went back to practising law after the merger with Fielding's, when I began to be involved in running the business. And I know he handled several firms' accounts, but apart from that . . . Why, is there something wrong?'

'I'm afraid so. Yes. I'm not sure quite where to start.'

'Try at the beginning,' she advised sharply. Her father's last words were fast taking on a more terrifying meaning. What if he hadn't been rambling? What if they hadn't been the product of a dying man's delirium as she'd thought?

'Well, ordinarily, my dear, your legacy from your father would have been quite substantial. This house alone would have fetched somewhere in the region of half a million pounds.'

'I'm quite aware of that. But what do you mean, *would* have?'

Marcus sighed deeply. 'Your father's practice had dwindled in recent years. He let several lucrative retentions slip until he only had one major firm left on his books.' He fiddled in his briefcase and brought out a wad of documents which he fingered nervously.

'Wasn't that rather stupid?'

'Oh, yes indeed, and I warned him about it, but Graham seemed quite confident that this firm, who paid him what I must admit was a very generous fee, would continue to do so. Perhaps because the firm was Hawaiian-based and run by some old Oxford friend of your father's. At any rate . . .'

The mention of Hawaii made her blood run cold. 'What happened?'

Marcus shifted uncomfortably on his seat and loosened his tie. 'Your father came to me about a month ago with a very tricky problem.'

'Yes?'

'Yes. It seems – well, your father said they had begun to fall behind with their retainer fee, and so he "borrowed" it from the corporate accounts.'

Rhiannon felt her fingers curl around the armrest, digging painfully into the highly polished wood. '*Borrowed* it?'

'Yes. Apparently he took rather more than he was entitled to, and since they didn't at first object . . .'

'He borrowed some more,' she finished. 'How much?'

'This had been going on over a period of almost twelve months. And you must understand that your father, as you know, was a generous man himself, and I'm sure that he saw it only as a fully justified – '

She cut across the waffle. '*How much?*'

'Nearly a million pounds.'

The words hit her in a single, shattering blow. 'What did you say?' she gasped.

'I'm afraid it was nearly a million pounds,' the lawyer repeated.

Rhiannon shook her head, licking lips gone painfully dry. 'Why didn't he come to me? He could have sold his shares in the advertising firm to either me or Ben.'

Marcus shrugged. 'He seemed confident he could sort it all out. He was sure it was a misunderstanding.'

Rhiannon shook her head. 'That doesn't make sense. And anyway, how did he manage to embezzle so much? Surely this firm, this. . . ?'

Marcus consulted the document resting in his lap. 'It's a subsidiary of Fairchild Enterprises,' he said, looking alarmed when she took a strangled breath. Walking numbly to the cabinet she poured them both a brandy. Marcus Fletcher sat miserably on the edge of his chair, looking very much as if he wanted to be somewhere else.

'Surely they employed security measures of some kind? My father was a lawyer, not an accountant.'

'I checked the books with him, of course,' Marcus admitted, glad that she had regained some colour. 'And I must say that Fairchild Enterprises were lax, very lax indeed. How they failed to notice what was going on I really can't say, especially when the firm has an excellent record in all other areas. Someone must have been very blind indeed not to notice.'

'But they eventually did,' she said, brandy and rage

beginning to make her blood boil as a clearer picture slowly emerged. Blind? Like hell! It had been cruelly thought out and deliberately planned. Her father had been right all along. And for years she had thought he'd been exaggerating. For years she had, in a sense, taken Dominic Fairchild's side instead of that of her own father. Just what kind of a daughter was she?

'Yes. Just over a month ago your father received a legal document listing the money he had borrowed, and demanding full restitution. It also demanded that the current interest rate be paid.'

'I see,' she said faintly, struggling to stay afloat in the tidal wave of guilt that washed over her. At last she understood what Graham had meant when he'd said that Dominic had killed him. It must have been the shock of that letter that had given him his heart attack.

'Can we . . . can I raise that much without selling my shares in the advertising company?'

'Yes. This house and the London flat should raise that much at an auction.'

Rhiannon nodded and took a deep swallow of brandy. Poor Daddy had been right all along. It had been a vindictive campaign from start to finish. His so-called 'old friend' must have known that Graham would 'borrow' the money. After all, Graham thought of it as his fee, his wages. Just what kind of man was this Dominic Fairchild? And why had he done it? Graham had said it was because he had loved her mother, but Jess had been dead for nearly thirty years, and surely no man held a grudge that long? Rhiannon sighed, angry at herself for the way her thoughts persisted in doubting her own father. What did it matter why? For most of her adult life she'd let Graham down. Firstly she had been unable to prevent his drinking, then she had not believed him until it was much too late about Dominic Fairchild. And yet still Graham had trusted her, on his deathbed, to seek justice for him. And she would not let him down. She could not, must not, let him down ever again.

RHIANNON slowly dressed and met her reflection in the mirror. Had it really only been three months ago? The pain and guilt, the burning desire for justice felt as new as if they'd just been born in her.

Her glance fell to her watch. Her flight was only two hours away. Before the sun set on another day she'd be on Oahu, the island of her birth.

The island of her enemy.

Chapter 8

Dominic turned his Ferrari into a deserted weed-strewn drive and switched off the ignition. Birds sang in the tangle of trees, oblivious to the loneliness of a house that had been boarded up for decades. The garden that had once been beautiful was now an overgrown tropical haven for local wildlife. He got out of the car and slowly walked to the front door, all the time wondering why he had come. He had awoken that morning feeling restless and unable to concentrate even at the office. It had been a spur-of-the-moment decision to visit the old house and one that he was beginning to regret.

On the porch roof honeysuckle had taken root, its fragrant curling flowers twining overhead, tendrils hanging down to curtain the door. The house seemed to be sleeping, and he stepped off the porch where the name *Kapuna* was engraved on a now-askew placard of wood. Following the wall of the house to the right, his eyes noted the boarded-up windows and a great wave of nostalgia engulfed him. He could remember this house when it was full of people and laughter with the aroma of good cooking emanating from the kitchen and the sound of a cheerful radio blasting out the latest pop hits. Yes, the old man was truly gone from this place.

Dominic paused by a wall where a yellow alamanda vine, freshly planted and still scrawny in his memory, was now a riotous mass covering the entire wall. Under his feet, what had once been an immaculately-kept lawn was now a meadow of grass and weeds. He smiled ruefully, thinking of the ear-bashing he would have got from the old man if he could see the place now. He'd have been mad as hell with him for not selling the place long ago and taking advantage of the soaring price of property and real estate.

Over his shoulder, he spotted the swing still hanging from the wili-wili tree. He could remember the old man fixing it up for him, and saying, 'It's a coral tree, boy. Speak bloody American when you're around me or I'll paddle your ass for you.'

Now Dominic stood by the side of the single-plank swing and looked up at the branch to which it had been tied, the knots still holding. He thought, 'I wonder,' and slowly sat down on it, expecting to fall on his backside at any moment, but the swing held. How old had he been when his grandfather had first pushed him on it? Five? Six? He sighed, a familiar ache of loss for what-should-have-beens creeping over him. Once he had looked forward to pushing his own child in this same swing. Once he'd felt, for all too brief a moment, the thrill of fatherhood, of holding a tiny body in his arms, of looking down into the face of a miniature human being who had sprung from his seed.

Looking out over the ten-feet-high stone wall he could still hear those long ago shrieks of delight as his small body swung in the air, anticipating the lunging thrust from the old man's arms as he travelled backwards, the jerk almost unseating him. But he had not fallen. No. He had not been unseated . . .

Dominic picked up a twig from the ground, turning it in his fingers, trying to concentrate on the new hotel in Hawaii's Volcano Park.

But time had a way of rolling back . . .

DOMINIC reached for the bottle of bourbon and raised it to his lips. He was half-lying in a chintz-covered armchair and swung his bare foot negligently, looking at the elongated little toe as if he hated it. The 'Fairchild foot' it was called – a generic deformity unique to the men in the family. He could hear Smith Flanaghan's voice in the other room but after a few minutes a door outside slammed shut and the sound of a car engine told him he'd left.

Through the open door he watched Tansie Chester, their housekeeper for the last twenty-two years, walk by, drying her eyes on the hem of her lifted apron. The old man was dead – for two days he'd been dead, and now nobody else seemed to be alive. He took another swallow of the raw alcohol and then put the bottle down. He was not drunk but pleasantly anaesthetized. On the table beside him the telephone rang, its intrusive noise in this so silent house of death sounding grotesque, obscene. He snatched it up and barked, 'Yes?'

There was a brief silence on the other end, and then her voice, accented and like warm syrup. 'Dominic! It's me. I've been waiting for you to call me for days.'

The petulance mixed with purring provocation made the bourbon sour in his stomach and Dominic groaned silently. 'Believe it or not, Akaki, I've had other things on my mind – like watching my grandfather die.'

The silence on the other end was telling. 'I expected you to call me the moment you got back, darling. Is he really dead?'

Dominic's lips curled into a painful grimace. 'Yes – really dead.'

'So you have all his money now?'

Dominic reached for the bottle again. 'Maybe.'

'Maybe?' The voice lost it purr and became an irritating squeal. 'What do you mean, maybe? Who else would he have left it to?'

Dominic laughed, a harsh sound that echoed around the empty house like a lost soul. 'Had you worried, did I, my ever-loving?'

'I don't like being teased, Dom. You're such a rotten bastard sometimes.'

'Yeah,' Dominic said. 'Rotten like you, Akaki.'

'What do you mean?' The voice was sharp and venomous and once, a year ago, he might even have been surprised to hear the ugliness in it but not now. Time and distance had made him wise and the suddenness of his loss and the staggering thought of his responsibilities had matured him considerably.

'I mean, darling, that you could have waited until the old man was at least cold if not buried before reaching with your avaricious little fingers for his money.' He could almost hear the wheels turning in her scheming brain as she weighed his words and decided a change of tactics was called for.

Right on cue, her next words held no sugar. 'I want to see you.'

'I don't think so. I've got better things to do – like burying my grandfather, for one. Not to mention finally getting together with Smith to discuss the transition of power. Shareholders are a little jittery right now,' Dominic said dryly in gross understatement. Shareholders didn't think a nineteen-year-old was capable of running Fairchild Enterprises and that was that. But Dominic had no intention of relinquishing power. No way!

'I want to see you now, Dominic. Don't think you can just cast me aside, Your Highness!' She sneered the last two words and in his mind's eye he could see her, the luscious lips thinned as she snarled, the eyes narrowed like those of a spiteful cat. He sighed, rubbing a hand over his face and shaking his head.

'It's over between us, Akaki. It was even before I left for Oxford.'

'No! You still want me, I know you do. Remember the Christmas vacation? You were like a starving dog. You still want me.' The confidence was almost monstrous and Dominic felt a twinge of pity for her.

'I don't. I've found another girl – in Oxford.'

'Some milk-and-water English Miss?' Akaki sneered, her voice thick with the local accent as her anger began to simmer out of control. 'You'll be tired of her within a month.'

'Look Akaki, it's over all right?'

He moved the phone away from his ear, the screaming voice getting fainter and fainter until it stopped abruptly as he replaced the receiver.

'Do you want dinner, Mr Dominic?' a soft voice asked and Dominic looked up to the doorway where Tansie stood like a wilted flower, her brown curls lying sad and neglected on her head.

'No thanks, Tansie. I'm not hungry.' He watched her leave then sighed angrily as the telephone began to buzz again. 'For God's sake,' he snapped in greeting, already knowing who it was. Akaki was not the girl to give up easily.

'Listen, Your Highness. You'd better come over here right now and talk to me or you're going to be sorry. And dress up – I haven't been out in ages and you're taking me somewhere good.' This time he was left with the dialling tone ringing in his ear and he stared at the instrument in his hand with a mixture of surprise and reluctant good humour. He was not in the least worried about Akaki's threats, but knew she would make a pest of herself until he'd sorted the whole mess out once and for all. And he didn't want her ringing or coming to the house and pestering Tansie. Not now.

In the kitchen he drank five cups of coffee and some of the numbness that had sheltered him for the last two days wore off. 'I have to go out, Tansie. I shouldn't be long but don't wait up.'

'No, Mr Dominic. Drive carefully now.'

He headed downtown towards the small bungalow by the ocean that he had leased for the past two years for Akaki. She had hinted and angled for him to buy it outright, but he had refused. Even at seventeen and totally smitten, warning signals had stopped him from making a complete fool of himself. Half an hour later he pulled to a halt outside the small, one-bedroomed dwelling and gave a short blast on the horn. He was not about to go in; she'd have been all over him in a matter of minutes, and the last thing he felt like doing was fighting off a sexy octopus. He saw the curtain twitch and waited. A few minutes later the outside light came on and she clicked the door shut behind her and walked down the path with that familiar, feline slink that was poetry in motion. She was dressed in an evening gown of gold lamé that glittered in every passing light. He could see that the dress was backless as she turned deliberately to shut the gate behind her, and the deep V at the front of the dress quite literally stopped at her naval. Her breasts looked fuller than he remembered, but her waist was smaller.

'Hello, Dominic,' she said and opened the door of the car. Sliding in beside him, the expensive Chanel perfume that he'd bought her as a going away gift filled the car with its fragrance. 'I'm starving. I thought we'd eat before we ... talked.'

In the moonlight her brown eyes looked topaz and he was relieved to feel no reaction in his loins at the sight of her breasts straining against the material, the nipples clearly visible. 'Why not,' he said mildly, feeling slightly more mellow now that he knew for certain he was finally free of her. 'How does Le Chien sound?' He named the most exclusive and snobbish French restaurant on the islands, knowing it would delight her. And it did, for her face lost its wary, sexy look and lit up like that of an excited child.

'Really? That's great!'

He pulled out, casting a quick look at her. 'You've lost weight since I saw you at Easter.'

Akaki's smile was pure cat-that-had-the-canary. 'Yes, I have. Eight pounds, six ounces to be exact.'

'Congratulations. I know how you hate diets.'

It took them only twenty minutes to pull up in front of the restaurant, a discreet, single-storey building on College Walk. Her eyes devoured him as they walked to the door. He looked magnificent in black, and she felt a familiar stirring of desire.

'Shall we?' She quickly looped her arm through his, her face flushed with pleasure. It had always given her a thrill to enter a room with a Prince on her arm. The Maitre d', a genuine Frenchman dressed in a black tuxedo, recognized Dominic immediately and rushed forward, giving a discreet bow.

'Your Highness. It is always a pleasure to see you,' he said, just loudly enough for the guests sipping drinks at the bar to hear. 'For you, we have the best table in the house.'

They walked through to a large but artfully constructed dining room. Every table had a three-sided trellis around it, carefully tended vines curling through the squares giving each table a delicious atmosphere of outdoor intimacy. Small pink lamps were incorporated into the walls and on each table a single candle burned in a delicate crystal holder shaped like a flower. Akaki knew that all eyes were on them and she could feel a delicious tingling all over her skin. She loved to be the centre of attention.

Dominic watched her with amused eyes as they were seated then he ordered and took an appreciative sip of his wine. 'All right, what's so important then?' he asked tiredly as they waited to be served. Akaki's eyes narrowed ominously. She didn't like it when she was not taken seriously. But for once she held the upper hand and planned to milk it for all it was worth. In spite of himself, Dominic felt a faint stirring of unease deep in his guts as her face fairly glowed in smug self-satisfaction.

'I have a surprise for you.'

'Oh?' he asked, barely impressed. 'Like what?'

She shrugged. 'It'll keep a little longer.'

'I see. We're playing this old game, are we?'

Akaki shrugged eloquently. 'You used to like this old game, Dominic.'

The first course was served on plates of finest bone china. His own appetite was still nowhere in evidence but Akaki ate heartily as she had always done. 'Not eating?' she murmured spitefully. 'Surely you're not mourning your grandfather?' she gibed, her long, gold-painted nails curling around the stem of her glass. 'He was a tyrant and you know it.'

Dominic gave a silent grunt. 'Yes. A tyrant. But he loved me in his way.'

Akaki stared at him, surprised by the sadness in his voice. 'Who are you trying to kid, Your Highness? You were always fighting,' she scoffed dismissively. 'Whenever you came to me your first words were nearly always about him, raging about this or that. I sometimes think the only reason you ever slept with me in the first place was because you enjoyed sticking up two fingers at the old man.'

Dominic sighed and pushed his plate away, uncomfortable with the idea that Akaki might just be right. Was his whole life just one long knee-jerk reaction to Fred Fairchild's bullying prejudices? He looked at her, for a second feeling guilty, then began to laugh. 'What a pair we make, Kaki,' he mused softly. 'The rebel and the golddigger.' As her eyes hardened at the mockery in his voice he saluted her with his wineglass. 'Well, at least we both got what we wanted, hm?'

Akaki drew in her breath sharply. He really had changed. He no longer spoke to her touchingly of love, the way he used to when she'd first met him. He'd only been a boy then, of course. But tonight he was not even bothering with the pretence of trying to please her. She hated to relinquish power and his smile vanished as he felt her hand on his knee, her nails splaying around his leg as it moved up his thigh. Holding her eyes with a cool stare of his own he reached under the table and lifted her fingers away, not even wincing as the nails dug into his palm in an attempt to draw blood.

'Cut it out, Kaki,' he said wearily. 'I'm too tired for all this. It's over.'

She pouted prettily. 'I want to go dancing. Can we go to that new place?'

Dominic sighed and put down his knife and fork. 'No.'

Akaki's smile turned spiteful. 'You should be nice to me, lover,' she warned softly. Her mouth curved upwards as he looked at her, his face expressionless as he wondered what she had up her sleeve. Was she bluffing? She could bluff well, but something told him that this time she wasn't.

Seeing the doubt in his eyes she laughed, a sultry pleasing sound that he noticed the waiter greatly appreciated as he collected their plates. Yes, Akaki was lovely – greedy, grasping, crude, but very, very talented. He felt a purely half-hearted stirring in his loins as she caressed his hand with her teasing fingers and watched the gold-tipped nails move in the candlelight with lazy eyes. At least she'd taken his mind off the old man for a little while and he supposed he should be grateful for that.

She wolfed down her dessert but he took only a few mouthfuls before pushing his away.

'I haven't been out like this in ages,' she said wistfully and Dominic grunted a disbelieving laugh.

'You've really changed,' Akaki said angrily.

'Yes. I know,' he said simply. The carefree teenager was gone and in his place stood the new owner of a financial empire and a man touched by grief for the first time in his life. Suddenly, as he paid the bill and handed over a generous tip, Dominic felt the last few days' lack of sleep and general misery catch up with him. Every bone in his body seemed to ache.

'Look, I'm beat. Why don't you just tell me about this damned surprise and let me take you home.'

'I want to do dancing, Dominic.'

'Then you'll go alone.'

Akaki let loose a string of foul four-letter words that left him totally unmoved. Eventually, recognizing she'd pushed him as far as he'd go she got ungraciously into the car but once they were on their way back to her place she began to test her

97

power once again. 'Princess Akaki Fairchild,' she said aloud. 'Sounds good, doesn't it?'

'You're dreaming, Akaki. It's not like you to let a bottle of wine, a little brandy and a smattering of kirsch make you this drunk.'

Akaki smiled viciously. 'I want a huge engagment ring, too – diamonds. No, that's tacky. I just want one *huge* diamond.'

'Uh-huh,' Dominic said, pulling up in front of her bungalow and turning to her. 'I won't switch off the engine – I won't be coming in.'

'Oh, but you must. The surprise is inside, waiting for you.'

His eyes narrowed as they took in her sparkling, almost feverish look and he felt a cold chill creep up his spine. Whatever it was she thought she had on him, she certainly placed great faith in it. Blackmail? But with the old man gone there was no one to go running tales to. What then?

'Come on.' She got out of the car and walked up the short path with her hips swaying hypnotically. Dominic opened the car door with exaggerated care and then viciously slammed it shut. Tonight he'd sleep – he was sure of it. He felt almost dead on his feet right now. Akaki took out her key and opened the door to a small hall. '*Aloha*, Liimi.' The door to the small living room opened and an old woman came through dressed in a floral-printed dress a size too big. Her hair was waistlength and grey, her eyes almost lost in folds of leathery brown skin. 'Pay her five dollars, will you Dom-Dom?'

Dominic dug into his pockets and gave the old woman a twenty-dollar bill, winking at her as she looked at it dumbfounded. Then he opened the door for her, letting her walk through before gently closing it after her. 'What did I just pay her for?'

'For looking after your surprise, of course, while we were out.'

'It needs looking after?' he asked as Akaki opened the door to her bedroom.

'Of course. Come on.' She hooked a beckoning finger.

'I thought I made it clear . . .'

'Don't you want your surprise?'

'No, I bloody well don't,' Dominic finally exploded. 'Why don't you find someone else to take you to bed?'

'But Dom,' Akaki said in mock shock. 'You know I've been faithful to you.'

'In a pig's eye.'

'*Komo mai.*' She repeated it in English, 'Come on. It'll only take a minute.'

'That's fast, even for you.'

'*Wikiwiki.* Don't you want to see your surprise? You've been such a good boy all evening.

Ignoring her demand to hurry up, he walked slowly towards her. 'I'm warning you, if this . . .'

'Ssh.' She reached up to lay a finger across his lips. 'Not so loud. See?'

He followed her inside, his eyes quickly taking in the small bedroom and coming to rest on a new piece of furniture: a crib, painted white and decorated with rabbits. A single shaded lamp glowed in one corner and he slowly shook his head in utter disbelief.

'You can't be serious,' he said, letting her lead him by the hand to look down into the sleeping face of a black-haired baby. 'You're not trying to tell me this is yours!' Dominic's shock gave way to anger. 'You think I don't know about all those abortions at old *Tutu* Luanna's place?'

Akaki looked momentarily disconcerted. 'I didn't know you knew about that.'

Dominic smiled, feeling on safer ground. 'I know you'd like to think so but you never did pull the wool over my eyes, Kaki. Now if this is all you've got . . .' He turned to go but she quickly grabbed him, her fingers like talons.

'You don't think I'd abort anything so precious as the Fairchild heir, do you?' she hissed. 'I never told you I was pregnant because I knew it was my meal-ticket for life, and I wasn't going to risk you making me get an abortion or taking it away from me when it was born. Now there's not a damned thing you can do about it, *Your Highness*!'

Disgusted with her cold-hearted reasoning, Dominic nevertheless felt an icy hand clutch his heart. 'You can't palm your bastard off on me!'

Akaki smiled and folded her arms across her breasts. 'You forget lover, I know you – every lovely inch. Including that strange toe of yours. All you have to do is take a look at the baby's foot. What's the matter –scared?' Her eyes glittered with anticipation as he stiffened.

He swallowed hard, then leaned over the cradle and gently pulled the soft blankets away. Taking a tiny foot in one hand, his whole body stiffened in a mixture of intense shock and pleasure as his finger ran gently over a little toe longer than its neighbour. 'Oh my God!' he whispered.

THE branch overhead creaked ominously and Dominic came out of his painful reverie and looked up. Seeing the branch sway and dip, he realized he'd been rocking the swing as memories caught up with him. He stood and walked slowly away from the overgrown garden back to his car.

Reversing down the drive he headed for home. Pulling up at red traffic-lights, the sight of the red light brought back the memory of a red lamp behind a well-stocked bar. He had stumbled from Akaki's place, her laughter and triumphant demands still ringing in his ears. He'd driven for miles before spotting a little bar tucked between a hamburger joint and a closed, dark shop. He'd pulled in on impulse, ordering a double bourbon from a bartender who'd merely grunted and complied. That double had been followed by two more, and then Graham was there, sitting by his side, his hand on his arm.

'Hello – celebrating alone? That's not very sociable of you.'

'*Aloha*, Gray-Gray,' he slurred, feeling ridiculously pleased to see his oldest friend, and Graham's hazel eyes had wandered to the barman, his small hand holding out a ten-dollar bill. 'You did right to call me. Thanks.'

Again the barman merely grunted and Dominic frowned at him, leaning back to try and get the man's face in focus and almost falling off the stool. It had been Graham who saved him from falling with a quick hand placed squarely in the middle of his back. 'Come on, Dominic. Time to go home.' Graham dragged him from the stool and out into the night. Taking nearly all of his weight, Graham half-walked, half-dragged his six-feet-four-inch frame to his own Ford car and drove him to his home a few miles away.

Jessamine, Graham's wife, was waiting for them, hovering anxiously in the doorway, her pretty figure bulging with the child she was carrying. Since the false labour that had brought Graham hurrying home she'd been having a difficult time, though she never complained.

'Get him inside. I've made up the bed in the spare room.'

'So kind. Isn't she kind, Gray-Gray?' Dominic asked, watching his own shaking hand reach out to pat her awkwardly on the cheek as she'd smiled that gentle, tender smile of hers. 'You're a lucky bastard, Gray-Gray!'

Graham grunted, almost choking on his hatred, and pushed him onto the bed in the spare room, wondering if his best friend and his wife had slept together in his bed? Dominic opened his eyes, seeing Graham watching him with a familiar, peculiar intensity and shook his head. Graham said, 'I didn't think you would take his death so hard.'

'Not old man,' he mumbled. 'Her . . .'

'Her?' Whom, Dom? Jess?'

'No – Akaki. My kid . . . Gray-Gray, I'm a daddy.' Dominic began to laugh, but felt tears on his cheeks and knew then that he was blind, stinking drunk.

Graham moved away when Jessamine came in with a bowl of cool water and a cloth, and watched as she bathed Dominic's face, his eyes flitting from one to the other and and monitoring every tiny nuance of expression on their faces. And they were good. Neither one gave even the smallest hint of . . .

'He's really sloshed,' Jessamine said, smiling fondly at the man who looked up at her and nodded wisely.

'Sloshed,' Dominic repeatedly solemnly.

Jessamine stood up and gasped, bending over as a pain sliced through her abdomen and the doctor's warnings came rushing back. Dominic, suddenly less drunk, watched as Graham took the bowl from her and helped her straighten up, his voice anxious as he said, 'You all right?'

'I'm fine,' Jessamine gasped, and smiled reassuringly at Dominic before slowly walking out, her face white with pain.

Dominic looked at her departing figure and then at the man staring down at him: his old friend's eyes seemed to burn holes right into him.

A car horn honked behind him and Dominic jerked back to the present. He moved away and desperately seeking distraction, turned on the radio, getting a loquacious disc jockey. He quickly switched channels until he found some music. Too much damned talk, he thought, and then shook his head, anger and frustration rising like bile in his throat. If he hadn't talked so damned much all those years ago, how different his life would be now. But then not even he, knowing Graham's strange, twisted nature as he did, had been able to foresee the viciousness of his attack or the devastation it would cause him and those he loved.

'Damn you Graham,' he said, his foot pressing down harder on the accelerator, the needle creeping up to the 100 mph mark. '*Damn you.*'

Chapter 9

Her paranoia had grown. It was nothing she could put her finger on exactly, but a steady feeling of being watched and of time running out, had begun to creep into the fringes of her life, making the crisis in her relationship with Richard all the more explosive. Over the weeks her hope of a quick resolution to her missing identity had slowly seeped away, leaving her depressed and ever more desperate. *Why didn't anyone know her?* Or was it just that nobody wanted her? She could drive herself crazy at night, creating possible past lives for herself, and in the morning be no further ahead. All she had was the here and now; and that was driving her as quietly mad as her amnesia. How many other women felt bound to a man they didn't love? Was she alone in feeling gratitude but nothing else for the man who was her lover?

She was just finishing the housework on Monday morning when the discreet chime of the doorbell interrupted her dusting. It was still only eight o'clock and she put down the duster and walked cautiously to the door. 'Who is it?'

'A candy-coloured clown they call a sandman . . .' a familiar voice sang deeply through the keyhole.

Vienna laughed. 'Too early – I'm already awake,' she said, opening the door. Farron smiled, his eyes slowly taking in the flush of pleasure on her cheeks and the sparkle in her eyes. For her part, she slowly took in the cut-off denim jeans that he was wearing, and suddenly became conscious of her own rumpled state. She pushed back her sweat-damp hair nervously. 'I must look a sight – I've been spring cleaning.'

'You look lovely,' he said simply, his eyes holding hers.

'Come in.' He smelt of sun and soap, warm flesh and a certain male essence that she recognized only on a primitive level. 'I really must shower.'

'OK. I'll wait. And change into something beachy.'

'Beachy?'

He selected the middle seat in the sofa and sank down on to

it, stretching out long tanned legs and crossing them at the ankles.

'Make yourself at home, why don't you?' she asked drily.

'Thanks.' Farron grinned and checked his watch. 'Come on –*wikiwiki*. We have to be at the beach by ten-thirty.'

'And what beach is that?'

'I told you,' he wagged a finger at her. 'Your memory must be worse than I thought. It's the freestyle windsurfing championship today – remember?'

'I remember,' Vienna said, ignoring his first comment which might have sounded cruel coming from someone else but not from him, and she decided that two could play at this game. 'I also remember saying I wasn't coming!'

'Did you?' Farron looked shocked. 'Amnesia must be catching.'

Vienna fought between outrage and laughter, and laughter won. She shook her head, smiling and heading for the bathroom. Farron made no comment when she came back five minutes later, but his eyes caressed her small, fair form and she felt her heart pick up a strange, taboo beat. 'So,' she said, folding her arms nervously across her chest. 'What makes you think I've changed my mind?'

Farron looked at her steadily and the air around them suddenly stilled. 'I mean about going to this surfing competition,' she clarified hastily, and Farron stirred on the sofa, letting his lips curve into a whimsical smile.

'Windsurfing, you philistine,' he corrected. 'Well – I got up this morning, saw the sun shining, thought of you all on your own and decided to take pity on you and rescue you from yourself.'

Vienna felt a shiver of desire slide into her stomach and uncrossed her arms. 'How gallant. But supposing I don't want to be rescued?'

Farron said, 'Aaahh,' very softly, and then, 'If you won't take pity on yourself, you might take pity on me.'

She took a deep breath and wondered why it suddenly felt as if the small flat was lacking in air. Farron hadn't moved yet she felt as if he was suddenly overwhelming her, sucking her into his eyes, his life, his body . . .

'After all, I am the reigning champion,' he continued, leaning forward and smiling into her wary eyes. 'And everyone knows it's harder for the champ to hold on to his title than it is for a hot and eager contender to snitch it away. I need all the support I can get. Come on – what do you say?'

'What if I see a gorgeous hunk and want him to win?' she asked, raising one eyebrow as Farron scowled ferociously.

'In that case you'll spend the entire afternoon trying to find your teeth in the sand!'

Vienna yelped in laughter. 'In *that* case I'll be your greatest fan!'

'THE beach looks crowded,' she said nervously an hour later, her eyes skimming over the groups of families and clusters of teenage friends.

'All locals – they can't wait to watch us make asses out of ourselves.'

Vienna laughed at his candour as he parked and grabbed two binoculars from the glove compartment. 'I mean it,' he insisted, laughing himself as he held out his hand to her. Vienna took it, the gesture so friendly and so lacking in threat that she hardly noticed what she'd done.

There were several mobile hotdog and icecream stands, and one van with an obviously home-made loud-hailer system that stood parked at the topmost part of the beach. It was to the latter that they went, and sitting in the back with the doors wide open was a smiling Korean woman of gargantuan proportions.

'Hello, Ma,' Farron said, reaching down to kiss her bulging cheek.

'Well, well. The reigning champ. People were beginning to say you weren't going to show up. Jimmy Kwan's been going around looking like he'd found heaven,' the huge woman grinned, her button-black eyes sweeping over Vienna in a knowing appraisal as Farron leaned closer to Vienna and whispered loudly, 'Jimmy's nothing like a handsome hunk.'

Farron signed himself in. 'When do I go, Ma?'

'Champ's privilege – you get the last fifteen minutes. Should be about one-thirty if everyone keeps to their time.'

'Should I bribe the crowd to cheer?'

'Nah.' Ma shook her head. 'You *kamaalna* – you'll be OK.'

'Thanks. Seen Kim and the others?'

Ma hooked a finger down the beach in a graphic gesture and Farron thanked her with a wink and another kiss, which she wiped off her cheek with exaggerated care as the couple walked away laughing. 'She loves me really,' Farron excused her, pretending not to hear the loud and rather obscene disclaimers that followed them for several yards down the beach.

'What did she just call you?'

Farron gave an evil chuckle. 'Quite a few things in her time. She used to babysit me and I got up to all sorts of things. *Kamaalna* means that I was born on the islands – not a tourist or immigrant. Most of the people here have their own man to cheer,' he looked sideways at her, blew on his nails and polished them on his shirt. 'But I'm their favourite, of course!'

'Oh, naturally!' She smiled, then frowned. Why didn't she know any Hawaiian words? It only confirmed her increasing certainty that she wasn't a native of the islands at all, only a lost holidaymaker. Vienna smiled, a touch bitterly. Some holiday!

They spotted Kim and Danny in a cosy little spot right at the front of the water's edge. Their girlfriends were conspicuously absent, and Farron told her that the lads took the championship seriously. In spite of herself, she couldn't help but feel a tiny thrill of pleasure that he'd broken the rules for her. They greeted Vienna with friendly smiles and handed over beers straight from a cooler. Farron sat close to her, his bare shins occasionally touching hers as they made themselves comfortable in the sand, the casual contact causing strange sensations under her skin.

'Hey, isn't that the boss?' Kim asked, shading his eyes and looking further along the beach where a lone figure walked barefoot at the shore's edge, hands stuck deep into cotton slacks which were rolled up at the feet.

Farron looked and then stood up, waving a hand. 'Hey, Dom! Dominic!' he yelled, his singer's voice cutting a powerful swathe through the beach chatter. Dominic saw him and raised a hand, changing direction to join them as Farron lowered himself to the ground again.

'*Aloha*.' Dominic greeted them but made no move to sit down. 'Quietly confident?' he asked, looking at Farron with a wide smile, his eyes travelling on to Vienna with friendly curiosity.

'Quiet my ar . . . foot,' Danny said, remembering just in time that he was speaking to his boss, and Dominic's grin widened. 'He's been telling everyone that Jimmy and Perry will be left crushed and broken men.'

'Lying toad,' Farron said mildly, his eyes on Dominic, knowing that business trouble was the reason he looked and sounded so withdrawn. 'Join us, Dom?'

Dominic felt a familiar painful longing clamour inside him but shook his head. 'Thanks, but I'm here with someone,' he lied. 'I'm also one of the judges again and it might smack of favouritism. But I'll be rooting for you.'

'Thanks,' Farron said, his brown eyes searching his older friend's face with an intense scrutiny that made Dominic inwardly wince. 'We were sorry to hear about the Princess Liliha chain, Dom,' he added quietly, taking the bull by the horns with his usual honesty coupled with genuine sympathy.

Dominic nodded. 'I know,' he said simply. Over the weeks he'd come to terms with the setback. Fairchild Enterprises, the towering giant that had ruled his life for so long, wasn't flesh and blood after all. Cut it, and he, Dominic, did not bleed. Oh, he was angry and determined that no one else would succeed in catching him unawares, but he'd managed to get the loss into perspective. Compared with losing his child, it was nothing more than a mere pinprick.

Just then the loudspeaker crackled and Ma's voice wafted over the assembled crowd. 'Welcome to the fourteenth annual Sunset Beach Rank — and I do mean *rank* — Amateur Freestyle Windsurf Competition.'

The crowd erupted into catcalls as Dominic said goodbye and walked back up the beach. Farron watched him go with troubled eyes, then sighed. Pointing to the blue sailboard just moving into the wind, he turned to Vienna and gave her a quick rundown on the sport.

'The sailboard is a simple enough contraption – just the board itself, the mast, the sail, and the boom – that pole that stretches from the mast to the end of the sail.' Squinting into the sun, her mind was more concerned with his nearness than his words. He handed her a pair of the binoculars and waited until she'd focused them before raising his own pair.

'Yeah,' Farron nodded. 'He's gonna start railriding.'

Vienna held her breath as the man on the sailboard began to manoeuvre himself so that he was skimming along the waves on one edge of the board, his hands positioning the sail artfully to catch the wind and keep his balance.

The wind was mild but the sails, expertly handled, picked up speed easily, and as she watched competitor after competitor do a ten-to-fifteen-minute routine she found herself becoming more and more intrigued with the sport. 'Here's Jimmy Kwan, folks,' Ma's voice rumbled across the beach. 'Two years runner-up to Farron Manikuuna, and he's *hungry* for the title.'

The clapping rose as Jimmy began his routine with what Farron called a 'water start'. Lying in the water, his head almost obscured by the gentle swell of the waves, the Chinese boy pushed the sail into the air and braced his legs against the board, slowly rising as the sail filled with wind until he was upright. Vienna felt a ridiculous thrill of fear for Farron: what if he couldn't beat him?

Sensing her scrutiny he lowered the glasses, his perceptive eyes noticing the worried look on her face. His expression altered, becoming infinitely tender. Vienna gasped, feeling as if someone had just hit her in the stomach, robbing her of all breath.

'Vienna,' he said softly, one hand beginning to rise to her face where her skin tingled in anticipation of the caress and she shuddered delicately.

'Hey! Hadn't you better get set up?' Danny said, suddenly turning around, and Vienna flinched away, as if she'd been caught out in some heinous act. She refused to look at him as he left.

'And now for the last contestant of the competition,' Ma said a few minutes later. 'Give a warm Oahu cheer for the reigning champ, the singing, the lovely, and he told me to say all this,' Ma lied outrageously, '*Farron Manikuuna!*' The crowd began clapping vigorously and Vienna's hands tightened on the glasses as she saw a bright scarlet sailboard heading past the line-up of judges.

To begin, Farron also did a water start and then went straight into a lying-down position, handling the sail with an ease that even Vienna could appreciate.

'What's he doing?' she asked anxiously, as he demonstrated a trick that had him jumping right off the board.

'It's called tacking,' Kim said. The crowd began to cheer as Farron leaned right over the sail, laying it almost flat in the water in a stunt that Danny told her had many names – including Sailor 360 and helicopter. 'So far I'd say he was level with Jimmy. I'll bet he's pacing up and down . . . oh shit!'

'What?' Vienna yelped, quickly looking back into her binoculars.

'He slipped – nearly went ass-backwards into the water,' Danny said in disgust. 'That's done it. That's finished him off for sure.'

But Farron recovered quickly and began to do a complicated manoeuvre of wheelies or tail-tappers, the sail falling forwards and hiding his head from view. 'Good, but not good enough,' Danny said. 'His time's almost up.'

'Bloody hell,' Kim whispered excitedly the next moment as Farron began to position himself for a stunt Vienna couldn't remember any of the others doing.

'What?' Vienna said, her fingers sweating as they held the binoculars still.

'A back somersault through the boom! Come on, Farron, go for it!' As she watched, dry-mouthed, Farron gripped the boom and hauled himself under it, his body totally leaving the board as he swung around and landed perfectly again, the sailboard hardly shuddering.

Vienna lowered her glasses as Farron waved a hand to indicate to the judges that he'd finished his routine. 'Does that mean he's won?'

'Won?' Danny yelped. 'The crowd will lynch the judges if he hasn't!'

And as all eyes turned to the score-cards of the judges and Ma read them out, it became apparent that Farron had won, with eight points to spare.

As they roared southwards on Route 83 half an hour later she couldn't remember exactly how he'd persuaded her to spend the rest of the day with him. What was it about this man that made her common sense desert her?

'Tell me about yourself, Farron,' she said quietly. 'You spoke of your grandmother before as if she took care of you. Is your mother still alive?'

'Nope.' Farron shook his head as he pulled back on to the road, and changed gear easily. 'She died when I was about eight or nine. I can't remember, really. I was living with my *tutu* even then.'

'Why? Was she ill?'

Farron smiled sadly. 'You might say that. She was a prostitute,' he said bluntly, feeling no shame. He'd come to terms with his mother a long, long time ago. 'She got into drugs and drinking and eventually died. *Tutu* never actually said what it was, but it could have been anything – a drugs overdose, liver or kidney failure – even VD.'

Vienna sucked in her breath. 'I'm so sorry. I had no idea . . . I mean, you're always so cheerful.'

Farron looked at her quickly. 'Don't go getting the wrong idea – I've had a great life. My *tutu* is a wonderful old gal. I had everything a kid could need – love, a stable home, friends my own age. In fact, I've been very lucky.'

'Lucky? What do you mean?'

Farron shrugged. 'In everything. I won a music scholarship to the University for one thing. Then I got a job at the Blue Hawaiian. Dominic's been great, and Kim and Danny are like brothers. Let's face it – if you've got friends your life can't be all bad.'

'No. But I don't know if I have any friends or not.'

'You must have. Somewhere.'

Vienna laughed hollowly. 'Yes. But where? I'm not from the islands, I'm almost convinced of that. But I like the country. Yet I don't know if that's because I was brought up in it, or if I'm a city girl responding to the peace and beauty of something I've never known before.'

The afternoon wore on as they explored her likes and dislikes, trying to find clues to what her past life might have been in a question-and-answer session that left her feeling much less alone.

He took her to Paradise Park, which was as lovely as its name suggested. The afternoon sun warmed them as they walked through bamboo forest trails past flamingo lagoons, where tall pink birds waded in the water, graceful necks swirling to and fro searching for food. Farron led her to fish-ponds alive with coloured fish and flowering waterweeds. The Park was big enough to take a large crowd that trooped to a Henri Hawaii Restaurant for tea and still leave enough room for couples to find shaded, private areas. It was in just such a place under a shower tree that Farron put down the picnic basket he'd retrieved from the boot of the car and unpacked it to reveal chicken legs and yams, a large breadfruit and crusty rolls. Cold fresh pineapple juice quenched their thirst as Vienna joined him on the ground and they ate the food with hungry relish. Finally replete they lay back on the grass.

Farron caught his breath as their eyes met in a rare moment of perfect understanding and leaned slowly closer, unable to resist temptation any longer. Vienna closed her eyes as his lips met hers in a gentle, tender and yet mind-blowing kiss that made her heart almost stop. Abruptly she pulled away and sat up looking straight ahead, her eyes catching a glimpse of something shining to her right. 'I'm sorry,' Farron said automatically, then added angrily, 'No, I'm not. I've wanted to do that ever since I first saw you. But you know that, don't you?'

Vienna sighed. 'I don't . . . Richard and I are . . . very close. I don't like myself much at the moment,' she added miserably.

'I can understand why you clung to the only person in a strange world who was there for you. Anyone would have done the same.'

'That's not true,' she cried, but her denial was unconvincing.

'Isn't it?' Farron said ruthlessly, refusing to let her look away as he captured her chin gently in his hand. 'Isn't it true, Vienna?'

'I don't know,' she mumbled.

'Liar,' he accused softly. 'You clung to him like a drowning man clutches at straws. But you're not drowning any more. You're stronger than you thought. You have a job, you have new friends . . . and you have me.'

'I have Richard too,' she said, and pulled her chin away.

'You don't have freedom though, do you? Do you know how many times you've looked at your watch this afternoon? You're so scared he'll get home from the hospital before you're there to greet him. It isn't your duty, you know. You don't owe him anything.'

'How can you say that?' She turned to him, her face bewildered and angry. 'He looked after me in hospital.'

'That is his job.'

'It wasn't his job to find me a place to live, though, was it? Or to keep the hospital administrator off my back, or help me get a driver's licence, or loan me money for clothes.'

'No. But do you really think he did all that out of the goodness of his heart? Do you?'

She looked away, doubts she had kept at bay about Richard now returning to haunt her.

'Your Richard is hardly the knight-in-shining armour type. I've been asking around after him,' Farron carried on grimly, 'and the nicest thing anyone has to say about him is that he's a social-climbing snob.'

Vienna opened her mouth to defend him, but Farron knew he had to reach her now, or it might never happen at all, so he pushed ahead, praying he was not going too fast. 'Now that you're out of shock, now that you've got a life, you can see that you made a mistake about him, can't you? Can't you?' he demanded urgently, his fingers tightening on her arms in his frustration. She remained stubbornly silent but her eyes brimmed with tears, making him groan softly. 'I didn't mean to make you cry. Don't, please.'

Vienna shook her head. 'Kiss me.'

Farron let out a long breath and then the world around them was fading into nothing as their bodies strained close, lips clinging together desperately. His hands clasped her as if to hold her to him forever and she pushed herself against him, needing to be held, to be convinced that what they were doing was right. Needing to know most of all that she was loved.

In the trees to their right the man who drove a red Volkswagen lowered his binoculars and parted his lips in a smile that looked more like a snarl. He wondered if the lovesick, pathetic doctor knew what was going on. She was really doing the rounds, this one. Bloody women, they were all alike. They all had the morals of alleycats and the greed of sharks.

RICHARD paced the flat and sipped neat bourbon. Looking out of the window he fought the urge to go downtown to the Blue Hawaiian and check that she wasn't there. But he already knew she wasn't as surely as he knew that she was beginning to slip away from him. He hadn't counted on Farron Manikuuna.

'Bastard,' Richard said softly, his large, strong fingers tightening on the glass. 'I know what you're up to, but you can't have her. She's mine!'

He drained the glass in one swallow and slammed it down on the table top, sitting heavily on the sofa. 'Where are you, damn you?' He took a picture out of his wallet and looked at it, his eyes slightly unfocused and unnaturally bright. The picture was of Vienna at the beach dressed in her striped bikini, leaning back on a blanket and smiling up at him. 'I made you,' he told her. 'Don't you understand that? I nurtured you, I took care of you. *I* did – not that bloody singer who only wants one thing from you.'

He stopped talking abruptly and leaned back, raising a shaking hand to push the dark-blonde hair from his forehead. Throwing aside the photo he stumbled into her bedroom and looking at the neatly-made bed there he pictured them in it together, making love. She wanted him – he knew how to make her writhe and moan. He could hear her breathless voice now, calling his name, pleading with him . . . No, the Hawaiian bastard wouldn't have her.

'Where are you?' he yelled again, a snarling anger growing

in his brain. He walked to the wardrobe, opening it and then slamming it shut, his eyes falling to her dresser. Roughly he opened the drawers, searching through the scanty things for evidence of her infidelity, his hands stilling as they found her bikini. He picked up the two pieces of cloth, his face clouded with an expression of pain. Suddenly he yanked his powerful hands apart, tearing the flimsy material with a loud ripping sound that seemed to echo around the empty rooms. Again and again he ripped the material until only tiny scraps littered the floor. Then he sank to the bed and hid his face in his hands, dry, rasping sobs tearing out of his throat. Eventually he brought himself under control. It was stupid to get so angry – there was no reason to think that she and that bastard were lovers. He knew her too well. She was too grateful to him to betray him. She needed him too much. Yes, that was it – needed him too much. He must make her realize just how much she really did need him.

He looked at the scraps on the floor and frowned. Quickly gathering them up he stuffed them into his pockets then drove to the shopping mall. Finding another bikini of the same design he purchased it and got back to the flat a scant five minutes before Vienna. He was in the kitchen making coffee when he heard her key in the door. Unobserved, he watched her come in, feeling a brief stab of pleasure and relief when he saw she was alone.

'Hi,' he said. She jumped, gasping as she spun around. 'Hey, it's only me.'

'Sorry,' she smiled nervously, fiddling with the beach-bag she had dropped on to an upright chair. 'I've had the feeling all day that someone was watching me. Raving paranoia, right?'

'Right, but not to worry – muggers hardly ever strike twice.'

A shadow passed over her face. 'What if it wasn't a mugging? What if it was deliberate? What if there is someone out there . . . someone whom I knew before, and he's trying to scare me?'

Richard walked over to her, catching her arms in his two hands in such a familiar gesture that she thought her guilt must be written across her forehead. 'Even if that's the case, no one's going to hurt you while I'm around.'

Vienna nodded, feeling dwarfed by his bulk and height but at the same time safe and protected. She leaned forward into his arms, resting her cheek against his chest and sighed. She belonged here – she must, or else nothing made sense. 'Why don't you have a bath and change,' he suggested. 'I've got a special treat in store for you.'

'Oh, Richard.' She wanted nothing more than a quiet night in but when she looked up at him, so familiar and kind, her words died in her throat. 'OK.'

'And wear your evening dress. I told you – it's a special treat.'

HALF an hour later the night scenery flew past as they drove to the harbour and he pointed to a large pleasure ship, its decks flooded with lights.

'It's beautiful,' she breathed.

'The *Rella Mae*,' he said. 'Just right for a sunset dinner, dancing and music.'

'Richard, it's lovely,' she said after they boarded, looking out to sea where the sun was just beginning to set. Minutes later they began to move slowly away from the quay, the deep dark ocean rushing past the bow as they began a short cruise out to sea. Above them silver stars began to appear along with a benevolent moon, and Vienna sighed deeply, telling herself she had to be one of the luckiest people around. A slow love song came over the loudspeakers behind them and Richard pulled her into his arms. 'Dance with me, lovely lady?'

They swayed in time to the music, but her eyes were open and unknowingly wistful. A man with deepset brown eyes and unruly hair sat on a chair at an empty table and watched them, his lips held back in a half-sneer that was hidden in the night shadows as he regarded the slowly dancing couple with febrile concentration. She'd rather be with the Hawaiian kid, he thought to himself – the lying, cheating little bitch. He shook his head, the sneer fading. He had to stay cool. He had to be calm, methodical, careful. Personal feelings couldn't come into a job like this . . .

The cruise lasted two hours, during which time Vienna ate the best food, drank the finest champagne and danced and strolled around the deck. But she was glad when the ship was once more berthed and they were driving home.

Back at the flat she quickly undressed and climbed into bed, knowing that Richard was watching her as he shrugged off his own clothes. She lay stiffly on her side as he got in beside her, tensing as she felt his hand on her bare arm. 'You must be tired,' he said softly. 'Why don't you get some sleep? I'll not wake you when I get up tomorrow.'

Vienna closed her eyes feeling unbearably guilty. He'd gone to such lengths to give her a lovely evening, and all the time she'd been wishing that it was Farron she was with, Farron's arms holding her, Farron's easy, teasing, potent presence surrounding her, warming her . . .

She sighed, slowly drifting away from all her problems and into another world, a world where she was with Farron, walking down a quaint, cobblestoned street with shop windows selling crinoline dresses and perfumed candles. Church bells pealed in the afternoon sun, and his fingers curled around hers as they held hands and windowshopped, laughing and teasing. In a doorway of a vine-covered shop he pulled her into his arms and kissed her with gloriously marauding lips. She closed her eyes in ecstasy then felt suddenly cold. When she opened her eyes again it was night, and the quaint street had changed into a dirty alley full of shadows and alive with rats and prostitutes who watched them and jeered. She pulled away as she saw a man with very short blonde hair, a square jaw and blue eyes. He was not tall but when he walked towards her she could see murder in his eyes. Terrified, she turned to warn Farron, then screamed as a round black object came spinning and hissing out of the night. She fell backwards as the object hit Farron on the head with a sickening crack. She heard his bones break and then there was blood . . . blood everywhere. She awoke screaming and the light snapped on.

'Ssh . . . It's all right. It was just a nightmare. Come on, now.' Richard comforted her, rocking her in strong arms as she sobbed out her fear, his voice deep and strong, pushing away the shadows. It had all been so real. So terrifying. And the blonde man – was he real? 'It was just a bad dream, that's all. Tell me,' he urged softly, kissing her hair and temples.

'I can't remember,' she lied, because now that the fear was gone all she wanted was Farron.

Richard fixed her a sedative. Kneeling beside her he held the glass to her lips, forcing her to drink in childlike obedience until it was all gone. He could feel her body trembling wildly in his arms as he gently lowered her and smiled down into her drowsy eyes. 'Aren't you glad I was here?' he asked softly, as she licked her dry lips.

'Yes, yes I am,' she said, her voice breathless and weak as the drug began to take effect.

'I've always been there for you, haven't I?' he asked, slipping the blanket over them, his arms cradling her as the fear began to recede.

'Yes,' she said obediently.

'And you know I'll do anything for you, don't you? Lie, cheat, steal . . . *kill*.'

Vienna closed her eyes, the world slowly fading. 'Yes,' she said, but she didn't know now to what she agreed. Her eyelids flickered as she felt gentle lips kiss her forehead and then she turned on to her side, resting her tearstained cheek on the pillow.

Richard watched her sleep for several minutes, his face intent as he gazed down at her, a satisfied smile on his lips as he considered his good luck. When he was sure she was settled he picked up the empty glass and rinsed it out in the sink. Tonight's nightmare couldn't have been better timed, he thought. And as long as she needed him, he was safe . . .

Stretching he walked to the window and opened it, breathing deeply of the fresh air, looking out over the streets scattered with traffic, feeling happier than he had in a long time. He did not notice the parked red Volkswagen on the street and could not see the lighted cigarette-end of the man who waited in the car, smoking with a slow deliberation, deepset eyes narrowed against the smoke as he watched, and wondered, and waited with snake-like patience . . .

Chapter 10

Rhiannon stepped from the plane on to her native soil, the excitement making her heart beat fast in her breast. For the first time since she was a baby she was on Hawaiian ground and she was very conscious of the warm bright sunshine as she walked to the airport building and approached passport control. She had sometimes wondered why Graham had never taken them to Hawaii on holidays, but whenever she'd asked him he'd always had some pat answer that satisfied her until the next time she'd wondered about it. He'd never talked much about their native home either, except when she'd questioned him. Dredging up memories of their infrequent conversations, she knew that the islands were a mishmash of white Americans, Hawaiians, Koreans, Japanese, Puerto Ricans, Chinese, Portuguese, Filipinos and Polynesians. She knew a smattering of the language, again courtesy of her father, and also a few of the old Hawaiian legends. But together with what she had learned from Ben's research department about the commercial aspects of the island and what she had read over the years about the unpredictable weather, the lush vegetation and the strategic importance of the islands to the United States, that was all she really knew about this strange new land into which she had just plunged herself so recklessly.

Once she'd passed through customs and walked into the airport lounge, a girl stepped forward and draped a *lei* around her neck, smiling widely in welcome. All the islands had traditional *leis* of different flowers – for Oahu the *lei* was comprised of ilima. On Molokai it would be made of kukui flowers, and on the Big Island, Hawaii itself, lehu flowers.

Ben had arranged for her to be met at the airport by a chauffeured limousine and from the back seat a man held out his hand to her and smiled, revealing perfect white teeth. 'Hello, I'm Jack Gunster.' His silver-blond hair contrasted sharply with his tan and electric blue eyes and she found herself wondering how many hearts he had broken in his thirty or so years. From all Ben's talk of Gunster's efficiency she'd been expecting a grey-suited man with grey hair and a personality to match. Jack's dazzling sexiness disconcerted her somewhat. To cover it, she slipped in beside him and smiled with what she hoped looked like professional friendliness.

'I could get used to this,' she murmured, looking out of the tinted windows of the black stretch-limo as they pulled away.

'Drink?' Jack offered, opening out an impressive bar.

'No thanks. Where are we going anyway?' she asked, her eyes on the skyscrapers and watching out for glimpses of the Pacific ocean. The city reminded her vaguely of Miami, a place she had visited quite a few times; they both shared a kind of sunny white holiday flavour.

'To your hotel of course,' Jack grinned. 'I have my orders from Ben.'

'We're booked at the Pink Palace?'

'Ben thought the Blue Hawaiian might be more appropriate.'

She caught her breath, realized that Ben had filled him in already, and slowly leaned back and let herself smile. 'Good choice,' she said softly. 'And I think I *will* have a drink — champagne, if you have it.'

Jack smiled. 'This car has everything. I hired it locally — it was easier than having one of Ben's shipped over.' He handed her a glass, his eyes running over her and coming back to rest on her mouth.

'Hm, lovely.' She took her glass of pale liquid and sipped it.

'How much do you know about the islands?' he asked lightly, and when she admitted to knowing very little, he spent the first part of the journey filling her in on what he knew, finishing off with a few items of trivia for good measure. 'Oahu can claim the only royal palace on American soil. It's home to the only major university for two thousand miles and it also has the world's purest water.'

Rhiannon looked away from his caressing blue eyes and sighed deeply. She knew he was sexually attracted to her but she couldn't afford to let that get in the way of her takeover of Fairchild Enterprises. She needed his expertise more than his sexual advances. Her business training had been extensive but was hardly in Dominic Fairchild's class. And if she was strictly honest with herself she was more nervous than she was letting on. Just the thought of being on the same island as her father's murderer made her skin shiver in a mixture of anticipation, dread and anger.

'Have you,' her voice was a little high and she coughed. 'Have you met Fairchild yet?' she managed as casually as she could, looking out over the Strip with unseeing eyes as highrise, white-painted hotels began to predominate.

Jack shrugged. 'No. I've just seen him around. I'm not quite in the rubbing-shoulders-with-royalty-class, not yet.'

Rhiannon nodded. 'Ben said you'd have his dossier ready.'

'I have it here. It makes for fascinating reading. He's quite some man, your Dominic Fairchild.'

Rhiannon bit back a hot denial and then settled down to read the report. It began with a copy of his birth certificate, listing his mother as a princess and himself as a prince. The word conjured up in her mind a fairy-tale man; tall and handsome, brave and noble, and she shook her head and carried on reading material that told her he was a brilliant scholar, leaving Oxford with a first-class degree in Politics, Philosophy and Economics.

'What's this note about the will?' she asked, as her eyes fell on the asterisk and several exclamation marks.

'Ah yes,' Jack said. 'I have a special treat for you there.' He reached into his breastpocket and withdrew a long white envelope which she took from him and quickly read, her eyes widening in shock and disbelief as she turned over the pages.

'The grandfather actually made up this will?' she said incredulously.

Jack nodded. 'And made sure it would be implemented.'

'Frederick must have been every bit as bad as his reputation. He's practically handed his grandson's head to us on a silver platter.' She looked at him quickly, a frown forming suddenly across her brows as a nasty suspicion hit her. 'Just how did you get hold of this?'

Jack smiled a smile of pure charm. 'I get by.'

She stared at him for a moment, fighting off a shiver of unease that ate its way into her spine, and then took a deep breath. 'I think we should get one thing clear right from the beginning,' she began quickly, noticing the way the smile slowly faded from his handsome face. 'I don't want any loose ends – legal ends – that might come back to hang me one day. I want Fairchild fair and square. It's his style to be crooked, not mine. Got that?'

'Got it.' Jack held up a hand in surrender, the smile once more back in place but not quite reaching his eyes. 'But don't get too excited about this,' he tapped the report on Dominic that she was still holding. 'The will was only the old man's way of keeping his grandson under his thumb. And Fairchild has kept strictly to its letter. And as long as he does, that,' he again tapped the folder, 'won't do us a bit of good.'

'Daddy talked about Frederick Fairchild sometimes. I don't think he liked him much.' She herself wondered what kind of a man could write such a harsh will, and even more, how Dominic Fairchild had reacted when he'd learned of it. She said thoughtfully, 'It must have hit him badly.'

'Of course,' Jack agreed callously. 'And there's something else I've got my research team investigating, also concerning the will. But it's taking time; the servants who were around in those days are hard to find. Some are dead and those that aren't won't talk.'

'Talk about what?'

'We're not sure it's anything at all. Just unsubstantiated rumours. Don't worry, the moment they find out anything you'll be the first to know. The investigative team I've set up is the best.' Jack looked at her curiously. He'd heard about Ben and a younger woman of course and had been surprised by Ben's request to ruin Fairchild, but now that he'd actually met the boss' mistress for himself he could well understand what prompted men to go out of their way to please her.

Rhiannon carried on reading but felt strangely dirty as the report became more personal, delving into a lifestyle that seemed more and more a lonely one, and less and less enviable. It was disconcerting to learn that the man you hated not only financed a children's hospital for the island's underprivileged, but also took time out from his busy schedule to regularly visit the children in the wards. But, no doubt, that was strictly for publicity purposes. Putting the papers away, she hesitated over the envelope of photographs.

'Inside is a smaller envelope of family pictures. The bigger prints are what the team took of him over this last week,' Jack filled her in.

She nodded and fished inside for the smaller envelope, turning over photos of school pictures in which Dominic's face had been circled. The odd family photo of Dominic and his grandfather along with newspaper clippings were the only other contents. 'A bit shy, weren't they?'

Jack shrugged. 'Some families don't care for publicity.'

'Can't stand up to the spotlight, you mean,' Rhiannon corrected grimly. 'And it must have cost Fred Fairchild dear to keep all those curious reporters quiet.' Just what had he been hiding? If there was something, she wanted to know.

Surprised by her sudden anger, Jack watched her carefully. He had worked for Ben Fielding for nearly ten years now, and the two men got on well. It had been a hard slog for Jack to become Ben's Chief Executive of the Oahu Branch but it had all been worth it. The money grew with the power, and Jack liked both. All he needed now was one more spectacular success – and crushing Fairchild for Ben would certainly be that – and he was sure to be London-bound. With a nice seat on the board to go with it, with any luck. And Jack, who was a closet Cockney, missed his home town.

Rhiannon shifted in her seat, unwilling to admit how the pictures of a small orphaned boy had affected her. He'd lost both his parents at Pearl Harbor, and she didn't want to be reminded that he'd had a tragic childhood, that he'd had a puppy as a youngster and became broken-hearted when it had died. What she wanted to see was a personification of evil, some dissipated old man with a cruel mouth and cold, unfeeling eyes. Eagerly she turned the first of the recent pictures over and gave a strangled cry.

'Miss Grantham, what is it? Are you all right?' Jack asked

sharply, his hand on her arm as he took in her pallor and wide, shocked eyes.

'These pictures,' she croaked. 'I thought you said they were taken this week?'

'That's right.' He stared at her, puzzled by her reaction, but she recovered in a moment, leaving him with no clue as to her real feelings.

She turned over photo after photo, seeing a man in the prime of life – jogging in a navy-blue tracksuit, his black hair damp from perspiration, his body lithe and graceful. Sitting in his car, bare arms stretched to the steering wheel, wind ruffling his hair. Walking along a sidewalk, dressed in a dark grey suit, looking the epitome of a successful businessman. And always the face was the same – unlined, classical, with green eyes that watched the world with a confident coolness that infuriated her. 'Damn him,' she said softly, then more forcefully, 'Damn him!' and shoved the photographs back into the folder. She'd assumed the women he'd known had been only after his money or the kudos of bedding a title, but now . . . now she had to admit that any woman would be attracted to such a man for his looks alone, and bile rose in her throat.

'We're there.' Jack interrupted her bitter thoughts but her show of anger was making him more and more curious.

'Good. And please,' she calmed down and smiled apologetically, 'call me Rhia.'

THE Emerald Suite was spectacular. Luxurious ivory-coloured carpets and walls of stark white created a perfect foil for the emerald-green velvet curtains that hung at wide French windows leading out on to a generous balcony. The king-sized bed was covered with an emerald satin bedspread and the cushions on the white leather sofa and chairs were also green. On a wooden, highly polished coffee table stood a huge fresh-flower arrangement of broad verdant leaves and orange-speckled lilies.

Jack tipped the bellboys generously as they left, having deposited the luggage just inside the door, and Rhiannon walked past the bed and looked into a bathroom complete with a jacuzzi tiled in cool green.

Jack grinned, showing perfect white teeth. 'Approve?'

'Oh yes, I approve. But I'd like to see his penthouse some time. And if I approve of that also I might just move in there permanently.'

'He has other hotels,' Jack pointed out, grinning at her cheek.

'But this was his first, wasn't it? The old hotels of Frederick Fairchild have long since been torn down.'

'Yes. He saw the hotel boom in the 1970s coming long before anyone else. By purchasing the sites early he could've made a fortune just selling them again.'

'But instead he built this,' she said, looking around her. 'Very stylish. That looks like a Mies van der Rohe chair.'

Jack wasn't about to be sidetracked. 'So now you've seen the lion's den, what do you think?'

Rhiannon shrugged. 'If his den had been a wooden shack in a jungle I'd still want it, just because it was his.' She kicked off her shoes and walked to the French windows, stepping out into late-afternoon sunshine. Below her a blue swimming pool lined with holidaymakers sweltered in a surprisingly colourful green garden. To her left Waikiki Beach curved and meandered out of sight – a creamy white expanse of sand, lapped by turquoise waters on one side, and overlooked by towering white hotels on the other. Palm trees grew in every hotel garden and Rhiannon breathed deeply of air now definitely redolent of ocean breezes and exotic flowers.

'I've booked dinner at his other hotel at Waimea Bay – the Princess Liliha.'

'Hm . . . he's fond of that name, isn't he?' she murmured thoughtfully, then angrily pushed away any thoughts of his vulnerability. It probably didn't have anything to do with love for the mother he'd never known. He was probably only using it to trade on his royal connections for advertising purposes. 'What time's dinner, by the way? I'm starving.'

'Nine. You'd better get changed – it's an hour's drive at best. I thought you might like to see something of his other hotels.'

'Good idea. After all, they'll be mine, I mean Ben's, one day.'

'Don't be so confident,' Jack warned hardily, his blue eyes growing cool. 'Fairchild has a far tighter grip on his hotels than he had on the boutiques – especially now. While you've been in London he's been consolidating and strengthening his position almost as if he knows what might be coming. He's a perceptive man – a tough fighter, too.' And if he was to win the day for Ben by destroying Fairchild, he had to make sure Ben was well aware not only that it was all his own work, but that it had been a hard and dangerous job too.

'Oh, I can wait until the time is right. Just so long as he sweats a little while I do it,' Rhiannon said, wishing she felt as tough and confident as she sounded.

Jack walked to the door. 'I shouldn't count on that. I don't think your Dominic frightens easily.'

'Stop calling him that. He isn't "my" anything!'

'OK.' He held out his hands in a pacifying gesture. 'But don't expect him to just lie down and play dead.'

'Oh, I want him alive,' she admitted softly. 'I want him to live so that he can suffer as my father suffered. To wait for the axe to fall, as my father had to wait. To face ruin, scandal, defeat and stare them in the eye as my father had to. And I'll show him exactly the same amount of mercy as he showed Daddy!'

Jack felt his skin chill at her unexpected vehemence and he shrugged to disguise the uncharacteristic shiver that ran up his spine. 'Try to civilize yourself for dinner, hm? I don't think I care to be seen out with a woman who eats raw meat off the bones.' And again he flashed his artfully charming smile her way.

'I got carried away, right?' she said ruefully.

'I would have said so, just a touch.' He held out two fingers, a scant millimetre apart to show just how much, and she laughed.

'I'll be on my best behaviour, I promise. Oh, one more thing. Can you arrange for my Norton motorbike to be flown over?'

'Sure . . . motorbike?'

'What can I say? I love them. I learned to scramble in a muddy field outside Cheltenham when I went to school there.'

Jack left to change, still shaking his head in disbelief. Rhiannon ran a bath, adding Floris gardenia bath oil to the steaming water and, stripping off, pinned up her long raven locks and sank into the water with a sigh of bliss. Damn! She'd meant to ask Jack if he'd managed to buy back her father's old house on the island. She'd been determined to reclaim his bungalow. Absolutely everything that Dominic had stolen from them, she was determined to get back.

Patting herself dry she donned a half-bra and close-fitting panties of flesh-coloured satin. A maid had unpacked whilst she'd been bathing and she selected a low-cut evening gown of a colour that could have been described as either silver, lavender or dove grey. Of finest silk it shone like a lustrous pearl and laying it out on the bed she walked to the mirror of a large dressing table and sat down. She smoothed cream on to her face and added the merest dusting of face powder to take off the sheen. On to her lids she stroked smoky lavender eyeshadow and painted her lips a light plum. Then she backcombed her hair into artful disarray, which made her look a little wild and very, very dangerous. The dress was simple in style. Leaving her right shoulder and back bare, it hugged her breasts lovingly and left the tops uncovered to show a discreet but intriguing cleavage. Pinched in tight at the waist it fell to her feet in subtle folds. Stepping into high, glitteringly silver heels, she added around her neck a simple pear-drop necklace on a fine silver chain, and donned a platinum and diamond watch. Into a silver lamé evening bag she dropped a comb and lace hankie. After spraying herself liberally with Yves St Laurent's Rive Gauche, she dropped the blue and black slim tube of perfume into the bag and snapped it shut.

When the knock came on the door, Rhiannon automatically checked her watch, smiling at Jack's punctuality. 'Come in.'

Jack, handsome in a black evening suit, opened the door and then stood quite still as his eyes travelled over her. 'Beautiful,' he said simply.

'Thank you.' She began to fidget under the intensity of his hot gaze. 'Hadn't we better get going?'

THE Princess Liliha Hotel was, she had to admit, quite lovely.

Sitting at their table, listening to a smoky-voiced woman singing love songs, they drank Kona coffee served piping hot after a truly excellent meal. She was just raising her second cup to her lips when the world seemed to jar to a screeching halt around her.

Dominic Fairchild himself, wearing casual black slacks and a loose-fitting black and white shirt, walked casually over to the bar and took a seat.

Rhiannon dragged her eyes away from the sight of him and swallowed hard, her mouth suddenly dry. 'He's here,' she said quietly, her hands perfectly steady now as she replaced her cup in its saucer. 'Wait for me in the car, will you? I won't be long.'

'You're not going to do anything foolish, are you?' he asked bluntly. He didn't think she was the stupid sort, but the last thing he needed was for her to mess things up for him.

'Don't worry – I'm not going to show my hand. I'll be all right,' she confidently predicted, giving Jack no other choice but to reluctantly make his way to the parking lot. Before her courage could desert her she headed for the bar, only then noticing that there was another room beyond a large glass doorway, and through it she could see dancing couples swaying to the music teased from a piano by a man with shockingly white hair.

Her heart began to trip in giddy anticipation of confronting him at last. She slipped on to the bar stool next to his with silent grace, grateful to relieve her trembling legs of her weight, but her face showed none of this inner turmoil as the bartender spotted her.

As Dominic saw Bill's 'customer smile' come into play he turned around casually and then froze at the sight of the vision next to him. Cascades of raven hair fell to delicate shoulders and he felt every muscle in his body leap into life as she turned to glance at him. Delicately arched black brows framed eyes of a deep jade green. Her cheek and jawbones were exquisite, her nose delicate and her lips ripe and full. Lips which now curved slightly in a polite, bored smile.

He turned on the stool to face her, his lean body tense with sexual interest.

Rhiannon ordered cognac from the barman. Even though she was no longer looking at him she could still see every detail of his face in her mind; the strong square chin, slanting bright green eyes, high intelligent forehead and the strong sweeping planes of his high cheekbones. She accepted the brandy and sipped it, admiring the dry taste on her palate. 'Not bad,' she told the barman, her smile friendly enough to take any bite out of her words. 'I've had better, mind.' She looked over the dining room and placed her silver bag on the bar, suddenly remembering that she had no money in her purse. For a second she felt dismay wash over her, but then could only smile ruefully at her own stupidity. So much for her *femme fatale* approach!

'Would you care for something else?' At the sound of his surprisingly deep and resonant voice Rhiannon drew in a sharp breath.

'No. Thank you, anyway. But after a mediocre meal you may as well have a mediocre drink to wash it down.' She didn't look at him as she said this, but behind her she could feel the barman bristle. Out of the corner of her eye she saw Dominic move a hand in a warning gesture to be silent.

'I'm sorry you didn't like the food,' he apologized, and Rhiannon shrugged the shoulder nearest to him in a delicate gesture.

'It doesn't matter — not when the entertainment makes up for it. The singer is good.'

'She'll be so pleased to hear it,' he said drily.

'I'm sure.' Her own voice was just as dry, and Dominic's eyes sharpened at the unexpected response. She knew instinctively that this man was used to women coming on to him, and she was determined to be different — *in every possible way*. She wanted to confound him; she ached to confuse him and yearned to lead him by the nose and taunt him with her triumph.

'Do you have any problems with the décor?' he asked and she looked around slowly, letting the moment stretch, before giving her verdict.

'Over the top,' she finally decided, and Dominic turned on the stool and looked around.

'The place seems to be doing a very good trade to me,' he said casually, his green eyes noting every move she made.

'It could do better — if it was managed correctly,' she proffered with such confidence that Dominic was momentarily startled.

'Really? I actually own this hotel and I thought it was doing quite well.' He watched her, expecting to see at least a flicker of discomfort cross her lovely face, but to his surprise the girl merely looked at him. Her eyes were cool as she slowly and deliberately examined him from head to toe in an impersonal gaze that made delicious tremors stir in every part of him. He found himself holding his breath as he waited for her next move.

Rhiannon sighed gently and took a final sip of her drink before placing it on the bar and collecting her bag. 'I can understand that,' she said finally with artfully insulting ambiguity, her voice husky and just slightly cold.

Dominic began to grin. He couldn't help it. He couldn't remember ever having been so successfully and so charmingly put down before. How could he protest or make anything out of that cruel little answer? Had he but known it, the effect of his smile on his tormentor had been enough of a come-back in itself. Rhiannon's heart leapt in her breast as something hot and unwanted lanced through her carefully constructed armour of cold determination, making her body tremble in an instinctively sexual reaction.

'I'll take that as a compliment,' he said, and turning to the barman told him, much to her relief, that her drink was on the house.

'Good answer,' Rhiannon said with annoying magnanimity. 'In the words of King Charles I, "Never make a defence or apology before ye be accused".'

'You're English, I take it,' Dominic said, and then could have kicked himself as he realized how gauche he'd sounded.

The woman paused, flicked him a look of almost pained disappointment and contented herself with a crushing, 'How very observant you suddenly are.' But Dominic was not a man easily crushed and he grinned widely as he chalked up an imaginary figure '1' in the air to sportingly acknowledge the direct hit.

Rhiannon walked towards the glass doorway, suddenly yearning to get away from the man, away from his voice that seemed to cut through her skin, away from his eyes that were clear and alive with undermining good humour. This was not how she had pictured their first encounter. The excitement of the parrying and fencing was too intoxicating for her liking, and much too distracting.

As he opened the door for her she felt her skin tingle in reaction to his proximity and to her horror, felt that secret place deep within her clench tight in unmistakable desire. She must be wrong – must be! She closed her eyes in brief panic and then stumbled into the room.

Dominic watched her move away and followed, knowing he was being led on by an expert but wanting to be led. It had been a long, long time since any woman had had such an instant impact on him and he sensed that there was more to her than just the obvious. There was something contrary about her – but was it only that, he asked himself candidly. Beautiful women had used every lure in the book, and he'd never bitten before, perhaps because he'd never been curious enough about what lay beneath their silky, feline veneer. But with this woman he sensed that he needed to know – that it was somehow important. Very important.

He tracked her across the room with infinite patience. Her back was warm honey, the indentation of her spine making him long to press his lips to her soft flesh and explore the ridges of her vertebrae with a seeking tongue.

She stopped at the piano as she recognized the song as *It's Impossible*. Dominic's breath caught and lodged in his throat as he saw the rueful but brilliant smile that suddenly transformed her face.

'Let's start again,' he said softly as she turned to give him an arch look, and he held out his hand with two fingers crossed. 'Pax?'

Rhiannon, totally disconcerted, let him lead her on to the dance floor where he pulled her with masculine ease into his arms. Angrily, she tossed back her head, feeling a frightening thrill of pleasure shoot through her as his lean body stiffened in response.

'Should I apologize for being so cavalier?' he asked, torn between a desire to win the cat-and-mouse game she insisted upon playing and an equally strong desire to gentle the whole thing down, find a quiet corner somewhere, and just talk, just explore who she was and who they could be together.

'I don't know,' Rhiannon said evasively, telling herself she was mad to think his eyes had suddenly become gentle. 'Do you make a habit out of bullying strange women?'

He frowned as he looked down into her eyes, a denial springing automatically to his lips when suddenly a memory from far away called to him. He said, almost as surprised as she by his words, 'We've met before somewhere.'

A wave of fear hit her and she tried to pull away. 'Oh, come now,' she said scornfully. 'The old haven't-we-met-somewhere-before routine is too much, even for you!' She attempted to step back but he totally defeated her by refusing to let go.

'I didn't ask if we'd met somewhere before,' he corrected her. 'I stated it as a fact. There's something about you I recognize.'

'Unless you've been in England recently, I can't see how. This is my first trip to the islands.' She stared past his shoulder, her stiff body a silent testimony to her disapproval and anger, but even so she was aware that whenever her breasts brushed the cotton of his shirt her nipples tingled and tightened ominously. She reassured herself that that meant nothing. They'd just met and, like people sometimes do, felt an instant sexual attraction. It was just chemical. It meant nothing. Nothing at all.

The music stopped and this time when she pulled out of his arms he let her go, but followed her as she made her way to the open balcony and stepped out into the moonlit garden. Down some shallow well-lighted steps and on to a soft lawn, she was attracted by the reflected moon's surface on some water nearby. Feeling calmer now she moved towards the pond. Play the game, she told herself. Play it, and win.

'I envy you your island,' she said softly, knowing that he had followed her.

'You shouldn't. Envy me, I mean,' he added as she looked

at him questioningly. 'You're the last person in the world who has to envy anyone.'

'It's getting late – I must go,' she said abruptly, suddenly feeling drained. Fencing with Dominic Fairchild was undoubtedly exciting and an experience unlike any other, but it was also exhausting.

'I'll give you a lift.'

She shook her head. 'I have a car – that one, in fact.' She pointed through the trees to where the black limousine waited, and Dominic raised a brow in silent acknowledgement of yet another score chalked up to her.

'Are you free for dinner tomorrow?'

Her voice was cool and mocking as she lifted her chin in a gesture of haughty challenge. 'Of course.'

Dominic's smile was every bit as dangerous. 'Of course you are. Where are you staying?'

'The Blue Hawaiian.'

Again he smiled softly. 'Where else?'

This time it was her turn, and her smile was pure devilment as she echoed softly, 'Where else indeed?'

He took time savour the moment, then murmured, 'I'll pick you up at eight. Suite. . . ?'

'I'll meet you in the lobby.' She neatly sidestepped giving him the information he sought and began to walk away.

'You forgot to tell me your name,' Dominic called softly, his eyes following every swaying movement of her body as she walked into the night. Slowly, teasingly, Rhiannon stopped and looked over her shoulder.

'I didn't forget,' she corrected. 'You'll know my name soon enough. 'And,' she promised with a dangerous edge to her voice that Dominic did not miss, 'believe me, you won't ever, ever forget it.'

Chapter 11

The city lights of Honolulu shone brightly beyond the windows of his penthouse as Dominic mixed himself a very mild gin and tonic and walked over to a large stereo unit. The majestic sounds of Dvorak's 'New World' Symphony flowed out of hidden speakers, the music suiting his mood of restless expectation. Something was in the air – something new; something magnificent was going to happen, and soon. He could feel it.

He stretched out on the sofa and using alternate heels to slip off his shoes, gave a tired sigh. Placing his glass on a table nearby his eyes fell on a large photograph of an old man. Seated on one of the benches in Kapuna's garden, Frederick Fairchild looked out at his grandson with eyes that both mocked and admired, and Dominic grunted, raising his glass to the picture. 'To you, you rotten old bastard,' he said and took a long, slow sip.

THE old man lying in the bed looked to his young nurse as if he were made out of wax. His skin was an unhealthy grey and shone in the filtered sunlight gleaming in through the open window. Outside, two of the gardener's boys were hoeing in the borders, whilst a radio played one of the hits of that summer of 1961, *Yakety Yak* by the Coasters, which competed with the sounds of *I Love Lucy* blaring from a TV set somewhere deep inside the house.

The old man didn't mind the noise – trivial though it was, it reminded him that he was still alive. His eyes opened to mere red-rimmed slits, his watery blue irises flicking yet again to his bedside clock. Hours – hours had gone by. The boy would be here soon. He had to be. He wasn't sure that he could hold on. No, dammit, he would simply refuse to die until he had his grandson by his side.

His eyes never wavered as the young and pretty nurse he'd hired personally only two months ago checked his pulse.

Once, Fred Fairchild knew, he could have snapped every bone in her body with the hands that now lay limp and unmoving by his side. Once he could have made the young girl, standing so stiff and prim in her starched, pale blue uniform, pant and moan with desire. Like his grandson undoubtedly could now.

The young nurse frowned as the old man began to wheeze, but when her eyes flew to his she understood at once that the old reprobate was laughing! She shook her head, her blonde curls bouncing under the white cap perched on her head, lips curving upwards in a smile that expressed her genuine fondness for her patient. She'd heard of Frederick Fairchild, of course, long before she'd seen the post of private nurse to him advertised in the local hospital newsletters. She could still remember her nervousness as she walked down the path of this very bungalow, wondering if the old man could possibly be as bad or as vivid as his reputation. It hadn't taken her long to realize that he was. Although confined to a wheelchair, Frederick Fairchild had a presence that was immediately apparent. Stooped though his shoulders were they remained broad and impressive. Similarly, in his prematurely aged sixty-five-year-old countenance, his eyes still held the all-seeing sharpness of a bird. The hooked nose had been broken some time in his youth, Judith Myers had seen immediately, but as his voice, weakened by his illness but still carrying that unmistakable tone of authority, had fired questions at her, she'd found herself somehow disappointed yet relieved that she'd never met this man when he'd been in the peak of health. It had been a sad job watching him slowly deteriorate, progressing from the wheelchair to complete bed-rest, from solid foods to liquids. And yet even now, with death surely only hours, maybe even minutes away, here he was, chuckling over some private thoughts.

'No sign of my grandson yet?' The voice was a tremulous whisper but Judith had had years of practice understanding and deciphering the strained, erratic speech of the chronically sick and dying, and she shook her head.

'But he won't be long,' she said quickly. Knowing he needed to have something to focus on she deliberately looked around the room, searching for something. And as her eyes fell on a portrait of a woman, lovely as any woman could possibly be, she knew she had the perfect opportunity to satisfy her curiosity as well. 'That painting – I've always admired it. Was she your wife?'

Frederick Fairchild's eyes slowly turned to look at the portrait of Princess Liliha Pelena, and shook his head. 'Daughter-in-law,' he said. 'My son's wife – lovely, wasn't she?'

Judith walked to the portrait and looked up into eyes of ebony, set in a face of total serenity and beauty, and nodded. 'Yes. She's dead, isn't she?' she asked curiously. The other servants never talked about the family except to praise the old man's grandson, Dominic, who was at Oxford University and it hadn't taken her long to sense a family mystery.

'Killed at Pearl Harbor,' the old man rasped, his eyes misting over as he remembered the moment he'd first set eyes on her. His words fluctuated and ebbed then rose more strongly as he talked about his son and his Hawaiian princess. 'I knew he was seeing her, of course. I could read Grant like a book – not like Dominic. Grant fell hard . . . yes . . . hard.' The eyes flickered from the portrait to the picture by his bedside of a man with short brown hair, green eyes and a kind smile. 'Not tough, either – not like I wanted him to be. Not like Dominic is now.'

'You're very fond of your grandson, aren't you?' Judith said, pulling up a chair by the man's side the better to hear him. Fred grunted a laugh and then caught his breath as the pain bit deep. Judith waited, knowing she could do nothing about it. He was already stuffed with morphine and she knew without asking that he didn't want, or dare, to fall asleep. 'He'll be here soon,' she said again, looking him straight in the eye.

Fred nodded and gave a shallow sigh, dragging his mind away from the interminable waiting. 'She loved him, though – I'll say that for her.'

'Who?' Judith asked, momentarily losing track of their conversation. 'Oh, your son's wife. She was a princess, wasn't she?'

'Yes. But none of us approved – not her father, and not me.

I had a little gal all lined up for Grant – Mary Hornskan. She was the daughter of old Dwayne Hornskan . . . but Grant was having none of it. Oh, he pretended, taking her out every now and then to keep me happy . . .'

'But you knew,' Judith finished for him as the old man struggled for breath.

'I knew. I thought it would blow over – all his other fancies had. But . . .'

'It was for real this time?' Judith prompted, looking at the portrait of the lovely Hawaiian princess again, her eyes misty at the romance of it all.

Fred grunted in impatience but his eyes were kind as he looked at the pretty young nurse. He supposed it was the way of women to hanker after romance. Romance – a load of bullshit! Still . . . his eyes strayed to those of his long-dead son and he wondered. Perhaps . . .

'And so they married.'

'Eloped,' Fred corrected, his voice holding a distinct snap. 'Knew damned well her dad and me would have stopped 'em.' He grunted a silent laugh, wheezing now. 'First and last time he ever disobeyed me. Just came home with her one night and s-said, "I'd like you to meet my wife." That was the first time I'd met her face to face. My God, she was lovely, and as cool and charming as any southern belle.'

Judith looked at the picture again, imagining the scene. 'What did you do then?'

Fred closed his eyes, feeling his body slipping away from him. He couldn't feel his toes or his fingers. He felt almost disembodied and he opened his eyes with a snap. No! No, he wouldn't go. Not until Dominic came back.

'What did you do then?' Judith prompted sharply, her hand reaching out to hold his. Fred's fingers tightened on hers in silent thanks, and he took a deep painful breath.

'What could I do? Rantin' and ravin' wouldn't change it. 'Sides, I could see why he was so smitten. I told Tansie to make up the big bedroom for them.'

'And they lived here?'

'Yep – her old man disowned her. Damned stupid thing to do; she was his only heir. Last of her line.'

'Except for your grandson. He's a prince, isn't he?'

Fred snarled, 'He's American!' The words were strong and clear and cost him much. For the next few minutes he concentrated just on breathing and staying alive whilst Judith made a mental vow not to touch on what was so obviously a sore point again. 'He was born here, in this house,' Fred continued a few minutes later. 'Dominic. He was the best thing the girl ever did. I think I forgave her for marrying my son the night Dominic was born. I held him after Grant took him off the midwife. Covered in blood, an' stuff. But he opened his eyes and looked up at me . . . didn't cry, neither. Never knew a baby like him for not crying. 'Course, the war was on then in Europe. And Grant and me – we both knew that America would have to come into it sooner or later. Should have done right at the beginning – I always said so. Leavin' England and Russia to fight alone so long . . . damned Roosevelt – always said he was a goddamned coward.'

Judith bit back a sharp retort at the slander, then found herself smiling. Opinionated was one of the kinder things she'd heard said about this man. 'And your son wanted to join the navy?' she guessed.

A look of pain crossed the old man's face and she quickly put a stethoscope to her ears and placed the cool disc on his sunken chest. His heart thumped, but it was a desultory sound and her face was blank as she removed the instrument. But Fred was thinking back over the years and missed the look.

'No. He wanted to join the army, volunteer to fight with the English. I made him stay. I thought he'd be safe at Pearl Harbor. God, I hate Japs! If I could I'd drop a hundred more H-bombs and wipe out the bloody lot of the slanty-eyed, yellow-skinned bastards!' He began to cough and hack, his eyes rolling back in his head and Judith stood up, alarmed. Reaching for an oxygen cylinder she placed the mask over his face and with firm hands pushed him back against the pillows. Coloured lights flashed behind his eyelids and for a few ugly moments he thought he was going to lose the struggle, that when his grandson came back he'd find him dead. But he had too many things to tell him. Too much to say. And he needed to see him just one last time. Oh yes, how he needed that.

Judith relaxed as the old man calmed down. Cautiously, she pulled the black rubber mask away. 'Feeling better?' she asked and Fred nodded, not trusting his voice to speak and for several minutes the room was totally silent.

'I was in bed when it happened. Most of us were,' Fred finally resumed the story. 'December the seventh, 1941. I'll never forget it. It was as if the world was ending . . . We rushed out of bed and into the gardens. We couldn't see the planes from here, but the smoke, the flames . . . I knew at once what was happening.' His eyes strayed to the portrait once more and tears glimmered in his eyes. 'I tried to stop her but I was too late. She was as fleet as a deer. Just screamed his name and took off runnin'.'

For a moment Judith didn't follow his meaning, but as she followed his eyes to the painting she suddenly understood. 'She went after him?'

Fred nodded. 'I lost 'em both that mornin'. Never did know whether they found one another but the chances couldn't have been good. I'd like to think they did, though. Yeah – I'd like to think so.'

'So you brought up your grandson?'

Fred smiled. 'Dragged him up, more like. Little bastard fought me every step of the way. Must have got it from her.' But although his voice was hard, the eyes that were fixed on the portrait of the young woman reclining on the chaise longue were bright and full of respect.

'He'll be here,' she said again, this time praying that she was right.

'I know,' Fred said, closing his eyes briefly, wondering if it were true that when a man died his whole life flashed before his eyes.

He'd been born in 1896 in Boston, Massachusetts, and the only thing he remembered about his childhood was the black poverty; his father coming home every night looking progressively more broken and his mother bent over a mangle where she seemed to be permanently washing clothes. Her hair had been grey at twenty-five and Fred could not imagine a time when it hadn't been. A manual worker at the docks, his father used up his body's strength loading and unloading crates, coming home at night with hands full of splinters that his mother would routinely extract with tweezers that she dipped in a bottle of rum from which his father had then drunk. Looking back, Fred could not place a specific time when he's sworn to have a different life.

To bring money into a family of ten kids, of whom he was the eldest, he'd spend six hours after a school day down at the docks, unloading, packing, hauling and bringing in a pittance that nevertheless just managed to keep the family from starving. One of his little brothers had died of influenza, but he couldn't now remember his name. Arthur, was it? Two others had died in an outbreak of cholera.

Despite the gruelling work, Fred still managed to win a precious and newly implemented scholarship to Harvard. His teachers had been delighted, his family despairing. He could remember the day he'd packed his suitcase and left. A single pair of trousers, three pairs of underpants, a darned shirt and a brand new cheap tie had been the cloth bag's only contents. He promised to send money every week, which he did, doing any job he could get but Harvard had taken up most of his time. And when news came that his father was dead, and most of his brothers and sisters had been taken to a local orphanage, he arrived just too late to attend the funeral. Taking one look at his mother, he predicted that it wouldn't be long before she joined her husband, and sure enough, she had died within a year.

This was the one and only time in Frederick Fairchild's life that he'd felt utterly helpless. With his family scattered and lost to him, he'd worked through the worst of his frustration by getting a top degree in business studies. During a summer job working at a prestigious hotel the fever had been born – hotel fever. And he finally knew how he was going to apply his education. His dedication was rewarded by a first-class degree. Newly graduated, he was conscripted into the last year of World War, I, an experience hammered into his memory as no other had been before or since, save for the loss of his son.

But as well as leaving him with the stench of death embedded in his nostrils and a raging anger at the injustice and waste of it all, the army, and the war also left him with an idea and the contacts to carry it out.

After his family's need for money had ceased, he'd saved regularly throughout college and with his army pay that he'd refused to squander on cigarettes, women and rye he leased a huge barn of a house that he converted into rooms for demobbed soldiers. Many men came back from the war to find their parents dead, or their wives gone. Alone and suddenly homeless, it was to these men that he rented rooms, taking the first sweet bite out of the cherry of success. The need for cheap accommodation boomed as post-war depression set in, and he made enough profit to allow him to open other boarding houses in New York. Within a year, Fred had more money than his father could ever have dreamed of, but Fred was the original man in a hurry. At the age of twenty-three, whilst gatecrashing a Boston society ball, he met Winifred Pagett, the nineteen-year-old heiress to an industrial machinery firm.

Seeing at once the potential of machinery in a future industrial boom, Frederick set about wooing the sheltered and pretty little socialite, much to her father's delight and her mother's horror. Johan Pagett, a Polish immigrant, liked the young man with gumption and brains and cared not a jot for his humble beginnings. And as their romance blossomed Fred began to feel a genuine, if diluted, love for his Winifred and he could remember her in her wedding dress to this day. Flame-haired, her blue eyes demure and downcast, she'd walked up the aisle like a queen. Attracted by Fred's brand of brash charm, influenced by his powerful charisma and excited beyond caution and all her mother's warnings by a man who'd known poverty and the horrors of war, Winifred had been easy and willing prey.

Determined to make a life of his own he left the States for Oahu, which was already becoming known as *The* place to holiday. Gauguin had started the craze with his paintings of the South Sea, and soon film stars like Mary Pickford and Douglas Fairbanks Jnr had followed Robert Louis Stevenson to the islands, rapidly setting a fashion that was soon to be copied by the world's wealthy citizens; Fred saw his chance to make his dreams of a hotel empire come true. His father-in-law, bitterly disappointed though he was by not having Fred take over the control of Pagett Parts & Machinery, nevertheless had sufficient confidence in him to give him a substantial loan to buy his first beach-front property.

From there he'd never looked back. The beauty of the place was an added bonus, but it was the pioneer spirit that appealed to his nature most. Raised on tales of how the Wild West was settled, Fred saw himself as a new breed of pioneer man, bringing good American know-how to the dark-skinned, easygoing natives. He thrived on challenge, but never really understood the native people, whom he slowly came to think of as lazy and sexually promiscuous. Slowly, a Them and Us gulf widened in his mind, and he began to give all the top jobs in his growing company to fellow whites.

Over the years the company thrived, as did his love for his wife. Even Winifred's mother had to admit that her daughter's marriage was a success, especially when Winifred gave birth to a healthy son.

Fred's second taste of tragedy came when Winifred drowned whilst swimming in the sea one sunny afternoon while her four-year-old son slept on a blanket on the beach. It had been Grant, wandering into his father's hotel unaccompanied, bewildered and crying for his mother, that had sparked the search that had ended with Winifred's body being dragged from the sea. Fred coped by pouring every ounce of his love, pride and ambition into his son, not stopping to wonder whether the boy could cope with it or not.

Several years after that, with the dual deaths of his in-laws in a train wreck, Fred had unexpectedly inherited Pagett's. Knowing his father-in-law would have guessed that he would sell it, Frederick did just that without the slightest qualm or feelings of guilt. The fortune enabled him not only to build his second hotel, but also to buy properties on all the islands. He knew that owning land was the greatest security he could hand over to his son, the often lonely only child who now meant the world to him.

Fred sighed now and opened his eyes, seeing the nurse standing by the window. He had not counted on losing Grant so soon. To outlive your child was an horrific cross to have to bear, and it had been Dominic who'd enabled him to survive. Dominic, a mere scrap of life, growing and developing, showing his grandfather character traits that simultaneously delighted and aggravated him. In the pugnacious jaw of a five-year-old he saw his own grim determination to succeed. In the battle of wills between the small boy and the older man, he had seen echoes of an earlier fight. In all aspects, he was the perfect heir.

Tansie tiptoed into the room to check on him and outside he could hear the gardener's boys talking lasciviously about Marilyn Monroe. Somewhere, a long way off, a dog barked. 'Did you know that Gloria's place has moved?' one of the boys said quite distinctly and Judith and Tansie both blushed, their eyes meeting involuntarily and then quickly moving away again in silent acknowledgement that nice women like them wouldn't know about such things. 'Really? 'Bout time. The other place was a fleapit.'

From the bed came a dry rasping chuckle; the nurse walked over to him as Tansie hurried out into the garden to admonish the two unsuspecting young men outside whilst Fred's thoughts turned to Dom and his Hawaiian whore. The boy had given him a bad few months there – months when he'd had the horrible feeling of déjà vu. He had pushed the boy towards Harvard knowing only that he had to get him off the island, away from the whore. Typically Dominic had rebelled, insisting on Oxford. Had the whore's attractions gone cold now? He knew Dom had visited her during both the late summer and Christmas vacations but he had seen a new maturity in his grandson at Easter. Easter, when he'd worked him so hard he knew damned well he hadn't the energy to go carousing to Gloria's place.

He might be bedridden but he had his spies. He knew about the leased bungalow the little whore was now living in, and chuckled silently in approval that Dom had not been so infatuated as actually to buy the place for the money-grabbing little bitch. He shifted slightly in the bed as his thoughts mulled over his latest information. The child: was it Dom's? Personally he doubted it; the whore had more men visitors than the rest of Gloria's girls put together. And his grandson was nobody's fool – hadn't he already proved that? Still . . . he thought about the will Arnold Grantham had just drawn up, amidst many dire warnings and complaints. Had he been too rough? He fretted then shook his grizzled head. No, it was justified. The boy needed a firm hand. Fred's lips twitched as he imagined his anger, not that he hadn't learned how to conceal and harness it. As a young boy he'd been passionate in his rage, but after Fred had destroyed his heated arguments with cold logic he'd quickly caught on. God he loved that boy, and secretly crowed with delight over his fighting instincts coupled with intelligence that would stand him in good stead in his later, professional life. If only he could knock it out of him, all this nonsense about his Hawaiian blood . . . And though he hated to admit it, the reverence the natives showed to his grandson because of his royal heritage irritated Fred, and only served to make him drum it into the boy's head more and more that he came from honest, dirt-poor, American beginnings.

Sitting in a taxi, his tense body held under rigid control, Dominic headed for Kapuna, his heart thumping hard. As the taxi pulled up the drive Koana opened the front door, his face strained as he watched the young Prince pay the driver and sprint up the path.

Alerted to his arrival by Tansie's delighted and loud greeting, the nurse stood back from the bed whilst her patient's eyes remained glued to the door, which soon opened to reveal the most handsome man Judith had ever seen. Expecting a mere schoolboy, the sight of the tall black-haired young man with the blazingly green eyes made her catch her breath.

Dominic stared at the old man lying on the bed and his hand curled on the doorknob, the metal biting into his hand. So it was true; it was actually, really true. 'Grandfather.' He said the single word, his young voice strong and sure in the silent room, for a glorious moment chasing away the presence of death that hung around the old man like a merciless cloud.

Fred wanted to hold out his arms but found they wouldn't move. Yet the small movement of his fingers and the look in his eyes galvanized Dominic into action. Crossing the room quickly he sat on the side of the large bed, ignoring the chair the nurse had recently vacated.

'Dominic,' the old man said, his voice as strong as the nurse had ever heard it during the last two months. Fred's eyes strayed to her, his chin jerking in a dismissive gesture. Nodding, Judith said a silent goodbye to her patient and left the room, softly shutting the door behind her.

'Scared ya, did I?' Fred asked.

'Like hell,' Dominic responded snappily and Fred nodded, satisfied. He did not want the boy crying all over him and he obviously wasn't going to.

'I'm about to die, boy,' he said simply, and Dominic's hand tightened on his. But he offered no meaningless denials, much to Fred's relief. 'I've got things to say. So don't interrupt . . .' He took a deep breath, the words rising and falling as he spat them out, using the last of his energy. 'I brought you up, tough. You helped – we were always fighting and scrapping.' The old man's lips curved in a whimsical smile. 'I wanted you to be ready to take over. Promise me you'll finish your education?'

'I will.'

'You'll go to Harvard after you've finished pussy-footin' around in Oxford?'

Dominic shook his head. 'Still got to have your own way, haven't you?'

'Damned right,' Fred said, knowing his grandson loved him too much to deny him. 'Don't think I'm gonna waste such a good advantage as a deathbed wish, do you?'

Dominic smiled. 'No, I've never known you pass up a golden opportunity. All right – I'll go to Harvard. But I'll do the course in two years – not three.'

Fred erupted into breathless chuckles, wheezing alarmingly for several minutes whilst his hand was crushed in his grandson's strong grip. He didn't try to shake off the painful clasp. The silent evidence of his grandson's love was too precious to lose just because it hurt.

'Can't wait to get your hands on my hotels, eh? Oh, come on – I know all about your high falutin' ideas, don't think I don't.'

'I don't want you to die, Gramps,' Dominic said, his voice thick.

Fred nodded. 'I know that, boy,' he said simply.

Dom shook his head. 'You're amazing.'

'You too – you're my grandson.'

'And proud of it.'

'Don't get mushy on me,' Fred snapped. 'Besides, you might not be so happy about our blood ties when Arnold reads the will.' Dominic stiffened, green eyes suddenly wary, and Fred smiled in approval. The boy was hungry for his inheritance. Good – that was how it should be. If he wasn't, Fred would be terrified he'd made a mistake about him.

'What do you mean?' Dominic asked. 'There's no way you'd leave it to those vultures in Chicago?' Years ago Fred had tried to find his family and hadn't been surprised that war, disease and poverty had wiped them all out save for two cousins on his mother's side, who now lived in Chicago. 'Gramps, what the hell have you done?'

'Don't worry, boy,' he gasped, his voice falling into a croak. 'I've arranged for a sur . . . surprise for you. That's all.' He coughed, his mouth falling open as he struggled for air and Dominic went cold.

'Gramps – don't,' he said desperately.

'I w-wouldn't if I could get out of it, boy. Never f-fear about th-that!' He began to cough again, the sound shuddering through Dominic like bitter poison.

'Gramps,' he said softly, sliding his arms around his grandfather's shoulders and holding the old man tenderly in his arms. Fred looked up at the green eyes and saw Grant. How he wished he'd had the chance to bid his son goodbye like this.

'Dominic.' His head lolled back on the strong arms holding him. 'L-love you.'

'I love you too, Gramps,' he said, but was never to know whether or not Frederick Fairchild had heard him. For long moments he stared down into the face of the man he had loved, and loved to hate. Then he slowly lowered the lifeless form on to the pillows and walked stiffly to the door and opened it. Tansie and Koana were in the hall, their eyes searching his face and finding the truth. Tansie delved into her apron for a handkerchief and pushed it to her mouth whilst Koana bowed his head and shuffled away. The nurse moved past Dominic and went into the room to perform her last service for her patient, and Dominic walked towards the housekeeper and hugged her heaving shoulders.

THE clicking of the stereo needle brought Dominic back to the present, and he rose, switching off the machine and walking with his half-empty drink to stare down into the photo of his grandfather. 'That damned will was a surprise all right, you interfering old bastard,' he said, his voice almost gentle. Swallowing the rest of the drink he put it down and walked to a grand piano at the end of the room and let his fingers play over the keys. Unconsciously, he picked out the tune of *It's Impossible* then hesitated, his eyes half-closing. With more careful attention he finished the tune.

For decades he'd been bound by Fred's will and he was sick of it. Heartily sick, and the advent of the woman into his life only made him resent it more. 'The Woman'. Yes – he'd probably always think of the green-eyed, raven-haired beauty of tonight as 'The Woman' even after he learned her name.

You really socked it to me, didn't you, Gramps, he thought, leaving the piano behind and walking to the window. You really stitched me up.

But more than that, the will had allowed Graham Grantham to add the final, finishing blow. Graham. At least he'd had the sense to run for cover to England, to get out of his sight if not quite out of his reach. If he hadn't . . . Dominic shook his head. Graham . . .

IT was two days until the old man's funeral. Time was dragging and Dominic was glad when Koana ushered Philip Pearce into the lounge. Philip, an old friend from High School, was welcome relief indeed. 'Phil! Good to see you, buddy. Want a drink?'

Philip gave his condolences on the old man's death and for a moment they both drank in silence. 'I saw Graham

Grantham in town yesterday. I thought he was still at Oxford?'

'He's supposed to be but Jess is having trouble with the baby,' Dominic said, a note of anxiety creeping into his voice.

'I'd heard that,' Phil admitted. 'Has he been around?'

Dominic shook his head. 'No. And I've given up trying to figure him out.'

Philip left half an hour later when Smith Flanaghan arrived. They spent the afternoon going over the specifics of the hotels and the transference of power and Dominic quickly realized that if his grandfather had any nasty shocks in store for him, then Smith, his most trusted business manager, didn't know beans about them. Smith had just left when the telephone rang, and he picked it up to hear Akaki's purring voice.

Meanwhile Graham was at home trying to read the paper whilst his father paced up and down growing steadily angrier. 'What the hell were you playing at? First you have to go to Oxford, in spite of the fact that there's a vast difference between English and American law. Then, when you do get there, you get a third in your first-year exams. What were you doing? Reading *Superman* comics all day long?'

Graham rattled the paper and sighed, and Jessamine, busy knitting, followed his lead and pretended not to hear. Since her false labour she'd promised herself not to get upset about anything. But she knew that Arnold Grantham's words were hurting his son, that every word was doing more and more damage. Why oh why didn't he keep quiet? Especially since he had no right to criticize him. His sins – no, *their* sins – far outweighed any shortcomings that might be laid at Graham's door. If only she hadn't got drunk that night ...

'Look, I have go,' Arnold sighed. 'There are certain formalities with Fred's will that I've got to see to. You coming to dinner on Sunday?'

'You shouldn't let him upset you like that,' she said mildly after Arnold had left, as usual unable to look her squarely in the eye.

'I know,' he sighed. 'Come here. I do love you, you know,' he said, looking into Jessamine's brown eyes, searching them for he knew not what.

'I know,' she said, believing it. 'And I love you.' Determined to believe that the baby inside her was his, despite what the calendar said, she smiled tremulously as she silently vowed to be the best mother in the world. 'It'll be a boy,' she said softly, holding her hand over his on her stomach. 'I'm sure of it. A son for Graham. Yes?'

Graham nodded. 'Yes,' he said with soft satisfaction 'That'll show my father . . . and Dominic,' he added, his eyes watching hers intently. Jessamine flushed in guilt and made a quick movement to look away. Graham frowned, his hand on her stomach tightening. 'I want this baby, Jess,' he whispered. 'I need it.'

'I know you do,' she mumbled softly and kissed his cheek. Then she walked back to the couch and resumed knitting, her dark head bowed over the needles.

Graham ambled to the window, pushing aside the curtain to look out, his thin body tense and restless. 'Jess?'

'Hm?'

'Have you thought about godparents yet?'

Jess shrugged. 'I don't know. I thought Tom and Ann would be a good choice.'

'Ye-e-ss,' he agreed, stringing out the word doubtfully. 'But they're family already. A godfather . . . godparents,' he corrected himself quickly, 'should be friends. Not blood kin at all. So how about Jean, for the godmother. She's your best friend – and then Dominic for the godfather?'

Jess smiled. 'Fine, darling. Whatever you want.' From now on she was going to be the best wife a man ever had as well. Anything to make it up to him.

Graham walked slowly around the back of the sofa and watched the busy knitting needles producing a baby's matineé jacket. Suddenly, he wanted to cry.

DOMINIC opened his eyes, looking at the plain blue-tinted ceiling above him and sat up, checking his watch. Nearly three o'clock. He'd better get some sleep. Rising, he stretched and yawned and walked through to his bedroom and sat on the edge of the king-sized bed unbottoning his shirt. His eyes fell on the walnut bedside cabinet and he paused in the act of undressing. Reaching across he pulled open the single drawer and took out the piece of paper he found there.

He could remember vividly the day he'd first read it. Years of careful planning and patience had finally paid off. But he had not expected that telegram. No. He'd definitely not expected that. The words were as stark, as final and as hollow now as they had been then. '*Graham Grantham died of heart attack, 4.45 p.m., Tuesday 6 June at John Radcliffe Hospital, Oxford Stop. Daughter in attendance Stop.*' It was signed Carl Lessing, the man in charge of the bogus corporation Dominic had set up two years before, and who had been keeping an eye on Graham for him.

Carefully, he refolded the message and put it back in the drawer.

Chapter 12

At the end of his song, applause rang out over the room. Vienna, just entering with a tray, looked at the scene with wide eyes and a feeling of sudden absolute knowledge. Farron and the band slipped into a mild rendition of *Aloha Oe* and she served her order with a sweet smile even as her mind grappled with the unmistakable truth. *She was in love with Farron Manikuuna.*

Dominic thrust back the starched white cuff at his wrist and checked the slim gold watch. It was only three minutes later than the last time he'd checked it. He tried to remember a time when he had waited for a date with such restless impatience, but no single occasion came to mind. Not even Akaki at her most skilful had been able totally to swamp his mind. Vienna approached his table nervously, her face now perfectly composed. 'Good evening, Mr Fairchild,' she said, not expecting him to remember her from the beach.

At the sound of the hesitant voice he looked up, his eyes crinkling at the corners as he smiled at her. 'Hello, Vienna. How are you this evening?'

'I'm fine, thank you. Would you care to order?'

'No, thanks. I'm dining at the Regent tonight. It pays to keep an eye on the competition.' She saw the almost boyishly mischievous grin he gave, and grinned in sympathy. 'Besides, I like to see the look of panic on their faces when I walk in through the door.'

From the stage Farron almost faltered at the sight of her bright, childlike smile and his voice warmed consciously as he continued to sing. 'Do you check up on the competition often?' she asked, listening to his answer with only half an ear, too aware with every atom of her being that Farron stood not ten feet away, his voice trickling through her blood like molten honey.

'Only when I'm in a spiteful mood.'

'Would you like a drink?'

'Perrier with a splash of lime. The bartender knows how I like it.'

'Yes, Mr Fairchild.' She told the barman the Perrier was for 'the boss', and took the drink back to Dominic's table. 'Is there anything else I can get you?' Dominic opened his mouth to say, 'No' as Farron began to speak on stage.

'And now, ladies and gentlemen, I'd like to sing for you a new song, with music by Danny Kanawa here,' he pointed to the guitar player who grinned widely, 'and lyrics by myself. I hope you'll like it. I want to dedicate this song to a lovely young lady who's with us tonight.' A ripple of curiosity shot through the crowd as Farron's unofficial fan club of female guests looked at each other with fake nonchalance.

Frozen at Dominic's side, Vienna knew without a shadow of doubt that he was talking straight at her. Farron smiled down at her and moved nearer to the edge of the stage. Dominic looked from the singer to the young waitress by his side, his face expressionless. The lights dimmed and the crowd disappeared, whilst the world diminished to Farron, alone in a pale pink spotlight. The music was a throbbing, poignant sound, the tune as beautiful as any she'd ever heard. When he began to sing, every word struck through to her heart like a searing but healing red-hot lance. Farron's eyes were dark ebony as they fell on her, his voice a rich, pulsating passion as he sang his song:

'Love for the lady of lost, Fills my soul to overflowing.
Love for her, at any cost . . . Forever growing . . .'

Vienna couldn't look away from the man on the stage, his bare chest with their darkened nipples beckoning her fingers, making them tingle with the desire to explore his skin and hear him drag in a sharp breath of desire as she touched him. She blinked and licked dry lips, her body trembling slightly in the sudden fierceness of her love for him and suddenly nothing else mattered – morals, right or wrong, sanity, decency. Nothing mattered but that she and he were one, as in tune as his song:

'Love for the lady of chains, Bound by promises unearned.
Love for her in my soul reigns. Unfettered, unlearned . . .'

Vienna closed her eyes briefly as the music rose to a
crescendo around her and then calmed again and when she
opened her eyes her lashes were wet with tears. He was right —
she must break free of the chains Richard had wound so
cunningly around her. She must and she would. For him. For
her. For them. He saw the promise in her eyes and his voice
became stronger, letting his song argue his love for him,
letting the music persuade, seduce and reassure her.

'Love for the lady of mystery, Will set her free.
Love decided by destiny, will bring her to me.'

He sang as he'd never needed to before, his voice an
extension of his soul. He did not see an audience, only the
woman he loved.

'Love for my lady of sighs, Broken by Fate's cruel whim.
Never withers or dies, Nor languishes within.
Love for the lady, Love from my heart. Love for my lady,
Will never . . . ever, depart.'

His voice trailed to a whisper and then into nothing as the
chords of the song vibrated, shimmered and then disappeared. When intrusive applause broke into her spell,
Vienna gasped, plunged back into the real world.

Dominic raised the glass to his lips and drank, eyes turning
speculatively to the blonde waitress as he told himself sternly
to keep out of it.

Vienna smiled absently at Dominic and walked away,
stopping to collect empty plates from a table and taking
orders for desserts with a slow deliberate care that belied the
turmoil broiling within her. On stage Farron nodded to the
group to begin an instrumental number. He stared at the
kitchen, wanting to go and find her but knowing that now
was not the time. She needed to be able to think. Instead he

walked to Dominic's table and sat down heavily, his legs feeling strangely weak. 'Did you like the song?'

'If it doesn't do the trick I'll be very, very surprised.'

Farron did not even pretend that he didn't understand the older man. But then, it had always been like this between them. Their instant rapport had grown over the years into a complete understanding of each other, a deep friendship that crossed the boundaries of age and status. 'I hope so. There are . . . complications.'

Dominic nodded and gave him a wise smile. 'There nearly always are.' He looked at his watch and saw that he still had a quarter of an hour to wait, but he was restless. He actually ached to meet her again. 'The Woman'. Would the magic have disappeared? When he finally met her again would she have become just another attractive female, no more and no less than that? 'I have to go,' he said simply. 'Want my drink?' He pushed the hardly touched water towards him and Farron took it with a preoccupied smile and a murmur of thanks.

Dominic walked away, his mind sharpening as he entered the lobby and saw her. She was standing by the fountain looking into the water, her eyes watching the flickering fan-shaped tail of a Yellow Tang fish. Her shoulders stiffened moments before she turned and looked at him, their eyes meeting.

She was wearing velvet of such a pale blue it was almost, but not quite, white. The lush fabric clung to her breasts, waist and hips whilst her throat and neck rose from the square-cut gown as graceful as a swan's, complemented by a blue velvet choker that housed a perfect sapphire and diamond cluster. Her hair was upswept into an elegant chignon and from her ears hung long strands of sapphire and diamonds that sparkled in the light with the slightest movement of her head. As she approached he saw the ferocious tiger-gleam of her eyes and she felt the raw virility, the almost overwhelming power of the man encloak her. When they met neither pair of green eyes faltered by so much as the flicker of an eyelash and around them the air became electrified. All the clerks and milling guests stopped in their tracks to look at the stunning couple, aware that something primeval was happening.

'Shall we go?' Dominic said, his voice low and especially for her.

Rhiannon tipped her head in regal, mute agreement. When he held out his arm she placed her hand on it, feeling the hard muscle and sinew clench in an involuntary reaction to her touch.

THE Blue Hawaiian's two dining rooms split the evening into two. From eight until eleven, one room and one act catered for the early diners whilst from eleven to one in the morning the other room and another act catered for the midnight owls. Tonight Farron had never had more reason to be overjoyed that his was the early shift. As the nightclubbing hour came round the diners disappeared, leaving the room to the silent army of staff who cleared away and restored immaculate order.

In the kitchen Vienna took off her white, lace-edged apron and put it with the others in the large laundry bin. In the lobby Farron walked forward to meet her, neither speaking as he held out his hand and she took it. Together they walked to the lift and rode down to the brightly lit garage, Vienna wordlessly slipping into the passenger seat as he held the car door open for her. Roaring up the ramp and out into the tropical night, he drove north past the Kewalo Basin and the Aloha Tower, and then headed inland. Each mile brought them closer to Richard Jago, and Vienna could feel her stomach muscles grow tight with tension.

'You have to move out of the flat.'

'I know,' she agreed softly, her hands clenching and unclenching in her lap.

He said gently, 'Tonight?'

'Yes.'

He wanted to ask her to move in with him but knew that it was too soon. 'You can stay with my *tutu* until you find a place. She has a small, two-bedroomed bungalow. You can have my old room.'

The thought of living where Farron had lived made her smile. 'I'd like that.'

They pulled into the side road and moments later he was

parking the car under the apartment block. Silently counting up and along Vienna saw that her own flat was ablaze with lights and she took a deep steadying breath. 'I'm coming with you,' Farron announced. 'I'm not going to let you do this alone. I don't trust him.'

She pulled away slightly and looked up at him, frowning. 'And what's that supposed to mean, exactly?'

Farron shrugged. 'Just what I say. To begin with, I understand why you feel so grateful to him, but don't forget he violated his medical ethics in beginning a relationship with you in the first place. He knew you were vulnerable – you're still seeing that psychotherapist from the hospital.'

'Not any more,' she said quickly, but without real conviction. She herself had felt as if Richard was steamrollering her on too many occasions to defend him more vigorously. 'Look, let's not argue, please?' She stepped with shaking legs on to the sidewalk and felt his steadying, comforting arms slip around her shivering shoulders, hugging her close. 'Oh God, I'm dreading this,' she whispered and Farron took her hand, squeezing it tightly. A few minutes later Vienna pushed open the door to her flat. Gently but firmly escorting her, Farron closed the door loudly behind him.

'Hello, honey. Just making you a coffee. Won't be a mo . . .' As Richard came through the door the sight of Farron, and the atmosphere within the room, made him jerk to a painful stop. And then he knew.

Ugly destructive anger flooded into him; silently he began to sweat.

'Richard,' Vienna said, the name sighing out of her in a tremulous mixture of entreaty and pain. 'Richard, I have to tell you something.' Involuntarily, she took a step nearer Farron and as he saw the compulsive movement, the rage turned hot within Richard, burning him with an unbearable pain. Agony ripped from him just one, explosive word.

'NO!'

Farron winced, understanding the anguish in the man's voice and for a brief but sincere moment he felt utterly sorry for Richard Jago.

'Richard, I . . .' In vain she struggled for words that would nullify the agony she could see in his face, words that would explain to him that she didn't want to hurt him. 'I never meant it to turn out like this. Please, please understand that,' she begged, moving forwards across the room, walking without fear to the man whose physical presence dwarfed her. Taking his large, icy-cold hands in hers, she looked up into his stunned eyes.

'You can't leave me,' he stated hollowly, shaking his head slowly as if he could force her to see how impossible that was. 'I love you.'

Tears brimmed in her eyes and she swallowed convulsively against the sudden tightness in her throat. 'I hate hurting you,' she said, letting the tears fall from her eyes. 'Please, Richard, please say that you understand that.'

Her pleading words unlocked his paralysis, loosing a natural cunning that fed like a starving wolf on his own fear. His whole world boiled down to the fact that he had to stop her leaving. He had to keep her unequivocally his.

'No.' He shook his head, his face deathly pale as he clasped her two hands to his chest in a pleading gesture. 'No, I don't understand that. You know how much I love you. You know I've never loved anyone before, nor ever will again. You KNOW that. How can you say you never meant to hurt me?' he whispered, his breath thundering out of his lungs as he watched the tears fall down her cheeks. 'How can it not hurt me? To let me love you and then just . . . just . . .'

Richard did not even look at Farron. All his willpower was directed at Vienna. I'll do anything, he thought. I'll do anything.

'I'm sorry, Richard.' Her voice was a strangulated whisper. 'But I love him.' She said it simply, and as he looked into her eyes he realized he'd lost.

And Richard Jago had never lost before.

'You love *me*!' he shouted, his voice raw and wild, and she trembled, her skin crawling where his hands touched her. For a moment she thought she saw some emotion flare fiercely out of control in his eyes and she shuddered.

'Richard,' she whispered, shaking her head in numb shock, her face tearstreaked and as white as a summer cloud.

'Richard, I don't love you.' Her voice was soft and sad, her words the simple truth.

Suddenly Richard screamed – a terrible sound. He felt bitter tears on his face and licked his lips, the salt tasting vile on his tongue. Finally he looked at Farron, his face contorted and ugly with hate and Farron could see murder in his eyes before he turned back to Vienna, his face softening. Looking totally lost and disbelieving, he looked down at her and whispered, 'You're mine, don't you understand that? Mine.'

Vienna shook her head. 'Richard, no,' she murmured, her hand coming up to his cheek to stroke the hair from his temple.

'Send him away. We'll forget all about this. Vienna!' He almost howled her name as he saw the denial and rejection flood into her eyes.

Farron decided enough was enough. 'That's it,' he warned, knocking Richard's hands from her shoulders. 'She's leaving with me and there's not a damned thing you can do about it.' With a gentle finger under her chin he made Vienna look at him. 'Go and pack. We're leaving,' he said softly.

Watching her slowly slipping away, Richard Jago suddenly cracked but his bloodcurdling yell of warning came too late for Farron. Swinging back to face the man who had made the awful sound he was unprepared for the huge body that suddenly lunged at him, nor did he see in time the large fist with all the power of a jackhammer slam into his stomach. With a 'whoof' of pain, all the breath left his body and he doubled over and lights flashed behind his closed lids. Dimly he heard Vienna scream.

'You bastard,' Richard yelled, moving on the stricken man with surprising speed. Just in time Farron's quick thinking enabled him to fall to his knees, thrusting his head forward to head-butt the on-rushing man in the abdomen. But rage, and a kind of destructive madness, enabled Richard to ignore the considerable pain; grabbing a handful of Farron's hair and pulling back his head, he slammed his fist into the young singer's jaw.

The sound of bone on bone flooded the room but even as he felt the pain shoot through his jaw and neck Farron brought up his own fist in a straight jab to the stomach that would have felled a man of his own weight and size. But Richard topped Farron by a good five inches, and his heavy-set, big-boned body seemed impervious to pain. Only a slight clenching of his teeth showed that he even acknowledged the blow as he brought his large knee up in a sudden vicious jerk, catching Farron under his chin and snapping his teeth together in a blunt crunching sound that made Vienna clap her hands over her ears. 'Stop it. For God's sake, Richard, stop it!' she screamed, running a few steps forward and then screaming again as Richard kicked the felled man viciously in the ribs.

'Farron!' Vienna moaned, throwing herself in front of the wide-eyed, heavily breathing giant. 'Richard, stop! For pity's sake, you're killing him.' She tugged at his raised, powerful arm. His vision fogged by a red-hot mist of murderous rage, Jago shook her off like a dog would a cat, only coming to his senses when she staggered backwards and collapsed into a chair.

Vienna's eyes widened as the room suddenly faded and she was in an alley, unlit save for a single light from a room somewhere high above her. She could hear a girl sobbing and moaning pitifully, and she shook her head helplessly.

Richard immediately recognized the unnatural brightness of her eyes and, forgetting the man at his feet, staggered quickly over to her. However the man Vienna saw coming towards her was not Richard, but the man in her dreams. The upstairs light illuminated his blonde hair and his mouth was a red, grinning, ugly slash. 'You whore,' he snarled. 'You're nothing but a cheap tramp – a two-bit pro who deserves to get this stuck in her instead of a cock.' He raised his hand and Vienna saw the wicked blade of a large knife glint in the light. As terror hit her she tried to scream, but only a pitiful croak escaped her lips. 'You whore, I'm going to kill you!'

Richard fell to his knees in front of the chair, medical experience suddenly coming to the fore. 'Vienna. Vienna.' He said her name clearly and strongly as behind him Farron lurched to his feet, each breath he took an agony as his cracked ribs expanded. 'Vienna. It's me – Richard.'

Farron staggered forward, every instinct intent on resuming the fight but a certain tone in Richard's voice made him stop. When he looked at Vienna, the terror on her face stunned him. 'Vienna, where are you?' Richard asked softly, his huge hands taking her trembling fingers and rubbing them gently. Vienna took a deep, sobbing breath and blinked, her eyes focusing again, first on Farron, swaying and bleeding from his nose and mouth and then on Richard himself. 'It's all right, darling,' Richard said softly, his thumbs caressing the palms of her hands. 'It's all right – I'm here. Nothing will hurt you while I'm here, remember?'

'I'm leaving, Richard,' she said shakily, but in a voice firm with resolve. She looked down at their hands and tugged her own free.

Sitting back on his heels as all his strength finally deserted him, Richard stared up at her. 'You can't. He doesn't know how to look after you like I do.'

'I'll look after her,' Farron said grimly, and wiped his bleeding mouth with the back of his hand. 'And if you ever come near her again, I'll kill you.'

Richard didn't appear to hear the threat, delivered in a voice that no one else would have doubted. Vienna stood up slowly, her heart pounding sickeningly. All she wanted to do was escape. Looking up at her from his kneeling position Richard said quietly, 'If you leave, you'll be sorry.' His voice held almost no emotion now, and as he said it the very rationality of his stare was suddenly more terrifying to her than his earlier, insane anger.

'No, I won't be sorry, Richard. Farron loves me.' As she walked around him into Farron's arms, Richard continued to stare at the empty chair, his eyes dull as pewter.

'He doesn't love you like I do,' he repeated softly as behind him Vienna ducked under Farron's arm, doing her best to support his weight as they turned and walked awkwardly towards the door. 'Nobody loves you like I do.'

Vienna opened the door and together they walked through it. 'Goodbye, Richard,' she said softly, and closed the door behind her. All alone, Richard shook his head. Goodbye? Did she really think she could just say goodbye and then leave him? How little she knew him. How little she understood.

'No. It's not goodbye, Vienna,' he softly contradicted, his unblinking eyes still staring into the empty chair. 'It's nowhere near goodbye . . .'

VIENNA sat in the casualty waiting room of a downtown hospital, waiting for someone to come and tell her what was going on. Farron's cheerful wink as they wheeled him into a curtained cubicle had done little to relieve her anxiety, and after the terrible scene with Richard she felt utterly drained. Her head throbbed, and she knew she must look washed-out and exhausted. Her one prayer was that Farron was not seriously hurt.

The man who'd wandered in from his Beetle car a few minutes ago now looked at her bent silver head, and smiled. She seemed so innocent it was hard to believe her little native singer had just been beaten up by her older lover boy. He settled down with a newspaper to wait and turned to the crossword section. He read the clue to one across but even though he knew the answer he had no pencil. Again he looked at the girl. She was like all women – loved to have men fighting over her, making fools out of themselves. You couldn't trust them. They were all rotten to the core.

Vienna shivered, puzzled by the sudden and hideous memory of the man with the knife. Was it an hallucination? Some product of the few drugs she still took, courtesy of the hospital? Or was it, God help her, a memory? And if it was, what could she do about it? Despite the combined efforts of the police, herself and Farron, she was no nearer to knowing her true identity now than she had been on the morning she'd first awoken in the hospital. But it could have been only a shocked reaction to the violence between Richard and Farron, couldn't it?

She walked shakily to the coffee vendor and bought a cup of strong sweet tea, which she sipped through slightly chattering teeth. She had never believed Richard could be capable of such brutality. What kind of doctor inflicted injuries on someone? And should she take his threats seriously, or was he just suffering from the pain of her leaving him and talking wildly?

'Hi.' A tall fair-haired doctor disturbed her near-hysterical thoughts, and she managed to give him a quick smile and at the same time take a calming breath. 'You must be the young lady Mr Manikuuna is so worried about.'

'How is he, Doctor? He will be all right, won't he?'

'Oh, certainly. He has a loose tooth that will need a good dentist, and some cuts and bruises. He'll be in X-ray soon. His ribs are only cracked but it's best to make sure. Why don't you stay here, and I'll get back to you once I've seen the X-rays?'

'Thank you, yes,' she breathed, relief evident in her every pore. 'His voice isn't damaged, is it?' she added anxiously. 'He's a singer.'

The doctor smiled. 'His voice will be just fine, though I doubt if he'll feel like singing for a few days.'

AT the Glorious Motel, a stereo pumped out the song *Smoke Gets in Your Eyes* while three men were dancing with women dressed only in see-through négligés. Madam Meow watched them with imperious orange eyes, her fluffy tail flickering in disgust. In the office the phone rang and Gloria, on her way to the door, strode back and reached for it impatiently, her eyes narrowing as she recognized the voice on the other end. 'When was this?' she asked, looking at her watch and sliding back into her chair. 'But the girl is all right?' She listened for a few more minutes. 'You're sure it was the singer? Yeah, OK. Right. Thanks.' She hung up, her face pensive as she stared at the closed door for a few moments, her active mind working overtime. Along with fences, cops and politicians, people in her profession had that curious habit of knowing within minutes everything and anything that went on. But she knew it was what you did with the knowledge that counted, and so she reached quickly for the phone and dialled the number of the Blue Hawaiian.

'Mr Fairchild, please – it's urgent. Damn! Do you know where he is? The Hawaiian Regent?' she repeated and wrote down the name of the hotel the clerk gave her and hung up abruptly. Ringing the number for the hotel she asked for Dominic Fairchild, only to be told he hadn't yet arrived.

'When is his table booked? Midnight?' she repeated, glancing at her watch, seeing that it was almost that now. 'Look – can you give him a message the moment he gets in. Tell him to ring Gloria immediately – it's urgent. Very urgent, got that? Thanks.' She hung up then leaned back in her swivel chair, rocking back and forth for several minutes until her hand wandered to the drawer and she pulled out the photograph of the baby.

She looked up as a loud burst of masculine laughter penetrated her office and quickly put the photograph away, drumming her nails on the desk top, a frown tugging at her plucked brows as she glanced at her watch.

MILES away, Dominic hung up in the phone booth in the Hawaiian Regent Hotel, his face white. Rhiannon, who had been waiting impatiently for him, suspecting that the phone call was about business, stepped closer.

'What's the matter? You look dreadful.'

'It's Farron. He's been hurt.' Dominic sounded dazed for a moment, but then shook his head briefly. 'I have to make a few phone calls. Why don't you order a drink and I'll join you in a moment?'

Rhiannon allowed the maître d' to escort her to a prominent table and then ordered a mineral water. She had a vague idea that Farron was the singer at the Hotel but she had no idea why Dominic should be so upset, unless of course he was worried about an insurance claim. She sipped her drink thoughtfully and reviewed the evening so far, which had been surprisingly pleasant. Neither of them had let their gentle sparring get out of hand, and she'd been surprised and delighted with the glimpses of the 'real' Oahu that Dominic had shown her, including natural waterfalls, ancient religious sites and even a small nature reserve. They had drunk traditional *okolehao* – a ferocious liquor made out of roots, in an authentic beach bar of thatched bamboo, then walked on a small, secluded beach that was as far removed from the commercially crowded Waikiki as it was possible to be,

Dominic pointing out and naming the wild flowers that grew beyond the sand.

In the phone booth, Dominic called the hospital and learned for himself that Farron would be all right, then he phoned Hua Lopan'ha, an old friend who ran his own Private Detective Agency. He was out, and Dominic left word for him to ring him at the Blue Hawaiian the moment he got in.

'You look angry,' Rhiannon commented as he joined her at the table a minute later.

'Not with you,' he assured her softly, very much aware of her beauty, of the clear accent of her voice, of the scent of her perfume which was fresh and yet just a touch sharp. It all suited her perfectly.

'Oh, you will be,' she said enigmatically, accepting a menu from the waiter who then disappeared.

'Sounds ominous,' he said mildly, not looking at all perturbed.

'You seem upset. Not more bad news I hope? Is the singer all right?'

'Farron? Yes. He was beaten up by . . . Never mind. It's nothing that can't be fixed,' he assured her, thinking of Richard Jago. His face and voice were so grim that for a moment Rhiannon felt a shimmer of fear slide down her own spine.

'You sound almost feudal. What's going on exactly? Some sort of Hawaiian vendetta?' She said it lightly, but underneath she was being eaten alive by curiosity. Farron was, she remembered, a native of the islands.

Dominic laughed. 'No. No vendetta. I look out for my people, that's all.'

'Your people?' You mean Hawaiians?'

'No.' His eyes narrowed at the slight sound of condemnation in her voice. 'I'm no racist. By "my people" I mean my friends, the people who work for me, people who trust me. People whom I won't let down – ever.'

She blinked, totally floored by the unmistakeable ring of sincerity in his voice. For a moment she floundered, unsure if she should try and say something witty or something placatory. And had her father, too, once been this man's

163

friend? She was saved from deciding when he beckoned the waiter over and gave their order.

'So,' he said softly, looking at her over a flickering candle. 'Are you going to tell me your name now?'

Rhiannon smiled. 'Why not,' she said just as softly, leaning forward and resting her chin on the back of her hand, watching his smoky, seductive eyes with a sultry look that she gradually let fade from her face. 'My name is Rhiannon.'

'Rhiannon?' he repeated, his browns drawing into a frown. *Rhiannon?* Suddenly he felt the blood chill in his veins and she saw his face turn pale. Her own eyes never wavered as she watched shock dilate his pupils into black circles that almost chased all traces of green from his eyes. Dominic only knew one person in the whole world with such an unusual name.

'Ahh, I see that you remember me now,' she purred softly.

Dominic saw clearly the hardness in her shimmering eyes and knew, with a despairing lance of pain, that 'The Woman' was his mortal enemy.

Chapter 13

'Well, well, well,' Dominic mused sardonically, his large lean body utterly relaxed now that the first moment of paralyzing shock had worn off, leaving him free to look at her with new eyes. 'So you're little Rhia – my own sweet little goddaughter, all grown up.'

Rhiannon, shocked both by the revelation that he was her godfather and by the speed of his recovery, grappled for her own composure as she faced a man who set about tasting the wine the waiter had brought him as if there was nothing else in the world that needed his attention. He smiled mockingly and slowly raised his glass.

Picking up her own glass she repeated his silent salute and their eyes clashed and held. 'Did you think I wouldn't grow up?' she challenged softly. 'That I wouldn't come of age?'

'I never thought of you at all,' he said, so conversationally that the insult was a masterpiece of understatement. Her breasts rose and fell several times as she silently battled with her anger, but eventually she managed a sweet and pure smile.

'So for all you know, I could be happily married with a couple of children?' she asked, eyebrow raised in question.

For a brief ugly moment the thought of her bearing another man's child made his hand clench on his glass. Forcing himself to relax yet again, he ate some of his Beluga caviar, but his stomach churned in protest at this nonchalant gesture.

Watching him, Rhiannon silently despaired. He was so cool, so unaffected. Delicately she nibbled on her own food but the pâté de foie gras Strasbourg might have been sawdust in her mouth.

'Are you staying on the islands long?' he asked casually, when all his instincts screamed for him to demand an explanation, to shake her by her lovely shoulders and find out exactly what she wanted, why she was here on the islands, and, most of all, *was* she married? *Did* she have children?

'Until my business is concluded,' she told him, pushing away her hardly-touched plate.

'And what business are you in, exactly?'

Rhiannon's lips curled into a wolfish smile, its dangerous quality so complementary to her beauty that Dominic felt his loins tighten and harden in helpless male reaction. 'Demolition,' she finally answered him, her choice of words rolling from her tongue in a soft, almost caressing whisper as her eyes wandered over his face to see if he understood.

'I see,' he said tonelessly, neither his eyes nor his expression giving anything away. The waiter replaced their plates with the main dishes and hastily left. There was something explosive about the two diners that made him feel distinctly jittery. 'Whereabouts in England do you come from?' he asked, elegantly cutting into his beef and chewing with every appearance of enjoyment.

Rhiannon, with a silver fork, flaked apart her salmon and then pushed the pieces around on her plate. 'Oxfordshire.'

'That's a coincidence. Oxford's about the only part of England I know well.'

'Yes, I know,' she said flatly. This wasn't going at all how she'd expected. Where was all the floundering, the blustering threats, the shamefaced denials or apologies?

Dominic finally pushed his plate away, took another sip of wine, and met her cold gaze steadily. She noticed that his own eyes were blank, like green mirrors, totally without expression. 'Did you go to the university there?'

She nodded. 'Somerville College.' She looked ready to kill him. He could see her hands curve around the handle of her knife, her knuckles white and strained. He wondered what she'd do if he told her the truth – here and now. She would not thank him for it, of that he was sure.

'Has my nose suddenly grown an inch?' she asked sharply, unnerved by his quiet scrutiny.

'Why?' he asked mildly, his eyes no less watchful. 'Have you been telling lies, Rhiannon?'

His reference to Pinocchio hit her on the raw and this time her rage leapt from her before she could recall and control it. 'I'm not some puppet you can make dance to your tune,' she hissed. 'You can pull all the strings you want, but I dance to my own tune and no one else's.'

Dominic's eyes narrowed, the only indication he gave that he had registered the warning in her tone. Yes, he thought, she hates all right. I think she can hate very, very well. Without knowing it he shook his head. She couldn't guess that he knew a fact that could annihilate her before she'd even begun to fight, and the ironic thought made his lips curl into a rueful smile.

'Something funny?' she demanded, her hand curling around the delicate stem of her glass in silent tension.

Dominic shook his head. 'No,' he said heavily. 'I take you very seriously, I assure you.' His eyes reluctantly fell to the angry heaving of her breasts and she felt his gaze like a physical caress. To her horror she could feel her nipples tightening and swelling under their cover of blue velvet and deep in her head she could hear warning bells tolling.

'How magnanimous of you,' she gritted, making Dominic smile broadly in response to her ill-concealed anger.

'Don't worry about it,' he advised. 'It's not catching.'

'I'm so pleased to hear it,' she flashed back. 'One never knows what one might catch from men like you.' The slur meant nothing to him, for in his time he'd been insulted much more inventively by men and women far more dangerous than she. But ancient wounds that were still not healed, were opening again, and he felt the barriers of restraint slowly crumbling.

'I understand your father suffered some financial setbacks,' he remarked, letting his eyes fall to the expensive jewels glittering at her throat. 'But I can see that I have no need to fear you won't be able to pay your hotel bill.'

The devastating attack, coming so unexpectedly and hitting so dead on target, momentarily dazed her. Dominic quashed the pity he felt when he saw her face turn as pale as that of a ghost. He quite simply could not afford to let himself feel sorry for her and as he watched her hands clutch her napkin, her lovely eyes flicker in pain, he forced his emotions into neutral.

Rhiannon took a deep breath and blindly reached for her

glass, sipping deeply of the wine, battling to bring her emotions under control.

Dominic knew that he could destroy her as surely as the sun would rise tomorrow. An enemy who was plagued with such strong feelings was a vulnerable enemy. But never, never, had he had so little heart for a fight. 'Go home, Rhiannon Grantham,' he advised softly. 'Go back to England now, before it's too late.'

As the words hovered between them, fatalistic and powerful entities, she fought off a sudden rush of fear and shook her head. 'I'll leave when I've done what I came here to do.' Her voice was as strong and as unwavering as the level green gaze she fixed on him.

Dominic sighed, even as he admired her rapid recovery, and lightly dropped his napkin beside the plate. 'You have lovely eyes,' he said, totally throwing her. 'Just like your grandfather's.'

Remembering her father's words as he lay dying, she leaned back in her chair, waiting until the waiter had removed the dishes and placed their desserts in front of them, before speaking with slow deliberation. 'I was told that I inherited them from my mother, Jessamine. Daddy said she was the most beautiful girl on the islands.'

Dominic's face tightened as he thought of Jess – that lovely girl who had died so needlessly, who had loved so unwisely.

Rhiannon saw the tense lines form around his mouth and the sudden dark shadow in his eyes, and let out a slow, painful breath. Daddy had been right – he *had* been in love with her mother. She didn't know why, but the thought of him loving her mother, of waiting so long and so patiently to take revenge on the man she had dared to love instead of himself, wounded her deeply and some masochistic impulse had her asking, 'Do I look like her?'

Dominic blinked and looked away from her, the past stirring painfully in his memory, people long since dead; Jess, his grandfather, Akaki, Graham, all suddenly rising up to haunt and mock him. 'Do I look like my mother, Dominic?' Rhiannon asked again, her voice sharp.

'Yes,' he said simply. 'Yes, you do. Perhaps that's why I

thought we'd met before.' She met his eyes, eyes that never wavered, and knew that something had happened. In the space of a second, he'd made a decision and she must find out what it was. More depended on her finding out than just the success or failure of her fight for justice, this she knew instinctively. The fight was no longer about fulfilling a deathbed promise. Now she was fighting for her life!

'You hated Daddy, didn't you?' she asked, weakly needing to have it confirmed by his own lips before she could continue the vendetta.

And Dominic Fairchild did not disappoint her.

'You'll never have your kid, Dominic. Never . . .' Graham's words rose from the past as clear and as viciously ugly as the moment he'd first uttered them, and the ever-constant pain bit deep. He met her eyes. 'Oh yes,' he said, almost casually, as if surprised she'd ever doubted it. 'I hated Graham all right.'

Rhiannon felt her chest tighten and struggled to take a calming, reassuring breath. 'Because he married Jessamine?' she probed, the words dragging painfully from her, like thorns being torn from her flesh.

'He told you that, did he?' Dominic mused sadly. He was not suprised – he'd long since been convinced that Graham Grantham had been capable of anything.

'Do you deny it?'

'I don't have to deny a damned thing to you, Riannon Grantham,' he told her harshly, his finger flicking the side of his glass with a musical 'ting'. 'Not one . . .' he lifted his eyes to her '. . . damn . . .' he strung out the words, to make sure she got the message loud and clear '. . . *thing*.'

After being raised by a bastard like Graham Grantham he understood only too clearly that he could never tell her the whole truth. Never. She'd only crucify him with it.

Rhiannon felt herself shivering, and to cover it she leaned slowly back in her chair. 'It really kills you, doesn't it?' she said softly. 'My father, a little nobody son-of-a-lawyer beating the great Prince,' she sneered the word, 'to the one thing in the world his spoilt greedy little soul coveted and couldn't have.'

Dominic felt rage at the injustice of it all suddenly uncoil within him, and he needed to hit out.

'I would have sent flowers to his funeral but I couldn't find a florist that sold poisonous orchids,' he said quietly, his voice lethal.

Rhiannon's head jerked up, her eyes fun of agony. 'You bastard!' she spat, her hand curling around the wine glass as she lifted it and tossed its contents fully into his face. He didn't even blink, but the green eyes were the deadliest she'd ever seen, making her skin crawl as if icy fingers had danced across every silken inch of her. She rose shakily to her feet and slammed down her napkin on to the table. Quickly she turned and walked away, not even aware that people were staring at her. Blood pounded in her ears as outrage, fear, and pain rippled over her in alternate waves. Now her father's desire for revenge suddenly made total sense. The man was a monster – a heartless, ugly monster. And to think that for a few moments she had almost allowed herself to feel sympathy for him.

She found herself on the sidewalk and hailed a cab. 'The Blue Hawaiian,' she said shortly, leaning back on the seat and quickly unwinding the window, taking in great gulps of air.

'You all right, lady?' the driver asked, checking in his rear mirror, his eyes widening in appreciation at the sight of his beautiful passenger.

'I will be,' she said grimly. 'I bloody well will be!'

INSIDE, Dominic slowly raised his napkin and wiped his face. His shirt was stained and obviously ruined, but the thought only vaguely crossed his mind. Lifting his spoon he slowly ate his dessert, his eyes narrowed and thoughtful.

I'm in trouble, he thought, nodding to the waiter who served the *après dîner* liqueur with an expressionless face. Dominic nodded to himself, a slow smile settling on his lips and attracting even more speculative glances that were now mostly envious. Not many men could weather such an embarrassing incident with such total aplomb.

Yes, Dominic thought, watching the waiter pour the coffee. I'm definitely in trouble. But not too much – and wasn't it good to feel so alive again?

BACK in her room, Rhiannon turned on the light and jumped as a figure rose from a chair. 'Oh, it's you,' she said to Jack, only then remembering that she'd asked him to wait for her in her room so that they could discuss how the evening had turned out. Removing her jewellery and letting down her hair, she tried to thrust the memory of Dominic from her mind. He wouldn't go.

Jack watched the transformation from sophisticated beauty to carefree loveliness in total silence, only the glittering light in his eyes offering a silent clue as to his feelings.

'It went badly, I take it?' he asked, and she gave a mocking laugh of agreement.

'You might say that. I ended up throwing my wine in his face and walking off. Dammit!' she exploded, pacing up and down in front of his chair. 'If I'd had a gun I would be in jail right now needing a bloody good lawyer!'

Jack chuckled softly, his laughter gaining in volume as he thought of the handsome Hawaiian dripping in wine.

'It's not funny,' Rhiannon snapped, but her lips quivered. 'I'm mad as hell at myself for losing my cool. I'm even more annoyed for not doing something more original.' She flung up her hands in self-disgust then stomped through to the bathroom. There she hesitated, glanced at the door then locked it before shrugging off her dress and stepping under the shower, turning the water deliberately to the 'cold' setting.

Shivering under the tingling needles of cold water, she hugged her arms across her breasts and took deep, calming breaths before drying herself and donning a voluminous peach silk robe. With a moisturing cream she removed what was left of her make-up, gave her hair a quick brush and walked back into the bedroom.

'Here. A margarita just the way you like it, according to Ben.' Jack Gunster offered her an elegant glass which she took with a grateful smile and sipped with a tired sigh. Walking to the couch she sat down, drawing her legs under her. 'So, tell me all about it,' Jack offered comfortingly, sitting opposite her and looking handsome and rakish in a casual white cotton shirt and pale green slacks. Rhiannon looked at him and wondered why she didn't find him physically attractive any more.

'Oh, I don't know. At first he looked poleaxed when I told him my name. But he recovered so damned quickly!'

Jack nodded and took a long swallow of whisky. 'I tried to warn you,' he said with well-concealed smugness. 'So what did he say, exactly, to make you baptize him in Chablis?'

'It was Bordeaux,' she corrected, her smile widening as Jack began to laugh.

'Bordeaux – much better. It stains more thoroughly, I believe.'

Rhiannon chuckled into her margarita but eventually humour gave way to a mixture of hurt and anger. 'I found out what I wanted to know, though,' she said softly.

Jack's right eyebrow rose an inch. 'Oh?'

'Yes. Daddy was right about him.'

'In what way?'

'In every way. I really touched a nerve when we talked about my father. He admitted that he'd hated him. And he said couldn't find any poisonous flowers to send to his funeral.'

'And that made you throw the wine,' Jack mused quietly. He still didn't know all the details but he could not fail to feel the cruelty of that remark. The man was obviously a bastard who was going to deserve all he got. 'Nasty,' he said, aware that she was watching and waiting for his reaction.

'I thought so,' she said, her tone as hard as concrete. 'If I ever had any second thoughts about what we're going to do, he shot them down in flames tonight.'

Jack watched her, but wisely kept his doubts to himself. 'Did you tell him about the boutiques?'

'No. I wanted to let that be a lovely surprise for him.'

Jack put down his glass on the floor and slowly stood up, walking towards her and placing gentle hands on the tops of her arms. 'Be careful, Rhia,' he warned softly, smelling the gentle perfume that rose from her skin and wishing vaguely that she wasn't the boss' property. 'He's a dangerous man.'

'I know,' she said wryly, looking up into his worried eyes. 'But I'm dangerous too.'

'You certainly are,' Jack murmured, and slowly moved closer.

Rhiannon knew he was going to kiss her and with the logical part of her brain she knew she should stop him. She needed a friend not a lover, an ally not a potentially jealous boyfriend. And yet the totally feminine part of her needed reassurance. Jack looked deeply into her eyes, asking silent questions and then his lips lowered a few centimetres more and found hers, cool and pliant to the touch. His arms slid around her waist, drawing her body further into him, his eyes closing in desire as he felt her supple form press against his. His tongue parted her lips and flicked against her teeth, using all the expertise he'd garnered from other women to excite her. His fingers stroked her spine, his mouth a teasing, testing extension of his manhood. But Rhiannon found the sensation at best mildly pleasing, and then, as the kiss became prolonged, intrusive and unwanted. Jack felt her withdrawal immediately and lifted his lips. Anger and frustration wormed their way into his guts and he sighed deeply and moved away from her. Best to stick to business matters after all. And who knows? She was bound to make some cock-up on the business end of things, a cock-up he'd be sure Ben got to hear about. Then it would be up to good old Jack Gunster to save the day. He smiled at the thought, caught his reflection in the mirror, and the smile widened. He lifted a hand and briefly finger-combed his blond hair.

Rhiannon walked desolately to the window, wondering what she could possibly say. Whatever reassurances she had craved had been denied her, and as Jack said a curt goodnight and left, she suddenly felt totally alone.

She ordered up some coffee and removed the boutique papers from her locked briefcase. The first document was a rundown on the stock that had been sold and the stock that was still remaining. She would be checking the shops tomorrow and needed to be prepared, but found she could not concentrate. Growling in anger she finally gave up. Shrugging off her robe she slipped naked between the cool green silk sheets. Turning off the lights she stared up at the ceiling, her body tensing anew as she remembered that above her was the penthouse and Dominic Fairchild's room. Was he in there? Or was he staying at his oh-so-famous Falling Pearls Palace, the edifice he'd had built as a monument to his mother and his own Hawaiian heritage? For long hours she lay silently staring up at the ceiling, wondering . . .

DOMINIC had just shut the door behind him when he heard the telephone ring. Sprinting across the penthouse he snatched up the receiver. 'Yes?'

'Hi, it's Hua. I just got your message.' Dominic picked up the phone and walked with it to the window, looking down into the traffic-lined street.

'It sounded urgent,' Hua said, knowing that Dominic only used his Private Detective Agency for matters that needed very discreet handling.

'It is.' Briefly he told him about Farron. 'I've heard second-hand who's responsible, but I want you to doublecheck who, and almost as importantly – why.'

'Right.' Hua was a little surprised. So far Dominic had only ever asked him to do standard but necessary checks on would-be business partners or discreet vetting of his personnel.

'I've got something else for you,' he said, ignoring the good-natured groan on the other end. 'Have you got any contacts in London?'

'Sure, one or two.'

'Good. I want you to have a complete check run on one Rhiannon Grantham. She was born here, but emigrated with her father to England when she was six months old.'

'Can you tell me anything more?'

'She went to Somerville College, Oxford.'

'How soon do you want it? I know, I know. You want it yesterday, right?'

Dominic grinned. 'How well you know me.'

'OK. Philip Marlowe was always getting this kind of aggro from his clients! I'll get back to you as soon as I can about Farron. Is he all right?'

'He'd better be,' Dominic said shortly, and after saying goodbye, rang off. Walking through to the bathroom he turned on the jacuzzi and stripped, lying in the bubbling hot water and closing his eyes with a weary sigh. 'Damn,' he said softly. 'Damn, damn, damn.'

This was not one of his better nights, and his concern over Farron was not the only thing that nagged at him. He felt as if he'd been cheated and for a long while could not figure out why. When he did, he swore again, even more loudly. He'd been looking forward to getting to know 'The Woman'. Looking forward to a leisurely, pleasurable, perhaps even loving, courtship. But now she was an enemy. A beautiful, dangerous enemy. And he was finding it hard to make the adjustment stick.

An hour later he was seated at his desk in the office, reading over the quarterly report on Dominic Tours. In the margins he made brief notes – queries for the MD on the performance of the new cruiser, requests for a complete rundown on stock valuations and movement. That done he walked back to the lounge and poured himself a stiff, imported Scottish malt whisky and added soda. When the phone rang, he pounced. 'Yes?'

'It's me,' Hua said unnecessarily. 'About Farron . . .'

'What have you found out?'

'Well, there's a pretty little blonde here that I've been talking to . . .'

'I know her, she's one of my waitresses,' Dominic interrupted, sitting down with his drink and sipping as he listened to Hua talk.

'Did you know that she'd been friendly with the doctor who'd treated her at the hospital?'

'Not until recently,' Dominic said, the whisky turning sour in his stomach.

'Well, she was. I've been asking around and you'd be surprised how the hospital grapevine . . .'

'Cut the waffle,' Dominic snapped, 'and get to the point.' A surprised silence reigned for a good few seconds, and Dominic sighed. 'Look, I'm sorry. It's been one hell of a night. In fact, it's been one hell of a year so far. Just . . . just get on with it, huh?'

'Sure, right. The doctor goes by the name of Jago – Richard

Jago. He helped set the girlfriend up with a flat – bought her clothes, the lot. Surprised the hell out of all the nurses.'

'Oh?' Dominic said, beginning to wonder if he'd read Vienna all wrong. Could she be a gold-digger? A faker? He didn't think so, or was it that he just didn't want to think so? 'Oh hell!'

'What?'

'Nothing. Why were the nurses surprised?'

'Because he's not known to be the charitable type. In fact, quite the opposite. He moved here on the skirt-tails of a model, dumping her as soon as he was settled. He's the sort to go to all the right parties and live in the right places. He has his own yacht which, incidentally, was a "present' from another of his ladies.'

'Sounds a real charmer,' Dominic said drily, taking another sip.

'Yes. Not very doctorly to beat up a man, is it?'

Dominic sat forward and said slowly, 'You're sure it was him?'

'No doubt about it. I've just got back from the good doctor's apartment block. A young couple saw a little blonde and a bleeding boyfriend leaving the apartment a couple of hours ago. It's my guess she gave the doc the royal kiss-off and he didn't take it too well.'

'About this Jago character . . .'

'I'm way ahead of you. He works at the Centre Hospital. Everyone agrees he's a bloody good medic but hardly likely to win any medals for personality or humanitarian of the year. I can do a wider check if you like.'

'No, that's not necessary.' After ringing off Dominic picked up the phone again, letting it ring for a good minute. Eventually a sleepy voice answered.

'Hello, do you know what time it is?'

'Uh-huh. Two-thirty. Look, Hank, I need a favour.'

'That you, Dom? What is it? Is it about the same kid?'

'Not directly. There's a doctor at the Centre Hospital by the name of Jago. Richard Jago. I want him out; out of the hospital and out of the islands.'

'This doesn't sound like you.' The voice sharpened, becoming wide awake. 'What's he done?'

Dominic grunted. 'Let's just say he's guilty of unethical conduct. He was shacked up with an ex-patient of his – an amnesiac girl. You might have read about her in the papers a few months back.'

'Yeah. Yeah, I vaguely remember. You think he used undue influence?'

'Had to have done. The girl was all alone and totally vulnerable.'

'It's borderline. I don't know that the medical revue board will push it.'

'From what I've heard, our Dr Jago is not particularly well-liked. I don't think you'll find anyone willing to go out on a limb for him.'

'OK. I'll see what I can do.'

'Thanks, Hank. I owe you one.' Dominic rang off and walked with his drink to the window, looking out at the city lights. Wherever he was, Richard Jago's days on the island were well and truly numbered.

RICHARD was vaguely aware that he had cramp in his legs from kneeling so long. The sound of traffic had stopped as the night had slipped by, and still he stared at the empty chair, his mind blissfully blank. Now he rose painfully to his feet, his legs tingling as his blood began to circulate again. Limping to the bathroom he stared at his haggard reflection in the mirror, raising a hand to where blood had dried on his chin. It was not his blood, but Farron's, and running the taps he quickly washed it off, shuddering. He hated the thought of the singer – hated even the stain of his blood.

Walking through to the bedroom his eyes travelled over the immaculately made bed to the dresser filled with feminine knick-knacks, hungrily eyeing the coloured tissues, vials of perfume, bottles of lotion and a golden tube of lipstick. 'Vienna,' he whispered, his lips stiff and cold.

Sinking on to the bed he picked up her apricot silk nightdress and crumpled it over his face, smelling the scent of her on the material and breathing it in deeply. Heavily he fell back on the bed, keeping the nightdress pressed to his face, his eyes screwed tightly shut. For long minutes his big body shuddered, sobs wracking his body and shaking his broad shoulders.

Eventually the tears ceased and he rolled over on to his stomach, his cheek pressed to the coverlet, grey eyes wide and blank as he stared at the scrap of silk in his large hand. 'One more chance, Vienna,' he said softly. 'I'll give you one more chance. And if you don't take it, I'll destroy you . . .'

Chapter 14

Shopping malls had sprung up in Honolulu with the tourist boom like mushrooms in overnight rain. The International Market Place on Kalakaua Avenue stayed open into the night as did the King's Alley just around the corner on Kaiulani Avenue, whilst the Waikiki Shopping Plaza at the Royal Hawaiian was ideal for early risers. Rhiannon hadn't been able to resist browsing around the fascinating New China Cultural Plaza on North Beretania Street even though she'd known that the morning was passing and that she should begin to inspect the Princess Liliha boutiques.

Dominic had opened a Princess Liliha store in every one of the four main shopping precincts and she'd already looked around three of them on the pretext of being a customer. The store in the Ala Moana Shopping Centre had been all but empty, but she liked the actual plaza itself. Situated opposite the park of the same name, it had been enlivened by local artists and the hundred or so shops and restaurants were both landscaped and pleasing on the eye. Within a Number 8 bus route from Waikiki Beach she knew that the boutique was ideally situated for the changes she had in mind that would form the new-look boutiques. The Hawaiian merchandise from 'Sears' attracted a great deal of attention, and had caused the germ of an idea to sprout in her mind.

In the Coral Grotto the Cracked Seed Centre was the most fascinating shop there, with its rows of jams, purées and masses of preserved fruit.

She'd paid particular attention to the rival clothes chains. Andrade and Liberty House proliferated, and for local designs there were McInery outfits available at the Watumull. She'd quickly skimmed her way through the fifty-eight-store Kahala Mall, and the third largest, the Windward Mall, which spread itself over thirty acres. Now, with aching feet and a rumbling tummy that reminded her she'd skipped breakfast, she arrived at the last stop on her itinerary, the

Pearlbridge Mall, which according to her papers housed the biggest and most profitable Princess Liliha boutique of them all.

The shopping centre itself was colourful and carpeted. Overlooking the historical and impressive Pearl Harbor it could also boast Hawaii's only monorail system. The Princess Liliha occupied one of the best sites, and as she approached, a man on a ladder was taking down the 'Princess Liliha' blue neon sign. She felt a thrill of satisfaction as the first letters of the new name were slowly inserted. In golden italics *Gray-Gray's* took its place. Her father had told her about his nickname long ago, a name he'd confessed he hated because he knew it was meant to reflect what others saw as his dull, nondescript character. Now Rhiannon smiled a victorious smile. For all the world to see Gray-Gray had now taken over from Princess Liliha.

She pushed open the glass door with the blue bar handle and walked in. A petite Hawaiian girl approached her dressed in a shocking pink kimono. '*Aloha.* May I help you?' Rhiannon knew that to take over a business about which she knew nothing and to run it sucessfully, it was imperative to retain at least half of the original staff. She also knew that as the biggest boutique, the manageress of this particular store was going to be very important. She asked to see the manager and the girl moved from behind the counter and quickly pushed across a blue partitioning curtain. A moment later Rhiannon turned to see a woman emerge, of medium height with short curly brown hair, her round face endowed with large light-brown eyes and a wide generous mouth. Aged in her late thirties she was dressed in a smart, tailored blue suit.

'Good afternoon, ma'am. Has there been some kind of misunderstanding?'

The voice took Rhiannon totally by surprise; it reminded her instantly of *Gone with the Wind*, the southern accent being so strong.

'Not really. I'm Rhiannon Grantham, the new owner of the boutiques.'

The manageress hid her shock well. 'How do you do.' The southern voice stressed the word 'you' with charming emphasis. 'I'm Clarice Meredith, and this is Holliani – Holli as we all call her.' She introduced the shop assistant who stood staring at her, open-mouthed. Rhiannon shook her hand and smiled, and Clarice said easily, 'Perhaps you'd like to come into my office?'

Inside a small neat room, both women took their seats and waited for the other to speak. 'Well, Miss Grantham . . .' Clarice began, and Rhiannon quickly interrupted.

'Please – call me Rhia.'

'Rhia. A lovely name, if I may say so.'

'Thank you,' Rhiannon said, very much aware of her responsibilities. These were her staff and they relied on her for their living. 'I've arranged to have letters sent to all employees immediately, stating that no jobs will be lost.' She took the plunge, meeting Clarice's wary brown eyes head on.

'Thank you,' Clarice said simply. 'I know a lot of people will be very happy to hear that.'

'I do hope there'll be no trouble about you staying on with me, Clarice,' she said, as coffee began to bubble in a percolator, and for long moments the manageress remained thoughtfully silent. Rhiannon could feel her nerves begin to stretch. She liked this woman in the way that women can take an instant liking to each other, and she sensed in her a camaraderie and personality that was highly in sympathy with her own.

'I'm not sure,' Clarice finally admitted, offering her a mug of steaming coffee that Rhiannon accepted quickly.

'Oh?'

'Dominic's been very good to me,' Clarice began in her lovely Southern accent, and Rhiannon felt her stomach muscles knot. Was it possible, she wondered, that Clarice and Dominic were more than mere employer and employee?

'I'm sure he has,' she responded, keeping her voice bland and free of nuances. 'But this is business we're talking now. Can I be frank?'

'Please do.'

'The boutiques are a brand new venture for me and I know next to nothing about shop management, consumer laws and regulations, or how to deal with staff or customers. I need people like yourself who know the ropes. So far, all the other managers to whom my assistants have spoken on the phone have agreed to stay on with a seven per cent rise in pay.'

Clarice took a casual sip of coffee but Rhiannon was sure she could feel some of the other woman's carefully concealed resentment beginning to waver.

'I'm well aware that people are not very happy with the change of circumstances concerning the shops, Clarice,' Rhiannon continued firmly, 'but this, as I said before, is business.'

'I know business is business, Miss Grantham – Rhia. But as I said, Dominic was very good to me. When I first came here looking for a job I was well, not the ideal candidate. Yet he gave me a chance.'

Rhiannon raised her brow in surprise at this. 'From what I've seen you're an excellent manageress!'

Clarice leaned back in her chair and a wistful smile crossed her face. 'I've never tried to put on a front, Rhia, so I'll tell you straight. When I first approached Dominic for a job, I was twenty-two and pregnant with twins. Their father . . . well, let's just say he didn't want to know. Needless to say, I wasn't married. Can you imagine a pregnant woman serving customers in a fancy place like this?' she asked.

'I see. Yes, I do,' Rhiannon insisted as Clarice looked her over sceptically, taking in the English girl's expensive Chanel suit of rich cream with black trimings. 'I can understand why you feel obliged to Mr Fairchild, but ask yourself this: did he get where he is today by letting personal matters influence sound business practices?' She shook her head, answering her own question. 'I can assure you he didn't. Besides, with children to support surely he can't expect you to resign from a perfectly good job?'

Clarice's mind was working furiously. 'Dominic rang me the other night. He . . .' she paused, unwilling to confide to his competition that he'd told her he was going to set up a new boutique chain. Instead she said, 'He asked me to hold on for a little while.'

'Until he's got another chain, you mean?' Rhia guessed accurately, shrugging with seeming nonchalance. 'Well you can, obviously,' she said mildly, deciding that now was as good a time as any to dangle a carrot. 'But that could be a long time ahead and it's not wise to be out of the fashion market for long. Can I tell you what I have in mind for the boutiques? That way you can make up your mind based on a lot more information than you have now.'

'All right,' Clarice said cautiously.

'I'm sure you understand that this is confidential?'

Clarice smiled. 'At the moment I'm still working for you, Rhia.'

Rhiannon smiled back, both trusting and liking the other. 'Well, to begin with, the exclusive top-market stuff is going to have to go. But don't worry,' she held up a hand as she saw a look of horror gradually creep on to the manageress' face. 'I don't intend to turn it into a tourist trap either. No – what I have in mind is a mixture of both worlds. I noticed in the other malls that the stores are either all muu-muu's and ghastly patterned shirts, or good ol' American casuals. What I am planning is a cross, a marriage if you like, of local native wear and elegant casuals.'

Clarice slowly leaned forward. 'A sort of exclusive teenage market, you mean?'

Rhiannon nodded. 'Yes, partly. But also simple summer dresses for the middle-aged customer. Look, what I'd really like is to find some local designers, youngsters with a sense of fun and adventure, but also older women, who know what appeals to the mothers of the teenagers.'

'I know a lot of girls, some of them our own sales girls, who just dream of a chance to design clothes. I've even seen some of their ideas made up.'

'And are they good?' Rhiannon asked, the excitement catching.

'Very, some of them. Nearly all of the girls Dominic hired are locals with a pride in their heritage.'

'Clarice, I need someone not only in the boutiques themselves, but at a corporate level. Someone with experience of how a boutique runs, to bring to the executive level common-sense and practicality. I need someone whom the girls who'll be designing the clothes actually know and trust, who can liaise easily with them. Someone with good taste, good sense and foresight. Someone like *you*, in fact.' Pushing home the advantage, she continued. 'Of course, the salary will rise accordingly – to roughly double your present rate of pay, but then you'll be taking on more work and responsibility. You may not want that, of course,' she said, with a sudden frown. 'Not with young children to care for.'

'My kids are at school now,' Clarice put in quickly.

'Of course I'll be busy with other things, which means that to a large extent you'll have carte blanche,' Rhia informed her, further coating the carrot with sugar. She knew instinctively that Clarice would do a good job for her and Ben with the boutiques, leaving Rhiannon free to pursue her real goals. 'You'll be the one who points the girls in the right direction and does the market research to see what might sell and what won't. You'll even have to redecorate the shops to suit the change of image and style.'

Clarice smiled, knowing exactly what Rhiannon was doing but also knowing that she herself was hooked. 'And I'm supposed to do all this on my own?'

Rhiannon met the older woman's gaze over the rim of the cup with eyes that sparkled. 'You'll be Managing Director,' she said simply. 'Hire yourself an assistant or two.' The carrot of power was a tempting one, especially for an intelligent, capable woman. Even today, women executives in positions of commercial, political and professional power were outnumbered more than fifty to one by men.

Clarice finished her coffee without hurrying, but her nerves were quivering with excitement. At last she would be stretched and have something to do, other than simply oversee a boutique that practically ran itself. And if she ever wanted to leave she'd have established herself on the corporate ladder. Dominic had been good to her, and she was by nature loyal. And yet she couldn't deny that this was a wonderful offer: the once-in-a-lifetime chance that she'd never thought would come her way. Could she turn it down? Could she *afford* to turn it down? The extra money alone meant that her kids could go to any school, within reason, that they wanted.

'All right – you've got yourself a deal.' She held out a slender hand and Rhiannon smiled broadly and reached across the desk to shake it.

'I'm glad,' she said simply. 'You won't regret it.'

'I hope not,' Clarice said quietly. 'Have you any idea how much it's going to cost to get these clothes manufactured?' Her mind was turning to practicalities straight away and Rhiannon smiled, sure she had made a wise choice in picking her MD.

'You needn't worry about that,' she said, deciding not to let Clarice know about the clothing manufacturing firm based in Hilo that she now 'owned', courtesy of Ben. 'I have a place on the Big Island. It's all arranged.'

Clarice looked her straight in the eye. 'I must telephone Dominic and tell him what I've decided.'

'I understand. But I'd appreciate it if you didn't tell him who I am. I mean, don't tell him that it's a woman who's taken over. Not just yet, anyway.'

Clarice's eyes glimmered in amused sympathy. 'Very well.'

'I'll have a look around the shop,' Rhia said diplomatically, rising to her feet and leaving the office with a sense of deep personal satisfaction. She needed a friend, a real friend. A woman she could talk to and trust. And although it was early days yet, she was fairly confident she'd found just such a person in Clarice Meredith.

DOMINIC pressed his intercom as it buzzed, a pen poised over a list of banking accounts. 'Miss Meredith on line five, sir.'

'Thanks,' Dominic said, putting down the phone and pressing the button. 'Clarice, good to hear from you,' he said cheerfully.

'Hullo Dominic. I'm calling about that offer you made me the other night.'

'Oh yes. You're staying on?' he asked, fiddling absently with the pen, rolling it between his fingers as he talked.

'Actually, no. I'm calling to say that the new owner is with me now and has made me an offer I really can't refuse.'

Dominic sat up abruptly. 'He's there, you say? Right now?'

'Ye-es,' she strung out the word doubtfully. 'I've been

offered the job of running *all* the stores, Dominic,' Clarice said almost apologetically. 'The offer, at double my salary now was too good for me to turn down. Can you understand?'

'Yes, I can understand,' Dominic said kindly, meaning it. 'Look, Clarice, can you keep him there for ten minutes? I'm on my way. Now that the cowardly son-of-a-bitch has finally come out in the open I want to meet him. I've been looking forward to this for months,' he added softly to himself.

Clarice heard the threat in his voice and felt a sense of deep unease: could it be that she'd backed the wrong horse? If so, it was too late now. 'Sure.' She rolled the word, making it into two syllables. 'I can do that. I owe you that much at least.'

'Thanks, Clarice. Ten minutes,' Dominic said, putting down the phone and sprinting to the door and through the office, telling his secretary he'd be gone for about an hour.

CLARICE walked back into the shop and Rhiannon paused in her perusal of a pleated full-length skirt in soft burgundy. 'You know, I think I'll take this – and the antique cream-lace blouse over there.'

'They'll look smashing on you,' Clarice agreed, and together they walked around the shop, bouncing ideas off one another, Holli shyly offering a suggestion of her own here and there. Rhiannon began to relax. It felt so good just to chat with other women, to talk clothes and business in a mismatch of humour and serious thinking. 'We could have murals painted,' she mused, 'of teenagers at a *luana*, wearing the clothes that are on sale.'

'Good idea – get them going on making up their own "look",' Clarice agreed, then suddenly stiffened as her eyes slewed over Rhiannon's shoulder. Rhiannon turned too to see what was going on then jerked stiffly to attention as Dominic Fairchild stalked through the door.

He was wearing a dark navy suit so deep in colour it was almost black. He looked lean and mean and Rhiannon had to stop herself from taking a hasty step backwards as he spotted her first and then Clarice. Walking over to them he looked at the bag of clothes next to Rhiannon's feet, Holli having carefully packed her purchases in the bags bearing the Princess Liliha motif. As he approached, he forced a polite smile on to his face. 'Hello, Clarice,' he said, voice cooling as he added curtly 'Rhiannon.' Beside her she felt Clarice give her a quick, sharp look.

'Dominic,' Rhiannon said sweetly, guessing that Clarice must have known he'd be hot-footing it over here and had purposely kept her talking. Not that she minded. In fact, she was rather glad that Clarice and Holli would be on hand when he learned just who had bought up the boutiques. A coward she was not — nevertheless, it was impossible to mistake the dangerous tension he had brought with him, and folly to underestimate the force of his anger.

'I see you've been busy,' he commented, looking down at the pile of bags at her feet. 'You must have excellent taste . . . to shop at my stores, I mean.'

She let this pass without comment and Dominic's eyes widened suspiciously. She felt a sweet anticipatory pleasure begin to creep through her bloodstream at the thought of what was coming next. Dominic looked at Clarice and then around the shop. 'Did the bas . . . has he gone?'

'No. The new owner's still here,' Clarice said softly, as Dominic spun away and strode over to the office. Looking at her new boss, Clarice shook her head. 'He's gonna be real mad, Rhia.'

Rhiannon nodded wrily. 'Don't I know it,' she said, with what she hoped sounded like a carefree laugh.

Dominic saw quickly that the office was empty and came back, his eyes falling on Rhiannon who looked at him with one brow raised. Swiftly his eyes travelled to Clarice who looked away, and slowly, very slowly, his gaze turned back to Rhia. She gasped under the green punch of his eyes as understanding quickly hit him and he snarled, '*You!*'

Refusing to be cowed, she shrugged eloquently. 'Yes. Little ol' me.'

Clarice looked at her in silent admiration. She was certainly fearless, this lovely Englishwoman who had dared to steal a possession belonging to the Lion of the Islands, as some of the more colourful inhabitants secretly called him.

Rhiannon's head tilted proudly back as he drew to a halt in front of her, mere suffocating inches away. 'What's the matter, Dominic – losing your touch? I'd have thought you'd have had it all worked out by now.'

'Oh, don't worry,' he said softly, shoving his hands deep into his trouser pockets. 'I'm beginning to see the light.'

'Oh, I'm so glad,' she said, so sweetly that even Clarice felt her teeth grind in reaction. 'After all, you've made it so easy for me . . .' she stressed the word 'easy' with insolence 'that I was beginning to get bored.'

Slowly Dominic shook his head. 'Oh, you won't be bored, Rhiannon,' he promised. 'I can assure you of that.'

Her heart was beating like a tom-tom drum, but her smile was as cool as an English winter. 'I haven't seen much proof of that yet, Your Highness.' She pronounced the last words with elegant scorn.

'Oh, you took me by surprise, I'll admit that,' he said, ignoring the taunt. 'And that's the only reason you've made it this far. But you'll get no further, I can assure you of that.' Their faces were now within a mere inch of each other. Rhiannon could see tiny black flecks in the irises of his eyes and feel his cool, clean breath on her cheek. She licked her dry lips and his black pupils darted to watch her pink tongue-tip's flickering movement.

'It's all downhill for you now that my back isn't turned. I must say, your family has a great propensity for sticking the knife into an unsuspecting back. But do you have the stomach for a real fight, I wonder?' he mused.

'Oh, I have the stomach for it,' she snapped, his reference to her father catching her on the raw. 'And it begins with this place.' She looked around, using it as the perfect opportunity to step back without seeming to retreat. 'We're going to create a whole new look – and it'll blow the Princess Liliha sales out of the sky.'

His lips pulled into a cold sneer. 'No way, lady.'

'Didn't you notice the new name above the door as you came in?' she asked coolly, watching his eyes flicker as he sensed another put-down. Taking his hands out of his pockets he turned and walked slowly to the door, all eyes watching him as he looked up at the stylish gold letters. She saw his lips curl derisively, and surreptitiously rubbed her damp palms against her thigh as he walked back in.

'A rather dismal name, I always thought.'

'As a replacement for Princess Liliha,' she said softly, 'I agree.'

Dominic jerked as if she'd hit him, then belatedly becoming aware of their open-mouthed audience, he took a deep calming breath and said quietly, 'I think we'd better continue this discussion in the office.'

Rhiannon coloured slightly, then tossed back her head and gave Clarice an apologetic smile. Once they were inside the office, Dominic shut the door with a muted click that sent little shivers tapdancing down her spine.

'You're playing with fire, Rhiannon,' he warned her impassively. 'You're on my turf now, remember? I dealt with your father and I'll deal with you the same way.'

Rhiannon tossed back her head, her raven hair flying free, and for a brief moment a few strands caressed his cheek with a silken touch. His skin tingled in instant reaction and at his sides his hands clenched into fists.

'You're not dealing with my father now; you're dealing with *me*.' She stressed the last word in a challenging whisper.

Dominic's eyes flickered in surprise for the briefest of moments and he found himself admiring her more and more. 'I've told you before,' he reminded her heavily, 'and I mean it even more now. *Go home*.'

'I am home,' Rhiannon pointed out. 'I was born here. Remember?'

'I remember,' Dominic admitted, his voice suddenly hollow. 'And the little girl grew up to be a rich, spoilt brat. I take it we have a wealthy boyfriend to thank for that? Let's see; the companies that fronted you were all Ben Fielding's. You must have been really something in bed for him to give you such a handsome payoff,' he mocked, but the thought of her in bed with Fielding made him itch to fasten his hands around her lovely throat and squeeze the life out of her.

Rhiannon forced back her anger, intuition telling her that it was exactly the reaction he wanted. Instead she smiled – a mere secretive lift of her lips – then, leaning forward and bringing those lips to within a centimetre of his, she whispered, 'You'll never know.'

The words hit Dominic like a hammer blow. Hating himself, but knowing he was fighting for his own survival, his voice was contemptuous as he shot back: 'I wouldn't *want* to know.'

For the briefest of moments something inside her died then burst back into sudden screaming life. 'Bastard,' she spat, her hand rising so quickly that he didn't have time to react. Her palm tingled painfully from the force of the blow on his cheek, but even as she raised her arm to hit him again his hand shot out and grabbed her wrist in a crushing grip. Wide-eyed they glared at one another.

He deliberately increased the warning pressure on her wrist but she wouldn't cry out – she wouldn't! She'd rather die than beg him to stop. Her muscles began to ache and with a sudden snarl that took him totally by surprise she quickly drew back her foot and kicked him on the shin. Dominic gasped in pain and pushed his free hand into her thick raven locks, grabbing a handful of silky hair and yanking her head back.

Rhiannon was catapulted into him and gave a soft moan of pain. With her breasts crushed against him, her arm and shoulder throbbing dully and her scalp tingling, she felt a sudden explosion of sexual tension deep in her vagina that made her knees go weak.

Dominic felt his loins tighten and ache as desire escalated unbearably. Suddenly, without either knowing who moved first, their lips were touching, sensations of fire and ice licking over them as their mouths fused and soldered themselves together. Tongues met and then began to duel as he dragged her body closer to his. Her nipples throbbed and ached with painful intensity, and her womb flowed with molten honeyed desire.

Eventually Dominic thrust her away from him with such force that Rhiannon staggered back. Dragging painfully huge gulps of air into her lungs, she wiped her mouth with the back of her hand in a graphic gesture of loathing.

'Get out of my sight, Grantham,' Dominic snarled, not

trusting himself with her a moment longer. Already the sight of her with her wild hair and red swollen lips would remain with him for the rest of his life.

'No way, Fairchild,' she almost sobbed in response. 'I'm here to stay – I'm in demolition, remember? And I've only just started. So enjoy you life while it's still good,' she finished, 'because I'm here to make it totally miserable!'

'You need much more than mere money for that, my darling Rhia,' Dominic drawled. 'You also need *influence* – the kind that I have and you don't.' His voice grew cold. 'You need the sort of power that comes from people in the know – the same people with whom I dine every day –people you've never even met. Just because you've managed to sneak this place from me,' he gestured towards the shop, 'don't imagine that you can do the same thing again because you can't.' He walked to the door, opened it and looked back at her, all fire and passion seemingly gone, leaving in their place a cold implacability that should have scared her, but didn't. 'You try anything else,' he said expressionlessly 'and you'll wish you hadn't.'

Rhiannon watched him stalk through the door and disappear, and for several long seconds total shocked silence reigned. Then she straightened and with shaky hands finger-combed her messy hair as Clarice tapped timidly on the open door and looked in.

'You OK, girl?' Clarice asked. 'Dominic just strode past us looking like thunder.'

Rhiannon nodded, then abruptly sat down. 'I'm fine. Really.' Finally she got her racing heart under control and looking up at Clarice's concerned face she suddenly smiled.

'Well,' she straightened her shoulders and took a deep breath. 'I'm starving. This morning's work calls for a jolly good lunch, I'm thinking. My treat – where can you recommend?'

'Recommend?' Clarice echoed blankly, then pulled herself together with a snap.

'Yes – my treat, remember, so pick somewhere fancy.'

Clarice hadn't understood half of what had just gone on, but she knew that any female who could stand up to Dominic

Fairchild like that deserved nothing but the best. Gray-Gray's would be a success or they'd die in the attempt! The two women stood grinning at each other in mute understanding. 'I've always had a fancy to eat at the Peacock room at the Queen Kapiolani Hotel,' Clarice drawled in her broadest Southern accent. 'It's real luxurious, so I've heard.'

'The Peacock Room it is then.' They walked into the salon, and Clarice told the younger girl where they were going.

'Holli, why don't you come with us?' Rhiannon asked with a reckless laugh. 'We'll shut the shop for an hour. What the hell!'

She stopped to pick up her bags then, eyeing the motif, said to Clarice: 'That's another thing you can get cracking on, Miss Managing Director. I want a new Gray-Gray logo and design thought up – pronto!'

Clarice grinned widely. 'Yes, ma'am!'

Chapter 15

Dominic looked out of his hotel window and squinted against the afternoon sun. Richard Jago had finally left the islands, and so far he hadn't heard a squeak from Rhiannon. But Dominic was not fooled – he was still up to his neck in problems. Problems that stemmed from decades ago . . .

BACK in Oahu, in 1961, Dominic had made a request that there would be no wake. He knew his grandfather too well to believe he'd have appreciated men and women he'd never had much to do with in life sitting around his house when he was dead, drinking his best port and eating his food. The only two men besides Smith Flanaghan who could call Fred Fairchild a friend, had died two and five years ago respectively.

'Tansie.' He looked anxiously at the housekeeper who stood in one corner, her face concealed by a thick black veil. 'Are you all right?'

Tansie nodded, her gloved hands curling even tighter around the old-fashioned black leather handbag that she had selected. 'The cars are here, Your Highness,' Koana said discreetly from the doorway, and Dominic nodded.

Together the three of them walked into the brightness of a sunny, summer afternoon. If the uniformed chauffeur thought it strange that the new heir to the Fairchild fortune chose to go to his grandfather's funeral with two servants, he kept the thought to himself and soon the black Cadillac was crawling at a decorous pace to the small, exclusive Haleani Cemetery, where Frederick Fairchild was to be buried.

The cemetery housed a small chapel and the graves of the island's élite. White marble slabs, sculpted statues of angels and tall, impressive obelisks were prevalent and as the car drew to a halt, Dominic saw the black-robed mob in one small, unpretentious corner and took a deep, deep breath. They reminded him of vultures gathered around a carcass and he fancied he could almost hear the old man's disparaging cackle. Drawing Tansie's hand to his chest, he patted it and began to walk forward, watching as the mob slowly parted for him. He did not know that his tall, dignified frame came as a shock to a lot of the people there, who still remembered him as a mere boy, and was equally unaware that they all saw in his level green eyes a cool strength that they had hoped would be buried with the man whose body lay in the flower-bedchecked coffin.

With dignity, Dominic looked at the coffin and then nodded at the priest. He'd been surprised to learn that Fred was a lapsed Roman Catholic, but had duly commissioned a priest to perform the simple ceremony.

As the words wafted over the mourners, Dominic looked at the headstone. It was almost plain compared with the more ornate and imaginative ones surrounding them, but somehow that seemed fitting. The pallbearers lowered the coffin into the ground. He felt a familiar penetrating gaze directed at him, and looked up to see Graham Grantham staring at him intently.

Dominic showed no emotion and those who watched for signs of weakness went home disappointed. Rumours had been rife about Fred's grandson from the moment he'd been born. His title alone had been the subject of much romanticism, for the Americans, with no royalty of their own, craved it in others. He had no intention now of satisfying the curiosity of any of them.

Despite his youth, he dominated them all as he shook hands politely, making no mention of a wake although several mourners angled for an invitation. As soon as he had thanked the priest, he lead Tansie away, Koana following closely by his side.

At the cars Arnold Grantham was waiting. 'Dominic – you all right, boy?'

'Yes. You're coming back to the house for the reading of the will, of course?'

The lawyer nodded, looking uncomfortable. 'First I have to meet two lawyers at my office.'

'Oh?' Dominic's eyes sharpened, the simple syllable demanding an answer.

'Representatives of your grandfather's cousins in Chicago,' Arnold Grantham said, and held up his hand. 'Not to worry — a mere formality.'

Dominic nodded, nothing of his thoughts showing on his face as he got into the car. The large bungalow looked and felt empty when they returned, and he ordered a tray of coffee which he took into the lounge, able at last to sit and think uninterrupted. Why were the cousins' lawyers here? What had the old man meant when he'd said there'd be a surprise in his will? And when a car bearing Arnold Grantham and two strangers pulled into the driveway half an hour later, Dominic realized that he was actually afraid. '*What have you done, Gramps?*' he whispered.

Walking out of the lounge he came face to face with Koana, who in many ways had been the exact antithesis of his grandfather: Hawaiian, not white. Gentle, not hard. Wise, not arrogant. The two men seemed to represent the two halves of himself. One white, American, rich. The other Hawaiian, with the bloodline of royalty.

'Are they all in there?' he asked, nodding at the impressive wooden door that led to the library. Koana nodded, and together they entered the silent room. The library was huge although Fred had not been an avid reader. Many of the tomes that lined the room were financial investments – in the shape of first editions, signed copies, or books that were bound with leather and gold inlays now worth a small fortune. A large fireplace dominated the room but it was hardly ever lit, and a huge floral arrangement of orchids, lilies and gladioli stood on its well-polished surround. Overlarge chairs of dull brown leather littered the room, but it was around an oval table of solid teak that the visitors had congregated. Dominic walked slowly forward, his eyes falling on the box of cigars resting on a walnut and onyx table. Arnold Grantham rose to his feet and coughed gently.

'Dominic, I'd like you to meet Samuel Goldblum and Vincent Marchetti.'

Dominic shook hands first with the short, round man with the bright black eyes and then with his greyhound-lean, hawkishly Italian sidekick who wouldn't have looked out of place in a gangster movie. '*Aloha*,' he said deliberately, noticing how both men looked quickly at each other in surprise and he could almost hear their minds ticking over. Was he an Hawaiian version of a country hick, or had he done it on purpose? Dominic smiled and walked over to a decanter of brandy on a silver salver. He poured himself a generous snifter in a bulbous glass of finest Venetian design, and ignoring the vacant chair at the table, sat on a low leather couch. Looking around at the understated luxury of the place he wondered how Akaki would fit in. Would it rub off on her, or would she pollute the gracious grandeur of the place? He supposed it didn't matter; it was the baby who counted. Arnold cast a surreptitious look at the off-balance lawyers and hid a smile. The boy had certainly learned his craft at his grandfather's knee, all right.

Dominic looked from the golden warmth of the liquid in his glass to Arnold Grantham's troubled eyes. Arnold sat down, disguising the large sigh that escaped him. Fred had been wrong to alter the will – he knew it, Fred had known it, and soon Dominic would know it. Damn Fred's stubbornness! He reached into the black leather briefcase and withdrew a document of surprising bulk. Opening it at the first page, he felt in the top pocket of his funeral suit for a pair of spectacles and slipped them on. 'Shall we begin?' he asked. 'With everyone's permission we'll skip the formalities and get to the salient points.' There was a general agreement and so he began the formal reading of the will.

' "*To Koana, my disobedient servant of twenty years,*" ' Arnold began, leaving no one but the two puzzled lawyers in doubt that the disobedience in question had come from his refusal to call Dominic anything other than 'Highness'; ' "*I leave the cottage at Malaena Beach and a cash settlement of ten thousand dollars.*" ' Dominic didn't need to look to know that the butler's expression hadn't altered one whit.

' "*To Tansie, the woman who drove me crazy with her fussing I leave an annual income of three thousand dollars and my Bentley.*" ' There followed other bequests to the rest of the servants, and Arnold paused to take a sip of water. ' "*To the charities who bugged me constantly while I was alive I leave nothing. Let them bug and bother my grandson."* ' Arnold paused to fight off the grin that threatened to disrupt his sober expression and coughed decorously.

Dominic took another sip of brandy, aware that he'd become painfully tense.

' *"To my cousins in Chicago I leave the sum of one hundred thousand dollars each. If either one decides to contest this will, this amount is to be withheld for the duration of the legal proceedings."* '

Arnold put down the document for a moment and looked at the two men, who stared back at him with bland faces. 'I needn't point out that Mr Fairchild took every,' he stressed again, '*every* precaution to ensure that there will be no legal means for the will to be overturned on the grounds of my client's mental condition. He had affidavits to his mental and even physical state registered by no less than ten different doctors. There can be no question of undue influence, either.'

Arnold looked quickly away from Dominic's gleaming green eyes and turned several more pages. ' *"The rest of my estate, including all real-estate properties, stocks and shares in Fairchild Hotels, capital investments, and the sum total of any and all items not bequested to the aforementioned people – in short my estate in its entirety, worth at the signing of this document five million, eight hundred thousand dollars, I leave to my grandson Dominic Fairchild, son of my son Grant and his wife, Liliha."* '

Dominic wasn't aware that he'd been holding his breath until it left him in a satisfied sigh. The five and half million would only be the beginning of a financial empire the likes of which this island had never seen, he promised himself. He'd take his grandfather's inheritance and turn it into a giant, a name that would lead the world, a name to be reckoned with.

Arnold harumphed, and coughed into his hand, causing Dominic to look at him sharply. ' *"There are, however, four conditions to the inheritance of my estate by my grandson Dominic Fairchild,"* ' Arnold read on sombrely, and Dominic felt rather than saw the Chicago vultures hum with alertness. At the same time he felt his own muscles knot painfully. Conditions! He should have known.

Arnold felt pity stirring within him. The boy wasn't going to like it. Hell, any decent human being wouldn't like it, but especially not this one. He cleared his throat again and began to read.

' "*The first condition being that Dominic Fairchild finish his course at Oxford and afterward completes a business course at Harvard or any other American university of the same calibre mentioned in the attached list.*" '

Arnold looked at Dominic. 'I understand that you've already applied to and been accepted by Harvard, Dominic?'

He nodded and Arnold bent once more to the will.

' "*The second condition is that Dominic Fairchild retains his inheritance only if he marries a Caucasian woman.*" '

'WHAT?' Dominic exploded, leaping to his feet, outrage and disbelief warring for supremacy. 'Is he mad? That's racial prejudice of the first degree!' The two lawyers leaned forward, smelling blood, and Arnold put down the papers and looked at Dominic levelly.

'I agree – and I told him so.' To give himself precious time, Dominic walked to the drinks tray and filled his glass as Arnold carried on reading. ' "*If he fails to comply, the inheritance will be split equally between my aforementioned cousins and my grandson will receive nothing.*" '

Slowly Dominic walked back to the sofa and considered his options. Did he really want to contest the will? He would win because the condition was so outrageous, but . . . He swirled the brandy thoughtfully in the glass. The two vultures would gain by a lengthy court case but what would he gain? Slowly he began to smile as he realized that Akaki would be furious but compliant. What she wanted was money with marriage as an added bonus.

Arnold watched him bring his outrage swiftly under control. Why couldn't his own son, Graham, be more like Dominic Fairchild?

Dominic could appreciate the irony of the situation; what the old man had thought of as a shackle to leash and chain him was, in fact, the perfect excuse to get out of a marriage that he did not want. And it wasn't as if he had a preference for Hawaiian women over white women – he found something beautiful in almost every woman he met.

'Am I to take it you do not wish to contest the will so far, Dominic? And I think it might be prudent if all but the interested parties left the room at this juncture.' Arnold courteously prompted him from his reverie.

Dominic gave a gentle gesture ordering the servants to leave. The Chicago vultures, he noticed as the others filed silently out, stayed firmly put.

' *"The third condition,"* ' Arnold continued once the room was cleared, ' *"is that, once married, Dominic Fairchild will not retain his inheritance should he for any reason whatsoever seek a divorce."* Here,' Arnold said, looking at a surprised Dominic over the rim of his spectacles, 'your grandfather added a personal note. Humph,' he cleared his throat. ' *"There has never been a divorce in our family, Dominic, and I don't intend that you should be the first."* '

Dominic shrugged. Since he had no desire to marry he could not see that that would be a problem.

' *"In accordance with this condition,"* ' Arnold read on: ' *"only the offspring of this marriage can inherit from my grandson, Dom . . ."* '

'Now he's gone too far,' Dominic snarled, the funny side of it totally swamped now that his baby's interests were being attacked. 'There's no way in the world,' and he pointed a finger at Arnold to emphasize his words, 'that I'm going to stand for that.'

Arnold looked at him, and slowly nodded. So the old man had been right – Dominic *had* fathered a bastard. Why else would he be so adamant about that particular condition? 'Your grandfather was a stubborn man, used to getting his own way, my boy,' Arnold warned him. 'And he made provisions for an army of lawyers to be called in if you decided to contest the will.'

Dominic opened his mouth to say that he'd win any case with such provocative clauses, and then paused, his astute brain searching for the catch. Akaki's baby had been born before his grandfather had died, thus anything to do with the baby could not possibly be connected with the will. But he knew his grandfather too well. Fred would have known the will couldn't be used to blackmail him about his baby, so what had he been playing at? Then he paled as the answer came to him in a flash. He slowly straightened up from his leaning position on the desk. 'And the lawyers will string it out for years,' he said softly, looking at Arnold and seeing the truth reflected there even before the older man nodded. 'And no doubt freeze the assets and all trading until it was settled,' he added, realizing how neatly he'd been trapped.

'I'm afraid so,' Arnold said regretfully.

'And a frozen company is a dead company. The competition would have a field day.' He swirled the liquor in his glass as he began to think. His baby would not suffer because of an old man's blind prejudice, he silently promised himself. He would diversify – build himself a separate empire that he could leave to his and Akaki's child. That way if he married and had more children, his legitimate heirs could inherit the two hotels, thus cutting off any chance of harmful legal action before it ever started. He looked at Arnold and saw the support in his unguarded green eyes before the older man blinked and looked totally poker-faced once more.

'OK,' Dominic said slowly. 'I don't contest. What's the final condition?'

Arnold sighed deeply, with such a look of embarrassed pity on his face that Dominic felt his heart plummet. 'The worst of all, I'm afraid,' he said, and Dominic gave a bitter bark of laughter.

'Worse?' he asked incredulously. 'What the hell could be worse?'

'The last is a morality clause,' the lawyer said heavily and for a moment Dominic was totally dumbfounded.

'A *what*!' he finally roared, feeling goaded beyond measure and not helped at all by the sudden look of glee that crossed, simultaneously, over the features of the two vultures.

'This clause is to be overseen by myself, a lawyer appointed by the two cousins who stand to inherit if you fail to comply, and two independent lawyers stipulated by Frederick Fairchild himself who will act as guardians of this clause. And the vote must be unanimous before you can be disinherited.'

Disinherited – there it was again, that all-powerful threat. 'And what, pray tell,' Dominic asked sarcastically, 'constitutes immoral behaviour in this enlightened day and age?'

Arnold looked deeply embarrassed. 'The usual sort of thing,' he muttered, 'covering the spirit of the law. Such things as undue or prolonged drunkenness, lewd or lascivious behaviour, drugs . . .'

'OK, OK!' Dominic held up his hands. 'I get the picture.'

'Of course,' Arnold began, then checked himself as he saw his two colleagues lean forward in anticipation. 'I'd like to speak to you in private about a few strictly personal matters.' He smiled coolly at the Chicago vultures and stood up. 'If you'll excuse us, gentlemen. I'll have my secretary draw up a copy of the salient points in the will for you and send them over to your hotel as soon as they are ready.' He walked to the door and held it open in a gesture of dismissal which the two men gracelessly accepted. Dominic waited until the door was closed then held up his hand to silence Arnold when he opened his mouth to speak. Walking to the door on silent feet, he opened it quickly, catching the two lurking men by surprise.

'Koana,' Dominic said, not even raising his voice, and the butler appeared in an instant. 'These two gentlemen are leaving.'

'Yes, Your Highness,' Koana said, making both men stare anew at Dominic who merely closed the library door and turned to his grandfather's lawyer.

'What the hell did he think he was doing?' he demanded, then laughed harshly. 'No – don't answer that. We both know exactly what he was doing. Can the will be broken quickly?'

'No – but you should get a second opinion. I am your grandfather's lawyer, after all.'

Dominic knew he could do just that, but he also knew that the will was rock-solid. Oh, not legally so – he could almost certainly successfully contest such a ridiculous document – but not without breaking Fairchilds as well. '*Shit!*' he hissed explosively.

Arnold gathered up his papers, took off his spectacles and snapped shut his briefcase. 'I have to get going. You know, lad, it's not as bad as you think.'

'No?'

'No,' Arnold said firmly. 'The two lawyers your grand-father picked were, I'm pretty damned sure, told by Fred to be very lenient with you. And I myself fully intend to be. You'll find the only people voting against you will be those two specimens who just left. Except . . .'

'Except?' Dominic asked warily.

'The third clause very specifically states that a legal heir must be produced by marriage. Thus the other lawyers and myself would have to vote with what your grandfather would have wished if you . . . er . . . were caught out with a child not . . . er . . .'

Dominic felt himself go cold. *He knows*, he thought. 'I understand,' he said, his voice like granite.

'I'm glad. And Dominic,' Arnold held out his hand, 'I tried to talk him out of it. But Fred . . . well, you know what Fred was like more than anyone.'

Dominic nodded and shook his hand without rancour. 'I do. And I appreciate your help, Mr Grantham. About everything,' he added softly.

Two pairs of green eyes met in a candid, man-to-man look.

GRAHAM was at his father's house when Arnold got back, ostensibly to visit his mother, who'd mollycoddled him since birth, but in reality to pump his father for information on the reading of the will.

'How'd it go? he asked casually, sitting beside his mother on the sofa, a skein of wool between his spread hands as she wound off it a ball of knitting wool.

'Fine,' Arnold said shortly, then stared at a wall. 'How's Jess?'

'She's OK. I've just come back from visiting her.'

'What do the doctors say?' he asked, licking his dry lips. Ever since the night of Melissa Hastings' party, when he had watched Jess get so drunk and done nothing to stop her, he found it strangely hard to meet Jess's knowing, guilty eyes.

'They're cagey. You know bloody doctors,' Graham said, more worry in his voice than he knew. 'Never commit themselves to anything.'

Arnold nodded and walked through to his study, unaware of the eagerness with which his son glanced at the briefcase in his hand. Taking the will out and locking it in his safe, Arnold checked his watch, and swore silently. 'I have to go out again,' he said as he walked through the room, his wife's mumbled, uninterested response barely registering.

Graham watched the door shut behind his father, a man he had long since stopped loving, and looked back at his mother. She was pretty, he supposed, in a faded sort of a way, and he forced himself to sit still with an almost animal-like patience as she rolled her ball of wool. Once his hands were free he got to his feet and asked if the *Book of Tort* was still in his father's study, knowing that she wouldn't have even the faintest idea that he was talking about a law book, let alone its location.

'I expect so, dear,' she said vaguely, already reaching for knitting needles as Graham quickly walked away and into the study.

Ever since the night Dominic had drunkenly told him about fathering yet another bastard, Graham had burned for a way of getting even. That he could sire children so easily whilst his own seed was useless, barren . . .

He went quickly to the safe, which was hidden unoriginally behind a painting by a local artist, twisted out the combination and removed the will. Walking to his father's desk he sat down and began to read, his legal training so far allowing him to quickly flick through the jargon and find the relevant details. At first he felt only bitter anger and disappointment when he read that the estate almost in its entirety was going to Dominic, although he had not really expected anything else. But then, as he read on with growing incredulity and blessed comprehension the conditions attached to the inheritance, he felt a great, almost orgasmic sense of pleasure wash over him.

Graham sat forward in the chair, the will that had given him glorious, much-sought-after power spread before him like a prize. He stretched his hands heavenwards, his slight body rocking with wild laughter.

Chapter 16

Richard Jago pulled away from the Crawfield mansion and drove quickly east. Cresting a rise he saw the grey blob that others called the Big Apple but which he had nicknamed 'rotten apple'. There was nothing about New York that he liked except the money that grew there.

It began to drizzle. He swore and clicked on the wipers with a savage chop of his hand. Still, things were improving. Old Lady Crawfield was a hypochondriac of the first order, a fact he'd picked up on when joining the most prestigious bridge club he could find in Manhattan. He'd visited her six times already and was making progress. Her regular doctor had begun to make noises but he'd managed to fob him off so far, insisting he was merely doing a favour to a relatively harmless old lady whose main problem was loneliness.

The drizzle turned to rain and he turned on the headlights. Up ahead New York loomed even closer, almost fading into the greyness of the day. An unexpected streak of bright red flashed by as a T-bird overtook him as if he were standing still. He watched it for the scant few seconds it was in view before taking a corner wide and whizzing out of sight, leaving him with the fleeting image of a woman with long blonde hair.

Vienna. Any blonde reminded him of Vienna. Sometimes, in the middle of the night when he lay staring at the ceiling, he thought the pain might kill him. After a while the rage would subside, leaving in its place the gnawing frustration of not knowing who had cast him into exile. How could he be expected to live in the rotten apple? It was ugly and grey, his nostrils picking up the carbon monoxide stench of the city even though he was still miles from it. He'd cultivate hundreds of Mrs Crawfields to get the money to go back. He'd even marry one if he had to.

He turned the corner and found his foot ramming on the

brake even before his mind had consciously assimilated what he was seeing. From the grey ribbon of tarmac, two tyremarks had been gouged out in the soft grassy bank to his left and halfway up the slight incline the red T-bird lay drunkenly on one side, its wheels ominously still. As he opened his door and slammed it shut he could see splintered glass littering the grass all around and as he approached he could smell the sharp tang of petrol. He stumbled up the incline, the wet grass slippery under his feet, and resting his hand on the underside of the car he made his way to the driver's side which was pressed against the damp earth.

Inside a woman lay limply, her face and blonde hair covered with blood leaking from a nasty gash on her head.

He put down his medical bag and walked to the passenger side, where he tugged on the dented door. Looking down into the car's mangled interior he saw the woman's eyes flicker open, but could not see their colour as she watched him. 'Come on!' he snarled at the door, placing both hands on the handle and heaving upwards. Slowly the door shuddered open and he went in awkwardly headfirst, crawling past the passenger seat and gear-stick to give the woman a preliminary check. Meeting shocked eyes that he could now see were blue, he forced a smile onto his face. The last thing he wanted was for her to start struggling in panic. 'Don't worry – I'm a doctor. You're going to be just fine.' The platitudes slipped from him automatically and the hands that he ran over her were expert but impersonal. He checked her neck first and then her back, finding no fractures or evidence of dislocation, and then he checked the arm and leg nearest to him. Satisfied that she could be moved, he slipped his arm behind her back and hoisted her out. She cried out but Richard ignored this and carried her a few yards from the car.

Placing her gently on the wet grass he quickly retrieved his bag and opened it, taking out a small torch. After checking her pupils and eye movement he noticed that the arm that had been lying pressed to the ground was bleeding profusely. He quickly ripped away the sodden sleeve of the sweater and the satin blouse underneath, and saw that a major artery had been severed. He looked back at her briefly as he reached into his bag for a hypodermic and found her watching him, seemingly alert. 'I'm just going to give you an anaesthetic in your arm,' he spoke matter-of-factly as he filled the needle and slid it into her arm. 'You have a severed artery which I'm going to have to tie off,' he continued, concentrating on the suture he was threading through a surgical needle. 'You haven't had time to lose much blood,' he lied competently, looking back at the blue eyes which definitely seemed to be understanding all he said. 'I'm a surgeon, so I'm used to stitching people up,' he carried on, letting his lips curl into a smile as he bent over her arm, working quickly and skilfully as he separated the artery from the flesh and stitched the two severed ends together temporarily with hands that he had doused in clinical antiseptic. He raised his head quickly as he heard an approaching car and stood up, waving both arms as a Ford came into sight and pulled to a halt.

'Are you all right up there?' a voice called.

'There's a phone in my car,' Richard yelled. 'Call my hospital – 5556878.'

He looked down at the girl who lay still and quiet and smiled absently. 'I've called them,' the voice came again a minute later and Richard looked down to watch a man get back into his own car and quickly pull away.

He crouched back down next to his patient. 'Can you nod or shake your head?' he asked, and after a moment the head moved downwards in a single nod.

'Good.' He ran his fingers over her ribs counting three broken ones, all on the side where the car had ploughed against the earth. 'It's only a few cracked ribs,' he smiled, needing to keep her calm. 'In fact,' he continued, pressing fingers into her stomach and finding no evidence of ruptures or internal bleeding, 'I'm probably in more danger than you are. I'm not, strictly speaking, supposed to be treating you. If . . .'

He broke off as she suddenly gasped and her hand reached out and clutched his arm in sudden fear. He saw the panic hit her at the same time as he heard the gurgling deep in her throat. Quickly reaching for his scalpel he cut away the polo neck of her cashmere sweater. Holding her clawing, panicking fingers away from her neck he immediately saw the problem. A piece of glass lodged in her throat had moved and was jutting into her windpipe, cutting of her air supply. Already her face was turning blue, her eyes rolling back into her head. As she lost consciousness Richard was able to remove the glass after he had performed a tracheotomy with his scalpel. He massaged her lungs, watching as her breathing returned to normal, then checked her pulse as her colour slowly returned. Finally relaxing, he sat down beside her, his fingers on her wrist.

He stirred as he heard sirens, the flashing red and blue lights appearing out of the misty rain a few moments later as the ambulance pulled to a halt behind his car, two paramedics sprinting to the rear of the vehicle and pulling out a stretcher, their movements economical and well-trained. Richard stood up as they approached, and watched them competently lift her onto the stretcher as he listed her injuries. Within minutes they were gone, sirens screaming and lights flashing, and Richard looked down, noticing for the first time the state of his clothes. He swore. He'd have to be more careful with his good stuff. He hated pennypinching. It reminded him too much of his childhood and his middle-class parents and their damned 'money ethic' mentality. He'd always known that money was all-important and didn't need to squander his time and talents doing manual labour for peanuts to 'appreciate' it. On Oahu he thought he'd finally laid all his financial ghosts to rest, but now it had all been wrenched away from him by some unknown, unseen adversary. Having been forced to leave his boat and car unsold on the islands, money had been tighter than ever. Such was the haste in which he had been asked to leave, that even now the thought of it made him feel physically sick.

As he knelt down to refill his bag with the scattered equipment, he noticed something other than glass shining in the grass a few feet away. A gold necklace, set with different coloured gems, it had slipped from the injured woman's neck as he carried her from the wrecked car. It must be worth thousands.

Looking around quickly he picked up the necklace and put

it into his pocket. He hesitated, one cool part of his brain telling him that if he didn't take it, the next carload of freebooting cretins would be sure to, but even so he had to fight off the guilty urge to drop the necklace back into the grass.

Going back to the T-bird, his heart beating a little faster now, he found her handbag and opened it. Delving deep inside his fingers curled around two cold objects. Removing his hands he stared down at a pair of dangling diamond earrings finished off with a single huge pearl and quickly put them in his pocket also. Cursing anew his parents for instilling in him a middle-class sense of morality he checked the glove compartment and found a sapphire and diamond ring which he added to his growing collection. Telling himself that anything would justify him getting back to Oahu and Vienna, he was just sliding back down the incline to his own car when a police vehicle pulled in. A sudden shiver of alarm made him jerk to a standstill before he remembered that it was standard policy for an ambulance called to a car crash to alert the police. Casually he walked to meet the patrolmen getting out of the car.

After giving them a competent and concise statement, omitting only his own thievery, he was once again safely headed towards the rotten apple.

NEARLY an hour later he pulled up in front of a large, rather squalid-looking apartment block that wasn't too bad on the inside. Five floors up, he let himself into his three-roomed apartment, locking the door carefully behind him before taking out the jewels. Lowering his large frame awkwardly on to the low couch that had come with the fully furnished flat, he reached into the black bag by his side and extracted a hooked, surgical implement. Working quickly and easily he prised all the gems from their settings, having already decided it was too risky to try and sell the items as they were. He knew no fences for stolen jewellery, and wouldn't have trusted them if he had. A small mound of stones —consisting of at least ten small diamonds, two pearls, three emeralds of small but perfect quality, four rubies and a fairly large and single sapphire sat in the middle of the table gleaming in a smug richness of colour. He had no idea of their precise worth, but they couldn't hurt his depleted bank balance. The gold settings he wrapped in a Kleenex, regretfully deciding he must throw them away.

He had a bath, since the antiquated plumbing in the tiny bathroom did not run to a shower, and afterwards changed into fresh clothes. Discreetly dropping the Kleenex into a street trash-bin a few blocks away, he drove halfway between his home and the hospital where he was working, looking out for a jewellery store. When he found a likely-looking place he pulled up and walked in, watching the man behind the counter serve a customer. He was small with a totally bald head and effeminate hands. Waiting until the shop was empty, Richard walked over and spread the jewels out onto the counter. Without so much as a word, the jeweller took out an eye-glass and examined each one and named a price which roughly tallied with Richard's most conservative estimate. Working on the premise that everyone was out to screw everyone else, he added another fifteen hundred dollars to the total, both men finally agreeing on one thousand dollars more. Richard was not surprised when the man came back with a wad of cash and as he quickly counted and pocketed it, the owner of the store never so much as glanced at him.

It took him another half hour to get to the hospital, by which time he was more than three hours late. Situated in a dirty little street not far from the Brooklyn Bridge, the place squatted its three-storey bulk on a site between a parking lot and a kids' computer amusement arcade where drug-pushers and porno reps hung out, and Richard found his spirits falling the closer he got. He hated its drabness, its lack of class and prestige. He hated the mixed Hispanic, Negroes and poor whites who were the inevitable patients, and he despised the doctors who in turn despised him. As he entered the antiseptic locker room and donned his white coat he pondered the possibility of setting up a private practice. With his looks and skill he shouldn't have any trouble finding clients.

'Nurse.' He acknowledged the woman sat at the reception desk as he passed by.

'Dr Jago – Mr Carew wants to see you in his office right away.'

Richard sighed. 'Didn't he get my message about the crash victim? I phoned before leaving my apartment.'

'I think that's what he wants to see you about. It's not hospital policy . . .'

'I know,' Richard snapped, attaching his ID badge to the pocket of his coat. 'I daresay he'd have preferred it if I'd stood by and let her choke to death rather than risk a lawsuit. Did the tracheotomy hold all right?'

'Yes sir, but the patient was transferred to another hospital.'

Richard nodded. That figured – a woman worth fifteen thousand dollars in jewellery wasn't likely to stay at the James Florance for long.

In Ross Carew's office Richard stood impassively while he was lectured on the consequences of a lawsuit. 'Do you know who she was, for chrissake?' Carew finally asked explosively, leaning forward in his chair as Richard looked at him sharply, for the first time actually listening to him.

'Who?'

'Odessa Vance, that's who. Good grief, you couldn't have picked anyone worse.'

'Oh? She's given to prosecuting hospitals is she? Hobby of hers, perhaps?'

Carew took a deep, deep breath. 'Odessa Vance is worth a fortune – and I'm not talking about the odd million. Her father was one of the pioneers of plastic, made millions before he was thirty. She . . .'

Richard stopped listening at that point, his eyes narrowing.

'Are you listening to me?' Carew all but screeched several hectoring minutes later, and leaping to his feet, he slammed a small fist down on to his desktop with an almost childish display of temper. 'I've also had a call from Carter Crawfield. He tells me you've been seeing his mother – prescribing pills for her.' At this Carew changed tack, subsiding into his chair and smugly anticipating cutting this arrogant oaf down to size. 'Needless to say, Mrs Crawfield's own doctor is most concerned. He's convinced there's nothing wrong with her.'

'She's old. There's always something wrong with an eighty-year-old.'

Feeling cheated by this reasonable reply, Carew blew his top. 'Mr Crawfield is threatening to bring legal action, claiming that you're using undue influence. He says you're using your medical training to ingratiate yourself into his mother's will. I need not remind you that such an action would not be tolerated by this hosptal . . .'

'So I quit,' Richard said softly, cutting into Carew's tirade with the same ease with which his scalpel cut flesh. Ross Carew looked at him, totally astounded, his little mouth hanging open as Richard sneered in disgust and turned towards the door.

'You have a month's notice to work out. You can't just walk away,' the administrator snarled, and Richard turned, his hand on the doorknob.

'So sue me,' he said softly. 'But I don't think Mrs Crawfield would like it if I told her I felt obliged to resign on her behalf. Doesn't she still donate rather heavily to this hospital charity?'

Carew went pale and his mouth snapped shut. 'Get out!' he snapped impotently and Richard laughed softly.

'I intended to – remember?'

Walking to the reception desk, he removed his name-tab and put it on the desktop along with his coat. 'Can you tell me to which hospital my road accident patient was transferred please, Nurse?'

Quickly she checked her records. 'Van der Valks, Doctor Jago.'

He'd heard of it. One of the city's première hospitals for the rich, it could probably boast designer needles! Wordlessly he turned and walked away.

Leaving the hospital he drove straight to a sports club not far from the Radio City Music Hall. There he ignored the changing rooms and made for the bar, finding it full of lunch-hour fitness freaks having an après tennis or badminton drink. Spotting Isaac Farnsworth, a passing acquaintance, he raised a casual hand. Nodding, the tall Jewish retailer of some of the priciest men'swear outlets in the city joined him at the bar. 'What's your poison?' Richard asked, ordering an Austrian lager for himself.

'Mineral water for me,' Isaac said and Richard paid the fifteen dollars for the two drinks and leaned an elbow on the bar.

'Busy day?' he asked and Isaac's dark, rather intense features creased into a smile shocking for its width.

'When isn't it?' he asked with a very graphic shrug and Richard gave a grunt of laughter.

'You can say that again. At least you're safe from your work until you get to the office. I had to start early. Some chick wrecked her T-bird out in the sticks. Beautiful car too,' he mused, 'preserved, pampered, lovely. Rather like its owner I gather, though she was too covered in blood for me to form an opinion at the time. Cheers.' He raised his glass and took a long cool swallow.

Right on cue, Isaac said, 'T-bird? Claudia Rychvik drives a model T.'

'Uh-huh.' Richard shook his head. 'This was some chick by the name of – oh hell, what was it? Olive Vance?'

'Odessa Vance,' Isaac gushed eagerly, nodding with the superiority that some drivers show when learning of some-one's else's accident. 'So she wrecked the car. She and my sister went to Bryn Mawr together. So – is she all right?'

Richard took another swallow, shaking his head as he did so, seeing from the corner of his eye that his quarry was on the edge of his seat by now. 'Wouldn't have been,' he said casually. 'I had to perform a tracheotomy.'

'Isn't that where you cut their throat?' Isaac asked, looking a little green around the gills, and Richard nodded.

'Yep,' he said with a slight shake of his head. 'If I hadn't come along when I did she'd have had it.' He drew his finger across his throat in a graphic gesture. 'Mind you, I had to quit the hospital because of it. My bastard of an administrater said the hospital could get sued.'

Isaac gave a cynical laugh, prepared to believe anything of the world in which he lived, and Richard took another sip before saying with just the right amount of trepidation. 'She isn't likely to sue, is she? Do you know her well?'

'Hell no,' Isaac said. 'Would you sue the man who saved your life?'

Richard shrugged, well-pleased. The story would soon be put about in Manhattan's expansive but élite little group, no doubt with the usual embellishments. When this Vance woman was up and about she'd be constantly hearing about his heroics from her own friends, and the fact that he'd lost his job because of her wouldn't hurt. Because he sure as hell wasn't going to tell her. That wouldn't be at all smart. 'Just so long as she doesn't have an irate husband to push her into it . . .' he shrugged. 'Do you want another?'

Isaac – who would always accept anything no matter what if it was free, nodded his head. 'Don't worry. She just got divorced last year. Her husband was someone in Detroit. Cadillacs, I think.'

Richard nodded. Anyone in Isaac's social sphere who came from Detroit had to be an auto-millionaire. 'I hear her father's a bit of a wizard.'

'Dead,' Isaac said. 'How bad is she?'

'I had to cauterize an artery that had been severed in her arm so she lost a lot of blood, but apart from that she should be OK. Actually I was thinking of going to see her later – do you know where the Van der Valk is?'

Isaac did, of course, for he had been there recently to have a nasty little social disease discreetly seen to and was happy to give his rather promising new acquaintance directions. Not that Richard Jago could be called a friend exactly. No one yet knew much about him, and party-crashers were a common hazard. But Richard's heroic profession made him intriguing, and his looks and size made him excellent material for any hostess with a spare female guest on her hands. Genuine heroes were hard to find nowadays . . .

Richard stayed with Isaac until he had to get back to the office, carefully hiding his contemptuous boredom, and then set to work. Seeing his landlord, he bullied him into giving back the rent money he'd paid in advance, and quickly packed his cases. Then he began to tour the hotels. What he needed was a quality hotel that was not too flashy. He didn't want to give the impression that he was trying to look rich. He needed the sort of hotel that a wealthy but not money-minded doctor might choose if he was new in town. He found just what he was looking for in the New York Helmsley, a fine forty-storey building situated in the fashionable East side of the city, adjacent to Fifth Avenue and the United Nations building. The room he was shown to after checking in was air-conditioned with a remote colour TV, telephone and radio. It was spacious and just right for a doctor who was rarely in. The bellboy recommended Mindy's as a good place to eat and Richard tipped him generously.

He quickly unpacked only the very best of his clothes, leaving the rest in the suitcases and locked the door behind him before walking to the elevator.

In the lobby, Harry's Bar, one of Manhattan's most sophisticated lounges, was plainly visible, but he ignored it. Time enough to make connections later.

Mindy's turned out to be a three-tier restaurant with a good selection of continental cuisine and a pleasant ambience. There he took his time over dinner, knowing that Odessa Vance would be groggy for a while even this long after coming out of surgery, and he enjoyed his food for the first time since leaving the islands, savouring his choice of cream of water-cress soup, salmon mousse, roast lamb and mint, with lemon pavlova for dessert.

IT was gone nine when Richard Jago pulled up in front of the Van der Valk hospital, a modern edifice that owed a great debt to the clever architect who had designed it. In the lobby a florist shop attracted his attention and he thoughtfully looked over the gigantic displays of roses, carnations, freesias, gardenias and orchids. Finally he purchased a single moon-daisy, its centre a golden yellow, its petals a pure brilliant white. At the desk he asked for her room, only to be told that all her visitors were screened.

'Are you family?' the nurse asked, her uniform of finest white linen, her face perfectly made up. If she ever emptied a bedpan in her life, Richard thought, I'll eat her designer cap.

'No, but I am the surgeon who treated her on the spot.' He

smiled gently at the redhead, whose hazel eyes sharpened with interest.

'I see.'

'I would just like to see how she is,' he said simply, but let his smile falter a little. 'I didn't realize I'd need an appointment.'

'Oh, I'm sure that Doctor Murrenbacher wouldn't mind in your case, Doctor. . . ?'

'Jago. Richard Jago.'

'She's on the tenth floor, room one hundred and four. There are elevators just over there,' she pointed a pink-painted fingertip to her left.

Richard smiled. 'You're an angel.'

On the tenth floor more luxury confronted him. The reception room wouldn't have looked out of place in a mansion, and he half-expected to see a chandelier hanging from the ceiling. The receptionist was obviously expecting him, her eyes running over him as he walked forward. 'Doctor Jago,' she greeted him courteously. 'Room one hundred and four is the second on the left.'

At the wooden door that bore italic gold numerals, he knocked softly and walked in. An expanse of rose carpet spread from wall to wall, whilst long, paler pink curtains hung at wide, closed windows. A television was in one corner, its screen at least five feet wide, and underneath was a video machine with a shelfful of tapes. Richard closed the door behind him carefully and softly approached the wide double bed. The sheets were white satin, the pillowslips edged in pink lace. The woman who lay amidst it all was looking away from him and had obviously not heard his knock. She wore a bandage around her forehead, throat and arm, and was hooked up to a drip.

Suddenly her peripheral vision alerted her and she swung her head around, long corn-coloured locks splaying out over her cheeks as she did so. Her hair looked a dirty colour to him, used as he was to Vienna's silvery strands, and underneath the covers he could make out a long, slender form.

By her side he noticed baskets of flowers and knew he'd been right to anticipate them. Stopping by her bed he made no attempt to bend down or minimize his height. 'Hello – remember me?' he asked softly, and as she parted lips that seemed to him almost shapeless, he held up a hand. 'Uh-huh,' he cautioned. 'You won't be able to speak for a few days yet.'

Odessa looked up a long, long way and saw again the most handsomely interesting face she could ever remember seeing. His hair was toffee in colour, and framed a face of such rugged power that it made her other lovers seem effeminate. Widely spaced dove-grey eyes smiled down at her, attractive crow's feet at the corners tagging him as older and more experienced than the men who usually courted her. With his slightly too-fleshy nose and a jaw that could have belonged on a boxer she found herself feeling very, very attracted.

'Well, you're looking a lot better than when I first saw you,' Richard said mildly, allowing himself to frown and forcing his voice up a notch. 'Just what the hell were you trying to do anyway?' he asked sternly. 'Kill yourself?'

Odessa had had many lovers, some of them macho types. Sometimes she'd played along, sometimes not, depending on her mood. But none of them had this man's . . . authority. Perhaps it was because he was a doctor, or because he was so physically big, but she could feel a distinctly feminine thrill of reaction snake down her spine as he loomed over her, and she shook her head slightly, unable to take her eyes off him.

Richard saw her eyes move to the daisy in his hand, waiting until she looked back at him before looking at the flower himself. 'Oh, yes,' he said as if he'd forgotten he'd been holding it, handing over the long-stemmed flower to her with an almost boyish embarrassment. 'This is for you.' He waited until her fingers had almost reached it, and then moved it away. 'But only if you promise not to sue me,' he added teasingly.

Her smiled widened, revealing teeth that seemed much too big to him, and not as white as Vienna's. Holding back his distaste he let her claim the daisy. She looked at it, intrigued by his choice and noticing for the first time how pure and how simply beautiful a daisy was. When she looked back at the banks of flowers beside her, they looked gaudy and meaningless.

Satisfied, Richard decided he'd done just enough. The

doctors would tell her when she asked that he'd saved her life, and her own friends would visit her, thanks to Isaac, with the news that he'd been fired for doing just that. The daisy would last long after the other hothouse flowers had wilted for weed-like flowers were always more hardy than their cultivated cousins. Oh yes, he'd done enough. Tomorrow he'd go on a shopping spree and blow at least half of the money her jewels had brought him on the finest wardrobe he could find.

'Well, I know how tired you must be,' he said, moving one step back, seeing the disappointment that took some of the sparkle from her eyes – eyes that were a dull blue and not at all like Vienna's azure gaze. 'I only wanted to make sure you were all right. You were gone by the time I'd changed and arrived at the hospital. Mind you,' he said, looking around, 'I'm rather glad that you were. This place is much more . . . right for you,' he let his voice drop an octave, and then shrugged, as if pulling himself together.

'Well, I hope you recover quickly. I know you're in good hands,' he added, as if nothing would have torn him away from her if it hadn't been so. 'And drive more carefully in future,' he warned, backing away intead of turning around, as if he couldn't bear to stop looking at her.

Oh yes, Richard Jago knew women all right. And after he had said goodbye, softly and regretfully, before turning and leaving the room without a backwards glance, he was smiling a predatory, anticipatory smile that he was careful to wipe off his face before approaching the reception desk.

In the lift he leaned back against the wall and nodded to himself. He would be hearing from Odessa Vance again, of that he was sure. And just to make certain he re-entered the florist, bought a small bunch of fragrant violets, and accepted a card and a pen. The florist assured him they'd be sent up immediately. He paused thoughtfully over his message, needing to set just the right tone, then wrote on the card, '*My daisy seemed a little lost amidst the beauty of your other flowers. Perhaps these will make up for my lack of gallantry. Richard Jago.*'

And on the back, in very small numbers as if embarrassed by his effrontery in expecting her to even want to call him, he wrote the telephone number of his hotel.

Chapter 17

Vienna knocked on the door, her heart pounding as Farron opened it and let her in. 'So, this is your lair, is it?' she mused, nodding wisely as she looked around the easygoing room. It was full of plants and mismatched furniture. In one corner, a canvas hammock swayed gently. 'Do you ever sleep in that?'

'Sometimes. But there are certain things that are easier to do in a real bed.'

She felt embarrassed heat touch her cheeks, even as a kick of sexual reaction to his provocative words sunk deep into her belly. 'I can't think what you mean,' she heard her voice come out light and teasing.

'Oh, such innocence,' he groaned. 'But I know you're very aware that the way to a man's heart is through his stomach — right?'

'Oh, right!' she agreed sagely, nodding her head solemnly.

'Good. Let's go shopping and then you can come back and feed me.'

She laughed and followed him to the door. 'It's a wonder you haven't starved to death.'

'I know,' he said pitifully, opening the door. 'Nobody loves me.'

The Belund international market, called by locals Kuhio Malls was a delight to see, hear and most of all, smell! As well as offering a vast range of Polynesian food, Farron told her it also gave customers a free show in the evening. Farron paid for the growing packages without demur as his chest and then his chin slowly disappeared under the bags of lichee and wild pomelos, Camembert cheese, oysters, crab and French bread that she selected. Eventually, with only his eyes peering over the tops of brown paper bags stuffed with oxtails and tongue, she called a halt. 'I think that's all,' she murmured, walking beside him as they made their way slowly to the exit, considerate fellow-shoppers giving them a wide berth. 'I only need a couple of things for a sauce or two . . .'

'Please don't,' Farron groaned. 'I'm saucy enough.'

A bag of cherries resting in the crook of his elbow popped open and a few of them fell out. She caught them and refolded the bag, watching him watch her bite into a cherry and lick her lips. 'Hm, lovely,' she whispered seductively and Farron made a choking sound from behind a plastic bag of fresh prawns. 'Want one?' Standing on tiptoe, careful not to jostle any of the bags, she fed him a cherry, watching as his strong white teeth bit into the fruit, feeling her womb contract in reaction. Without a word they walked back to the car.

'I'll drive back,' she threatened.

'Oh no,' he whined. 'One of the most dangerous creatures alive is a woman who's just passed her driving test.'

She did her fair share of donkey work back at the flat, her arms aching and full even before the elevator drew to a smooth halt at the fourteenth floor.

'Oh-oh,' Farron said ominously as they stood outside his door and she looked at him curiously. 'Keys,' he said succinctly and glanced down over the mound of his groceries to his trouser pocket. She followed his line of vision and then met his exasperated eyes in a moment of total silence before she began to laugh helplessly. She became hysterical as she watched him gyrate and swivel, trying to work a hand free, his clumsy juggling act going astray when the crabs landed on the floor and scattered.

'Here,' she finally spluttered, taking pity on him. 'Let me.'

Juggling her own parcels she pressed herself close to his side and then with careful fingers traced his thigh until she found the pocket. Farron tensed and looked stonily at the door, a fine sweat breaking out on his forehead as she wriggled her fingers into the tight pocket of his shorts and worked her way down. 'Oh God!'

'What?'

'Nothing. Got them yet?'

'Not yet ... ah yes.' She curled her hand into a fist as she found them, her knuckles brushing lightly against his shaft as she did so, and he shuddered.

She watched him fiddle to open the door, wishing her hand didn't tingle so much. She could feel her breasts, tight and ultra-sensitive straining against the material of her dress and could feel every warm inch of him still throbbing against her hand. She said quietly 'Crabs.'

'What?'

'Crabs – in the corridor,' she nodded in the general direction and he snapped to with a decided effort. As he retrieved them, Vienna walked into the kitchen, exploring the food processor, microwave and conventional oven, timers and gadgets. 'This place really is something.'

'Yeah – the landlord reduced the rent for me,' he confided as he began to put away the groceries, hoping she didn't notice how his hands shook.

'Why would he do that?'

'Said I was doing him a favour living here. It gives the place a bit of panache having a megastar like me in residence,' he teased, casting her a leering look out of the corner of his eye as she snorted sceptically.

'Oh yeah – Bruce Springsteen watch out,' she said dryly. 'Still, it doesn't sound reasonable, does it? I mean, how many landlords do you know go about reducing the rent?'

Farron considered. 'Not many. Just another case of Manikuuna luck, I guess.'

Two hours later they sat down to a meal of oysters in lemon sauce, stuffed crab and macadamia nut pie. 'Not bad,' Vienna complimented herself cautiously. 'But I still think when we go to *Tutu*'s place for Sunday dinner, it will be put in the shade.'

Farron decided not to tell her how very much it pleased him that she and his grandmother had taken to one another at first sight. 'That was deeee-lish-ous,' he murmured contentedly, patting his stomach with gastronomic satisfaction. 'You ought to take up cookery classes.'

'Hmm, I did enjoy it,' she admitted, glad that the food had turned out so well. There was something satisfying about creating a meal, about smelling and mixing. It made her feel capable. Was she a cook? Was that how she'd made her living? It didn't seem likely, though. No matter how much Farron complimented her on getting on with her life she still felt useless to a large extent, like a computer without a programme. But each new triumph made her feel a little more real. The police had all but given up on her, and now no longer even called to give her progress reports. It was all up to her now.

'Then why don't you? Take classes, I mean. There's always ways around the shifts,' Farron pointed out, interrupting her thoughts.

'I wish. But with rent, bus fares and taxes I doubt if I could afford it.'

'Leave the dishes, I'll do them tomorrow,' Farron said as she rose and picked up her plate. 'Coffee?'

'Yes, please.' She wandered slowly to the couch and sat down, listening to the sounds of clinking cups that emanated from the kitchen before he brought in two steaming mugs.

'How are you, Vienna?' he asked, sitting beside her and looking deep into her eyes. 'I mean, how are you *really* doing?'

She shrugged. 'Sometimes, when I'm busy, or happy, I don't realize that the past is gone. Then, at other times, I don't know,' she shuddered. 'I get so scared, so – spooked. I keep thinking there's something, something I'm missing. Something important. I don't know – it's as if there's something dangerous out there, waiting to get me.'

His hand curled around her shoulder and she rested her cheek against it, her eyes closing as he watched her, fascinated by the curling lashes that cast minute shadows on her skin. 'Listen, I've been thinking,' he said cautiously. 'If you didn't have to worry about money, you could take those cookery classes you want.'

'But I do have to worry about money. I told you, rent . . .'

'You wouldn't if you lived with me.' He felt time stop as he waited for her answer, his breath locked in his lungs, his heart pounding. Damn! After all his promises not to rush her, why couldn't he keep his big mouth shut? It was obvious she didn't like the idea because her silence was long and total.

'Here you mean?'

'No – not here,' he said quickly, hoping to salvage something. 'I meant if I could find another place . . . one with two bedrooms. That way you wouldn't be alone. You'll have someone to talk to when you need it most.'

She opened her eyes, her gaze falling on a large plant in the corner of the room, its green leaves curving towards the sun. 'All right,' she said quietly.

Farron jerked his head back to look at her, half-inclined to believe he was hearing things. 'You will?' he asked, then could have bitten off his tongue. He sounded like a kid being offered the chance to feel under a girl's skirt for the first time. 'I mean, OK. That's great.'

'But I'll have to pay half the rent. I don't . . .' she bit her lip and then felt him hug her reassuringly.

'I understand. You don't want to fall into the same trap of dependence as you did with Jago.'

'No. Not that I'm comparing you with him,' she said quickly.

'Good. I'm going to profit from this deal too, you know. I get meals – cordon bleu standard, mind,' he wagged a finger at her, 'every day. No more starving to death for me.'

'Just meals?' she teased, then gasped as his brown eyes smouldered.

'Oh, I might,' he raised a finger to trace the delicate bones in her shoulder 'be able,' he ran his finger down her throat, 'at a push,' his hand stopped just short of her breast, 'to think of something else.'

Vienna took a shaking breath and licked her lips.

'Please,' Farron startled her by moaning. 'Don't do that! It drives me nuts.'

'What? Oh, does it?' she asked, her voice dangerously low and husky as she ran her pink tongue to the farthest corner of her mouth. Farron watched her, fascinated. She was seducing him and he loved it. He loved it even more when she sat astride him, knees on either side of his thighs. Sitting on his lap, feeling the hardness of him pressing helplessly against the cloth-covered entrance to her very core, she was aware of the way the muscles in her stomach contracted eagerly, causing molten rivers to stir deep in her womb.

'What else drives you nuts?' she asked softly and felt a strictly feminine, age-old power thrill through her as his shaft hardened and pressed even more firmly against her, seeking to enter her inner place that was still sheathed and safe. He raised a finger to his ear, but could not have spoken to save his life. Leaning forward she blew gently into his ear and felt his whole body tremble. Farron swallowed hard, his eyes closing.

'Vienna,' he groaned warningly, his hands curling impotently into fists by his side. She could feel the heat coming from his skin and felt an answering excitement deep inside her, spreading outwards, giving her a confidence that she'd never been aware of before. He wanted her, and that felt wonderful.

'What else?' she asked, sitting back on his lap, feeling the hard shaft underneath her leap in response to her proximity once again.

He crossed his arms and pulled the T-shirt off his head, letting it drop from his hand and fall behind the sofa. Taking her hand, he brought her fingers to his nipple, dark brown and as hard as any pebble found on the beach. Obediently, she caressed him there, raising her other hand to his other nipple, nipping them between her thumb and finger, plucking at the tiny hairs that grew there, half-hurting him. The tiny spasm of pain shot straight to his groin. Holding his eyes with her own for as long as she could, she closed her lips around one button of flesh, instinct driving her on as she tasted the slightly salty flavour of his skin. 'Oh sweet Jee . . .' Farron moaned, his back arching and his hands splaying helplessly against her ribs as she suckled greedily, a warming flash of triumph heating her to fever pitch.

'Does this drive you nuts too?' she asked, her hand falling down between them, resting against the denim of his jeans and rubbing against the hard mound between his thighs.

Farron jerked helplessly, bucking hard. 'Yes,' he moaned. 'Yes!'

Sliding backwards she moved to the very end of his knees and with shaking fingers found his zip and worked it carefully down, pulling the jeans off and leaving him proudly naked. For a long, long moment she looked at him, taking in the beauty of his lean, tanned body, the quivering of his sensitized skin, the throbbing, up-stretching eagerness of his shaft. She swallowed, aware of her own crazily pounding heart urging her to act. Without pausing to think she pulled down and stepped out of her panties and straddled him again, her thighs shuddering as they slid past his.

'Vienna!' He cried out her name as she impaled herself upon him, her breath leaving her in a shaking moan as she felt him inside her, hot and strong, filling her. His hands cupped her back as she began to move up and down on his penis, feeling the muscles of her vagina contract and expand to take its girth. As he felt her tense and close around him, squeezing him hard and relentlessly Farron moaned. Rolling his head from side to side in helpless ecstasy he dragged in deep shuddering breaths as the world around them burst in an explosion of jerking and harshly uttered love words.

She felt the orgasm hit her like a tidal wave as she collapsed around him, her lips pressed to his lips, her legs holding him a willing prisoner. She slid sideways on to the sofa and he followed her, his hands gentle on her breasts.

'Are you OK?' he asked softly, long minutes later, their bodies slowly cooling and pulse-rates returning to normal.

'Hm, lovely,' she murmured, smiling lazily into his brown eyes.

'You're amazing.'

'So you said,' she teased, and then frowned. Perhaps he hadn't liked it that she'd been so bossy? 'Farron, was it,' she balked at saying the corny words. 'Did you enjoy yourself?' she finally blurted out boldly, and Farron stared at her.

'Oh Vienna, couldn't you tell?' he finally admonished.

Vienna gave a relieved laugh and sat up. 'I could do with a shower.'

'Now there's an idea,' he said, eyes twinkling, and together they walked naked to the shower, which he turned on to cold and then dragged her squealing under the spray to join him.

THAT evening they went to the famous Kodak free show in Kapiolani Park, holding hands and kissing each other's knuckles. They ate fruit picked from wild trees growing near the tiny beach they found afterwards and casting off their shoes, walked along the shore where the sea came in, the warm water caressing their ankles as they splashed and strolled.

When they went back to his flat there was no question of her going home, although he offered to drive her, and in his big bed they learned their bodies by braille. Questing fingers and sensitive lips sought out the love areas that made the other squirm and gasp, all the while his whispers telling her he loved her, her own whispers repeating the same. The next morning, arriving at eleven-thirty for the lunch-time shift, they walked hand in hand into the lobby, the coolness a welcome relief from the growing summer sun outside.

'Isn't it funny how our shifts keep coinciding,' she commented as they walked into the opulent luxury of the dining room and Farron shrugged.

'I told you – it's better to be born lucky than rich.'

'Well, you certainly seem to have your fair share.'

'*Wahini*,' he teased, patting her rump as she walked away laughing, heading for the kitchens. Half-turning to the stage where Kim sat alone fiddling with the mikes, a movement at the bar caught his eye and he turned, his smile widening as Dominic raised a glass of iced papaya juice at him. Farron walked quickly to join him. Lord, the world was good today!

Watching him approach, Dominic recognized the look in the younger man's eyes and a mixture of emotions washed over him. Fear for the young singer, because being in love was a very vulnerable state. Envy, because he knew that he himself had never truly known what it was to be so vulnerable. Happiness for him, and hope that it all turned out well.

'Drink?' he asked as Farron sat on the stool next to him and nodded. 'Pineapple Toni,' Dominic said, accurately anticipating Farron's choice.

'Cheers,' Farron accepted the glass, moist with ice-water, and saluted Dominic who obligingly clinked glasses and took a long swallow. 'I don't suppose you know of any bigger flats on the market, do you?' Farron surprised him by saying abruptly.

Dominic looked at him, crow's feet deepening attractively at the sides of his emerald-green eyes as he smiled and looked pointedly at Vienna. 'You mean a flat big enough for two?'

Farron laughed, not at all offended or annoyed. 'That's right.'

'Can she cook, that's the thing,' Dominic said facetiously.

'Like a dream. She wants to take some cookery classes actually, and I think it's a great idea. She has such a real flair for it, we thought she might have been a professional chef. We thought about hiring a private detective, to see if he can get a trace on Vienna from that angle, but it seems such a hopelessly huge task.'

'She's really that good?' Dominic said thoughtfully. 'I have a guest-house up near Nanakuli, just up the west coast from Waianae. I need a good cook for when I have guests, which is often enough to justify a full-time employee. Up until now I've been hiring a local woman as and when needed, but she's getting old and hinting that retirement won't do her any harm. Do you think Vienna would be interested?'

Farron nodded, fighting back a growing excitement. 'I think so. But . . .'

'Of course the job is live-in, and if you moved in with her you could housesit for me. There's a one-bedroomed bungalow in the grounds that would be just right for a young couple.' He kept his voice businesslike, but Farron was already nodding.

'It sounds perfect. I think it will do Vienna a world of good to get away from the bustle of the city for a while. She's still a little . . . nervous. Not that she hasn't coped,' he added hastily. 'She's much stronger than she looks.'

'I don't doubt it,' Dominic said quietly and could feel warning words hovering on his lips: *'Be careful. Take it slow, watch out.'* But he could not say them. 'I'd like to pay for the cookery classes too. She'll need them to impress the sort of people who'll be staying there. We'll see how her first weekend's catering goes, and if we're both happy with it, we'll see about making it permanent,' he added before Farron could protest, knowing that in making it too pat the singer might suspect some sort of charity.

'I'll go and ask her.'

'Take your time. Room and board for the both of you will be part of her salary,' Dominic advised, draining his glass and checking his watch again. 'I've got to go; got a board-meeting of ravenous bank managers and accountants to oversee. See me later about the job.'

Farron laughed. 'OK. A bad audience can be nasty, but I don't think I'd swap you jobs,' he admitted and Dominic's mouth twisted wrily.

'I can't say as I blame you. *Aloha*.'

Farron watched him go and shook his head. He sometimes wondered how Dominic found the time to breathe! Although he knew that Fairchild Enterprises were a huge part of the man, Farron did not envy him. With money came power, and power corrupted unless you were very careful. No, he didn't envy him the money, or title, or the corporation.

Spotting Vienna with a tray of green-tinted wine glasses, he lithely slipped from the stool and went to talk to her.

'I can't believe it,' she said finally after he'd finished. 'You really do have the luck of the devil. I can't take it all in. It's very generous of him, though, isn't it? It hardly sounds a strenuous job.'

'Dom's like that. He supplies an army of local old women with the materials for them to weave mats and then buys them off them. God knows what he does with them – they're too plain to be sold to the tourists and I can't see it would pay him to export them. Still, to them he's their king. Literally.'

'Sounds as though he takes his responsibilities seriously.' Vienna had already sensed the close bond between her employer and her lover, and she was curious.

'He does. Most people respect him for it too. Except for this Grantham woman.'

She was about to ask who he meant, but caught sight of the head waiter's disapproving eye. 'Look – I've got to get busy. See you at three, OK?'

In the garage, Dominic got into his car and groaned silently. He was not in the mood for hours of wrangling over interest loans, bad debts and dividends for profit-sharing. Picking up the phone he dialled the number of Grant Mannings, the next best thing to Philip Pearce, and told him to chair the meeting. Hanging up, Dominic turned the key in the ignition and pulled out of the garage, having no clear idea where he was going. He felt curiously rudderless. He knew why, of course. 'The Woman'. Rhiannon Grantham.

Swearing viciously, he turned his car towards Chinatown. To hell with caution. Even he needed to talk sometimes. And the person he felt most comfortable talking to was Gloria. Over the years they had occasionally met on mutually neutral territory to reminisce over old times, catch up on each other's news and laugh about life.

The girl who opened the door to him was a reed-slim Filipino, her eyes widening as they recognized him. Quickly she showed him in. 'Miss Gaines is through there,' she whispered, padding in front of him through the lounge where another girl was sprawled in an armchair, her brows creased in concentration as she studied the crossword puzzle.

Watching the Filipino's derrière wriggling in front of him, her buttocks blushed peach by the pink see-through wrap she wore, he didn't notice the grey cat that found men's trouser legs irresistible. As a consequence he nearly tripped over the animal when it wound its tail like a monkey up his leg. Standing on his shoes with padded feet, its orange eyes looked upwards in feline invitation. As the girl knocked on the office door, he scooped down to pick up the cat and with an absentminded finger, stroked it under its chin.

'Please, go right in Mr Dominic, sir.'

'Thank you.' Dominic smiled and walked into the office where Gloria was standing behind her desk, pouring out coffee.

'Dominic! This is a surprise,' she said. 'I never expected you to show up here, of all places.' What might have been bland, clichéd words were instead blunt and straight to the point.

'I know,' Dominic nodded, hearing the door shut discreetly behind him. He hadn't visited the brothel since that damned will. 'You can blame it on the old man.' Gloria raised an eyebrow but didn't comment, and Dominic shook his head ruefully. 'Private joke,' he said simply and then held the cat firmly away from him, leaving pumping claws dangling in midair. 'This cat of yours is trying to puncture me.'

'Madam Meow is all cat,' Gloria informed him judiciously.

'Madam Meow?' His voice cracked into laughter as he met

Gloria's deadpan face and then looked back at the outraged Persian cat, whose ears had flattened to the side of her head in haughty disapproval.

'Do you want something in your coffee?' Gloria asked, lips twitching as she reached into her drawer and pulled out a rounded bottle of finest cognac.

'Not for me, thanks.' Walking forward he pulled out a chair and plopped the cat back on to his lap with total disregard for her ruffled feline dignity.

'Looking good, Dom,' she said, her eyes travelling over his figure dressed in white shirt and cool grey slacks with the experienced look of a connoisseur.

'Only on the outside,' he surprised her by saying rather grimly, and then reached for his mug. 'Hell, Glory – I thought I'd gotten over crying into my coffee in front of you.'

Gloria's lips twitched. 'I don't recall you ever doing that,' she said. 'You always were a self-possessed little bastard, even when you were totally infatuated.' Madam Meow began to dig her claws rhythmically into his legs, fixing him with an imperious stare as he winced and she purred softly. 'To the *Alii*.' Gloria raised her glass and drank.

Dominic smiled, never having felt less like the Hawaiian chief she'd just called him than he did at that precise moment. 'To business,' he corrected and took a sip. 'You always did make good coffee, Glory,' he confided, settling into his chair. 'You know, I've missed this place.'

Gloria smiled, but understood what he meant. In the old days her place had represented freedom and rebellion to the young Prince. Freedom from the old man, freedom from his ever-present and ever-growing responsibilities of money, power and status. In many ways she felt like a surrogate parent. When he'd been hurt in a knife-fight, stopping a potential bloodbath between two drunken sailors from Pearl, it had been to Gloria he'd come, watching without comment and enduring without flinching as she'd patched him up. It made her feel doubly bad about Akaki being one of her girls. 'So – what's up?' There was something in the strained green eyes that she couldn't ever remember seeing before. 'Are you all right?'

'Yeah, I'm all right,' Dominic said, running his hand over the cat's head and shoulders, and a loud lawnmower purr suddenly filled the room. 'Hell, Glory, what kind of animal is this?' he demanded, looking at the cat suspiciously as it yawned widely, revealing vicious teeth.

'A real one. So don't waggle anything. She's likely to pounce first and ask questions later.'

He looked at her, lips twitching. 'A bit dangerous, considering your line of work, isn't it? Youch!' he added as claws dug even deeper. Lifting the cat off his lap he dumped her ignominiously on to the carpet. Dominic liked Gloria more than he'd ever let on. There was an honesty about her that was missing in most other aspects of his life and just to talk to someone who knew him and didn't expect anything from him was like a taste of heaven.

'Do you know who was behind the boutique takeover?' he asked unexpectedly.

'No.'

'Rhiannon Grantham.'

'*What?*' she exclaimed with an uncharacteristic loss of composure.

'Yeah. That's how I took it.'

'Oh, Dominic – I'm sorry. I only heard yesterday that Graham was dead.'

'He is.' Meeting eyes that never probed, he confessed simply: 'After twenty odd years of blackmail I'd had enough. So I gave him some rope . . .'

'. . . and he hanged himself. Yes, he would,' Gloria commented briefly, sipping her coffee slowly and thoughtfully. 'Does she know he was blackmailing you? Or why?'

'Hell no! It would be a bloody disaster if she did,' he added grimly.

'Yes, I can understand that. Does she look like her father?'

'No, thank God. She's definitely her mother's child.'

Gloria remained silent for a long time, jumping a little as the cat leapt on her lap and immediately curled up into a ball. 'Do you think Jessamine knew?'

'No. I'm convinced she didn't have a clue what that bastard was up to.'

'I agree. It was terrible – the way she died.'

'Yes. Just something else we can lay at dear Graham's door.'

'I'm curious,' she drained her cup. 'Just how did this Rhiannon Grantham finance the takeover?'

'With the help of an English billionaire. She's out for blood,' he said flatly.

'And you're afraid of hurting her.'

Dominic looked up into her knowing eyes and cursed inwardly. He should have remembered how astute Gloria was. 'If she tries another stunt like that last one, I'll have her neck before she knows what's hit her,' he said quietly.

Gloria nodded. 'You really think she'll push you that far?'

Dominic shrugged. 'I hope not.'

Gloria smiled. 'Then you have nothing to worry about, do you?'

Her visitor grinned. 'You know, Glory, if I'd had half the sense at seventeen as I do now, I'd have fallen for you instead of Akaki.'

Gloria laughed. 'Now wouldn't *that* have been something!'

'Wouldn't it, though.' Dominic stood up and walked to her side, looking down from her friendly eyes to the grey cat and giving it a perfunctory stroke. 'I think,' he said, looking at the huffy cat, 'that I've burned my bridges.'

'There's always the fire department,' Gloria said bluntly, and Dom leaned over and kissed her forehead.

'Don't ever change, Glory,' he said softly.

'I won't. How's Farron doing these days?' she asked in what she hoped was a tone of casual interest.

'Ah, now there's a question. He's either the luckiest, or unluckiest man in the world – depending on your viewpoint. He's In Love.'

'Seriously?'

'Very, I think. He's talking about setting up house.'

'With that girl who lost her memory?'

'Yes. You're well-informed,' he commented, his eyes sharpening, and it was Gloria's turn to curse herself.

'It helps,' she said mildly.

'Do you know something I don't?' Dominic probed.

'No,' she denied, meeting his gaze head-on without blinking.

'If you know anything you should tell me,' he pressed.

Gloria shrugged but her shoulders felt tense. 'You're being a bit overprotective, aren't you?'

Dominic slowly rose. She was hiding something – he knew it. He could *feel* it. Softly he said, 'I'm fond of Farron. I want to see him happy. Vienna seems to do that, but if there's something I should know . . . I'll find out, Glory.'

'I don't know what you're talking about, Dom. Make sense, huh?'

Dominic straightened, looked her in the eye and said, 'You know I'd do anything to help if you were in trouble.'

'I know,' she said more warmly. 'But really, you're the one who's in a better position to know what's going on. I only hear things, and second-hand at that.'

She's protesting too much, he thought. Or was he just getting paranoid? He sighed and ran a hand through his hair. 'OK. I'd better be going anyway.'

Gloria watched him turn to go, regret warring with caution, but caution won. In her position it had to, much as she wished she could return his compliment and confide in him. 'Come any time,' she offered, and meant it despite the danger. He was clever, this man, and if she had to trust anyone besides Frank with her secret, it would be Dominic Fairchild – in spite of his own personal stake in it all.

'I might just take you up on that. I never did thank you properly for all you tried to do for Akaki.'

'You still feeling guilty about her?' she added accusingly.

'Can't help it, I guess. Glory, was there anything more I could have done?'

'No,' Gloria said bluntly. 'After a while she forgot she'd ever had a kid.'

'But I knew. Damn Graham to hell,' he said quietly, the nearest thing to defeat in his voice that Gloria had ever heard.

'I imagine he already has been.'

Dominic's eyes focused sharply on her before he slowly nodded. 'Yes. How many of us haven't?'

Gloria said heavily, 'Not many.'

After the door had closed behind him she dialled the Avant Garde Casino and was put through to Frank.

'Yeah?'

'Frank. Dominic was just here asking questions.'

'About what?'

'What do you think?'

'He doesn't know anything?'

'No, but he's clever, Frank,' Gloria said, her voice hard. 'Very clever. He's rich, and he's powerful. In fact he's about the only man on the island who could find out.'

'You're worrying too much.'

'No, I'm not. With your muscle and my little dossier of names we have our backs fairly covered if anything does go wrong. Except for Dominic Fairchild. He's the only one who could sink us.'

'But why should he? He's got no reason to see you go under.'

Gloria sighed heavily. 'The girl has moved in with Farron Manikuuna. You know what that means?'

'Fuck it!' Frank sounded rattled, but when he spoke again he was calm. 'There's no need to panic. If it looks like Fairchild is getting too close then we'll just have to find a way to get the girl off the island.'

'All right. Frank, you won't do anything without consulting me first, will you?' she asked as an unnamed, ugly fear suddenly leapt out from the hidden corners of her mind.

'Course not,' Frank said impatiently. 'Don't worry. We'll cross any bridges when we come to 'em.'

'I think I've burned my bridges', Dominic had said, and Gloria closed her eyes briefly before pulling herself together. 'OK. I'll see you Tuesday, then.'

She could almost feel his relief on the other end of the telephone wires as he said with mock cheerfulness, 'Right – and don't worry, OK?'

'I won't,' Gloria lied and hung up. Then, 'Keep out of it Dominic,' she pleaded to the empty room, in such a harsh whisper that the grey cat on her lap crouched in sudden fear. 'For all our sakes,' she hissed. 'Keep the hell out of it!'

Chapter 18

The limousine glided to a silent halt on the crest of a hill and Rhiannon stepped out on to lush grass. She could smell sun, sea and flowers, but most of all, she could smell pineapples. 'Where exactly are we?' she asked Jack.

'The Leilehua plâteau. Nearly all of it is taken up with pineapple growing.'

'It's fantastic,' she breathed, looking over the vast panorama of the crops growing close on the ground, their tall, cruel leaves thrusting up in the air. 'What happens when the fruit is ripe?' She moved closer to the crest of the hill and looked down a giddying fifty-feet drop without flinching. Birds sang in the flaming royal poinciana trees and a gentle breeze lifted her long dark hair from her neck and face. She breathed deeply, unaware that as she did so her breasts thrust innocently against the cool white silk of her sleeveless summer dress. Nor was she aware of Jack watching her with the same intensity that a dog watches a juicy but forbidden bone. But the chauffeur saw. With his window wound down to catch the breeze that he found so much more pleasant than the car's expensive air conditioning, the middle-aged Hawaiian was very much aware of the blond American's feelings. And who could blame him, Billy Hoki thought. The *wahini* was lovely.

'After it's picked it's taken to the cannery on Iwilei Road,' Jack began, his voice a little strained now, 'which covers fifty-six acres and can process three million pineapples a day. Dominic's fruit company is even bigger. He was also one of the first to catch on to the boom in fruit juices, producing a wider variety of choices than just orange juice. It made him his third fortune, after the hotels and boutiques.'

She looked out over the vast ocean of fruit and shook her head. 'So many fortunes,' she said quietly.

'Naturally, Lanai Fruit Company is more diversified than this one, dealing in bananas and papayas which grow all year round and also in the seasonal fruits – mangoes, guavas and, from February to April, avocados. He's made millions in avocados,' Jacked moved slowly closer, his eyes glued to her lovely profile.

Billy surreptitiously lit a cigarette and dragged in a good portion of fragrant smoke, watching his two passengers with carefully concealed curiosity.

'And of course,' Jack murmured, his arm rubbing very casually against hers as he turned to admire the view, 'passion fruit.'

She didn't respond to the sexual innuendo and Jack winced inwardly at the blow to his ego. Used to easy conquests he wasn't sure he liked her continuing cool-and-businesslike attitude. 'Of course Lanai is virtually impregnable,' he added spitefully.

'What?' she asked sharply, her voice making Billy Hoki perk up considerably.

'At the moment Fairchild has forty per cent of all stock which, in a company the size of Lanai is or rather should be, almost inviolate.'

'Except?' Rhiannon pressed grimly.

'Except that you have twenty-two per cent which we purchased at the same time as the Liliha stock. It gives you a seat on the board automatically when it becomes known.'

'I want more than a seat on the board.'

'You need another nineteen per cent to gain controlling interest and hoist Fairchild out on his ear.'

'So who has that much stock and – more importantly – who'll sell?'

'I've unearthed several likely candidates,' Jack said, retrieving a file from the car, which she read with growing interest.

'Tom Fletcher with eight per cent and Gavin Phelps with five look promising,' she said, thinking of the private information Jack's team had been able to sniff out, the results of which were precisely catalogued in the pages she held in her hand.

'I agree. I already have an army of agents out buying the other six per cent you need.'

She nodded but her eyes were cloudy. Once, reading such highly personal information about a complete stranger would have been beyond her and she still felt nauseous and dirty about it. Sighing she forced herself to focus painfully on the grey face of her dying father and to hear again his broken words and last request. It was the only thing that made her feel better about herself at times like this. 'Will they sell?'

'They will if I apply the right pressure.'

'Fletcher's rich wife won't like to be informed of the mistress he's keeping on,' she quickly checked the papers again, 'Punahou Street, any more than she'll like to know the parentage of the little six-year-old boy who attends school there.'

Jack drew in a sharp breath. 'You've become hard all of a sudden. And cold.'

And because she knew he spoke the truth she felt herself cringe inside. 'I'm dealing with a hard and cold man,' she finally said defensively.

Inside the car Billy Hoki ground out his cigarette into a black steel ashtray.

'Are you sure about Phelps' gambling debts?'

Jack gave her a strange look and said, 'I'm sure.'

'But he owns so much stock.'

'On paper – he needs cash to pay off Gillespie and his other creditors.'

'You'd better put the word around with the banks that he's a bad risk. I don't want him getting a loan.'

'You soon learned how to play dirty,' he said.

'I had a good teacher,' she said, Dominic Fairchild's image rising up to torment her. 'Can we tour the cannery? I want to get as good an idea as I can about how the processing works.'

'Of course. I anticipated your request and cleared it with the manager.' He opened the back door for her and only Billy Hoki was aware of how he slammed it shut with controlled savagery behind her.

DOMINIC looked up from the list of transactions for the quarterly returns on Fairchild Real Estate when the intercom buzzed. 'Mr Hoki to see you, sir.'

'Send him right in.' Dominic closed the folder out of habit and returned the pen to its beaten silver stand, rising and smiling as Billy Hoki walked in and looked around self-consciously. Both men sat down simultaneously.

'How's life treating you, Billy?'

'Fine, Mr Dominic – just fine.' He fiddled with his cap and coughed.

'Been busy?' Dominic asked, helping him out by getting straight to the point.

'Yes, sir – that's why I'm here.'

'And for that I'm more than grateful,' Dominic said quietly.

Billy fidgeted on his chair. 'I don't mind. I was glad when you came to me the other night to ask for my help. I often used to lie awake wondering how I could ever pay you back for what you did for me and Amii.'

'Forget it,' Dominic said tersely.

'I can't do that, Mr Fairchild, sir,' Billy was already shaking his head. 'I would have done anything you asked, you know that.'

'I know spying stinks but I don't have many options left open to me.'

'No, sir,' Billy said quietly. 'I can see that.'

'Oh?' That sounded ominous.

'They went out to the Leilehua Plâteau this morning. I only just got through dropping them off at your hotel. They were talking about your fruit company.'

'Lanai?' he asked sharply. He'd known that the past month had only been a breathing space, but Lanai? How the hell did she think she was going to get her claws into that? He soon found out when Billy related all that he'd heard.

'She suggested cutting off Phelps' access to a bank loan, you say?'

Billy nodded a head gone prematurely grey. 'Yes, sir. She's a *huhi* woman, that one.'

'Yes, I know,' Dominic said grimly, applauding Billy's choice of words. An angry woman. Yes, that described Rhiannon perfectly.

Billy nodded and got to his feet, anxious to be out of the fancy office and back with his car once more. Dominic smiled and stood up, holding out his hand which Billy took with a wide grin and shook warmly.

'Thanks, Billy. I appreciate it.' He didn't insult him by offering him money.

'I'm glad. It was useful information, yes?'

'Oh yes,' Dominic said meaningfully, and Billy's grin split his face in two.

After the chauffeur had left, Dominic ruminated on what he had just learned. He didn't like it. Oh, the crisis at Lanai could be prevented easily now that he knew her intentions, but it didn't give him the satisfaction it should have. Billy had called her a *huhi* woman, but was that all she was? She was showing signs of becoming a first-class streetfighter and he wanted her. Oh God, how he wanted her.

And she'd tear him to ribbons if he gave her half the chance.

Chapter 19

SAN FRANCISCO

Richard pulled his maroon Mercedes convertible to a halt outside the gravel-lined front porch of Odessa's mansion and checked the time on his new Cartier watch. He was greeted at the massive oak doors by Hopcroft, her English butler and directed to the east lounge. The opulence of the Vance mansion was matched only by the style of her staff. The reigning queen of San Fransisco society not only had an English butler, but a French chef and Swedish masseuse as well. The gardeners, naturally, were Japanese.

He had learned early on, that Odessa had only been in New York on one of her many shopping trips and, for the first time in his life, he was glad that he had been born and raised in San Francisco, thus giving him the perfect excuse to travel west with her.

He walked quickly through the hall and strode confidently towards Odessa's favourite lounge, scanning it quickly, passing over the Pembroke tables and coming to rest on her seated figure lounging in a Hepplewhite chair. The scar on her throat had all but healed and her voice, which had been grating on his nerves, had returned to normal. 'Hi,' he said, coming to a deliberately awkward halt in a parody of a shy little boy suddenly confronted by a vision of feminine beauty.

Odessa went to him with a lithe grace that Richard Jago did not even see, let alone appreciate. All he saw was that she was taller than Vienna by a good seven inches. She was thinner, not more slender; she was flat, not less curvaceous. The fact that she was Odessa Vance, a woman in her own right, did not even occur to him.

'Richard,' she said, her long white hand coming out to curl around his forearm, aware of its power and as usual feeling a delicious thrill of ownership and desire. After he'd first visited her at the hospital and she'd been forced to watch him leave, she'd spent ten minutes silently cursing and plotting and then the violets had arrived. Odessa's smile widened now as she led him forward, feeling like a woman confidently leading a lion around on a lead. When, after six impatient days, she'd been able to put enough words together to call him, she'd done so, asking him to come and see her again and he had – looking every bit as big, handsome, and wonderful as before.

When his muscles tensed beneath her fingers she felt it immediately, as she noticed every single thing about him. The way he spoke so softly for such a huge man and with an amount of shyness which was totally unnecessary since he always conversed intelligently. He was also witty in an unassuming manner, and quite naturally charming. And the fact that he was gauchely unaware of it all, thrilled her as nothing else had ever done. Now, seeking the source of his unease, her eyes swivelled back to her forgotten visitor.

'Oh, Jonathon is here with things for me to sign,' she said airily, her vagueness very deceptive, as Richard was well aware. Instinct told him she was a tough cookie where business was concerned.

'Hello Jago,' Jonathon Hannel said crisply. Of average height, he was aware that next to Richard he appeared small. Around Richard's age, his caramel-coloured hair was already streaked with grey, framing features that were nice but unremarkable. Richard had never seen him in anything but a navy-blue business suit.

He smiled. 'I didn't realize I would be interrupting . . .'

'You're not,' Odessa said quickly, relinquishing his arm to walk to a drinks cabinet. 'What would you like, darling?' She glanced at him to see if he heard her endearment, one she hadn't dared use until now.

'Er, a scotch will be fine,' he mumbled and Odessa nodded. Richard rarely drank, and so far never during the day. In his corner Hannel was fidgeting.

'She has a lovely and unusual name, doesn't she?' Hannel surprised them all by saying, and Richard looked at him quickly, his animal instinct sensing a set up. And he should know one when he heard one, for how many of his own had he instigated? 'Wasn't her father right to give it to her?'

Hannel continued, his small, perfectly manicured fist tightening on the handle of the black leather briefcase he seemed perpetually to carry.

'Johnny,' Odessa said warningly, biting back the swearwords that she'd like to let loose at him. At times, as all her friends and the gossip-column journalists knew only too well, she had a tongue that would make a navvy blush, her colourful vocabulary learned from a father who had grown up on the wrong side of the railway tracks in a small Nevada mining town. So far, in front of Richard, she'd kept a very firm hold on it, so she contented herself with a killing glance at her lawyer who was wise enough not to push it.

'My father had Russian ancestors. Before the revolution they were quite wealthy, having made their fortune at Odessa, the city,' she explained now, walking towards the tall and silent man and handing him his drink – a drink he obviously did not want by the way he looked down at it and swirled it absentmindedly in the glass. 'Daddy had made a vow to himself on his fourteenth birthday to be rich one day,' she continued, taking a sip from her own daiquiri. 'Which he did, of course, naming me Odessa as a sort of salute to his ancestors. It was his way of saying he was as good as any of them.'

'I should have guessed,' Richard said, allowing his voice to break just a little, and then uncomfortably clearing his throat. 'That's why you always look especially lovely in red.'

'Really?' Hannel's voice interrupted the moment. 'I personally never thought red suited her. In fact I don't think you have many red outfits, do you, Odessa?'

Richard looked at the man over Odessa's head, allowing a look of only mild annoyance to cross his face. In reality, Richard loathed Hannel because he was an obstacle to getting what he wanted. Odessa's money.

'I love red,' Odessa said, when in fact she didn't, and gave Hannel another look that would have felled a bird from the sky.

'I wondered, if you're not too busy, whether you'd like to go out on the boat this afternoon,' Richard asked nervously, looking around for a place to plant his drink, even though he could do with a good swift shot of it, finally electing to hide it behind a Brancusi sculpture. Odessa opened her mouth to agree, when Hannel once more interrupted, making Jago despise him even more.

'I think Odessa's yacht needs an expert seaman to handle it.'

'I know that,' Richard replied with total mildness. 'And I can handle boats. I still have my own boat at Honolulu which I haven't sold yet.'

Jonathon Hannel looked away, an incredulous sneer on his face which Odessa saw; her face tightened ominously. It had not taken her a second to know she wanted Richard Jago. But in the weeks following her release from hospital he'd made no move to bed her and she had quickly come to see with a shocked incredulity that had quickly turned to delight that he was, as her aunt would have said in prim tones, 'just not that kind of man'. At first, she'd been determined to seduce him, to peel away his shy innocent exterior and make his eyes bulge in sexual gratification. But although that desire was still with her, Odessa was aware that it had changed and matured since she'd got to know him. She'd since spent hours probing him about his work, fascinated and not at all repelled as he talked about surgery, describing medicine and the human body in ways she'd never even thought about. Now she saw his large, manly hands as powerful, life-saving appendages, and not just objects that she wanted on her body, although want them she did. So much so it kept her awake at nights. He was quiet much of the time, a vast contrast to the men she usually dated, who filled every moment trying to impress on her how clever and accomplished they were. He was also a very far cry from her garrulous husband, who'd spent their entire marriage practising his speeches on her whilst running for the State Senate. Richard made her laugh in a way none of the other San Franciscan sophisticates had. He was cultured deep in his soul. When he took her to the opera or theatre, he really knew what was what. He was sexy, and didn't know it. He was big, and handsome. And she, quite simply, was head over heels in love with him.

'How is the job-hunting going?' she asked softly and he looked at her, a slight frown marring his forehead and creating interesting wrinkles which reminded her once again that he was a good decade older than her. It was another thing she found exciting.

'Not too well. I don't know,' he shrugged. 'I don't think my heart is in it. I keep thinking that instead of looking around all these fancy places, I should be working where somebody needs me.'

The job had been the only thing over which they had ever argued. She wanted him to find a good position in a good hospital. He deserved the best, and with her influence, which he'd firmly ordered her not to use, she knew she could take him to the top. But still he persisted in talking about working at one of the hospitals far away from Nob Hill, in some seedy, ugly little place. Oh, she loved him all the more for it, of course. The thought of him sacrificing his working lifestyle because of personal ethics was thrilling to a woman used to the shallow, give-me attitude of the born rich, but she had no intention of letting him work all the bloody awful hours she'd heard about and was confident about her ability to control him.

'How very wonderful of you,' Hannel snapped, then could have bitten his tongue out for letting his savage hatred of the man show so openly. Richard looked at Odessa, his lips twitching helplessly, and then deliberately crossed his eyes, making her choke on her daiquiri.

'John, let's get these papers signed, shall we?' she asked, still disinclined to forgive the man for his sarcasm even though Richard always took it in good part. 'We'll get it over with in the library. Darling, you will excuse us for a few minutes, won't you?'

'Of course.'

'I'll hurry, I promise. Make yourself comfortable, hm?'

'I'm sure you can manage that,' Hannel said drily. Richard retrieved his drink and saluted the closed door. After finishing it he refilled it and put it back behind the sculpture.

In the library, Odessa Vance snatched the documents from her lawyer and quickly scanned the contents of the sheets, approving the blue-chip stock purchases by signing her name on the dotted line with an angry flourish and thrusting them back at him.

'If you speak to Richard like that again, you're fired.'

Jonathon flushed, his sallow skin mottling like marble. At his temple a blue vein throbbed tellingly. 'The man's a phoney – anyone can see that,' he stated stiffly, despite the threat striking cold fear into his heart. 'I know he acts so nice and puppy-dog clumsy, quoting all that philanthropic claptrap, but he's a goddamned phoney, Odessa. He's after your money!'

'You said he was lying about staying in that hotel in New York, didn't you?'

'He was living in a little flat that wouldn't fit into your hall before he moved there,' he got in quickly, feeling again the shaft of self-righteous pleasure he'd experienced after tracing Richard's first address.

'He told me about that. He was new to the city. And if you really knew Richard you'd know that he was more interested in getting a job than in living in a fancy apartment.'

'He soon moved out of it though, the moment he found out who you were. And the cops still haven't found that missing jewellery someone stole from your car.'

'He was fired from the hospital because of what he'd done for me!' Odessa corrected sharply, her eyes spitting dangerous fire, 'so don't you fucking come that bullshit with me! And the cops said anyone could have taken the jewellery. The car was left on the side of the road for hours before the tow-truck arrived.' She moved away from him, throwing her pen down against a marble-topped coffee table and snapping it. 'You don't really think a doctor like Richard would have stolen a few baubles, do you? And did my doctors confirm he'd saved my life, or didn't they?'

'They did,' Jonathon agreed tersely. 'But Odds, I promised your father I'd look after you – protect you from guys like him.' He jerked his head in the direction of the lounge, and Odessa bit back her anger.

'I know you did,' she said softly, mention of her father always mellowing her. 'And I married a man you and Daddy approved of, and look how that ended up. And Richard's a fine doctor, one who saved my life. And it isn't as if he's a penniless nobody – look at his clothes, his car.'

'Yes – look at them,' Hannel repeated grimly. 'And if he owns a bloody yacht in Honolulu, I'll whistle *Dixie*.'

'Oh fucking hell, Johnny, what do we have to do . . . Look, I'll tell you what,' she said with a sigh of exaggerated patience. 'You check out his story about having a boat. If it turns out he was lying, I'll stop seeing him,' she lied without blinking. Nothing was going to stop her marrying Richard Jago. 'But if he does, you'll stop creating waves – deal? What's the matter?' she mocked his dubious expression. 'Not got the courage of your convictions?'

'All right,' he agreed, thinking of the cocksure s.o.b. in the other room. 'You've got a deal.'

'Good – and while you're at it, why not check out the hospital where he worked in the islands? See what kind of a doctor his colleagues thought he was. And if they don't think he was at the very least excellent, *I'll* whistle *Dixie* – stark naked, in front of the Mayor.'

Hannel laughed. 'I don't think his heart will stand it.'

'I don't think his heart will have to.'

'We'll see,' Jonathon Hannel said, smugly pleased. At last she'd given him the opportunity to get rid of his hated rival.

'Yes, we will,' she agreed, watching her lawyer nearly skip out of the room. She herself was curious but not really worried. Still . . .

She found Richard standing by the pool looking down at the blue-tiled, Olympic-sized rectangle of water with his usual brooding intensity. She was well aware there were hidden depths to this man, and she yearned to let loose some of the dark forces she could sense lurking in his psyche. He was the most excitingly different man she'd ever met. Slipping off her turquoise silk robe she walked over to him in a brief matching turquoise bikini that showed her slender and firmly muscled figure to perfect effect.

He noticed a slight frown sulking on her face as she rejoined him, and turning quickly he let his eyes wander over her in apparent approval, inwardly finding nothing at all appealing in her almost straight, athletic frame. 'Has he gone?'

'Yes.'

'Good. I don't . . .' he hesitated just enough '. . . really like him.'

'Such honesty,' she mocked gently, and he was wise enough to smile and shrug.

'In fact I hate his guts.'

'Oh?' she asked, raising her brow. She liked the sound of it, but it was a little surprising coming from him.

'He's in love with you,' Richard stated.

'Rubbish.'

'Don't laugh – I mean it. A man can always tell when someone else is in love with his girl.'

His girl. How delightfully old-fashioned, she thought. With anyone else it would have sounded ridiculous. Odessa felt a thrill shoot through her. After frustrating dates that ended in progressively heavy necking but nothing more, the words held a ring of possession and intent for which she had long been waiting. He saw her eyes glitter and rewarded himself with a self-congratulatory smile. He was right to be so patient. He knew this type well – a rich, bored bitch. Only by playing out-of-reach had he kept her interested, thus giving himself time to capitalize on it. 'I like that,' Odessa said softly, and walked towards him, stretching up on tiptoe to link her long arms around his neck.

'Like what?' he asked, letting his eyes linger on her lips.

'Being your girl.'

Richard looked at her, letting just enough uncertainty show in his eyes and voice as he said, 'You are, though – aren't you?'

'Of course,' she said dreamily, their mouths meeting in a kiss that grew gradually bolder, Richard finally letting the heat she'd been waiting for seep into their embrace as his hands travelled down to cup her buttocks firmly. She stirred immediately, her vagina tightening in reaction to his first openly sexual caress. Simple though it was, it turned her legs to jelly.

'It seems a pity to put on clothes over that pretty outfit just to go sailing,' he said, allowing his voice to drop an octave as he pulled away.

'I agree – let's stay here instead.'

'Sounds good to me,' he smiled, clumsily pulling off his shoes and socks.

'How's the suntan?' she asked, looking at his silk shirt as if she hated it.

He pretended ignorance. 'Suntan? Oh, I don't know.'

'Then take off the shirt and top it up,' she suggested casually, putting on a pair of sunglasses. Walking to a red and blue patterned sunlounger of canvas and chrome, she lay on it invitingly before reaching for a tube of sunscreen cream, wiping it sparingly on her arms as he shrugged off the shirt. Lying on her back she thrust first one leg and then the other high in the air, her hands sliding over the tanned skin with caressing movements designed to arouse him. His shoulders were wide and powerful, as was his chest. He was not too hairy, and she was glad. She didn't like hairy men much, and her critical eyes instantly noted that although he was big, he was not fat.

His shadow loomed over her as he approached and sat on the neighbouring sunlounger which dipped and groaned ominously beneath his weight, making him laugh. 'I don't think anyone makes garden furniture with my size in mind.'

She laughed and, leaving her own lounger, perched herself on his lap. With a snap the lounger collapsed, throwing them sideways. Rolling over on the grass they came to rest in the shade of a huge rhododendron in full pink and white flower. She waited tensely as he gently pushed a few strands of wayward blonde hair from her cheek and rubbed her skin almost thoughtfully with his long, sensitive fingers. She found herself liking the feeling of being loved and cherished by a huge, gentle giant. He lowered his head and kissed her, leaving her wanting more, much more, as he lifted his head. 'I want you,' he said, as if puzzled by it. 'Right here – and now. To hell with servants, or patients, or surly lawyers.'

'To hell with them,' she agreed, her voice more reckless than his, hands rising up to link behind his head. 'But why did you wait so long?' she asked, her voice suddenly losing much of its bravado. 'Didn't you want me enough?'

'Oh, Dessie, of course I did,' he murmured, his hands warm on her bare flesh. 'I just couldn't really believe that you'd want *me*.'

'You idiot,' she accused tenderly, then her fingers were caressing his sunwarmed hair, applying enough pressure to bring his lips once more to hers.

Slipping his fingers under her bikini top he gentled her breast, bringing on to his closed lids an image of Vienna. He began to caress and kiss, his hands light yet full of passion on Vienna's substitute as he cast aside her bikini and with remarkable grace shed his own remaining clothes. Spreading her long legs, Richard plunged into her, making her fingers dig deep into his shoulders, her back arching in sheer delight at his size and power. Quickly she hooked her strong legs around his thighs and moaned loudly. With the sun and dappled shadow playing over their naked bodies, Odessa thrust towards him, her eyes opening to a vista of sky and overhanging pink and white flowers before Richard's head, large and handsome, intense and passionate, blocked out even that view.

There was something about his lovemaking that surprised her and left her unprepared to cope. She had expected him to be a little shy, clumsy even, and had readied herself for his huge body to maybe even hurt a bit, but there was an expertise about his lovemaking that both annoyed and thrilled her. Annoyed her, because it spoke of many other women, and thrilled because it was so consummate and so all-reaching. '*Yes!*' she screamed in triumph as one orgasm followed another and then another. Still he pounded within her, strong and hard, his large body pinning her to the crushed fragrance of the grass, driving her into a world of pleasure to which no other lover had ever taken her with such complete abandonment. Richard moaned, his head lowering to Odessa's shoulder as he grimly bit back the name that yearned to escape him, and groaned instead, 'Odessa! Odessa!' But as he exploded, his sweat-slick body finally finding its own release, there was only one name ricocheting and echoing in his head. And it didn't belong to the woman who held him tenderly to her breast as she drew in ragged gulps of air.

'Oh baby,' she gasped, her fit body gradually calming to a more dignified breathing pattern as she swallowed hard. 'You were fucking marvellous.'

Richard slowly slipped out of her hot, tight body and lay on his back, raising a forearm to cover his eyes, massive chest still rising and falling deeply. Eventually he asked, 'Did I hurt you?'

Odessa sat up, leaning on one elbow and idly tracing with her fingernail the circumference of his nipple. He'd given her no time or opportunity to take even a minor seductive role in what had just happened, and she promised herself that in the future she would have that seduction scene she'd imagined for so long. Only now the spice would be greater in knowing the hugeness of the reward that would be hers. Just the thought of having him helpless and moaning beneath her knowing hands made her want him all over again. 'Not a bit,' she said, licking off a trickle of sweat that slipped down his neck. 'Let's swim – the pool is nice and cool.'

HE was the first to climb out of the pool ten minutes later, wrapping a huge bath towel around his waist and watching her as she approached him. He kissed her with just the right hint of renewed passion before handing her her turquoise wrap. In the pool anteroom she poured two glasses of iced lemonade and flopped down in a rounded rattan chair.

'You said you grew up here. Are your parents still alive?' she asked.

'No.' Richard shook his head. 'They lived over on Lexington Street, in one of those large suburban houses of the not-quite wealthy. I attended the local highschool here.'

Odessa shook her head. 'Just imagine – all the time I was growing up here I didn't even know you existed.' She reached forward and with one mobile foot ran her toes up his still-wet shin, smiling when he dragged his breath in loudly and took a large gulp of the innocuous drink. He thought longingly of the scotch hidden in the other room. 'Did you get a scholarship?'

Richard shook his head. 'Not as such. My dad, who was an architect, put me through Med. school but I had to give piano lessons to help get myself the necessary extras.'

'Really? There's a piano in the music room. Play for me!'

Richard ignored the bite of command in her voice and laughed lazily. 'Oh, Odessa! I haven't played in years – I haven't had time. I must be as rusty as hell.' And he had been, but in the last month he'd been practising like a demon so he let her lead him, protesting vociferously, to the music room.

He had practised in particular his best-remembered piece from his school years – a flowing, easy Rachmaninov Piano Concerto that sounded a lot harder to play than it actually was. After casting her another hangdog look he shook his head and commenced to play, beautifully. Odessa was not surprised to hear the lovely sounds rising and falling around her. She'd already recognized that Richard Jago was the kind of man who could do anything, and everything, well. He let his large hands rise and fall with elegant rather than technically correct, movements and when he'd finished she clapped loudly. Laughing they walked back to the pool where he determinedly put back on all his clothes, Odessa sighing as she lay back down on her lounger.

Sitting on the grass at her side, twidling a blade of grass, he told her of his early career and his move to Hawaii. 'I knew the moment I saw the place that I belonged there,' he said truthfully, his words holding a sincerity that impressed itself on her greatly.

'How come you left?'

Richard tensed, knowing that this moment had been inevitable. He could not trust that bastard Hannel not to go digging around in his past and it was imperative that he get his version in first. He shrugged, looking at her almost guiltily, and then stared straight ahead, taking a deep breath. 'You deserve the truth, I know,' he began, letting his voice soften, 'especially now.' It didn't hurt to remind her of how he'd just satisfied her. 'In December last year, there was this patient. She came in as a simple mugging case, but it became apparent the moment she regained consciousness that she had amnesia. She couldn't remember a damn thing – nothing at all about herself or anyone else, let alone who attacked her.' Richard shook his head, letting pity and sympathy thicken and soften his voice. 'Poor kid – she only seemed about eighteen or nineteen, but from medical evidence I guessed she was a few years older.' He shook his head.

'What happened?' she urged impatiently.

'It's hard for us to imagine what it must have been like for her. The cops ran her picture in the papers but no one recognized her, and everyone assumed she was holidaying alone in the islands. She . . . she clung to me, I guess, because I was treating her. She was scared, alone, no money, no friends, nothing.' Again he paused and sighed, scratching his head in his adopted gesture of absentminded thought. 'She was paranoid, of course, but that was only to be expected. I helped her out. She was almost hideously grateful, poor kid. I don't know . . . When the time came for her to be discharged, she still had nothing and no one, so I got her a flat in the same block as mine, loaned her some money for clothes and stuff like that. The thing is, instead of getting her life sorted out she still clung to me. I tried to get her to make other friends but she was scared, I guess. Looking at it from her point of view, I was the only thing in the whole world that was familiar to her.'

'I see,' Odessa said, beginning to relax. It sounded just like him. Generous and too kind for his own good.

'Anyway, I insisted she get a job. Not so that she could pay me back but to get her out of the flat, back amongst the real world. And she did, eventually, becoming a waitress in a fancy hotel. And then things got worse.'

'Worse? How?'

'An Hawaiian kid who sang at the hotel sometimes took a fancy to her. Naturally she rebuffed him, and he blamed me. One night . . .' he trailed off and lay back on the grass, covering his face with his hands. 'One night he came at me, yelling and screaming, fists flying. I had no choice but to fight him off.' For a long while he was silent and then he sat up and looked at her, meeting her gaze head-on. 'The upshot was, he got hurt. I never meant to hurt him Odessa, honest to God I didn't. But – ' he shrugged helplessly.

Odessa smiled, cupping his cheek with her palm as he made to look away, watching as he closed his eyes and kissed the mound of her thumb, sighing deeply like a little boy being comforted by a gentle touch. 'But you don't know your own strength, hm?'

'I guess,' he shrugged. 'Anyway, to cut a long story short, the Hospital Board decided my conduct towards an ex-patient was not ethical, and so I left. What I still don't understand is, *who* was behind it.'

'Behind it?'

'Hm. I mean, everyone must have known that I wasn't . . . I mean, the girl and I weren't lovers, poor little kid. The Board wouldn't have even bothered unless someone with clout had put them up to it.'

Odessa frowned. The thought of someone being so grossly unfair to the man she loved was enough to raise her ire to dangerous levels. She was accustomed to getting what she wanted and for the first time she was in love. Gloriously, dangerously in love. She drew his lips to hers, kissing him with an expertise that was wasted on him although when she drew away his eyes looked suitably dazed and hot. 'You've had a rough time, haven't you?' she whispered.

Richard shrugged. 'Well, if it hadn't been for that I wouldn't have left the islands . . . or met you. I won't lie to you, Odessa. I've had other women. They keep cropping up in my life, but none of them have made me . . . none of them are like you. I can understand why you might not believe me though,' he added, taking her by surprise. 'I mean, look at all this,' he waved a hand at the house. 'You being so rich I bet you've had gold-diggers sniffing around you all your life. And I'm nowhere near being in your range. Not that I'm poor. By a lot of patients' standards, I must seem very wealthy, but . . .'

'Richard,' Odessa interrupted softly. 'Shut up and kiss me.'

He did so, feigning mounting passion with an ease that was fast becoming automatic. Then, with seeming reluctance, he pulled away from her.

'You know, I hope you were right about that yacht, because I just made a deal with Jonathon not to see you again if you were lying about it.'

Richard laughed and stood up, lifting her from the sunlounger and swinging her around with easy strength. 'Don't worry,' he chuckled. 'When he comes back all hangdog and apologetic, I shall be suitably magnanimous.'

'I can't wait,' she said as he put her down and looked miserably at his watch.

'Look – I've got to go. I promised the old lady who works in the bakery on El Morocco that I'd take a look at her varicose veins.'

'Richard!' she wailed, but he shook his head.

'I'll pick you up at seven.'

'All right. Don't be late.'

'I won't be,' he promised, his voice smouldering.

AFTER leaving Odessa's place he drove straight to Lynens, the most exclusive jeweller in town, where he bought a tiny silver ring, the least expensive they had. It was not the ring he was interested in, but the famous red velvet box embossed with golden letters that was bound to make any feminine heart flutter. From there he drove to a jewellery store near the wharf and purchased a good-quality diamond and sapphire engagement ring, all but emptying his bank account. Transferring it to the Lynens box, he then drove to his rented bungalow on the outskirts of town. After showering and changing, he waited impatiently for the time to pass, going over in his mind his plans for that night.

At seven o'clock prompt he pulled up in front of her mansion and blasted on the horn. A moment later she ran happily down the steps, a slender vision in orange tafetta that suited her tanned skin and dark blonde hair and got in beside him. Richard kissed her tenderly. 'You look lovely.'

'Thank you. I haven't had someone drive up to the house and pip his horn since I was a teenager.'

'You still look young enough to be a teenager,' he teased, slipping the car into gear and driving quickly to the bay area. 'Did Hannel get back to you?'

Odessa tugged down her strapless evening gown to reveal the tops of her firm but small breasts. 'Yes he did – he said the boat was only a tiny one.'

Richard laughed, relieved when she joined in. 'I never said it was the *QE 2*. Up until now, a boat big enough for one was all I ever needed or wanted.'

He was glad Hannel had been taken down a notch but knew he'd have to keep a watchful eye on him until after they were married. After that, in any divorce, he'd have community property to fall back on, and Hannel would be welcome to her.

'I don't deserve you,' she said softly, leaning against him as he cruised for a parking space near Fisherman's Wharf. 'I'm spoiled, lazy and possessive, and sometimes not at all nice.'

'How come I've never noticed all these glaring faults, then?' he teased, pulling into a spot and turning to kiss her.

After dinner he drove to an isolated hill with a superb view overlooking the famous Golden Gate Bridge. The sun was setting in a hazy red and pink beauty, and he turned to her, reaching into his pocket and drawing out the box.

'Odessa,' he said and he swallowed hard. So much depended on the next minute that he did not need to pretend gut-wrenching nervousness. 'Odessa,' he moved the box so that she could see it, and let it rest in the palm of his hand. 'I got this for you.' She didn't hesitate to open it and stare down at the simple, tasteful ring. 'I thought of a single diamond,' he lied, 'but when I saw the sapphires, I was instantly reminded of your eyes . . . so I got that instead. You don't mind, do you?' he asked anxiously. 'I can easily replace it.' Slowly he slid the ring on the third finger of her left hand, and whispered, 'Will you marry me, Odessa Vance?'

'Yes,' she said, her voice sure and confident. 'I'll marry you, Richard Jago.'

Richard pressed her back in her seat and kissed her with savage, eager abandonment before becoming seductive and artful, his hand just below her breast, his thumb almost but not quite rubbing against her straining nipple.

'The wedding will be just however you want it,' he vowed, thinking nervously of the cost as he pulled away. Without a father to pay for the wedding, going dutch seemed the logical choice, and knowing how lavishly Odessa liked to spend, Richard might have to arrange a loan to cover his share of the expenses. And wouldn't Hannel crow then. Looking out over the bay he said softly. 'It's pretty here but not as pretty as over there. Let's honeymoon in Oahu, Odessa.'

Odessa laughed, never having felt so wonderfully happy in all her life. 'This wedding's on me,' she said, not seeing the glitter of relief that lit up his grey eyes. 'And we won't just honeymoon in Hawaii,' she carried on in a sudden burst of generosity, 'we'll stay on for a year, and find out who was responsible for making you leave in the first place!'

'Odessa,' Richard said softly, taking her hand and kissing her palm. 'You don't know how happy you've just made me.'

Chapter 20

Philip pulled up in the drive of Falling Pearls Palace and was greeted by Koana. 'Good evening, Mr Pearce,' The butler bowed as Philip smiled and stepped through the door. 'His Highness is expecting you?'

'Yes,' Philip said. Inside the briefcase he held, were complete dossiers on the men mentioned by Rhiannon Grantham as the weak links at the Lanai Fruit Company.

'Very good, sir. His Highness is busy upstairs at the moment. Where would you care to wait?' Philip selected the poolroom where he shrugged off his jacket, racked up the pool balls, took down a cue and began to pot.

Upstairs Dominic stretched and checked his watch, yawned lazily and rolled on to his side, reaching out to trace the bare thigh of the girl who lay next to him. 'I have business to see to,' he murmured regretfully. The girl was in a dreamy mood, satiated from an afternoon of the best sex she had ever had. The Palace, the man, the once-in-a-lifetime romanticism of the moment had been something special. But it was over now and she was wise and experienced enough not to ask or push for more. Showering and dressing they made their way downstairs, Dominic feeling absurdly guilty.

Alerted by the sound of footfalls on the tiled hall, Philip walked to the door in time to see a lovely redhead kiss Dominic wistfully on the mouth and say goodbye. Five minutes later, Dominic joined him at the table.

'*Aloha*. Been waiting long?'

'Nah,' Philip said, and with the cue ball hit the eight ball in the left corner pocket.

'Got it?' Dominic asked as Phil nodded, missed the next ball and watched his friend pot three perfect shots in rapid succession.

'It's exactly as you said on the phone yesterday. Phelps and Fletcher are all sorted.' Walking to his briefcase he retrieved several documents and handed them over. 'These are the gambling markers we bought off Gillespie.'

Dominic took the rest of the papers, glancing at a receipt for rent on a small flat. 'Did Fletcher's girl kick up much of a fuss about being moved?'

'No. She wasn't about to argue with the goose who lays the golden eggs for her boyfriend.'

'OK. Let's get it over with.'

Dominic drove what Philip always thought of as his no-bullshit car, a Silver Ghost Rolls Royce, to Tom Fletcher's home whilst Philip filled him in on the rundown of Lanai company stock. 'What it boils down to is that without Fletcher and Phelps, your Ms Grantham can't get control,' he summarized as they pulled up in front of a sprawling bungalow that was now ablaze with lights and the sound of music and chattering people. 'Looks like we interrupted a party.'

'And we weren't invited,' Dominic said with mock self-pity.

'Al-ahh-oh,' the young girl who opened the door smiled beatifically at them and tried again. 'I mean Al-oh-al-oha. Oh shit! Hi, come on in.'

Inside, the noise of disco music beat loudly against their eardrums, making conversation impossible. They split up and searched for their unsuspecting host among the groups clustered around coffee tables laden with vol-au-vents and smoked-salmon canapés. Martinis abounded and it was Dominic who first spotted Tom leaning by a French window, chatting to a girl wearing a lowcut cocktail dress. Seeing a tall figure towering over the rest of the mob, Tom's thin face paled considerably at the sight of his powerful chairman wending his way towards him. He could feel sweat trickle down his back as the voice of the pretty little blonde he'd been contemplating screwing suddenly began grating on his nerves.

'Hello, Tom,' Dominic mouthed above the din, pointing to the open French windows to his right. Philip spotted them and followed them out into the cool quiet night. 'Didn't know you had a party on, Tom,' Dominic remarked as they eventually settled beside an artfully rustic bench beneath an umbrella tree.

'That's OK. We're glad to have you drop in. Any time, you know that.'

'I'll come straight to the point,' Dominic began. 'We know the Englishman, Gunster, has been to see you about selling your shares to him. We also know that it hasn't gone through yet, because of the Bank Holiday yesterday.'

'I don't . . .' Tom said, then fell silent.

'You will not sign the papers tomorrow morning when he comes around with the cash but sign these papers now.' He waited as Philip pulled the contact from his briefcase and handed it over to Fletcher, reaching into his shirt pocket for a pen.

'What is it?'

'Your shares, sold to me at current market value. Not the extra good deal the American offered, but I'm sure you can see the advantages in dealing with me.' Dominic leaned casually against the umbrella tree, his hands stuffed deep in his pockets in a gesture that should have looked easygoing, but didn't.

Tom Fletcher was basically a rabbit. A clever rabbit, but a rabbit. It took him only a moment to sign on the dotted line.

'You needn't worry about your mistress and the child. If Gunster tells your wife she'll find no evidence of your supposed infidelity. No house, no record of a kid at the school, nothing. I've hidden your tracks well, Tom.'

Tom Fletcher stared at him, open-mouthed.

'Here,' Philip said, handing over the keys to the new flat and its address.

Tom took them wordlessly and watched the two men walk as swiftly and as silently away as they had entered. His mind was reeling. He didn't understand Dominic Fairchild, not one bit. Anyone else would have thrown him to the wolves. Realizing that his mouth was still hanging open he quickly snapped it shut and wandered back to the party, avoiding his wife and the blonde, and finding the bar.

THAT was easy,' Philip commented once they were back in the Rolls. 'Much easier than I'd thought. I'll be glad when it's all over, though.'

'Yes,' Dominic agreed tersely, not liking it any more than his MD.

Gavin Phelps turned out to be a different proposition altogether. His flat occupied the prize, ground floor site in a prestigious new condominium block, a place he could not afford but would never give up. When the door opened at their knock, the words on Dominic's lips choked as he was met by the sight of the naked blonde girl who answered. However, he recovered in a second. 'I need to see Gavin.'

The girl shrugged skinny shoulders and opened the door wider. 'Sure. *Gavin!*' she yelled in a voice that would have made a wonderful substitute for a foghorn. By his side Dominic saw Philip jump and fought back a smile.

'What!' The voice was impatient and came from behind a slightly ajar door.

'Some men to see you.'

For several seconds there was silence and then a slight creak. Dominic frowned, then swore, taking both Philip and the girl by surprise as he quickly ran around the side of the building. Philip wasn't far behind him when they spotted the half-naked figure of Gavin Phelps sprinting along the pathway between two swimming pools. Seeing a broken branch lying under one of the bushes, Dominic bent down and with an athletic few skips tossed the stick through the air. It fell just right to catch the running man on the back of his knees and topple him. With a yelled curse, Gavin sprawled forward and sideways into a pool.

'Shit, Dom,' Philip breathed heavily as they pulled up at the poolside. 'Where'd you learn that?'

'Playing rugby at Oxford.'

'I'm beginning to feel sorry I missed Oxford,' Philip admitted conversationally as they looked down on Gavin doggy-paddling, his bare chest white in the moonlight.

'Dominic?' Gavin said incredulously. 'What the hell did you do that for?' Swimming with vicious strokes to the laddered steps, he climbed out, his trousers dripping comically, depositing small puddles of water at his feet.

'I wanted to do some business,' Dominic explained jovially, 'and you seemed in a hurry. So . . .' he shrugged.

'Business? At this time of night? I'm soaked. Let's go back to my place. What kind of business can't wait until the morning?'

'The same kind as Gunster had in mind yesterday.'

Gavin looked innocent as he opened the door and stepped inside. 'Who?'

'Cut the crap,' Dominic advised, his voice making even Philip flinch. Walking into the house they found the blonde had gone.

'I gotta get dry. I still have no idea what this is all about,' Gavin lied. 'But I'll learn quicker if I'm not dripping chlorine all over the place.'

'Sure, I'm a reasonable man. After all, if I had been the heavies you were expecting, you'd have two broken legs by now. Gillespie has quite a reputation, doesn't he? Or did you think your gambling was a secret?'

Gavin felt his guts clench but his puzzled look remained in place. 'Still got no idea what you're talking about. Make yourselves a drink. I won't be long.'

'No, thanks – and leave the door open,' Dominic said softly as he went to shut it. Gavin gave him a sharp look, then reluctantly lowered his eyes.

Philip put the briefcase on a wide-leafed table, ignoring the small pane of glass and its mound of white powder that lay openly in the middle of it. A small glass tube and several needles lay neatly in a leather-bound box resembling a pencase. Gavin came back rubbing a small towel over his hair. He walked to a drinks cabinet and poured himself a stiff bourbon.

'What's this?' He took the contract from Philip who gave him a cold look the like of which Gavin had never seen before on his usually affable features.

'Read it,' Dominic advised.

'No way,' Gavin said after skimming the details. 'The Englishman offered me nearly a hundred thou more than this.'

'This is the exact amount your shares are worth. Sign it.'

Gavin smiled, his round face looking so smug that Philip found himself fighting off the desire to lay into him. Gavin had one of those faces that belonged on a slightly overweight, mischievous schoolboy. His rather lanky brown hair, squat figure and wide mouth could easily repel, or charm. 'Exactly,' Gavin said now. 'I'd be a fool not to sell to the Englishman.'

'You'd be a fool not to sell to me,' Dominic corrected so mildly that a less cunning man than Gavin Phelps might have been fooled. Again Gavin felt his guts begin to shiver in cold juices, but he was not a compulsive gambler for nothing.

'I don't think so,' he said slowly.

Dominic looked at Phil, and nodded. 'Show him.'

Philip produced the receipts. 'From our mutual acquaintance, Mr Gillespie.' Gavin took the papers and read them, his face paling slightly but the grin remaining in place.

'I should thank you,' he drawled, draining his bourbon and pouring another. 'Frank was a nasty customer. But you, Your Highness, are a civilized man.'

Slowly Dominic shook his head. 'Mistake number one,' he said softly.

Gavin took a quick swallow of the raw alcohol. 'You don't scare me,' he lied. All his life he'd used a mixture of bluff, cunning and bullying to get what he wanted, avoiding work and seeking pleasure with the dedication of a true sybarite. The thought of missing out on a lucrative deal was unthinkable.

'Mistake number two,' Dominic continued inexorably, and although he did not move and his voice did not alter, the other two men felt the atmosphere change, and darken with menace.

'Never kid a kidder, Your Majesty,' Gavin sneered. 'Haven't you heard that?'

'Indeed. But who's kidding?'

'What if I don't sign?'

'Easy. You go to jail.'

'What?' Gavin laughed increduously. 'I've done nothing illegal.'

'So?' The one syllable was so blasé that even Gavin was momentarily thrown.

'So,' he recovered, blustering with the arrogance of a born bully, 'there's no way I can get sent to the pen!'

Dominic shook his head, his smile almost pitying. 'Gavin, grow up,' he said tiredly, sickened by the whole sordid mess. 'Remember who you're talking to, will you?'

'You're bluffing,' Gavin's voice wavered now. 'You wouldn't do it.'

Dominic looked slowly at Philip, shaking his head. 'You hear this?'

Philip shrugged. 'I hear it. I don't believe it, but I hear it.'

Dominic turned back to Gavin and sighed elaborately. 'Let me spell it out, so that even you can understand. A few phone calls, and a cop comes and sees that nasty little pile of powder on the table. Your source is found and persuaded to confess that you traffic – *traffic*, mind – and hey presto! A five-year stay free of charge in a nice little prison somewhere in . . .'

'I hear New Mexico is nice,' Philip said helpfully. 'Plenty of sunshine and scorpions.'

'I agree. New Mexico then,' Dominic said, looking surprised as Gavin stared at him. 'You didn't think we'd let you stay in one of our own pens, did you? You're not thinking, Gavin. You've got to stay with us, kid,' he admonished with bitter sarcasm. 'Just think,' he carried on. 'You get to work laying roads. I hear there's a lot of cattle-ranchers out there who pay the government a small subsidy to get their roads tarmacked. Now won't that be nice? Not to mention finding yourself a nice, big – *really big* – cellmate who'll keep you exclusive.'

'Exclusive?'

Dominic looked at Philip, and shook his head sorrowfully. 'So naive,' he murmured, turning back to Gavin. 'But then, he's so pretty he's bound to find protection from a con soon, don't you think?'

'Oh yeah,' Philip agreed, leaning against the table and folding his arms.

Catching on at last, Gavin growled, 'I'm no faggot.'

'Gavin, do you really think you'd have a choice?'

'You're bluffing. You forget, I know you,' Gavin said, walking away but sinking down quickly on to the nearest settee. 'You're the original good guy.'

'You don't know me at all,' Dominic said, voice totally

emotionless. 'If you don't sign, you pay, and pay big. I don't think a man like you *can* survive in the joint, Phelps. But if you think you can, that's your choice I guess.'

He walked to the door and Philip straightened up and joined him.

'Hold it. Raise the price twenty thou and you have a deal.'

'You've heard the deal, take it or leave it.'

They were almost out of the door when Gavin snarled, 'All right – I'll sign.' A gambler he was, but only with money. When it came to his own safety and comfort, it was totally different. He signed angrily, the pen biting deep into the paper as he wrote out his name and handed it over. Dominic checked it and nodded.

'I'll have my lawyers subtract what you owe me for the gambling debts.'

'*What?*' Gavin yelled, jumping to his feet.

'The gambling debts,' Dominic reiterated calmly. 'You owe *me* now, not Gillespie.'

Gavin spluttered. 'I thought . . .'

'Thought what?' Dominic asked coldly, one eyebrow raised.

'You bastard,' Gavin snarled with feeling.

Outside, Philip took a deep breath. 'I'm glad you're on my side,' he confessed with a grin, opening the passenger door of the car and slipping inside gratefully. 'What would you have done if he'd called your bluff?'

Dominic drove on to the main road, then looked at Philip. 'What bluff?'

Back at the Palace, Philip made straight for the bar and poured himself a stiff vodka and Dominic a scotch. Watching his friend walk moodily to a large black-leather armchair and sit down heavily, he commented matter-of-factly: 'You have her now.'

Dominic leaned back in the chair and his eyes narrowed, a habit of his when he was thinking hard. 'Yes,' he agreed, his voice rich with satisfaction.

'Looking forward to the meeting, boss?'

Dominic looked up and smiled wolfishly. 'That I am,' he admitted. 'Cheers.'

'Cheers,' Philip raised his glass and drank deeply. What a night, he thought, then caught the small but savage smile that played with Dominic Fairchild's lips. His eyes glittered as green as any cat's watching a mousehole. Yes, he'd had a rough night, Philip thought. But not half as rough as the afternoon Rhiannon Grantham was soon going to have.

RHIANNON crossed the lobby en route to the elevator but the sound of music coming from the Sunset dining room changed her mind. Most of the lunch-time customers had left and she chose a table near the stage, ignoring the menu as she looked up at Farron.

Used to opera and the resonance of trained singers, Rhiannon knew a good voice when she heard one. The song he was singing was one she hadn't come across before and she was not surprised when a woman seated at the next table told her ogling daughter that he wrote all his own lyrics. Watching him as closely as she was, she saw his eyes sharpen on one particular girl, a pretty little blonde waitress who was serving iced tea two tables away. Rhiannon waited until the girl was passing and then raised her hand slightly.

Vienna saw the movement immediately. It was not showy like those performed by men with first dates to impress, nor was it the imperious, superior kind favoured by rich middle-aged women. As she turned and encountered the friendly smile of the almost stunningly lovely woman seated there, Vienna found an answering smile came easily and genuinely to her face. 'Hello,' Rhiannon said, and glanced at the menu. 'I'll have the iced pineapple juice, please.'

'Certainly,' Vienna, getting good at guessing nationalities, immediately placed the accent as English. The girl gone, Rhiannon turned her attention to the stage and received something of a shock. Farron Manikuuna was looking directly at her, and although he was too professional to show hostility she knew immediately he was not her number one fan. Deciding to play dumb she waited, her eyes curious as they watched Vienna approach.

'Thank you. I don't know if you're aware of it or not, but the singer up there can't take his eyes off you.' She accepted her chilled glass and took a delicious sip. Her voice was naturally friendly and just a little teasing, and Vienna blushed. Rhiannon's smile widened. 'He has a very good voice. I was rather surprised, actually,' she continued chattily. 'You know, you come to a place like Hawaii and expect – not amateur entertainment exactly, but certainly nothing as fine as this.'

Vienna nodded, needing no stranger's praise to make her proud of Farron. 'Mr Fairchild is very particular about the quality of his entertainers.'

'So I heard,' Rhiannon said mildly, then looked around. 'Looks like the place is emptying fast. I bet you're relieved. I always thought waitressing must be a lot harder than you ladies make it look.'

'Ain't that the truth!' Vienna smiled, sensing their mutual compatibility. And the thought of finding a friend made her ache longingly.

'When does the show finish?'

Vienna checked her watch. 'He should be coming up to the last number now.'

'Pity. Do you know if he has a recording contract lined up? A singer of his talent must have attracted a few talent scouts.'

'I don't know,' Vienna said cautiously. 'He's never talked about it.'

'Well, I have a few contacts in the music business. If he's interested, tell him to give me a call. I'm staying at the hotel.'

'Thanks,' Vienna said, warming even further to this lovely Englishwoman. 'I'll do that.'

Dominic jolted to a halt at the sight of the two women talking, his eyes slewing to the stage and noting that Farron too was watching them uneasily. Vienna was the first to see him striding towards them, and she straightened automatically. Although she had grown to like her boss and was able to relax around him more and more, she still felt reticent when working. 'Hello, Mr Fairchild.'

'Vienna.' Dominic smiled at her, then let the smile fade as he addressed Rhiannon. 'Miss Grantham,' he used her surname for Vienna's benefit, nodding down at the seated woman with polite but cool hospitality.

Rhiannon saw Vienna look back at her quickly, dismay and rather painful disappointment evident on her face, and sighed inwardly. 'Hello Dominic,' she said, and smiled regretfully as Vienna excused herself and left.

'Not interrupting anything, I hope?' he asked, drawing out a chair and sitting next to her. Lying sod, she thought silently, even as she shrugged. Jack had told her about Farron's relationship with Vienna and when he'd explained about the mugging as well and the girl's consequent amnesia, Rhiannon had dropped any ideas of getting to Farron via Vienna. Not that Dominic would understand scruples like that: he used anybody and everybody, regardless of such minor details as compassion or decency.

'Not at all,' she finally answered him sweetly. 'Do you always foist yourself, univited, on to your guests?'

He smiled sweetly. 'I make an exception with you.'

'I'm flattered,' she sniped. Dominic paused to applaud with the few remaining diners as Farron wound up the act, then blatantly took a large healthy swallow from her drink. 'I trust that'll be on the house,' she snapped, and Dominic looked at her, tut-tutting.

'Such a lack of style,' he commiserated. 'You've disappointed me.'

Unbidden, an image of their last meeting flashed across her mind, and she felt a cold blush stain her cheeks. 'I'll endeavour to cultivate some,' she said mildly. Taking a handkerchief from the pretty bag that perfectly matched her scarlet gypsy skirt and white, peasant-style blouse with delicate lace, she carefully wiped the glass where his lips had been and took a delicate sip of her depleted drink. Dominic watched, furious at this graphic insult.

'About this Extraordinary Meeting you called for tomorrow. I hope you haven't got anything up your pretty little sleeve.' His fingers enclosed her wrist and raised her arm off the table. He ran his hand up to her elbow, his fingers warm and caressing over the tight-fitting, full-length lace sleeves.

Rhiannon's heart somersaulted at the warm questing touch of his fingers on her forearm, the delicate blue vein in the bend of her elbow leaping desperately as he travelled over it and came to a rest on the curve of her shoulder. Belatedly, very belatedly, she snatched her hand away. 'I always play my aces close to my heart,' she said, her voice annoyingly husky and breathless. Dominic dropped his eyes to that region of her anatomy and wished heartily he hadn't started this damned conversation.

Rhiannon was relieved to look up and see Farron Manikuuna gazing from one to the other of them with curious caution. 'Aloha,' he said, and Rhiannon sensed rather than saw the slight tightening and wariness that crept into Dominic's stance. More than ever she was convinced that a possible weak spot lay in the mystery. The singer was the reason he had flexed his muscle to get the Jago man banished from the islands. Ignoring Dominic she smiled brightly up at him.

'Aloha. I enjoyed what little I saw of the show immensely. Please join us.' She did not miss the quick questioning look Farron cast his employer, nor the almost telepathic communication that passed between them. Farron pulled out a chair and sat down. 'I was just speaking to Vienna,' she said, making sure to keep anything that might even hint at flirtatiousness out of her voice. The last thing she wanted was to give Farron more reasons to distrust her. It was already blatantly obvious where his loyalties lay. 'She's really very brave.'

'Yes, she is,' Farron said, admitting to himself that he was surprised. Whatever he had expected Dominic's enemy to be like, it was not this.

'I can't begin to imagine what it must be like for her so I won't try. I only hope that she soon regains her memory.'

'So do I,' Farron agreed. She was beautiful, but not as glossy as he'd imagined. Dominic watched her tactics, shifting restlessly on his chair.

'I was wondering if you have any plans for a recording contract.' Rhiannon repeated her earlier question, testing the ground. Could she woo him away from Dominic with a valid business deal?

'We've already discussed that,' Dominic lied.

Farron picked it up immediately, saying with a hard voice, 'I'm completely happy with things as they are.'

Rhiannon met his brown eyes head-on, smiled and nodded. 'I understand,' she said, and Farron knew immediately that she did.

Dominic leaned back and smiled. In a way she'd done him a favour by mentioning a recording contract. He should have thought of it long ago. He'd have a word with Tim Roath, the island's resident record producer.

'Well, I'd better be off. We still have a lot of crating up to do,' Farron said, referring to the move. This week was Vienna's last as a waitress, and things were getting hectic. 'Aloha,' Farron nodded to Rhiannon politely. As he walked swiftly away towards the kitchens, Dominic reached forward and drained her drink, rattling the ice cubes in the glass and deciding that the time for fencing was over.

'I take it this Extraordinary Meeting you've called for at Lanai means you still intend to fight?' He changed the subject so abruptly Rhiannon almost faltered.

'Certainly,' she recovered crisply, letting him know he was a total fool if he thought otherwise. 'I'll fight you and City Hall on King Street if I have to,' she said, remembering the luckless Doctor Jago's ousting by Dominic's friends in that department. Jack Gunster was nothing if not a mine of information.

'I'm the King around here, remember?' he said softly.

Rhiannon breathed in sharply. 'Why you arrogant, big-headed, miserable . . .'

'Ah, ah, ah,' Dominic wagged a finger at her. 'Temper temper. What you need is cooling off.'

She didn't argue as he took her hand and led her outside to the garage; she was too intrigued. With the top down on his car the wind felt glorious against her face as they drove through Tantalus Drive, winding past lush forest rife with ferns and enormous philodendrons. Their destination turned out to be The Foster Botanic Gardens, and by the time they'd turned on to the North Vineyard Boulevard and pulled up into a parking space most of her anger had fled. The garden, said a notice, was open daily and entrance was free. Orchids abounded, as did tropical palms which whispered in a high breeze. The grounds proliferated with flowering trees, and when she innocently asked him what one was, he told her in a deadpan voice that it was called Cannon Ball. She didn't ask again. They did, however, manage a halfway civilized conversation and things didn't go wrong until they had toured the complete gardens.

'I hear you've applied for membership of the Oahu Country Club,' he commented as they walked back to the car.

'Yes. My father was a keen Country Club member back in England.'

'Couldn't have been much of a club – or did he buy his way in? That was one of his preferred methods, I seem to remember. Nobody would want him other . . .' He jerked to a halt as he caught her flying hand headed for his face and two sets of blazing green eyes clashed in silent fury. 'Not again you don't,' Dominic promised grimly, and remembering how their last physical fight had ended in those disturbingly brutal kisses, Rhiannon froze.

No, her brain panicked. No, not again! But something else, some traitorous thing deep inside, was saying 'Yes! Yes, yes, yes!' and in a moment she was defeated. His lips were hot on hers, burning into her subconscious and branding her in a way that no one had ever done before. She wanted to pull away and to kill him, to be free of his tenacious, dangerous spell at the same time as she wanted to melt into him and drag him kicking and screaming into her soul to join her.

Dominic moaned against her lips, the sound making her skin tingle and leap on her bones. They dragged themselves from each other's arms simultaneously, denying both of them the comfort of saying they were the first to put a stop to the madness. Rhiannon backed away and then turned and ran out of the gates, ignoring the parked car. She'd only gone a few hundred yards down the road when she heard the purr of a car behind her.

'Get in.' The voice was curt.

Staring stonily ahead she said grimly, 'I'd rather walk.' She'd walk a hundred miles if it meant she didn't have to sit next to Dominic Fairchild. Especially when her body was still clamouring for him with such longing.

'Suit yourself,' he snarled and, to her complete amazement, rammed his foot on the accelerator and drove away.

Chapter 21

The *Hokunani* was slowly sailing out of the harbour, a white cruising vision on the azure ocean. On the stretch of white sandy beach opposite the Blue Hawaiian an ambulance, white and silent, waited on the road. A crowd had gathered, heads bobbing and straining to see the cause of all the excitement.

A car pulled to a halt on the beach road, a single red light flashing on its roof. The man who got out was about forty. His hair was an untidy brown blob, his face only slightly tanned. Lt Perry Clements was an islander of twenty years and people in the know predicted he was going far, although their idea of 'far' might not be the same as Perry's own. Pale brown eyes, almost amber in colour, surveyed the scene as the driver of his car joined him. His shoes sank into sand and quickly filled with the fine, hot grains that irritated him as he made his way through the crowd easily. There was nothing in Perry's physical appearance to account for the way the crowd parted. He stood only five feet ten, was slender and ordinary-looking in black trousers and plain white shirt. Nevertheless, most people recognized him instantly as the man in charge. Patrolmen straighened as Perry arrived on the scene.

It didn't take long to learn that the body had been discovered by an early-morning jogger, and that there was no ID on the body. Already Vic Quintero, the police surgeon, had been called to the scene and Perry knelt beside the stooped, grey-haired doctor and glanced at the corpse which had probably been in the water for months – it was bloated, fish-nibbled, eyeless and a shade between blue, green and mauve. Relieved when the surgeon replaced the black plastic, he straightened up, his jaw tightly clenched.

Perry had gained a psychology degree from a prestigious college stateside before joining the force, but had not taken the penpushing route to his present lieutenant's job, much to his recruiting officer's surprise, and the surprise of his superiors at the precinct to which he'd been assigned. It didn't take long before his arrest and conviction record was second to none.

'What can you tell me, Vic?' Perry asked as the police surgeon got slowly to his feet and began to brush sand from his trouser-leg.

'Male, Caucasian, between thirty and forty years old,' Quintero said, with the unemotional voice most police surgeons acquired after a few years on the job. 'Blond, probably blue eyes. Six feet and fair musculature, I'd say.'

'Cause of death?'

'Unlikely to be drowning. A blow to the left side of the head, corresponding with a blow by a heavy blunt instrument probably finished him before he hit the water, but until the autopsy, don't quote me.'

'We'll need a dental ID,' Perry commented, walking slowly away from the monstrous corpse. 'How long would you say the guy's been in the water?'

'Since December, maybe January.'

Perry nodded. That was hard luck on whoever dumped him. With the tides on their side they must have thought he'd be safe enough. It had to be just sheer bad luck that the capricous seasonal tides had washed him back before sharks or a school of fish had picked the bones clean.

Hell, this was just what he needed – a possible homicide at the beginning of the tourist season. Perry's eyes scanned the scene as the crowd gradually dispersed, the holidaymakers drifting back to their bars and swimming pools. He looked across the road, his eyes resting thoughtfully on the nearest hotel. Perry continued to look at the Blue Hawaiian for a long, long time.

INSIDE the Blue Hawaiian, Dominic Fairchild stood on a paved patio, his eyes focused on the blue flashing lights that had first arrived over an hour ago. Raising a glass of iced tea to his lips he frowned. Behind him he could hear some of his returning guests whispering in awed, avid tones, and he smiled mirthlessly.

'What's going on?'

Dominic looked around quickly, smiling as Farron came to

a halt beside him. 'A drowning, I think. Want some?' He offered the ice-cube-filled glass and Farron took it with a murmured, 'Thanks,' taking a few long swallows, and keeping hold of it as he watched the coroner's car pull away.

'One of ours?'

'Hell, I hope not,' Dominic said with feeling. 'How's the move going?'

'That's what I came to see you about. We're ready to move in this afternoon.' Farron and Vienna had decided to take up Dominic's offer and move into his beach-house on the west coast.

'Fine. You can get the key from the manager's office.'

Farron nodded, his eyes still on the flashing blue lights. People drowned in Hawaii all the time, just like they did in any other holiday spot. So why did he feel so cold?

'How is Vienna?'

'What? Oh, she's fine. She's looking forward to classes on Monday.' She'd talked of nothing else since she'd been accepted by one of the island's most prestigious culinary colleges.

Dominic nodded, but he too was staring at the beach thoughtfully.

GLORIA looked at the new girl with assessing eyes, taking in her long-legged, ultra slender figure, and wondered if she was on something.

'You had five customers last night. Four the night before that, and six on Monday. A new face is always sought after,' Gloria commented now, leaning back in her chair and looking the girl straight in the eye.

'Si,' the girl nodded, all smiles, but in the black eyes Gloria could sense the unease. Unease, Gloria understood and didn't mind. Cheating, she did. 'I thought I'd made the financial arrangements perfectly clear,' she carried on now. 'The house's cut is not negotiable.'

'I understand, Madame.'

She watched as the raven-haired girl hung her head and wrung her hands in a graphic gesture. She was obviously South American, probably Nicaraguan. She got on well with the others, the doc had passed her as clean and she'd had no complaints from the customers. As soon as the petty fiddling was sorted out, Juanita – as she called herself – could be taken off probation.

'Look. You know and I know that I offer the best deal in town but if you want to go back on the streets, all you have to do is keep holding out on me,' Gloria said, her voice hardening just slightly, knowing instinctively that this was the only language the girl could understand. No doubt she had brothers and sisters back home who ran into double figures. Without having asked a single question of her, Gloria could accurately guess the girl's life story. Working at the age of ten in some child-related slave-labour industry, her looks had attracted the boss. Urged by her family to comply, she'd probably spent a few months with him and then, ruined and unmarriageable, a life on the streets was the only alternative.

'Look, kid. We're not a bloody bank here. There are no hidden charges. What you pay to me is all you pay. And for that you get the room for as long as you want it, meals and medical expenses. You won't have to pay anyone anything more.' Leaving her chair to put a hand under the girl's chin she saw Juanita flinch, obviously expecting a physical beating. Gloria raised her chin until she was looking into the frightened brown eyes. 'I take the house cut, and the rest is all yours. You don't have to hold out on me. But if you do you're out. Now,' she moved away, took out a black-bound book and checked the entries. 'You owe another hundred dollars.'

The girl's lower lip trembled. '*Si*, Gloria.' She reached into her cleavage and withdrew some bills, counting them out slowly and carefully like a child might, and then handed them over.

'Good. Now, all the rest is yours. Do you have a bank account?'

The girl shook her head, already looking sceptical, and Gloria sighed. 'Fine. It's yours to do with as you like,' she spread her hands in a placating gesture then stood up and walked to the door. It would take time, but eventually the girl would come to see that no one was going to take what was rightfully hers. In the lounge Juanita glanced at the other girls

273

nervously and walked quickly up the stairs. Three pairs of eyes looked at Gloria knowingly and she smiled, shaking her head slightly, words unncessary. Just then the radio that had been playing Country and Western music switched to a news programme.

'*The main news story today is the discovery of a body on Waikiki Beach* . . .'

'Leave it!' Gloria ordered sharply, making all three girls jump and freezing Janice in the act as she went to change stations.

'The body, found by a jogger early this morning, has not yet been identified, but is believed to be that of a Caucasion male. Although not yet confirmed by the coroner's office, the body is thought to have been in the water for several months. So far, the police have not indicated if they are treating the case as an accidental drowning, or homicide. In the other news, a motion to allow billboards to be used on the islands was again defeated . . .'

'All right,' Gloria smiled, knowing she had gone pale. 'You can turn it over now.'

They knew of course, she thought pensively as she walked back to her office. They knew whose body that was. Not that any of them would ever talk, but still . . . How long before they'd start to get scared?

Gloria felt like crying, but as she slumped in her chair her backbone was already stiffening. Picking up the telephone she called Frank and, as usual, launched straight into what was troubling her. 'Have you been listening to the news?'

'No. What about it?'

'The police have found a body on the beach. It's been in the water several months, they said. A man.'

'It can't be him.'

'Why can't it? How many men do you think got tossed into the sea last winter, Frank?'

'OK – so perhaps. There's no need to panic.'

Gloria smiled mirthlessly. 'Who's panicking?' she asked. 'I just thought I'd keep you informed, that's all.'

Frank laughed heartily. 'You're an original, Gloria, know that?'

'Yeah,' she said heavily, rubbing the aching bridge of her nose with a tired hand. 'The only thing we can do is sit tight.'

'Agreed,' Frank said crisply. 'The cops can't know who he is, and even when they find out there's nothing to connect him with us. Unless . . .'

Gloria tensed. 'Unless what?'

'Unless the girl gets her memory back.'

'She won't. And even if she does, you're safe enough.'

'Meaning?'

'Meaning you're to leave her alone. She's doing all right now. She's got a man, a job, a good life. I mean it, Frank,' Gloria warned, straightening in her chair. 'If the worst comes to the worst I'll take the heat. And you know I won't let you down.'

'You're crazy,' Frank said bluntly.

'Nevertheless, if anything goes down, I'll take the rap.'

Frank's sigh sounded loud and clear in her ears. 'I don't understand you. Even after all these years when I think I know you inside and out, you go and say something stupid.'

Gloria laughed, but wouldn't let go. 'Promise me, Frank.'

'OK, OK! But I still think you're mad.'

'Probably,' Gloria agreed then rung off, and sat staring into space. But she was not mad. She knew precisely what she was doing. And why.

VIENNA wiped her perspiring forehead with the back of her hand and grimaced at Farron. They'd borrowed a van from the band's banjo player, taking three journeys to transfer all their belongings to the small bungalow and at last they were nearly finished. Boasting a tiny living room, a large bedroom, adequate bathroom and kitchen, the bungalow was a young couple's dream. Set in a lush garden with their nearest neighbour a good thousand yards away, the little dwelling was now beginning to look like home. An hour later, they were finished. Only a vase and a model car had been broken, with one chipped casserole dish rounding off the casualty list.

'Did you know, apart from divorce, moving house is supposed to be the most stressful thing a normal family can expect to endure?' Farron asked as he collapsed on to the sofa.

Vienna smiled. 'If the shower doesn't work, I'm going to scream.'

'Now there's an idea,' Farron said, his eyes lighting up as he rose from the settee and Vienna's grin widened.

'I don't know,' she said moments later as they stood looking at the shower cubicle. 'It looks mighty small.'

'That's a contradiction in terms,' he said smugly. 'Mighty means big, as in . . .'

'Yes?' she said archly, as he stuttered to a laughing halt.

'Well, I was going to make a comparison with . . . but my natural modesty forbids it.' His eyes dropped to where her small fingers were working free the buttons of her shirt, all laughter draining from him as those buttons came apart. Slowly she rolled the fabric off her small creamy shoulders to reveal pert, pink-tipped full breasts that made his mouth go dry and his fingertips tingle. Next she undid the zip at the front of her jeans and wriggled out of them. Clad only in brief white panties she opened the shower door and turned the knob, thrusting her hand under it. 'Brrr . . . cold,' she said, daring to look back at him over her shoulder.

He was shaking his head. 'The way I feel now,' his voice was strangled and not its usual clear self, 'it might be just as well.' Every time they made love he lost himself completely, she was so fantastic. He couldn't help but wonder if it was love alone that made their lovemaking so wonderful, or if it was because she had known many men in the past. Sometimes he could lie awake at night, satiated in her arms, and his suspicions would run like demented mice through the convoluted maze of his mind.

'Are you going to go in like that?' Vienna teased, one eyebrow raised. 'I know the clothes need washing, but . . .'

Farron stripped himself quickly, watching as she rolled the panties down her thighs, the material twisting into ropes. Her body was tanned pink and cream, the hair at the juncture of her thighs as silver and golden as that atop her head. She held out her hand and together they stepped under the spray which immediately darkened their hair.

Through the water that streamed down her face, she watched him reach for the soap and slowly turned around, moments later feeling a well-lathered hand run down her back following the indentations of her shoulders and spine before rounding out over her buttocks. She gasped as her breasts brushed the cold tiles in front of her and her legs trembled as she saw his hand reach for the pink bar of soap again. She breathed deeply as he bent down, his soapy hands wandering caressingly over her calves, rising slowly higher to her thighs. She bit her lip, just managing to stop the moan that rose to her throat as he teasingly slid his hands around her to wash her concave stomach. Her head tipped back to rest against his shoulder as he slowly straightened up, his hands at last gliding in soap-smooth intimacy over her breasts, where her nipples burgeoned painfully. This time she could not stop the moan of desire that escaped her, and Farron murmured something in throaty Hawaiian, the prominent vowels rolling off his lips in a passionate message.

She felt the arch of his foot press against the inside of her ankles, sliding her legs apart, and his hands on her breasts held her tighter as her balance became more and more precarious. 'Farron,' she gasped as she felt his penis slide down the crack of her buttocks and slip through her parted legs, her hands flying out to flatten against the cold tiles in front of her as he lifted her slightly, slipping almost half of his length into her hot and eager core. Lukewarm sprays of water cascaded on to her stomach, trickling down to where their bodies joined. He moved inside her, his shaft rubbing with ever more friction her sensitive clitoris, making her legs twitch in helpless reaction. She could feel the tightness begin to grow with helpless, almost shocking pleasure as his hard shaft moved ever faster within and against her. She swallowed hard, her eyes opening as she heard his voice, hoarse and husky, whispering native words to her. The ceiling of the shower tilted and swirled above her as her body began to jerk helplessly, Farron's hold tightening on her as she began to arch in climax.

She cried out as orgasm claimed her, dragging in sobbingly deep breaths for long moments. Giving her no time to feel disappointment he slipped out of her and turned her around, his hands coming under her to cup her buttocks as he lifted her off the floor. The cold tiles against her back made her gasp, but her legs fastened eagerly around his waist as he thrust fully and deeply within her, making her cry out in renewed pleasure. This time she looked him straight in the eye as he drove into her, his jaw clenching as her tightness enveloped him, squeezing him in a delicious vice. 'You could kill me, doing this,' he gasped, 'and I wouldn't care. I'd be glad . . . glad . . .'

He rested his forehead against hers, the shower spray hitting his shoulders and rolling down his back and through the crack of his buttocks before falling to the floor. Her nails dug deeper into his back as she clung to him, her leg muscles straining as she gripped him. For long minutes they strained together, their moans and cries echoing within the empty space, before they climaxed in perfect unison. Vienna slid slowly to the floor as Farron leant weakly against the wall for support.

Reaching for the soap beside her, she lathered her hands and then looked up to find his eyes on her. Starting on his feet she worked her way up his calves, her fingers finding the indentation at the back of his knees and smiling as he dragged his breath in sharply. Stopping just above his knees to re-lather her hands, she massaged and soaped his thighs, finally curling her hand around his shaft, already grown turgid and stiff. Farron closed his eyes, moaning as her fingers, soapy smooth, curled around him, pulling and caressing him. The sweat that accumulated on his brow was washed away by the water as he thrust his face under the jet stream of it. His mouth was open and gasping, his eyes tightly shut as his fingers scraped helplessly against the tiles as her exquisite torture drove him slowly mad.

IT was half an hour before they finally left the shower and dressed. 'We'll have to get some food in tomorrow,' he said, looking into the empty fridge and equally empty cupboards. 'How does eating out sound?'

They drove to the Waimea Falls Park not far from the north beaches of the island and wandered amidst lush grounds which they shared with peacocks, displaying their magnificent tail feathers to bored and dowdy peahens. Farron pointed out a rare and native ne-ne geese, the state bird. In a flowering jacaranda tree rife with bell-shaped blossoms gathered in clusters, a Kona nightingale began to sing as they kissed, breaking them apart as they looked upwards, trying without success to spot the small bird amidst the flowering foliage. Glancing at his watch as they reluctantly strolled away, Farron headed towards a meadow where a traditional hula dance was being performed.

'The hula was performed originally in honour of Pele's sister, Laka, goddess of dance,' Farron whispered to Vienna as they sat crosslegged on the warm grass, holding hands and looking at each other more often than they did the dance. Afterwards they watched *ulu manka*, an old form of Hawaiian lawn bowling being taught, laughingly trying a few shots themselves.

'I'm starving,' she confessed as they walked back to the exit, stopping to let trams, each with its own guide pointing out rare species to a captive audience, trundle by, looking over her shoulder as they waited for the track to clear. Suddenly, although she could see no one, the hairs on the back of her neck bristled.

'You all right?' Farron asked, looking at her anxiously. She shrugged, peering around again as she waited for him to unlock the car doors and let her in.

'Yes,' she said, but her eyes scanned the crowd.

'*Honi*, the mountains look lovely tonight,' he said romantically as they drove back, and Vienna glanced at them, about to reply. Suddenly she froze. Into her mind flashed the picture of other mountains, taller and all around, covered in snow. In the surrounding meadows she could see cows and goats with enormous bells around their necks and she reached out, compulsively grasping Farron's forearm in a tight, excited grip. Then the vision faded, leaving her frustrated and wanting to cry.

'What's wrong?' Farron asked sharply, quickly pulling to a halt on the side of the road. A battered Volkswagen Beetle behind nearly rammed into them before it swerved out just in time and continued on down the road.

'I remembered something,' she said, looking at him with stupefaction. 'I remembered seeing other mountains – higher than these,' she pointed to the Konau's, 'and in the fields the cows all wore huge bells,' her hands went to her own neck and she talked, her eyes brimming over with excitement. 'I saw it, Farron – I remembered it!'

Farron was already grinning widely. 'That's great. It sounds like Switzerland, or maybe Austria to me.'

'Do you think this is the beginning of getting my memory back? Should I see a doctor?'

'I'm sure it is but I don't think a doctor will help. You know what the hospital said? It's just a matter of time.' She nodded, fighting off the harsh arrow of disappointment that lacerated her. Still, she told herself firmly as Farron once more put the car into gear and drove them into Pearl city in search of a restaurant, she was beginning to remember at last.

Spotting a Zippy's – a fast food chain with the Hawaiian touch – Farron thought better of it, eventually finding a little Italian place that was all red wine, candles in bottles and pasta. He ordered ravioli for both of them.

'Hmm, delicious,' Vienna commented, spearing another pasta envelope in its thick, delicious tomato sauce and popping it into her mouth, gazing idly out of the window as she did so. A traffic warden wandered suspiciously around the parked cars, stopping to chat to a man in a disreputable-looking Beetle. A necking couple stood under a street lamp, kissing voraciously. A woman walked her dog. And still she shivered. It was as if her memory, while precious and joyful, also sparked off renewed fear.

She reached for her wine and drank deeply, a squeal of delight from a child at the next table making her glance over at them. As she saw the two teenage heads bend close together she took a deep breath. She was once more in the shadow of those huge mountains, walking across a grey-tiled floor with a book balanced precariously on her head. The image wavered and changed to one where she was sitting in a classroom, listening to a woman by a blackboard, who was describing something that she couldn't quite catch . . . But that didn't matter, because suddenly she knew. 'Finishing

School,' she said, quite clearly, making Farron stare at her blankly.

'It was Switzerland,' she said, putting down her knife and fork. 'I just remembered something else – a classroom and . . . elocution lessons, I think. And fashion magazines . . . other girls and make-up lessons. Finishing School.' She said the two words with total conviction, and then began to laugh.

Farron called for the bill as, food forgotten and unwanted, they left the restaurant hand in hand. 'What you have to do,' he mused as they drove to their new home, 'is to write to the Swiss School Board Authority and ask for brochures on all the Finishing Schools. You might recognize one.'

Vienna nodded, too excited to talk, but her eyes shone brightly at the city lights speeding by.

'You know what this means, don't you?' he said, beginning to think about it rationally, and there was a serious undertone in his voice. She shook her head. 'Think about it,' he said quietly, taking his eyes off the road only long enough to glance at her but for the first time she could remember, she saw in his eyes, something . . . withdrawn?

'A Swiss Finishing School,' Farron prompted, his voice tight with a note she'd never heard before.

'I don't understand,' she said, her voice tinged with fear.

Farron signalled right, changed gear, sighed and then told himself not to be an idiot. His eyes softened as she fixed him with a pleading blue gaze and he felt blissful relief was over him. She loved him, and he loved her. Nothing else mattered – he wouldn't let it. So, taking a deep breath he blurted out exactly what was on his mind.

'Only rich kids get to go to Swiss Finishing Schools, Vienna.'

Chapter 22

Rhiannon was dressed all in white. A white pencil skirt fell to just above her knees, whilst white silk stockings clung to her tanned legs. Her shoes were strappy and showed off her ankles to perfection. Her jacket too was white and of the finest cotton, with long narrow lapels that reached almost to her waist. White gloves and handbag completed the ensemble. Later she was to wonder whether the choice of colour had been prompted by an unconscious vision of impending disaster; white being the colour of a sacrificial victim.

The offices of Fairchild Enterprises were located in a twenty-storey modern block of glass and steel. Giving her name curtly to the receptionist in the classy lobby, she walked to the elevator looking cooler than she felt. Where was Jack? On the quick journey to the top floor her gloved hands ran nervously over her long and loose hair making sure it was in order. Her face was made up lightly but classically. When the doors of the elevator opened she felt suddenly afraid. A young blonde girl dressed in a smart grey pants suit smiled brightly at her and said cheerfully, 'Miss Grantham? This way – the board is convened and waiting for you.'

Rhiannon's nerves threatened to snap. Damn it, where was Jack? He was supposed to have met her before leaving the hotel with the signed Phelps and Fletcher documents. Rhiannon had overseen many board meetings, but that had been from a position of power with friendly executives. She'd never before had to face a hostile board at a takeover bid and her nerves were tight.

Led to an impressive wooden door, Rhiannon paused, eyes swivelling to a portrait of an old man with white hair and fierce eyes who glowered at her with a mocking superiority.

'That's Frederick Fairchild,' the young girl beside her said.

'Rhia! Rhia, wait!' The voice was like a pistol shot in its unexpectedness and she whirled around, her heart leaping into her mouth as she saw Jack sprinting towards her at the same moment as, behind her, the door opened. She looked over her shoulder and into the face of Dominic Fairchild.

'Miss Grantham,' he murmured, his hand on her arm in a polite enough gesture that nevertheless reminded her of a jailer leading a condemned man firmly to his execution. She looked at Jack and saw his desperate look but Dominic's quick actions gave them no chance to talk or plan strategy.

The boardroom was huge. The carpet underfoot was beige and restful, the walls a corn-coloured yellow. The table was a huge rectangle slab of ebony at which set seven men who stared at her with varying expressions.

'Gentlemen, this is Miss Grantham, and her associate, Mr Gunster,' Dominic announced, leaving her with no choice but to walk forward when all she wanted to do was speak privately with Jack and find out what the hell was going on. She cast Dominic a sideways glance through her lashes but his face was inscrutable. He led her to a vacant chair then resumed his place at the head of the table.

Philip glanced at her and whispered to Dominic, 'She looks even better close to. You have to admire her poise, I suppose.'

Rhiannon sat back in her chair and put her handbag in front of her on the table. Her movements were as quiet and graceful as those of a ballerina, and her natural elegance suddenly had the murmuring board members falling silent. With infinite care, she pulled off her gloves to reveal long, pale, pink-tipped exquisite hands and every man suddenly recognized that here was a woman to be reckoned with. Curiosity and speculation grew. Rumours had been rife amongst them since the notice of the meeting. All of them knew of her takeover of the Liliha boutique chain and now they'd had a chance to become used to her physical beauty, caution and hard-nosed intelligence once again became the order of the day.

She let her eyes slide across the table to where Gavin Phelps and Tom Fletcher sat staring down at the notepads in front of them.

A mere lift of a fingertip from the man at the head of the table brought the meeting to immediate order and even Rhiannon could feel his power. 'As you all know, Miss

Grantham, through the offices of the Company Secretary . . .' he nodded to a man seated next to Rhiannon '. . . called for this meeting, so perhaps she'd like to tell us what she has in mind?'

Rhiannon stood up and looked Dominic straight in the eye. 'My associate is better placed to explain the details to you than I am, gentlemen,' she said, her voice as cool as an English frosty morning but her lips curled just enough to make all eyes fall to her mouth. Dominic felt disappointment bite deep into his innards at her very neat little ploy. She'd caught on that something was amiss, damn her!

Jack leaned forward and opened his briefcase, extracting documents which he gave to the man next to him and asked him to pass around. 'As you can see, Miss Grantham's name appears as the owner of the companies ringed, companies which own over twenty-two per cent of Lanai Fruit stock. In addition, if you will look on page three . . .' there was a rustle of paper as eight men turned a page, 'Miss Grantham also owns . . .'

Jack's words went on, smoothly outlining details but Rhiannon did not hear him. Her eyes were unable to escape the man seated at the head of the table. He was dressed in a black suit that sat on his lean frame with classical panache. His shirt was white and contrasted sharply with the darkly tanned skin of his wrists and neck. His tie was a deep, blood red. Black and blood red. And she was in white. She almost laughed aloud. But as the meeting went on she grew colder and colder, which allowed her to sit stiff and emotionless throughout the next nightmare five minutes.

Jack finished outlining the stock report and could feel sweat trickle between his shoulderblades. He knew what was coming and was torn between the urge to get up and drag her out of there before it came and the desire to see what would happen. But more than anything, he wanted to know if he could turn it all around to his advantage. Ben Fielding wouldn't like it if he let his precious little mistress suffer a humiliating setback.

'It looks as if we have a new stockholder,' Dean Gregson, a respected lawyer and longtime board member finally broke the silence, and Jack, aware that Rhiannon was giving him the silent message to go ahead, spoke again.

'Not merely a stockholder, gentlemen. According to your articles, Miss Grantham is entitled to a seat on this board.'

Aware that something had gone badly wrong, Rhiannon was prepared to settle for just that, but Gavin Phelps had different ideas. Burning to humiliate the man who had robbed him of a good deal, he decided he'd never get a better chance than this. 'Considering Miss Grantham's awesome reputation,' he commented, his smug voice making all eyes swing his way in varying degrees of surprise and interest, 'I'd like to motion that not only does she get her seat on the board but that she also takes over as chairman.'

The board table erupted in noise. 'What? Are you mad, Phelps?' 'I don't see . . .' 'Oh, come on!' 'Don't be an asshole.'

'An excellent idea,' Jack said over the commotion, fascinated by it all and wondering at Phelps' motives. He'd been adamant only hours before that he was not selling, and close-lipped as to the reason for his change of mind.

Rhiannon sat silent and watchful, looking lovely and lethal all in one, both seducing and scaring the pants off many of the men now in uproar around her. At the head of the table, Dominic Fairchild remained expressionless, watching them with an aloofness that only those with the upper hand can use with such confidence. Jask asked loudly, 'Is the motion seconded?'

Rhiannon looked across at Tom Fletcher whose head dipped, if possible, even lower. Next to him, Gavin Phelps looked at Dominic and winked cockily.

The men fell silent, as if totally flabbergasted by Jack's presumption, and Dominic looked around the table at the faces of his board. 'What, no one wants to champion the cause of such a lovely lady?' he asked with exaggerated censure. 'Such lack of gallantry,' he accused, lips twitching. 'It looks as if I shall have to come to the board's rescue and salvage our reputation.' He waited until all eyes were on him, save for Rhiannon's, who now stared at the blank wall opposite her. 'I'll second the motion. Shall we vote?' The words were light-hearted, and all the men, save Jack and Gavin Phelps, laughed.

'All those in favour of Miss Grantham becoming chairman . . . er chair*person*,' he corrected himself with a false pleasantness, 'raise your hands.'

Rhiannon didn't look. Instead she leaned forward and slowly began to don her gloves again but doubted that anything could warm her chilled hands except several hours roasting in front of a fire. Again all eyes were on her as she smoothed the silk gloves on, her face as exquisite as when they'd first seen it.

'It looks as if your motion is defeated, Mr Phelps. Which reminds me,' Dominic continued in that smooth voice that she so hated, 'while the board is convened, now is as good a time as any to inform the board that Mr Phelps and Mr Fletcher have signalled to me their intentions to resign . . .'

There was a brief murmuring, which another fingertip gesture from Dominic silenced. 'I have purchased their joint stock. I trust no one objects?'

Rhiannon knew he was looking at her and she reached forward to retrieve her bag, needing to do something, anything, but just sit there. With brief, economical movements she removed a tube of red lipstick and without the aid of a mirror, expertly applied a light layer of colouring on to her lips. The air became tight as all eyes looked at her. Men began to shift uncomfortably on their chairs as they stared, unable to take their eyes off her delicately moving lips as she coated them. To the man at the head of the table, the gesture was one of mocking defiance, but in fact Rhiannon was totally unaware of the stir such a mundane act had caused. Feeling more in control now, she put away the lipstick and snapped shut her bag. Looking around the table she smiled politely, and prayed her voice would not let her down. It didn't.

'Gentlemen, I look forward to joining this board immensely. Mr Gunster will take care of the paperwork,' she turned to the small man next to her. 'I hope that's convenient for you, Mr Secretary?' The man nodded wordlessly. 'Excellent. I'm sure,' she turned and looked at Dominic openly now, and her eyes glittered with either unshed tears or boiling rage, he was not sure which, 'that I can bring fresh and invigorating new ideas to the company.'

In other words, Dominic thought sourly, she's going to cause as much trouble and do as much damage as she damned well can.

'Gentlemen,' Rhiannon said sardonically and walked from the table towards the door, her back ramrod straight and her chin held high.

Philip Pearce let out his breath in a slow exhalation, and then looked up as Dominic got to his feet and followed her. 'Let me walk you out, Miss Grantham,' he said, and held open the door. She tensed at his nearness and he enjoyed the way her body stiffened. In his veins he felt his own blood stir traitorously.

'Thank you,' she accepted coolly. The freezing numbness was beginning to wear off, letting her assess the situation more fully. Thank God she hadn't made a complete fool of herself, although it had been a near thing.

Dominic closed the door on the babbling occupants of the boardroom, and the Secretary's vain attempts to calm the members down and move on to the next item on the agenda.

Rhiannon took a deep breath. 'How did you know?' she asked almost casually as she stepped aside to let a squadron of efficient-looking secretaries disappear into a lecture room.

As they entered the elevator, Dominic pressed the ground-floor button and shrugged eloquently. 'This is my island. Nothing goes on here that I don't know about.'

The small space was closing in on her. He was at her side, robbing her of air, of space, of will, and she could feel her knees threatening to buckle. 'Are your board meetings always that frenetic?' she asked faintly.

'Not usually. But then I've noticed you do add a certain . . . verve . . to my life.'

Rhiannon smiled grimly. 'That is the intention,' she reassured him, almost groaning with relief when the elevator doors opened on to the spacious reception room.

Once outside Rhiannon began to tremble in reaction, and at the realization of her near humiliation. Still, she did have a seat on the board now and the partial victory wasn't something she could afford to ignore. As they walked across the car park to where her limo waited, she said, 'You realize of course that I shall do as much damage to the company as I possibly can?'

'Naturally. But I have the majority of stock – and winning friends on the board will not be easy.'

'We'll see,' she said, wondering if Ben knew any of the board members personally. She had long since come to understand that the world of finance was, in many startling ways, very small.

Dominic felt a strong urge to take her by the scruff of the neck and shake her like a dog shaking a rat. Like all of the men back there he'd been transfixed by that little lipstick ploy she'd pulled.

As the chauffeur got out to open the door, Rhiannon smiled her thanks at him and then – out of the blue – the truth hit her. She looked from Billy Hoki to Dominic and slowly nodded in grudging respect. 'Very clever,' she said simply, looking at Billy without malice and tossing her handbag on to the back seat. 'I should have been more careful.'

Jack walked rapidly towards them, his blue eyes speculatively observing the pair who stared at each other so intently, both simmering with animosity and something more pagan. She and Fairchild were hot, whether they knew it or not. Perhaps things were not well in paradise after all. And how would Ben react to that? And would he blame him, Jack, for not putting a stop to it . . .

Rhiannon was the first to spot him. 'Ah Jack,' she smiled. 'When we get back to the hotel, have an English driver flown over, will you? I think it might be prove to be . . .' she glaced at Billy again who was looking uncomfortable, '. . . prudent.'

Jack caught on in a flash. 'Certainly,' he promised, then got in the back of the car.

'Dinner tonight?' Dominic asked softly, and her head snapped back to look at him incredulously.

'Love to,' she said sweetly, accepting the challenge then sliding into the back seat. 'Eight o'clock. Don't be late.'

'Eight-thirty,' Dominic corrected softly, shutting the car door for her. Through the glass their eyes met, clung and communicated for the merest instant. Then he strode away, his long-legged pace easily eating up the ground as he walked to his Ferrari and slipped behind the wheel. For a moment she felt explosively angry, and then abruptly she relaxed. Looking out of the window to where a ten-year-old green Ford was parked on the side of the road, she nodded to the young man who was seated behind the wheel, then looked pointedly at the Ferrari that was pulling out of the lot.

The man in the Ford was about twenty-two years old and looked like any one of the many blond beach bums who frequented the resorts, except for the equipment that lay on the passenger seat next to him. An expensive camera fitted with a telephoto lens lay glinting in the sun and, as she watched, the driver moved the Ford expertly into the traffic stream three cars back from the Ferrari which roared away into the distance.

'I couldn't warn you in time,' Jack apologized as the limo pulled away.

To his immense surprise she merely shrugged and said tiredly, 'It doesn't matter,' her voice drained and dispirited and the drive back to the Blue Hawaiian was made in gloomy silence. In her suite, she kicked off her shoes, threw down her handbag and collapsed on to the settee.

'Damn him,' she said, her voice flat. 'He had me well and truly set up.'

Jack walked to the bar. 'Martini?'

'Please.'

As he poured, he kept his voice deliberately light and cheerful. For the time being at least, he needed to keep on her good side. 'I do have some good news for you. Your father's old house is finally yours – I received the deeds from the lawyers today.'

'Really? That's great.' She was looking forward to living in the house in which she'd spent the first few months of life. 'Is it habitable?'

'Perfectly.' Jack tossed her a set of keys. 'For the house,' he told her, then held up another, much smaller set. 'For the motorbike.'

Rhiannon smiled widely. 'My Norton's here?'

'Parked downstairs, even as we speak.'

AFTER Jack had left she made her way to the bathroom, rejected the idea of a shower and ran a soothing bath instead, collapsing into it with her third martini, which she then decided not to drink. God help her, she still had this evening and Dominic Fairchild's brand of torture to get through yet, and getting drunk would not help her, no matter how tempting the thought.

The phone was ringing when, half an hour later, she stepped from the bath, and she sighed deeply. Even in the paradise islands of the world, the phone still miraculously rang just when it was most inconvenient. 'Hello,' she snapped grumpily into the receiver after winding, sarong-like, a huge white fluffy bathtowel around her.

'*Aloha*,' a masculine voice said softly. 'I just called to ask if you wanted to go anywhere special tonight?'

'Nowhere with you in tow could possibly ever be special,' she snapped, then could have kicked herself for being so obviously upset.

'My, my, you are in a bad mood. Still, I can understand that,' Dominic commiserated insincerely. 'I'm reading a report right this moment about Jack Gunster. I'm sure he told you he's married, with twin daughters?'

Rhiannon blinked, feeling absurdly betrayed and hurt, and she struggled with herself not to slam down the phone. Don't give him the satisfaction, she warned herself fiercely. Don't do it! Besides, why shouldn't Jack have a family? Just because he'd flirted a little . . . 'Your grapevine *does* hum quickly,' she said sweetly, winding the telephone cord in her hands, wishing that it was his neck.

'Poor little Rhia,' he purred into her ear. 'It just hasn't been your day, has it?'

'I was going to say the same about you,' she rejoined sweetly. 'After all, I have a foot in the door at Lanai's, your spy is out on his ear . . . It's not exactly been one of your bumper days either, has it?'

In her ear, his rich delicious laughter made her shiver violently in reaction. 'Oh, I don't know. For a bad day,' Dominic mused, 'I quite enjoyed it.'

Rhiannon's teeth snapped together. 'Look,' she asked grimly. 'Did you just phone to gloat?'

'Me? Gloat?' The voice was raised in scandalized hurt. 'As if I would. No, I just called to check if you wanted to beg out of our dinner engagement tonight. After all . . .' that tormenting voice lowered once more into bogus sympathy, 'I would understand if you wanted to stay at home and lick your wounds.'

'I'll be ready,' she snapped. 'Eight o'clock. Sharp.'

'Eight-thirty,' the voice corrected gently, and this time she did slam the receiver down. 'I hope it deafens you!' she screamed at the innocuous telephone, breathing deeply. She ran a shaking hand over her forehead, forcing herself to calm down. Walking to her wardrobe she looked over the vast array of clothes hung there, trying to decide on her dress and her strategy for tonight. At the renewed brrrr-brrrr of the phone she marched over and yanked up the receiver. 'Look, you,' she snarled, 'didn't you know that talking on the telephone can ruin your teeth?'

'Teeth?' a bemused voice asked.

'Yes, teeth,' Rhiannon hissed. 'Because if you call me again, you supercilious bastard, I'm going to ram them right down your throat.'

There was a startled silence, then crackles, and then laughter. Rhiannon sank down on to the settee as a voice, undeniably not Dominic Fairchild's, said faintly in her ear, 'I don't think I'll bother to ask how things are going.'

'Ben?' Rhiannon said, her lips parting in a wide, embarrassed smile. 'Oh, Ben, I'm sorry! I thought it was . . . someone else.'

'So I would hope,' Ben said jovially from his yacht in the middle of the Pacific Ocean. 'Things aren't going well, I take it? Never mind, perhaps some fresh input from a third party will help, hmm?'

'I hope so,' she sighed, then laughed drily. 'Oh Ben, it's been one of those days. When will you be here?'

'Hard to say,' Ben said aggravatingly. 'Expect me when you see me.'

'OK,' she said gloomily, suddenly missing him like mad.

'You sound . . .' Ben paused, obviously struggling diplomatically for the right words, and she supplied them for him.

'Down? Blue? Depressed? Miserable? Angry? I'm all of those, and more.'

'Sounds interesting. I shall urge the captain to sail faster. Don't worry, we'll soon have your dragon slain.'

'You'll get no arguments from me!' she said, then wondered why she suddenly felt so cold.

They talked for a few more minutes then said goodbye. She felt better knowing she'd soon have Ben's company for as long as his vacation-cum-business-stopover lasted, and knew she'd been in need of cheering up. Yet she couldn't help but notice that an ominous chill had crept into her bones. It was almost as if . . . she was afraid of something Ben might do. But that was ridiculous! All Ben wanted to do was what she herself had instigated and fiercely wanted. Namely, *to give Dominic Fairchild a taste of his own medicine.*

Shrugging off the feeling of anxiety, she walked to her open wardrobe doors and pushed back the garments on the rails, her face thoughtful as her eyes fell on one particular outfit. Her hand paused.

Well, why not? she thought, a mischievous smile lighting up her face as she pulled it from the rack.

Yes. Why the hell not?

Chapter 23

'Is this it?' Odessa Jago asked as her husband pulled their Mercedes into the parking space opposite the John Dominis restaurant.

'This is it – a seafood-lover's paradise.' He smiled but his thoughts were miles away. Vienna had moved out of the old woman's house but he was meeting the ex-cop he'd hired to find her new address tonight. Nevertheless, he was worried. He didn't like being out of touch, even for a moment, not knowing what she was doing and where she was. Or, most importantly, who she was with.

Since they'd flown in three days ago, staying at a beach-house belonging to a friend of hers, Odessa had seen a vast change in her husband, one that she liked enormously. There was an added glow in his eyes, a more eager spring in his step, a readier smile on his face. They made a striking couple as they entered the restaurant and she felt a glow of pride and smug possessiveness as eyes turned their way. The menu, as he'd promised, was extensive, imaginative and delicious. He opted for the mussel cocktails, followed by lobster patties and mayonnaise of turbot. Sipping a pre-dinner Martini, she slipped off her high-heeled shoe and ran her toes up his shin. 'What do you really think of that last house we saw?' she asked and he bit back a sigh. She'd been on about the damned house all afternoon.

'I think it's perfect for us – but the final choice has to be yours. You're the one who'll be living in it, holding parties there . . . sleeping there.'

'I like the sound of that,' she purred. 'I'll call the agent tomorrow then, and tell him we'll take it.'

'Here – try this,' Richard said, spooning a piece of delicious mussel into her mouth, forcing himself to smile tenderly as he did so. He'd arranged to call the cop later this evening and time was dragging.

'*Hmmmm.* Why does somebody else's food always taste better than one's own?'

Richard shrugged. 'It's a mystery.'

'Talking of which, I've found out who was responsible for your exile. Conrad Mynheer was a pal of Daddy's way back in the old days. He works in City Hall now. In fact, Jonathon says he's tipped to be the next Mayor. Isn't it funny how small the world is? Anyway, he says it was a man called Dominic Fairchild. Apparently he's the bigwig around here ... Richard?'

Richard was staring at her as if she'd suddenly broken out in warts. He shook his head to clear it. 'Bigwig is the understatement of the year. Dominic Fairchild? Are you sure?'

'Positive. Mynheer was pulling my leg. Told me he was some kind of prince and richer than Daddy!'

'He's right – on both counts,' Richard said shortly. It didn't make sense. Why would Fairchild want him off the island? True, the Hawaiian punk sang for him but that wasn't enough, surely?

'A real prince? I didn't think any of them still existed,' Odessa said, more and more intrigued as she watched her husband's dazed face fall into a frown. 'Do you . . .' she began then stopped as Richard's eyes sharpened on the couple just walking through the door.

'Well, well, well,' he drawled coldly. 'Speak of the devil.'

Odessa turned in her seat, her eyes immediately finding the man who towered above all the others and slowly whistled between her lips. He sure was good-looking. Mynheer had said Dominic was in his late forties, but this hunk looked no more than thirty-five, tops. As the couple passed their table Odessa took a long female look at his date, and had to admit she was easily the most beautiful woman she had ever seen. Dressed in silver lamé that shimmered in every light, she was tall and slender but well-curved, graceful and perfectly formed. Her dress-top consisted of two wide bands of material that criss-crossed from an elongated diamond-shaped waistband over her breasts, leaving the sides of them exposed and tying behind the nape of her neck. Silver ribbons fell provocatively down a bare back where the dress was cut cleverly to hug her rounded bottom. The girl's hair was raven-black and shaped on her head in a high, classic chignon. Emerald and diamond earrings dangled from small ears, a perfect match for startlingly green eyes.

'He's very handsome. And he certainly doesn't stint on himself, does he?' Odessa commented waspishly, and Richard, who had been half-turned in his chair to get a better look at them, turned back now and shrugged.

'Don't forget, he's the one who hounded me out of paradise.'

'True. And if he tries anything again I'm going to stick Jonathon on to him so fast he won't even see him move until it's too late.'

Richard could not see Hannel doing him any favours. The man had looked like he was facing his own firing squad when he'd sat in the church, watching them getting married.

'That couple seem rather interested in us,' Rhiannon commented briefly, and Dominic turned to glance over his shoulder, his face tightening as Richard Jago looked up and their eyes met. Rhiannon immediately sensed the crackle of anger between the two men. Something was up – she could smell it. 'Who are they?' she asked with the utmost non-chalance.

Dominic shrugged. 'No one important,' he said dismissively, opening the menu and pretending to read the contents.

Rhiannon said no more but ate her dinner with appetite.

'Feeling less grumpy now?' he asked, smiling at her over the rim of his bourbon and ice. He was wearing black again, this time an evening suit that fitted his lean body with perfectly tailored elegance.

'I haven't been at all grumpy,' she denied. 'I have the boutiques, and a foot in the door at Lanai.'

'But not control of the whole company like you were expecting,' he quickly stuck the knife in. 'I told you things had changed. It's a pity you're being so stubborn,' he mused. 'Despite what you may think, I won't enjoy myself when I scatter your broken bones all over the islands.' His silky, almost casual tone belied the savagery of his words. She reached for her own drink, looking at him over its rim and, when their eyes met her stomach lurched in a primitive reaction.

'Really?' she commiserated, tasting her excellent wine before looking him straight in the eye. 'Because I'm rather enjoying breaking your bones.' She stressed the present tense slightly, reminding him that whilst he only dreamed of her destruction, she was actively causing his. His pupils dilated and his lips curled, and she felt her body quiver.

Three tables distant, Odessa pushed her plate away, feeling full and a little annoyed. She sensed she'd lost Richard's attention and she didn't like it. 'Shall we go?'

Richard shrugged. 'Why not. Unless you'd like dessert?'

Odessa smiled whimsically. 'I have dessert in mind,' she said slowly, 'but not of the ice-cream variety.'

'Uh-huh,' he said with what he hoped sounded like feverish anticipation as he beckoned the waiter and paid the bill. It was marginally easier to weather their lovemaking when she made all the moves, which she was very fond of doing. Then all he had to do was lie back, close his eyes and pretend the hands and lips that were all over him belonged to Vienna.

Rhiannon watched the couple leave but said nothing. Dominic noticed their absence only when a waiter came to ask them if they wanted dessert. Meeting Rhiannon's mocking, knowing eyes. Dominic felt his lips twitch reluctantly. 'The lady will have the raspberry fool and I'll have the *bombe surprise*.' Rhiannon couldn't help laughing softly at his artful message, and raising their glasses they touched them together in a mutual salute.

THE Neal Blaisdell Centre boasted a theatre with two thousand seats and a concert hall with an eight-thousand-seat arena. Rhiannon looked about her in open admiration. Getting tickets at such short notice had probably been easy for him, but she couldn't help being impressed and just a little honoured that he'd gone to so much trouble. 'Who's playing?' she asked as they walked up the wide steps amidst the genteel crowd, waiting for her answer as Dominic purchased a programme.

'The London Philharmonic.'

'Really?' Rhiannon asked, totally surprised. 'I didn't know they were on tour.' She shrugged off his hand as he guided her up the carpeted steps to a private box and, as she sat down she was conscious that below, far more faces looked up at them than at the still-curtained stage.

'What are they playing?'

'The Dvořák in E and a selection of other classics.'

The lights began to dim, the conductor took the podium and the curtains parted to reveal the huge orchestra. The great hall fell totally silent and Rhiannon almost forgot the man by her side as the music began. Almost, but not quite, for the music seemed to speak to them. The first movement of Dvořák's Symphony No. 9 in E Minor seemed to echo the sense of homecoming she'd felt on setting foot on Hawaiian soil, its soothing music lulling her into a cruelly false sense of security, for the next item was an expressive melody from Tchaikovsky's *Romeo and Juliet*. The thought of those doomed lovers released in Rhiannon all the repressed doubts that had begun to plague her. In her restlessness, her every sense became attuned to the man seated next to her. The way his tall shadow fell over her lap. The scent of his aftershave. When he moved she could hear the rustle of his clothes and when he breathed she could see out of the corner of her eyes his upper torso moving rhythmically.

When the interval finally came she let out a breath in relief, like one who'd just survive torture, and accepted his offer of a drink. She remained in her seat, too drained to move then looked up into his eyes as she took the glass from him. Mistake. Bad, bad mistake. For long, endless moments they looked at each other, aware of a mysterious force that mocked their carefully cultivated hatred of each other, that laughed at their puny efforts to fight each other. Until that moment, Rhiannon had never come face to face with Fate, but in that second when their hands touched and an anonymous crowd murmured below them, she confronted its power and was terrified.

Dominic resumed his seat, breathing erratically. If I had any sense at all, he thought grimly, I'd run like hell. Right now, anywhere in the world. Canada, New Zealand, Borneo. Anywhere, as long as it was half a world away from her.

The curtains then parted to reveal a world-famous choir,

who raised their voices with the orchestra to sing the famous extract 'Prima Verve' from *Carmina Burana*; the music and voices started low but threatening, like a sea before a storm, then slowly rose to a crescendo of almost demonic volume and power. The music made Rhiannon's hands shake, the emotion suffocating her. She had to get out of there! She stood up blindly as the final chords died away and applause erupted all around them.

Outside, Dominic watched her in silence for a moment, then said: 'Would you like to go for a walk?'

Rhiannon laughed hollowly. 'I want to run.' She echoed his own earlier thoughts with eerie fatalism. 'But I'll settle for a walk.'

'OK. I know a place . . . it's quite far away, though.'

That suited her just fine, for never had she felt so badly in need of time to think and regain her lost balance. As they drove they made polite conversation, avoiding all but the most trivial of topics, until he finally parked on the side of a deserted road and pointed to a narrow, overgrown path that led into a wood. 'It's through there,' he said, voice strangely awed. 'The most magical place in the world.'

The night air was welcome after the enclosed concert hall and equally claustrophobic car, and Rhiannon quickly found the path, aided by the moon which was high and full in the sky. It was midnight, and patterns of moonshadow danced on them as they walked beneath the trees' canopy. 'Where are we?' she asked quietly as some creature rustled in the undergrowth to her left, and Dominic's voice behind her, quiet and deep, sounded as much a natural noise of the night as those others around her.

'Sacred Falls Park.'

A few minutes later, a clearing in the bushes revealed a scene so idyllic and mystically enchanted that she felt like crying. From a rock about thirty feet high a cascade of silver water fell into a still pool, its silver stream sparkling in the moonlight. Cool dew-wet grass tickled her ankles as she walked towards it, aware of the humid air on her skin. Dominic watched her stop at the pool's edge and look up into the sky, and felt drugged. Her dress, sparkling silver, seemed a human version of the waterfall, her eyes as she turned to look at him, the green equivalent of the grass. Her hair, as black as the midnight sky above them, her skin the creamy colour of the mella flowers that bloomed all around, their rich fragrance scenting the air.

Stories of ancient times wafted into his memory. According to old Hawaiian law, if a condemned man managed to reach certain designated and sacred places, he was pardoned for his crime and allowed to live free without the fear of punishment. He wanted her so badly, even knowing he would have to pay for it dearly: could he escape the consequences of his desire here?

As he walked towards her on silent feet, the air around them fell into stillness. She watched his hand as it rose to caress her cheek and her eyes closed helplessly as his fingers brushed her skin. Tipping her head back he lowered his mouth to hers. Yearningly with a force that paid no heed to common sense, her fingers clutched his back with passionate desperation, her nails sending tiny lines of electricity through his flesh where they gouged compulsively.

Then his mouth left her clinging lips with a moaning sigh and he dipped his head lower, his lips on her throat, his black hair feeling like silk on her jaw. The sensation of his warm, sipping, drugging kisses slowly travelling lower and lower made her knees threaten to buckle, and her hands dug ever-more painfully into his shoulders.

Desire was hypnotic, passion was drugging, turning the night into a kaleidoscope of silver stars, sparkling water and encircling, black trees. She was not surprised to feel her bare back press on to the cool grass or his weight pinioning her to the ground. Her fingers slipped under his jacket and roved up his chest to shrug the material from his shoulders, leaving it rucked around his back. Transferring her attention to the buttons of his shirt, they strained and then broke as her fingers rent the material apart in their urgent, impatient quest for skin.

Dominic groaned, closing his eyes as she lifted her head from the earth, her lips like tiny suckers on his skin, tasting and licking him, sliding to his left nipple with unerring accuracy and curling around his hard button of flesh, nipping almost painfully. Either side of her head his hands dug into the ground, tearing aside the grass, his fingernails embedded in the cloying brown earth as his body shuddered in terrifying reaction, the strength of it bringing back his sanity.

Rolling off her and lithely getting to his feet, he left her feeling stunned and cold. Shrugging his jacket into position, his back was turned towards her as he ran badly shaking fingers through his hair. 'I must be mad!' he yelled into that enchanted, treacherous clearing with such hopelessness that Rhiannon flinched and slowly dragged herself to her feet.

'I must be insane,' he said more quietly. 'After all that Graham did to me . . .'

'After what *he* did to *you*?' she queried, her voice harsh and hysterically high now that shock was wearing off and shame was taking its place. 'What could he possibly have done to *you*?'

Dominic shook his head and swung around to face her, ironic laughter grating painfully from deep within him. 'If only you knew,' he said simply, then shuddered. 'No – thank God you don't.'

'He did nothing to you,' Rhiannon spat. 'He's the one who's dead. And you killed him!' she accused, fighting back her own feelings of guilt over her less than ideal relationship with her father. Her lipstick was smudged, and one of the silver bands that covered her breast was askew, not quite revealing the nipple.

He shook his head and turned away, leaning wearily against a tree trunk.

Rhiannon dragged the pins from her hair and shook it free, fingercombing it as she breathed deeply, trying to regain some semblance of control. Readjusting the bodice of her gown, she looked up just in time to see him wiping her lipstick from his lips with the back of his hand, and something inside her snapped. The next instant she launched herself at him. 'You bastard!' she screamed, her nails catching him in a vicious swipe across his chest where his shirt still gaped open. Her teeth, savage and sharp, sank into the hand he'd raised to hold her off and he swore sharply in Hawaiian. Spinning her around he rammed his knee in the bend of her back, forcing her first on to her knees and then fully on to the ground where she thrashed in bitter rage, oblivious to the pain. Finally she lay quiet, all emotion spent, her cheek pressed to the cool grass where silent, hot tears slid unnoticed into the stems.

Then slowly, with arms that shook, she levered herself off the ground, her mind floundering in circles. Confusion gave way to pain and a sudden, ugly fear. The next moment she began to run.

Greenery lashed against her arms and face as she plunged recklessly ahead, her breath beginning to tear painfully from her lungs. She could hear him behind her, getting closer and closer and then she was on the road. She literally flung herself into the car, her fingers fumbling with the keys.

'Oh no, you don't!' Dominic snarled and she screamed as his hand shot through the open window and snatched the keys from her. Bundling her into the passenger seat he got into the car, slamming the door shut. For a long moment they sat in a tense silence, and then he gunned the engine and drove at gut-churning speed to Honolulu where he pulled into the hotel's well-lit car-park and turned off the ignition. Still without speaking a word and studiously avoiding eye-contact they walked to the elevator, and from there into the lobby.

At the desk she managed a trembling smile. 'Do you think you can have my bill prepared, please? I'll be moving out in the morning.'

'Certainly Miss Granth ... am.' The pause came when Dominic began a slow sarcastic handclap that had a middle-aged couple on the way out to a casino staring at them curiously.

'Don't get your hopes up,' she warned him, feeling unbearably weary. 'I'm only moving out as far as my new house. Well, not so new house, actually. You might know it. It's Dad's old place.'

THE bag of groceries was heavy, and Vienna was grateful to dump it in the boot of her small car, a present from Farron. 'Not exactly the car of a rich heiress,' she'd teased as he'd led her to the second-hand, lovingly preserved Buick. 'But I love it.'

As she closed the boot, a man got into a battered Volkswagen Beetle several cars behind her, pulling out and following her as she drove home. There, parked discreetly under a shady tree, Richard Jago watched the Buick stop, his hands tightening on the wheel as Vienna got out. Waiting until she was inside, he left the car and crossed the road, walking quickly up the driveway.

So *he's* back, the man inside the Beetle thought, his eyes narrowing thoughtfully. Now that was interesting. Very interesting indeed. Carefully and quietly he got out of the car and made his way through a small gate in the back. He'd checked the layout thoroughly beforehand and as he moved, his slight frame left no footprints to testify to his presence. He was a pro. Slinking along the side of the hedges he slowly made his way to the patio windows, flattening himself against the wall and peering around into the room. The girl was in the kitchen putting away groceries.

Vienna heard the tuneful tones of the doorbell and put the jar of coffee she had in her hand on to the kitchen counter top before opening the front door.

'Hello Vienna,' Richard said softly.

'Hello,' she responded automatically, her hand clutching the door in acute misery and shock. How had he found her?

'Can I come in?'

'No,' she said sharply, suddenly pulling herself together. 'What are you doing here, Richard?' She licked her lips in an anxious gesture, looking behind her but seeing only bright sunshine and an empty, lovely garden.

'You look surprised to see me,' he said, moving his large bulk forward, giving her no choice but to back away and let him in.

'I am,' she said, leaving the door open and hovering nervously a good three feet behind him as he looked around the luxurious interior.

'I don't see why.' When he finally turned to look at her, his face was wearing that smile again; that gentle, pleading, ruthless smile that had once fooled her so completely. 'It's a nice place you have here.'

'It's Mr Fairchild's,' she said, relieved that the conversation was so normal. 'I live here as part of my wages. I work for him. I mean, as housekeeper. For his guests. There are guests here at the moment,' she lied, knowing she was talking too much and that her words were jerking out of her in unnaturally staccato sentences.

The man outside on the patio frowned. They were tiptoeing around each other like dancing boxers. Go on, he urged malevolently. Give it to her.

Richard walked to a high, upholstered leather couch and sat down. 'I wouldn't mind a drink.'

'Of course.' She stopped rubbing her fingers nervously together and cleared her throat. 'What would you like?'

'You know my favourite.'

She said nothing but went quickly to the bar and poured him a tumbler of chilled pineapple juice, adding to it a liberal dash of Malibu. Walking towards him she extended the drink as far as she could and backed of the moment he took it from her. 'Thanks,' he said mildly and took a sip. He looked relaxed and normal, but she yearned for Farron to come walking through the open door and hold her in his arms, chasing away all the bad things . . .

'I'm glad you're here actually,' she said, walking to her handbag and extracting a chequebook. 'It's the money I owe you,' she said awkwardly, writing out a hasty cheque and pressing it into his palm. 'I never have felt right about you leaving, and me still owing you money.'

Richard let the cheque fall to the floor. 'You owe me more than that, Vienna,' he said softly, shaking his head. 'Much more.'

'No!' she denied sharply, moving back and tensing visibly as he stood up and began to walk towards her. She turned rapidly, making for the conservatory where the illusion of freedom lay behind the glass walls and the man hiding there scrambled back and around the house, cursing as he furtively made his way back to his car.

'I owe you nothing more,' she said, opening the window and wondering how far it was across the lawn. Could she slip out without him catching her?

'Vienna.' She winced as his large hands fastened around her

shoulders and dragged her towards him; there was an insane look in his eyes. She began to struggle in earnest.

'No, no!' she moaned as he bent towards her, a look of disgust on her face, but all he did was let his lips slide along her cheek. She struggled again but was no match for his immense bulk or strength, and coloured lights flashed across her vision as his arms squeezed around her like the killing coils of an anaconda. Thinking she might pass out if he kept it up, she lay still in his arms, her head thrown back and hanging to one side as she breathed in deeply. His hold on her immediately lessened as she lay passive in his arms. Unbelievably he mistook her capitulation for consent, and smiled, his hand sliding around her cheek to turn her face towards him.

'I knew you would miss me,' he murmured, leaning forward to kiss her.

His nearness, the touch of his breath and the scent of his body was more than she could bear. Groping behind her she found a pile of letters and her fingers closed around a carved letter opener. Bringing it quickly around, knowing only that she wanted his filthy hands off her, she sliced the instrument across the hand that still held her cheek, cutting him in a short, deep wound. His hand jerked back as he recoiled instinctively and she took quick advantage of his retreat to bring the bloodied weapon between them. Richard stared down at his hand, bleeding and throbbing, his face totally stupefied.

'My hand,' he said blankly. 'You know I have to be careful of my hands.'

At his stricken words, Vienna felt nausea hit her. Oh God, he was a surgeon! How could she have forgotten? 'I'm sorry,' she gasped, shaking her head, tears coming into her eyes. 'But you . . . *I love Farron!*' she screamed at him, goaded beyond endurance. 'Why can't you understand that? I never loved you – never!'

Richard touched his wound with a fingertip, his mind snapping into focus as her words ricocheted like bullets round his head. Following his movements as if hypnotised, she looked once again at his bleeding hand then down at the letter opener, gleaming wet with his blood. Appalled, she dropped it. There had been a knife there too, in that dark back alley that smelled of death and fear. A glint of a knife in a grubby light, and a girl screaming. She stared down at the bloodied thing now lying on the thick blue carpet and then back at Richard, shaking her head in nameless fear, her eyes glazed and confused.

Richard's clever, opportunistic brain leapt into overdrive. Reaching into his pocket for a handkerchief, he bound his hand. 'So you *are* capable of great violence,' he muttered, as if she'd just confirmed something he'd long since suspected. 'I always knew, but I . . .' He looked at her cautiously then slowly bent down and gingerly picked up the instrument. 'I'll keep this,' he said in a voice an adult might use to a retarded child. 'All right?'

She found herself nodding. 'I'm not violent,' she denied desperately, her voice hollow. 'I'm not. I just thought you were going to hurt me. You scared me,' she accused, trying to convince herself. She felt sick – ill. He was so sure she was unbalanced. He'd always been sure. Why hadn't she guessed? All she wanted was some quiet corner where she could curl up and die.

Richard shook his head sadly. 'But you know I love you. You know I would never do anything to hurt you.'

She looked at him pleadingly but still backed away. Yes, it was true – she knew he loved her. God, what had she done? The old nameless fear was back again. What did she know of herself really? She could be anything . . . anyone. She could have done anything.

'Vienna,' Richard said, casting his mind back for ammunition and finding it with a flash of inspiration. 'Vienna,' he said again, as if searching for the right words, 'the police found a body on the beach a little while ago. A man who'd been in the water since around the time when you lost your memory . . .'

'No,' she said, her voice cracking. '*No.*' The final word was a groan of pure pain because she did remember hearing that news item on the radio. And she did remember the chill of fear that had her bent double over the sink, retching painfully into the aluminium bowl as Farron had shaved in the bathroom.

'Vienna. Listen to me. I can look after you. I'm a doctor, I know about these things . . .'

But Vienna was already shaking her head. 'Not again,' she vowed. 'No matter what, never again! Get out of here, Richard,' she warned him, her voice stronger now, 'before Farron comes home.' Then she lifted up her chin and, firmly quashing the hysteria that bubbled within her, told him, her voice ringing out with pride and love: 'We're living together here.'

Richard's face transformed itself into a sneer, produced more from heartache than disgust. 'I know,' he spat out the words. 'But I'd forgive you even that. I'd forgive you anything,' he said sadly, and meant it. 'I wonder if your Hawaiian singer-boy could say the same?' He closed his eyes briefly, and then snapped them open, holding out his left hand to her. 'I've already forgiven you for so much,' he said simply, but the flash of gold on his hand distracted her and she stared at the ring on his finger dumbly for a few seconds.

'You're married!' she said disbelievingly.

'She means nothing to me,' he reassured her quickly. 'Nothing. She's rich, that's all, and I needed her to get back here, to get back to you. I'll divorce her – you know it's only you I love. I'll get a good settlement and we can move from here to another island. The Seychelles, perhaps.'

'I don't believe you,' Vienna said. 'I just don't believe you could be so coldhearted. What do I have to say to make you understand?' she finally shouted, frustration taking over from fear. 'It's Farron I love, not you. It was never you. I wish you hadn't been my doctor in the first place!'

'Don't say that,' he roared, his powerful voice like an explosion in the quiet house, making her jump half out of her skin. 'This is your last chance,' he warned her. 'Your very last chance If I can't have you, no one will.'

'Oh please,' Vienna said scornfully. 'Spare me that, at least. Get out of here, Richard, before I call the police.'

'Call them. I'm sure they'll be interested in what you know about that murdered man.'

'I know nothing about him,' she said, then laughed hysterically. 'I can't *remember anything* – as you well know!'

He stared at her for a long moment, thinking about the promise he'd made to himself if he couldn't persuade her. He didn't want to do it, though. 'Don't make me destroy you,' he pleaded, his face crumpling. 'Don't, please.'

'If you don't leave,' she warned, taking a deep breath, 'I'm going to call your wife and tell her.'

'You've changed,' he said, his voice weak now with despair. 'You've changed.'

'I'm sorry,' she said softly. 'But that's the way it is.'

'You will be sorry,' he corrected her. 'Oh Vienna, you will be.' He turned and stumbled out of the house, staggering across the road as if drunk, unaware that brown eyes watched him with a mixture of curiosity and contempt. What a wimp, the Beetle driver thought, ducking to lie across the front two seats of his car as Richard's Mercedes pulled out of the trees and passed him. He sat up again, lit a cigarette and grunted in scornful laughter, his eyes resting thoughtfully on the rooftop of the house behind the hedges.

The job had seemed like a godsend at first, but he was beginning to grow bored with all the waiting. Soon, he thought. Soon . . .

Chapter 24

'The figures are in on the first week at Pearlbridge and they're great,' was the first thing Rhiannon said to Clarice that morning when the two women met amidst the chaos of a shop still in the throes of change. Despite the mess, the boutique showed signs of what was to come. Oystershell pink paint gleamed on the walls whilst white-coated decorators set up planks in preparation for painting the ceiling a soothing lilac.

'Gawd, the girls are just gonna flip over this,' Clarice declared laughingly as she read the report, and Rhiannon nodded, enjoying the way her friend elongated the last word of every sentence she uttered.

'With good reason. You certainly pulled it off.'

'Let's go into the office,' Clarice suggested, watching suspiciously as lilac paint began to be rolled on to the ceiling. It was supposed to be non-drip, but she was taking no chances. In the office three girls were poring over design plans and looked up as Clarice whooped, 'Pearlbridge is a success, girls.' But Clarice knew as well as Rhiannon that the figures were hardly a guarantee of success; however, keeping up enthusiasm and confidence was very important to these untried girls who were obviously nervous and worried about their first big break. 'Gina and Kiluni are settling in well over there,' she continued, 'but it's still up to us to work the same miracle here.'

'Are those the lines?' Rhiannon asked curiously.

'Yes, Miss Grantham.' Hali, a lovely, willow-slim Japanese girl with enormous black eyes, nodded shyly and moved aside for her to take a better look. Squeezing behind Yoki, until recently an art student, she studied them hard.

'These are good,' she said sincerely. Shorts, halter-tops and sundresses were the order of the day, but mix-matched accessories that could transform a look by a simple addition, subtraction or inside-out design added a touch of novely that would immediately impress the teenage girl who, above all, worshipped experimentation. 'I think it'd be a good idea to sell cosmetics here, too – perhaps hire a trained beautician who can make up some sketches of special ideas for some of the more outrageous outfits,' Rhiannon said, looking around, and then adding deliberately, 'What do you think?'

Clarice kept silent, forcing the girls to do the talking.

'I think it's a good idea,' Hali finally said, her long black hair rippling as she nodded her head. 'My little sister is always pinching my make-up.'

After the laughter eased, Rhiannon said, 'Good – that's settled, then. And whatever you do, don't forget you're designers now. Be creative! And this is not Liliha any more,' she added grimly. 'We're not pandering to the rich, like my predecessor,' her voice chilled very obviously, 'but to working-class people who come here for a holiday away from driving taxis or working in factories.'

'Er, honey, can I talk to you outside a moment? About the business end of things?' Clarice asked as the girls looked at each other in miserable silence.

Once more amidst the nauseating smell of paint, Rhiannon said, 'What's wrong? Are you having trouble with that accountant? Because if so, you hired him so you can fire . . .'

'The accountant's just fine,' Clarice interrupted. 'It's you I want to talk about. You were doing so well in there with those girls, but then you went and blew it. Look,' she began earnestly. 'You must realize that these girls all worked for Dominic before working for you. And without exception they all like and respect him. He even paid for Hali's mother to be treated by a plastic surgeon when her face was burned in a factory fire a couple of years ago.'

Rhiannon went pale. 'Is she all right?'

'Oh, yes. Thanks to the surgeon Dominic flew over from Switzerland her face isn't even discoloured.'

Rhiannon looked away to absently watch a roller slowly coating the ceiling above her. 'I don't believe it,' she said at last, and Clarice clicked her tongue impatiently.

'You just don't *want* to believe it, and that's something different altogether. If you begin to see for yourself that Dominic Fairchild is not the big bad wolf you want him to be

'. . . Oh, I'm sorry. All I'm saying is that you should maybe cut out the criticism in front of the girls.'

'It was me who gave them the chance to break into the designing world,' Rhiannon snapped, 'not their precious Dominic.'

'I know, honey,' Clarice soothed. 'You don't have to convince me. I'm on your side, remember? I'm just saying that Hali especially adores the man. And what's more, I don't think that you believe he's really a blackhearted monster any more.'

'Now there you're wrong,' Rhiannon denied, stabbing a finger at her. 'Dead wrong.'

Clarice shook her head. 'The sparks sure do fly when you two get together, but I'm not certain they're for the reason you think they are. When you two meet,' Clarice blew out her cheeks, 'hoowee! You can *feel* the electricity in the air — pagan, if you know what I mean?'

'Bullshit,' Rhiannon dismissed inelegantly. 'The man may have saved Hali's mother's face, but he killed my father. And there's no way he's going to get away with it.'

Clarice stared at her, her jaw hanging open. '*Killed*? I had no idea. I can't believe it,' she said slowly. 'Are you sure, Rhiannon?'

Rhiannon gave her a speaking glance.

Clarice looked miserable and argumentative, but spotting something over her employer's shoulder, she was promptly distracted. 'Isn't that your gorgeous friend?'

Rhiannon turned and saw Jack beckoning outside the window. 'Yes, I have to go. Look Clarice, I'd appreciate it if you just forgot what I said.'

'What was that, honey?' Clarice's face was a blank mask. Rhiannon laughed, stepping forward to hug her in a spontaneous gesture of gratitude and friendship, one that Clarice immediately reciprocated.

'Now,' Rhiannon said decisively. 'About the girls . . .'

'Don't worry.' Clarice backed away. 'I'll sing your praises to high heaven.'

'Not that far, I hope! See you later, Clarice. You're doing a wonderful job.'

'So you keep saying!'

'I'll keep in touch. Bye!'

'Bye. If you and that gorgeous friend of yours are going out to chow, you ought to try the crêpes at L'Auberge. I hear they're just outta sight.'

THE crêpes at L'Auberge really were superb. Artfully using her fork-edge to spear a piece of crêpe stuffed with a mixture of raspberries, almonds and a smidgeon of grated mandarin rind, Rhiannon summed up the contents of the information Jack had brought her. 'So Dominic definitely was behind this Jago character getting forced off the islands.'

'Definitely.'

'Hmmm. I think we saw him and his wife at a restaurant the other night. The pictures you managed to get on Jago weren't all that clear, but it certainly looked like the same man to me.'

'I've got an updated report on him. He almost certainly married this Odessa Vance for her money. By all accounts, he gave the amnesiac woman a very bad time when their relationship turned sour.'

Rhiannon nodded, her own appetite deserting her at mention of the plucky blonde girl she'd met only briefly but who'd had such a profound impact on her. She didn't like the thought of dealing with a man who had hurt her.

'We might make use of him,' Jack mused, his blue eyes looking thoughtful. 'Any enemy of Dominic's is a potential ally for us,' he added.

'True. But it might be better to wait until we can find out what's going on. So far we've come up with no possible connection between Fairchild and Jago,' she put in quickly. 'Besides, I think it has more to do with the singer, Farron Manikuuna. I'm sure of it.'

'Yes,' Jack said, thinking about the last, vague report from their private investigator. 'I'm sure you're right. Manikuuna does seem to be the key.'

'What have you heard?'

'Nothing concrete. Nothing even substantiated. Just very vague rumours. You'll be the first to know when I have something. Anyway, getting back to Jago. He has a reputation for . . . not living off women exactly, but certainly supplementing his lifestyle at their expense.'

'I can imagine,' she said, bringing to mind the image of the man in the restaurant. She'd know more about him once she'd spoken to him and sized him up from first-hand experience. 'Arrange a meeting between Dr Jago and myself,' she requested flatly and then wondered if it was all worth it.

THE coffee doesn't get any better, Perry Clements thought ruefully as he drained his polystyrene cup. Swivelling in his chair he neatly and accurately threw it into the galvanized tin waste basket in one corner of the tiny office. His desk was battered but its surface, unlike those depicted in the many TV cop shows, which he hated with a passion, was clean and tidy. Pens and pencils clustered in a wooden beaker made for him by his eldest son Jake in woodwork class. A telephone sat on the right-hand corner, and in the left was a picture of his wife Carla. The case file of his most recent investigation, the John Doe washed up on the beach, sat open in front of him. Around him, books on law, criminology and psychology sat on shelves Jake had proudly erected for him less than a year ago, whilst a pot plant, lovingly tended by a green-fingered Carla, now wilted and slowly died on the window-ledge that overlooked the busy streets below. For years his colleagues and juniors had watched him take out the pathetic remains of dead plants, only to come in the next day with a doomed new one to take its place. 'It's Carla's traffic-cop mentality,' Joe Hines, his now-dead partner, had told everyone.

Perry smiled now in remembrance of the first time he'd met his wife. She'd given him a ticket, and was just placing it under his windscreen-wiper when he'd come dashing out of the bookstore. The sight of a perfect pair of legs clad in black stockings with a pristine straight seam down the back of her calves had transfixed him. She'd turned, flushed from the warm sunshine and her restricting uniform. Looking up at him with big grey eyes it had been love at first sight, but she'd still given him the ticket! The smile left his face quickly as the glass-fronted door opened and Rolnalski, an up-and-coming detective, walked in. 'You were right, Lieutenant.'

'That's nice to know,' Perry said mildly. 'But about what exactly?'

Rolnalski grinned at the gently sarcastic response, revealing crooked teeth. 'The M.E. just confirmed it. It was an anchor tattoo on John Doe's forearm.'

Perry nodded. He'd gone down to the morgue to inspect the body thoroughly and discovered a discoloured shape on its arm. That it was an anchor had been a guess more than anything. 'You've checked with the port authorities for crew listings of all ships docked between October and December last?' He took the proffered wad of computerized paper from his subordinate and glanced at the top sheet. The strident ringing of the telephone interrupted him. 'Clements here. Hi, Carla. What's up?'

Rolnalski looked away, his eyes falling on the suffering plant in the window. Too much sun, he thought but he, like everyone else, never bothered to say anything. No matter what the Lieutenant did, plants died on him.

'It's Sally's play tonight,' Carla's voice informed her husband over the wire, sounding unusually harassed. 'And the damned car's broken down.'

'I'll fix it when I get home.'

'But I need it this afternoon. I promised the Principal I would collect the costumes from Mrs Myers' and I'm supposed to be collecting the refreshments from Gilly's at three.'

'Borrow Pete's. He's on nights, so he won't be needing it till seven.'

'You know I hate borrowing from the neighbours. It's so . . . tacky.'

'What do you want?' Perry asked, smiling. 'To be tacky or take a bunny suit, five fox-heads and a Little Bo Peep outfit on the bus?'

'Tacky,' Carla said shortly, and hung up. Laughing Perry put the phone back and continued looking over the list of names.

'There must be a hundred on here. Hmm . . . now there's an interesting coincidence,' Perry commented thoughtfully. 'Gary Lyons. Left the *Philadelphia* in November, giving the

Princess Liliha Hotel up in Waimea as his next job. Doesn't that belong to the Hawaiian fellow who owns the Blue Hawaiian?'

'Dominic Fairchild – yes sir.'

Perry nodded. A mere coincidence, yes, and they happened much more often in his line of work than people thought. Still . . . 'I'll take this one,' Perry decided, picking up his dark blue tie from where it hung on the back of his chair and putting it on. 'Give me the ideal excuse to get out of here and sample a bit of the high-life.'

WHEN Perry was shown into Dominic's office and introduced himself, he came straight to the point. 'It's about the body that was washed up on the beach several days ago. It's possible, but by no means certain, that he may have been one of your ex-employees at the Princess Liliha Hotel.' He watched the man for signs of reaction, seeing only the expected ones. Surprise first, then a hint of worry.

'Oh?'

'Yes. A certain Gary Lyons, who worked at the hotel in Waimea.'

'Doesn't ring any bells,' Dominic said, 'but then it wouldn't. The hiring of staff is nearly always done by the hotel managers.' Leaning forward he pressed the intercom buzzer with a long index finger and spoke briefly into it. 'Cynthia, have the personnel file on Gary Lyons from the Princess Liliha sent up, will you? And make it priority.' He leaned back in his chair and looked at the Lieutenant thoughtfully. There was an aura of quiet confidence and ability about the policeman that informed Dominic that Perry Clements would have been a success at whatever he had chosen to do.

Perry was thinking much the same thing, and in the few minutes it took for the file to appear, both men had arrived at a certain feeling of mutual respect. Dominic indicated to Cynthia to give the folder straight to his guest and Perry read it through in silence. The age and physical description all fitted. He closed the file and looked across the impressive desk at the equally impressive man.

'It looks promising,' he said mildly, watching him closely.

Dominic's expression didn't alter an inch. 'If I remember right, Chuck, our barman downstairs, transferred from the Princess Liliha not long ago. Would it help you to talk to him?'

Perry nodded, and smiled slightly. Very cool. Either Fairchild had nothing to hide, or he was very confident his tracks were covered. 'It would, yes.'

The bar was located in a discreet alcove off the main dining room, and as Dominic accompanied him through the restaurant, Perry looked around with admiring eyes.

'Chuck.' Dominic beckoned to a rather florid, overweight man with wispy blond hair and curious eyes. 'This is Lieutenant Clements. He wants to ask you about a man called Lyons – Gary Lyons, from the Liliha. Remember him?'

'Yes, sir, I do,' Chuck said grimly. He's not surprised, Perry thought at once, that a cop should come asking about this Lyons character.

'OK. Tell him all you can. I have to get back to the office,' Dominic lied, guessing that the policeman would prefer to question his bartender alone.

'Thank you, Dominic.' Perry held out his hand. 'I hope we meet again.'

'So do I,' Dominic said, and meant it. He asked: 'Do you play golf?'

Perry grunted. 'I try.'

'Then we'll have to get together for a game one Sunday. Ring me here any time during the day and we'll fix it.' He turned and left them, his face thoughtful, a small frown tugging at his brows as he walked quickly away. Perry watched him go and wondered why a man of Dominic's wealth and status should want to cultivate a mere police lieutenant. It worried him.

'Chuck, isn't it?' Perry asked, casting aside these thoughts to be mulled over at a later date. He hoisted himself on to a bar stool and pointed at the refrigerator. 'Can I have an OJ?'

'Sure,' Chuck said, glad to have something to do.

'So, what can you tell me about Lyons?' Perry asked casually, his quiet voice and easy face inviting confidences.

'He was OK,' Chuck said cautiously. 'Not all that good a bartender, though. Too busy chatting up the girls to pull his weight.'

'Good-looking was he?'

Chuck shrugged his fat shoulders. 'He thought so.'

'Bit of a poser?' Perry's tone was full of sympathy and Chuck nodded, his red rimmed blue eyes glittering now that he was relaxed.

'Yeah. Always had his sleeves rolled up showing off his tattoo.'

'Of what?'

'A ship, or anchor – something like that. Fancied himself as a sailor.'

'When did you last see him?'

'Must have been, oh, mid- to late December. That's right, he didn't bother working out his notice.'

'Any idea where he went?'

'To work? Nah. I know where he'd have liked to spend all his nights, if he could have afforded it, but as far as I know he only went there once or twice, after pay day. Gloria's. Down off Hotel Street. Know who I mean?' Chuck grinned lasciviously, then remembered who he was talking to. 'Not that I've ever been there, mind.' He wiped the bar top vigorously with a towel, the rings of fat around his neck glowing a deep pink. 'But one of our customers, a chap Lyons got talking to, mentioned the good time he'd had there . . . not that he was a hotel guest,' Chuck spluttered hurriedly. 'Mr Dominic's clientele here is spotless. Really, only the best . . .'

'I'm sure,' Perry said coldly, watching the man's reaction closely. 'What makes you think Lyons went there?'

'The way he was talking, drawing this guy out, getting the address and asking him to describe the girls.'

Perry nodded. 'And you never saw him after that?'

'Nope.'

'Nor heard anyone who had?'

'Nope.'

'OK. Thanks.' Perry pushed his half-full glass away and made for the exit, his face thoughtful. He was now pretty sure his coincidence meant something. If so, Lyons' murder was going to be harder going than he'd thought. He wouldn't be surprised if the man had a rap sheet a yard long. And a man like that had a lot of enemies. And if one of them was Dominic Fairchild for some reason, Perry knew he was in for a rough time. Taking on the likes of Fairchild would be no easy matter. Not that Perry would hesitate, if it proved necessary. But he found himself hoping that it wouldn't. He rather liked Fairchild.

In the lobby he noticed that the singer who had been on stage had now finished his stint and had his arm draped around the shoulders of a little blonde. He stopped to kiss her playfully on the lips but Perry, being well versed in body language, could see that she was tense, and suddenly he recognized her: the amnesia victim. One of the lads in the precinct had been talking about her. Following them out at a discreet distance, he walked down the pathway of the lovely gardens, stopping under a shady ginger tree as they climbed into a sports car. Perry's eyes narrowed when he noticed her chewing her lip. Her face under the suntan was pale and strained, and the way she twisted a few strands of hair between her fingers was a sure sign of nerves.

On the drive back to the precinct, his thoughts were once more on Gary Lyons and the unpalatable but reasonable question that nagged at him, asking if there could be any possible connection with his murder and Dominic Fairchild.

IN the sports car, Farron was frowning. 'You're still worried about him.'

'No,' Vienna denied automatically.

'Good, because with a new rich wife he'll get bored with bugging us. He's the kind who wants yachts and silk ties. He won't risk losing his meal-ticket.' For a few minutes, until the worst of Honolulu traffic was behind them, Farron kept silent but the air shimmered with words unsaid, and when the countryside began to open up around them he asked quietly, and not for the first time, 'What's the matter?'

'Nothing.'

'You've been having nightmares?'

'I've always had them.'

'They've been getting worse this last week,' he pointed out. 'And you're not eating. What's the matter, baby?'

'It's just . . . silly.' She sighed painfully. 'It's something he said.'

'Jago?' Farron said sharply. 'What did he say exactly?'

'About that body. On the beach. And something else. I had that . . . vision, hallucination, whatever you call it, again. The same one. About being in an alley, and a knife, and . . .' she began to shiver. 'I know something awful happened in that alley, but I can't quite remember it.'

Farron swore softly under his breath. 'It's Jago,' he said harshly. 'Every time he starts hounding you, it upsets you. That's all it is, darling. Believe me.' He reached across the seat and lifted her hands to his lips, kissing the knuckles tenderly, trying to hide how much Jago's return to the islands bothered him. Not least because he couldn't help but wonder if Vienna was, in some part of herself, glad he was back. It must do a woman's ego an awful lot of good to know someone loved her with such obsessive strength, and Vienna was a girl who badly needed to be loved and to belong. Although logic told him his fears were based only on his own insecurity, it didn't help.

Vienna smiled tremulously. 'I love you,' she said simply.

'I love you too. The question now is: do you trust me?'

'I trust you with my life, Farron,' she murmured lovingly and told him all that Richard had said about the murder.

'Bullshit,' Farron scoffed, then promptly wondered if he'd done the right thing in stopping her from carrying on. 'Listen, darling, he's just trying to scare you, to make you dependent on him again. He's not right in the head.'

'I know. But, when I first heard about it on the radio . . .'

He glanced quickly at her and pulled the car into a layby. Turning off the engine, he twisted in his seat to look at her. 'Go on.'

'I don't know. Something happened. I felt cold and sick, and . . . *awful*.'

Gently he pulled her to him, fingers stroking her hair. 'Darling, that's because you're you. You feel sad every time you hear bad news. You're special.'

He kissed her deeply then drove on, teasing her gently.

They both laughed but her eyes were still strained and she still twisted her hair. And Farron's own eyes were strained and his fingers gripped the steering wheel tighter than necessary because he, too, was scared. Something was happening to her. He could feel it, sense it – almost see it. And the most ugly and insidious of all thoughts wouldn't go away. And he knew that this thought, which could be summed up in two simple words, could, and often did, destroy anything and everything that was good. It was sitting between them now in the car, hovering over their laughter like a raincloud. And those two simple words were: *'What if. . . ?'*

Chapter 25

The motorbike felt familiar and exhilarating beneath her as she coasted down the gears to approach a red traffic-light on Kahlili Street. She was wearing tough denim jeans and a hefty black leather jacket and matching black crash helmet. Safety had been something her scrambling teacher had drummed into her repeatedly, which is why her visor was made of darkly tinted glass, keeping the strong sunlight out of her eyes.

The day was hot, and after coming to a perfectly controlled stop at the lights, she removed her gloved hands from the wide handlebars and pulled down the zip of her jacket an inch, allowing a cooling breeze to play over her throat. It was good to have her Norton back, to feel its powerful 749 cc engine rumble underneath her with a snarling power that was a mere fingertip touch away. Suddenly a flash of silver blue pulling up alongside her commandeered all her attention. With the top down and the mournful tune of a single saxophone wafting from twin speakers, Dominic Fairchild waited patiently, fingers drumming absently on the black steering wheel. With a featherlight touch on clutch and gear pedal, she nudged the large bike a few feet over the line so that her exhaust pipe was level with the driver's door of the Ferrari and began to rev strongly.

Dominic scowled as the powerful roaring of the bike's engine drowned out the sound of Elijah Canton's saxophone solo and coughed as the carbon monoxide exhaust fumes rushed into his face.

Nudging the Ferrari forward, its silver-blue elegance in direct contrast to the almost ugly black power of the old Norton, he yelled: 'Cut it out, will you?' He cast his eyes curiously down the length of the bike which was bulkier, older and more powerful than the modern Japanese models he was used to seeing. As he glanced over the spoked wheels, powerful engine and the impressive sweep of the handlebars, a shaft of jealousy pierced him. Sitting in his comfortable cream leather seat surrounded by luxury, he felt hemmed in and envied the young punk sat atop that gleaming, snarling, superior machine for the sense of freedom and originality he must feel.

Again the motorbike engine revved and he coughed on the sharp stench of petrol fumes in his throat. The gap between them was no more than inches and he could see his own face reflected in the black glass of the punk's visor.

Rhiannon grinned behind her helmet and leaned back on her bike, looking the sports car over from tail-light to front fender, making her disdain of it obvious. She revved harder, her gloved hand turning on the black tube of the throttle in an almost teasing series of rolls.

Dominic was half-amused, half-angered by the snub. Did the punk really think a bike – any bike, could beat his Ferrari? Like hell! 'You've got nothing to be so damned proud about, kid,' he roared. 'This baby could leave that hunk of black metal standing.'

Rhiannon laughed. Like hell it could! The traffic light turned to amber, and he was just going into first gear when she suddenly whipped off her helmet. A look of sheer incredulity met Rhiannon as she looked over at him and with an easy snap of her wrist, tossed the helmet squarely into the passenger seat of the Ferrari. Momentarily distracted, Dominic glanced down at the helmet. With the light now on green she stopped revving and, every muscle ready, yanked up on the handlebars at the same time releasing clutch and shifting gear. Performing a perfect wheelie she sped away from the lights, the honking cars behind her falling silent at the awesome sight. With her front wheel in the air above her and her lithe body perfectly balanced on the back, she silently blessed Jim Spchiele, the younger brother of her friend at College, for teaching her how to do wheelies. Accelerating even faster, about fifty yards down the road she leaned forward, letting the front wheel bounce back on to the tarmac, and then rapidly changed gear, looking in her rearview mirror to see what was happening.

Dominic, after a moment of stunned disbelief, had

promptly shifted into gear and was away, his heart in his mouth. Every second she drove on her back wheel he expected her to lose control and the black monster slip from under her, throwing her beneath the wheels of oncoming cars. His hands on the wheel were cold and sweating. 'You stupid bloody bitch!' he yelled, his foot pressed on the accelerator as he rapidly drew up behind her. He almost groaned with relief when she righted the machine and it was only then that he relaxed and grudgingly appreciated the skill she had displayed.

Rhiannon's eyes narrowed as she found the silver-blue car right up her chuff. Damn, but he was good. Slowly she began to smile.

Steadily increasing speed, she came up behind a Chevrolet and easily overtook it, sliding between the two lanes with ease, a car no more than a foot away on either side of her. Like threading a needle, she thought with satisfaction, watching as the blue Ferrari fell further and further behind. With the merest pressure on her left hand or right, she swayed gracefully through the trundling traffic like a big sleek black leopard amongst fat cattle. Built originally for the British Police to chase and catch speeding cars, the Norton was, to Rhiannon's mind, the King of bikes.

Dominic swore viciously as he saw her pulling away, passing between lorries whose jetstreams would have made a normal bike wobble like a winding-down spinning top. But not that monster. It looked as if it weighed a ton. How the hell did a mere slip of a girl have the muscle power to control that thing? And, by God, Dominic thought, swinging out to overtake a truck with bare inches to spare, she could drive that thing. But then, he could drive too. An amateur rally-driver for over ten years, his own personal choice of car a Ford Escort, he was grimly determined to catch her up. And as the city was left further and further behind, and the traffic diminished, she was unable to make such good use of her advantage and slowly but surely he began to gain on her.

Rhiannon, cruising along at a steady ninety, blinked back tears from the wind and wished she had goggles on. She felt guilty now about having discarded her helmet so recklessly. Still, her challenge had been impulsively made and she hadn't been prepared. The four-lane road dwindled to two as the last of the buildings fell away and she was heading south-east out of Honolulu, Highway I well behind her.

She checked the mirror, gasping when she spotted the silver-blue frame of the Ferrari closing up the gap behind her. She was grinning even before she realized it. He could really drive that thing! OK, she told herself and her fingers tightened on the accelerator, the bike responding immediately by nudging the needle to ninety-five. Rhiannon laughed, her movements easy and speaking of years of experience and practice as the bike ate up the miles.

At the sight of the black monster in front of him, Dominic allowed a small but very grim smile, to cross his face. He checked his speedometer: ninety-five. His green eyes narrowed as they looked out from behind the windscreen. When he caught up with her he was going to beat the living daylights out of her! And that's a promise, Dominic, he told himself. A promise that looked to be coming his way sooner than he'd anticipated, for ahead of him the huge bike seemed to be . . . no *was*, slowing down. Rhiannon knew the road ahead well since moving into her father's house a week ago, and anticipating its highspots she smiled thoughtfully to herself as Dominic pulled out alongside her.

'What the hell do you think you're doing?' he roared. Her cheeks were whipped pink by the wind, her eyes made even brighter by the tears in her eyes, while her hair streamed behind her like ebony gossamer, and the fierce, taunting expression on her face prompted a reaction in him that was totally primitive. 'Pull over!' he yelled. '*Now.*'

Rhiannon then proceeded to put his heart firmly back into his mouth. Raising the hand that had been poised ever ready on the brake, she held it up, driving and steering with only one hand. 'Rhiannon,' he screamed, checking the road ahead was clear. 'For pity's sake . . .' She waggled her fingers at him in a cocky wave, her lips pulling into a wider grin before putting her hand back to the handlebars and clenching her fingers. Like a pouncing cat, the machine leapt in response under her clasping thighs and suddenly moved ahead of him like a hot knife through butter.

A car coming around the bend headed straight for Dominic who was still on the wrong side of the road. She heard a silent scream of agony ricochet in her head, and with eyes glued to the mirror felt her breath thunder out of her in an enormous sigh of relief when he swerved the car back into position, the oncoming driver honking furiously on his horn as he passed harmlessly by.

The road ahead began its zigzag curves as it climbed and she pushed up the speed to take the first corner, bending her knees and leaning low into the curve. Behind her, Dominic felt his heart stop and then begin to pump crazily again. Her lovely body leaning low to the ground reminded him of the motorbike champions in a similiar position on posters in teenage shops. Then, and now, he wondered how the hell they managed to stay on. When he caught up with her he was damned well going to kill her! The wheel under his hands became her velvet-soft, silky smooth white neck and his hands tightened on it pleasurably. Gaining on her steadily and surely as the Ferrari purred confidently around the bends, he could drive with the minimum of effort. Rhiannon, on the other hand, could feel the strain on her thigh muscles and shoulders beginning to tell.

It had been over a year since she'd done any serious riding and in the mirror the Ferrari was still right on her tail. But there was no way she was going meekly to give up. No way! As they crested a hill, the steep incline on her left gave way to scorched grassland, the road twisting visibly away and down and a triumphant voice screamed 'YES!' inside her as she saw her opportunity. Lifting the front wheel just slightly off the ground so as not to be thrown by the transaction from tarmac to dirt, she left the road, taking to the grass like a duck takes to water.

For the merest instant, Dominic thought that she had lost control, and a scream of anguish, terrifying in its intensity, ripped through him bellowing forth into the air in a strangled, outraged demand: 'NO!' But then, as she slowed down visibly, her body shifting forward in natural, practised ease, he realized that the manoeuvre had been deliberate. The relief was as sweet as anything he'd tasted before in his life.

Leaning into the steep decline, the bike bouncing on the uneven surface, Rhiannon sped down the hill, regaining the road way in front of the Ferrari that was forced to stick to the winding route. 'Eat my dust, sucker,' she yelled with wild exhilaration, repeating a line she'd heard from some movie or other, its corny taunting flavour making her laugh.

Dominic took the bottom corner at a hundred and ten. His hands were as easy on the wheel as her own had been on the handlebars, his skill equal to hers.

Looking in the mirror she was dismayed at how promptly he'd caught up. Still, the amount of pleasure to be gained in any challenge became sweeter as the skills of one's opponent climbed higher. It wasn't any fun, after all, to shoot fish in a barrel. The road ahead turned sharply in an almost hairpin bend, and as she accelerated recklessly, determined to beat him to her house, where she'd been originally heading, she was forced to take it far wider than she'd have liked. With the greenery speeding by in her peripheral vision, the grey ribbon of tarmac flashing by below her, a huge, utterly unexpected flash of yellow in front of her had her heart flipping in her breast.

A huge lorry carrying pineapples trundled sedately around the bend, its bored driver totally unprepared for the sight of a speeding black bullet heading straight at him. GOD! She reacted instinctively, her brain working super-fast. She couldn't head into her own lane again, for the impetus would either have her slamming into the rockface that bordered it, or sliding like a demented crab under the huge oncoming wheels. The driver of the lorry didn't even have time to brake as the bullet suddenly altered course; she yanked the handlebars to her right, where the road ended in a dangerous dip down into the grassy verge, applying the brakes only marginally, knowing it would be fatal to ram them on as her first instinct had demanded. She felt and saw the huge lorry lumber by with mere inches to spare as the bike dipped and rattled beneath her. Battling to keep it straight on a gradient that dipped terrifyingly away from her, it was only a combination of her skill, years of practice, luck, and probably divine intervention as well, that saved her life. Regaining the road moments later, still with the latter half of the hairpin bend to contend with, she shot across the road mere yards in front of the silver-blue car that had begun to brake in a squeal of burning rubber the moment the lorry had appeared.

Dominic was beyond anger. The sight of that huge juggernaut bearing down on a suddenly very flimsy-looking black bike had taken away all rational thought. Quite simply, he believed he'd lost her, sure that no one could have escaped from that situation alive.

As her house came into sight at last, her stomach churned nauseously with relief. Suddenly the Ferrari overtook her, sweeping elegantly through the narrow double gates and turning in a controlled spin to stop in front of her. Her wheels turned to spit up gravel as her legs came out to steady the machine as she came to a halt. Her fingers shook as they turned off the key in the ignition. The sudden silence was utterly terrifying.

Dominic didn't bother opening the car door. Leaping lithely out of the Ferrari his eyes never left the girl who sat trembling on the bike. Rhiannon felt the air around them ripple with the waves of fury and incredible passion that emanated from him, like the ever-widening circles created by a stone recklessly tossed into a calm pond.

Her tongue darted out to moisten her lips as he began to stalk inexorably across the ten yards of gravel between them. *Run*, a voice piped up from somewhere within the shocked treacle that was her brain, but she could not heed it. Her body felt paralyzed. Her legs ached with the remembered vibrations of the motorbike engine, while her hair, stirring in the silent breeze, caressed cheeks that were icy-cold. Minutes ago she had stared death in the face, and was still alive. Now she stared Dominic Fairchild in the face and didn't think she was going to be so lucky twice. He looks white, she thought inconsequentially. Under that gorgeous tan, he looks absolutely white.

The feeling of time suspended came to an abrupt end as his hands reached out and curled around the top of her arms, his fingers biting deep into her flesh. She could hear the sound of his harsh breathing and the squeak of her leather jacket under his hand. She could feel the sickly hot sun beating down on her head and she parted her lips to draw in a shaking breath.

Yanking her viciously from the bike he dragged her away from it, holding her up by the scruff of her neck like a dog. 'You could have been killed!' he screamed.

Her eyes widened and then blazed as she spat back with venom: 'You won't get rid of me that easily!'

Dominic stared at her speechlessly for a second, then, taking the two flapping edges of her leather jacket in a vice-like grip he lifted her off her feet and all but threw her on to the overgrown lawn, her shoulders connecting painfully with the grass in a dull thud. Her booted legs sprawled untidily as she lay, winded and panting on the grass. Looking up at him as he moved closer, his face tight with fury and something else less simple, she tried to sit up but he straddled her with his knees, bending down to kneel over her stomach as she leaned awkwardly up on her hands, arms bent at the elbows.

Holding her eyes with his own he put his hand on her sternum and with near-brutal force, pushed her back on the grass. With a hand on either side of her head he leaned over her, his face only inches above her, eyes glittering down at her like emeralds – rock hard. His black hair hung attractively down and away from his face and his nostrils flared.

'Get off me, you bastard!' she snarled, frightened by the melting feeling that was trickling from her stomach and into her womb, making her vagina itch and ache in a way that terrified her. Bringing up her hands with curled nails, they were quickly knocked away with a stinging blow that shot pins and needles up her arms. Hissing in her breath and determined not to yelp, she clenched her hand into a fist but he read the intention in her frustrated eyes. Grabbing her two wrists in one hand, his grip tightened ominously.

Rhiannon gasped and her eyes filled with threatened tears. Her lips fell open on a tiny sob and Dominic made a low sound deep in his throat. Then he was kissing her, or she was kissing him, she was not sure which. With lips grinding against teeth, tongues clashing, duelling, fighting, loving, he lay atop her, his hands no longer hurting but holding her immobile. Her breasts were flattened against his chest, but even through the leather of her jacket and the cool cotton of his dark green shirt, she could feel her nipples tighten and throb.

Her mouth opened wider and her head raised from the ground to press against his. It was all the encouragement he needed. With a snarl that was also a groan, his hand cupped the side of her face as he dragged her head back to the earth and stretched on top of her. His lean, pleasantly heavy body pressed her down, scorching her with its heat. As his tongue found its way past hers, his kiss thrusting deep into her mouth, she brought her hands up to his head, her fingers caressing his scalp and pulling the hair from his forehead to reveal his vulnerable temples. She massaged his skull in a frenzied, almost clumsy caress that drove him mad. With a few muttered Hawaiian words that she didn't understand, he found the large gold zip of her jacket. Pulling it down, his flushed, desire-tight face fell into stillness as he saw that she wore nothing underneath. Her body quivered like a bowstring as his hand slowly slipped under the leather. With his fingers curled around the sides of the jacket he yanked her into a sitting position and the material stretched tight against her back, supporting her weight.

Breathing hard, Dominic watched the pink-tipped mounds of flesh rise and fall. Then, with a graphically violent gesture, he dragged the leather down over her shoulders, leaving it rucked halfway down her arms, binding them to her sides. Her eyes closed and her head went back with a low moan as his palms closed squarely over her nipples and slowly caressed them. The flesh beneath his hands moved and rippled around his fingers whilst its single button became harder and harder. She heard a sighing, whimpering voice, soft and weak in her ears and it took a few moments to realize that it was hers.

Lifting her up and supporting her limp body in his strong hands, he sat back on his ankles and pulled her forward, her bare breast falling like easy prey into his parted, waiting mouth. The reaction in her body was explosive. Her head lolled back on her shoulders, all strength leaving her at the erotic sensation of his mouth on her breasts. His teeth danced around her flesh, his tonguetip pressing into the very tip of her nipple and her vaginal muscles clenched in helpless spasms of desire.

Dominic could feel blood pumping into his penis, engorging and enlarging it until it pressed and throbbed against the restricting white corduroy of his trousers. Her scent intoxicated him. She filled his mouth with her flesh, and still he wanted more, wanted to gag on her beauty and drown in her body. No woman had ever, ever done this to him before. No woman.

Except Rhiannon Grantham. *Grantham* . . . Against his closed lids he saw the man's face, contorted in triumph, eyes glittering with febrile hatred, lips pulled into a sneer. Above the moaning of their voices, he heard that other voice, thick and ugly crowing: '*You'll never have your kid . . . never . . .*'

With a moan of combined disgust, regret, desire and pain, Dominic once again pulled away from her and without his strength supporting her, she fell away from him, rolling on to her side. Dominic staggered to his feet and turned away from her, walking like a drunk to his car.

On the grass Rhiannon opened her eyes, watching for several moments as a small yellow and black beetle climbed up a grass stem in front of her. Then she put a hand on the grass and sat up, pulling with weak hands at her jacket, slowly fitting it back over her shoulders. Drawing up her knees to her chin she clasped her arms around her legs, locking the screaming pain within her.

She must not let him see. She must not! With her back to him, she picked up a small twig and prodded the beetle gently with it, watching as the small insect began to crawl up the stick towards her hand. 'Do you remember this place, Dominic?'

Dominic wiped his sweating upper lip with his fingers and cleared his throat. 'Yeah. Yeah, I remember this place.'

'Has it changed much?'

'Not really.' Dominic looked at her back hunched protectively against him, and felt himself begin to rally, that immense stamina of his rising up from the wellspring of his strong character to save him yet again. Straightening up and walking to a point just a yard behind her, his shadow fell in front of her on the lawn, warning her of his presence. He stuffed his hands in his pockets and asked grimly, 'Just what were you trying to prove back there?'

She tossed away the stick and looked over her shoulder, raising a hand to shield her eyes from the sun. 'That I could ride a bike?' she said innocently.

For a second he stared down at her and then began to laugh. 'You certainly proved that. How the hell you missed that damned truck I'll never know.' The words came out mildly in direct contrast to the killing rage that had just pulsed through him like quicksilver. Damn it, what was it about this woman that had him climbing the walls?

'Neither will the driver,' Rhiannon commented guiltily, feeling sorry for the man. She hoped he'd recovered by now. 'This place needs a good gardener.' Feeling stronger now, she got to her feet.

Dominic pushed his hands even more firmly into his pockets. 'Those trees are ohia trees. Graham planted them. They're said to be Pele's favourite.' He looked at her then, his face totally immobile as he said softly, almost to himself, 'The fire goddess.'

Rhiannon felt again the looming spectre of fate. She snapped: 'I hope you don't imagine that what just happened meant anything,' looking down moodily as she spoke, her black leather boots digging into the grass and leaving it flattened as she walked.

Beside her, Dominic gave a rueful grunt of laughter. 'Don't worry, I won't. I already know how warped your character is, remember?'

'Warped? Me?' Rhiannon gasped, spinning around to stare at him. 'I'm not the one who deliberately ruined a man I once called a friend, and then hounded him into his grave.'

Dominic gritted his teeth almost audibly. 'He'd been blackmailing me for years,' he grated, then could have kicked himself – hard.

Rhiannon laughed scornfully. 'I don't buy it, Fairchild.'

'I couldn't care less, Grantham.'

Ignoring him, she stalked into the small house. It was a funny mixture of brand new furniture and carpetless floors, rather grubby curtains and square patches of darker colour on the walls where pictures had once hung.

'Lovely,' Dominic said drolly as they entered the small square lounge.

'It will be when I've decorated it,' she said defensively, then added with a shrug, 'besides, it's only meant to be a holiday cottage. For my main residence, I have in mind a certain palace, built of pearls.'

Dominic's smile flashed white and wolfish in the dim interior of the house. 'You're dreaming again,' he warned softly. 'No Ben Fielding, rich or not, is going to find your charms – lovely though I know they are,' his voice husked, 'worth that much.'

'And you're being complacent again. I thought at least I'd cured you of that by now.' She sighed elaborately. 'You must be a very slow learner.'

Looking around at the rather grimy fireplace, the window edged by a creeper that Graham had forever been pruning, memories came flooding back to Dominic. 'It seems so long ago,' he murmured. 'Graham and me.'

'Conscience troubling you?' she gibed as they walked back to the garden and Dominic opened the car door before turning to look at her, his eyes unwavering.

'Not a jot,' he told her, his voice as hard as her eyes became.

'I was there when he died,' she said, and Dominic looked at her, biting off the words, 'I know' that hovered on his tongue and he slipped behind the wheel. 'He told me it was your doing, and asked me to get even,' she went on quietly, looking over the top of his head, her eyes filling with pain.

'He isn't worth it, Rhiannon,' he said softly.

'He was my father!'

'No, he . . .' Dominic quickly bit off the angry words and turned the ignition key abruptly. 'Why don't you take that black monstrosity and yourself back to England, before things begin to get really nasty?'

'Nasty for you, you mean?' she said scornfully. 'Running scared, are we?'

Scared, he mused? Yes, he was scared. But not for the reasons she thought.

Chapter 26

Rolnalski tapped briefly on his superior's door then entered. 'Hi, boss. Thought you'd like to see this straight away.' Perry looked up and held out his hand, scanning the print-out quickly. So it *was* Lyons, he thought, looking over the dental records and X-rays. 'And,' Rolnalski said, hazel eyes twinkling as he produced a second sheet, 'The great Madame Fortuna strikes again.' Perry grinned. 'Madame Fortuna' was his nickname – one that had sprung from his growing reputation as a mindreader. 'The rap-sheet. Tah-dah!' Rolnalski whipped a report out from under his shirt and handed it to his boss. Ignoring the damp patch caused by sweat, Perry opened the folder and leaned back in his swivel chair. Before he could start, however, Rolnalski began to recite its contents.

'Seems our people in Maine wouldn't have minded talking to our Mr Lyons about the murder of two of their ladies of the night last year. The physical description fits,' he carried on, glancing across at the pot plant in the window with a vain, half-hearted hope that it might be recovering. It wasn't. 'And the murder weapon, a particularly nasty stiletto, was found in his apartment.'

'No kidding?' Perry said mildly, still reading the report for himself.

'Disappeared in October. They knew after he'd already split that he'd forged a passport and got a job on a cruise ship bound for Oahu as a bartender. According to the report he jumped ship before they'd radioed the captain to hold him. His past record is rather boring. Grievous bodily harm, both girlfriends, and two dismissed cases of attempted rape.'

Perry closed the folder and handed it back. 'Looks like the tip about him being seen at Gloria's is getting to look more and more likely.'

'Uh-huh. Gonna check it out?' Rolnalski's colourless eyes lit up.

'Yes. What's the word on where he worked after the Fairchild hotel?'

Dipping into the pocket of his rather dirty shirt, Rolnalski took out a piece of card ripped from a cigarette packet, turned it around, and squinted at it.

'Er ... El Dorado's. That's a seedy little joint on the outskirts of Chinatown. By the way, if you want some volunteers to do the legwork at these B & Bs there's a waiting list outside on the noticeboard.'

'B & Bs?'

'Bars and brothels. Old Jack says it's good for 'em. Learn more in a night down in Soho then you can five years at Harvard. According to Jack.'

'I can imagine. You drive.'

El Dorado's was a sleazepit. Located in the basement of a sweatshop factory, it was dirty, cramped and smelled of decay. Perry didn't mind. The threat of a visit from the Department of Health would work wonders. In one corner a drunk lay with his head on the table, snoring loudly. By the door a girl lounged, half-in and half-out of the sunlight, her hair lank and dry, her eyes blank. Sitting at the bar was a motley group of humanity, all of which Perry ignored. Rolnalski skipped lithely on to the barstool next to his boss, as Perry beckoned the waiter with a simple crooked finger.

Cops, the bartender thought, wiping his hands on a cloth that was a definitely unhealthy grey. 'What can I get yah?'

'Beer,' Rolnalski said promptly, and Perry shook his head. Knocking the metal top off the beer bottle, the bartender sat it squarely in front of the younger man along with a squat glass. And if he drinks from that, Perry thought, eyeing the smeared tumbler with deep suspicion, he's either a better man than I, or a complete moron. Rolnalski drank from the glass.

'Gary Lyons,' Perry said simply, and the bartender visibly relaxed.

'Ain't been here since December. He only worked her a few days anyhow.'

'How come?' Rolnalski asked, taking a hefty swallow of beer, his Adam's apple bobbing up and down as he swallowed.

'The man was a sleaze,' the bartender commented with forthright honesty. 'Even for this place.' A crowd barged in and their leader, a tall and gangling black youth, demanded food. Perry waved the bartender away and waited. 'Hey, Flick,' the man yelled through the door behind the bar. 'Get going with the lunch-time act!' A female grumbling reply filtered through the door in answer, and Perry watched as greasy fries, rather flat burgers and spare ribs swimming in red sauce were slapped on to the tables in front of the gang who sneered at it, mocked it, then ate it hungrily. A far cry from the Blue Hawaiian, Perry thought drily, and watched as a girl came into the room dressed in a harem outfit and walked to a record player where she put on a sixties number: *Don't Throw Your Love Away*. As the psychedelic electronic music pulsated into the room she began to sway, whipping off the veil from her face, her belly undulating as she began to strip. Nobody paid the slightest bit of notice. 'You still here?' the bartender asked pointedly as he resumed his position behind the bar.

Perry sighed. 'Where did Lyons go after leaving here?'

'Don't know.'

'Did he have any special friends?' Rolnalski asked.

'Don't know. He had one guy though he tried to slip free drinks to.'

'Know why?'

'Nah. But he was always going on about Gloria's girls.'

Perry nodded. 'Anything specific?'

'Nah – just the usual. Thought he was some sort of sexy sod, though. Last time I saw him he was real pissed because Gloria had given him the boot. Word is he was too rough on one of the girls.'

Perry nodded. It fitted. 'Thanks.'

'Uh-huh.' To Rolnalski he said, 'That's a dollar for the beer.'

Back on the street where the air was a lot cleaner, Rolnalski walked slowly to his ancient car and leaned on the top. 'Gloria's place, boss?'

Perry nodded and got into the car, his face thoughtful.

'I don't think anyone's gonna cry if we don't find out who topped him, Lieutenant.'

'Probably not, but while we have leads, we carry it through.'

Rolnalski honked on his horn as a little Toyota cut in front of him, and the grey-haired old woman who was driving stuck her hand out of the window and raised two fingers into the air. Perry grinned. 'What do you know about our Gloria?' he asked as Rolnalski opened a packet of gum and began chewing noisily. Perry hated gum. He never let any of his own kids use it, and if he caught them out he told them they looked like stupid goats, chewing the cud. It never failed to cure them.

'She's got quite a reputation.'

'That bad?' Perry asked. He had never worked vice, or wanted to.

'No – the reverse.' Rolnalski blew a bubble and sucked it in. ' "The Pimps' Despair" they call her. They started off laughing at her, cracking jokes about her medical plan, her baby crèche, her free room and board policy . . .' Perry looked across at his subordinate, wondering if his leg was being pulled. 'I'll tell you one thing though,' Rolnalski finished. 'The pimps ain't laughing no more.'

'Any more,' Perry corrected automatically.

'Nowadays,' Rolnalski continued as if he hadn't been interrupted, let alone corrected, 'every girl on the street is trying to get into Gloria's. But if they've got a habit or the clap they can forget it. She's taking the cream and everyone knows it. Rumour is she's going to expand into a second motel.'

'Who's her muscle?'

'Frank Gillespie.'

Perry's mouth formed into a silent whistle. Now that was what he called muscle. 'She sounds very interesting,' he mused, feeling a sudden spark of anticipation at the thought of visiting the famous brothel. And when they pulled up outside and he read the name on the awning, his anticipation multiplied. *Glorious Motel*. Yes, any woman who could think up that handle *had* to be a character worth meeting.

A spyhole slid back, a heavily-fringed eye peering out at them. 'Yes?' a high musical voice asked and Perry took out his badge. The door was reluctantly opened to reveal a tall, dark-haired girl with wide brown eyes. 'Please come in.' She led the way into a lounge where five pairs of eyes turned in their direction. Gaudy, Perry thought, the word leaping immediately into the forefront of his mind. But then, what else could it be? And was it his imagination or was there humour in this place, evident in the saucy calendars of cartoon characters that hung on one wall, the cheeky ashtrays shaped like bottoms, the furniture itself looking as if it came from Mae West's boudoir? 'Just a minute,' the girl said, glancing anxiously at her companions before walking quickly through the lounge to a door at the far end. Rolnalski stared at a blonde who lay on a couch, absently stroking a fluffy grey cat, her blue eyes ironic and come-hither. As Rolnalski began to blush, Perry thoughtfully looked away. It was all tongue-in-cheek and over the top. No doubt it made the wealthy men who came here think they'd found something out of history, but Perry was pretty damned sure, without even meeting the owner yet, that Gloria Gaines was secretly laughing at the lot of them.

In the office, Marie quickly filled Gloria in. 'There's a cop outside. Wants to see you.'

'Brightman?'

'No – not the regular boys. I've never seen this one before.'

Gloria stood up, not missing the sound of panic in the younger girl's voice. 'Don't worry. We've paid this month's dues. Send them in.'

Perry nodded at Rolnalski as Marie beckoned them over. 'Wait here.'

'Yes, boss.' Rolnalski didn't look away from the blonde.

The woman in the office was the second person in one week to surprise Perry. Dressed in a simple brown skirt and white blouse she looked to be in her late fifties, but was remarkably well-preserved and attractive. Her naturally blonde hair was short and curling, revealing a fine face almost bare of make-up. A lady was the first description that popped into his head, and he smiled at her briefly, but made no other overture. 'Sergeant. . . ?'

'Lieutenant Clements, Miss Gaines. May I sit down?'

'Please do.' Gloria pointed to the simple padded chair

tucked neatly into her desk which was every bit as tidy as his own back at the precinct. Gloria immediately dismissed the two possibilities that had sprung to mind when Marie had told her the cop was new. He didn't want a girl, gratis, or otherwise. And he didn't want a cut. Honest cop. It had been so long since she'd met one, she'd almost forgotten what they smelt like. An honest cop meant trouble. The face was pleasant, the manner easy, but it was the eyes that Gloria immediately sought out when meeting any stranger. And these eyes, neither blue nor grey, neither gullible nor mean, meant a lot of trouble. 'Is there some kind of problem, Lieutenant?' she asked politely, and Perry shook his head. She's nervous, he thought. Her shoulders were too tense, although she sat well, almost covering it.

'I want to ask a few questions about a man called Gary Lyons. Do you know of him?'

Gloria's eyes never flickered, but in her chest her heart began to thump sickeningly. 'Yes. He was a guest here once.'

'A guest? Oh, yes. When was the last time he . . . checked in?'

Gloria pursed her lips thoughtfully. 'About January, or it could have been earlier. No, it was earlier, I think. December time.'

Perry waited, but she said nothing. Now that was unusual. Almost anyone else would have added, 'Why?' to that last statement of hers.

'Before or after Christmas?'

'Before. Yes, I remember. His idea of a Christmas present wasn't the same as some of our other female guests here.'

Perry nodded. 'I see. Did you know that Mr Lyons was wanted in connection with the murder of two prostitutes stateside? Or that he had a history of rape and crimes of violence against women?'

Gloria felt the blood drain from her face, but her voice was perfectly steady as she said, 'No, I didn't. But I'm not surprised.'

Perry nodded and began to wonder anew about that nervousness of hers. She was too cool and too damned good to get nervous about another cop on the take or a horny little

337

sod out for free nookie. And he was pretty sure now she must have had him pegged from the moment he came in. So why the nerves? Interesting, that. 'You don't seem to be very curious,' he commented mildly. 'Most people would be asking all sorts of questions by now.'

Gloria smiled. 'I find a lot of my guests, quite a few incidentally who are in your profession,' she slipped in the knife almost pleasantly, 'don't like to be asked questions. My lack of curiosity is probably just a habit.' She smiled as she said it, and Perry couldn't help but laugh softly.

'Have you seen Mr Lyons since he . . . checked out?'

Gloria tensed then forced herself to relax. Damn, but she'd fallen for that one. This was one clever cop. 'No.'

Perry nodded. That double-meaning 'checked out' had hit home. She knew something. It might only be street rumours that the body on the beach was Lyons. Then again . . . 'Well, I thank your for your time, Miss Gaines. It's been . . . educational.'

Gloria rose and held out her hand. 'Goodbye, Lieutenant.' She walked him to the door and called softly, 'Marie, show the Lieutenant out, will you please?'

Perry looked across in time to see a red-faced Rolnalski leap guiltily from the sofa. Outside Perry chewed his cheeks and when he was sure he could keep a straight face, looked at the man who was getting in behind the wheel.

'Get some men checking out her girls, will you, especially any who might have either disappeared around Christmas-time or fallen down some stairs.'

'You think Lyons got to one of them?'

'Could be.'

Back at the station, Johnson at the desk waylaid him. 'Got a call for you, Lieutenant. Man asked for the cop in charge of the body-on-the-beach case.'

Perry walked to the desk. 'Leave a name?'

'No. No number either. Said he'd call back.'

'Any clue?' Johnson, a large black man with more years' experience than anyone could guess at, nodded tnoughtfully. 'White, well-educated. Sounded pretty damned sure of himself.'

Perry nodded thoughtfully. What at first had looked like a routine, no-hoper case was turning out to be very, very interesting indeed.

RHIANNON looked around the Hawaiian Hall, cooling down slowly as she escaped from the hot June day outside. She walked slowly to the wall where feather cloaks were splayed out in all their finery.

'Lovely, aren't they?' a voice asked behind her and she spun around, looking at the shoulders of the huge man who loomed in front of her. He seemed a hell of a lot smaller when he was sitting down, she thought wryly, taking in at a glance the toffee-coloured hair, the large grey eyes, the handsome face.

'Looking at these, it's not hard to imagine the ancient Hawaii, is it? Especially when their *aliis* wore garments like these,' she added softly.

Richard looked at the cloak on the wall and then back at her. '*Aliis*?'

'Yes – their chiefs wore them on special occasions, during a festival of the gods. These lesser robes,' she continued, walking a few steps further along the wall to where smaller but still fabulous feathered creations were hung, 'were worn by the Kalaimoka, the tribes admin. officers and the Kahuna Nui, or high priests.'

Richard was not interested, but for a few minutes they continued to walk the circumference of the room as Rhiannon played for time. Although she hated to admit it, the man's rather overpowering size unnerved her. A doctor of medicine and skilled surgeon did not equate with an image of a six-foot-six man with a body that looked as indestructible as concrete.

'I was rather surprised when Mr Gunster phoned and asked me to meet you here. We haven't been introduced before, I'm sure,' Richard smiled smoothly.

'We saw each other at John Domini's, but didn't speak.'

'Oh yes. You were with the fair Prince.'

Rhiannon laughed rather hollowly. 'Yes.'

Richard didn't miss the grim yet wry tone of her voice, and

reminded himself to be careful. If even half the rumours his wife had told him were true, this girl had masterminded the takeover of Liliha boutiques and wangled a seat on the board at Lanai. Odessa had her uses, he admitted. There was nothing more a woman liked than to feel needed. Consequently, he now knew a great deal about this girl because his wife had called in markers, putting out gossip feelers and coming back with all kinds of interesting titbits. But not, alas, the most fascinating thing of all; why she was out for Fairchild's blood.

'I'm sure,' Rhiannon said cautiously, pausing in front of a shark's tooth necklace safely laid out in a glass case, 'that you must realize by now that our ... goals may, in certain respects, be very similar?'

Richard recognized the cleverness of the question. She didn't admit to anything but left the door wide open. The question was, did he want to walk through it? Yes, he wanted Fairchild off his back, but only in so far as he affected the singer and Vienna. 'I don't believe either of us has a great love for a certain businessman, no.'

He's a weasel, she thought. A big, handsome, well-disguised weasel, but one nonetheless. A shiver of distaste crept over her flesh. Without really knowing why, she decided then and there that there could be no collaboration between them. There was nothing definite that she could put her finger on, just a feeling. A repugnance that increased the longer she stayed within his orbit.

'I must congratulate you,' Richard said mildly, 'on your successes so far. They've been quite spectacular. I trust you mean to carry on?'

'I do,' she acknowledged reluctantly.

Richard nodded. Good. If he could leave it to her to take care of Fairchild, it would leave him free to concentrate on Vienna. That suited him just fine.

'Do you know why Fairchild had you thrown off the islands?' Rhiannon asked bluntly, looking at a display of rough rings, made mostly out of carved coral and chunks of turquoise and quartz.

'No. Do you?'

'No.'

'If you find out, will you tell me?'

Rhiannon did look at him then, her green eyes unflinching under the onslaught of grey granite that looked back at her. 'That depends,' she finally answered. 'I believe it has something to do with that handsome singer who works at the Blue Hawaiian.' She saw the explosion of raw emotion take place in the deepest centre of his eyes and felt her own blood run cold. He's not normal, she realized with a dawning horror. He's not right in the head! She looked away, hoping she sounded calm. 'Of course, I have people working on that and other things.'

'Naturally,' Richard said, glad she didn't linger on the subject of the hated Manikuuna. 'If there's anything I can do . . .'

'I'll call you,' Rhiannon lied firmly. 'Well, I have another appointment, so it's goodbye for the present.'

Richard nodded. 'It's been a pleasure meeting you at last, Miss Grantham. I hope we both achieve our goals soon.'

Not if I can help it, Rhiannon thought, even as she smiled briefly and held out her hand. Her flesh crept as he shook it, but her face retained its polite expression. In one corner a museum guide working part-time to relieve the boredom of retirement, watched them shake hands and leave, then walked quickly into the offices to make an urgent telephone call.

Outside Rhiannon walked quickly to her chauffeured limousine, driven now by an Englishman, and allowed herself a graphic, uncontrolled shudder.

'Where to now, madam?'

'I'm not sure, Sam,' she sighed, then shook her head. No – she *was* sure. She was after Dominic – but no one else must get hurt on the way. Otherwise she was no better than he was. Lifting the phone from its niche in the back of the driver's seat she checked her portfolio on Farron Manikuuna that Jack kept regularly updated and dialled the number of Vienna's new house.

'Hello?' the clear voice sounded a little scared.

'Hello, Vienna? We met in the dining room of the Blue

341

Hawaiian when you served me a drink. Rhiannon Grantham?'

'Oh yes, Miss Grantham.'

'Rhia, please. Miss Grantham reminds me of my granny.' Vienna's laughter held a trace of relief in it and Rhia wondered if that odious creature she'd just met had been the cause of the fear she had heard in her voice. 'I was wondering if you were free for lunch.'

'Well, I'm not sure.'

'Please, let me get things out in the open. It has nothing to do with Mr Fairchild, or Farron, I promise. But I really do need to talk to you.'

'OK.' Vienna accepted more readily now, and Rhiannon nodded, aware that the other girl was in something of an awkward situation. She was glad, but not surprised, to find Vienna having the guts to make a choice that her boyfriend probably wouldn't approve of. She'd been right when she'd guessed the little blonde girl was made of fine and sturdy stuff.

THEY met an hour later in the Monarch Room of the Royal Hawaiian Hotel, and ordered two iced teas. Vienna folded her hands in her lap, and smiled shyly. 'I was surprised to hear from you.'

'I understand,' Rhiannon said, then decided to get the preliminaries out of the way. Until they were, she knew Vienna would not relax. 'Look, it's no secret that Dominic Fairchild and I are . . . rivals. And, working for him like you do, and Farron as well, I can understand why meeting like this could feel awkward for you. But if I don't talk about him, and you don't, there'd be no reason why we couldn't be friends, would there?'

Vienna shook her head. 'None at all,' she agreed firmly.

'Good.' Their iced teas came and the women fell silent until after the waiter had gone. 'The reason I asked you here . . .' Rhiannon paused, wondering how best to broach the subject, then decided there was nothing for it but to take the bull by the horns: 'I've just met Richard Jago.'

Vienna went white, her large blue eyes widening with an almost haunted expression.

'I don't know if you're aware of it or not,' Rhiannon said urgently, 'and I know it's going to sound melodramatic, but I think he's ... touched.' Vienna looked up quickly as Rhiannon tapped her forehead. 'You know – in the head. He gives me the creeps.'

Looking up into the earnesat and sincere green eyes opposite her, Vienna smiled weakly. You must learn to trust your instincts, she told herself. And they said that there could be nothing but good coming from a friendship formed with this lovely woman who was warning her even when, Vienna guessed shrewdly, it might have paid her not to.

'I don't mean to scare you, but I think you should watch out for him. He's up to something.'

'Did he say anything?' Vienna asked sharply.

'I'm afraid not. He's very close-mouthed and cautious.'

Vienna nodded, slumping back in her chair. 'Yes. I know.'

Rhiannon didn't know what to do or say next. She felt helpless and despondent. 'Look, Vienna. Perhaps you should think about leaving the islands?'

Vienna shook her head. 'No. I still need this place. It's all I know.'

'You still haven't got your memory back?'

'No.' Vienna didn't mention the glimpses of Switzerland or school. While she liked this woman and was beginning to trust her, she still held back. Perhaps I'm naturally cautious, she thought grimly. Like Richard. And although she never mentioned it, she could tell by the way he looked at her sometimes, that Farron wondered about her. 'Why . . .' she began crisply, then softened her voice somewhat. 'I don't mean to sound ungrateful, but why should you try and warn me? I'm practically a complete stranger, after all.'

Rhiannon stared at her for a second, totally caught out. 'Well, because I thought you might need it, I suppose.' For a second the two women stared blankly at each other, and then Rhiannon laughed. 'That sounds crazy too, doesn't it? I don't know,' she shook her head. 'Perhaps madness *is* catching.'

Vienna laughed. 'I hope not,' she said fervently, then thought about her own problems and added in a much more subdued voice, 'If so, you'd better stay away from me.' She shuddered as an image of a flashing knife in a dark alley superceded her tea cup, and then determinedly shrugged it away. She had told no one but Farron about these waking nightmares but had begun to wonder if she shouldn't seek some professional help.

Rhiannon saw her sudden pallor, and instinctively reached across the table and squeezed her hand. 'Its going to all right. I mean it – I really think you'll get your memory back.'

Vienna smiled, but was glad that Rhiannon had misunderstood. It was no longer not remembering that worried her, but what she *might* remember . . . 'Thanks. I mean it.'

For another second they smiled at each other in mutual understanding, then Rhiannon sat back and withdrew her hand. 'I'm glad you agreed to meet me,' she said. 'I felt I had to warn you.'

'I'm glad I came too,' Vienna smiled then looked down at her watch. 'But I have to go. I'm meeting Farron after the show.'

'Oh well, in that case,' Rhiannon raised her glass, Vienna followed suit, and together they clinked glasses. 'Cheers.'

I LIKE her, Farron,' Vienna told him defiantly a scant half hour later as they left the Blue Hawaiian.

'What did you talk about?' he asked suspiciously. 'Dominic?'

'No,' Vienna said. 'In fact, she admitted quite openly that we were on opposite sides of the fence about him, and it was her suggestion that neither of us mention him – at all.'

'So what exactly did she want?' Farron probed.

'Nothing. We just . . . talked. You know, all-girls-together kind of thing?' Vienna was not about to mention Richard Jago. She knew Farron was jealous of him and she didn't think she could stand a cross-examination right here and now. 'Oh, let's forget it,' she sighed wearily. 'OK?'

Farron looked at her out of the corner of his eyes, a smile beginning to appear as she continued to gaze at him chidingly until eventually he began to laugh and hold up his hands. 'OK, OK.'

'Admit it,' Vienna teased, slipping into the car beside him. 'She's not as bad as you thought.'

'No, she's not. I suppose,' he added dubiously.

Vienna giggled, but let it pass. For some reason her liquid lunch with the other woman had made her feel better. Perhaps it was just knowing she had someone else on her side that helped. Or perhaps it was getting out of the house for something beside cookery classes or meeting Farron. She needed a friend to talk to – a good female friend. And, in spite of all the odds against it, Rhia Grantham still seemed the most likely candidate. 'She's quite a lady,' Vienna mused. 'But don't worry. I won't do anything to hurt Dominic.'

'Good.'

'Where are you taking me?'

'To Chinaman's Hat. Or Mokoli'i, as we natives call it. It's a little island – not far. You can wade to it when the tide's out. Did you bring your bikini?' Vienna prodded the large beach bag resting on the floor between her feet. 'Good. We'll rent some surfboards and I'll teach you to surf.'

At the beach she changed in the car while Farron rented out some boards. Walking to the water's edge, Farron carrying both boards, Vienna sighed dreamily. 'It's so lovely here. I don't think I'll ever want to leave.'

'I'm glad.' He stopped to kiss her, a friendly kiss that quickly developed into something far more potent.

'Get to it, my man,' a laughing voice drawled a few feet away, and they broke apart, laughing.

'Right – surfing lesson coming up,' Farron said firmly.

'Help!' Vienna warbled weakly.

'Don't be chicken,' he accused, dropping the board to the sand. 'Surfing is an ancient sport, once called *he'enalu*. 'Course the best surfing month is November, or *Ikuwa*, but these little rollers will do.' Those little rollers looked gigantic to Vienna, but she wisely kept her mouth shut. Farron was talking with the enthusiasm of a zealot. 'I belong to the Hui Nah Club, the oldest. But the Outrigger Canoe Club has a few good members.'

'When are we going to get on the board?' she teased, feigning impatience.

He put a playful fist under her chin. 'First of all, do you know what it is?'

'It's a board.'

He shook his head. 'You can have boogie boards, lightning bolts, bungie cards, fishpin and swallow-tails. Most weigh about thirty-five pounds and are ten feet long.'

'Yes, Teacher.'

'Watch it! Here,' he shoved one board further away. 'Stand on this. Surfing is a question of balance and foot pressure. See?' He moved behind her, his arms encircling her bare waist as she leaned back in his arms.

'Oh, Teacher, are you sure this is part of the lesson?'

'Pay attention, Wright, or it's detention and one hundred lines.'

'Yes, sir.' Vienna began to laugh, Farron quickly joining her.

'You'll never progress to Sandy Beach or Makapu Beach Park at this rate,' he growled playfully, nibbling her ear. 'Look at my feet and do what I do.'

'Yes, sir.' Vienna looked down, following his foot movements.

'When the wave comes you brace your knees like this,' they crouched down, his arms firm and strong around her, but she went too far, sending them sprawling sideways on to the hot sand.

'Ouch,' she wailed, sitting up, then slapped his legs playfully. 'Hey,' she looked down at him as he lay beside her, his dark eyes dancing with laughter, his hands tender on her back as they rubbed her skin. 'I never noticed that before,' she said, her voice surprised.

'What?' He sat up and looked to where she was pointing, at the little toe on his left foot which was longer than its neighbour. 'Oh, that . . .'

Chapter 27

The Sea Life Park looked out over the Makapuu headlands. Rhiannon, who'd spent a pleasant half hour at the Hawaiian Reef tanks, now sat in the stands in front of a small three-masted sailing ship that bobbed in a lagoon so blue it almost hurt her eyes. Children squealed and laughed as they were splashed by jumping dolphins and overhead the sun beat down mercilessly.

She turned to Sandy McNally, the phographer she'd hired to follow and photograph Dominic Fairchild. 'So what you're saying is, he's too clever to be indiscreet?'

Sandy nodded. 'Much.'

Rhiannon sighed deeply. She'd been prepared for this, but nevertheless experienced a feeling of distaste for what she was about to ask. 'What I need,' she began cautiously, 'is a man who is not too choosey about the jobs he takes on.'

Sandy shifted nervously in his seat. 'What do you mean, exactly?'

Rhiannon gave what she hoped was a casual shrug. 'Someone prepared to bend, shall we say, the law? Do you know anyone like that?' From her briefcase she withdrew a wad of green bills, neatly encircled by a band. 'If you do, there's a bonus for you.'

He looked at the wad with yearning eyes. 'I might know someone,' he said reluctantly. 'But I'm not sure if he'll get in interested. He's expensive.'

'Money's no problem,' she said dismissively, wanting only to get the whole sordid mess over with.

'I'll tell him, but I can't promise he'll get in touch.'

'Fine,' she smiled and added softly, 'thank you, Sandy.'

Rhiannon watched him go, feeling acutely miserable. She didn't like herself much these days. She was getting in deeper and deeper and it scared her.

SHE saw the notice in the paper over breakfast the following morning, and read it with growing incredulity.

'*The Party of the Year, the birthday celebrations of His Royal Highness Prince Dominic Hua Fairchild, will again be held at his fabulous home in Kalena Heights, Honolulu, the famous Falling Pearls Palace, on 9 August. Sources have told this reporter that the guest-list will include all of the island's most prominent figures from the world of politics, sport and business, not to mention a host of celebrities from stage, film and music. Definitely an occasion of last-minute panic visits to your dressmaker for that "original" ballgown, ladies, so all you matrons of society should polish up your best diamonds and daughters. Don't forget that the Prince, after so many years of careful bacherlorhood, is still by far the greatest catch for 5,000 miles!*'

Good grief, she thought savagely, what snivelling moron could write such sickening piffle? Whatever doubts Rhiannon had had about her behaviour yesterday were now pushed firmly to the back of her mind. Picking up the phone she punched out a number, held it to her ear, and waited.

'Hello. Gray-Grays.'

'Clarice, it's me.'

'Rhia, darling. What's wrong?'

'Nothing. I was just wondering if two of your best girls could get your heads together and design a ballgown for me in time for the ninth of August.'

'The ninth? Isn't that Dominic's birthday?'

'Uh-huh. I'm going to the party.'

'No! I never would have thought that you'd be invited.'

'What makes you think I have been?' she said lightly, then frowned in sudden anger. She might be all right to take out to dinner now and then, but he obviously had no intention of asking her to come to his home.

From the other end of the line came a wave of soft, almost helpless laughter. 'Oh Rhiannon! Do you have a death wish or something?'

'Or something,' Rhiannon agreed drolly. 'Can you do it?'

SHE'D just returned from the Hilton Hawiian Village

Rainbow Bazaar, where she'd bought some interesting one-of-a-kind curios and novelties for Ben, who was due to dock soon, when she noticed Jack's car parked outside the bungalow.

Shrugging off the unease she was beginning to feel whenever Jack was around, she walked in and deposited her purchases on the hall table then entered the living room. Jack was seated on the sofa, idly leafing through the paper. She opened her mouth to ask him sarcastically to make himself at home, then thought better of it, and merely smiled a cool greeting.

'I've got a present for you,' Jack said, slowly uncrossing his long legs.

'Dominic?' She said the word quietly, and Jack nodded.

'Dominic,' he confirmed. 'We were right about the reasons for Jago's exile. It was because of the singer. Fairchild has been behind the kid all the way – paying for the nonexistent music scholarship that Farron thinks took him through university, picking up the tab when the kid had to have his appendix out and didn't have any insurance. We know he masterminded the boy's singing career, but he's also the well-hidden landlord of the house where he grew up, which is now the grandmother's.'

Rhiannon frowned. 'Why so generous?'

'The kid's mother was a prostitute by the name of Akaki Manikuuna. She died of VD and drugs-related diseases of the liver and kidneys in 1969. The grandmother brought him up. His mother was working for a brothel madam called Gloria Gaines when Fairchild met her. Afterwards she left the brothel and moved into a small rented bungalow, keeping her favours exclusively for him. When he returned from Oxford for his grandfather's funeral, she had a baby son. She was seen for a few days wearing a huge diamond engagement ring, until after the funeral.'

'And the will!' she yelped as realization hit her. His son! Farron was his son. She could see it now – the likeness in the high cheekbones and the way he tilted his head.

'So,' Jack said slowly, watching her reaction like a hawk, 'we have another knife that we can stick into his back and twist.'

She walked to the window and stared out at the ocean, fighting off a terrible chill. She'd won. With this information, surely she held the winning card? As a personal weapon to use against Dominic, Farron could be devastating. And if she offered to pay the Chicago relatives considerably more than the hundred thousand dollars bequeathed to them by Fred Fairchild, she could surely persuade them to contest the will, thus freezing enough of Dominic's inheritance to cripple the rest of his companies. With the morality clause, coupled with Fred Fairchild's obvious intention that no illegitimate child should benefit from his money, the lawyers could make enough of a case that Farron *had* benefited from Fred Fairchild's will. The job at the hotel for a start could be seen as breaking the spirit of the will. Oh, the argument might be rocky, and Dominic would almost certainly win it, but it would still take years in the court to sort out. Years that Dominic could ill-afford to waste.

Yes, both personally and financially, she surely had a much stronger hand now than when she had first arrived on the islands. So why did she feel so miserable?

THE phone on his desk rang stridently, and Perry lifted it quickly. 'Clements.'

'You're the man in charge of the murder of Gary Lyons?'

'Yes,' Perry admitted, stopping what he was doing and listening intently. Caucasian, well-educated. His desk sergeant had been right.

'I have some information for you.'

'And you are?'

'Doesn't matter. If you want to find out who killed Lyons, ask the girl with amnesia. The one who so conveniently lost her memory around the same time that Lyons was dumped for the fishes.'

The receiver went dead in his ear and Perry thoughtfully hung up. He stared at the dead plant on the windowsill and sighed deeply.

TWO miles away Odessa walked through her breeze-swept lounge just as her husband was putting down the phone. She looked at him sharply. 'Who was that?'

'An old friend of mine, Larry Craine, wants to know if we can get him into the Country Club. He's been trying for years but he's only an anaesthetist, with a salary to match. And the snobs there . . .' he shrugged.

'I'll get him in,' she promised, walking in front of the open french windows that led out to perfectly landscaped gardens, and sat quickly on his knee.

'I've got a surprise for you,' she whispered in his ear, then nibbled it and Richard slowly slipped his hands around her waist, gently rubbing his thumbs teasingly below her breasts. She stood up, tugging on his hand, leading him outside to where a brand new Maserati waited.

'Where are we going?' he asked, not commenting when she walked to the driver's seat and got in, but smiled and got into the passenger side.

'You'll see,' she said teasingly, slipping the car into gear and roaring away, checking her make-up in the mirror. Ever since she'd seen the PI's pictures of Vienna Wright she'd been taking extra special care with her appearance. She looked across at her husband, who was smiling softly at her, and told herself not to be stupid. After two weeks of purely innocuous reports, with Richard not going within miles of the girl, she was beginning to think that her suspicions were ridiculous. Just because he seemed to be spending more and more time away from home when he was not at the hospital didn't mean he was having an affair. And so what if she had to make all the moves to get him to make love to her? That was just his way. He was so shy and sweet he probably thought it was insensitive to demand sex all the time. When she'd parked the car, she leaned over the gearstick and kissed him hungrily.

'Hm. We're being stared at,' Richard laughed, using two gawping teenage girls as an excuse to pull away and open the door.

'Look,' she said, pointing to the end berth where a large 900-tonne, ocean-going yacht gleamed brilliant white in the afternoon sun.

'Lovely,' Richard admitted with genuine praise, his experienced eye running from bow to stern, the powerful engine indicated by the numbers on the hull.

'It's ours,' she announced, feeling like Santa Claus at Christmas when Richard's grey eyes widened and swung to her, a mixture of shock and pleasure on his face.

'You're kidding?' he breathed, genuinely stunned.

'No I'm not.' Odessa shook her head. 'I hired the crew this morning. Want to go for a ride?'

'A cruise,' Richard corrected, then took her by surprise by lifting her high in the air with powerful ease and swinging her around. She revelled in the physical strength of her husband. She truly had it all. A man who was strong yet tender. An honourable man, a real husband at last. And a wonderful lover. She couldn't wait to show him the yacht's master bedroom. On board she introduced him. 'Captain Williams, this is my husband, Dr Jago.'

Richard shook hands with the captain, a fiftyish, very capable-looking man.

'Welcome aboard, Doctor. What do you think of her? Your wife tells me you're a sailing man.'

'Oh, not in your class. And certainly never a vessel like this. Tell me . . .'

'Let's sail to Lanai,' Odessa enthused, cutting them off before they could get the bit between their teeth. 'We can stay on board for a few days then sail on to Hawaii. Anything you like, darling,' she offered, her mouth pulling into a sexy smile. The captain took the hint, excusing himself to check the bridge.

'Lanai's fine,' Richard agreed, pulling her to him and kissing her firmly and thoroughly. 'It's a magnificent yacht,' he added, taking her hand and kissing her knuckles. 'Thank you.'

Odessa said huskily, 'Have a look inside. There's everything down there – a cinema, a games room, a lounge, a huge galley, a dining room, a bedroom.'

The bedroom was obviously all her creation. The bed was circular with black satin sheets, its headboard a fan-like shape of pink and black silk. Within moments her loose-fitting red silk dress slithered off to reveal her totally naked body. Walking to the bed she agilely wriggled into the middle of it and stretched. He shrugged off his T-shirt and slacks and her eyes slid hungrily to his upswelling organ, her heart pounding. She'd never had a lover as well endowed as her husband before, and her thighs parted eagerly as he loomed over her, his face tight with desire. There was no need for preliminaries. Pushing her thighs even further apart he lunged almost perfunctorily into her. Odessa cried out, feeling hot velvet steel pushing up, up, past her vagina, past her womb, up higher into her belly. Her legs locked around his in compulsive reaction, her back arching up, her head thrown back, eyes wide open and glazed.

Richard closed his eyes. He saw Vienna, her body twisting under his, her eyes huge and crying as he lunged deeper into her. He felt fingernails digging into his back and he pushed harder, faster, and now Vienna was behind bars, in a dingy, dirty dungeon, a judge pronouncing sentence in the background and she was turning to him, her arms outstretched pleadingly. But he ignored her. Laughing he turned and walked away.

'Richard!' Odessa screamed as orgasm followed orgasm and still he pounded away inside her willing body, his eyes closed, his breath gasping from his mouth. Odessa moaned again, her body twisting and bucking with the force of agonizing pleasure that rippled through her. 'Richard, I can't take any more!'

Richard moaned, hearing the words come from another mouth, for another reason. 'Stop,' Odessa moaned, even as her hands and legs clutched him even further into her body, yearning, straining for more, always for more.

'No,' Richard moaned, his big body shuddering as his own climax swept him into a shaking, shivering release. 'Never. *Never!*'

Chapter 28

Gloria looked up from her desk as Angela, a petite brunette, quickly popped her head round the door. 'It's that cop again,' she whispered.

'Hell!' Gloria quickly folded away her graphs of projected earnings and slipped them into a drawer, locking it with a snap before looking up at the girl and nodding. 'Show him in.'

Angela did so, her hazel eyes spitting venom at Perry Clements who noticed but didn't take it personally. Dressed in a simple pair of dark brown trousers and wheat-coloured shirt with brown tie, he looked very bland. 'Miss Gaines,' he smiled slightly as he nodded, crow's feet appearing attractively at his eyes. Gloria rose slowly, a cool smile on her artfully made-up face.

'Lieutenant,' she said pleasantly. 'It's so nice to see you again,' she lied, offering him a chair. 'Please, sit down. Can I get you a cup of coffee?'

'That would be nice,' he dismayed her by accepting, and walking to the door Gloria opened it and called to no one in particular for two coffees. Perry watched her walk back to her desk, his appreciative eyes taking in the still-trim and neat figure in a simple maroon dress tightly belted at the waist and curving over slender hips. Like all men, Perry knew class when he saw it.

'What can I do for you, Lieutenant?'

'I've heard that one of your girls is missing. Has been, in fact, since — oh, December last?'

Gloria shrugged coolly but was glad when a knock came at the door and Angela walked in carrying a loaded tray. She put it down in front of Gloria, turned to spit more venom upon Perry's head, and left.

'I don't think she likes me,' Perry commented idly. He smiled as she handed him a cup, knowing that he liked her. It was a simple enough thing — some people you liked on sight, like Dominic Fairchild, others you didn't. It did not hinder him in any way. During the course of his career he'd arrested and even convicted a number of people whom he'd liked well enough on a personal level. Gloria didn't say a whole lot, he realized ruefully, and that was smart. The amount of people who hanged themselves by talking too much was too incredible for Joe Public to believe. 'The missing girl, Gloria?' he prompted, taking a sip. It was good coffee. He had known it would be.

Gloria shrugged, looking very much at ease. 'My girls are not obliged to stay here. Many of them go back stateside with a man they've grown fond of and have several kids.'

Perry stirred the dark liquid in his cup thoughtfully. 'I've heard that old chestnut before – of prostitutes making the best mothers.'

Gloria winced quite openly and reached for the sugar cubes to add one to her own drink. 'Some do. Some don't,' she finally responded noncommittally, and although she kept her breathing even and normal, her chest still ached. Something there, Perry thought. Has she got a kid herself somewhere?

'The rumour on the streets has it the girl had to retire for health reasons.'

'Oh? I don't walk the streets any more, so I wouldn't know.' Perry smiled. 'Perhaps you could get to the point, Lieutenant?' she asked sharply, her voice strained for the first time.

'Certainly,' he agreed mildly enough, reaching forward to deposit the cup and saucer on the table. 'I think Gary Lyons . . . you remember him? Of course you do. Because I think it was Lyons who was chucked out of here for roughing up your girls. And I don't think a man like Lyons would take it very kindly.'

'I know all that,' Gloria snapped, then could have kicked herself. 'More coffee?' she added with total cordiality.

'I also think,' he continued remorselessly, with a voice kept deceptively low, 'that Lyons came back and tried to murder one of your girls. He made a habit of that stateside, as I think I told you.'

Gloria went white and Perry felt sorry for her. It must have been a very nasty scene for anyone to witness, even one as self-possessed as this woman. 'You know,' he said softly, 'I can't see any court in the world taking a hard line with a woman who killed a suspected murderer and convicted felon and rapist in the course of self-defence.'

Gloria could feel the kindness of the man begin to sway her and she fought it off fiercely. Hell, he was more dangerous than she'd at first thought. He saw her lips firm and her eyes harden, and knew what was coming. Damn! She was not going to make it easy.

'I suppose so, Lieutenant. But since your ... theory, is totally wrong, I don't see what that has to do with us.'

'I hear Bunny works for you.' Perry mentioned the pet name of the struck-off doctor who'd been on Gloria's payroll for years. 'I wonder if he remembers a patch-up job around about Christmas?'

Gloria shrugged. 'I can't imagine. Why don't you ask him?'

'You sound very confident, Miss Gaines.'

'I'm a very confident – and competent – person, Lieutenant.'

'I'd noticed. But perhaps you're so confident because it wasn't good ol' Bunny who did the patching at all. Could it be that a local hospital took care of it?'

The effort it took Gloria to stay outwardly calm began to make sweat trickle down her back. 'It's your fantasy – have it whatever way you like,' she offered, sweetly magnanimous.

'Let's see. A local hospital in December ... Of course!' He clicked his fingers. 'That was the time that poor girl with amnesia was admitted into the Memorial, wasn't it?'

Gloria felt a tunnel closing in around her, darkness invading her vision with a roaring wall of blood that seemed to thunder into her ears. Her throat and mouth were suddenly as dry as the Sahara. She blinked hard, once, twice, three times. *Think!* a voice screamed with panic-stricken stridency in the back of her mind. *For God's sake think!*

Perry, who saw every drop of colour drain from her face, also saw the slight swaying motion of her upper torso as she leant against the table and his body was poised to leap forward if she should faint. But she suddenly snapped out of it, her back straightening once more in the chair, her pupils shrinking back into sharp focus. In a voice that wasn't quite steady she said, 'That's a big leap. Still, as I said, it's your fantasy.'

She finished the coffee quickly, uncaring that the liquid burned her tongue whilst Perry sighed in relief. Manlike, he'd never felt comfortable around women who looked ill. 'You don't recall the amnesiac case?'

'No, Gloria lied shortly. 'I don't read the papers much – except for the financial or political editorials. A lot of my short-term tenants are in office, and after all, my girls have their own Republican and Democrat ideals.'

Perry laughed. What a recovery. She was now looking every inch the confident and competent woman she had called herself. 'If you say so,' he allowed, checking his watch. Twenty minutes he'd been here and she hadn't let slip a damned thing. Hadn't even admitted her girls were pro's. Very clever, Perry thought. But not cold. Not hard.

Gloria tensed. At that moment she'd have given half of her business to know what he was thinking. 'Well, thank you for your cooperation, Miss Gaines. I appreciate it.'

'Is that all?' she asked, caught offguard, then could have bitten her tongue out.

'Yes, that's all,' Perry stated abruptly, turning to walk to the door.

There, with his hand on the handle, he paused as she said coolly, 'I wish I could have been of more help to you.'

'You were of immense help, Miss Gaines. It's been truly,' he searched for the right word, knowing he was dealing with a lady of intelligence, 'informative.'

Her eyes narrowed in annoyance before a slight rueful smile crossed her lips, a silent salutation at an enemy who had trounced her, fair and square. Perry found respect being added to liking for this woman. 'Lieutenant,' she said simply.

'Miss Gaines,' he said, just as simply, and left.

ROLNALSKI tossed away a cigarette as his superior emerged from the motel door. 'Did she bite?'

'Hard. When I mentioned the blonde I thought she was going to pass out.'

Rolnalski whistled silently. 'Our anonymous tipster's on to something, then?'

'Looks like it,' he admitted, getting into the passenger seat.

'Do you think the madam herself might have topped Lyons?' Rolnalski asked, starting the engine and revving it.

'Possible,' Perry admitted. 'But not, I think, probable. It's more likely the blonde did it. To kill someone and almost be killed yourself would be enough to make anyone lose their memory . . . if it's for real.'

'You think she might be faking it?'

'Could be. How could anyone know? Quit revving the engine, will you?'

Rolnalski sighed deeply. 'Where we goin' then?' he asked testily.

'The Honolulu Memorial. I want to know the details before checking the girl out herself.'

THE hospital was large and squat and the moment he stepped inside he felt uneasy. He hated hospitals. There was something about the smell of them and a quietness that unnerved him. By his side Rolnalski chewed gum. Walking to the reception desk, Perry took out his badge and asked to see the administrator. The woman showed them the way at once without so much as a word.

The administrator's office was very different from the sanitized wards. Large and airy with wide windows that were framed by curtains and not blinds, the walls were a pale eggshell blue, the carpet underneath a navy blue with grey roses. A grandfather clock, totally out of place, ticked ponderously in one corner. Perry dragged his eyes from the carpet to the man sat behind a large desk cluttered with photographs, a vase of flowers, books, papers and paperweights. Dr Matthews was a small, dapper man, who looked as if he'd been born in a navy-blue suit, white shirt and black tie. His hair was grey and combed so neatly on his head and smothered in so much oil that it almost resembled a plastic skullcap. The eyes were watery blue, the moustache on his upper lip another plastic-like expanse of neatly-trimmed hair. 'Lieutenant Clements. There's nothing wrong, I hope?' The voice was thin and nervous.

'Not at all. We're investigating a homicide case.'

'Homicide? I trust this hospital is not involved in any malpractice case, because if so . . .'

'It's nothing of that nature,' Perry interrupted firmly, his voice raised to cut in across the high-pitched, outraged squeak of the other man.

'Oh. That's all right then.' Dr Matthews relaxed, wilting in his chair. Perry almost expected him to reach for a pristine white handkerchief and wipe his face. He glanced across at Rolnalski who looked bored and half-asleep. 'I need to see the files of an ex-patient of yours, Dr Matthews. For our investigations.'

'Oh, now I'm not sure about that,' the little man began to demur at once. 'This hospital has a strict policy of patient confidentiality.'

'I understand. I can, of course, get a search warrant issued,' Perry confided, then added meaningfully, 'but I had assumed that this hospital, like all the others, would want to cooperate with the Police Department.' It was a dirty trick, he supposed, but it worked like magic.

'Oh, of course. In that case, which patient file do you need to see?'

'It concerns an amnesiac case you had in December last. A young woman. I believe she chose the name Vienna Wright?'

'Oh yes, yes. I remember. I understand now. You think you know who she is, yes?' As he pressed the intercom buzzer and asked for her file, Perry did not bother to correct him. 'I'm not sure that I can let you have copies of the file, mind,' Dr Matthews warned now, obviously having second thoughts.

'That won't be necessary. In fact, I don't even need to see it. If you could just answer one or two medical questions for me, I don't think we need take it any further.'

Rolnalski blew a gum bubble, the flat 'pop' immediately making two pairs of eyes swing in his direction. He promptly went pink. A knock at the door saved him when the same receptionist walked in and handed over a very thin, large square folder. Dr Matthews pulled out several black plastic X-ray sheets and studied them. 'Hm, all very straightforward. What exactly did you want to know, Lieutenant?'

'Oh — just general things. Can you tell me what the test results indicated, for instance?' For ten minutes Dr Matthews talked them through the brain scan, its negative reports, heart graphs, indicating a perfectly functioning organ, and a variety of blood tests, showing only that she was the very common O-type, with no disorders. Perry let him have his head until he came to the nitty gritty. 'Did she have any tests done on her . . . er . . . I mean, was she for instance a mother?'

Rolnalski grinned as his usually erudite boss stumbled for words, and Dr Matthews quickly checked the relevant results. 'That will be indicated in the gynaecological report. Ah, here we are.' The man's eyebrows rose and disappeared under his hairline. 'Now that's interesting.'

Rolnalski and Perry exchanged looks. 'The results show excessive sexual activity?' Perry guessed confidently. But the small man shook his head.

'No — exactly the opposite. The girl was *virgo intacta* — that is to say, she was still a virgin. Her doctor gauged her to be roughly twenty-two to twenty-six years old. Not many virgins still around of that age, I suspect.'

Perry was completely floored. He stared at the doctor for a long, long while, before pulling himself together. 'No — er no, indeed. Are you sure about those results?'

'Oh, quite. Yes, no doubt about it. You see, there is a membrane that is broken when sexual intercourse first takes place, and in this case . . .'

'I see,' Perry cut in quickly, already on his feet. 'Thank you, Dr Matthews. One more thing: was there any sign of drug or alcohol abuse?'

'None. Her blood was very clear, her liver and kidneys perfectly healthy.'

'Thank you. We won't take up any more of your time.' Perry reached over to shake hands, not surprised to scent a body cologne waft over the table at him.

'Any time, Lieutenant. The Memorial is always eager to help the police,' Matthews gushed, relieved that it had all been so simple and painless. 'Of course, if you want to know more about the young lady you should talk to the doctor who treated her.' Matthews' voice hesitated in mid-sentence as he remembered just who that was, and when sharp grey eyes turned on him he wished miserably he'd kept his mouth shut.

'And that was?'

'Dr Jago. Richard Jago,' Matthews admitted.

Perry hesitated halfway to the door. There was something there. 'Can I have his address?'

'Er, well, he did go back to the States shorty after he . . . er . . . left here.'

'Left?' Perry ignored the questioning look Rolnalski gave him, walking back towards the desk and the man who was beginning to look very uncomfortable.

'Yes. Well, actually, he was asked to leave. Oh, not on medical grounds, you understand. My surgical team tells me that Dr Jago was one of the finest surgeons we had, I suppose.'

He didn't like him, Perry thought and wondered why. 'He was asked to leave?'

'Well . . .' Matthews began to sweat. The orders for the dismissal had come from on high and had been suggested in very vague terms that had, nonetheless, been unmistakable. Self-preservation dictated that he never said as much to the police, though. 'It became apparent that Dr Jago's relationship with Miss Wright was not, er, strictly within the moral bounds of doctor-patient. You understand?'

Perry nodded. 'I see. His address?' he prompted and Matthews sighed.

'Dr Jago recently got married, I believe. His wife is apparently from San Francisco. She's very wealthy. I know Richard is living in a large house near Diamond Head somewhere. My receptionist can give you his address. On your way out,' Matthews added hopefully with as much gumption as he'd ever been able to manage in his timid existence.

Perry nodded. 'Don't worry, Doctor. I'll be discreet.'

Outside Rolnalski surreptitiously threw his gum into a wastepaper bin. 'That blows it,' he predicted gloomily and Perry nodded.

'I could have sworn that she would be a pro. I don't get it. When I mentioned her name I thought our local madam was going to keel over.'

'But she's not a pro. A virgin! Jeez. There must have been something wrong with her. Ugly perhaps.'

'No,' Perry shook his head. 'She's a lovely little thing. I saw her in the Blue Hawaiian.'

'Blue Hawaiian?' Rolnalski repeated. 'Dominic Fairchild again, eh'?

'Yes,' Perry said reflectively. He did keep cropping up. In the car he sat in silence as they headed for Diamond Head. 'The girl's mixed up in it somewhere – I know she is.' The trouble was, Perry thought wearily, he could find no connection between the mugging that had left Vienna Wright without a memory, and Gary Lyons. His officers hadn't been able to come up with a single witness who had seen Lyons and Vienna Wright together, and with so little to go on he was not optimistic of finding a connection.

Rolnalski didn't comment but slowed down to check the numbers on the street until they found the Jagos' residence. 'Here it is. Hell, what a place,' he ejaculated, looking out over the landscaped gardens, the twinkling sunlight on a large pool, hibiscus, rhododendron and lilac bushes foaming flowers and scent into the street. They got out of the car and walked to the front door of the large, white-painted two-storeyed building. It was opened by a woman in a simple navy uniform.

'I'd like to see Dr Jago, please.'

'Just a moment, sir. I'll see if he's available. Who shall I say is calling?'

Wordlessly Perry showed her his badge. Her face did not falter. 'If you'd care to wait in the library?' She opened the door wider, showing them in to a large, airy room stacked with books, real walnut shelving, overstuffed black leather chairs, and an antique Chippendale table.

'I think that's what they call a perfect servant,' Perry said drolly was the woman disappeared. Wandering around the shelves he looked at the book titles. The most well-worn were all medical books and sailing and boating manuals. The rest had that well-preserved look of antique bindings and first editions designed for show and investment rather than reading. A scant minute later the maid came back and showed them into a large lounge, where a series of french windows, all of which stood open to let in a cooling breeze, revealed a perfect ocean view. A man walked towards them, his sheer size for a moment making Perry readjust his thinking. 'Lieutenant?'

'Clements. And this is Sergeant Rolnalski.'

'What can I do for you?' Richard asked, ushering them to a sofa, glancing across at a woman who watched them with hard blue eyes. There was something about the simple orange and cream sundress that looked expensive. She wore a gold chain around her slender throat, and a tasteful engagement and wedding ring on her left hand. Her long hair was the colour of Kansas wheat. Her face was thin and interesting rather than beautiful, but the eyes were unfriendly. A rich bitch, Perry guessed, was how most people would label her. But Perry did not label people. There was something ... vulnerable about her, and he wondered if, but doubted it, she was aware of it herself.

'Is there something wrong, gentlemen? Can I offer you a drink?' The large man with the handsome face and long, sensitive hands walked to a globe-like drinks cabinet stocked with the finest booze money could buy but Perry shook his head. 'Darling?' Richard looked at Odessa. 'This is my wife, gentlemen.'

Perry nodded at her and smiled, but his mind was on other things —such as where he had heard Richard Jago's voice before. 'Mrs Jago. It's your husband I've come to see ... about hospital matters.'

Odessa smiled and walked forward. 'I'll have a G and T, darling,' she requested, deliberately ignoring the hint to leave. She was a woman used to doing what she wanted. His eyes once more went to Richard. Just what kind of man was this? A fine surgeon – yes, probably more than fine, for Matthews hadn't liked him but still admitted he was a good doctor. His grey eyes smiled softly as he handed his wife her drink, but there was something ... It looked genuine enough. Perhaps too much so? Yes – that smile looked very practised.

'You say it's about the hospital? I don't work there any more, so I don't ...'

363

'My husband now works at the Fairbourne, Lieutenant,' Odessa cut in, coolly dropping the name of one of the island's première medical centres as if it were no more than a place for her husband to practise his hobby. 'In fact, we've had to cut short a yachting trip to Lanai because he was needed for an emergency heart operation. Sir Raymond Blake – you may have heard he was visiting the islands?'

'Indeed I have,' Perry said, getting the message loud and clear that Richard Jago was very much on the rise as *the* surgeon in the islands. 'But it's about an ex-patient of yours. Miss Vienna Wright?' Neither policeman missed the sharp, almost bitter look Odessa Jago cast her husband, but the man himself either missed it or ignored it.

'Oh? You've found out who she is? That's good news.'

'No, no we haven't. It's about another matter altogether. As her doctor, you know her well?'

Richard shrugged. 'As well as anyone, I suppose. Unless she's got a boyfriend by now or something.' He sat down in a chair next to his wife, leaning his long arm across the back of her chair. Very casual, Perry thought. But Matthews was right about him. He still very much cared about Vienna Wright's lovelife. He thought about that tiny girl, a girl that this man knew to be a virgin. Wouldn't that prove an irresistible combination to any man? 'What can you tell me about her?'

'Surely the hospital records . . .'

'Yes, I've just seen Dr Matthews.' Was it his imagination or had the man frozen then? 'It isn't medical data I need but your opinion as to her emotional state. Was she, for instance, violent?'

Richard's face looked disconcerted for a moment, uneasy. 'No – I don't think so. Why should she be?' He kept his voice deliberately vague. He glanced at Odessa, who was staring at him, her eyes beginning to darken, a sure sign of anger.

'You don't sound too sure, Doctor,' Perry pressed, and Richard shrugged.

'She was angry a lot of the time, frustrated. But that was only natural.'

'I'm sure. Do you think her memory loss is genuine?'

For the first time, Richard looked sincerely surprised and

his answer was totally spontaneous. 'Yes. Yes, I'm sure it was. Why do you ask?'

Perry ignored the question. 'Did she ever tell you about any flashes of memory she might have had?'

Richard's eyes slid away. 'No,' he said.

He's lying, Perry thought, and then he wondered – was he? 'Nothing at all?'

'No – I told you.'

'How did Miss Wright adapt to life once she left the hospital?'

'Very well. She was . . . paranoid of course, but that was only to be expected. She was mugged, and the feeling of being watched, of someone being out to get you, is common amongst amnesiacs. She underwent psychiatric counselling whilst in hospital to help her get over that.'

'I see,' Perry nodded. 'And there's nothing more you can tell me?'

'Nothing,' Richard said, after the merest hint of hesitation.

'Well, thank you for your help, Doctor.'

'Certainly.' Richard rose and showed them to the door.

Outside, Rolnalski gazed enviously at the pool. 'Nothing much there.'

'You think so? I thought our Doctor Jago was being very cagey.'

Rolnalski snorted. 'So would you be if you had a wife like that. Hell, I could feel the daggers her eyes were sticking in him even from where I was sitting.'

Perry smiled slightly. 'If he did marry her for money he's certainly earning it. Did you notice anything odd about him?' he added and Rolnalski shook his head.

'Nope.'

'He never asked why we wanted to know about her. That's another person with an unnatural lack of curiosity. And I've heard his voice, or one like it, somewhere before.'

Inside, Odessa tossed back the last of her gin and tonic, watching her husband walk back through the door. 'What was all that about?' she asked sharply, her eyes watching his every movement as he walked to the French windows and looked out over the ocean.

'Your guess is as good as mine,' he said indifferently, but he had difficulty keeping his voice neutral, for triumph was eating away at his innards. He hadn't expected it to work so soon. Had they called on her yet? Was she pacing the floor at this very moment, or crying on that faggot-singer's shoulder? It wasn't enough. He had to think of something more. Something worse. Far worse.

'Are you seeing that girl?' Odessa's sharp and ugly voice made him look around, an expression of surprise-turning-to-anger flashing across his face.

'Don't be stupid,' he denied harshly. 'Why should I want to see *her*?'

Odessa got up, slamming her empty glass on to a walnut shelf next to a stereo unit. She strode over to him, her long fingernails digging into his arm as she tried to yank him towards her. He turned obligingly, and she stood on tiptoe, her long face white and pinched, making her look even uglier. But Richard was feeling too good to let anything ruin his day.

'I'm warning you, Richard,' Odessa hissed. 'If you cheat on me, I'm going to make you so damned sorry . . .'

'Cheat?' Richard cut in, his voice harsh and hurt. 'What the hell are you talking about? We're still on our honeymoon, for God's sake. What sort of man do you think I am?' The accusing tone and stricken eyes had her anger and suspicions yelping way, cowering back into the darkest corners of her mind where they crouched, ready and waiting for another chance.

'Oh baby, I'm sorry,' she crooned, her hands coming up to the side of his face. 'I didn't mean it like that. It's just that I'm a jealous bitch, and you're such a catch, any woman would want you.'

Richard smiled and shook his head. 'You're a nitwit,' he told her, reaching down to lift her into his arms. 'What are you?'

'A nitwit,' she echoed, pushing open the bedroom door with her foot. But as he laid her on the bed and his large hands went caressingly to her breasts, there was a bright light burning at the back of his eyes and a sharp voice hissed in her head that it was not desire for her that had put it there.

DOMINIC was in the restaurant when he spotted Perry Clements. He greeted him easily, nodding to the man's sergeant as Clements introduced Ronalski.

'Sit down and join me. Is it about Lyons?'

'Not really,' Perry hedged, his eyes straying to the stage where the band was playing *Moon of Manakoora*, and Farron was singing softly. 'I'm looking for another employee of yours, a waitress. But I don't see her.'

'Oh? Which one?'

'The girl who lost her memory.'

'Vienna?' Dominic said sharply, green eyes boring into him with sudden pentrating scrutiny.

'Yes. Miss Wright is the name she chose, I think.'

'Yes. Named after the alley in which she was found.'

Perry summoned up a mental map. Wright Alley was some way away from Gloria Gaines' motel. But then, it would be, wouldn't it? 'Isn't she working today?'

Dominic felt uneasy. 'I've given her another job – promoted her, if you like,' he said finally, looking the man straight in the eye. 'Why do you ask?'

At last, Perry thought. Someone who was curious. 'We have a possible lead about her identity,' he lied.

'I see,' Dominic commented, not fooled for a second. 'At the moment,' he checked his watch, 'Vienna should be at Julian's – that's a gourmet school. Someone . . .' his eyes flickered briefly to the stage where his son was singing, 'informed me that she was an exceptional cook. I had need of a cook at a house I use for entertaining so I enrolled her at the school and asked her if she'd like to live in.'

'And she accepted? Does she live alone?' Perry probed, and saw the flash of irritation in the green eyes.

'No. She lives with a man.'

'That one?' Perry looked at the stage where Farron was singing expertly and with great emotion. He was also watching them closely and as they all three looked at him, Farron felt a sudden chill in the air. For the first time ever whilst on stage he shivered and his fine voice quavered. Luckily it was at an auspicious line of the lyrics, but Farron was aware of Kim flashing him a worried sideways glance.

'Yes. She's living with Mr Manikuuna,' Dominic agreed quietly. 'Is there anything more I can do for you?'

'I think that's all for the moment.'

'Glad to be of help.' Dominic stood up and held out his hand, which Perry took. Farron watched them leave, his eyes swinging back to the man he thought of as his best friend and found his green eyes fixed penetratingly on him. Something was up. Farron could feel it. He'd trust Dominic Fairchild with his life, but what the hell was going on, and why did Dominic suddenly look as if he carried the weight of the world on his shoulders?

VIENNA was adding the fresh tomato sauce to her Prawns Magenta dish when Mrs Freeling, the tall, super-elegant and very French woman tapped her lightly on the shoulder. 'Meeez Wright, there are the gentlemen from the police waiting outside to see you.'

She froze for a moment, then nodded and walked to the door, aware of her fellow pupils watching her go. Her first reaction was panic. Then hope. Her first words caught Perry Clements on the raw, accompanied as they were by wide, hopeful and utterly innocent blue eyes. 'Lieutenant?' She looked at Perry automatically, almost ignoring the younger, scruffier man by his side. 'You've found out something about me? Has someone filed a missing person's report?'

Perry blinked. 'Er . . . no, miss.'

There was something almost dejected in the way he looked away from her, and after a few seconds she suddenly understood the reason for it. 'You've stopped looking, haven't you?'

Perry cleared his throat. 'Yes, miss, I'm afraid we have. We just don't have the manpower any more, and until the Government does something about it . . .' He aired the genuine and very frustrating grievance with regret.

Vienna nodded, trying to smile but looking dispirited. 'I understand. You must have much more important things to do. So – how can I help you?'

And, despite her obvious disappointment, both men were struck with the feeling that she was sincere and Perry began to feel like a prize fool for ever thinking that this girl could have been a prostitute. 'Well, we're just following a routine line of enquiry about the murder of Gary Lyons – you might have read about it in the papers?'

Vienna went as cold as death. 'Lyons?' Her own voice almost hurt her ears. Did it sound normal? She couldn't tell. 'I don't . . . oh, isn't that the man who was washed up on the beach, about a month ago?'

'Yes, miss. Er . . .' Perry dug into his pocket for the copy of Lyons' photo. 'Do you remember seeing him anywhere?' Vienna turned slightly away as she took the photo and was glad she had, for as she stared down at the photo her nightmare suddenly became reality. The blond man, the man she could never remember when she woke up, now stared back at her.

'No – I don't think so. But then, Lieutenant, there's an awful lot I don't remember.' She swallowed hard as she handed the photo back. She must act normally. What would a normal person do now? Ask why. But her lips felt glued together and they took some opening. 'Why . . .' she cleared her throat. 'What makes you think I'd know him?'

'Nothing specific, Miss Wright,' Perry said kindly. She was obviously upset and struggling not to show it, and Perry's psychological training made him realize more than most just what a trauma she must have been through. 'It's just that we're obliged to pursue any lead, no matter how small, in a homicide investigation,' he said, but did not sound convincing even to his own ears.

'I'd better get back,' she said, though going back to the kitchen was the last thing she wanted. 'I expect my Prawns Magenta are burnt to a crisp by now.'

'Sorry about that.' Perry smiled widely at her feeble joke. 'Good luck with the rest of the course.'

'Thank you.' Vienna opened the door behind her and smiled goodbye to the two men who turned and walked away.

'She's a nice kid,' Rolnalski said quietly, and Perry nodded. But he was deeply troubled. For once his head and his heart were in direct opposition and he didn't like it one little bit.

Inside the hot classroom, Vienna smiled at her teacher and

walked to her own table, picking up the first wooden spoon she found and stirring a saucepan whose contents she couldn't name if her life had depended on it. Outside, the sun shone, children played and seagulls swooped, but she felt as cold, as hard, as numb as rock. What had she done? *What had she done?*

Chapter 29

Vienna was on a boat filled with pleasure-seekers. Party games were being played and tinsel decorations were draped over chandeliers. Huge circular fans whirled high overhead. The women had on 1920s sleeveless dresses that fell to just below the knees, and many strands of beads. Their hairstyles were all the same – short, sharp and chic, with pert little hats that hugged their skulls and sat snugly on their ears. The men were all dressed in white tuxedos, with well-greased hair parted in the centre and wide, mannequin-like grins. As she walked amongst the tables, moving through a sea-fog that was drifting into the dining room from the open French doors that led on to the deck, she heard a band strike up.

Looking behind her she saw a tuxedo-clad bandleader conduct the jazz band, Glenn Miller's *In the Mood* wafting with maniacal speed and tempo into the room. A waiter, who was also a fox, served a live chicken to a couple who loudly told everyone they were from Arkansas. As she continued to look for her own table, which she couldn't seem to find, everyone stared at her and she didn't know why. The laughter got more strident and the chickens began to squabble from the tables, clucking loudly as the fox-waiters chased them. To her right, in a dark little corner that looked like a haven, she saw a deserted bar and walked towards it, her feet as light as feathers under her as she floated towards the darker corner. A gorilla asked her what she wanted to drink and she chose a frozen daiquiri, sipping it and then blinking as her lips froze together. The gorilla turned into Gary Lyons, who began to laugh and pointed at her. When she looked around all the diners were laughing at her too. She got off the stool and ran through treacle that tried to slow her down, heading for the decks where the fog was coming in from the sea. The crowd faded behind her, the fog cleared, and she was looking out over green meadows where black and white cows grazed. The huge pleasure ship continued to sail easily over the undulating

371

green fields as, in the distance, she could see amidst a frothing green copse of trees the square tower of a church and she knew she was in the English countryside.

The little village she saw had a picturesque humped-back bridge spanning a rippling stream that led to a village pond where she could hear ducks quacking. She slipped under the rails and jumped from the ship's deck, which was only a foot high, landing and then bouncing on lush grass like an astronaut skipped weightlessly over the surface of the moon. Turning around, the ship was already a long way off, the diners hanging over its decks, laughing and waving. The sun shone overhead in an ultra-violet ball and birds sang as she walked through the village. A robin was singing *When the red, red robin, goes bob, bob, bobbing along*, whilst in the trees a crow sang *Bye, bye blackbird* with a mournful voice. There was a big oak tree showering acorns in front of a decrepit tin school where little children swung on an old swing, catching butterflies with their long sticky tongues that shot out and dragged the fluttering insects into their mouths.

Vienna smiled and walked on past an old grandmother seated in the doorway of a picture-postcard thatched cottage with roses around the door, honeysuckle bowers and lupins in the garden. The woman was winding wool from a huge wicker basket, and when she looked inside she saw a decapitated head in there which turned to look at her. It was Farron, and he winked and smiled at her.

She smiled and winked back and walked on, finding a lovely little pub with oak beams and a sign that said 'The Swan'. She stopped to look at the painting of a majestic swan, and saw that it was covered with little black fleas. She walked through the garden, past rustic benches and saw Rhiannon Grantham and Dominic Fairchild sitting at a big cider barrel feeding each other snails, smiling at one another like lovers. Rhiannon saw her and opened a purse from which spilled hundreds and thousands of dollars, offering it to her. Vienna smiled, but shook her head. She walked into the inn where it was cold, the tiles a dull red and flat beneath her feet. Her six-inch high-heeled shoes tapped on the floor like bullets and with every step she took, an old man looked up and watched her. The pub was filled with old men wearing flat cloth caps with unshaven, white whiskery chins. They were all playing dominoes, darts, or Russian roulette. She walked to the bar and Gary Lyons asked her what she wanted. She asked for a Bloody Mary, and he nodded, getting to his knees on the bar in front of her. He withdrew a long, thin stiletto and slit his wrist holding it over her so that the blood trickled down on to her head, running in tiny rivulets down her forehead, nose, cheeks and on to her lips . . .

Vienna sat up with a jerk, the last echoes of her own gasping cry still resounding in the room, her hands wiping furiously across her face as a light snapped on, hurting her eyes.

'What is it?' Farron asked urgently, his hands curling around the top of her arms. 'Another nightmare?'

Vienna blinked against the sudden fierce light, then nodded miserably, her lips trembling and her throat hurting as tears clogged her eyes. She sighed, telling him everything in a husky, wavering voice. After she'd finished, Farron drew her head back to rest on his chest, his body-heat warming the chilled flesh of her arms and small hands.

'That was a real corker. I like the bit about Dominic eating snails!'

Vienna laughed weakly, suddenly seeing the ridiculous aspects of it. 'I liked the kids eating butterflies myself.'

'Ugh.' Farron pulled a face and sat up, swinging out of the bed and walking to the TV at the foot of it, knowing that it would be impossible for her to sleep again that night.

'Oh no,' she groaned. 'Not Elvis Presley – *again*.'

'Made in 1961,' Farron commented, 'and shown as many times on Hawaiian TV.' She giggled as the opening credits for *Blue Hawaii* began to roll. 'Want some coffee?' he asked, rubbing his eyes and stretching.

'Hm. Strong and black.'

Farron made no comment until he came back with a tray and climbed into bed. 'Here. Careful, it's hot.'

'Thanks.' Vienna took the cup and stared blankly at the TV screen. 'I've been thinking,' she said cautiously. 'About the nightmares.' She felt his hand massaging her back, and closed her eyes, sighing softly. 'I love you,' she whispered. 'I don't know what I'd do if you weren't here.'

'I'll always be here,' he assured her softly. 'Now – what about the nightmares?' It was the first time that she'd wanted to talk about them and bring it all out into the open, and he was anxious to let her talk it through now that she had started.

She sipped her coffee. 'I think I should see someone about them. A doctor.'

'You mean a psychiatrist. Don't be afraid to use the word, honey.' He put his coffee mug out of the way on the bedside table and sitting cross-legged in front of her, put a gentle forefinger under her chin and lifted her face so that her eyes looked straight at him. 'Lots of people see shrinks, you know. It doesn't mean they're loopy.'

Vienna laughed. 'What a way you have with words!'

'I'se a songwriter, baby. It's what I do gooder than anythin' else.'

'With grammar like that how can you miss?' she teased, leaning forward and kissing him, needing his laughter, his common sense and his touch to chase away the bitter residue of the dream. Farron cupped the back of her head with his hand and prised her lips open then pushed his tongue between them, understanding her need and giving her what she craved. Her fingers bit compulsively into his shoulders as she lay back against the pillows, her eyes tightly shut as his hands found her breasts under her white cotton nightdress. She moaned softly as her nipples hardened, and lifted her hips from the bed when his fingers delved beneath the sheets to find the hem of her nightie and lift it up. She held her arms out like a child as he pulled the garment over her head and let it fall to the ground. He himself always slept naked, and now he wriggled back under the sheet, coming to her side quickly as she opened her eyes to watch him and fill her mind with his image. As he parted her legs with his hands and lay between her thighs, his face was tight with desire, the black eyes burning as he looked down into her flushed face.

He kissed her neck and shoulders with hot, fast little kisses then dipped lower, his mouth fastening with greedy need over first one hot pink nipple then the other. Vienna moaned, her eyes closing as he slipped beneath the sheet, his head disappearing from view as he slowly slid down her body. His tongue dipped into her navel, making her gasp before he went lower still. With slow, artful, almost tormenting thoroughness, his hands were firm and hard as he held her thighs apart, exposing her innermost and vulnerable core to his probing tongue as he explored her there. As his mouth found her femininity, loving her with a merciless skill, her eyes shot open to stare up at the white ceiling with a glazed expression. Her arms lifted above her head and clasped the headboard with knuckles that turned white as Farron continued to nibble and suck at her engorged clitoris. Gasping hard now, her legs flailing helplessly either side of his head in knee-jerk reaction to the spasms that overtook her, Vienna arched her back off the bed, her open mouth dragging in great gulps of air as she writhed helplessly, her head tossing from side to side, spreading her golden hair into tangled disarray on the pillow. Her cry of orgasm split the room and she slowly relaxed as Farron began the return journey back up her body, pausing to pander to her painfully tight breasts before he emerged from below the sheet and kissed her passionately. Her hands came to the back of his head to hold him as their hungry mouths met. His penis head nudged urgently against that place where his mouth had been so recently, and her vagina clenched and coiled in intense reaction, her legs parting even further to allow him entry. With one sure stroke he was within and filling her. She moaned, her ankles rising and crossing to hook over his calves, holding him a willing prisoner within her. He began to withdraw and then surge into her again, faster and faster, driving her to the brink of endurance over and over again until one orgasm followed another and her brain ceased to function on any level save that of savouring the ecstatic pleasure that exploded repeatedly in her body.

Long minutes after it was all over Vienna raised a hand and stroked his damp hair. 'Thank you.'

Farron smiled weakly, his cheek still cushioned against her breast, her nipple making a little round indentation in his cheek. 'Any time.'

Vienna laughed softly. 'I mean, thank you for chasing away the nightmare. You knew, didn't you?'

Slowly Farron rolled from her and lay on his back, catching her hand and dragging it to where his heart still thundered in his chest. 'I love you and always will. And the nightmare can be explained. That visit from the cops got you thinking about Lyons. And you'd read that he came over on a cruise ship. Hence, the ship part. And Rhia Grantham is English, so you went to England. You know dreams – they're all mixed up and crazy. At the time that you dream them everything that's bad seems normal. Like my head in a basket. Do you suppose I was a beheaded French aristocrat in another life?'

Vienna thumped him playfully. 'That doesn't explain the other dreams, though. When I'm in the alley. And there's that man, and a woman screaming and Gloria stood in the doorway. You remember her? The madam. You told me about her.'

'It's just another dream,' Farron said, sharply, turning to lean on his side and look at her. 'You read his movements had been traced to Gloria's, although that was barely mentioned. Good ol' Gloria probably had something on the paper's editor.'

'But I had that dream about Gary Lyons before the papers told the story.'

'Did you see his face?'

'Well . . . no. Not until after that detective showed me his picture.'

'There you are, then. You just transferred Gary Lyons to fit the shadowy man in the dream.'

'What's that round object I keep seeing? Like some . . . I don't know – macabre frisbee? And I know it was Gloria in the dream,' she finished positively, reluctant to abandon her chain of thought. She was getting tired of waiting for the Swiss Finishing School brochures to come. Perhaps that was why she still had the dreams. Until she knew who she was, how could she know what she had done? 'And then there was that other girl, screaming all the time,' she added, shivering beneath the covers despite her still sweating body.

'I can't see our local brothel-keeper as another Lucretia

Borgia somehow,' Farron teased as, in the background, Elvis Presley began to sing. Vienna gazed at the film in silence for some minutes, then turned to Farron once more, who'd never stopped watching her. He loved to look at her – when she was hoovering, when she was washing her hair, when she was weeding the garden, all sweaty and mud-streaked. It was his favourite pastime.

'I don't know why I was born this lucky,' he said softly, his finger coming out to gently trace her brow and nose. 'I love you. Did I tell you that?'

Vienna smiled coyly. 'I think your body was saying it for you not so long ago. It's funny that Gloria came to the hotel so soon after I started working there though, isn't it?' she asked, determined not to let it go.

'Gloria and Dom are old friends.'

'Does she come to the hotel often?' she half-asked and half-challenged.

'Well, no,' he reluctantly admitted. 'But that could be coincidence.'

Vienna sat up, determination written all over her. 'Coincidence my eye!' she denied. 'Let's go and see her – talk to her. She knows something. I thought so before – but well, everything was so new and different and I thought I was just imagining it.'

'You still are,' he warned.

'No, I'm not. Farron – please. Come with me.'

'What – now? It's two-thirty in the morning!'

'Does a brothelkeeper work from nine to five?'

Farron was forced to laugh. 'Good point.'

THE oriental girl who opened the door recognized him. 'Mr Manikuuna. Hello. We haven't seen you here before.' She hesitated in mid-sentence as she spied Vienna behind him and her slanted almond eyes turned puzzled and a little wary.

'We're here to see Miss Gaines,' Farron explained, feeling just a little nervous and off-balance.

'I see. Please come in.' Both Farron and Vienna looked around them with avid curiosity as they walked into the lounge.

'It's rather too much, isn't it?' Vienna whispered in his ear, feeling very inhibited now that she was actually here. Before he could reply Gloria and the girl came back. The madam was dressed in a loose-fitting kaftan of burnt orange, and once again Vienna was assailed by a feeling of *something*. Not déjà vu, exactly, but definitely something. Gloria looked at her, her blue eyes bland and friendly enough on the outside, but Vienna could feel the strength of the woman's gaze boring into her and wondered if Farron could feel it too. It was not, strangely enough, an unpleasant sensation.

'Hello. Farron, isn't it?' Gloria asked, holding out her hand.

'Yes. And this is Vienna Wright.'

Gloria felt her heart trip as she turned back to look at her lovely blonde daughter but she inflected her voice with just the right amount of puzzlement as she asked, 'Haven't we met somewhere before?'

For the first time, Vienna felt unsure. The woman acted so naturally. 'Er, yes. I served you a drink one time. At the Blue Hawaiian.'

'Ah.' Gloria allowed the slight frown to clear from her forehead. 'That must be it. What . . .' The doorbell rang and the oriental girl left them to answer it. 'Why don't we step into my office for a moment?' Gloria suggested discreetly as a deputy mayor was led upstairs by the hand.

'Yes. I think that would be better,' Farron agreed, struggling hard to wipe the grin off his face.

Inside the quiet office all three sat down and an awkward silence followed, broken by Gloria offering them coffee. 'No thanks – not for me,' Farron declined. Vienna, too, shook her head, unable for the moment to speak.

'Well, what can I do for you?' Gloria asked, looking from Farron to Vienna then quickly away.

'Good question,' Farron laughed, just a shade embarrassed. 'You might have read about Vienna in the papers,' he jumped in with both feet, sensing that Vienna was tonguetied. 'She lost her memory back in December.'

'Oh yes. Yes, I did read something about it.'

'Well, the thing is, she thinks she remembers something,' he began, and then his eyes sharpened on her. Was it his imagination, or did the older woman suddenly look downright scared?

'Well, I'm glad your memory is returning, my dear.' Gloria forced herself to look at Vienna, keeping her voice brisk and cheerful, whilst she eagerly took in every detail of her appearance. She did not miss the shadows under the wide blue eyes nor the rather strained expression within them, and a mixture of guilt and overwhelming maternal instinct battled for supremacy. She wanted nothing more than to take her in her arms and tell her everything, but it was impossible. As a mother her first duty was to protect her child, come what may. So she said blandly, 'I still don't see why you've come to me.'

'I think I remember you. From somewhere.'

'Oh? Let me see.' She stared at Vienna openly, her heart aching but her mind made up. Whether her beloved Pauline knew it or not, it was for her own sake that she said what she did next. 'I don't think so. No – I'm sure I would have remembered you. Look, I don't mean to be rude, but someone should be out front in case a customer calls.'

'Please,' Vienna said quickly, rising to her feet along with Gloria, who froze as if turned to stone. 'Please,' she said again. 'I keep hearing a girl screaming, and a man – the man in the papers, with a knife. And you're there. I know you are.' Vienna took a deep breath and felt Farron by her side, his hand sliding to her waist, offering silent, total support.

Gloria licked her suddenly very dry lips but she was too strong to falter at the most critical moment. 'You remember all this? Why don't you go to the police?'

Farron shifted uncomfortably as Vienna admitted miserably, 'I don't remember it, as such. I dream about it.'

Gloria relaxed slightly. 'Well, I don't see why I should play such a leading role in your dreams, but I can assure you, that's all they are. Dreams. And if there were anything to them, surely the police would've found out by now?'

Farron looked up at Gloria then, his eyes looking thoughtful. Yes, she said all the right things but he was not convinced. Before, he'd been almost sure Vienna was on a wild goose chase, but now? Suddenly he went cold, and his stomach churned. Did Vienna know Gloria from before the mugging? Had she, in fact, been one of her girls? Was she a *prostitute?* Farron swallowed hard, finding his breath had become trapped in his throat. She had moved into Richard Jago's apartment block, not to mention his bed, within days of knowing him. He'd always thought before that it was simply because he was the only one she could turn to. But had she really only been reverting to instincts – instincts that told her to sleep with a man. Sex for money, position, status, security?

Farron shifted in his chair, sickened by his thoughts, guilty for thinking them but unable to deny that they made sense.

'Look P . . . – Vienna,' Gloria said, walking around the desk, her voice genuinely kind. 'I can't help you, I really can't. I would if I could,' she promised, and thought silently: If only you knew, darling – I'm already helping you. 'But there's nothing I can do for you.' She looked across at Farron speculatively. It made her feel infinitely better to know that Vienna had found a man of worth at last. 'You love her very much, don't you?' she asked him now, and both women looked at Farron, who, after a startled second nodded and said with simple truth, 'Yes.'

'Then take her home. Love her, and look after her.'

'Gloria. Please, I need to know.' Vienna tried one last time, but Gloria spread her hands in a helpless gesture.

'But I don't know your story, honey,' she lied. 'How can I help?'

Filled with bitter disappointment, but not at all sure she believed her, Vienna nodded. 'OK,' she said, her head hanging with tiredness and defeat so only Farron saw the impulsive gesture of comfort, almost immediately checked, that had Gloria reaching out her hands towards her. Meeting his questioning black eyes, Gloria shrugged. 'I hate to see anyone hurting.'

'Perhaps you should see that psychiatrist after all.' Farron played a hunch, and Gloria turned white.

'A shrink?' she asked sharply. 'Honey, what do you want a shrink for?'

Farron took a deep, shaky breath. Gloria was obviously

rattled. But why should she be if, as she claimed, she and Vienna had never met? Farron suddenly wanted to get out of there. Get out of that 'Glorious Motel' filled with whores and men willing to pay for their love. He and Vienna had nothing to do with this place. They made love because they were in love. He didn't pay her, and she didn't ask. So what if Vienna did have a dark or scandalous past. What did it matter to them now? Farron licked his dry lips, wondering if he was convincing himself or just fooling himself.

Vienna looked up at Gloria, her eyes full of tears, and unknowingly twisted a knife of torment into the older woman's heart. 'I just don't know what to do any more!'

'Take my advice,' Gloria urged now, her voice earnest and intense. 'Live your life for today. You have a man who loves you. A place to live, a job. That's a hell of a lot more than most girls have.'

Vienna smiled weakly. 'I know. Look, I'm sorry we bothered you. We obviously made a mistake.' She tugged on Farron's hand and he responded to her unspoken plea gratefully, nodding his head curtly as he said goodbye.

'Goodbye,' Gloria said miserably, accompanying them to the door, watching then walk out of sight down the long dark alley at the side to where Farron's car was parked out back. Farron breathed deeply, battling his twin demons of suspicion and doubt.

Vienna's head was leaning on his shoulder and she did not look around her at the alley with the garbage that would have been familiar. Nor did she look back at the woman framed in the doorway, watching them go out of sight with eyes that suffered as much as they worried. And later, much later, she was to wonder why Fate played such cruel tricks.

Chapter 30

'Is it my imagination, or has the fire for revenge dampened a little?' Ben asked her quietly as they were sitting in the limo heading for the Royal Mausoleum. Rhiannon, delighted by Ben's arrival at last, had promised him a cultural tour, but now she sighed, not knowing how to answer his question.

'I'm a little tired, I suppose, and a little impatient. I'm working on the hotel angle right now, and I've learned something of a personal nature that I can use as a last killing blow.'

Ben shrugged graphically. 'It sounds as if it's going well. So what's wrong?'

'Nothing. What on earth could be wrong?'

'You tell me,' Ben said mildly. 'How's Jack Gunster working out, by the way?'

Rhiannon felt her lips twisting into a grimace and quickly looked away. 'He's very efficient, and keeps me updated on everything.'

She managed to avoid Ben's searching eyes and, as the afternoon wore on, determinedly acted the teacher, relating the stories of Hawaiian gods, history, art and culture whilst trying unsuccessfully to keep Ben's more difficult questions at bay.

'I've been fascinated by the sound of the Blue Hawaiian,' he confessed on the way back to her place and Rhiannon made a face.

'Oh, not now! I want to forget about him for one night. What say we take in the Maile Restaurant at the Kahala Hilton?'

'OK,' Ben said, with a wise and knowing smile.

'I won't be ten minutes,' she promised a few minutes later as they got home and he made himself comfortable in her newly decorated living room.

'I've never known any woman take less than an hour.' Ben blew her a playful kiss.

She laughed, running up the stairs and into her bedroom, already stripping for a quick two-minute shower. A brisk rubdown was followed by the donning of a matching peach-coloured bra and panties set, sheer flesh-coloured tights and scarlet, high-heeled shoes. Reaching into her wardrobe she pulled out a scarlet cocktail dress that stopped halfway from her thigh to her knee, showing off her lovely legs to perfection. The dress was off-the-shoulder with a wide trouncing ruffle that teasingly hid the shape of her breasts but hugged her waist and hips like a lover. She left her hair loose and long, adding only a silver eyeshadow to her lids and a scarlet lipstick to her mouth. Reaching into her jewellery case she brought out and donned a beaten silver and garnet necklace that was chunky and pagan-looking and added a dab of Nina Ricci's L'Air du Temps to the back of her ears, on her wrists and at her throat. After slipping on a silver and garnet Cartier ladies' watch she checked the time. Nine minutes exactly. Picking up a sparkling, silver-beaded envelope handbag and putting into it a comb, her lipstick and a lacy white handkerchief, she skipped lightly down the stairs.

Ben stood up and slowly looked her over. 'You look lovely,' he said gruffly, and swallowed hard.

The head waiter at the Maile greeted them like royalty, seated them immediately at the best table in the house, fawned and fussed and promptly phoned Dominic Fairchild, anticipating a huge tip for his trouble.

Rhiannon was the first to see him and the lovely girl who accompanied him, just over an hour later. Now seated at the bar with Ben and just about to sip a delicious *après dîner* Martini, her frosted glass paused in mid-air. Her eyes flickered with an expression that Ben just caught, but didn't understand. Turning on his stool to look in the direction of her eyes he spotted the tall raven-haired man immediately, but it wasn't until he saw the look that passed between them that he realized who the man was and his heart sank.

Dominic looked at and promptly dismissed Ben, his gaze moving to Rhiannon, who silently saluted him with her glass and took a sip, her scarlet mouth curled into a smile that made every muscle in his body clench with the effort of preventing

383

himself from going over there and strangling her. The report from Hua had come in long ago, telling him all about Ben Fielding and the business partnership with the Granthams. At first he'd been puzzled by Rhiannon's swift rise to executive status in the giant Fielding organization, but then he'd remembered that the bedroom was often a quick way to the boardroom. The thought of her in bed with Ben, her lithe, lovely body squashed under the other man's weight, his fingers on her lovely breasts and his vile body within her made him want to throw up.

Both Rhiannon and Ben saw the undisguised look of sheer revulsion cross his face before he turned abruptly, muttering something to the waiter before handing over what looked like a fair wad of cash and dragging his protesting partner quickly towards the door again. The girl's words could be clearly heard. 'But Dom, I'm hungry. What's the matter?'

Ben turned back to his companion. 'If looks could kill,' he commented casually, his mind working overtime. If Graham wasn't Rhiannon's natural father, who was? Until meeting Dominic Fairchild's green eyes head-on, he'd barely given it a thought. Now he wondered. Why, exactly, had Graham Grantham hated Fairchild so deeply?

'You and I would be on our way to the nearest cemetery. But perhaps you can see what I mean now. The man's a menace,' Rhiannon muttered angrily.

'Oh yes,' Ben agreed with quiet sadness. 'I can quite see that.'

FARRON was in the final stages of his late-shift, his powerful, emotive voice singing the song of an Hawaiian boy begging his love not to leave in the visitors' big ships, nor sail away from him to a distant land. In his favourite chair, at his favourite table, Dominic, alone now, drank more brandy than he should and silently cursed both himself and life more than he did when he lost the Liliha chain. Both Ling and Farron noticed his unusual lapse, but not even the brandies blotted out the thought of Rhiannon and the Englishman together. It was almost one in the morning, according to the ornate clock on the wall. Were they in bed? He rubbed his eyes tiredly and looked up as the audience began to clap the singer on the stage.

Never before had the desire to confess to his son who he was and what he had done been so strong. And never before had he looked at his son with such longing or pain, and for a second, catching that stricken look, Farron faltered over the words of the opening lines of his next song, and then quickly recovered. Dominic looked away, taking a deep breath. '*Oh, shit!*' he swore, his voice lost in the music and conversation, but his hand tightened compulsively on the exquisite cut glass of his goblet and shattered it. The glass cut his fingers in several places, the alcohol stinging the cuts, but he barely noticed. Dropping the glass pieces on to the table, he took a napkin and carelessly bound his hand in it, then raised his free hand for another brandy.

Ling silently brought it and cleared away the broken glass, his face impassive, but his eyes sought the stage as he poured the drink, and a silent message passed between him and Farron. In all the years he'd known him, Farron could never remember seeing Dominic in this state.

The brandy wasn't helping. Bleakly Dominic admitted to himself that he knew of only one thing that would take his mind off her – at least for a while. But was the alternative any less painful? Grimly, he supposed it must be, and so with a sigh of tiredness, he let the years drift away.

IT was July, 1961. When he woke up it took a while for the hangover to clear and for him to remember where he was, and why. As he lay looking up at the ceiling, thinking about Akaki and his baby son, Graham walked in with a large mug of coffee. 'Morning. You look awful.'

'Thanks', He sat up gingerly and only then was he aware that he was naked in the bed. He knew he'd been in no fit state to have undressed himself. Idly he rubbed his aching forehead, then reached for the mug.

Graham looked vacantly out of the window. 'You were totally pissed.'

'I know. Hell, I know,' he groaned ruefully, the pounding in his head sounding like several discordant drummers having a whale of a time. Then he felt a memory tug at him, nagging and worrying. 'Jess? Is she all right?'

'Yes – she's going into hospital this afternoon,' Graham gritted, his voice curiously cold.

'Ah.' He sipped the coffee, and sighed. 'That's good.'

'What are you going to do, about the whore and your kid?' Graham suddenly asked and Dominic bit back the groan. So he had spilled his guts; he'd had a nasty idea he had ever since Graham had first entered the room. Sighing deeply, he leaned back against the headboard and shrugged.

'I don't know. I'm not sure.'

'You'll have to be careful,' Graham said, his voice expressionless. 'My old man won't approve of a bastard. He'll follow through to the letter your grandfather's wishes in the will,' he carried on with savage satisfaction. Not only would he not have Akaki's baby, he was also sure that Jess hadn't told him he was the father of their soon-to-be-born baby either. To be robbed of both children seemed to Graham to be the height in poetic justice.

'Will?' Dominic said sharply. He didn't remember telling him about that.

'Yes, you told me all about it,' Graham lied. 'About the morality clause – the lot. Jeeze, Dom, Freddie really socked it to you, didn't he?'

Dominic watched the brown eyes swivel briefly in his direction and didn't miss the glitter of something other than sympathy in their depths.

'Yes,' he agreed shortly. Hell, he'd spilled more than he knew. That wasn't like him. Damn, he'd never get drunk again – never!

'What was it, a girl?' Graham asked hopefully, not at all surprised when Dominic shook his head and quickly stopped as the room spun around him.

'A boy,' he corrected, his voice already thick with pride and Graham sucked in his breath against the vicious pain that kicked in his chest. 'There must be a way out of it,' Dominic muttered, more to himself than anyone else, his young face frowning in concentration.

'Well, you can't marry Akaki, that's for sure. And I can't see how you can adopt him either. Dad'd never go for it. He and your old man were pretty close, and Fred obviously wouldn't have approved if he'd lived.'

Graham's words only confirmed Dominic's own suspicions, but to have them voiced aloud made him wince. He leaned back against the headboard, his eyes closed against the pain he could feel building up inside him, unaware that Graham was watching him with an expression of pleasure on his face.

'Wait a minute!' Dominic's eyes shot open. 'I *can* adopt the kid.'

'But Akaki . . .'

'No, no. Not Akaki – I can marry Mandy,' he said, referring to the English Literature student he'd met at Oxford. 'It would be the perfect gesture – to adopt a native Hawaiian from a poor background. The baby would obviously be in danger in the environment he's in now, and I've got pull with the welfare people. And there'd be no question of the child inheriting, so the lawyers couldn't haggle. It's bloody perfect!'

'Will Amanda agree, though?' Graham asked weakly, the thought of his revenge being snapped away making bile rise in his throat.

'Of course she will.' Dominic dismissed his friend's fears with a confidence that was fully justified. Knowing a good catch when she found one, and not caring a jot for the reasons behind his sudden proposal, within two days Amanda was in Oahu shopping for her trousseau and Jessamine had given strenuous but successful birth to a bouncing baby girl they'd named Rhiannon, after Jess' grandmother.

Farron was firmly ensconced in a discreet bungalow in one of Honolulu's more prestigious suburbs, Akaki agreeing to forsake her baby for a price of nearly a quarter of a million dollars. A wetnurse and nanny were looking after him full-time. Although he hadn't yet gone to see his son's grandmother, that was next on Dominic's list, following an interview with an adoption agency that he'd scheduled for the following day.

It was towards the end of a bright, sunny afternoon when it

happened. He was at Kapuna reading the briefs from his solicitor. His lawyer had done a good job with the pre-marital contract, Dominic acknowledged as he read through the clauses, most of them having to do with Farron. Amanda was to agree to adopt the boy as soon as they were married, and in the event of Amanda forcing a divorce, would make no claims to sue for custody. There were other, financial clauses that he checked but didn't consider important. Money was not the issue.

At first, when he heard the car, he thought it was Mandy, but a quick glance out of the window revealed Graham walking up the path. The sun was just beginning to sink, the coming evening holding that end-of-day hush, and something in his friend's face, or maybe just instinct, made a shiver of foreboding rattle up his spine. Walking to the door, before Graham could knock he held it wide open. He'd long since learned that the only way to handle trouble was to face it, head-on.

'Come in, Gray-Gray. Want a drink?'

'No.' Graham shook his neatly brushed head. 'But you'd better have one,' he added, breezily defiant now that the fear was slowly being replaced by anticipatory pleasure. He saw Dominic hesitate, those amazing green eyes flickering for the briefest of moments and the pleasure bit deep. He turned away and walked to the window and looked out.

'How's Jess and the baby?' Dominic asked, cautiously feeling his way and unknowingly hammering nails into his own coffin.

'Fine – they're both fine,' Graham snapped. 'Rhiannon's going to be a real beauty, just like her mother.'

'I know,' Dominic agreed. 'I visited them both earlier today. She's a real charmer, Graham. Congratulations. You're not sore because it wasn't a boy, are you?'

Graham looked at him with genuine surprise. 'No,' he said truthfully enough. After all, what did it matter? The baby was not his, but he'd bring her up as such. Yes, he would make the baby love him. It was all that Dominic deserved.

'All right Graham,' Dominic said softly, the air around them stilling like a boiling ocean suddenly gone flat as a sheet of glass. 'What is it?'

Graham looked at him. Only yards apart, Graham knew that in reality they were whole worlds away. Dominic was the great success, himself the great failure. Except this time, just for once, *he was going to win*.

'I want money. A lot of it,' he said abruptly.

'Money?' Dominic echoed, for once totally stupefied. Whatever he'd been expecting, it hadn't been that. 'You don't mean to say that all . . .' he waved a hand in the air, 'all this time we've been friends you've jealous of my money?' His voice was raised on octave in disbelief.

Graham smiled with a mixture of anger and contempt. 'Jealous, yes. But of money?' He shook his head. 'No. The money's just a means to an end – a fringe benefit.' His voice was thick with twisted hate and Dominic swirled the drink in his glass and took a long sip, realizing the man was close to breaking point. He'd no idea things had got so bad.

'How much do you need?' he asked cautiously.

'Need? None. But I'll take a thousand dollars – every month.'

'Are you crazy? Graham, what the hell's the matter with you?'

'Don't you know? Can't you guess?' Silently he added, 'Did the affair with my wife really mean so little to you?'

Slowly Dominic shook his head. 'I won't give you the money,' he said finally. 'Whatever the problem is, money won't solve it. Look, why don't you see someone,' he began, walking towards the smaller man with a hand stretched out, still in friendship, but Graham backed away. 'Graham,' he finally warned, his voice firm. 'What the hell do you want from me? Ever since we were kids I've watched you, day in, day out, struggling through life when everyone else, myself included, just breezed through it so easily. What happened to make you so damned miserable? Have you ever been happy? Even now, with Jess and your new daughter: are you happy, damn you?'

'No!' Graham's control snapped 'No, I've never been happy. I can't remember a time, not even a minute, when I was. But I'm about to be.'

They stared at one another, Graham as taut as a bowstring,

his face taking on a febrile and ugly smile that was in no way an expression of happiness. '*You're* going to make me happy, Dominic. Because you're never going to have your kid. *Never.*'

Dominic stopped walking towards him, his priorities shifting rapidly. He wanted to help his friend if he could, but suddenly, without warning, Graham had become the enemy. He could see it in the hot brown eyes burning with pain and hate. He could sense it in the air, the stench of an animal drawing blood – his blood. 'What the hell are you talking about?' he asked dangerously, but with a hint of insecurity in his voice that was like nectar to a man who'd always felt overshadowed and inferior. Graham had never seen his friend unsure of himself before and it was giddying stuff.

'I mean,' he said, his voice thick with triumph, 'if you try to adopt that bastard son of a whore I'm tell my father and those Chicago lawyers of your dear cousins'. They'll have you in court so fast your oh-so-high-and-mighty feet won't touch the ground.'

Dominic's head tilted fractionally to one side, his powerful body as still as a hunting lion's. 'You wouldn't dare,' he breathed softly. 'You don't have the guts, Graham. You never have had.' He didn't bother to explain that he was bound to win any court case concerning Farron anyway, because winning was not the point. The only way he could win now was keeping out of court for the next ten years or so. Just long enough for him to become financially independent of his grandfather's will.

Graham laughed then, his neat nondescript face almost radiating pure joy. 'You never knew me, Dominic,' he said, truthfully. 'Never. You thought you could beat me any time you wanted. You thought I'd be happy with crumbs tossed from your princely table. You didn't think I would even object when you slept with my own wife!'

'*What!*' Dominic roared. 'I've never slept with Jess,' he denied, appalled and totally astounded by the allegation. He loved Jess like the sister he'd never had, like a good and trustworthy friend to whom he could always turn. Even if she hadn't been his friend's wife, Dominic would never have ruined their relationship for something as fleeting as sex, casual or otherwise.

'You're lying, as usual,' Graham sneered. 'But it doesn't matter, because this time you're not going to get away with it. Well, how does it feel, Dom?' he taunted. 'How does it feel to have the worm turn on you and take it all away?'

A cold sensation of dread was settling in his guts, in his chest and in his brain. He could feel the colour drain from his face, could feel horror, for the first time ever – true, real, ugly horror – widen his eyes.

'You mean it,' he said, his voice barely a whisper as he stared into the face of the man he'd always regarded as a friend. 'You really mean it!' Triumph nearly killed Graham then and there. At last, at long, long last he'd done it. He'd finally bested him.

'Oh yes, Dominic,' he said softly. 'I mean it. I'm really screwing you, and what's more, you'll pay me for doing it to you. Every month, one thousand dollars, or else you can kiss goodbye to Fairchild's.'

Fairchild's, for money's sake, meant little to Dominic. But Fairchild's as a means to change the lives of his own people, to provide fair employment, decent wages, pensions – Fairchild's as his just heritage . . .

The past few days flashed through Dominic's mind in a blur – holding Farron in his arms as he left Akaki behind, staring at her cheque. Of meeting Mandy at the airport, discussing the marriage and the adoption. She must have known, or at least guessed, that Farron was his, but like the sophisticated, 1960s freethinking woman that she was, she hadn't demurred. But now the dream was gone – shattered and in ruins. And it had been Graham – *Graham* – who'd done it to him.

'You bastard!' The words echoed like shots in the room, taking both men by surprise. And then his hands were at Graham's throat and he could feel the younger, smaller man's fragile bones under his fingers and the convulsive movement of his adam's apple under Dominic's palm as he squeezed. Graham's back bent under the pressure, his slender body sagging as he fell to his knees, and still Dominic didn't let go. Looking down into his flushed face, turning bluish now and watching the brown eyes fade and yet still burn with some hideous nameless emotion, Dominic felt disgust rise within him.

Yanking his hands away, he backed off until he felt the wall behind him. For several seconds he stared down at his hands and then back to Graham, who was still on his knees breathing deeply, slender shoulders and body shaking in reaction. 'Get out of here, Graham,' he said, his voice dead and flat. 'And if you ever try to contact me or my family, *especially* Farron, I'll kill you.'

Slowly Graham rose to his feet and stood there for several seconds, swaying weakly, his eyes never leaving Dominic's face as he drank into his soul and memory the defeat that he saw there. He'd won. 'You'll never forget me, Dom,' Graham said simply. 'Whatever else you might do, you'll never, ever forget me.'

They were the last words they ever spoke to each other.

But for the first fifteen years of Graham's exile to London, Dominic had paid money to keep him silent, even though the capitulation had gone against everything in him. He stopped paying the blackmail money only when he finally admitted to himself that at fifteen and still ignorant of his parentage, Farron was lost to him as a son. Living with his grandmother and perfectly happy as he was, Dominic hadn't been able to risk wrecking his young son's life with the publicity that would surely follow if he publicly acknowledged him. So he wrote the last cheque and informed Graham he would counter-sue for blackmail if he actually contacted the Chicago relatives. Confident of Graham's cowardice, Dominic had then set about exacting repayment . . .

Now, as Dominic slowly dragged himself back to the present and looked around the crowded dining room, his eyes skimmed over the dancing couples and waiters and waitresses and then inexorably, he looked to the stage and at his beloved son.

It was incredible to think that so much time had passed and that back at the palace he had a filing cabinet full of reports about Farron. Every aspect of his life Dominic had followed and been a silent, unknown part of. Oh God, Farron, Dominic thought, raising the glass to his mouth and draining its contents. You'd hate me if you knew.

He saw then that the white napkin around his hand was stained in two places with his blood, and his lips twisted into a savage smile. Farron, not a foot away now after singing his last song and leaving the stage, stopped dead in his tracks, a cold chill running down his spine.

'Dominic,' he said softly, and the dark head snapped up, his green eyes meeting the younger man's then looking swiftly away again, but not before Farron had seen the expression in them, an expression that cut him to the quick. Slowly he sat down beside him. 'God Dom, what's the matter?'

The worried voice of his son very nearly broke him, and he visibly fought for several seconds to keep from going under.

Farron asked simply, 'Can I do anything? It's her, isn't it?' he said, his voice going vicious on his behalf. 'It's that English bitch, isn't it?'

Dominic's smile turned into a helpless grin. 'Her too,' he admitted wrily, his words slightly slurred. He got painfully to his feet, and found himself staggering as the full power of the brandies hit him. Luckily the room was now almost empty. Farron turned and beckoned to a hovering Ling. Slowly and in complete silence, all three men made their way to the elevator where Farron nodded wordlessly to Ling, who turned and left them to ride to the penthouse alone. At his door Dominic reached into his pocket for the key and turned it. 'You should get back to that pretty lady of yours,' he warned him, his voice wise and sad. 'Don't let her get away from you.'

'I won't,' Farron promised, pushing the door open and gently propelling him in. Walking through the office and into the lounge, Farron guided him to the bedroom. Sitting him on the mattress, he swung his legs on to the bed and took off his shoes. Dominic flopped back on to the pillow, aware that he should say something or do something, but couldn't remember what.

'Farron?'

'What?'

'Nothing. Goodnight.'

'Goodnight.' Farron pulled up a single blanket over him, half-turned and then found that something in the green eyes made him hesitate. 'Tell me,' he urged.

Dominic stared at him steadily for a few seconds, then blinked. He'd made a promise to himself years ago to live up to the title of Prince – the sole thing his mother had left him. And to keep that promise, he'd sacrificed his only son. Had he been right? Had he been honourable, or just plain stupid. He didn't know. After all this time, he still wasn't sure. 'I . . . I'm in a hell of a mess,' he finally confessed, his lips curling into a wide, helpless smile.

Farron's smile was equally sad as he said grimly, 'Aren't we all?'

Chapter 31

'Good morning, Lieutenant,' Gloria greeted him crisply. 'If we keep meeting like this, certain other factions of your fair profession are going to think you've joined the club.'

Perry, not waiting for an invitation to be seated, made himself comfortable before replying to her jibe with total certainty, 'No, they won't.'

No, they won't, Gloria echoed silently. No one would ever mistake this one for a bent cop. 'But word might get back to your wife.'

'It might. But it wouldn't matter if it did.'

'Oh? Trusting sort of soul, is she?'

'She knows me, inside and out,' he corrected, sure that the words would tell this woman all she needed to know. It did. She gasped in exaggerated shock.

'You're actually a faithful husband?'

'Guilty.'

'I never thought I'd actually see one this side of heaven,' Gloria admitted whimsically, playing for time.

'You live and learn. Talking about learning, I've been learning all about an ex-girl of yours called Wanda.'

Gloria blinked and she felt a nasty lurch in her stomach. 'Wanda?'

Perry shifted on his seat, suddenly tired of the game. 'Uh-huh. Went missing about last Christmas.'

'She's on vacation.'

'A long one, isn't it? Seven months?'

'A girl can get very tired in this business.'

'Where is she?'

She shrugged negligently. 'Offhand, I don't know. She said when she was ready to start work she'd call. For all I know she could be honeymooning at Niagara Falls with a millionaire.'

'I went to the hospital to check on Vienna Wright's hospital records. Very interesting gynaecological results she had.'

'Oh?' Gloria raised a brow in arch boredom. Not biting,

Perry thought. But did that mean she already knew, or didn't care? 'About Wanda,' he changed tack suddenly. 'Is she alive or dead?'

Gloria shrugged her shoulders. 'I told you. She went on vacation. She was certainly very much alive the last time I saw her.'

Very good answer that, Perry thought, both his respect and irritability shifting into fourth gear. She was telling him precisely nothing, whilst at the same time seeming to co-operate. 'Look, Gloria, why don't you make it easier on both of us? Just tell me what the hell happened.'

'Oh come on, Lieutenant. That's not worthy of you.'

'You think we're playing a game?' he asked quietly, but his eyes were a darker grey and his voice a darker tone. Some quality in his gaze, something very human, caught her on the raw and made a wave of guilt shift somewhere deep inside her.

'No,' she said shortly, angry at him, at herself and at the whole damned stinking world, but she remained stubbornly silent.

'All right – if that's the way you insist on playing it. I'll be seeing you.'

She watched him turn and walk to the door, expecting a last parting shot that never came. But she felt cold in her small office after he'd gone as if he'd come with a block of ice and left it there. Honest cops always had given her the jitters. Dedicated cops gave her even more of the same. But honest, dedicated and bloody clever cops made her bones rattle. Quickly she rose and took her bag off the coat-stand in one corner of the room and walked through to the lounge, calling to Nancy that she'd be gone an hour or so.

Outside, Perry walked to the car parked behind his own and bent down to talk to the two occupants through the window. 'Stake the place out. Get Neall and O'Donnell to spot you tonight.'

'Right. Hey, isn't that our mark?'

Perry looked around just in time to see Gloria step from the door and in a second he hit the deck. When Gloria came out she looked around the street for cops. And Gloria knew an undercover cop when she saw one – the formula was simple. Pick the least likely character – a bum, a traffic warden, a mother pushing a pushchair, and there you had a stake-out cop.

'I'll follow her,' Perry whispered, crouching around the car and clumsily scrambling on his haunches towards his own car. Getting inside and keeping low over the gearbox, Perry felt a back muscle twinge spitefully and winced. He was getting too old for this sort of thing.

Gloria edged the car on to the road, her eyes taking in and memorizing every parked car she saw. Starting up the moment she'd turned off at the bottom of the road, Perry radioed Rolnalski at headquarters, giving terse and precise orders. About ten blocks away Gloria spotted his car and slowed down, biting her lip. Looking in the rear mirror she nearly ran down an old dear crossing the road with a bag of shopping, and felt her nerves stretch as she quickly turned the wheel to avoid her. Hell, she was getting too old for this.

'I think she's spotted me,' Perry talked into the radio receiver in his hand. 'Where are you now?'

'Coming up on Kua.'

'Good. Park there, she's heading that way. Let's just hope she makes a break for it and we can switch cars.'

Luck, for once, was on Perry's side. Spotting a narrow turning across the line of traffic, Gloria suddenly put on speed and cut across the honking line of cars. Taking the opposite turn, Perry screeched to a halt in front of Rolnalski's car. 'She took the old alley between Fourth and Pele Drive,' he said curtly, getting in. Rolnalski knew the streets well, but they still had a barren few minutes before they picked her up again, heading back the way she'd come. 'She's been backtracking,' Perry commented, his blood still racing with excitement. Old or not, fieldwork could still be fun.

'I think she's headed for Gillespie's,' Rolnalski observed, sitting tense and eager behind the wheel, his eyes glued to the economic red hatchback that was always three cars in front. 'She is,' he said with certainty a few blocks later. 'What do we do?'

'Park out of sight. She's a crafty cautious cat, that one.

She'll be on the lookout for any car she sees parked outside.'
Rolnalski pulled in round the corner and Perry checked his
watch before saying, 'Get out and watch for them.'

'You don't think they'll stay long?'

'No, I don't.'

Rolnalski shrugged and got out, walking to the corner and
looking out over the entrance to the casino. At the bottom of
the stone steps Gloria knocked on a steel-reinforced door and
faced the spyhole that was immediately slotted open. Within
minutes she was inside where she made her way quickly to the
back offices, the man standing guard outside the door
recognizing her immediately and making no move to leave his
chair as she knocked on the office door and walked in.

'Hey!' Frank greeted her warmly as he saw her, standing up
and walking around his desk to give her a quick peck on the
cheek. 'Looking good, as always. What's up? Trouble?'

'Yeah – but from cops, not pimps.'

'Oh? Same man?'

'Clements, yes. He mentioned Wanda by name – and he's
been digging into the other girl's hospital records. He was
hinting, good and strong.'

Frank scratched his chin. 'The blonde's no problem, not
while she's walking around with no memory. But we'd better
do something about Wanda.'

'We'd better do it in person; the last thing we need is to
spook her into bolting into the open. Not with that damned
cop about.'

Rolnalski was beginning to be a believer in Perry's psychic
abilities. Quickly nipping back into the car a scant five
minutes after leaving it, he turned the ignition and looked
across at his mindreading boss. 'You were right. They're off.'

It took Frank half an hour to make it over a ten-minute
distance, and it was a mute testimony to Rolnalski's skill that
they weren't spotted. The apartment block they disappeared
into was the large, cheap and anonymous kind that could
have been located in any American city in the world. Waiting
only a few minutes, they then followed the other couple in and
had a discreet and none too friendly chat with the manager
who sat behind a little glass screen assuring them righteously

that he minded his own business and didn't know who came or went. But after a flashed badge and a little friendly blackmail they learned that the 'black chick with the re-arranged face' was on the fifth floor. Perry didn't bother to knock, but attempted to open the door. It was on a chain but he could hear an inside door open and then muffled whispers.

'Come on, Gloria – open up,' Perry yelled.

Gloria swore, coming to stand by the door but making no move to open it. Frank joined her and called, 'Let us see the warrant.'

'I could get one, Frank,' Perry said mildly. 'You don't really want to make an enemy out of me, does he, Gloria?'

Gloria sighed. 'I told you about him,' she whispered grimly, and Frank looked at her thoughtfully, his dark eyes blank mirrors behind which a creative and steely brain worked rapidly. Slowly he opened the door and stood back. 'Lieutenant Clements, I presume.'

'Mr Gillespie.' Perry walked firmly into the room, taking in the handsome, middle-aged man who looked back at him with a diplomatic smile that wouldn't have been out of place in Washington. 'I don't think you've met Sergeant Rolnalski.' The two men sized each other up as Perry looked around. The flat was small but clean and nicely decorated. Guessing that the door leading off to the left was the bedroom he made for it, his supicions confirmed when both Gloria and Frank moved in unison to follow closely.

Inside, the room was gloomy, made so by heavy curtains drawn across the window. A girl sat up against a headboard, plucking nervously at a sheet. Perry nodded at the curtain with a wordless command and Rolnalski walked quickly across to draw it back. The girl blinked in the bright sunlight as Perry walked closer to the bed, sitting down on the edge as he took in the girl's face. She had once been very pretty, with that smooth-cheeked dark chocolate colour of mixed African and Caribbean blood. But now her cheeks were criss-crossed with pale scars and her nose, although reset, had obviously been broken. Her thick lips were misshapen and even after seven months, Perry could imagine what a pathetic mess she must once have been. Back at HQ he had seen pictures of

Lyons' last victims, the list of their injuries horrific to even the most inured of cops. Broken ribs, shattered cheekbones, dislocated shoulders and even, in the murder case, a gouged-out eye. By those standards, this one had been lucky. Dark eyes looked nervously across to Gloria for reassurance, and her fear made Perry's gorge rise. That bastard Lyons had got all he deserved, no matter who had actually done it. 'Hello – Wanda, isn't it?'

'That's right,' the girl replied, her voice husky, her open mouth revealing broken teeth that would look much better after a good dentist had been around them.

'You feeling better?'

'Sure – thanks. Cop.' The final word was determinedly defiant. His kindness had taken her by surprise, leaving her feeling unsure and obliged to defend herself. She'd never had sympathy from a cop before. Watching his gentleness, Gloria felt a shiver of something long-since forgotten snake down her back. Pity he was a cop. And ironic!

'What happened?' Perry asked softly, his voice soothing enough to talk a teething baby into going to sleep.

'A car crash,' Frank's voice cut in quickly and firmly from behind, and the girl nodded vigorously, her damaged lips pressed firmly together.

'I see. Did you report it?' The girl shook her head. 'That's illegal, you know,' he chided softly.

'There wasn't another car involved,' Frank's voice again, and Perry finally turned around to address him.

'And which hospital did she attend?'

'She didn't have insurance,' Gloria took up the tale. 'So I paid for a doctor to treat her here.'

'I see.' His eyes rested briefly on Gloria, giving nothing away, and then he turned back to the girl in front of him, still twisting the sheet in her fists in a pathetic gesture that made him inwardly wince. 'Remember him?' he asked, taking out the picture of Lyons and holding it up in front of her. The girl shuddered and looked away.

'Only as a john.'

'He was murdered. Had his skull crushed in by a heavy blunt object.'

Wanda shrugged and looked back only when Perry had put the photo safely away in his pocket. 'I don't carry heavy blunt objects around with me.'

'I never said you did.'

'And even if I did, I wouldn't have been in any fit state to do him in. Oh, I know that's what you're thinkin',' Wanda sneered with more desperation than defiance. 'But I didn't do nothin' to him.'

Perry was inclined to believe her. That bastard had worked her over good – he'd be willing to bet his entire month's salary that she'd had broken ribs and probably concussion as well. Definitely not able to crush in a physically fit and much taller man's skull. That left Gloria. He looked around and up at her, his eyes so speculative and questioning he might just as well have voiced the question aloud. Gloria's blue eyes were so bland they couldn't have offended a vicar. 'You know, Wanda,' Perry glanced back at the woman who was looking less frightened now, 'if you cooperated with us, I'd guarantee that nothing would . . .'

'If you have any proof,' Frank interrupted quickly, 'then make an arrest. If not, then Miss Jenkins would like you to leave her apartment. Wouldn't you, Wanda? The Lieutenant has no warrant, and he's here only at your invitation.'

'Yeah,' Wanda said, then slewed her eyes away as everyone looked at her.

Perry sighed and got up. 'Can I speak to you in private, Gloria?' He made the question an order with the merest alteration in his tone and she nodded, stepping back a few paces and holding out her hand to Frank in a silencing gesture as he looked about to object.

'See you later, Wanda,' Gloria promised softly, and all three left the room, Rolnalski and Gillespie reluctantly stepping into the corridor to lurk and cast each other suspicious glances.

'He really did her over, didn't he?' Perry said almost to himself, and not expecting Gloria to answer. She didn't. 'Gloria, why don't you level with me? I don't give a toss about Lyons – as far as I'm concerned the murdering son of a bitch got what was coming to him.'

Gloria glanced at him quickly. Was it true? She couldn't take the risk. Too much was at stake. 'I don't know anything,' she said flatly.

'You know,' Perry said with a small wry laugh, 'I've always hated mysteries ever since I was a kid. They've always seemed to be some sort of personal insult, put there just to annoy me. That's one reason I became a cop, believe it or not.'

Gloria believed him. 'I don't know anything, Lieutenant,' she repeated, her voice as flat as glass.

Perry sighed. 'Is the girl, the amnesiac, involved?'

Gloria made sure she wore her best surprised look, then quickly concealed it. 'How could she be, Lieutenant? You keep insisting on dragging her into it for some reason of your own. That's fine by me of course,' she held out her hands in a submissive gesture. 'You're the cop after all,' she finished with a truly brilliant challenge that made him smile briefly.

Perry walked slowly to the door where Frank immediately pounced. Perry looked from one to the other. 'You two are good friends, aren't you?'

'The best,' Gloria stated.

'I imagine he could come in very handy in a messy situation, hm?'

'Sorry?' She blinked innocent baby-blue eyes at him.

'I mean, I bet Mr Gillespie here knows a lot of people and a lot of things. Like how to get rid of unwanted . . . garbage, for instance?'

'Lieutenant!' Gloria shook her head, mockingly.

Perry smiled broadly. 'You know, I really like you, Miss Gaines.'

Gloria inclined her head graciously, whilst Frank leaned against the doorjamb, folded his arms across his chest and looked from one to the other with a half-smile. 'The feeling is mutual, Lieutenant,' she assured him.

Perry nodded. 'I'll be seeing you.'

'I don't doubt it,' she said tiredly. Frank waited until the two cops were out of sight, then turned a speculative look on Gloria.

'You two seem to have started up a mutual admiration society. Am I interrupting anything?'

'Don't be an asshole, Frank,' Gloria chided. 'He's trouble.'

'Funny – I didn't think so myself. Compared to some of the bastards, he's a milk-and-water college boy.'

'He's trouble,' Gloria corrected. Frank heard the certainty in her voice and for the first time felt the stirrings of real fear deep in his own gut.

'Why are you so sure?'

Gloria looked at her oldest friend and one-time lover and then back down the now empty corridor. 'Because he's a clever. And because he's a real cop.'

VIENNA rubbed her damp palms on the crisp white apron she wore and checked the hors d'oeuvres tray once more. Tiny vol-au-vents stuffed with crab, cheese and shallots nestled against their neighbours, which contained salmon mayonnaise and caviar. Tiny truffles, pâté de foie gras and Melba toast made up the rest of the entrées. Lifting the tray which was lined with lacy serviettes, she carried it into the large lounge where Dominic was standing at the bar talking to the two men who were watching him mix the drinks. Smiling at the two women sat on the Mies van der Rohe chairs, wearing Paul Gotthard and Saint Laurent designer dresses, diamonds and Chanel No. 5 perfume, she offered them the choice morsels. She waited politely as they made their selections and arranged them on the delicate Wedgwood plates that were attractively stacked on the right-hand side of the tray. Walking to the bar, her eyes flickering away from Dominic who winked reassuringly at her, she offered the snacks to the men who looked first at her and then at the delicacies she'd spent all day preparing.

'When would you like dinner served, Mr Fairchild?' she asked Dominic softly, and he glanced at the gold watch on his wrist.

'Half an hour all right with everyone?'

There were polite murmurs of consent and Vienna retreated to the dining room to check for the tenth time that all was in readiness there. The oval table was covered with the finest pastel-green linen tablecloth, smooth and stiff. Wedgwood china with the 'Kutani Crane' design added elegance and sophistication to the outdoor flavour of the room, as did the large flowered centrepiece that she'd arranged in colours of lilac and cream. Silver candlesticks containing lilac-coloured candles, and fluted wine goblets sparkled in the light from the overhead crystal chandelier. Back in the kitchen she brought the turtle soup to a final gentle simmer and checked the stuffed shoulder of lamb in the oven. Everything seemed to be going well. She wasn't sure what she'd do if she burnt something, or if a guest complained about a sauce or the temperature of the wine. But although she was nervous, she was also happy. At last she felt as if she were earning her keep. And soon all the plates she collected as they progressed through the meal were satisfactorily empty and she began to relax. The dessert, a lemon Pavlova with real cream, seemed to go down very well too, as did the Irish coffee she served afterwards in the library.

'It was a superb meal, Vienna,' was the first thing Dominic said to her when, his guests gone, he found her in the kitchen. 'Everyone said so.' He watched her heart-shaped face flush and her shy smile come and go. 'I think you deserve a glass of wine and a little relaxation on the patio. White or red?'

'White, please. But I can get it.'

'No, no. You've worked hard enough for one evening. Go and stretch out on a lounger. I won't be a minute.'

She rejected the lounger in favour of a comfortable chair, but she did kick off her shoes with a grateful sigh. Dominic handed her a glass then folded his long body on to the chair next to her. 'Feel better now the first hurdle is over?'

She laughed. 'Was it very obvious?'

'That you were scared stiff? Only to those of us who know you well. You were a big hit – with the men especially. Cheers. To your first dinner party, and long may they continue to be such a resounding success!' They clinked glasses and drank, the silence amiable and relaxing.

'I think that's Farron,' Vienna said some fifteen minutes later after a meandering, none-too-serious chat about nothing in particular.

'That's him,' Dominic confirmed without opening his eyes, recognizing both the sound of Farron's car and the rhythm of his footsteps as he walked up the path and followed the sounds of their voices into the back garden.

'Hi. How'd it go?'

'Terrible,' Dominic said dryly. 'All the guests are in the local hospital with botulism. It's only by an immense effort of will, and by collapsing in this chair, that I'm still in the land of the living.'

Vienna laughed and stood up, reaching to loop her arms around Farron's neck and kiss him lightly on the lips. 'He's terrible,' she whispered and Farron grinned, his hands resting lightly on her hips.

'I know. He's an awful man.'

Dominic slowly swung his legs to the floor and looked discreetly away. 'Well, now that you've arrived, I should be going.' he yawned widely.

'Oh, no, please stay a while.' It was Vienna who spoke, moving away from Farron and towards the French doors. 'I was going to take a bath anyway.'

Both men watched her leave in silence, then Farron lifted Vienna's glass and took a long draught, slowly sinking into her chair with a sigh. 'It was good of you to stay with her till I got back.'

'My pleasure. Besides, after the other night, I owe you.'

'You owe me nothing,' Farron denied sharply.

'Tough night?'

Farron shrugged. 'The audience wouldn't let us go.'

'Speaking of which, you'd better arrange with Burke to have three days free next week starting Tuesday. I've booked you and the boys in with a recording studio. Someone called Pete Adams is doing the mixing. Pete assured me he was good.'

'Good? He's only the damned best,' Farron accused happily.

'Ahh. He should be able to make the sow's ear sound like a silk purse then?'

'Thanks!' Farron laughed then sat on the edge of the chair, his smile disappearing. He'd just been handed the chance of a lifetime and as usual he didn't know what to say, except the obvious. 'Thanks, Dom,' he finally managed, his voice simply genuine.

'Any time. I'm mad at myself for not thinking of it before.'

'I wasn't ready before.' Farron immediately defended him. 'Singing at the hotel, having fun, taking it easy, all that was what I wanted – all I needed.'

'And now it's different.' Dominic nodded, looking around at the light shining in from the bedroom window. 'I understand. She's lovely.'

'You really like her, don't you?' Farron probed, sure that he did and yet still a little nervous about his answer. Of all the people in the world, only his *tutu* and this man's opinions mattered to him and he felt a stringing out of time as he waited for him to answer.

'I do. Very much. She's come a long way, I think, since you first met her.'

'Yes, she has. Although . . . she still has bad dreams.'

Dominic leaned forward to rest his elbows on his knees, looking down at the paved patio floor as he said quietly, 'We all have those. The trick is to make real life more than a match for them.'

'I try to make sure it does for her,' Farron agreed softly. 'But who does the same for you?'

The question caught Dominic on the raw and he looked away, a bleak smile already on his lips. 'I'm old enough, and mean enough, to look out for myself.'

Farron nodded but didn't push it. 'We were discussing Vienna seeing a shrink,' he changed the subject instead. 'Someone with a history of good hypnotherapy behind him. We've reading up on that, and Vienna's keen. It might also help her to get her memory back. Thing is, the best around is someone called Drake, and we simply can't afford him.'

'No problem. I know someone in Welfare. I can work out a subsidy. Don't look at it as charity, look at it as justice. Her problems, in a way, were caused by Oahu. Let Oahu help rectify them. That's only fair, after all. I'll get on to him straight away. It was time I left, anyway.'

Farron nodded and rose with him. He wasn't proud when it came to helping those he loved. He held out his hand. Dominic looked up at his son then stepped forward, drawing the younger man into a brief but firm embrace. Farron was stiff and surprised at first, but then quickly relaxed. The mutual and masculine back-slapping made both of them feel better.

Dominic smiled. 'I'll see you tomorrow.'

'OK.' Farron nodded, feeling a little shy. 'Goodnight.' Farron watched him walk out of sight, thoughtful and happier than he'd been when he first arrived.

Once back at Falling Pearls Palace, Dominic got on the phone to Dr Vincent Drake and made it abundantly clear that his prospective patient was never to know that he would be exclusively paying her bills.

Chapter 32

The drive was full of cars illuminated by the bright lights spilling from the multitude of windows incorporated into the renowned Falling Pearls Palace. Rhiannon leaned forward and said softly, 'Drive past the main gates and go around the back. I want to see if there's a side entrance.' The driver nodded silently and slowed down once they'd passed the huge, wrought-iron double gates positioned between two impressive stone pillars which bore the Fairchild crest and the car's headlights created double white beams on the tall, thick green hedge that skirted the entire five acres of grounds.

'Stop here a moment,' she urged, as she spotted a single wrought-iron gate in the middle of all the greenery, but a large black padlock signalled the end of her hopes. Hugging a full-length black velvet cloak around her she slipped back into her seat and quietly closed the door. 'Carry on, Sam.'

She craned forward, eyes concentrating intensely on the green expanse of hedge that seemed to go on and on without ending. Finally, on the north side at the back entrance to the Palace they found another gate, still padlocked, but a mere six feet in height. It was, she was damned sure, the best chance she'd get. 'I won't need you again until later. About two o'clock.'

The long black car pulled away with a silent purr and she watched the cheerful and somehow comforting red tail-lights until they'd disappeared into the night. Well, she was committed now. She turned and looked up the expanse of patterned black iron, then down at her white-gloved hands and delicate slippers. Luckily the loose pattern of the ironwork gave her several easy footholds as she climbed but the spikes on the top required some tricky manoeuvering so as not to catch her dress. Climbing down the other side, her feet touched gravel and she turned to face the Palace, a smile of pure devilment on her face. She stripped off her soiled gloves to reveal slender hands with nails brushed in a clear polish with the faintest tint of silver. On the third finger of her right hand an emerald and diamond ring glinted softly in the moonlight.

Even the back view of the Palace was impressive. The shimmering white moonlight had given it a fairy-tale-castle look and she felt something stir deep inside her. All week she'd been looking forward to this occasion, but last night a touch of apprehension had kept her awake, the morning bringing with it not a return to confidence but an almost paranormal foreboding. The air was soft and the breeze full of moisture, wafting to her the smell of rain. Suddenly she shivered and trying to shake off the feeling of Fate closing in, she began to walk briskly across the lawn, keeping a sharp eye out for guards who might mug her for an invitation she didn't have.

Inside, the Palace was full of human voices, clinking classes, cigar and cigarette smoke. Vienna carried a tray of delicately fluted glasses filled with the best champagne with the careful fear of a novice, looking progressively relieved as anonymous hands reached out and slowly emptied the tray. Politicians rubbed shoulders with Care workers, who badgered them for more money for the handicapped, the mentally ill and the old, whilst up-and-coming actors fawned over movie producers, directors and screenwriters. Businessmen ignored all but each other, and wives headed for the celebrities or Dominic Fairchild, whichever happened to be nearest.

Outside, Rhiannon walked through the rose garden, the fragrance of the blooms heavy and intoxicating in the sultry pre-storm air. She paused beside a bush of pale yellow blooms and picked one, carefully holding the stem between the thorns and twirling it thoughtfully in her hand. Turning abruptly, she wandered along the side of the Palace where borders of anthuriums, orchids and bird-of-paradise thrust colourful heads into the air. Climbing the Palace walls themselves were clinging vines of yellow alamanda, orange trumpet vine and stephanotis. Looped through the Lehua and glorious shower trees were colourful Chinese lanterns of red, blue, gold, green, pink, mauve and white, their small globes of colour casting patches on the lawns and flowers, adding to the fairy-tale atmosphere of the night.

'The guest-list is now completed, sir.' Koana spoke quietly into Dominic's ear and he turned with the last of his guests and walked with them through the large entrance lobby and into the main ballroom. Six french windows opened off on to a semi-circular terrace, letting in the cooling night breezes and fresh air. Off to the left of the ballroom was the grand dining room, laden with food, ice-sculptures and flowers. Uniformed men stood in every room, ready to guard anything that needed guarding, from lap dogs to jewel-encrusted handbags, real fur coats of mink, fox and sable, ivory walking sticks, jewelled cigarette-holders and video cameras. Overhead in ballroom and halls, chandeliers shone forth brilliantly, whilst on the elevated dais a twenty-piece orchestra played inoffensive classics. On the patios jugglers, mime-artists and novelty acts entertained the blasé or the young, whilst in the grounds themselves plenty of shaded bowers and dark nooks and crannies pleased the more adventurous or romantic element.

Rhiannon made her way to a paved area and slipped off her all-encompassing cloak, draping it over the back of the nearest chair. Straightening her bare shoulders, she walked into the room. Dominic, who was talking to Franklin Benny, his doctor since childhood, felt a shifting in the air, a silent touch that needed none of the normal five senses to alert him to her presence. The fact that she would dare to gatecrash his party didn't surprise him in the least, and he felt a shaft of ridiculous pleasure lance through him.

Rhiannon paused at the top of the five steps, her glittering green eyes sweeping the room. Out of all that movement a mere turning of the head caught her gaze like a magnet catches iron, and they were looking at each other. Dominic felt his mouth go dry at the sight of her, stood ten yards away and up to his right. Her hair was swept up in a gentle but high chignon, a glittering diamond band shimmering in it, meeting over her forehead to drop a single emerald on to her white skin just above and between her eyes. Her dress was of sea-green – not silver, not blue and not emerald, but somewhere in between, while the finest of silver lace covering the full skirt gave her a mermaid-like, ethereal look. Hugging her waist in a tight embrace, the misty skirt swirled to a stop just above her ankles, whilst her shoulders and arms were left bare. A diamond and emerald necklace, a web-like, ruinously expensive creation, added delicacy and fire to her throat and he felt the room around him ebb like a receding wave.

Rhiannon could feel herself trembling. He was magnificent and dressed almost outrageously. His chest was bare, showing well-formed muscle tone, his skin a lovely dark tan that revealed darker nipples. A flowing feather cloak tied by simple leather bonds across his shoulders flowed down his back and just swept the floor, the bordering feathers of black and white, whilst layer after layer of speckled and dyed feathers overlapped each other. His trousers were black and close-fitting, his shoes simple sandals made by an old woman who lived on the east coast. At his neck a single strand of sharks' teeth, a tribal emblem of an *alii*, gleamed whitish yellow against his skin. His black hair was combed back from his face, revealing the high cheekbones and firm jaw that was clenched tight now as they stared at one another. Desperate to break the spell, she reached out blindly for a passing tray and clasped a glass.

Dominic excused himself from the doctor and Rhiannon's muscles began to tighten as his foot lifted the first step and she took a quick swallow of her drink. She looked over his head, her desperate eyes fixed on the orchestra until his face blotted out even that. He was stood three steps below her and his eyes were on a perfect level with her own. '*Aloha*,' he said softly. 'I should throw you out.'

Rhiannon shrugged one shoulder. 'You could,' she admitted. 'But just think how boring the party would be then.' She looked out over the rest of the room, crammed with elegantly-clad bodies. Other eyes than those of Philip Pearce's and Farron's were turned in their direction, and a few whispers, like undulating waves, slowly circumnavigated the room.

'That's true,' Dominic murmured as she looked down at the rose, still in her hand. Silently she offered it to him.

'For you.'

'From my garden, I suppose?' he asked drily, and she laughed.

'Where else?'

He took it, then winced as a thorn pierced his thumb. He looked at her, whispered something savage in his native tongue and turned abruptly away. Rhiannon let out a long shuddering breath then looked across the room, aware now of all the eyes that were upon her. She felt a moment of panic and then slowly walked down the steps. Her eyes began to wander over the room, narrowing as they spotted the famous freshwater pearls that had given the Palace its name. Embedded into the pale pink plaster on the walls, the lonely white drops formed patterns of fountains, flowers and swirling curlicues.

She began to circulate and to accept invitations to dance; her smile was artful, designed to make her partner of the moment think he was the only man she'd noticed, her questions designed to lead him into talking about himself, impressing her with his talents, his skills, his acumen, and leaving her mind free to wander.

Once or twice she spotted Vienna and smiled and nodded at her, and then, spying Farron, she threaded her way towards him. He straightened as she approached, his eyes dark and cold.

'Hello, Farron.'

'Miss Grantham.'

'Rhia, please. I was hoping you'd ask me to dance.'

Farron opened his mouth, not sure whether to admire her cheek or put her down, then shrugged and held out his arms, holding her a good five inches away as they began a slow waltz.

'I'm surprised you were invited,' he said stiffly.

'I wasn't. I climbed over a side gate at the back.'

That caught his attention. He looked at her quickly, then began to grin. No wonder Dom was fascinated by her. But it was a lethal attraction – like a moth fluttering around an open flame. Dom was already singed if their potent meeting tonight had been anything to go by. He was damned sure he was not the only one who'd felt the electricity spark between them.

He wasn't. Perry Clements, for one, had seen it. His invitation to this party, to the party of the year, had been a total shock, especially to his wife with whom he was dancing. The Palace, even he'd had to admit, was overwhelming and Carla's eyes were not the only ones to swivel like pivots, bulging with interest and admiration at the sights and sounds of high society in full swing. Suspicious as ever, Perry wondered about the reasons behind the invitation. Tomorrow he'd start re-searching Dominic Fairchild in earnest . . .

'You climbed over a gate in that get-up?' Farron asked, artfully steering them through the throng that seemed intent on closing in on them, diamond-studded ears straining for every word.

Rhiannon grinned. 'I did. I was a champion tree-climber as a girl.'

'There are dogs patrolling the grounds, not to mention security guards.'

'I know,' Rhiannon said airily. 'I saw them.'

Farron was fascinated in spite of himself. Stepping back another small pace he looked her straight in the eye. 'What are you really after?'

Now there's a good question for you, a little voice said in her head, and before she could stop herself a bittersweet smile flickered across her lips. 'If I told you I don't think you'd believe me.'

Farron slowly shook his head. 'I just don't understand you.'

'No? Well, don't worry about it. Dominic does, and that after all is what matters, isn't it?'

Farron slowly nodded. 'Yes, it is. He'll do for you, though, you know that, don't you?'

'So people keep saying. So far he doesn't seem to be doing so well.'

'You think so?' Something in his voice made her eyes swivel back to him, narrowing sharply.

'What's that supposed to mean?'

Farron half-shrugged. 'It seems to me that you both have a knife in the other, and neither will break the deadlock. You'd better be careful: one of you could bleed to death.'

'So . . . it's a question of whose endurance will last, is it?' she said faintly, unwilling to acknowledge that his graphic imagery had sent a cold wave flooding over her.

'His will.' Farron said the words with total conviction.

'I wouldn't bet on it if I were you,' she said quickly, the words a purely defensive gesture. Then she took a deep calming breath and told herself not to be such a rabbit. She'd heard from Sandy McNally only yesterday: the man he'd mentioned at the Sea Life Park had returned to the islands, and Sandy had put out the word that he wanted a meet. If everything turned out as anticipated then Farron would have to eat his words.

Farron smiled sadly and shook his head. 'But it's not me who's betting on it, is it?' he reminded her softly. 'I'm not the one standing to lose everything. You are.'

At midnight there was a slow shifting into the dining rooms where a buffet was laid out on every inch of available top space. Nestled on lettuce leaves, decorated with shaped wedges of tomato and cheese were delicious concoctions of cracked crab, lobster mayonnaise and patties, quenelles of pheasant, slices of roast lamb with mint, tiny slices of turbot and dover sole with shallots. In squat crystal dishes were rows and rows of *pommes soufflées*, cream of watercress, tomatoes *à la tartare* and prosciutto and figs. On silver platters were roulades of beef, smoked salmon with capers, Beef Wellington and turbans of chicken and tongue, while tasty titbits including caviar and canapés of every kind were constantly being offered from trays. Large Royal Worcester plates in dark green and gold leaf were quickly snapped up and piled high, guests either migrating into small lounges converted into dining rooms or headed for the informality of the garden furniture on the terraces and patios. Rhiannon looked, but had no appetite. The air outside was stilling in preparation for rain and time seemed to hang as heavy as the thumping of her heart. Dominic had selected a plateful of food, piling it on generously so that his quests wouldn't be embarrassed at their own amount of food, but no one actually saw him eating.

'Would you care for some gâteaux?' a polite voice beside her asked and she turned to look at Vienna, who was smiling widely.

'I would,' she said, looking over the Swiss-style gâteaux of walnut, chocolate, strawberry and lemon, all topped with whipped cream, sprinkles of nuts, chocolate and fruit. 'But I don't think I dare. I wouldn't like to have to count up the calories in that little lot.'

'Me neither. But I wouldn't mind cooking them.'

'Yes, I'd heard you'd changed jobs. Congratulations. Enjoying it?'

'Yes, I am. Did you enjoy dancing with my boyfriend?' Vienna wondered how Rhiannon knew so much, and then pushed the thought aside as unworthy. Lord, she had to start trusting someone! Her paranoia was getting worse and worse.

Rhiannon laughed and held out her hands in a submissive gesture. 'One dance only, and there were at least six inches between us at all times.'

'So I noticed! Everyone's talking about you,' she added more hesitantly, her blue eyes sympathetic, and Rhiannon laughed a trifle grimly.

'I know. Nothing good, I hope?'

Vienna shook her head. 'I'd better go,' she said regretfully. 'The head caterer's motto is "Circulate" with a capital "C". Good luck,' she added charmingly.

'Too late for that,' Rhiannon whispered under her breath then felt her sensitive skin prickle.

'Not eating?' Dominic asked a moment later, drawing to her side with quiet grace, one eyebrow raised questioningly.

'Not hungry.'

'Me neither. What do you think of the cloak? It's my grandfather's on my mother's side. The royal cloak of the Hunaakalii tribe.'

'It's very lovely,' she agreed, reaching out a finger to stroke over the feathers that lay across his shoulder and feeling a current of desire threaten to suck her under. 'Which makes me wonder,' she pulled her hand away quickly, 'how it comes to be worn by an unworthy *haole* half-breed.'

Dominic never took his eyes from hers. 'I'm not rising to the bait, Rhia.' His voice was soft and seductive as liquid gold. She took a quick step backwards and then the lights dimmed, all talk coming to an abrupt halt as through the door a seven-tiered cake, alight with candles, was carried by two waiters. The orchestra struck up the tune *Happy Birthday* and all the guests save for herself, began to sing. As the clapping began the waiters placed the cake on a trolley and wheeled it over to him. 'You need a seven-tier cake to hold that number of candles,' she commented with sugar-sweet bitchiness.

The waiter nearest to him handed over a wide, flat knife which he took, balancing it testingly in his hand and looking tellingly at her, his meaning clear. Rhiannon's grin widened.

Dominic made a short, witty speech, and took a wedge of cake in his hand.

'*Hauoli la hanau*,' Farron called out 'Happy Birthday' in Hawaiian, the impromptu toast taken up by others who raised their glasses. Dominic turned to Rhia until their green eyes met with all the force of two steel swords, and then he stepped deliberately closer, a hush falling over the crowd as he moved the slice of cake to touch her lips. Still not taking her eyes from his she opened her mouth and took a fair-sized bite, chewing defiantly. Turning slowly from her, Dominic took another bite, and waved a hand to the cake. 'First come, first served. So if there's not enough you can fight each other for it – but outside on the lawns, if you please.' There was more laughter and a surge towards them and she took the chance to slip away, wandering instead to the now-empty ballroom.

She was startled when the orchestra began to play *Save the Last Dance for Me* and gasped as strong arms came around her waist and turned her into his arms. She could smell his naked skin and feel its heat and she licked her lips nervously. 'You should be . . .'

'Be quiet.' The two words were a command that she simply could not disobey. His hands around her felt capable of crushing her every bone, and every breath she took seemed to be dragged past hot coals before they reached her lungs. Her bare shoulders touched a combination of feathers and skin, and over the small of her back she felt his fingers span and press against her.

She closed her eyes and let her head fall forward, her cheek resting against his shoulder where she could hear the drumbeat of his heart echoing her own. His strong, long legs brushed against hers as they moved whilst his hand migrated from her back to caress her shoulderblades. Her breasts tingled and blossomed against his bare skin.

Below his chin, her black hair was soft against him, and he could smell its perfume. Every sinew in his body was stretched, waiting, every sensor on his flesh attuned to the cushioned softness of her breasts with their hardening nipples pressing into him like tiny, deadly sword-tips. '*Kokua*,' he whispered softly, then closed his eyes, dipping his head to rest his cheek on the top of her soft hair, their bodies barely swaying in time to the music that ended on a whispering, regretful sigh. It hurt them both, that ending of music, and as they pulled away, it was as if each left a vital part embedded in the other.

Swiftly Rhiannon walked away towards the patio, stepping into the night with a sigh of relief. It was cooler now, the breeze in the trees harsher, the sky deprived of all stars by thickening clouds. She retrieved her cape and wrapped it around her shoulders as she walked far away from the lights and the party to where a protecting brick wall against which grew apricots and pears rose ten feet into the sky. She placed the cloak on the ground and sat down, slipping off her shoes and all her jewellery before pulling the pins from out of her hair, the tresses falling to warm her cold shoulders. Stuffing the jewellery into the cape pocket, she lay back against the warm velvet. She was alone and waiting for him and she knew it.

The party slowly began to wind down. The orchestra played their last song, and Dominic, once more in place in the hall, said goodbye to his last guests.

Outside, the first rumble of thunder rolled across the sky and warm, fat raindrops flew in the wind. Rhiannon felt them on her skin, but still did not stir. Instead she sat up and, with the aid of the rain and a handkerchief, removed her makeup, leaving her face as fresh and innocent as the moment it had been born. Lying back again, she let the now pouring rain wash over her.

Inside Dominic wandered into the now-deserted ballroom,

his eyes hurt by the lack of her. The dining rooms were empty of all save the catering staff. Abruptly he told them to leave it till morning.

After they'd gone it was deathly quiet save for the splattering of rain on the windows, and his footsteps echoing eerily against the tiles as he aimlessly wandered around. When had she gone? He could feel her absence but could not understand it. Wearily he reached around the back of his neck and untied the necklace, an heirloom that he hardly ever wore, and reverently placed it on a Chippendale sideboard of glowing mahogany. Slipping out of his sandals he caught sight of his reflection in the glass; half-naked, half-white, half-Hawaiian, and suddenly he realized. Without her, he was only half a man.

Drawn to the french windows, to the sighing breeze that blew out a long lace curtain, he stood framed in its doorway, a tall, black silhouette.

Rhiannon, who had slowly walked forward to stand under the spreading branches of a shower tree nearest the patio, let the cape fall to the damp earth and Dominic stepped outside, listening to the rain hit the protecting porch roof overhead. Suddenly a movement, a merest shifting of light, brought his head down and around with the speed of a hawk, and he saw her. The silvery-green dress was darker in colour from the rain, sopping wet and plastered to every inch of skin it touched, clinging to her thighs, her breasts, her waist and her calves. Her hair was loose and wet, darkly rich and clustered around her neck and shoulders. She raised a hand to brush a few strands from her cheeks but other than that she did not move.

With a simple pull of a leather thong, the feather cloak slithered from him, revealing large and powerful shoulders. He stepped on to the grass, the rain eagerly falling on his skin like tiny warm kisses but his eyes never left hers, nor did he pause as he joined her under the spreading, dripping limbs of the tree. Without effort or thought his lips sought hers as overhead lightning flashed and illuminated the sky for a scant second. Electricity crackled all around and through them.

Her back bent like a supple reed as his hands dragged her to him, her bare feet slipping on the black velvet beneath her. His mouth was hard and warm, as undeniable as his tongue that slipped between her lips to find and duel with her own. She gasped, opening her lips wider, her fingers curling into the firm muscled flesh of his shoulders, her nails scoring tiny red lines on his skin. A molten explosion between her thighs radiated white-hot heat into her blood. 'Dominic,' she groaned his name, a plea, a curse, but the thunder rumbled and roared, drowning out her pitiful human voice with contemptuous ease. His lips slewed across her cheek, his teeth and tongue attacking her ear, sending shafts of sensation down the chords of her neck to her shoulders and then lodging in her breasts, tightening the nipples into a painful bud.

Her legs collapsed under her but he took her weight easily, holding her arched back against his arms as his lips moved to kiss the side of her neck, then her throat, his mouth a hot coal on her skin. Sinking to his knees, allowing her slowly to fall on the sodden black cape beneath them, his hands came from around her back to splay over her breasts, his palms directly over her nipples thrusting against the wet silk that covered them.

She cried out in inarticulate need as his fingers curled around the material, pulling it down to her waist, baring the firm white mounds with their pink aureoles to the rain, the breeze and his lips. 'Dominic!' she moaned again as his lips encompassed one pulsating nipple, her arms stretching out on the cape, his fingers digging compulsively into the material, curling into helpless fists as her back arched from the ground with the fierce power of desire that spiralled within her.

He was intoxicated by the hard peaked softness of her breast within his mouth, his nostrils breathing in the scent of her skin and her passion, making his penis swell harder and harder against the tightness of his pants. Sitting up abruptly, his hands dragged the silk from her body as if he hated it, his hands stripping her of her panties at the same time, leaving her naked, glistening pale and perfect in the night, her skin made silver by the flash of lightning that split the sky. She lay panting, watching him through half-closed eyes, her harsh breathing making her breasts rise and fall rapidly.

His fingers were hot and firm as they curled up and slid over her calves, and she jerked on the cape as lines of fire shot up her leg from the contact and lodged in her womb. She felt hot tears mix with the cool raindrops falling on her face, but she could not take her eyes off him. There was a look of intense concentration on his face as he moved his other hand to her other calf, both hands then moving up in a slow, five-fingered snake-like movement to the backs of her knees, then around, travelling up her thighs to where the black triangle of hair glistened with the rain and a hot waiting juice, juice that tempted him to drink of her.

She screamed as his head dipped low, his lips parting her lips there to allow his tongue to dart into her like a flame-tipped arrow, his teeth finding her clitoris and nibbling with a delicacy that was torture. Words exploded in her brain but were never uttered as his hard hands kept her legs apart, her head falling back to the earth and then thrashing from side to side as she jerked helplessly as orgasm claimed her. She was sobbing when she felt him stand up, and a low rumble of thunder like a dark explosion sounded directly overhead. When she opened her eyes a flash of lightning revealed him standing over her, naked and strong, his penis hard and rigid, large and powerful. Her breath clamoured like fluttering iron-winged butterflies in her chest.

'Spread your legs for me, Rhiannon,' he demanded, his voice low and yet stronger, louder than the thunder around them. She felt her thighs part, baring that gateway to her very womanhood for that pulsing shaft that strained towards her as he fell to his knees. With his hands either side of her head, his eyes glittered like jade above her, the breeze pushing his damp hair off his forehead. She felt the hairs of his thighs against her skin as he sank between her legs and then the hot tip of his penis slowly sliding down, finding its way with unerring skill to that feminine place that waited. Her eyes opened wide as he stopped, his face a scant millimetre from hers, their eyes so close their lashes almost collided, and then he pushed down and into her.

They came together in a perfect, pagan, age-old mating dance that made them both cry out. She could feel him pushing further and further into her belly, filling her, tormenting her with ecstasy and as she watched, a look of pleasure-pain crossed his face as her body, so starved, tightly cradled him, her internal muscles squeezing him, sucking him, making his body simmer to a broiling heat. He lowered his head to her shoulder, her hand coming to caress the back of his head as he thrust into her, her legs jerking and thrashing helplessly either side of him as he speared her.

Her fingers dragged down his back and drew blood as he began to withdraw, then push forward again, slowly, slowly, then faster and faster. It seemed to her as if he were trying to pound her into the ground, burying her in an ecstasy that came, pitilessly, in wave after wave until the thunder around her and the thunder of her heart were one, until the lightning flashing in the sky and the lightning in her blood merged and mated.

Dominic could feel her hot velvet strength draining him, demanding, sucking, drinking him dry like a perverse, passionate leech, and his face contorted helplessly as he felt his defeat drawing near. '*Rhiannon!*' He uttered her name on a hoarse cry as he climaxed, his body becoming a liquid that poured into her. She screamed, her arms holding him tight enough almost to break his back as she felt pouring fire flood inside her. Her muscles spasmodically clenched, the final pleasure so intense she could almost feel her consciousness slip away. Breathes were dragged into lungs with gasping cries, their bodies joined together with a fiery sweat that was relieved only by the large, fast and furious raindrops on his back and her face, legs and arms. Slowly, weakly, he withdrew from her and fell away on to his back on the wet green grass, the rain washing his body, the receding ecstasy leaving his mind empty.

Tears fell from her eyes and slowly dwindled before drying altogether as she stared up into the branches overhead, green leaves dripping water on to her face whilst over her heated body the night breeze blew cruelly cold. Shivering, she sat up and dragged on the clammy green silk, her legs unsteady and shaking uncontrollably. Picking up the black cloak she huddled into it, as if its midnight blackness could hide her 'rom what she had done, could cover the self-treachery and regret now rising up inside her, threatening to choke her.

'Stay with me,' he begged, but with one forearm thrown over his eyes for he knew that she would not, and to watch her go would kill him. 'Please, stay with me.'

But she did not stay. At least, not that part of her that could walk away; her body, her brain, her reason. But her soul and her heart – they stayed with him, tormenting them both through the long, lonely hours of the many nights that were to follow.

Chapter 33

The battered red Beetle pulled in a few parking spaces in front of the second-hand hatchback, the driver turning off the ignition. Keeping deepset brown eyes fixed to the rearview mirror he watched the small blonde-haired girl alight and lock the car doors, then glance apprehensively up at the modest five-storey redbrick office building. But as he followed Vienna discreetly into the small lobby of the building, it was a case of the watcher being watched. In an open-topped Mercedes convertible, Richard Jago was gazing at the man's back with curious, vigilant eyes. His keen memory began summoning up the other times that he'd noticed the battered car and the weedy, shifty man hovering on the fringes wherever Vienna had been. Who the hell was he? And more importantly, what the hell was he up to?

Richard followed them in and walked to a list of businesses hung on one wall. He read through them: there were several individuals that had possibilities, and his grey eyes read down the list; De Regis, Pyke & Appleton, Attorneys at Law, Rooms 215, 216, 217. Dr Vincent Drake M.D., Ph., Psych., Room 310. Clancy Farmer, Interior Decorating Services Inc., Room 312, M.D. Lakehurst, Dentist, Room 401, Paul Williamson & Associates, Literary Agents, Room 420. Zachary & Pitt, Attorneys at Law, Room 422, 423.

The dentist looked the most likely, but Vienna wasn't in the waiting room. He left and descended to the third floor, reviewing the other possibilities in his mind, then paused in midstep as a thought occurred to him. All he had to do was find the scruffy driver of the Beetle. Wherever he was, Vienna was close by, of that he was damned sure. And he was right. He spotted him several minutes later hanging around the office doors of Dr Vincent Drake. But although he crept silently towards him, it was a stunning testimony to the small weasel-like man's uncanny sense of survival that he heard him, and after the briefest of startled glances, ran like hell.

Seeing the little worm sprinting down the corridor, Richard took after him, but while the small spiral fire escape was a perfect escape route for the driver of the Beetle, it was a hindrance for a large man. Two floors from the bottom, Richard saw it was useless and stopped the chase, leaning over the barrier to watch the smaller man leap to the ground, glance up at him and then run down the alley towards the main street.

Richard slowly walked back up the stairs, along the corridor then paused outside the door, reading the brass nameplate there with a half-puzzled expression. A shrink. Drake .. Of course! Vince Drake from the Yacht Club. The man owned the *Pacifier*, a small, one-masted yacht that was berthed three boats along from his own. Drake's speciality was hypnotherapy, so obviously she was seeing him in the hopes of getting her memory back. Now *that* had possibilities. As Jago's memory sharpened he began to smile. He'd once lent the supposedly happily-married Drake one of his girlfriends, thinking at the time it might come in useful to have Drake owe him a favour. And even more useful to have something on him . . .

He walked quickly back to his car and made a telephone call. It was an extension of his character that Richard should know people who knew people, and after only five minutes of casual gossip with a fairweather friend, he knew more about Vincent Drake than the man himself would ever have thought possible. Hanging up, an almost beatific smile on his face, Richard quickly checked his watch. He was meeting Odessa and some of her new friends at the Tennis Club. He'd have to go and dance attendance on the possessive bitch – at least for the moment.

He drove quickly to the Tennis Club where his wife was seated with two other couples and bit back a groan of impatience, forcing a smile to his face. Over lunch he made the standard charming conversation, and afterwards even changed into shorts to play two matches, one singles with Odessa that he won, and one doubles. He was teamed with the wife of Morton Norris, one of their dinner companions, whilst Odessa played with Morton himself. Richard diplomatically let his wife and partner win that one. After a quick shower and an even quicker drink, he firmly said his goodbyes, Odessa looking less than pleased, but hiding it well.

'Sure you got me out of there quick enough?' she asked sweetly in the car as they headed for home.

'Nope.' He pressed his foot harder on the accelerator as she pouted.

'You could at least have let me shower and change,' she commented, pulling away her sweat-soaked shirt from her small breasts. 'I stink.'

'I love the way you stink,' Richard lied, overtaking a straining hatchback crammed with kids and dogs. 'It turns me on.' He pulled into the drive and left the car parked haphazardly, walking around to open the door for her and pulling her roughly into his arms, his lips on hers almost brutal.

She felt her heart bump erratically against her ribs. Her legs dangled in midair as he quickly carried her, past a startled housekeeper and up the stairs. With quick efficiency he stripped them both of their clothes, the frame of the bed creaking as the mattress bounced them once and then twice as his large frame covered hers.

'Richard!' she accused, thrilled and then crammed as his large penis slammed into her, her long supple body arching under him in a mixture of pleasure and pain that no man had ever given her before. The bed creaked and groaned in a rapid succession as they fought and twisted on it with the mating frenzy of wild animals. Richard was angry and he was excited and Odessa found it infectious. Only ten minutes later they were both exhausted, bruised, bleeding and satiated. Rolling off the bed, he walked sluggishly into the bathroom and stood under a shower. Then, refreshed and invigorated, he went to the built-in wardrobe and removed an Adolfo suit of cool caramel-coloured cotton.

'Where are you going?' Odessa demanded, abruptly raising herself on one elbow as she watched him walk fully dressed back into the room and shove his feet into shoes from Maxwell's and add onyx and gold cufflinks to the sleeves of his Turnbull's shirt.

'To see a friend.'

'What friend?'

Richard leaned down and kissed her hard on the lips. 'I'll bring him back for dinner, OK?'

Odessa lay back on the bed, satisfied and reassured. 'OK.' She watched him go, her head telling her that no man who had wanted her so viciously and who had taken her with such wild and fantastic abandon could be unfaithful. But as she heard his car pull away she was frowning.

RICHARD pulled up once more in front of the redbrick building. It was exactly four-thirty and if he remembered correctly, Drake was not the kind of man to work long hours. The medical community was a small one, and Richard, with his habit of hoarding any possibly useful information, had no difficulty recalling the kind of man Drake was. Namely, a high-roller without the means to keep up the lifestyle to which he'd like to become accustomed.

Ten minutes later his thickest figure stepped through the doors and headed for a car that was surprisingly small and economy-minded. Richard got out and began to walk towards him. The car fitted; yes, the information he'd asked around for earlier that day had to be correct.

He deliberately collided with the stocky figure, letting out an injured yelp as the half-opened car door caught him squarely in the ribs. 'Hey, watch out! Why don't . . . Vince!' he let his voice rise in pleasure. 'Vince Drake, isn't it?'

'Yes. Dick! Dick Jago. It must be all of . . . six months?'

'At least.' Richard held out his hand. 'Since Babette's party. How's the yacht?' Richard remembered that they had spent most of their time talking about the merits of various yacht clubs.

Vince Drake's face flickered. 'I sold the yacht some time ago. Well, my practice has done nothing but expand and I just never had the time to sail her. You know how it is.'

'That's tough. She was quite something. Say, why don't we stop some place and have a drink? My treat.'

Vince didn't need to be asked twice. 'Well, I was on my way to Keo's for some Thai.'

'Forget that,' Richard demanded heartily. 'Come back to my place for a meal and meet the wife.'

'You married now?' Vince asked, his surprise genuine.

'A few months.' Richard let a rather sheepishly pleased look cross his face.

'Strange – I never thought you were the marrying kind.'

'It happens to us all. Besides, she's loaded.'

'Here?' Vince held his cupped hands over his chest. 'Or in the purse.'

'Both,' Richard laughed, clasping a firm hand on the car door and slamming it shut. The bar they went into was dark but that suited Richard fine. It wasn't the kind of place where he was likely to run into anybody he knew. Drake ordered neat whisky, Richard deciding on beer. It wouldn't hurt to get him a little plastered. 'So how's life treating you, Vince? Good, I hope?'

Drake took a long swallow of the powerful liquid and leaned back a little on the stool, his blue shirt straining at the buttons across his ample belly, the brown serge of his jacket falling unevenly off his shoulders. 'OK I guess, but not as well as it's been treating you. Just how rich is this wife of yours?'

'Seriously,' Richard laughed. Jealousy was good for him and would put him in the right frame of mind. There was no one easier to manipulate than a man who thought life had done the dirty on him.

'Lucky bastard,' Vince said enviously.

'I am. You know, I thought I saw you at a casino one night last week. But I wasn't sure, or I would have come over then and said hello.'

Vince's eyes looked at him from under bushy eyebrows. 'Oh? Which casino?'

'Oh, I don't remember. Some fleapit or other – Gillespie's place, I think.'

Vince shrugged. What was the point in denying it? Jago was a man of the world, a predator, a man who knew what was what. 'It probably was me. If he was losing then it *was* me.'

'Run of bad luck, huh?'

Drake snorted. 'A stampede more like.'

'Owe much?' Richard asked softly and Drake shrugged,

still not seeming to scent the trap. He raised his glass to his lips and drained it before looking at Richard with a wary jaundiced eye.

'Curious, aren't you?'

Richard nodded to the barman for refills and waited until he'd finished before turning on his stool and raising his glass. 'Cheers.'

'Cheers.' Vince took the drink but didn't take his eyes off Richard. He'd known Jago for years, and could sense that there was something more than idle curiosity lurking behind the cleverly-concealed third degree. Drake was a bad gambler but a good shrink – one of the best – and careful questioning was his forte. Richard should have remembered that.

'I was just wondering if I could help an old friend out, that's all,' Richard shrugged. 'As someone once said, it's easy to be generous if you're rich. And I've heard about Gillespie – he's not a patient man.'

Drake went a little pale. 'I wouldn't say no to a helping hand. Mind you . . .'

'How much?' Richard asked again, in that soft bland voice that would make any man's blood run cold.

Vince Drake looked down at the drink in his hands. What did he have to lose? 'A hundred and fifty thousand.'

Richard already knew that, but he let a soft whistle escape him. 'Pheeeew. That's quite a sum.' Drake said nothing. Richard caught on at once. It looked as if it were going to be easier than he thought. 'You know, you could do me a favour.'

'What – one worth that much?' Drake asked, his voice ironic but scared. A fine sweat appeared on his forehead and he took another sip of his drink.

'Most definitely.'

Drake swallowed hard, but could see no way out. 'Is it illegal?'

'Only if you get caught. And that's so unlikely it's laughable.' Which was true, in a way. The only possible danger came from Dominic Fairchild, who had his fingers firmly on the island's pulse. But the likelihood of his knowing, or caring, about smallfry like Drake was remote. Besides, outwardly, Drake was eminently respectful, and Fairchild had no reason for keeping tabs on him.

Drake ran a trembling hand over his mouth and drained his glass. Richard lifted his finger for another refill. 'I don't know,' Drake finally said.

Richard shrugged and slipped off the stool. 'That's a shame. Wasn't it Gillespie's men who were responsible for that merchant banker's son getting his legs broken, supposedly when his Porsche came off the road on the Kalena bend, a few months back?'

With hopeless eyes Drake looked slowly up at him. 'What do you want?'

THE elevator opened on to the lobby of the Blue Hawaiian and Dominic and Philip Pearce emerged, heading for the large lounge next to the pool. 'When can they start construction?' Dominic asked, nodding to a waitress as they walked into the light airy room and ordering coffee for two.

'Beginning of October.'

'Too late for next season.'

Philip laughed and stretched out into a comfortable chair, contemplating his toes as he tapped his feet together. 'Not even you can snap your fingers and have a ten-storey luxury hotel built in the wink of an eye.'

Dominic smiled vaguely and absently loosened his tie. 'Is it me or are the board meetings getting longer and longer?'

Philip grinned widely. 'You're getting old, friend.'

Dominic thanked the girl who placed a tray on the table in front of him. On it were two bone-china cups filled with freshly ground coffee, a jug of ice-cold cream, raw and potent brown sugar and chocolate mint sticks. Ignoring the chocolate, knowing how Phil liked to indulge a sweet tooth, he added a single teaspoon of sugar to the black liquid and took a sip.

'You don't seem too thrilled about the hotel,' Phil commented lazily, grabbing a handful of sticks and chewing blissfully. 'I thought a rival to Volcano House on Hawaii was the final dream?'

'I'm thrilled, I'm thrilled,' Dominic assured him drily, then yanked off his tie altogether and stuffed it into one of the pockets of his black jacket.

'Yeah, you look it. I can . . .' Phil's open face flickered in a disconcerted frown, his blue eyes swivelling over Dominic's shoulder. 'Isn't that . . .' he began, and Dominic turned abruptly.

'Yes,' he agreed tersely. Walking by, dressed in an elegant white cotton suit, Ben Fielding swept past them and on to a free table.

'So that's him,' Phil murmured thoughtfully. A typical Englishman.

'You sure those specifications for the foundations are adequate?' Dominic asked sharply, and Phil snapped back to attention.

'Positive. Those foundations go way beyond what's legally necessary.'

'To hell with legality,' Dominic swore. 'What the government calls legal and what's safe are two different things, as you should bloody well know. I don't want the damned thing collapsing into the crater killing a thousand guests.'

'It won't,' Phil said, his voice just hard enough to get through, and Dominic cursed silently.

'You see too much, Phil,' he accused. 'You always did.'

The waitress arrived with Ben's order and Dominic watched broodingly as she unloaded a cream cake and pot of tea on to the table.

Ben looked around, very conscious of twin lasers boring into his back and spotted the reclining figure immediately. Dressed all in black, Dominic Fairchild reminded Ben very much of the black panther that he had back home in his private zoo in Cheshire. Although his wild cat's eyes were blue, and the ones staring at him were green, the expression was the same.

Ben turned back to pour out his tea, his eyes thoughtful. For five minutes Phil watched in silence as the two men cast each other measuring glances, the mutual weighing-up so obvious he wondered if they realized how ridiculous they looked. 'You remind me of two dogs meeting in the street, both wanting to sniff the other's backside, but not sure which end to approach,' he said finally. Dominic shot him a startled glance, then began to chuckle.

Ben observed this and nodded almost imperceptibly to himself. A handsome man – tough, rich and dangerous. And Rhia should be here any minute.

'He doesn't look exactly like a raging bull,' Philip commented mischievously. He liked to stir it now and then. 'But perhaps the English aren't all that cold beneath their stiff-upper-lip and horsey accents?'

Dominic felt the old agony in his guts and swore under his breath. The memory of the night of his birthday was going to stay with him for life. Already it felt like a jail sentence, condemned to love and want a woman whose sole aim was to deny and destroy him.

'This is ridiculous,' he snarled as Ben glanced once again in his direction, and he abruptly stood up, some decision obviously made. 'Stay put,' he advised Phil. 'I won't be long.'

Ben's pleasant candid face turned bland as Dominic approached.

'Good afternoon, Mr Fielding,' Dominic said smoothly. 'Is everything satisfactory?'

Ben inclined his head. 'Most, thank you. You have a first-class establishment here, Mr Fairchild. Or do you prefer your title?'

'I prefer Dominic,' he heard himself say, and was as surprised as Ben, who was too quick and too wise to look the gift horse in the mouth.

'Dominic it is, then. I'm Ben.'

Dominic's lips twisted. 'I know.'

'Of course you do,' Ben said with brisk dismissal, as if two civilized men shouldn't waste their time fencing. 'Won't you join me for a few minutes?'

Dominic inclined his head and drew up a chair. Catching the eye of a passing waiter he nodded. 'Champagne for two, please Kiko. Grende, I think.'

'Certainly, Mr Fairchild.'

'I've wanted to talk to you for some time, Ben.'

'Oh?'

'Yes. Several of your companies have been trespassing on my territory recently. Do you smoke?'

'No, thank you. Which companies are these?'

Dominic shut the lid on the box of best Cuban cigars that rested on every table in the lounge and told him the names of the firms.

'Ah, I knew there must be some error.' Ben shrugged philosophically. 'These are no longer mine. I sold them last year.'

'Really? The new . . . owner – ' he had trouble spitting the word out 'must have paid a high price for them?'

Ben looked at the outwardly composed face and did not respond.

A few tables away, Dominic heard Phil's distinctive warning cough and turned slightly in his chair, his eyes meeting those of his friend and then following them to the doorway where Rhiannon stood, for a moment shocked into immobility. Damn – she should have tried harder to talk Ben out of meeting her here! She should have known Dominic would find them. No, be honest, she told herself. You did know all along that this would happen. Even as she silently cursed, her eyes were drinking him in, remembering the beautiful strength and power of the naked body hidden by those expensive clothes. As their eyes met she moved forward, glad that her dove-grey dress was feminine and silky but also very nearly businesslike. Her hair was loose but combed into obedience, her make-up light.

'Hello. You two look very cosy,' Rhiannon greeted them. She would not think of that night. Not ever again.

'I'm sorry you missed my birthday party, Ben,' Dominic drawled suddenly. 'I'm sure you would have found it a very interesting, not to mention informative, evening. Don't you think so, Rhia?'

Rhiannon managed to shrug a bored shoulder. 'I doubt it. Ben is used to dining with real politicians, world-leaders, and true stars. Your guest-list was a little . . . provincial.'

Meeting Ben's eyes Dominic could not miss the amused but slightly sad expression that sparked within them and he felt his confusion grow. No man could have missed the hint he was giving out that they'd become lovers. Was it possible he could be so lacking in jealousy? Or was he tired of her already? But no man in his right mind would ever tire of her. Not a night had gone by when he hadn't dreamed of their lovemaking. Damn it, it was getting bloody farcical, and he felt renewed anger at himself and his own weakness. He stood up. 'Well, I must be going. Hotels don't run themselves.'

'I'm looking forward to finding that out for myself,' Rhiannon couldn't resist giving the dig – or reminder – and smiled sweetly up at him.

'I did hear that there was a motel down in Chinatown up for sale. Usual rent five dollars an hour, I believe,' Dominic shot back with killing contempt.

Rhiannon's smile slowly froze. 'Go to hell, Dominic,' she requested sweetly.

'It'd have to be warmer there than it is here at any rate,' Dominic shot back just as pleasantly and nodded at Ben who was furiously chewing his lip. 'Ben.'

'Dominic.' Ben nodded back just as curtly. Rhiannon watched him leave, then readily accepted Ben's proposal that they forget drinks and go back to her room. He was strangely silent during the short trip, and when they arrived, Rhiannon kicked off her shoes and made them a drink, before tackling him about it.

'OK, Ben. What's troubling you?' she asked, sitting on the sofa and tucking her legs beneath her, ready to thrash out whatever snag he had discovered.

Ben took his whisky and walked to the window, looking down on Waikiki Beach. He had such a troubled air now that, for the first time, Rhiannon began to feel uneasy. 'Ben?'

He sighed and turned back. 'Rhia, I wasn't ever going to mention this before, but now that I've met Dominic Fairchild for myself, I think I should. It's about Graham, your father.'

Rhiannon tensed. 'What about him?'

'You know he began to drink – oh hell, of course you do! Let me just blurt it out. One night he got drunk, seriously drunk, and told me, well, he told me that he wasn't your real father. I mean, he wasn't your *biological* father. He said he couldn't be, that he'd had mumps before you were born and it had made him sterile.'

Rhiannon very carefully put down her drink and took a deep, shuddering breath. For several seconds she digested this in silence, then asked quietly, 'Did you believe him, Ben?'

Ben hesitated, but could only answer honestly. 'Yes. Yes, I did.' He watched her anxiously, knowing that although she seemed calm, she must be feeling as if she'd just been poleaxed.

Rhiannon slowly unfolded her legs and leaned forward. She did indeed feel very shocked, but was also thinking very clearly. 'Well, even if that is true, it doesn't really alter anything. I loved my father . . . I mean, I loved Graham as my father, so . . .' She shook her head. 'I just can't believe my mother had an affair with someone else. Daddy always told me they were so much in love.'

'Yes. I know,' Ben said, then realizing that he had still to tell her everything that was on his mind, he took a large gulp of whisky. 'The thing is, Rhia . . .' he hesitated as she looked up at him, obviously confused, her face pale and pinched but nevertheless perfectly composed. 'Your real father might still be alive.'

Rhiannon blinked, struggling to come to terms with this. Eventually she nodded slowly. 'You're right. But it still doesn't matter. Graham was my father in every way that counts. I don't need to try and track down some stranger. He might not even know he has a daughter. My mother probably never told him.'

Ben moved to the sofa and sat beside her, taking her hand in his and rubbing her cold fingers with his thumb. 'The fact is, Rhia, your true father might not be a stranger. I mean, think about it. I know it's hard, and you probably feel you've been knocked for six, but look at the facts. Graham hated Dominic, for some reason we've never really fully understood. And he did tell you that Dominic was in love with Jess. And look at Dominic, then at yourself, Rhia. You both have raven hair and green eyes. Rhiannon, I think it's highly likely that Dominic Fair . . . *Rhia*!'

Ben never had a chance to finish the sentence. With a

stricken glance in his direction and an anguished half-cry, Rhiannon fainted.

EMERGING from the dim-lit bar on to a busy sidewalk, Vincent Drake staggered just a little on his feet. The large man by his side escorted him slowly past his own car and on to a large Mercedes convertible. 'I can't do it,' Vince said, looking pasty and pale in the bright sunlight.

Richard said nothing until they were both heading into the early evening rush-hour. 'Sure you can, Vince. You and me – we're not the usual yes-men. We do whatever the hell we want.'

Vince stubbornly shook his head. 'It's not just unethical, although God knows . . .' He let his voice trail off. 'It's ugly. That's what it is – ugly. I always knew you were a warped bastard, Dick.'

'I'll give you an extra twenty grand on top of paying off Gillespie. Playing money if you like. That'll keep the roulette wheel spinning for a few days.'

Vince closed his eyes as if in pain. 'If I get caught I won't just be struck off, I'll go to the pen. I'm not cut out for that, Dick. When I first got started I used to take some prisoner cases under that government scheme a while back. Shit, it's a nightmare in there.'

'You won't get caught. How the hell do you think a court of law would be able to prove anything? The human mind is a minefield, you said so yourself. Even a lawyer just a week out of Harvard could get you off.'

Vince swallowed hard. The car drove real smooth, but he felt sick nevertheless. 'What have you got against this girl anyway? What did she ever do to you?'

Richard's face went statue-still and even in his slightly inebriated state Vince had the sense to go cold with fear. 'That's none of your business. Don't ever attempt to find out from the girl and don't ever ask me again. Got it?'

'All right. Forget I mentioned it,' Vince appealed quickly, unaware that he'd already accepted the situation as a *fait accompli*. But Richard knew, and slowly he began to relax. The thought was giddy. He could string it out for months, watch her lose weight, become white and pale as her life collapsed around her. He wanted to watch, to listen, to see her suffer. The next time she went to her good Dr Drake he'd be there after she went under – he'd watch. And then, at the very end, he'd let her know that it had been him, all along. Oh God ... The thought was like potent wine. 'When's her next appointment?' he asked sharply, dragging himself with an effort back into reality.

'Tuesday. Why?'

'I want to be there. To watch.'

'No way. I'm not sure I'll even do it. I'll have to think about it.'

'Gillespie's not the waiting kind, Vince,' Richard commiserated softly and Vince looked away, recalling his last chat with Frank Gillespie in his poky, smoke-filled office. So pleasant, and so filled with menace.

'All right,' Vince spat out the word on a single breath, his flabby body shuddering. 'All right, I'll do it. You pay off Gillespie and I'll do it.'

'Uh-huh.' Richard shook his head. 'You already sold the boat and car. If you suddenly hand him over a hundred and fifty grand he'll get very curious. And I don't want that. I'll pay him in instalments.'

'You're a bastard, Jago.'

'I know.'

Vince felt even more sick. Instinct and wily cunning alone had prevented him from telling Jago about Dominic Fairchild's involvement. Fairchild! Hell, what would *he* do if he ever found out? Talk about being between a rock and a very hard place. Fairchild's reputation was every bit as terrifying, albeit in a different way, as Gillespie's.

'Relax, Vince,' Richard advised, taking his eyes off the road for a moment to give Vince's shoulder a patronizing pat. 'Everything's going to be just fine. You get what you want and I get what I want. And I do want it, Vince, so don't let me down.'

Whatever else he was, Vincent was a damned good psychiatrist. 'You should see a shrink yourself, Dick.'

'Yeah?' Richard smiled cruelly. 'And why don't you try and

436

cure yourself of the gambling fever, Vince? A classic case of physician heal thyself, don't you agree?'

Vince looked away, sick at heart, and noticed the street sign. 'Hey, where are we going? This isn't the way to my place.'

'It's the way to mine. You're coming to dinner, remember? I have a very suspicious little wife at home who's just dying to meet you.'

Vince closed his eyes briefly, then swallowed hard. Looking out over the sidewalks he saw a young laughing blonde accept a cigarette from her friend as they walked down the streets, dressed in party clothes. So young, so carefree. Vince himself had forgotten what that felt like. Or had he ever felt it? The gambling bug had bitten him in college, so perhaps he'd never been young and carefree. But *she* was. Remembering her visit this morning, her nervousness, her open face and trusting blue eyes, he felt a wave of shame and self-pity wash over him.

Her story had been touching and tragic. And he'd been looking forward to helping her. And now . . . 'God help her,' Vince whispered.

Richard looked at him quickly but saw in the darkened brown eyes of the psychiatrist the defeat that was plainly written there and was reassured. Leaning back in his seat, his hands light and sure on the steering wheel, Richard took a deeply satisfied breath and smiled a happy smile.

'God might help you, but no one's going to help her, Vince,' he said softly. 'That I promise you.'

Chapter 34

The *Desert Mirage* was well-named. A huge 2000-tonne oceangoing yacht, two storeys high, Ben had bought it from an Arab sheik, hence its name. Gleaming white in the sunlight, the mammoth boat boasted crew quarters, dining room, lounges, a gym and games room, extensive kitchens and ten luxury bedrooms. As Rhiannon watched the crew stow her luggage aboard she felt suddenly glad that Ben had insisted she get right away from everything for a few days. She went straight to her lavishly decorated stateroom where she showered and changed into an apricot chiffon sundress. She arrived back on deck just in time to help Ben greet their other guests.

Marion and Stewart Stoppard were visiting from the South of France, where Stewart had retired three years earlier after selling his shoe manufacturing company. Rhiannon liked Marion on sight. There was an unpretentiousness evident in the short unfussy cut of her curly grey hair and a friendly warmth that instantly attracted her. The two women chatted happily over a glass of Bucks Fizz before going in to eat.

Following lunch the yacht began to fill with a deluge of other guests invited for afternoon drinks. Rhiannon was sipping a daiquiri and on her way to the rails on the deck when she saw a familiar dark head towering above the dancing throng. No, she though for a paralyzed second, it can't be. But it was. Chatting in a group of five men, dressed casually in an open-necked shirt with navy trim and snug-fitting navy-blue slacks, Dominic Fairchild glanced casually her way and smiled at her, raising his glass in a mocking salute.

Rhiannon went white. For a second the world around her tilted and faded and the deck beneath her feet rolled ominously. She didn't notice Dominic's expression change to concern as she turned and grappled her way to the bridge lounge where Ben took one glance at her stricken face and left the game in mid-rubber. Apologizing briefly to his guests he took her arm and steered her to her stateroom, closing the door firmly behind him.

'Did you know that Dominic was here?' she whispered.

Ben nodded. 'I invited him.'

'You did what?' she asked, her voice almost failing her completely.

'I invited him.'

'But you know I . . . You know I can't see him, Ben.' She reached for his hands and held them tightly as Ben sat beside her on the bed. 'Please. You know it's impossible.'

'I know no such thing,' he contradicted gently, then took a deep breath. 'There's more to it than just the fact that the man you hate and are planning to ruin could be your father, isn't there? You know I . . .' He shook his head sadly, knowing that now was not the time to tell her of his own feelings for her. 'You love him, don't you?' he said instead.

'No!' Rhiannon said sharply. 'It's not that. It *isn't*,' she insisted, as Ben continued to watch her silently. 'Oh Ben, it's awful. I just can't face him.'

'Rhia, don't you see? You have to meet him, face to face, and sort all this out. For days now you've been acting like a zombie. You're not sleeping, not eating. It can't go on. Whatever is bothering you, you have to deal with it. Surely you . . .'

He stopped as there came a sharp rap on the door, and a moment later Dominic walked in.

'Oh God,' Rhia said, and buried her face in her hands. Dominic took a half-step towards her but Ben quickly moved between them.

'What's going on?' Dominic asked grimly, his eyes travelling from Rhiannon's averted head to Ben's tight face.

'Rhia?' Ben softly turned to her and knelt beside her, prising her hands away from her face and holding them gently in his palms. 'Do you want me to stay?'

For a second Rhiannon's hands tightened on his, then she glanced at Dominic's questioning face, and shook her head. 'No. We have to talk. You're right, Ben. Dominic and I do have to . . . get things straightened out.'

Ben slowly got to his feet. He nodded briefly at Dominic then walked to the door, but once there, he hesitated. Although he spoke to Rhiannon, he looked straight at Dominic. 'I'll be right outside if you need me, my darling.'

Rhiannon nodded, and when Ben left, closing the door softly behind him, she took a deep, shuddering sigh.

'What's wrong, Rhia?' Dominic asked quietly. 'When you looked at me just now, out there on the deck, you looked, God, I don't know. I've never seen anyone look so wounded before.'

Rhiannon couldn't look at him. She stared down at her feet, at her hands, at the clock ticking on the wall, anywhere but at his face. 'Graham wasn't my real father,' she blurted out at last, the words sounding alien and strange in her ears.

Dominic walked to the porthole, staring out over the marina. 'I know. But how did you find out?'

Rhiannon's head shot up and she stared at his back. 'You *knew*? How?'

'Jess told me. In a note.' Dominic turned back to her, his expression still wary. 'Her solicitors handed it over to me when she died.'

Rhiannon stared at him, her eyes as round as saucers, her face going, if possible, even more ashen. 'How could you?' she breathed at last. 'My God, how could you?'

Dominic shook his head. 'How could I what? Something's obviously very wrong here, but I don't understand what it is.'

'Very wrong?' Rhiannon echoed, standing up, her hands clenching into tight, shaking fists. 'You make love to me, you let me make love to you – knowing all the time that I'm . . . that we're . . . that I'm your daughter, and you say something's *wrong*!'

This time Dominic went white. '*Daughter*? What the hell are you talking about? You're not my daughter.'

Rhiannon stared at him, the blood pounding in her head, thoughts tumbling crazily across her mind. 'You're not my father?'

'No. Of course not!' Dominic repeated, shaking his head. 'I never had an affair with your mother, though Graham was convinced that I had.'

'But I don't understand,' Rhiannon moaned, collapsing on to the bed, all strength leaving her limbs. 'You said my mother told you that Graham wasn't my father.'

'So she did. I think she guessed that Graham knew he couldn't be your father. And I think she also guessed that he suspected me of having an affair with her. I think she wanted to protect me, in case anything happened to her and she could no longer control Graham.'

Rhiannon stared at him. 'I don't get it. Did you love my mother or not? Did she love you, is that it?'

Dominic shook his head. 'Your mother loved only one man in her life – and that was Graham.'

'But if he wasn't my father and you're not my father, then who was?'

'Arnold Grantham.'

'My grandfather?' Rhiannon whispered.

'Yes. Jess got drunk one night at a party. It was so unlike her. She rarely drank. And Graham wasn't there, he was up at Oxford with me. I guess Arnold was drunk too. I know he and his wife had never had a particularly good marriage. I don't think Jess ever told him that he, not Graham, was your true father. And I know Graham certainly never suspected that Arnold was responsible.'

'Are you sure? Are you really, really sure?'

'Of course I'm sure,' he said coldly. 'We can have blood samples taken, if it will make you feel any better. Genetic fingerprinting will prove beyond a doubt that we're not related.'

'Oh, thank God.' Rhiannon fell sideways on to the bed and buried her face in the pillow, weak and exhausted. 'Oh, thank God,' she murmured shakily. 'I thought it was you.'

She closed her eyes as tears of relief trickled from beneath her eyelids, unaware that Dominic watched her with an expression of fury mixed with pity.

WHEN she awoke, everything sounded reassuringly silent. She washed her face and changed into a peach-coloured swimsuit with a matching beach jacket that she carried over her arm to the now-deserted deck. Checking her watch she saw it was still only seven o'clock and the sun, whilst slowly sinking, was still pleasantly warm. She felt as if a huge weight had been lifted from her shoulders, and that her sense of balance was gradually being restored.

As she relaxed and sunbathed, she could even begin to straighten it all out in her mind. Her father was actually her half-brother, but it made no difference. Graham Grantham was still the man who had raised her and loved her like a father, and she was still going to keep the promise she'd made to him.

She heard the clanking of the anchor being lifted, and then the throb of the mighty engines. She left the deck lounger and walked to the rails, watching as the mighty vessel began to pull away from its mooring off the south-east coast of Oahu and head east towards Molokai where she and Ben were due to spend a few days.

The boat was so big it barely undulated as they headed out into the open sea and Rhiannon returned to lie on the lounger, at peace with herself for the first time in days. Dinner wouldn't be until much later, and with any luck she'd have the spectacle of a setting sun at sea all to herself. But just then a cloud passed in front of the sun, making her shiver. Opening her eyes to see how big the cloud was and how long before it passed, she gasped, sitting up jerkily. Dominic, clad only in brief black trunks, looked away from her only long enough to gaze out to sea. 'Looks spectacular, doesn't it?'

'We're sailing!' Rhiannon finally managed to get out, reaching for the peach jacket that lay next to her. 'What are you doing still here? Everyone else has left.'

'Everyone but me.'

'Are you crazy? We're going to Molokai,' she snapped out, thrusting her arms into the jacket and hugging it more securely around her.

'I know. It's been some time since I went. I'm looking forward to it.'

Rhiannon groaned. Ben again. Just what did he think he was doing?

'It'll be nice to have a break – leave all the grind and all my troubles behind me for a while,' Dominic mused now, stretching out in a neighbouring lounger, and she snorted inelegantly.

'You biggest trouble is right here beside you,' she corrected sourly.

'I don't think so,' Dominic denied, closing his eyes on a blissful sigh.

'How do you figure that out, genius?'

'Even the nights here are so warm that you can sleep outside totally naked if you wanted to.'

'Go to hell.'

'You know, good ol' Ben didn't seem to pay much attention to you today,' Dominic tormented. 'He obviously didn't tell you he'd brought me along for the ride. Hardly the actions of a loving partner, now is it?' he murmured tauntingly, and she laughed softly. He still thought they were lovers. Good – she hoped the thought killed him.

'I'm not worried about Ben.'

'Perhaps you should be. Your charms are obviously on the wane. And he obviously has no idea we're lovers.'

'We're not lovers,' Rhiannon denied hotly. 'That was a mistake. It won't ever happen again.'

'If you say so,' Dominic said politely, and taking a deep, almost yawning breath, he stretched out on the lounger, his arms rising above his head to show the muscled ripples in his chest.

Rhiannon caught her breath sharply. 'Don't do that.'

'What?' He looked at her, a knowing grin on his face, and she could have kicked herself for being so stupid.

'You're too tall for those things,' she said waspishly. 'You'll break it.'

'Good ol' Ben will have another one.'

'He's not old,' she snapped.

'He's running to middle-aged fat, though.'

'So are you – between the ears!' Standing up abruptly she walked to the rails where the sun was now hovering over the blue horizon, a globe of glowing red. 'It doesn't make any difference, you know. About Graham not being my true father, I mean. I'm still going to make you pay for what you did to him. And when the crunch comes, Ben is going to be firmly on one side – mine.' With the last word she tapped her chest with a thumb, and Dominic slowly sat up, his superb physical fitness painfully obvious. Not that she needed the reminder. She already knew just how strong and athletic he was. 'All his money,' she pressed on without mercy, 'all his power and influence – I'll have it all. And I'll bury you with it.'

Dominic didn't seem to take her words to heart, for when he stood up he was not angry. As he approached her slowly she could see in the gathering dusk that his eyes were glittering with other feelings – ones that made her begin to tremble. She dragged her eyes away, seeking out a pale moon high and anaemic in the sky. He swore softly at her evasiveness and walking to a drinks trolley poured himself a stiff shot of Napoleon brandy, swirling it in the giant glass.

'Turning to the booze?' she gibed. 'I can look forward to the day, then, when I step over your drunken body in the gutter outside my Blue Hawaiian?'

'Rhia,' he said softly, shaking his head. 'Don't think that I'm fooled for a minute by your waspish little recitals.'

'I think I'll rename the Blue Hawaiian "Granthams".'

'Dream on, if it pleases you.'

'Not dreams – future reality. You bastard!' Desperation had her spitting the last word at him in a vain attempt to regain some of her old determination. The emotional scene of only a few hours ago had left her feeling extremely vulnerable and offbalance. It was imperative that she put the last few awful days behind her and get on with her plans. He wasn't her father, she hadn't committed incest, and nothing had really changed. She must remember that, and not let him undermine her ever again. She had to get things back to normal as quickly as possible, and she was determined to do just that.

Dominic walked lazily towards her and rested against the rails a few feet away, looking out across the inky-black ocean. 'Hurts, doesn't it?' he asked softly.

'Does it? I've never felt better myself.'

'You're a really rotten liar.'

'Bastard!'

'We could both end it all right now – the pain and the fighting.'

'Shut up.'

'Just walk down to your room, or mine. It wouldn't matter which. Lock the door, take off these damned clothes and make love until the sun rises tomorrow.'

'Now who's dreaming?' she said, but her voice was huskier than it should have been.

'You're sadly deluded if you think that all we are is enemies,' she heard him say softly, and he moved closer.

'What do you think then?' she demanded scornfully. 'That we could be friends? Chums, best buddies – pals?'

Dominic shook his head. 'Uh-huh. I like to choose my friends and you're not made of the right material.'

'Bastard!'

'So you keep saying, but both my parents were legally married, I assure you. Unlike yours.'

Rhiannon gasped. 'That's a rotten thing to say.'

'Good,' Dominic said shortly. 'You don't think it's rotten to think me capable of committing incest? That is what you thought, isn't it? That I made love to you knowing you were my daughter?'

'I never . . .' Rhiannon began to deny it hotly, and then was forced to hesitate as she realized that, for just a few scant seconds back in her cabin, she had thought exactly that. 'I wasn't thinking straight. I'm sorry. Oh God, Dominic, I am sorry,' she said, feeling truly appalled and utterly guilty. She reached out to him, her hand clutching his arm and wordlessly rubbed her face against his bare bicep, her eyes closing softly.

Dominic drew in his breath on a silent hiss as he felt desire and a ridiculous urge to protect her from life's bombshells shoot through him in almost equal proportions. Hell, he'd almost forgotten how very dangerous she could be. The situation was potentially explosive and he knew it. For both their sakes, he had to defuse it quickly.

'I didn't get the chance to thank you for my birthday present,' he said mildly, and, still preoccupied by her guilt, she fell for it. Pulling away, she looked at him in genuine puzzlement.

'I didn't give you one.'

'Oh, I wouldn't say that,' he drawled drolly.

Rhiannon gaped at him for a brief second and then couldn't help but burst into laughter. Bent almost double, hugging her arms round her waist, the tension of the last few hours was suddenly released. Dominic watched her in almost tender silence for the first few seconds before he too became infected and his rich deep laughter joined hers, their combined mirth becoming lost on the Pacific Ocean as they let their mutual relief, anger and fear pour out of them.

Ben stood in the shadows, watching them. He had gone in to her mere minutes after Dominic had left the room, but she had already been sleeping. Reluctant to wake her, he'd left, controlling his intense curiosity only with great difficulty. Now, listening to their laughter, he knew it could only mean one thing. They were not father and daughter, and he wasn't sure whether to be relieved or depressed. He was glad Rhiannon was no longer in so much pain, but he was sad, so very sad, to finally admit that any chance he still had of winning her for himself was now gone. Feeling like a Peeping Tom, Ben reluctantly turned and left them alone, returning to the empty lounge where he poured himself a cognac and began to do some serious thinking.

Rhiannon's ribs were aching when their laughter finally died away. She rubbed her cheek with her palm and gulped in some calming breaths. 'Isn't life funny?'

Dominic's smile was pure irony, his voice as dry as the desert the yacht beneath his feet was named after. 'Oh, it's a real scream,' he agreed.

The small coloured lights clicked on, stretching from bow point to the top roof of the vessel, giving the yacht a party-like look. No doubt passing ships would see the pink, orange, green, white and lilac lights and think there was a celebration going on. Some party, Rhiannon thought miserably, and her misery must have been reflected in her eyes for when she dared glance across at him, his lips parted in a silent gesture of sympathy or regret, and his hand reached slowly across the space that divided them to touch her cheek. 'You want me every bit as much as I want you,' he informed her softly. 'Admit it.'

446

'Why? To make you feel better?' Almost sorrowfully, she shook her head.

Slowly his hand fell away, and after a fraught few seconds of total stillness she turned and walked away. Dominic watched her go, his face bleak. Then the bleakness disappeared so abruptly that anyone who had been watching him would seriously doubt their own sanity in suspecting they had seen it in the first place.

Dominic stayed on deck watching the night pass by and within the hour, Ben joined him.

'You and Rhia have things sorted out?' Ben asked, and Dominic nodded.

'Yes. She thought I was her father. I put her right.'

'So you're not her father?'

'No,' Dominic said flatly. 'Like I told Rhia, I can prove it, if need be.'

Ben slowly turned back to look out at the passing ocean. 'I love that young woman, you know,' he said calmly. 'I won't let anything hurt her, if I can prevent it.'

Dominic's jaw tightened, but after a second he nodded. 'I know. Is that why you're backing her?'

'Yes. But it's also a good business move. The Gray-Gray chain is already showing a profit.'

Dominic nodded. Turning to look at Ben he decided to lay at least one of his cards on the table. If he didn't, he could see that he wasn't going to get anywhere. 'What do you know of Rhiannon's reasons for this ridiculous vendetta?'

Ben pursed her lips. 'She's positive that you were responsible for her father's death. Well, Graham Grantham's death.'

'She's right, in a way. I was responsible for Graham's death. Oh, not directly. I had no intention of killing the man. And any trouble Grantham was in was all of his own doing. I merely provided him with the rope – he was the one who chose to hang himself with it. Of course Rhia is quite incapable of seeing that.'

'Understandable. But why did you give Graham the rope in the first place? If it wasn't because you tried to steal his wife, as he'd hinted to Rhia, then why?'

'He was blackmailing me.'

Ben blinked, totally stunned for a moment. 'Now that,' he finally said, his voice as hard and openly sceptical as Dominic had ever heard it, 'I find very hard to believe. You're just not the kind of man who would allow it.'

Dominic smiled grimly. 'For myself, you'd be right. If I'd done something wrong I'd face the music and be damned before giving in to some snivelling blackmailer. But Graham knew me well,' Dominic continued softly, turning to look out to sea, his voice becoming thick with memories. 'We'd been friends,' he laughed bitterly over the word, 'since we were kids. So, it wasn't me he threatened but . . . someone else. Someone very close whom I loved with everything I had in me.'

Ben, with typical English reticence, looked towards the moon and coughed. 'Now I believe you,' he said simply, his thoughts going to his own family, for whom he'd do anything. 'Love makes the strongest of us vulnerable. Does Rhia know of this?'

'I told her he was blackmailing me but she didn't believe it.'

'You don't have proof?'

Dominic laughed. 'Not on your life. All the proof I had, I destroyed. I wasn't going to risk it getting into the wrong hands.'

Ben frowned. 'And you can't tell her the whole thing, even in broad terms?'

Dominic shook his head. 'If she didn't believe me, and you have to admit that she is blindly loyal to the kind of man she thought Graham was, then I'd be well and truly up the Swanee with paddles in short supply.'

'I see your point. Well, I can get people on to it in England,' he surprised Dominic by offering. 'Graham wasn't the sort to have been too careful.'

Dominic looked sceptical. 'I don't know. He may not have been clever, but he was cunning. Like a damned fox.'

'If Rhiannon delivers a plan that will finish you before my people in London come up with proof that Grantham was nothing more than a dirty blackmailer, then I help her put that plan into operation. I want that clearly understood.' Ben knew that if Rhiannon pulled out of her attempts to takeover

Fairchild Enterprises at this stage, no real damage to her or the companies would be done. But the longer it went on, and the more entangled her companies and those of Fairchild became, the harder it would be to call a truce with both financial empires intact.

'If she discovers that Graham wasn't the man she thought he was, it'll hurt her badly,' Dominic pointed out, ignoring his threat completely.

'Yes, it will. And if she finds out about him after she has seriously hurt you – it will almost kill her,' Ben added. 'I don't want to watch you two tear each other to pieces, Dominic. As I've said, I love that woman and I'm not going to abandon her now. And besides anything else, I have my investments and my company to protect. If it does come down to a drag-out fight between Fairchild Enterprises and Rhiannon, there's no question as to which team I'll be fighting on.'

'I hope it doesn't come to that,' Dominic said bleakly. 'But no matter what the circumstances, if she ever does genuinely threaten me or mine, I'll have no choice but to protect myself.'

Ben nodded. 'Then we understand each other,' he said crisply.

Chapter 35

Vienna waited nervously in the peaceful, pastel-shaded waiting room and jumped when a static, disembodied voice crackled over the intercom. The redheaded receptionist pressed a pink-painted fingernail on to a button and answered in the affirmative. 'Dr Drake will see you now, Miss Wright.'

Her legs felt stiff and awkward as they carried her into Vincent Drake's office, but she smiled bravely at the man who rose from a comfortable-looking settee and held out his hand.

Vince did not wear a suit. He'd learned very early on that a suit intimidated some of his women clients and immediately set him up as a rival against the men. So, as she shook hands with the rather podgy man dressed in simple flannel slacks and a plain white shirt, opened at the collar and tie-less, Vienna's smile became more natural.

'Miss Wright, you're looking very nice today. How are you feeling?'

'Fine, thank you.'

'Please, sit down. The chair will be fine,' Vince added, seeing her cast an anxious glance at the infamous psychiatrist's couch. 'So, I've been reading over the notes we made last week. That visit, of course, was barely half an hour. From now on we'll be working through one-hour or two-hour sessions, depending on how things go. All right?'

Vienna nodded. 'Fine.' Anyone else like a Dr Frankenstein than this man was hard to imagine. His face was chubby and friendly, and even the moustache suited him. She looked briefly about the room at the brightly coloured and bound books lining the walls and the collection of brass animals and tiny porcelain vases that lined the window-shelves. A model ship, obviously handmade and quite magnificent sat in pride of place atop a cabinet that obviously contained medical supplies. Following her glance Vince shifted in his chair.

'Do the sight of those pills scare you?'

Not sure how to reply, and afraid of offending him by

seeming to question his competence, she shrugged. 'Not really.'

'Vienna, you mustn't lie to me,' Vince gently rebuked her, his voice a cross between a kindly schoolteacher scolding a favoured pupil and a doctor telling his patient he had to eat less and exercise more. 'The whole relationship between us must be based on mutual trust and understanding, otherwise you might just as well leave now, because we'll accomplish nothing.'

'I'm sorry. You're right, of course – I can see that it makes sense. It's just difficult,' she found herself apologizing the moment he finished speaking, and again felt like all kinds of an idiot.

Vince smiled, his friendly face creasing into folds that reminded her of a happy St Bernard. It was impossible not to trust him. 'You shouldn't be worried about either shocking me, because after fifteen years as a psychiatrist I'm unshockable, or hurting my feelings, because I'm a tough old coot, or making me angry. I *never* get angry. Well – I did have a child once with a dog fixation, and every time I saw him he would insist on biting my ankles. That did make me a little sore!'

Vienna laughed. 'OK. And that was an atrocious joke.'

'Who's joking?' he wailed playfully. 'Also,' he carried on, his tone serious now, 'I'm not a judge. I don't have a God complex so you can tell me anything.'

'OK,' she said again, a little less sure. What if she told him something truly awful, something so ugly whilst under hypnosis that when she woke up he couldn't look her in the face?

'Oh dear,' Vince smiled. 'I know that look. All my patients who opt for hypnosis get *that* look,' he stressed the word with a wise nod and knowing smile. 'I call it the "What-if-I'm-a-transvestite-vampire-and-didn't-know-it-look".'

Vienna began to laugh in spite of herself. 'Transvestite vampire, huh?'

'That's the one. Most people are scared to death of what they might say or do whilst under hypnosis. People have the wrong idea about hypnotism, no doubt from all that awful television stuff where horror writers have people go out and

451

commit murders or something. So let's get a few things straight. I don't have any interest in exploiting you or digging anywhere that you don't want me to. In point of fact, I couldn't if I wanted to. People will not, I repeat, will *not* do anything under hypnosis that they would not normally do whilst fully conscious. Do you understand what I'm saying?'

Vienna nodded.

'I mean, I couldn't tell you under hypnosis to go out and murder somebody unless you had, if you like, a naturally homicidal personality. On the other hand, I can, with several sessions and a lot of patient cooperation, cure people of things. A lot of my patients for instance come to me to help them give up smoking or lose weight. Some come to get over their fear of flying or water, or whatever. That I can do because problems like these are basic and simple matters – I tell the smoker that he'll gradually grow to hate the taste of nicotine, that it'll make him feel sick and ill and he won't want a cigarette, and so on. But your case is very different. According to your medical records, the problem is definitely psychosomatic. It means you don't really want to remember and it's that that we have to deal with.'

'I understand. But I do want to remember – you can't imagine how much.'

Vince smiled. 'So it shouldn't be too difficult then, eh?'

Vienna felt her nerves come back as he stood up and walked to the desk, watching him closely as he reached into the drawer for what looked like a flashlight. On his way to the windows where he drew the blinds, he glanced anxiously at a closed door, then quickly away again.

'Now,' he said, his voice soft and reassuring as he approached her. 'All I'm going to do is test the waters, so to speak. No two people are ever alike – some are very susceptible to hypnosis, some so-so, and others are very hard work. See this?' The doctor's flashlight, she saw on closer inspection, was more like a kaleidoscope, flashing shifting coloured patterns out over the room as he flicked a switch. 'All I want you to do is to look into the pattern . . . there, that's right and just watch it.'

'Just watch it?'

'That's all. You don't have to do a thing . . . just relax. I know it's hard. It's something new, something different, and that's usually exciting, and you really don't want to relax. Just feel the chair beneath you – yes? Feel it against your back . . . now, take a deep breath and feel how your diaphragm moves . . . yes . . . keep watching the patterns. Follow the movements with your eyes, good.'

Vienna was not aware of feeling drowsy, and then suddenly she was wide awake, so she knew she must have dozed. Abruptly she sat up and Vince clicked off the flashlight. 'Hm. You're a so-so.'

'That's nice,' she heard her own voice, slightly tremulous, drift into the darkened room. Vince reached for a jade-coloured table lamp and turning it on, the whole room was cast with a restful green light. 'Are you OK?'

Vienna nodded. 'I think so. I'm just nervous.'

'You shouldn't be. I haven't put you under yet. Check your watch.'

She looked; barely a minute had passed. Questioningly, she met his eyes.

'As I said, I was just testing your reactions. In a few minutes I will put you under, but only for a short while. Is that all right with you?'

Vienna licked her lips, aware of her heart thudding in her breast. 'I don't know. I mean, you must think me a real coward,' she laughed nervously. 'I don't quite know how to say this. It just seems so farfetched, like something you see in a black and white film on TV or an article you read in a trendy magazine.'

Vince nodded. 'Hypnosis doesn't happen to normal people, right?'

Vienna shrugged. 'I guess.'

'But it does. All the time,' Vince said. 'Otherwise I'd be out driving a truck or delivering frozen chickens or something.'

'I feel like a real coward,' she said softly.

'Well, hypnotism is scary at first. Until you trust me and feel confidence in me, it may stay that way.'

'Oh, it's not you,' Vienna said quickly, and Vince held out his hands.

'Look. We don't have to do this today,' he said softly, a fine sweat breaking out on his forehead. He had to fight to keep his eyes on the girl's face and not turn to look at that door again. 'You don't have to do this, at all. You're free to go and walk out that door and forget all about it. Most people I know would give up their fortunes to wake up and find the past gone, along with all their troubles. The chance for a brand new start is something so few of us ever get, you know.'

Vienna listened, his words making perfect sense. She was under no pressure – it was silly to be so scared. It had been her idea in the first place, hadn't it? 'No, I'll go through with it,' she said, her voice firm now, the decision made. 'I have to know.'

'Why do you have to?'

'I'm in love. That's the main reason, I suppose. I must know that there's no one else. No other man, out there somewhere . . . I'm not making much sense, am I?'

'On the contrary, you're making perfect sense.'

'I'm glad you think so,' she said. 'Sometimes I think I'm having a very very long nightmare and one day I'll wake up.'

'Speaking of nightmares – how are yours?'

'Mine?' she echoed nervously. 'Oh, they come and go.'

Vince nodded. Very tense. Yes, those nightmares were a real worry to her. He turned away abruptly as self-disgust hit him, his eyes going to that door once again, but his hand was already reaching out to turn off the lamp, and when the room was once again dim and anonymous, he felt a little better. Not much – but a little. He couldn't stand the sight of her eyes, those beautiful, trusting, innocent blue eyes, looking at him like that. 'All right,' he heard his voice, soft and gentle and as sly as a snake's hiss. 'We'll try it again, shall we. Just relax . . .'

Vienna swallowed, but not nervously. She felt in fact very comfortable. The chair did feel nice underneath her – funny how she'd never noticed before how her body folded and fitted perfectly into a chair. And the room was warm and yet cool, and the colours so pretty. Colours . . . how dull and dim and ugly the world would be without colours. And Dr Drake did have a nice voice. Nothing special, nothing Richard Burton-ish or James Mason-ish, but a nice, nice voice . . .

'You've got a nice voice,' she complimented him, and Vince snapped on the light and smiled at her. She watched him with surprised eyes as he walked to the blinds and slowly opened them, both of them blinking in the bright white sunlight that filtered into the room. 'What's the matter?' she asked, alarmed. 'Aren't you going to put me under, Dr Drake?'

'Vince, please. I thought we agreed on first names,' he smiled at her as he approached and slowly sank into his chair. 'But to answer your question, I have already done so, Vienna.'

'What? But it's . . .' she looked down at her watch, her eyes widening at the passage of time indicated by those innocuous hands. 'Half an hour?' she breathed, looking up at him, and suddenly paling. 'I've lost half an hour!'

'You're scared,' he said, his voice neither an accusation or question, and Vienna leaned back in her chair, fighting down the rapid drumbeat of her heart and the slight nausea in her stomach. 'You shouldn't be. We went through nothing more than some of the things you did since waking up in the hospital, and stopped with your first visit here.'

'Oh.' Vienna wasn't at all reassured. 'Did I talk about . . .'

'Farron?' Vince helped her out. 'Yes, you did – a lot. He sounds a very loving and helpful mate.'

'He is,' Vienna immediately admitted, but was puzzled by the way the doctor seemed to raise his voice just a little as he said it.

'The first time, all I do is make a few observations; make out a kind of emotional guideline so that when we begin to take you back in time, to try and find out what trauma caused the amnesia, I'll have some idea of your basic emotional make-up to help me. The human mind is a very delicately balanced organ, you know. I'm not just going to go charging in there like a bull in a china shop.'

This time her smile was brighter and less tense. 'OK.'

'And remember – the relationship between psychiatrist and patient is every bit as sacrosanct as that between priest and confessor. Do me a great big favour and never forget that, will you?'

Again Vienna nodded. She was beginning to feel like an

idiot again and suddenly all she wanted to do was get out of there. Vince saw it at once.

'Well, I think that's enough for today, don't you?'

Vienna almost wilted with relief as she quickly stood up, and then hesitated, not sure what she should do next. Vince held out his hand and she took it gratefully and he led her to a large door that opened out into another corridor. The discretion of that second door, together with the doctor's obvious sensitivity and understanding, made her feel infinitely better.

'When can you come again?' Vince asked simply and without pressure. 'I'll make the appointment with Vera whenever you say. If you want another appointment, that is. You may have decided hypnotherapy is not for you?'

Looking into the large, friendly face, Vienna shook her head. 'No – I want another appointment.'

'Good. How about in two days' time? Say ... three o'clock?'

'Fine. And thank you, Dr Drake.'

Vince forced himself to take her hand, his lips feeling like twin wires as he pulled them into a smile. 'You bet. And it's Vince! See you then.'

'Yes. Goodbye.'

He watched her walk a few steps away then quickly shut the door. Leaning against it he wiped his forehead with the back of his sleeve. He felt sick. At the sound of another door clicking open he moved away, taking deep breaths. 'Satisfied?' he asked, spitting the word out as if it were cobra venom, and Richard watched him through thoughtful eyes as he walked to a cabinet and reached for a whisky bottle. Pouring out a good shot Vince shuffled wearily to the window and looked out. There he saw Vienna emerge from the doorway directly below him and stand for a second on the sidewalk. He took a large swallow, the alcohol raw and bitter on his tongue. Her step was almost jaunty as she turned and walked to a small car parked a few yards down the street, and he could almost feel her relief and happiness from where he stood. He took another large swallow. Pulling out in front of a battered red Beetle, the small car and the girl drove away and he had no more excuses. He turned at last to face Richard. 'She's a very nice girl, Dick.'

'Yes. Isn't she?' Richard mused.

Vince made for his chair. His legs felt weak, suddenly, and his fingers tightened on the glass in his hand. 'She's very pretty too.'

'Yes. Just what the hell were you trying to pull? Asking her if she wanted to leave – almost prodding her into it. Not getting second thoughts, I hope?'

Vince sighed. 'It's a well-known psychological ploy, Dickie my boy,' he snapped out the words savagely. 'The very fact that I don't seem to care one way or another relieves them of any paranoia they might have and has a contrary effect on them. Most people are contrary, you know. By almost pushing them out the door, it makes them dig their heels in further.'

Richard made himself a drink and watched Vince's dark brown eyes light up when he pulled a wad of cash out of his pocket and ostentatiously began to count it. It hurt him that he had to mediate with this lizard but he knew he needed Vince's skill. Nevertheless, he wished he could have found a way to destroy her himself, personally. It was, after all, very, very personal.

'This will keep Gillespie off your back for a while.'

'Only a short while,' Vince snapped.

'Then hurry up,' Richard advised. 'The sooner I get what I want, the sooner you get free of your gambling debts.'

'I can't hurry the girl. Besides,' Vince said slyly, 'I'm surprised you're in such a hurry. Surely you'll get more pleasure from it if you string it out?' But although he watched the man's face closely for telltale signs of reaction, Richard's face remained like granite.

'I'll see Gillespie gets this,' Richard said, patting the wad of cash in his jacket pocket at the hip. 'Just so long as you keep up the bargain.'

'I will, don't worry,' Vince said bitterly, and drained his glass.

'You didn't seem to do much today.'

'I did enough, God help her. By the way, she likes cats and dogs.'

'I heard. What was that about the knife, though?'

Vince shrugged, a puzzled frown coming to his brows. 'The image of the knife was already there,' he said, his voice vague and absentminded, as if he'd forgotten Richard's presence and was merely talking it through with himself. 'There could be any number of reasons for it – she might have cut herself with a knife when she was little. But whatever the reason, the knife image was so strong all I had to do was build on it. It'll have more impact than a purely fictitious one of my own making so I was sure you'd approve.'

Richard nodded. 'I do.'

Vince felt another wave of nausea hit him. The trouble with being a shrink was that you couldn't fool yourself. He was weak, and he knew it. He also knew just how much damage he'd already done to that poor girl – a girl who trusted and liked him. Reaching for the whisky bottle, it was snatched out of his hand the moment he grasped it.

'Keep off the booze,' Richard warned, his voice straight from the Arctic. 'Don't you have another patient? Then leave this stuff alone,' he warned when Vince nodded. 'The last thing either of us wants is for you to get struck off the register for being a bloody drunk.'

'Go to hell.'

'Just so long as you make sure that little girl joins me there.'

Vince looked at Richard with a mixture of puzzlement, hatred and pity. 'You're not normal, Jago. You know that, don't you? You're not even a complicated case,' Vince carried on as Richard walked to the door. 'You simply don't have a heart.'

At the door Richard turned and looked back at him, but there was no anger on his face. 'No,' he said simply. 'No, I don't. And do you know why? Because she ripped it out of me. That's why.'

The door closed softly behind him and Vince crouched over and covered his eyes with the palm of his hands. He wished that Jago had slammed the door violently, but he hadn't. He'd been in perfect control – unnatural control, and it worried him. Gillespie worried him. The girl herself worried him. Everything worried him.

OUTSIDE, Richard turned the ignition of the car and then sat still; he had nowhere to go. He couldn't face Odessa again – not after seeing Vienna. He stared blindly out through the windscreen, his grey eyes becoming dreamy with remembrance. She had looked so lovely, so peaceful, sitting in that chair, her head leaned back against the headrest, her small white hands dangling over the arms. Her lashes were long and incredibly dark against her cheeks, and his hands had twitched with the desire to touch her hair. But Drake had been watching, and he'd been inhibited. Damn Drake. Abruptly pulling out on to the street he headed for the west coast, the impulse too powerful for him to resist.

The battered Beetle was parked a good hundred yards away and in a stand of umbrella trees. Its driver's dirty fingernails twisted the focus knob on his binoculars, bringing the bungalow into sharp relief. There she was, vacuuming the lounge. The man licked his thick lips. He'd bet she was humming something. The sound of a car made him turn around, and from his hiding place in a thick clump of hibiscus bushes he saw the Mercedes convertible pull over. He nodded thoughtfully: that bastard doctor was back.

Richard shut the car door softly and walked across the empty residential street. He passed within yards of the crouching figure. Intrigued, the Beetle driver trained his binoculars on Richard, focusing them on his retreating figure.

At the beach's edge, Richard took off his shoes and socks and walked slowly down to the waves and stared out to sea. One of the most engaging things about Oahu was that once you got off the main tourist beat you could always come across deserted little coves like this. You could always find solitude and sun, sea and surf. And she was not far away. Richard was tired. He could feel it seeping into his bones like a cancer. Weariness. It was a worse killer than pain. Walking back from the waves he dropped his shoes on to the sand and sat down, watching a large cruiser on the horizon.

In his mind he could see her coming down to the beach, dressed in a bikini, ready to swim. Then she'd see him, and be scared at first, maybe take a few backward steps. But she'd see how miserable he was, see how tired he was, how sad and alone he looked, and she'd slowly get closer. Her kind heart and her soft blue eyes would be filled with sympathy and she'd call his name softly.

Then he would turn his head, slowly, very slowly, and look at her, and say hello. She'd ask him if he was all right, and he'd shrug and say 'Sure,' but she'd know he wasn't, and come and sit beside him. Then he'd ask her if she was happy, and she'd say, 'Sure,' but he'd know, like she did, that it wasn't the truth. He'd look at her knowingly. 'Don't lie to me – remember?' His soft words would bring tears to her eyes and she'd admit she'd made a mistake, and he'd stroke her hair and kiss her, gently . . . gently . . .

Richard closed his eyes. She'd lie down on the sand and raise her arms to him, telling him over and over again that she was sorry, that she loved him, and not Farron, and asking him to forgive him. And he would – even now, even after all that she'd done to him. After all the agonies of rejection, the pain of despair and the lonely emptiness of sleepless nights, he'd forgive. And call off Drake. And her hands, her small white hands, would be soft and caressing as they slipped under his shirt and stroked him, her arms strong and sure as they looped around his neck and pulled his head down to her. She'd sigh and squirm in the sand, and take his hand with her hand and guide it to her breast. She'd moan and cry out when he fondled her. And he'd ask her if Farron had ever made her feel that way, and she'd shake her head, and say over and over again, 'No, no, no.'

Richard's eyes snapped open. He'd give her another chance! He was a fool to do it, but he didn't care. He loved her – and hated her. *One more chance . . .*

In the bushes, the Beetle driver lowered the binoculars and licked his lips, a savage smirk of satisfaction on his face. He eyed the lowslung sports car which had pulled up not half a minute ago, and then looked back at the house. Raising his binoculars once more he found them in the kitchen, the Hawaiian kid stood with his arms around her waist while the girl fixed some kind of drink. Crouching even lower as the huge shadow of the doctor fell on the ground nearby, the Beetle driver held his breath as the doctor stood statue-still by the gate, his grey eyes fixed on the car. That got you, didn't it, your horny bastard? the Beetle driver thought. She's already got another on the go. What do you think of that then, you overgrown blubbering bastard?

Richard backed away a few steps his face, though in profile, obviously screwed up into an expression of either extreme pain or extreme rage, the Beetle driver wasn't quite sure which.

The front door of the bungalow opened, and the driver and Richard quickly crouched down, both of them watching the couple as they walked hand in hand over their back garden and through a gate in the now neatly-mended fence.

Nice for some, the Beetle driver thought with bitter envy. His own place was a tiny one-roomed apartment in Chinatown. No flower-bedecked, swimming-pool-equipped back garden for him that led on to a private and pretty little beach. Shit, he hated the rich. Hated them.

Richard moved parallel to the unsuspecting couple behind the bushes, and then cut across the neatly-mown lawn to stand behind the huge trunk of a milo tree. There was something hawklike and dangerous about the stance of his body, held rigid and yet fluid against the bark of the tree as he watched the pair walk on to the burning white sand of the beach. With furtive eagerness the driver raised the binoculars again, dirty fingernails working furiously as he focused first on the couple on the beach, and then on the man watching them. There was something extra delicious about the situation. Watching a couple, being watched. Would they get down to it? He'd like to see that. It'd drive the big man crazy to watch her give it to another man.

Vienna's laughter wafted clearly on the breeze as she took off her blouse and skirt, revealing a white bikini that showed off her tan to perfect advantage. Farron too wriggled out of his jeans, showing bright red trunks. Fairly well endowed by the looks of it, the Beetle driver thought. Not as good as his own organ, but not bad.

Vienna took the blanket she'd carried and spread it on the sand and lay down, holding out her hand to Farron who looked down on her for a moment and then joined her. Slowly he trailed his hand up her calf. The Beetle driver sweated behind his binoculars, whilst Richard slowly froze to death.

When Farron reached over and kissed her, her hand ran over his back with a fervent pleasure. The driver licked his lips then swung his binoculars in the direction of the milo tree where he was just in time to see Richard Jago smash his hand into the tree, the force of it clearly visible and tangible even over that distance. It made the Beetle driver's own hand twinge in sympathy.

Incredulously he slowly lowered the binoculars to dangle unheeded from his hand. 'That guy's nuts,' he whispered. 'Really nuts!'

The bar was pure sleaze. She turned on her stool, her fishnet stocking-clad legs crossed at her knees revealing a large amount of her thighs. Her black leather miniskirt rode even further up her hips. Vienna reached for her screwdriver and took a long sip. A man watching her grinned lasciviously and a wave of sweet power and cutting contempt exploded in her belly. The fool was hers — she could do what she liked with him. But her body was already satiated after her last trick's performance so she slowly slipped from the stool.

Outside, the alley was dark and littered with garbage cans that stank with the leftovers from the Chinese restaurant next door. A cat dodged in front of her path and disappeared into the night. A large rat whisked quickly out of sight. 'Here puss puss puss,' she called softly and the cat, a black one, came back, inquiring green eyes looking at her. She pointed to the shadow behind the garbage can and the rat ran out, stopping to stare at her accusingly. The cat pounced, and with the broken-backed rat hanging from its jaws turned to give her a thank-you look before skulking off up the alley, green eyes swivelling from left to right in a wary lookout.

Vienna laughed and walked up the alley, her high silver heels clicking on the slippery cobblestones. She heard footsteps behind her and looked around but it was not the grinning man from the bar. 'Well, hello there,' she said, looking at the handsome, blond, square-jawed man who stood there with an anchor tattooed on his arm.

He grimaced a smile. 'Hello, whore.'

'Now that's not nice. Come here and be nice.' She held out her wrists, where ten silver bangles dangled from her arms. The blond man came to her, his strong arms slipping around her. He smelled of sweat, bay rum and aftershave. 'My, you're a big boy. Are you big where it counts too?'

The colourless eyes smiled down at her. 'Sure am, whore. Want to see?'

Vienna pouted. 'I don't think so – not tonight, big boy.'

'Hey, come here!' He yanked her back as she moved to pull away, and she felt hot and bitter anger seep into her stomach. She gave no show of it, letting instead her lips curl into a sweet, sweet smile.

'Can't take no for an answer, huh, sweetmeat?'

The blond grinned. 'My name's Gary – and I'm a lion.'

Vienna laughed. 'Is that so, sweetmeat?'

'Yeah – feel, whore. How'd you fancy some of that?'

She pulled her hand away from his groin. 'Not bad, but I've had better.'

'Why you dirty little tramp. You're nothing but a cheap tease.'

Vienna shook her head sorrowfully as the man suddenly stiffened, his colourless eyes going round and shocked. 'You shouldn't have been so persistent, sweetmeat,' she told him as he began to buckle against her, his mouth falling open. 'I'd have gotten around to you tomorrow, if you hadn't been so impatient,' she said with regretful irony as he sank to his knees in front of her, slowly slumping sideways on to the filthy cobbled ground. She looked down at him then at the blood-soaked stiletto knife in her hand. 'You were a messy boy, sweetmeat,' she told the dead body, and knelt down to wipe the knife and her bloodied hand on his pristine white shirt. She stood up and slipped the knife back into the pocket of her leather mini-skirt, and slowly walked away, humming 'Polly-wolly doodle all the day'.

The light snapped on in the bungalow and the Beetle driver suddenly perked up from his semi-doze, reaching for the ever-present binoculars. He saw her filling the kettle. She looked awful – pale and haggard even at a distance. She spooned hot chocolate mix into a mug, added hot water and went back to the bedroom, the kitchen light snapping off. Starting the car, he first checked the time – 3.30 a.m., then pulled the Beetle from under the trees and drove to the nearest phone booth on the corner of the main street. Carefully locking the car and pocketing the keys he walked into it and punched out a numiber.

'Yeah, it's me. I wanna speak to the boss . . . *now*.' He only had to wait a moment. 'Yeah, I thought I'd better call in and tell yer that the doctor is back. No, you don't get it, he was watching 'em on the beach. He's mad, I tell you – like a cuckoo. Totally crazy.' The man turned in the booth as he listened, sighing deeply. 'How much longer have I just gotta watch? Don't you want me to . . . OK, OK. But if you want her to go the same way as Lyons . . . OK, I said. You don't have to get so excited! I won't do nuthin'. Yeah – fine. No, no, all right. Yeah, yeah.'

He held the phone away from his ear, looked at it, muttered a few graphic curses and then slammed it down. He could wait. It was just a matter of time, after all. And he was a patient man. Mostly . . .

Chapter 36

MOLOKAI

The *Desert Mirage* shimmered in the early morning sun as it cut cleanly through the aquamarine waves sweeping past Pali shore, a dramatic expanse of wave-lashed rock. On deck Rhiannon watched the awe-inspiring sights with a sigh of wonder. Molokai, she knew from the literature she'd read, was an island steeped in fable and history, a mysterious place that she had been looking forward to visiting for a long time.

The skin on the back of her neck began to prickle, and she slowly turned around, her face impassive. Dominic smiled as he joined her at the rails, and nodded at the scenery. 'Did you sleep well, Rhia?' he asked, his voice soft and suggestive.

'I slept fine, thank you,' she lied coldly, then turned back to the mist-shrouded mountains in front of her. 'It looks like an island out of time.'

'It is, in some ways. King Kamehameha was raised on Molokai; the nobility of the islands is of the highest strain. My great-grandfather and grandfather were born here.'

'Just goes to show that there's an exception to every rule,' she commented cruelly, and heard him drag in a sharp breath.

'You never change, do you?' he said after a moment's silence, sounding half-angry, half-amused.

Ten minutes later she learned that Ben intended spending the day at the Sheraton Molokai playing bridge, and when she tried to talk him out of it he merely suggested she let Dominic show her around the island. When she fumbled for excuses not to go, Dominic whispered, 'Scared, Rhia?' and that settled the matter.

AFTER agreeing to a mutual truce, and hiring a four-wheel drive Landrover for the day from the hotel, they drove through some of the loveliest scenery Rhiannon had ever seen, culminating in a stroll along a tiny beach, bordered by trees and vegetation on both their left and right sides. Gulls dipped and turned overhead, and she lazily followed the flight of one over the trees where a giraffe slowly emerged, long neck craned to browse the leaves off the lower branches. Rhiannon couldn't have been more surprised if her head had fallen off her shoulders and rolled to a standstill at her feet. Quickly she glanced at Dominic, who was looking out to sea, totally oblivious. No – no it couldn't be. She turned her head slowly and looked again. The long-legged, long-necked creature still browsed, the big brown eyes watching them without fear, the ears flicking off persistent flies from its soft velvet little horns.

That's it, she thought. I'm cracking up. 'Dominic,' she said conversationally. 'There's a giraffe in those trees.'

'Hm? Oh yes, so there is,' he looked briefly in the giraffe's direction then turned, bent down and picked up a shell from the beach studying it with suspiciously minute detail.

Yes. Definitely cracking up. 'Are there a lot of giraffes around here?'

'Quite a few,' Dominic told her, his lips twitching helplessly. 'They roam free all over this part of the island – we're in the giraffe and wildlife park.'

Rhiannon slowly nodded. 'You dirty, rotten . . .'

Dominic began to laugh. 'You should have seen your face – that double-take you did was a classic.' He did a good imitation of her incredulous second glance and a helpless grin spread over her face. She never could resist laughing at herself.

'I'll get you for that,' she warned, her eyes dancing with laughter as she pointed a warning finger at him. 'Just you wait and see.'

'Promises, promises,' he taunted then held out his hand, his gesture so normal and friendly that she took it without thinking. 'Come on, we'll take the tour around the park. They mainly breed endangered species here, but there's plenty to see. They even have a dancing ostrich.'

Afterwards they drove to the village and stopped outside a coffee shop called Kanemitsu's Bakery. 'This place is famous for its cheese and onion bread,' Dominic told her, ordering the speciality before they made their way to a rustic wooden table. It was then, without warning, that the sky came crashing in. Emerald eyes met, clashed, caught fire.

'Rhia,' he said softly as he reached for her hand, and fear bit deep into her stomach.

'This bread does look delicious,' she interrupted hastily, her voice as bright and false as coloured glass. He looked away angrily for a moment then reached for his coffee cup.

The conical volcanoes just waiting to spew forth molten lava were not as potentially explosive as the silence between them as they drove away from the village and into the countryside once again. Rhiannon could feel her body aching. She wanted him – oh, how she wanted him! Her hands trembled in her lap, her breath did likewise in her throat. She licked her lips that tasted faintly of coffee, and shifted in her seat.

He turned off the gravel road just after the junction of Maunaloa Highway and Route 46, taking them past the extinct volcano of Kauhako and on to Waikola Lookout, one of the island's most spectacular views. Looking down on a majestic valley three thousand feet below, veined with waterfalls, Rhiannon found all words failing her.

'There's another place like this one not far from here. Do you want to see it?' His words were ordinary enough, but they reminded her that she was all alone with him and her heartbeat began to accelerate.

HE took her to Kalaupupa Lookout, the sun beginning to sink in the sky as they gazed out over fields as green as their eyes, over terrain as wild as the need in their hearts, over waterfalls whose combined weight of cold water could not drench or douse the passion that was theirs.

'What's up that trail?' she asked, pointing to a narrow path, and he looked up to where she was pointing and nodded with a strangely fatalistic smile.

'Come and see,' he invited softly.

The grass beneath her feet felt like a springing green carpet and as they walked the sun began to bathe them in a red-gold light. It would be dark soon.

Suddenly, up ahead, she saw a rock, about six feet tall and shaped like . . .

'Phallic Rock,' Dominic said softly. 'In ancient times, the women believed the rock had fertility powers, so they came here to pray for children.'

She wished he hadn't brought her here but then acknowledged that she'd brought herself. And now she couldn't get back.

'The women used to bring their lovers here,' he continued, his eyes no longer on the rock that cast its ancient shadow over them, but on her. 'Queens from bygone ages would take a lover of their choosing, right here, and seduce them, making love, knowing that they would be impregnated.'

She backed away, her legs feeling weak underneath her, his words affecting her in a way she'd never have thought possible. The sun began to drop behind the stone which became a huge black shape, casting its shadow further upon them. Meeting his eyes for a breathtaking moment, Rhiannon turned and ran.

But she did not run fast enough. He clutched her shoulders, dragging her back, his hands slipping almost immediately to cup her breasts as she leaned against him, her head on his shoulder. His fingers slipped beneath the cowl neckline of her dress, his hands abrasive and arousing on her bare breasts, his thumb and forefingers teasing the swelling nipples to painfully aching attention. A long low moan escaped her, a moan of helpless need but also of desperate denial.

He turned her around, his lips hot and possessive, covering her own before she could draw breath, her body folding into his like liquid cream as his hand found the zip at her back. She struggled briefly, but the cream and lemon dress fell to the grass and he lifted her from its circle around her feet. Carrying her to the base of the rock they lay down on the cool grass, her face bathed in the red light of the setting sun. Her eyes were dazed with wanting, watching him as he stood up and tore off his clothes, revealing dark nipples in the tanned brown expanse of his chest, the straining power of his penis rising from the black hair that gathered there. She closed her eyes for a moment, not sure if it was all real or if the magical island had plucked her up and sent her spinning back in time.

Then he was beside her, pulling down her panties. His head

468

dipped to her breast, lips suckling so strongly on her nipples that she arched in helpless arousal. Slipping his hands under her and cupping her buttocks, he slipped between her thighs and nudged them apart and she welcomed him with hot and wet eagerness. His hands ran up her arms, anchoring them firmly above her head as he lay over her, his weight and strength subduing her as he slipped into her body with a cry of triumph that must have been echoed by other men in that ancient place a million times throughout the centuries.

She moaned as she felt him inside her, his hot, velvet, iron-hard presence demolishing all opposition and thoughts of denial. 'I hate you,' she screamed as her nails dug into his back, dragging him closer to her, propelling him further into her body, her legs linking behind his thighs to make sure he could not escape until she was through with him. 'I hate you!'

Dominic buried his head in the mass of raven tresses spread out on the ground and lunged into her again and again, driving himself and her to their utmost endurance. His physical superiority kept her thrashing body pinned to the ground as she bucked and cried out with the orgasms that exploded in her body time after time.

Eventually, in the final rays of the setting sun, Dominic lost himself in her, his heaving body shuddering as he emptied his seed into her. His arms collapsed as male strength deserted him, leaving him panting weakly on to her breasts. And like all those ancient queens, Rhiannon smiled with satisfaction, knowing that men, for all their power, would always end up like this – as helpless, weak and spent as newborn babies, reliant in a woman's arms.

The stars were out above her when next she opened her eyes – silver twinkling dots of light so far away that it defied imagination. Dominic lifted his head, but his face was in shadow, his expression impossible to read as he sat up and away from her. Only his hand cupped her calf, the simple contact beyond price. 'Rhia . . .' he said, and she knew she must stop the words quickly.

'Shut up,' she moaned, her voice exhausted, 'and take me back to the yacht.'

'You think you'll be safe there?' he asked, his voice amused and sad.

No. She didn't think that. But what else could she do? Dragging herself to a sitting position, her body full of aches and pains reminding her of just how completely and passionately she had been loved, she pulled on her dress. Her panties gleamed white in the moonlight as she snatched them from the grass and stepped into them. Her shoes took some finding, but eventually they were both walking back down the trail. She stumbled over a rock, and his hand was there, preventing her from falling, but as soon as she was steady again she pulled it away.

'Be honest,' his voice came to her in the darkness. 'You know what you want.'

'Yes,' she lied. 'I do. And don't think I've changed my mind because of . . . what happened back there.'

His hand dropped from her shoulder at the first hard word she uttered, and nothing could stop her from feeling cold and bereft.

Later, she had never felt so relieved nor so miserable at the sight of the brightly-lit yacht bobbing at anchor. The launch waited at the pier and sitting on its leather bench she hugged her arms around her. In silence he steered them to the yacht where a mercifully empty deck awaited. Not looking around to see if he followed, she ran quickly below to her cabin and locked the door. Snapping on the light, she looked around her room with something akin to panic in her eyes. Walking to the bathroom she turned on the shower to its coldest setting and dragged off her clothes, standing under the needle-point spray and shivering like some lost, whipped dog before wrapping a towel around her. Throwing herself down on the bed she stared up at the ceiling dry-eyed.

'You really did it this time, didn't you?' she asked herself aloud, and feeling more and more angry at herself she got up and rubbed herself dry. A frantic need to do something – anything – drove her and she walked to the wardrobe and dragged out a black rubber skindiving suit. The clammy cold rubber made her shiver until her own bodyheat warmed it.

In the equipment room on deck, she fished out flippers and

collected around her the proper gear; regulators, which regulated the pressure of air in the cylinders, and on the cylinders of air themselves the compressors, to recharge the air. She clipped herself expertly into the tanks, checking that the pressure gauge which told a driver how quickly he was using up air was working and accurate. Into a weightbelt she also checked that she had a diver's knife, depth-gauge, diver's compass, a watch, harness and torch.

She knew how to skindive and handle the equipment, and also knew that she was committing the ultimate diving sin by breaking the biggest and baddest taboo of them all – diving alone. If she got into difficulties she could die.

DOMINIC couldn't settle. At his porthole he stared at the sky, then looked down quickly as someone snapped on the underwater lights. Powerful bulbs illuminated the water around the yacht for several yards. In stupefied amazement he saw a figure dressed in full diving gear walk to the unroped gangway.

With one hand holding her mask and demand-valve firmly in place and the other on the cylinder, she checked behind her, ducked her head forwards, relaxed and rolled over backwards. With a tuck dive she slowly descended, checking for signs of discomfort or trouble, but finding none. Snorting gently down her nose to clear her ears, she began to relax.

The ocean outside the *Mirage*'s lights was pitch-black. Most fish were daytime denizens, but there were still a few nocturnal species who were startled or made curious by the lights. It was a ghostly feeling. The water, which became buoyant the further she sank was like a warm caress, the only sound that of her own breathing.

When she looked around minutes later, he was there. For several moments she watched him approach her, his air bubbles silver columns in the powerful lights, heading for the surface. Treading water easily, she waited until he was alongside her and then moved slowly down, where the light faded to dimness and half-seen fish and slow-moving crustaceans darted amongst the ghostly fingers of coral and rock. It was a magical few minutes. There could be no talk and no reprisals, no human tantrum to cloud the cool dark water, the silence of the ocean or the beauty of the marine life.

Yet, like all good things, it had to come to an end. Checking his gauges, Dominic tapped her on the shoulder and pointed up, his eyes glittering greenly behind the glass. Rhiannon sighed but looped her fingers into a circle, giving the internationally recognized 'OK' sign. Then as he looked up, she saw his arms jerk in reaction to something, and her own face turned up to the bright surface where the most feared of all outlines slowly circled above them. *Shark*.

The single word was enough to make the most experienced and stalwart diver's heart falter. In fact, there were plenty of sharks that were not dangerous, from the smallest, pike-sized shark, to lazy basking sharks, and the biggest of all, the whale shark, which was very gentle and very whale-like, as its name suggested. But she saw at once that this shark belonged in none of those categories. Her eyes turned to Dominic, who was watching the creature but also looking around him for any possible escape route. Taking the knife from her belt she tapped his shoulder. His face-mask turned in her direction and his hand came out and took the knife from her.

Her heartbeat drummed loudly in her chest, but she kept her breathing steady – the very last thing they needed was for her to start hyperventilating. The shark, she knew, must have seen them. It was a fair size, about twelve feet in length, gleaming bullet-grey and silver in the light. It was circling above almost lazily, and didn't seem overly interested, but that didn't stop her from being scared to death.

Slowly they began to ascend, as far away from the shark as they could get and still be in the light, careful not to ascend faster than their air bubbles. She could feel her nerves stretch and scream, but forced herself by sheer willpower into being patient, and above all, calm. Calm? The thought, for some reason, made her want to laugh.

Dominic looked at her just at that moment and saw her smile, his eyes widening in disbelief as he gave his head a brief shake. Still the shark circled above them, its powerful body capable of turning on a coin by the mere flick of its powerful tail or fin. It was, Rhiannon acknowledged in a totally detached part of her brain, a beautiful creature. Sleek, silent, graceful. And deadly.

At last they broke the surface, but now the shark was out of sight, lurking somewhere beneath them. 'Swim quietly,' she heard his lovely voice close by. 'Don't splash.'

Using a slow but very smooth breast-stroke she headed for the yacht, clasping the steel ladder with a heartfelt sigh and clambered up, her limbs, the suit and airtanks, feeling as if they weighed a ton. Dominic's hands on her waist helped her up and urged her on silently until she reached the deck where she fell to her hands and knees, gasping and shivering.

She heard the thud as his cylinders were dropped on to the deck, and then sat back on her heels as he crouched beside her and unfastened the harness, pulling the tanks from her back. Gently but firmly he pulled the sticking wet suit off her body and ignored her shivering nakedness to drape a huge and warm fluffy towel around her shoulders.

'Come here,' he commanded softly and she walked into his arms without a second thought, pressing her cold cheek to his shoulder, only then feeling the hot tears that coursed down her cheeks.

'Oh, Dominic,' she whispered, swallowing hard. 'I've never been so scared before in my whole life.'

'Haven't you?' he asked, his voice unbelievably smiling. 'I have.'

She pulled away and looked up at him, his wet hair leaving trickles of water to run down his forehead and over his nose. 'When?'

'The day you nearly came off that bloody motorbike of yours.'

'Oh, that,' she dismissed. 'That was nothing – but that was a shark down there!' she accused, as if only now realizing it, and looking out over the swelling waves of the ocean she shivered convulsively in his arms.

'Hm. Good job he wasn't hungry.'

Rhiannon laughed weakly and pulled herself reluctantly out of the blissful security of his arms. 'Don't joke.'

'I wasn't,' he said, his voice hardening as anger took over. 'I

473

don't suppose it would do either of us any good to point out that you don't go diving alone?'

'I know that,' she snapped, relief turning, as it often does in reaction, to annoyance.

'Do you?' he accused, standing with his hands planted firmly on his hips.

'Yes,' she snapped back, goaded beyond endurance for one day. 'You also don't have to point out that you may, just may,' she stressed, 'have saved my life.'

'I wasn't going to,' he surprised her by saying. 'Most women I know would have panicked down there, but not you. You didn't make a mad dash for the surface either, thrashing about and stimulating the damned thing into attacking. And at least you had a knife with you, although what good that would have done you if the fish had been hungry, I don't know.'

It was the 'fish' that did it. Referring to that multi-toothed vicious predator capable of biting a human being in two as a mere 'fish' totally destroyed her and she began to laugh. Softly at first, but then with growing hilarity as she collapsed on to a deckchair, clutching the towel firmly about her as she rocked with uncontrollable mirth tinged with hysteria.

'You're crazy,' he accused, rubbing his hand through his hair in a gesture of a man who'd just reached the end of his tether. 'A certifiable and hopeless mental case.'

'Who is?' The voice was Ben's, puzzled and amused, and both of them turned guiltily at the sound of it. They had forgotten his very existence.

'She is.' Dominic pointed at Rhiannon.

'What's she done this time?' Ben asked indulgently, walking further on to the lighted deck.

'Nothing drastic. Just tried to feed the fish,' Dominic said, and both men turned to stare at Rhiannon as once again she collapsed into helpless gales of laughter.

'Feed the fish,' Ben echoed, totally lost. 'With what?'

'With herself,' Dominic said drily. 'Excuse me, I must go and change.'

Ben watched him go. 'It sounds as if you've finally driven him bananas.'

'Not quite. I just went skindiving, that's all.'

'What – now?' Ben looked at the night, and then noticed for the first time the powerful underwater lights illuminating the sea beneath his yacht. 'You went down alone?' he asked, his voice scandalized and stern.

'Dominic was with me.' She cleverly chose her words as she walked away. 'And so was a shark,' she added, almost as an afterthought, tossing the words carelessly over her shoulder, leaving Ben standing on the deck with his jaw dropping open.

In her cabin her fingers shook as she dressed simply for dinner, but before she reached the dining room the First Mate found her and told her she had a call on the bridge. 'Just press the button down whenever you want to talk, ma'am,' he demonstrated the use of the radio, then thoughtfully left her alone. Depressing the switch, she said cautiously, 'Hello?'

'Hello, Miss Grantham, it's Sandy. I hope you don't mind me calling you, but the woman at the dress store gave me this number.'

'Oh, no. That's fine. Have you got news.'

'Yes. It's about that . . . request you made at the Sea Life park.'

Rhiannon swallowed hard, then said in a businesslike voice, 'I remember.'

'Well, the man we talked about just contacted me. I told him what I could, which wasn't much, but he's agreed to meet you. If you've got a pad and pencil I'll tell you where and when.'

Five minutes later she stepped out on to the deck and the First Mate straightened up, walking to meet her. 'You finished, ma'am?'

'What? Oh, yes,' she said, her voice grim with desperate humour. 'Yes, I think I am. Quite finished.'

Chapter 37

Vienna opened her eyes to a feeling of well-being and pore-deep relaxation that she had not felt for a long time. Sitting up and swinging her legs from off the couch on to the floor, she smoothed back the hair at her temples. 'What happened?' she asked quickly, before she had time to lose her nerve.

Vince walked to his armchair and sat down. 'We had an interesting conversation,' he said, knowing it was an unsatisfactory answer at best.

'Oh? About what?'

'Things that have happened to you since you woke up in hospital. Things that have worried or upset you.'

'Richard?' she hazarded a guess, her voice turning out sharper than she had expected.

Vince looked up at her, a professionally bland look on his face. 'Dr Jago? Yes, we talked about him, but not as much as you seem to think. So, let's take a look at the other things we discussed.'

'Like what?'

'The nightmares, for instance.'

'You really come straight to the point, don't you?'

'I have no other choice. In your case we have no childhood memories to refer to, so until we break through the amnesia we only have the brief period between the hospital and now to work with. And the most interesting feature of that is . . .'

'The nightmares.'

'Yes,' Vince agreed. 'They all seem to stem from this murder case a few months ago. Why is that?'

'I don't know. I suppose it was the police visiting me at cookery class.'

'But you had those dreams before that. And they always took place in a dark alley.'

'They told me I was found in an alley.'

Vince nodded. 'Yes,' he agreed thoughtfully. 'But have you

476

'. . . I don't know just how to put this without worrying or scaring you.'

'Just come right out and ask. I'd prefer that.'

'OK. Have you ever lost your temper? With Farron, Dr Jago, friends at work, the mailman. Anyone?'

Vienna frowned, a little puzzled. 'Well, I get mad with things sometimes. Who doesn't?'

'No. I mean, have you ever violently lost your temper? Thrown a carton of milk down because you couldn't get it open, that sort of thing.'

A frisson of fear made her shudder. 'No.'

Vince let his suspicion show plainly for a split second before he nodded and wrote something down.

Vienna asked the inevitable question. 'Why do you ask me that?'

He smiled vaguely. 'I'll ask a lot of questions that don't seem to matter or make sense or even be relevant. Humans think and react and feel things in chainlink. Like the story of the lost nail, leading to a lost horseshoe, leading to a lost horse, lost message, lost battle, lost war, that kind of thing? So it is with human beings. One tiny little thing can lead on to other things, even though you may never associate one with the other.'

'I see,' Vienna said slowly, but even so wondered why he wanted to know if she had a violent temper. What had she said to make him suspect that?' Then, as a thought hit her, she paled and swallowed hard. 'Does it seem likely that I do have a nasty temper, Dr Drake?'

Vince looked deliberately evasive. 'Oh no, there's nothing concrete to indicate that. It's early days yet. The resistance to remembering is very deep-rooted. It will take us some time to break down the barriers, I'm afraid.' He hesitated skilfully. 'That is, if you still want to carry on, of course.'

'Of course I do,' she said, her face paling even further. 'Why shouldn't I?'

'Oh, no reason.'

His open, friendly face told her nothing. Only instinct warned her that he was hiding something; that for some reason he was urging her to quit now. 'Vince, I want you to

477

tell me what's happening and what you're thinking. It's my head and my problem, after all,' she demanded, sitting on the edge of the couch, her hands locked together as her knuckles showed white with the strain.

Vince silently cursed his own skill then sighed. 'I didn't tell you, Vienna, because I was afraid you might misconstrue the significance of it. You see,' he seemed to struggle for the words, and Vienna felt her whole world suspend itself. 'All people, *all* people,' he stressed, 'have one thing in common, in that they are all capable of doing things that they thought they were not. Also, the vast majority of the human mind is given over to subconscious activities. For all our exploration of the stars, the depths of the ocean, our own minds remain uncharted. Our own selves are almost as much of a mystery to us today as they were to our caveman ancestors. Even now, our subconscious affects us in ways we haven't yet discovered.'

'Please,' she interrupted, too agitated to worry about being rude. 'Can you get to the point?'

'I'm sorry. The point is this: every one of us is capable of violence, of self-sacrifice, or bravery and depravity. But most of us, luckily, have our conscious minds to act as a kind of safety valve. You can see when sometimes this fails – incest or child-molesting for instance show us clearly the baseness of depravity that we can sink to, whilst the heroism of men who give their lives saving others in fires or shipwreck demonstrate the nobility of which we are also capable.'

'Are you saying that my safety valve as far as violence is concerned is shot to hell?' she asked, her whole body bathed now in a cold sweat.

'No,' Vince said forcefully – and that was not in the plan. He was supposed to say it without conviction. But, ironically he saw that the very nature of his vehement reaction made her think that the opposite was true. Like an unfaithful wife overdoing the denials. Like an alcoholic telling everyone he could handle it.

'I don't understand.' She shook her head miserably, and Vince sighed.

'I was afraid of that. I can't explain it in layman's terms

because it's too complicated. Can't you just take my word for it that just because I come across things in your subconscious, it doesn't necessarily mean that they'll emerge into your conscious mind?'

Her head nodded, but it felt stiff on her shoulders and, although hope struggled valiantly within her, sparking off a tiny flame of optimism, she had never felt so wretched, alone, scared or confused in all her life. 'OK,' she finally said, her voice pathetically small.

'Good. Vienna, we mustn't stop now,' Vince said softly. 'If we do you're going to go away from here misinformed.'

Dully she looked at him, then managed a weak smile. 'I won't stop,' she promised him. 'It's gone too far.'

Vince winced. You poor kid, he thought. If you only knew how right you are. 'We're coming up with several interesting and promising factors already.'

'Yes?'

'Were you aware that you are afraid of the police? Not that that's significant,' he hastened, much too fast, to reassure her. 'Most people are. It has to do with guilt complexes created by things you wouldn't believe. Pinching ten cents from your brother's piggybank when you were four would be enough to do it!'

'And I suppose I'm scared of the police because they were there when I was in hospital and that was a bad time for me. Then later, asking about the murder. Another bad time.'

'Hm, I see what you're getting at. You associate the police with a bad, or troubled experience. Yes, that might account for it. Probably does, I should say,' he corrected himself, and scribbled something more into his notes. Walking to his desk, he took out a form and filled it in, then handed it over to her. 'This is a prescription. I want you to get it filled immediately.' She took it gingerly, as if it might bite her. 'It's for sleeping pills. You look exhausted and you simply must sleep.'

The thought of a nightmare going on and on because she could not wake up made her hand shake so badly that the piece of paper fluttered like a giant butterfly in the air and she hastily folded it into a small neat square. 'All right.' She would fill the prescription but she hadn't promised to take them.

'Good. Now don't be afraid to take them. They contain a strong sedative, and,' his sharp, well-trained psychiatrist's eye had not missed the defiance in her blue gaze, 'they also have a reputation for being dream repressives.'

'You mean I won't dream?' she asked, the thought so heady it almost frightened her.

'It means you probably won't remember it when you wake up,' Vince corrected. 'There's a theory, a very viable one in my opinion, that all people dream every time they sleep. But some people remember them better than others.'

She slipped the piece of paper firmly into her bag. Yes, Vince thought sadly. She'll take the pills. 'Thank you for all you're doing for me.' She unknowingly heaped burning coals over his head. 'I really appreciate it.'

'Don't be so grateful,' Vince shot out before he could stop himself, then recovered quickly. 'After all, it's my job and I'm getting paid for it. We shrinks have a saying to ensure we get paid. It goes, "If you don't pay, you don't get well". It's blackmail of the cheapest kind,' he leaned forward to whisper confidingly to her. 'I think if you can wangle something for free it always makes you feel marvellous.'

Despite her misery, Vienna laughed. She liked this man, and yet . . . There was something about him that she was beginning to mistrust. At first she had liked and respected him, but now a whisper of doubt entered her mind. What exactly did he do and say when she was under hypnosis? Slowly she shook her head. Face it, she told herself. It's the syndrome of shooting the messenger because you didn't like the message. Well, to hell with that! She wasn't some petty, emotional quitter. You didn't get anywhere in this life if you didn't see things through.

'So, I think that's all for today. Some time soon I want to do some tests . . .'

'Tests?'

'Oh, not medical tests. Don't worry, no needles or anything.'

'No, of course,' Vienna quickly backtracked, feeling like an idiot again. 'Well, I'll see you tomorrow then.'

Vince looked up from his scribbling. 'Yes – tomorrow.

Goodbye, Vienna.' He let her get to the door and then gave the parting volley. 'Oh, my dear. Between then and now I want you to think back and try to remember all the times you have lost your temper. Then I want you to make a list of roughly when it was, and why. Can you do that for me?'

Vienna paused, her hand on the door, and slowly turned around. 'OK.'

'Fine. Bye – till tomorrow.'

'Yes. Bye, Dr Drake.'

Vince waited until she was gone then walked to the bathroom door and opened it. Richard walked in and glanced at the closed door.

'Do you have the money?' Vince asked abruptly.

'I have it. It's not necessary for you to see it, though. Don't worry – if Gillespie doesn't get his next instalment you'll be the first to know.'

Vince turned away in self-disgust.

'The session went well today.'

'Yes. If you're a twisted son of a bitch, it did.'

Richard ignored him. 'When you do those tests, I want to see the results – the real ones I mean. And write them up in plain English.'

'What I don't understand is why you want all these extensive records kept,' Vince looked at him closely. 'They're all false. Fictitious answers that she's supposed to have given me, totally untrue . . .'

'Just keep the records like you would if she really had killed that man. That's all. And those tests you're going to do – make them fit in with the picture. Just give me the true results.'

'You're not going to use these records to have her committed, are you, Richard?' Vince asked suspiciously, the ugly thought making him turn pale. Richard walked to the door, obviously not intending to answer and Vince got rapidly to his feet. 'Because if you are, then let me tell you now I won't go along with it. There's nothing seriously wrong with that girl and I'm not going to be a party to anything that . . .'

'Relax,' Richard warned him. 'You'll end up doing just what I want you to in the end, and you know it.'

'Why else do you want me to keep those damned records if

not to be used in some sort of legal proceedings one day?' Vince pushed, all his psychiatric training telling him that Jago was suffering from some kind of psychopathic disorder. It was obvious that he could not distinguish from a moral viewpoint what was right and what was wrong any more. Just how far had it gone?

'I'll make sure Gillespie gets a little 'more cash, Vince,' Richard ignored the question. 'Whether or not he continues to get it, depends entirely on you. Remember that whenever your selective conscience takes a bite out of your ass.'

Vince watched him go with helpless frustration then sat down heavily. The man was unstable. There was only one person he knew who needed to be locked up in an institution, and it wasn't Vienna Wright — God help her. And God help her boyfriend too. Would he stick by her through the hellish months to come? Could any man, no matter how strong or how much in love? As he drank his scotch, Vince thought about that last session. Just how much could he find out about her if he really was trying to get past her amnesia? He'd been truthful in telling her that her mental block was strong. Perhaps even too strong to break down. His glass was empty, he saw with something of a surprise, and slowly he refilled it.

WHEN Farron stepped down off the stage after his lunch-hour stint, Vienna was waiting for him, her face alight with excitement. In her hand she was clutching a brown paper envelope. 'Hi,' he kissed her lingeringly, then glanced questioningly at the envelope in her hand.

'The Swiss brochures have come,' she half-laughed and squeezed his hand tightly in her own. 'Farron, some of them strike a chord.'

'They do? That's great!'

'The thing is, it's the area that looks familiar — not any school, so I've got to write to all of them — eighteen in fact.' She opened a brochure to show him some scenery as they walked to their cars, and Farron grinned at her excitement.

'I have to go to the post office to get some stamps. Follow me?'

'I'll follow you anywhere, sweetheart,' he gushed

dramatically, then chuckled and lifted her feet off the ground, swinging her around in the air, his laughter loud enough to attract several indulgent and envious glances from passers by. 'It's all coming together, honey,' he said softly, letting her body slowly slide down his. If she really had gone to Finishing School then surely the probabilities of her being one of Gloria's girls were lessened. Not many prostitutes went to a Swiss Finishing school, of that he was sure. His hands on her waist were firm and possessive, and she smiled with deliberate enthusiasm.

'Yes.'

'You don't sound too sure.'

'Oh, ignore me. I'm just impatient, that's all. And I have to figure out what to write to these schools. How do I tell them what I want without sounding, I don't know. Crazy?'

'We'll think of something,' he reassured her, then noticed the white lines of strain at her mouth and eyes and the bruised expression in their blue depths and an arrow of apprehension shot through him as he opened the car door for her. 'How did the doc's go today?'

'Oh, so so. We never thought it was going to be quick or easy though, did we?' Her voice appealed for patience but also for him to leave it alone. Farron hesitated, but went along with her.

They drove in their separate cars downtown and after getting the stamps, realized that the schools would need a photograph of Vienna to check against their records so they found a passport photo booth and Farron made wisecracks as she fed coin after coin into the machine, waiting endlessly for little reams of neat square photos to slide out of the slot.

'Is that the last?' she finally asked.

'Yep,' he smacked his lips together on the word. 'Now for some fun pics!'

'Farron!' she squealed as he bundled her into the booth, sitting on the chair and dragging her into his lap, contorting his face monstrously as the flash illuminated the booth. 'You're an idiot, you know that?' she laughed, but stuck a leg up in the air as the flash went again, crossing her eyes as she did so.

After five hilarious minutes of this, and another ten hilarious minutes laughing over the results, they nipped into a Zippy's for a takeout then drove with it to Waikiki, which was still a human sardine can. Tossing a good bit of their meal to marauding seagulls, they paddled in the surf hand in hand, dodging laughing children and topless sunbathers.

On Kalakaua Avenue, Vienna spotted a chemist and told Farron about the prescription and he browsed whilst she talked to the pharmacist. It was good just to have him so close. He never crowded her, but never left her lonely either. 'I love you,' she whispered when, her prescription filled and a brown bottle of pills safely zipped into her bag, she walked up behind him and slipped her arms around his waist. Putting a tube of toothpaste back on the shelf he covered her hands with his own. 'You already told me that,' he teased softly and turning her around, oblivious to any watching eyes he kissed her tenderly.

'Hm,' she murmured, a beatific smile on her face. They turned away, almost bumping into a slight blond man who was loading a basket full of baby food.

'Sorry,' he muttered, although the fault was theirs, and as she met the innocuous blue eyes the world around her faded. Gary Lyons stood in front of her, and in her hand was a knife. A knife that she plunged into his chest, again and again and again. Around her a dark alley stank of decay, and in the air a woman's sobbing screams echoed off the dirty brick walls.

'Hey? Do you fancy a new spot-free face?'

'What?' She blinked, licked her parched lips and stared at Farron who was holding a jar of cream. 'I said, do you want a new, spot-free face. Because if so, *ipso facto* Zit-Zap Wonder-cream will do it for you.'

The cheap and cheerful chemist's shop swam around her for several giddying seconds before she could pull herself together. 'Are you saying I need it?' she heard her remarkably light and teasing voice and she saw him grin.

'I wouldn't dare.' The noise of tills opening with a small 'ping', the creaking wheels of trolleys and the muted sounds of voices were all around, but she shivered violently. It had been so real, so vivid. Nor had it been just a thought or memory. The whole chemist's shop had disappeared; she'd really been in that alley! What was happening to her?

'Hey – are you all right? Darling?'

'Of course I'm all right,' she lied, linking her arm through his. 'Come on, let's go home.'

Farron said nothing, but on the way to the cars he kept glancing across at her, forcing her to keep up a flow of chatter that seriously undermined her nerves. She was very badly scared. She was seeing things. Ugly things. She needed Dr Drake. She'd call him – tell him. No, that was silly. She would be seeing him tomorrow morning, she'd tell him then.

'Are you OK to drive?' Farron asked as she fished for her keys and unlocked the doors.

'Course I am,' she said briskly. 'I'll follow you.'

'No – I'll follow you.'

'OK.' She reached up and kissed him, and Farron's arms tightened on her, but when she pulled away he forced his face into a smile. Shutting the door for her he walked almost blindly to his own car and got in, sinking slowly behind the wheel, his heart pounding with fear. Her lips had been so cold. It had been like kissing ice. Vienna pulled away and overtook him with a cheerful toot on the horn and he pulled out immediately behind her, never letting a car get between them. She had gone so pale back there; looked so strange. He took a deep breath and told himself not to get jittery.

Vienna drove automatically, her actions coordinated and careful whilst her mind raged in first one direction then the other. Consequently, when she got home she was so tired that when Farron handed her a coffee cup and sat beside her, asking her quietly to tell him what was wrong, she didn't have the energy to lie. Briefly she told him about Dr Drake asking her if she had a violent temper, but kept the incident in the chemist shop to herself. It was as if saying it out loud would make it true.

'That's nothing to worry about!' Farron found himself relaxing, relieved that it was nothing more serious. 'You're the sweetest-natured person I know.'

Vienna gnawed her lip. 'But what if I'm not? What if that Police Lieutenant knew more than he was saying?'

'Look.' Farron took her hand, trying to reassure her by the sheer strength of his own belief in her. 'A pimp probably knocked off that guy. That's the theory the cops are working on – the papers said so. Hell, the story isn't even in the papers any more. The case might be closed for all we know.'

'And what about those nightmares? Where I kill people?'

'Everyone has nightmares like that,' Farron said with a mixture of amusement and reassurance. 'When I was ten I dreamt that I was drowning my gym teacher in the pool. How I detested that man!'

It wasn't the same. She knew it, but she didn't know how to explain it – or even if she should. Why should he suffer just because she was? Slowly she smiled and leaned her head on his shoulder, but even as she felt his shoulders relax beneath her, her own eyes were full of fear and pain as they stared at the wall.

'Let's go to bed,' he whispered.

'OK.'

But there another nail waited to be hammered into her coffin. When he touched her she felt nothing. Worse, when he continued to touch her she felt a small knot of rebellion and reluctance stir in her belly. Moving away from him in the bed a bare inch, he felt her withdrawal. And although it cut him to the quick, giving him more pain than he'd ever felt before in his life, he hid it from her. 'You've had a rough day,' he whispered in her ear. 'Go to sleep.'

He turned slightly away from her and she closed her eyes in relief.

For a long time Farron stared up at the ceiling, his dry eyes burning, a sense of helplessness gnawing at his innards like maggots. Something was coming between them. Something sly, cunning, something he couldn't see or hear but only feel. Feel in the stiffening of her body when he touched her. Hear in the small sigh of her relief when he turned away from her. And fight it as he might, he couldn't help but wonder if this was how Richard Jago had felt many months before. Was she about to find another man again? Leave him, as she had left Richard? His heart told him no, but his cynicism told him it was possible. After all, how likely was it that he alone had the magic formula for true, everlasting love when so many others had failed?

Long into the night, the memory of her cold, cold lips plagued and hurt him. For the first time in his life, Farron Manikuuna began to pray.

Chapter 38

MOLOKAI

The lights of the yacht competed for beauty with the myriad lights of the stars that scattered silver diamonds over a navy-blue velvet sky. Rhiannon stood on deck dressed in a luminous pale-green silk that clung to her high full breasts and fell in a foaming wave of pale green to her feet. Her midnight black hair was piled on her head in a careless array of gentle curls that allowed little wisps to cling to her high intelligent forehead and in her earlobes, around her neck and at her wrist, her diamond and emerald jewels sparkled.

She lifted her glass of Chandon champagne to her lips and slowly sipped it, turning her head as a line of lights in the distance caught her attention. The SS *Constitution* sailed on past them as she slowly disappeared around the other side of the island. Other green eyes watched the *Constitution* slip by, and then returned, as if dragged by magnetism, to the woman who stood so still and silent by the rails. Dominic raised his eyes to the stars, impressed but not overawed by their vastness. He had other things on his mind.

'Rhiannon.' He whispered her name softly but the word might easily have been a curse, and she stiffened before slowly turning around. He was wearing black and seemed to melt into the night as if he were part of it. Only his deep green eyes glittered with colour in his handsome face. The glass in her hand began to tremble, and she felt her lips part. And then . . . salvation.

'Miss Grantham? Mr Fielding asked me to tell you that dinner is ready.'

She smiled and said with more fervent appreciation than the crew member had expected, 'Thank you, Andy. Will you be so kind as to escort me in to dinner?'

Andy was more than happy to.

Ben had invited to dinner several people he had met at the

island's exclusive hotel. Earlier that evening Rhiannon had talked with a painter named Brian O'Keefe, a charming man who unfortunately suffered from 'wandering hand' trouble. It was only in deference to his need to be careful of them that she hadn't slammed them in a door some place. His wife Carole, a pretty and longsuffering brunette, was a keen and moderately successful amateur photographer. Sally Durnfield was an ex-model turned professional actress and doing very well in spite of severe attacks by scornful critics. Her escort of the moment was a plastic surgeon named Hal Conrad who spent more time talking to Rhiannon than to Sally, a fact that had not gone unnoticed.

The dining room was big enough to seat twenty people comfortably, and on an original Sheraton table, exquisite arrays of Waterford crystal wine goblets, Royal Worcester china and silver cutlery had been laid. In a crystal vase, exotic bird-of-paradise flowers, orchids, sweet-smelling jasmine and orange blossom cast their shadows on the snowy-white linen tablecloth. Light came from pale mauve candles secured in silver candlesticks.

'Shall we take our seats, ladies and gentlemen?' Ben asked formally, watching with benign interest as the men seated their ladies and then themselves.

Dominic, as a prince of royal blood and honoured guest was seated at Ben's immediate right. From hidden speakers the soothing sounds of a Chopin Étude – the 'Tristesse', filled the room, a perfect accompaniment to the excellent meal that followed. A French chef had come along for the ride and was earning his money. Giant prawns, stuffed with a mixture of lemons, sage, shallots and a tiny sprinkling of wild mint were served with a delicious tomato and courgette sauce as an entreé. This was followed by swordfish, duck à l'orange, quenelles of pheasant, and for dessert, kirsch-soaked cherries flambés. Over Irish coffee and cognac the mood mellowed and even the blonde-haired model stopped sending poisoned barbs across the table at her plastic surgeon boyfriend.

Something of a poker enthusiast, Brian O'Keefe proposed a game, which was immediately accepted by Ben, who loved card-games of any description. Too polite to do anything other than go along with their host, the small group retired to the lounge and seated themselves around a circular, green-baized table.

'I'm not sure I know how to play,' Carole O'Keefe confessed with a sheepish grin as she sat down.

'Don't worry, angel,' her husband comforted. 'I'll see you're OK.'

'You mean you'll see that you're OK,' Carole corrected him with a laugh. 'I know you – you'll milk me for every cent I've got.'

'Andy,' Ben smiled enigmatically. 'Do we have gambling chips in the safe?'

Andy nodded and moved away. 'So gentlemen,' Ben rubbed his hands together. 'Who wants to play?' Naturally, none of the men could resist the challenge, and Rhiannon set the precedent for the women by reaching into her bag and writing out a cheque for ten thousand dollars. As she did so, aware of being surreptitiously watched by everyone, she raised a brow and cast Dominic who was seated directly opposite her, an arch look.

'Nothing ventured nothing gained, I suppose,' Sally muttered and not to be outdone by the woman who rivalled her for beauty, made out her own cheque for fifty thousand. As she did so, she looked across at Brian and grinned waspishly. 'Prepared to lose your pants, darling?' she challenged, making everyone laugh and leaving the painter with no choice but to join in.

'You ladies have the advantage over us men,' he moaned, but his hazel eyes glinted at her with anger. 'We're all too gallant to take your money.'

Rhiannon felt her lips twitch when Dominic, who was watching her with knowing eyes, suddenly chipped in with an ironic, 'You speak for yourself.'

Andy came back with the chips and, not surprisingly, Rhiannon had the smallest pile. 'Not feeling adventurous this evening, darling?' Sally asked spitefully, pulling her own large pile of chips in front of her.

Rhiannon shrugged. 'The object of the game is to start with as few chips as possible, but leave with a whole sackful. So my Daddy told me anyway.'

Sally flushed, knowing when she'd been bested and the whole table began to laugh and applaud her reasoning. 'She sounds dangerous,' Hal commented, but kissed Sally's hand in a loving gesture that soothed the blonde's temper somewhat. But Rhiannon's remark had been meant more for Dominic than for anyone else. Glancing across at him, she raised a brow.

Yes, now he remembered. Graham had been an extraordinarily capable poker player. Not only had his nondescript face allowed him to bluff with cunning ease, but he also had an uncanny knack of knowing almost to the card what other people were holding. But had he really taught his daughter how to play? Dominic's eyes gave away none of his thoughts. Even as Ben dealt the cards, his face turned into one of statuelike implacability.

The men, their competitive instincts aroused, looked at one another and all, without fail, picked out Dominic Fairchild as the man to beat. Glancing at her cards, Rhiannon opened the bidding with a hundred, the calls going round in easy rhythm apart from Carole, who looked to her husband for guidance. Rhiannon threw out two cards and received their replacements, her face as blank as that of Dominic, who took none. Dominic bet; Hal dropped out. When Ben called and cards were displayed, Dominic held a flush, beating all of them. Rhiannon never batted an eye. The next game went to her. The third to Brian, the fourth to her.

After an hour of play, Rhiannon had more than trebled her original pile, whilst Sally Durnfield was down to her last thousand. Carole was dipping into her husband's reasonably well-stocked pile, and Hal had written out another cheque. Dominic's pile had grown almost as much as Rhiannon's. Intent as they were on their own games, only Ben, a deceptively clever player, noticed the private war going on between the two raven-haired, green-eyed players. It was, he saw, very much an even battle, although she might just have the edge. Or was Fairchild only allowing her to think so? One thing was for sure – Ben himself would never underestimate the Hawaiian.

Which was just as well, for Dominic was determined to

win. Never had Graham seriously beaten him, although they'd had a few close calls, and he was determined that Rhiannon wouldn't either. Opposite him, handling her cards with graceful hands, looking beautiful enough to hurt the eyes, Rhiannon was equally driven to win. Somehow, in the last hour, the battle of poker had become a symbol for that other battle. She could not lose now. She could not. It was time to move in for the kill. All she needed was the opportunity.

When Hal, currently dealing, handed her the ten, queen and king of diamonds, along with the three of clubs and seven of spades, it was possible that the chance she'd been waiting for was there. Although she knew the odds against getting the jack and ace were astronomical, she was confident she could bluff better than any of her opponents at the table if need be. However, nothing on her face showed her thoughts. Throwing out a thousand as an opening bid, listening to the murmurs of interest and groans of pain spread around the table, she watched the two cards she'd requested land in front of her and then picked them up. Dominic's eyes were glued to her but her eyes never flickered and he had to rely on instinct alone. Were the cards what she needed? If they were, she could have a spectacular hand. Had it paid off, or was she bluffing? Damn it, he couldn't tell. His instincts were being waylaid by the sight of her. The memory of her. The scent of her. Damn it! Keep your mind on poker, Fairchild. Looking down at his own cards, Dominic stared at three eights, the deuce of diamonds and four of spades. He'd decided to stick with the cards he'd been dealt. It always created interest when a player played the cards he'd been handed. He upped the call by five thousand. Now the rest of the table began to shift uncomfortably in their seats, but Ben, always a stirrer, immediately followed suit and cast the men bland looks that acted as more of a spur than any smug smile would have done. Both Hal and Brian cast in their lot. Sally hesitated, but unable to follow suit, reluctantly dropped out, her chips totally gone. Carole also backed out.

Dominic looked across at Rhia, his eyes narrowed. Looking steadily back at him, then down at her cards, Rhiannon tossed ten thousand on to the table. Hal immediatley folded, Ben followed, but Brian was stubborn.

Dominic saw Rhiannon's ten thousand and raised the bet. Brian promptly folded. Leaning back in his chair, Ben smiled. 'It's become an interesting game, hm?' he asked of his guests, who smiled and muttered comments. But they were all on the edge of their seats watching the pair.

Rhiannon could feel a trickle of sweat run down her back, but her eyes were blank as they looked at Dominic. She longed to ask him if he wanted to back out, but could not. Her father had told her time and time again that the one who started speaking first was the weakest player because he felt a need to boost his own confidence. So she merely gazed back at him, her eyes as limpid as a garden pool, and raised the bet yet again. She had no other choice. Dominic looked at her pile, then at his own. Piling the chips into the centre of the table, he called it. Hal let out a low whistle, whilst Carole went a little pale.

Rhiannon looked down at her cards again and then up at him. Dominic felt his guts tighten, his mouth go dry with the taste of excitement and risk. His body was flushed in the sweat caused by facing defeat or victory, but his eyes never moved from hers. Slowly he spread his cards on the table. The men let out long breaths and began to laugh nervously.

Dominic continued to stare at Rhiannon and soon all eyes turned back to her. Her face was inscrutable – as unreadable as that of an oriental, and suddenly the atmosphere changed. Sally's blue eyes sharpened on Dominic, a handsome specimen that she'd been contemplating going after, and then swung back to the English girl. Ben's chest began to ache and he let out his breath quickly.

When she laid down her first card, the ten of diamonds, you could have heard a pin drop. She never looked down at the cards as the jack of diamonds followed, then the queen. Her green eyes were fixed on him, eyes that were as hard as the emeralds they resembled, eyes that gave nothing away. Dominic glanced down only long enough to see her possible hand. A coldness invaded his guts, an awful fear seeping into his heart, but when he looked back at her his expression had not altered. Rhiannon lowered the king of diamonds, and the room began to hum with tension as she laid her final card – an ace.

Of hearts.

Everyone sagged except the two players involved. He could tell by the reaction of the others that she had lost, but only by that. Her eyes did not admit defeat but that, had he but known it was mere self-defence, for inside she was bleeding. She had begun to bleed on watching him lay down those eights.

'Goddamn if that isn't the best poker game I've seen in years.' Brian broke the silence, his lazy American drawl releasing the other guests from the spell of the game and Ben forced a smile to his face.

'So much so I fear any game after that will be something of an anti-climax.'

Rhiannon used the opportunity to look away from Dominic and forced her face into a natural smile. 'I only lost ten thousand, remember?' she said with a cheeky grin. 'Everyone else lost much more than that.'

'That's one way to look at it,' Sally said spitefully as Ben stood up and murmured politely, 'Shall we retire to the hotel for some dancing?'

'Wonderful idea,' Carole said.

Rhiannon turned to Ben and smiled sweetly. 'I think I'll change first. Ben, darling, can you have Andy bring me the jewellery case?'

Ben met her gaze with an admonishing look, but not for anything would he let her down in front of all those watching people whose interest had once again sharpened. He'd agreed back in London that it was imperative she appear super-rich and had agreed to loan her the family jewels.

Rhiannon smiled at the room in general and said graciously, 'I won't be long.'

She walked, stiff-backed and gracefully from the room and only when she was in the corridor did she begin to shake. Back in her room she took a deep, shuddering breath and collapsed on to the chair in front of her dressing table. *She'd lost.* How had she done it? And had she lost on purpose? Would she, in another game with another man, have held back on seeing that ace of hearts and waited for another hand? They had both been bluffing, but Dominic had been bluffing from a much stronger position. Why, suddenly, did that seem so ominous? Was it some sort of portent for the future?

Shaking off the eerie thought, Rhiannon accepted the jewellery case from the steward, asking him to wait outside, then she began to undress. All she wanted was to find a private hole somewhere and creep in it to lick her wounds in private. But she couldn't. And besides, the glint of fury in Dominic's eyes as she'd asked Ben for the jewellery had almost put salve on the wound. She'd needed to regain the upper hand quickly and asking Ben for the jewellery case had been an inspiration too good to pass up.

Wearily she sorted through her dresses in search of the most sumptuous, and found it in a shimmering snow-white satin dress that was reminiscent of Ancient Greece in style. Taking off her bra, she slipped on the dress that fell from one shoulder only, cutting a diagonal path across her breasts to drape loosely around her waist and fall to the floor in rippling waves. Rhiannon then stepped into high white-heeled shoes. Opening the jewellery case, she caught her breath at the sight of the gems within. Replacing the emeralds she found the necklace she was looking for in a large flat box: a web of platinum containing no fewer than twenty sparkling diamonds. It hung around her bare neck like the web from a fabulous spider. Adding matching tear-drop diamond ear-rings, she walked to the door and handed the box back to Andy, who returned it to the safe.

After a quick touch up of her make-up she headed back towards the voices, and stepped on to the deck with careless bravado. Carole was the first to see her, her voice stopping in mid-sentence, making her husband turn, his hazel eyes heating at the sight of her. Sally Durnfield went white, then said something very vicious to Hal which, mercifully, no one else heard. Ben smiled and walked towards her to take her hand. 'You look spectacular, Rhiannon,' he said softly, but loud enough for all to hear. Then under his breath he added for her ears only, 'You're playing with fire.'

'Is everyone ready?' Carole asked.

'I think I'll give the hotel a miss.' It was Dominic's voice, and Rhiannon felt herself go cold.

'Oh?' Ben looked around, about to object and attempt to persuade him, but one look into the green eyes killed the idea dead. There was a polite shuffle as they all descended into the launch and Rhiannon felt slightly nauseous as they powered over the waves, but it had nothing to do with sea-sickness.

At the hotel she danced with Hal and Brian, talked with Carole and fenced with Sally, but she was aware of being beaten. Not just in the poker game either. She was bored without Dominic. She had to admit it, even if it killed her. The night had fallen flat now that he was not there. After just two hours, she'd had enough. Leaning over she yelled to Ben above the live music that she was going back to the yacht. He nodded and watched her go whilst the other couples were on the dance floor, thus sparing her the humiliation of saying goodnight. Outside she walked through the moonlit gardens and on to the beach where she took off her shoes and dropped them into the tied-up launch.

'You're not going already, Miss Grantham?' a young Hawaiian who had stayed with the boat asked, and she shook her head.

'Not yet. I think I'll walk up the beach.'

She walked back along the sand which was still warm from the day's sunshine. She was being a coward not returning to the yacht straight away and she knew why, of course — because he was there and she just didn't have the guts to face him.

Once the lights of the hotel were behind her, she had the deserted beach to herself. Overhead a full moon illuminated the night, casting white light on to the rippling waves of the sea. A breeze rustled through the palm fronds and teased her hair. Pulling out her hairpins she let her hair blow free.

Dominic, who'd been too restless to stay on board, and had decided to go ashore for a walk, had watched her from the tree line until she was almost parallel, then he stepped out into the moonlight. She saw him at once and turned to run. He followed quickly, and as his hand came out and caught her arm in a grip that was firm enough to hurt if she struggled he said with soft menace, 'Oh no, you don't. I want a word with you.'

Rhiannon turned on him, attack being the best form of defence.

'Go to hell,' she spat, twisting her arm in an attempt to get free, and then gasping as pain shot up into her shoulders.

'You and Ben,' he snarled. 'You're not lovers. Are you? Are you?' he added, shaking her hard as she stared mutely up at him.

'No! That was just your filthy mind! If you must know, he's like a father to me . . .' Appalled at giving away so much, and even more appalled by the way it sounded so disloyal towards Graham she watched his face go ominously pale.

Slowly, Dominic nodded. 'All this time you let me think you and he were lovers. Did that please you, Rhia?' he asked savagely, and she allowed herself a triumphantly smug smile.

'Yes,' she admitted proudly. 'As a matter of fact it did. I laughed myself sick over it.'

Dominic growled — there was no other word for the guttural sound of anger that escaped him, and abruptly Rhiannon's hackles rose. It was like listening to the growl of a hidden tiger in the undergrowth, closer, much closer than you'd thought and getting ready to spring.

'I sometimes wish I could kill you,' he said softly, and ran a light finger across the delicate line of her jaw. 'Or even just want to.'

Her heart leapt in her chest as his hands curled around her waist and pulled her gently but relentlessly down into the surf with him. She felt the waves swirl around her, soaking her dress as he knelt over her. A primitive excitement began throbbing deep inside her, and panicking at its strength, she made to get up. But he was prepared, and his hands curled around her shoulders, his fingers warm and firm against her skin as he pushed her back down on the sand, his face hovering only inches above hers.

'Dominic, please,' she began, but never got the chance to say more, for his head swooped and his mouth fastened on hers with such sweet passion that she felt desire explode in her womb. An indistinct moan escaped from her mouth as her hands came up to grasp handfuls of his hair, yanking upwards but failing to dislodge his mouth from hers. Pain tingled in his scalp, but Dominic ignored it. There was no room for pain – only for blind, driving, irresistible need. The need to be inside her, the need to lose himself in her, to pound into her again and again until they both screamed.

Moments later her white dress was washed to shore, and they lay naked in the surf, the cold waves washing over her breasts, eagerly replaced by his scorching hot lips. The cool salt-water caress of the waves over her legs gave way to the rasp of his legs as he forced open her thighs with his own.

The rocking of the pounding waves accompanied the powerful thrust of his loins deep inside her, pushing into her womb, throbbing hot velvet inside her. Her back arched from the sand and thrust her tight-nippled breasts into his chest, her necklace digging into both their skins. 'Dominic,' she screamed into the night as the sky swirled above her, the silver stars flashing into streaming lines as tears filled her eyes. No one loved her, or could love her, as fully, as overwhelmingly as he did then. Her nails scored red marks into his back whilst his lips scorched her cheeks, her eyelids, her nose, her lips as he kissed her over and over again with desperate urgency.

His green eyes feasted on the sight of her face, flushed and dazed with desire as she reached orgasm, his spirit rejoicing in the way her eyes lost all sense of sanity and reality as she felt her mind float away on a bucking tide of ecstatic pleasure. And then it was his turn to melt and flow into her, his turn for bones to liquefy as his muscles collapsed and his seed spurted from him in helpless passion.

The waves took over again, washing them, rocking them, cooling molten blood until sanity once more returned to reclaim the ground it had momentarily lost. Rolling apart, they lay panting in the surf and for a long while silence reigned. Then Dominic moved his head and looked at her.

He reached out and gently pulled a strand of hair from her cheek, leaning over her and cradling her softly against him. 'You're tired of fighting, aren't you, Rhia?'

The question hit her like a thunderbolt, and quickly she

pulled herself from the drugging, addictive warmth of his body and sat up, her body stiff and aching, then rescued her hopelessly wet and ruined dress from the surf. Listlessly she pulled it over her shoulders, even that small exertion making her arms ache.

'No more than you're tired of fighting me,' she told him as he dragged himself into his own soiled clothes. His face, when he turned it back towards her, looked grim and strangely defeated and she had to fight the urge to go to him, to kiss him, to . . .

She turned and walked briskly back to the pier and told the young steward to have the night off. Dominic, who had matched his steps to hers, watched as she pushed her dripping hair off her forehead with a shaking hand. 'Is it so impossible for us to stop fighting?' he asked her as the young man happily jogged away. 'Even now?' But his voice was not hopeful.

'How can we?' she asked, in what was meant to be a scornful voice. 'Nothing's changed. Or are you trying to tell me you love me now?'

'Damn you!' he erupted angrily. 'I could never love you. You're nothing but a cold, vengeful, ignorant . . . *witch*,' he spat. Suddenly Dominic was furious with her. Did she have to mock the possibility of love between them so . . . so . . . *unthinkingly*? Was it so hard for her to contemplate that love was possible between them? But wasn't it, a little voice deep inside himself mocked his anger. And wasn't he being the biggest idiot around, letting himself fall for her so completely?

He took her totally by surprise when the glinting of her necklace speared his eyes and became a symbol of all he hated, reminding him of the fool he'd been – and still was. Reaching out he yanked it from her, the chain digging into her skin before it broke, leaving a tiny red weal on her nape. Flinging it far away from him, as if it were contaminated with some ugly disease, the necklace hit the sea with a tiny splash and then sank, its million-dollar brilliance destined to shine only for the fish. Rhiannon looked to where the tiny splash still caused ripples on the surface, but her brain was incapable of working. She supposed she should be afraid of what Ben would say. Or should she be ashamed of herself for wearing it? Or mad at him for throwing it away? She was too tired to know. Or care.

'Just get into the boat, Rhiannon,' he sighed, unknowingly mirroring her own soul-deep weariness. With a mechanical grace she obeyed him, sinking into the padded chair and wondering how she was ever going to find the strength to get out again. Her body throbbed with the remembrance of shattering pleasure but her head throbbed with a headache born of despair.

Steering the boat towards the yacht, Dominic took a deep calming breath. 'Graham always was a twisted bastard,' he said irrelevantly.

Rhiannon, with total disregard for her own safety, smiled grimly. 'Like father like daughter?'

'Ahoy there! Welcome back.' The cheerful voice belonged to Ben, who was leaning on the railings watching them. Hurriedly she clambered up the stairs, taking Ben's proffered hand and walking to the furthest side of the deck. 'Your dress . . .' He never completed the sentence. Dominic, who was similarly bedraggled, oozed elemental, tightly controlled rage and Ben took a step backwards as Dominic set foot on the deck.

Ignoring Ben he stared at Rhiannon's back. 'You'd better keep away from me,' he warned, his voice tired but quite lethal, 'while you still can.'

Apart from her back stiffening even more she gave no other sign that she had even heard him. It was not until his footsteps had receded and disappeared altogether that she slowly collapsed into the nearest lounger.

Ben stared at the doorway through which the tall Hawaiian had disappeared then turned to look down at her. 'What on earth happened?'

Rhiannon looked up at him with bruised eyes, and remembered the necklace.

'I lost your necklace by the pier,' she said simply. 'I'm sorry.'

'It is not important. The water's shallow over there, and the divers will soon find it tomorrow. Are you all right?'

Rhiannon's grin was pure irony. 'Not nearly,' she responded with total truth.

'You did something to him tonight,' Ben said sharply. 'What?'

Rhiannon looked up at him, her blank mind struggling to work, but for the life of her she couldn't find the answer, although she knew Ben was right. Something *had* happened tonight. 'You know,' she said with a wobbling smile, 'I really haven't got the faintest idea.'

'He looks like a man ready to hit back,' Ben warned her. Never before had he felt a man's anger more palpably than just now. Yet there had been more than rage in the Hawaiian's eyes. Much more. 'Be careful, Rhia,' he said softly.

Rhiannon looked out across the ocean, a breeze making her chilled skin erupt into gooseflesh. 'Don't worry – I will be,' she said, thinking of Sandy's radio call, thinking of Farron and the will. 'I have it all under control.'

In his cabin, Dominic lay on his bunk, staring at the ceiling with burning eyes. He knew she was going to give him no other choice but to destroy her and he felt his heart crack and splinter in his chest.

Chapter 39

'Hello – you're looking chipper this morning.' Vince looked up and smiled as Vienna walked in, immediately searching her face for signs of strain, and found instead that her eyes were shining brightly in excitement.

'So I should be.' She put down her bag and sat in the chair opposite him, her movements relaxed and familiar, a sure sign that she had begun to trust him.

'Oh?' He let the syllable do the asking.

'Do you remember I told you about a memory of a place that we thought was Switzerland? Well, I sent off for some brochures and they came yesterday. I couldn't believe it when I thought I recognized a place.'

Vince sat up and she quickly waved a hand in the air, misinterpreting his sudden sharp interest. 'Oh, not a specific place, and not a memory exactly, more like a feeling of familiarity. You know what I mean?'

'Yes. But I . . .' Vince swallowed the saliva that fear had brought to his mouth, but was interrupted before he could say more to bring her down.

'I've written to all the schools in the Oberland, enclosing a photo of myself, and if any of them writes back then we'll probably be going over there.'

'No!' Vince shot up in his chair. 'You mustn't!'

For the first time, Vienna noted his intense unease. After a good night's sleep Farron had woken her with a breakfast in bed, a loving kiss, and the admonishment not to worry about them not making love. 'It's only stress,' he'd whispered. 'I can wait.' His understanding, and his patience and loyalty had made her cry, and they had spent almost an hour just hugging and kissing, the closeness without passion spreading a warmth and feeling of well-being throughout her body and soul. Now her euphoria slowly evaporated with the look of near-panic on Vince Drake's face.

'Why not?' her voice was both defiant and yet obviously

scared. 'Is there some reason I shouldn't go abroad, Vince?' Her hands wrung tight in her lap as the fear escalated.

'Well, travel at this time might be inadvisable,' he said mildly. Any attempt to forbid her outright would only make her dig her heels in.

'But why do you think I shouldn't go?' she pressed.

'Well, to stop the hypnosis now might be detrimental.'

'But we'll be coming back after a week. And if I know who I am, and can tell you a name, surely you can use that to trigger off something in my memory if I still haven't recovered it when I'm over there?'

Vince licked his lips. Her logic was faultless and a change of tack was needed. Hints – they would to the trick. Innuendo, enough to plant seeds of fear and self-doubt in her mind. 'I think it will be best if you don't leave the islands – just for a little while longer,' he began earnestly. 'You must understand that you've been through a very harrowing time, and during hypnosis, the emotions involved have been brought closer and closer to the surface of your conscious mind.'

'Are you saying I might *flip* while I'm in Switzerland?'

Vince shifted in his chair. 'Think of this: what if finding out who you are brings everything back – and it's bad. You'll be in a foreign country, scared and without proper help. It could do a lot of damage, to yourself and . . .' He deliberately let the words trail off, as if angry at himself for nearly slipping.

She picked up on it instantly. 'And?' she prompted, her face paler than he'd ever seen it. She was sitting on the very edge of her chair. In the face of his continuing silence, she pressed, 'And what, Doctor? Come on, spit it out, please, Vince! This tiptoeing around is driving me crazy!' Then, as she realized what she'd said, she felt a half-hysterical smile flash on to her face. 'Sorry, I didn't mean to put it quite like that.' Vince smiled, but without humour, and she took a deep, calming breath. 'Please, Vince – tell me.'

With seeming reluctance he asked, 'You'll be with Farron, yes?'

'Yes.'

'Then perhaps you should think of the . . . strain on him,

too? All I'm asking is that you think it over. Just think about postponing, not abandoning, any trip.'

Strain, he'd said. But she had the sudden conviction that he'd meant to say danger. Was she a danger to Farron? To anyone? Was that what he was getting at? Vince saw her eyes widen in shock as she picked up the hint with almost uncanny intuition, and he looked down, swallowing hard.

'You said it could be bad, if I remembered. What did you mean by that exactly?'

Vince made himself look uncomfortable. He cleared his throat and didn't quite meet her eyes as he began to speak. 'Well, trauma is a very emotional and unpredictable thing, Vienna. Farron for all he loves you, wouldn't know what to do if you went into shock, for example.'

'I see,' she said, but her voice was cool. 'They do have doctors in Switzerland, Vince. I believe that modern psychiatry was more or less founded in that country, wasn't it?'

'Yes. But they . . .' He was arguing with her, the worst possible thing he could do, so he shrugged and began to backtrack a little. 'Well, it's up to you, of course.'

'Yes, it is,' Vienna reiterated. 'And nothing is going to stop me from finding out who I am. No matter how much it hurts, or what I have to do.' She looked at him hardly, and in spite of the exhaustion written clearly on her face, Vince knew determination when he saw it. He broke out in a cold, cold sweat.

'So long as you come to me straight afterwards, Vienna. Please.' Vince was the kind of man who would take whatever he could get.

'I never thought of doing anything else.' She smiled tremulously at his words, relieved that the nearly-unpleasant scene was over. Not that she felt she needed his permission – she was in charge of her own life. But the reasons behind his objections worried her. Nagged at her. And more than that – they scared her.

'Good.' Vince smiled, but he was nearly as pale as she was by now. 'You know,' he carried on, his tone thoughtful and yet firm, 'there's a great gap between how we see ourselves and how others see us.'

'Yes, I can imagine. Sometimes I'm scared of finding out who I am in case – and I know this sounds funny – but in case I don't like me.'

Vince nodded. 'That's a common fear, even amongst those of us with perfect memories. It's nothing to concern yourself about.' But he didn't sound sure and again her skin broke out in a cold sweat.

'Vince – you have told me everything, haven't you?'

'Yes, of course I have!' He dismissed this airily and much too quickly, then compounded it by rapidly changing the subject. 'I know what I meant to ask you. Do you have that list I asked you to jot down of all the times you lost your temper?'

Her lips tightened but she reached silently into her bag and handed it over. Vince glanced at it with total absorption and when he looked up at her, his face was blank. 'Well, shall we begin?' he asked heartily, reaching for the kaleidoscope torch as Vienna got up and lay down on the couch. It took him longer than usual to relax her and put her under. When she opened her eyes again she had the usual few minutes of feeling totally relaxed, happy, and confident. But it did not last. The first time the feeling had lasted all day. The second time, only all morning. Now, sitting facing him, after that last session, the feeling of well-being had already gone.

'It's still only half-past ten,' Vienna said in surprise when she noted the plain and simple clock on the wall behind his desk.

'Yes. I wanted to spend the last half hour on those tests we talked about.'

'Oh. Yes.'

'Is something wrong?' he asked innocently. 'You don't look very eager.'

Vienna made herself laugh. 'I'm just chicken.'

'Don't worry. It's nothing too heavy, I promise. We'll start off with word association.' He reached for a tape recorder and switched it on. Vienna stared at it for a second, but made no objection. What was the point? Her lethargy was getting daily more pronounced, and she promised herself to do something about it soon.

'Right – I want you to clear your mind. I'm going to say a word, and I don't want you to think about it at all. I just want you to say the first word that comes into your head. So if I say "Sun" I don't want you to think "Sun . . . hm, sun is hot" and say "Hot". If the first word that comes into your head when I say "Sun" is something totally strange, like . . . oh, I don't know – "shoelace" then say shoelace, OK?' He smiled to illustrate the ridiculousness of the answer, and Vienna slowly relaxed back in her chair.

'OK I'm ready.'

'Good. Black.'

'White.'

'Funny.'

'Sad.'

'Bird.'

'Air.'

'Candle.'

'Light.'

'Dog.'

'Cat.'

It went on for ten minutes, the words becoming less and less innocuous, with less obvious opposites. Some of her answers amused and intrigued her. When Vince said 'School' she said 'Curtains'. Why, she hadn't a clue. But towards the end she became more and more nervous when he began to come up with words like anger, danger, fear and death.

'All right, that's enough of that.' Vince finally called a halt when her answers got slower in coming. 'That wasn't so hard, was it?'

Vienna shook her head, but wondered just how much she had revealed during the seemingly innocent game.

'These are ink-blots.' Vince withdrew some stiff cards from his desk drawer, laying them face-down on the table-top between them. 'They're just shapes, but I want you to tell me what they remind you of. All right?'

'What if they don't remind me of anything?'

'Then say so.'

'OK.' The ink-blots were less harrowing than the word games as she turned the cards this way and that, seeing in them pictures of baskets of flowers, flying birds, fighting cats, rivers with trees and watering cans.

It was eleven o'clock when she left, in very much of a mixed mood.

'You sure she won't remember me being present when you put her under?' The voice made Vince spin around as he closed the door after her, and he walked quickly to the intercom and told Vera to hold his next patient until he called her. 'Positive,' he said crisply, wishing Jago would quickly leave.

Richard walked to the window and looked down. The profile that was turned to him was almost classically handsome. But inside that head – Vince could only suspect what horrors were there. 'You didn't do a very good job of keeping her here,' Richard commented, almost mildly.

'No. And I don't have much hope that the hypnotic suggestion that she should not go will have much effect, either. As I told her, you can't make someone do something under hypnosis that they really have a strong objection to doing in a conscious state.'

'Whatever. But it does mean we'll have to step it up a little from now on.'

'We can't go much faster than we just did,' Vince said sourly. 'We ran her through that fictitious night over and over.'

Richard grunted, fighting a silent battle with himself. Ever since he'd first thought of using hypnosis in order to destroy her, a question had been burning in his mind and only his reluctance to share the thought with Drake had kept him silent for so long. But now he could feel time running out – for her, and for him. Naturally, it would happen to them both. How could it not? They were bound together by things that she didn't see and wouldn't admit. Why, Richard wondered with both burning anger and harrowing sadness, did she not see that? If only she would then they could both be so happy. He sighed deeply and closing his eyes ran his fingers over them, seeing coloured lights flash against the darkness. Opening them again, he saw Vince watching him closely, and drew himself up to his full height, his eyes flashing as cold as arctic steel. 'Drake.'

'What?' Vince looked at him warily, alerted by the tone and intimidated by that arch look he was getting.

'Can you make her love me?' He spat out the words reluctantly, making them almost vicious, but Vince knew how much they had cost him.

Consequently he was not as smug as he might have been when he shook his head. 'No, I can't. I'm sorry.' He wasn't sorry, not at all. The thought of that lovely girl loving this maniac was painful.

'If I find out you're lying to me,' Richard walked to the window and looked out absently, 'I'll kill you.'

'I know.' Vince amazed himself with his own courage. 'But it's a romantic fallacy that a hypnotist can make people fall in love. It goes with love potions and magic spells – it's all totally unreal.'

Richard looked out over tall buildings 'shimmering in the heat haze, feeling blissfully numb. He had known, or at least guessed, what the answer would be. Vince watched him and shivered. There was something tragic and yet terrifying about Richard Jago. For a second Vince could almost wish he'd never met the man and was now safely ensconced in a hospital somewhere with a couple of broken legs, courtesy of Frank Gillespie.

'You're warped, Jago,' Vince told him, without heat. 'Totally warped.'

'That intense desire you're giving her to confess,' Richard began, ignoring the other man's words. 'How long before it becomes irresistible?'

Vince sighed. 'Not long. Tell me, what will you do if the cops arrest the real killer in the meantime?'

'Then I'll think of something else, of course.'

VIENNA was on the bus heading for home since the car was in the garage with a busted fuel pump. The sun shone brightly through the window, making her perspire and squint her eyes, but she was miles away.

In spite of Farron saying it didn't matter, her coldness in bed had worried her. Worrying her too was the reason why Vince had been so against her going to Switzerland. And then it happened. One second she was on the bus watching shoppers go by with laden bags and the next second she was assailed by a feeling so intense it made her reach out and grab the headrest of the seat in front of her. Pure misery seemed to have been injected into her bloodstream like a poison. How she knew, she was not sure, but suddenly she knew: she had done something terrible, horrible, unforgivable.

'Hey, dearie, you all right?' The voice belonged to the overweight, middle-aged woman seated next to her, and as Vienna looked across at her the woman's kind and concerned face grew even more alarmed. 'You're white! Are you sick?'

'Sick? Yes,' Vienna said weakly, grasping the excuse offered her. 'I have to get off,' she said, standing up on legs that shook badly. Staggering up the aisle, she stood behind the driver praying for the next stop to come soon. When it did she staggered on to the sidewalk where the heat immediately attacked her. Stumbling to the brick wall of the nearest building she rubbed her forehead and closed her eyes against the sun's glare. A mistake. Instantly Gary Lyons was there, and she saw a hand raised, fingers curling around the handle of a wicked blade. But it was not he who held it, but herself. Vienna pressed herself against the wall as she felt her hand push the knife into his flesh and winced as she heard the squelching sound it made as it dug into him. She forced her eyes open and looked at the world of reality revolving around her; she saw couples walking hand in hand and kissing, several busy women with loaded grocery bags and others who watched her briefly with curiosity before passing by and going on to homes and children or jobs.

Spotting a café two stores down, she walked inside on trembling legs, paid for a coffee, sat at a table and stirred the spoon around absently.

'Would you like anything else?' A blonde, gum-chewing waitress hovered over her, notebook and pen at the ready.

Yes, she thought. I'd like to confess to a murder, please. With a monumental effort of will, she shook her head. The waitress wandered away, her heavily-mascaraed lashes not even blinking. Raising the cup to her mouth, Vienna's hands shook so much that she spilled coffee into the saucer. She forced herself to drink it, then quickly left. She had to think logically.

She hailed a taxi but once inside it took her a moment to remember her own address. Turning her pale and tense face into the breeze she told herself, 'I'm all right, I'm all right, I'm all right . . .' The three words became a litany that she silently repeated over and over in her head as she waited to get home.

Farron looked up out of the kitchen window as the taxi pulled to a halt, frowning as Vienna alighted, looking like a sleepwalker. She swayed as she closed the door, looking ready to fall in a heap as she searched her bag for money to pay the fare. He left the small bungalow at a run, meeting her half-way up the path, his footsteps faltering as he saw the dazed, uncomprehending look in her eyes. He smelt fear in the air — his own. 'What happened?'

She shook her head mutely, and Farron's arms came around her as they slowly walked up the path towards their home. 'That damned doctor,' Farron muttered angrily. 'How could he let you leave on your own when you were like this?'

'It wasn't his fault,' Vienna found her voice at last but it sounded almost disembodied, as if she was hearing it from a long long way away. 'I was fine when I left his office. It happened on the bus.'

'What happened, darling?' he asked softly, his arms hugging her tighter as he opened the door and slowly guided her into the house.

'I don't know.' She shook her head, her blonde hair flying in the air, caressing his cheek as it touched him. 'I just suddenly . . . knew.'

Farron swallowed hard. He'd never seen her so vague before, or so out of it. 'What did you know, sweetheart?' he probed softly and with infinite tenderness as he sat her on the settee. Quickly he was beside her, swivelling his body towards her, one leg under him as he gently put a finger under a chin and turned her to face him. 'What did you know, Vienna?'

'That I'd done something terrible.'

'You haven't done anything terrible, my love. You're only scared that you have — that's different. How can I convince you?' Reaching forward he kissed her, his mouth comforting and warm. Vienna clung to him, her small body leaning into his with fervent need. For a long while he just held her, rocking her back and forth in that age-old, wordless expression of comfort. 'Why don't we get married?' he whispered at last, and when she pulled away to look at him, the vacant expression was gone.

'Married?' she breathed, her face smiling with uncertain joy and then clouding again, seconds later.

'Why not?' Farron urged. 'We love each other.'

'What if I'm already married?'

'You didn't have a ring.'

'Oh, that doesn't mean anything. Can't you see, Farron? I don't KNOW. I'm supposed to guess. And what if I guess wrong?' Her voice was tight with angry frustration, her eyes bright with unshed tears, and in them Farron saw the answer written as clearly as words on paper.

'And until you do know, the answer's no, isn't it?'

Miserably she pulled away, and nodded. 'It has to be, you must see that?'

'All right,' Farron said slowly. 'I can wait.' But he wondered if she was using her loss of memory as an excuse. If she didn't really *want* to marry him, what could be easier than to put him off?

'It's not that I don't love you,' she assured him. 'I love you more now than I've ever done. It's just that we can't marry until I know what I've done.'

'You haven't done anything!' Farron said sharply, then forced himself to relax. Getting impatient, even when it was only because he was so worried about her, would only do even more harm. 'I have a surprise for you.'

She smiled weakly. 'A surprise? What?' She was glad, more glad than she could say, that Farron was taking it all so well and that he wasn't going to argue with her. She didn't think she could have taken that.

'Come on.' He stood up and crooked his finger, leading her into the kitchen. Lifting a small cardboard box from the floor and putting it on the table, Farron took a step backwards. 'Take a look.' Glancing at him questioningly and then unfolding the top of the box, Vienna looked down, her face softening instantly at what she saw.

'Oh, Farron!' she breathed, reaching in with gentle hands

and cupping the black and white furry ball that was sleeping inside. The kitten that emerged into the daylight blinked wide blue eyes and yawned slightly, white whiskers twitching, still-soft claws coming out of tiny paws and digging without pain into her hand. Drawing it to her breast, her fingers soft and gentle as they stroked the downy-soft black head, Vienna felt her eyes mist over. 'He's lovely,' she said, her voice wobbling precariously.

'I got him from an animal rescue centre. Someone saw a bag in the river and it was moving. When they hooked it out and looked inside they found this little tyke and six of his brothers and sisters.'

'Oh no! How can anyone be so cruel?'

Farron shrugged and said quickly, 'What do you want to call him?' He didn't want her to dwell on the kitten's near-death. Her emotions were too precarious, her moodswings too wild and sudden for him to chance setting off anything else.

Vienna looked down as the kitten mewed. 'Oh it's all right, precious,' she whispered, rubbing the kitten's head with her cheek. 'He's a demanding little fellow, isn't he?' Farron smiled as the kitten began to purr loudly in appreciation of the caress he was receiving.

'Yes,' she mused softly. 'Like a professor.'

'Professor?' Farron said, then smiled. 'Hey, that's not a bad name. Cats do have the same snooty, know-it-all looks that professors have. Ever noticed that?'

'Professor.' Vienna looked down at the kitten which stared back at her, baby blue eyes loving and innocent. 'Professor you are then.' And Farron leaned forward and kissed her in spite of the fact that her lips were still cold.

THE huge military ships anchored at Pearl Harbour were giant grey monoliths, war-machines of awesome power. Frank took another bite out of his hotdog and looked out over the famous harbour whose destruction had finally brought the US into World War Two.

He turned to look at his first real love, who'd changed easily into his best friend over twenty years ago, and offered her a bite. Gloria smiled and shook her head. 'Not just now, thanks. You forget – to me this feels like the middle of the night.'

He grunted and took another bite, chewing thoughtfully. 'So, how are things?'

Gloria shrugged. 'Fine.'

'Has Wanda called you yet?'

'Hm, this morning. She's happy to be back stateside and settling in well apparently. I recommended her to Madge McGinty – she'll take care of her.'

'Good. I feel safer with her out of the way. Especially with your Lieutenant Clements still sniffing about.'

Gloria smiled. 'He's not my Lieutenant as you kindly put it.'

Frank gave her a sly grin. 'Admit it – you fancy him rotten.'

'I like him – in a way,' Gloria corrected, almost primly.

Frank laughed. Gloria still had to be the least likely madam he'd ever met. 'Did you know he was at Fairchild's birthday party?' Frank dropped the bombshell casually into the conversation, and Gloria did a quick doubletake.

'You're kidding?'

'No.' Frank shook his head and contemplated his hotdog, overflowing with onions and ketchup.

'Good God Almighty.' Gloria strung out the words tellingly as Frank licked some ketchup from his hands.

'He certainly gets about, that nice Lieutenant of yours.'

'Shut up, Frank.'

The casino-owner grinned, then tossed a piece of his bread to the seagulls, before asking more seriously, 'How's the girl doing?'

Gloria bit her lip. She knew this was inevitable but she was not looking forward to it. If she didn't tell Frank someone else would, and that would do irreparable harm to their relationship. She sighed and said shortly, 'She's seeing a hypnotist.'

Frank nodded. He already knew. And although he had not really doubted she'd tell him, he did feel his mind settle more easily. For the first time ever, he'd actually wondered about Gloria's loyalty. It just went to show how protective she was of the girl. It annoyed Frank that she refused to give him any real explanation for it. 'You know that if she gets her memory back,' he began warningly, and by his side she stirred restlessly.

'Yes.' Her voice was raised sharply, anger palpable on her face. 'I know. You don't have to keep reminding me. And I'll deal with it, Frank.'

He held up his hands in surrender. 'OK, OK. No argument here.'

'Besides, nothing might come of it.'

'True,' he agreed then asked carefully, 'Do you know something I don't, Glory?'

'Like what?'

'I just get the feeling you're playing with an ace up your sleeve.'

Gloria smiled a trifle sadly. If only you knew, she thought wistfully. Oh Frank, if only you knew. 'You have nothing to worry about, Frankie,' she teased him with his childhood and much-hated nickname. 'If the worst comes to the worst, I'll confess to *my* Lieutenant,' she stressed wryly, 'that I killed Lyons.'

Frank sighed heavily. 'You're not still talking that rot are you?' he asked, disgust written clearly on his face. 'I'd have thought you'd gotten over that by now. No one but an idiot confesses to a murder she didn't commit.'

Gloria shrugged, but wouldn't argue. 'The point is, you're in the clear, no matter what. So leave the girl alone, Frank.'

'I got the message loud and clear. You don't have to keep ramming it down my throat,' he grumbled and Gloria smiled.

'Hurt your feelings, have I?' she teased, and in spite of himself Frank felt his lips curl.

'You know me so well,' he drawled, attractive crow's feet forming around his eyes.

'From shit-poor Bronx punk, to whizkid businessman, kiddo.'

'I can't say the same for you,' Frank said moodily, disinclined to let it go. 'I can't understand why you want to take the rap for Lyons.'

'Don't, Frank.'

But Frank wouldn't back down. 'Just because you confess, it won't change the facts.'

'It was an accident,' Gloria said sharply.

'Not much difference.'

'All the difference in the world,' Gloria snapped back, her face becoming flushed. 'Lyons was beating up Wanda; for Christ's sake he had a knife and was going to kill her!'

Frank looked at her thoughtfully. 'What I can't understand is what a tourist was doing in that alley in the first place.'

Gloria looked out over the huge ships, and shrugged her shoulders. 'Lost, probably,' she lied. 'But lucky for Wanda. If he hadn't been hit with that garbage can lid, she'd be dead – of that you can be sure.'

'I'll take your word for it,' Frank said. 'That garbage can lid must have caught him one hell of a clump, though.'

'It did.' Gloria shuddered. 'You should have seen her face when she heard it crash against his head. Ughh ...' she shuddered at the remembrance of it, the horror still very much alive in her mind.

'Accident, self-defence, call it what you like,' Frank said briskly. 'It doesn't change the fact that Vienna Wright killed Gary Lyons.'

Chapter 40

Rhiannon eased her hand on the throttle of the powerful Norton, came to a rolling stop and cut the engine. Taking off her helmet she let her hair fly loose around her head before pulling off her gloves and tossing them into the helmet. Spread out before her was the vista of the Punchbowl, one of Honolulu's three heights. In the olden days the Punchbowl had been the site of human sacrifice and she had chosen it deliberately for that very reason when Sandy had spoken to her on the yacht.

Human sacrifice – in this case Dominic Fairchild. It was, she thought with a hurtful wrench in her chest, the only fitting place for a Prince of Hawaiian blood to have his fate sealed. She saw Sandy immediately and beside him was a man of medium height with short dark hair and watchful brown eyes. As she walked towards them the stranger half-turned to Sandy.

'She's stunning,' Bryan Canon said quietly. 'Why the hell didn't you tell me?'

'Don't let the looks fool you,' Sandy advised. 'She wouldn't want you if she was a veritable angel now, would she?'

Bryan already knew that and his compliment in no way meant that he'd been smitten. At twenty-two he was both intelligent and streetwise, the combination serving to both keep him out of jail and make him comfortably well-off.

'*Aloha*,' Rhiannon said softly as she drew level with them, her voice pleasant and English. Walking to a rustic-looking wooden bench she sat down, crossing her booted legs at the ankles.

'*Aloha*,' Sandy responded, walking towards her with his hands thrust deeply into his pockets. 'This is Bryan.' Sandy was careful not to give her his last name.

'Bryan,' she nodded. 'I'm Rhia.'

Bryan sat down beside her. 'I know.'

It was simply said, but it told Rhiannon all she needed to

know. The man had checked her out – for all his boyish good looks and innocent air, he probably knew as much about her as documentation could tell him. Yes – he was just what was needed. Smart, cautious, and hungry. She had not missed the gold gleam of his watch, nor the gold and onyx signet ring that he wore on his right hand.

'Sandy,' she turned to look at the photographer who was hovering in front of them, obviously ill-at-ease and feeling out of place. 'I believe this is yours?' She zipped down the front of her jacket and extracted a tightly-padded envelope.

Sandy's face cleared as he reached for the package, slipping it into the back pocket of his own jeans without even opening it. Bryan found that interesting. It meant he either trusted her, or wasn't prepared to argue over it if it came up short. Somehow, Bryan did not think she had undercut him. The woman had an air of confidence and also of class that boded well for any future business dealings. Whilst not prepared to commit himself until he was totally satisfied, Bryan sensed a good feeling coming on. He always felt good when a challenging well-paid job was on the cards.

'Thanks, Miss Grantham.' As both of them continued to watch him in silence, he nodded, turned and quickly walked away. Until he was out of sight, neither of them said a word.

Bryan smiled. 'I like a discreet woman.'

'I thought Sandy was your friend?'

'Whatever gave you that idea?'

The voice, she noted, sounded as young as he looked. But in his line of work she could well understand how a fresh-faced innocent look and guileless voice might well come in very handy. 'I see you like the good things in life, Bryan,' she commented casually. 'The job pays well.'

Bryan lit a cigarette and said nothing. He was in no hurry. Many of his colleagues had copped out by rushing in too quickly, letting greed get in the way of common sense. He was sitting easily on the bench, his cream cotton shirt hanging loose and coolly on his slender shoulders, the black cotton trousers crisp and stylish.

His appearance was deceptive and that went a long way towards helping her make up her mind. Anyone but the best and Dominic would spot him. Dominic was no fool. 'How did you come to be a . . . how shall we put it?' she smiled almost whimsically. 'Less than law-abiding citizen?'

'What makes you think I'm not totally law-abiding?'

For a long second Rhiannon looked at him, green eyes meeting brown with mutual understanding and the glimmerings of mutual respect. Then she slowly shrugged her shoulders. 'If you are,' she pointed out with quiet regret, 'then you're not only the wrong man for the job, but you're also the man who isn't going to get paid twenty thousand dollars for a single night's work.'

Bryan's eyes never flickered at the mention of the sum, but by then Rhiannon had not expected that they would. The younger man looked away from her, facing forward for a few seconds as he digested it. He hadn't expected twenty thousand. Five to ten had been his estimate, but since Sandy couldn't tell him what she wanted him for, he'd been guessing blind. But twenty thou was very handy. Very. Of course, it all depended on what she wanted him to do. 'That's a lot of money,' he agreed sensibly. 'But I'm not a hired killer.'

'I'm very glad to hear it,' she said, suddenly feeling cold.

'So – what is it you want done?' Bryan asked simply.

There it was, she thought. As simple as that. *What do you want done?* The fencing was over, the weighing-up over, and both had silently agreed they could do business. Now, at this site of human sacrifice, all she had to do was say what she wanted done, and that was that. She was not aware that she had gone a little pale, but Bryan's sharp eyes missed nothing. With a flash of insight that had extricated him from more trouble than bribes to the right people, he realized that whatever it was she wanted, she wasn't looking forward to having it done. And that did surprise him, for every indication was that she was a lady who knew exactly what she wanted and how to get it.

'If you're not sure, don't do it.' The words, and the advice they contained, surprised her. Not to do it would mean a loss to him of twenty thousand dollars, and she was sure Bryan Whoever-he-was didn't give up that much money easily.

'Don't worry, I'm sure,' she reassured him. 'OK – the

situation is this,' she began quickly, anxious to get it all over and done with. Bryan didn't move but his ears pricked up, like a cat catching the sound of a rustling mouse. 'There's a certain man who is kept under strict control by a will which contains a morality clause. Needless to say, the inheritance is huge and he's been very careful·and very discreet.'

Bryan nodded. 'Sounds like something out of the Ark.'

'The will was written nearly thirty years ago.'

Bryan whistled. 'And the poor sap's lived with it for that long?'

Rhiannon couldn't help but smile at the thought of Dominic being described as a poor sap. 'He had no choice,' she said drily, 'or believe me, he would have smashed the will in court.'

'Go on.'

'It's simple,' she shrugged, and glanced at him out of the corner of her eye, 'and I'm sure you've already guessed what I want.'

'Yeah,' he admitted, dropping his cigarette on to the concrete beneath him and stamping it out with the toe of his shoe. 'You want the will blown wide open.'

'Wide,' she nodded. 'Really wide.' She stretched the word to emphasize it. 'I need strong, irrefutable evidence that will stand up in court so that when the will is contested no lawyer, no matter how slick, can save the day.'

'That's easy enough,' he said and Rhiannon felt a chill run through her.

'How can you get the evidence?'

Bryan didn't usually discuss his methods with clients, but he had a shrewd idea it was best to handle this woman straight. 'First I follow him and see if he plays with anyone. Is he gay, by the way?'

Rhiannon blinked. 'Er, no. No.' She smiled at the thought after she'd recovered from the shock, and shook her head.

'Hm. In this day and age, nookie with a chick might not break a morality clause. What was immoral thirty years ago isn't so immoral today.'

'What do you suggest?' she asked, fascinated by her glimpse of the seedier, darker side of life in spite of herself.

'There is a simple way,' Bryan said thoughtfully. 'Follow the mark until he goes to a bar or nightclub, slip him a mickey, then rush in to save the day and take him home. Home being a little well-known *lomi-lomi* parlour where the ladies have been known to solicit customers. Strip him, get a couple of girls to pose, and there you have it.'

Rhiannon felt sickened by this coldblooded recital, but made herself continue. 'What's *lomi-lomi*?' she asked, to give herself time.

'Massage parlour.'

A thought suddenly hit her, and she straightened quickly on the bench, all traces of nonchalance gone. 'He mustn't be hurt,' she warned, her lovely face suddenly menacing. 'If he's hurt you'll be so sorry you won't . . .'

Bryan frowned, for the first time getting angry. 'Look lady, I told you I'm no hit man. Hurting people isn't my business. If you want someone worked over you go to the clubs and hire some bouncers. All right?'

'What kind of drug would you give him? If you had to follow him?'

Brian shrugged. 'Standard knock-out drops – I have a contact at a hospital. No side-effects apart from a headache, no chance of respiratory failure, or heart failure, or anything else.'

'Is that guaranteed?' Her voice was still as hard as granite.

Bryan nodded. 'It is.'

'It had better be. Just because I don't know your last name doesn't mean I won't be able to find you if something goes wrong and you hurt him.'

Bryan looked into her pale face with its fierce green eyes and slowly nodded. 'I believe you,' he assured her. 'And you should believe me. I'm a professional – I'm good at what I do. If I wasn't I'd be out of business. And besides all that,' he leaned back against the bench, holding her eyes with his as he did so, 'Do you think I'm stupid enough to risk a murder charge? No way would I do that, ever. Not for twenty million, let alone twenty thousand.'

Slowly she relaxed. 'So long as that's clear.'

'It is,' Bryan told her. But her vehemence had pleased him.

In spite of his work he did not like violence. He'd turned down more jobs because he didn't like or trust the client than because the money wasn't good enough. In many ways, Bryan Canon had strict moral standards. 'You're something of an enigma, you know that?' he challenged her now, and Rhiannon smiled.

'So I've been told.'

'Often, I bet.'

'Often enough.'

'Most of the people I work for don't give a fig for their victim,' Bryan commented in all innocence, but his choice of words was unfortunate. It was 'victim' that did it, catching her totally on the raw.

'Let's get one thing straight. I'm the victim here – not him. Got that?'

Bryan looked momentarily surprised then shook his head. 'I don't really want to know. It's none of my business, after all. Just tell me when, and who.'

Rhiannon licked lips gone suddenly dry. It was no longer a game; it was ugly and mean and she hated it. It was only by remembering Graham, reminding herself of the binding qualities of a promise made to him on his deathbed that allowed her to carry on. Her voice was bleak and cold. 'I want it done within two weeks at the most. Is that possible?'

'It's a bit tight, but I can do it. Do you have a picture of the guy?'

'You won't need one,' Rhiannon said grimly. 'His name is Dominic Fairchild.'

Bryan's eyes rounded. 'Dominic Fairchild? Shit!' He'd known she and Fairchild had a running business battle going on but it had not occurred to him that it was personal. And whatever else this set-up was, it was deeply personal, of that he was sure. It was written all over her. But Fairchild? 'If I'd known who it was I'd have upped the price,' he joked, giving himself a chance to adjust. 'Hitting Fairchild is like taking on the mafia.'

'I'll give you another twenty thousand after the will is broken in court,' she offered temptingly, but her voice was dead and toneless and he cast her a quick, searching look. She didn't have to do that, but he wasn't going to argue with her. For forty thousand dollars he'd do even Dominic Fairchild. He was good – the best. He was careful. No one would trace him, of that he was confident. But a gallant streak he wasn't aware he possessed, made him hesitate.

'You know, the feud between you is fairly common knowledge.'

Rhiannon almost laughed. 'After the pieces in the gossip and financial columns, I'd say it was widespread public knowledge.'

'Exactly. After the will thing comes out he's going to guess it was you.'

Rhiannon saw the concern in his brown eyes and felt strangely touched by it. 'He won't have to guess, Bryan. I'll tell him.'

'Tell him? Are you crazy? Do you know who he is?'

'Oh, yes – I know who he is,' she said, rising slowly to her feet. At the bike's side, she reached into a second pocket and withdrew another envelope, silently handing it over. Bryan looked at it, then at her, and counted the money out. Ten thousand.

'I'll get in touch with you only when I have the pictures,' he warned her, for the first time ever feeling sorry for both his mark and his client. Whatever was going on between those two it was real heavy. Heavy enough, perhaps, to crush them both? Straddling the huge bike, Rhiannon turned the key and the Norton roared into earsplitting life. Kicking off she raced away from the Punchbowl as fast as her beloved machine would take her. Five minutes later she pulled off on to the side of the road under some octopus trees, and leaning over the wide handlebars she cried her heart out.

Her hand rested protectively over her stomach as she sobbed, as if she could comfort the new life growing inside her. Although she had not yet had her pregnancy confirmed by a doctor, she knew in her heart that she was carrying a child. And she knew when she had conceived it, of course. Through her tears she managed a hiccoughing laugh of irony. How appropriate that it had been at Phallic Rock, the place where Dominic's ancestors had come to ask the gods for fertility, that Fate had chosen to deliver this wonderful, terrible blow – bequeathing her Dominic's child.

Her hand tightened briefly on her abdomen then slowly fell away. She couldn't let the baby affect her decision about its father. She simply couldn't. Rhiannon shook her head, her mind in turmoil. *But, oh God, what did she do now?* She'd been deliberately denying the truth about her condition for days now, refusing even to think about it. Now she once more determinedly pushed the problem to the back of her mind. Time enough to deal with that later. She was only human, after all. She could only deal with so much at a time.

HALF an hour later she pulled up outside her fully restored and decorated home. Taking off her helmet, her eyes focused on two men getting out of a parked car and walking towards her. She could feel her hackles rise as they approached her, for their faces had that look of polite determination that only officials with bad news wear. Getting off the bike, she removed her gloves and waited. One man, in his mid-forties, was dressed in a navy-blue suit with sober tie and sober eyes, set in a face that was almost handsome. Grey hair sat attractively on his head and it was he who spoke first. 'Miss Grantham?'

'Yes,' Rhiannon confirmed warily, standing lightly on the balls of her feet like a suspicious cat. The second man continued to move closer. He was younger, fitter and dressed more casually in denim jeans and a fairly thick caramel-coloured suede jacket. 'What can I do for you gentlemen?' she asked, her voice as polite as his had been.

'My name is Dixon. I'm from the Civil Bureau of Noise Pollution.'

Rhiannon blinked but looked at the documentation and identification he showed her. Whatever she had expected, it wasn't this. 'Yes?' she prompted, her eyes following him as the younger one advanced on her bike and began to look it over with professional thoroughness. 'We have received several complaints from your near-neighbours about the noise from your motorbike. This is yours, I believe?'

'Of course it is. You saw me pull up on it.' She didn't like playing games. 'But I have no near neighbours,' she felt her mouth pull into a smile at the ridiculousness of it. 'Look around – there's not a house in sight.'

'This is a residential district, Miss Grantham. I know you haven't been in the islands long, but certain desirable districts are protected by particular statutes of the traffic law as well as others, designed to keep the desirability of these districts at a very strict level.'

Rhiannon was pretty sure she was being fed verbal whitewash, but she had absolutely no experience with obscure zoning laws or whatever they were, so couldn't tell for sure.

'Naturally, high noise levels are not desirable and might lower the value of real-estate in this area. For that reason we have been authorized to inspect your vehicle.'

Rhiannon opened her mouth to say something, but didn't get the chance as the younger man behind her commented, 'There's a violation here I can see concerning the muffler system incorporated into the exhaust. Were you aware, Miss Grantham, that we have strict codes about mufflers on the islands?'

Dixon nodded. 'We'll have to confiscate the vehicle, Miss Grantham.'

'Confiscate?' She stared at him, aware that her mouth had dropped open and quickly snapped it shut. 'You can't be serious.'

'We are, Miss Grantham. Very much so. Until this vehicle meets the correct requirements according to US law, it's impounded.'

Rhiannon stared at him for several seconds, fighting off amused outrage. 'I don't suppose Dominic Fairchild had anything to do with this by any chance, did he?' she finally demanded, her hands planting themselves on her hips, her legs spread slightly apart, her gesture one of pure defiance.

George Dixon lifted an eyebrow in what was supposed to pass for surprise. 'Mr Fairchild of Fairchild Enterprises? Good grief no,' he said with patent insincerity. 'What makes you think that?'

Rhiannon slowly nodded, a helpless grin coming to her

face. Unaccountably, the whole episode seemed to be lifting her spirits, erasing the tension that had formed after her interview with the mysterious Bryan. 'OK, take it – but don't think you'll have it for long,' she warned them. 'You'll be hearing from my lawyer before the sun sets.'

She went back into the house humming. Taking her bike was a nasty, mean thing to do. Why, it smacked of . . . Slowly she began to grin as an idea formed in her mind.

THE intercom buzzed and Dominic reached for it. 'Yes, Cynthia?'

'Mr Dixon on line four for you, sir.'

'Put him through. Hello, George. You got the bike?' Dominic listened for a moment, a wider smile coming to his face as he heard the details.

'Now remember, I want you to hold on to that bike for as long as you can,' he instructed. A knock at the door interrupted him and he put a hand over the mouthpiece as the door opened and Philip came in. Wordlessly he took a seat as Dominic removed his hand from the phone and carried on. 'Pull whatever stunts you like, George – search the codes for ancient clauses if you have to, but keep that Norton locked up.' The thought of that monster that had nearly killed her being safely locked up did a lot for Dominic's peace of mind. 'Yeah – OK. Bye.' He hung up and looked at his chief right-hand man. 'I thought you were in Hilo?'

'I was, but we . . .' The intercom buzzed yet again and Dominic jabbed it a little impatiently. 'Yes?'

'A package for you, sir. Special delivery.'

Dominic raised a brow at Philip, who shrugged. 'Send it in.'

His secretary came in with a white cardboard box. 'It was delivered by courier just a moment ago, sir. No message.' After putting it on his desk, she nodded and left.

'Expecting a present, were you?' Phil asked.

'Not exactly. A bomb, perhaps.'

'Oh?' Phil sat up a little straighter. 'You haven't been rubbing our Miss Grantham up the wrong way again, have you by any chance?'

Dominic gave a very satisfied grin as he admitted

cheerfully, 'I'm afraid so.' While telling him about the bike, he lifted the lid, peered in curiously then reached in and lifted out a tiny whicker basket of grapes.

'Grapes?' Phil was as surprised as Dominic.

'Grapes,' he confirmed, then popped one into his mouth. As the small fruit split he screwed up his face and spat it out into the wastebin by his side.

'What's up?' Phil asked, not sure whether to laugh or worry that his friend had just been poisoned. Dominic stared at the fruit, then began to laugh, slowly at first, and then louder, throwing back his head, his white teeth flashing in his tanned face. 'What is it?' Phil repeated, hating to be left in the dark.

Dominic shook his head, still laughing. 'She's something else, that girl,' he managed to get out, rubbing his streaming eyes with his hands. 'They're sour.'

Rhiannon was very cleverly telling him exactly what she thought was behind the bike escapade.

Sour grapes!

Chapter 41

The envelope was postmarked Switzerland. Looking across at Farron on the other side of the breakfast table, Vienna ripped it open with shaking hands and began to read the letter.

The school secretary had matched her snapshot with an old school photo but they were reluctant to deal with the matter through the post, as records were, in the strictest sense, totally confidential. They hoped she'd understand that a school that boasted amongst its pupils the rich and famous had to be careful, and was it possible that she could fly over and talk to the school's headmistress in person? Frustratingly, they did not mention her name or any other personal details, saying only that they would need to see Vienna in person before they could consider giving out what would otherwise be privileged and private information. Wordlessly she showed it to Farron.

'I'm so *Hauoli* for you. Happy,' he corrected himself in English. 'Oh God, I'm so happy for you!' He laughed and scooped her out of the chair, swinging her around and kissing her again and again. She closed her eyes, relief pouring through her, but also fear. At last, her identity was within her grasp.

'We must go,' she said, struggling to be put down. 'Farron, we must go.'

'Damned right we will. As soon as we can make it.'

Vienna took a deep breath, aware now of the cold fear in her heart. 'I'm scared,' she admitted softly.

'I know – but who wouldn't be?' He lifted her chin with his finger and smiled tenderly down into her white little face. 'We've got to get busy – arranging a visa, flight schedules, Swiss francs. The lot!'

THE telephone was ringing as Rhiannon got out of the limo and she quickly dashed up the path, fumbling for her key. As she rushed into the hall, she tripped and almost fell, swore and picked up the receiver to say a rather breathless 'Hello?'

'Could I speak to Miss Grantham, please?'

'Speaking.'

'This is the Immigration Department speaking, Miss Grantham I'm afraid we've come across a problem with your passport.'

'Oh, yes,' she said drily, drawing out a chair. 'Do tell.'

'We've been reviewing your visa and your application for official US citizenship in regards to settling permanently in Oahu.'

Rhiannon closed her eyes. Dominic's handiwork again. They were looking, and would find a way, to get her thrown off the island. Only over my dead body, she thought grimly as she let the voice drone on and on, not even bothering to protest that she had always held joint citizenship, nor even that she had business interests in the islands.

'The problem, you see, is that it has come to our attention that your father applied for, and received, a United Kingdom passport, and this . . .'

Rhiannon sighed and closed her eyes. Another call to Jack with another plea for a good lawyer was once again on the cards.

'We shall get in touch with you as soon as we've reviewed the situation further, Miss Grantham.'

'Wonderful, you do that. In the meantime could you give me the name of the officials involved? I shall be contacting my lawyer.'

She jotted down the name and rank given her by the anonymous male voice on the other end of the line. 'Have a nice day,' the voice said and she stared at the phone that was now buzzing with the disconnected signal. Have a nice day? Shaking her head she hung up, made the call to Jack, dithered with herself, and then dialled another number.

'Blue Hawaiian, Dominic Fairchild's office.'

The cultured female voice escalated her anger even more, and she took a deep breath, asking ever-so-sweetly, 'May I speak to Mr Fairchild, please?'

'Who's calling?'

'The owner of Gray-Gray boutiques,' she singsonged, even more sweetly than before, and was greeted with a startled silence and then a wry, 'I'll see if he's in.' There was a pause, a click, and then his voice. She decided there was no point in giving him the satisfaction of exploding over the telephone.

'Hello, Rhia. Thanks for the grapes.'

'My pleasure.'

'They're in the greenhouse at Falling Pearls at the moment, ripening off. A few days in the sun and they'll be as sweet as sugar.'

She bit back a scream of outrage and just managed a polite, 'Really?'

'Yes – I'm looking forward to eating the juiciest sweetest grapes the island has to offer. Did you know you had selected the best variety?'

'Of course. I never do things by half,' she shot back, although in reality she had just picked out the sourest bunch at a local market store.

Dominic laughed. 'I'd noticed. What can I do for you?'

Rhiannon smiled. 'Now there's a leading question. There are several things I'd like you to do . . .'

'Ah, ah, ah,' he warned. 'Not over the telephone. We might have a crossed line with a little old lady, and we wouldn't want to shock her now, would we?'

Rhiannon could feel her muscles tensing as rage began to boil her blood. The damned man was laughing at her. 'I don't know what makes you think I'd shock her,' she said now, her sweetness as ripe as the grapes would be. 'All I called to say was that you are wasting your time. I have US citizenship, a business in the islands and friends every bit as powerful as your own. If you think petty inconveniences are going to wear me down, you're very much mistaken.'

Dominic laughed. 'Now why would I think that?'

'I'm not sure what goes on in that convoluted, sadistic, petty, bestial . . .'

'Ah, ah, ah. Remember the little old lady.'

'Go to hell!' she finally screamed, and heard him laugh softly in her ear. Helplessly she closed her eyes.

'I'm very busy at the moment Rhia,' he said smoothly. 'In fact, much too busy to deal with such a minor problem as yourself. So, much as I enjoyed the chat, I'll have to say goodbye.'

Rhiannon blinked as for the second time in ten minutes a final parting shot left her speechless with the dialling tone buzzing in her ears. Slamming down the receiver she let out a frustrated growl and stomped into the lounge.

The evening loomed ahead, boring and lonely. On impulse she picked up a phone and dialled Vienna's number. 'Hello, it's me, Rhiannon.'

'Hello yourself. I didn't expect to hear from you quite so soon.'

'Sorry! The reason I called was to ask if you were doing anything tonight.'

'Tonight? No, I don't think so.' Vienna glanced across at Farron and putting her hand over the receiver told him who it was.

'Great. How'd you like to listen to the Hawaiian Symphony tonight at the Blaisdell? My treat – you and Farron both.'

'We'd love to,' Vienna said immediately. She was restless and any distraction would be welcome. Besides, she'd heard Farron talk about the orchestra and knew he'd jump at the chance to hear them.

'That's wonderful. Can you meet me at the Centre, about half seven?'

'You bet. See you then.'

Rhiannon dressed in a black silk kaftan shot through with threads of gold and added chunky gold earrings to complete the outfit. She arrived in plenty of time at the theatre and found Farron and Vienna waiting. Putting a confident smile on her face, she approached the ticket office with crossed fingers and hoped that her little scheme would work.

It did, and she left a minute later with three tickets for the second box that Dominic had permanently reserved in his name. The ticket vendor had already informed her that Dominic and his companion had arrived and taken their seats in the Premier box which was, she saw at once, located immediately below and in front of them. As she took her seat her eyes bored into the back of his black head. Beside him she could see the bare back and cascading curls of his redheaded companion, and as she watched, his latest conquest leaned over to whisper something into his ear, her red lipsticked-mouth all but nibbling on his earlobe.

She bit her lip viciously and dragged her eyes to the stage where the orchestra was beginning to tune up, the notes mellow and harmonious even then.

Dominic slowly became aware of the hairs standing up on his neck—which meant only one thing. He was being watched. Listening with only half an ear to Moira's sultry voice he looked slowly around but no one seemed to be taking undue notice of him. Then, as the hairs on his neck quivered he suddenly half-turned in his seat.

He saw Vienna first, for her pale blonde hair stood out against the darkness in the box. Surprised, his eyes flew to the man seated beside her, relief flooding through him when he saw it was Farron. For one awful second he'd thought she was out with another man. Then he realized the box they were sitting in was the one he had permanently in reserve. He knew damned well Farron didn't know about the box, so how . . . A glitter of gold caught his eye as Rhiannon moved her hand to brush a strand of hair from her cheek, and his gaze fixed on hers. He felt a jolt of sexual electricity go through him, tightening his chest and heating his blood. In despair he knew it would always happen that way.

What the hell was she up to now, he wondered, a smile crossing his face.

A responsive grin spread over hers, then the lights went down and the music began. The orchestra started with one of the Strauss waltzes, progressing for stark contrast to Wagner, but Rhiannon paid little attention to the music. Her whole mind was attuned to the interval and the possibilities it offered. After what seemed like ages, the half-hour interval was announced.

'Fancy a drink, ladies?' Farron asked, but Rhiannon rose. 'I'd like to stretch my legs, too. You Vienna?'

In the bar, Farron battled for the drinks but Rhiannon was looking at the redhead who sat in a chair in one corner. She was wearing a backless white evening gown and had the figure to show it off. Jealousy was a new sensation for Rhia, and for a second she was unable to place the harsh clenching of her stomach. Dominic saw Farron and joined him at the bar. 'Hey – hello,' Farron said, his surprise genuine and confirming what Dominic had already suspected. The minx had been at work again.

'*Aloha*. You here with Vienna?'

'Yes, as a matter of fact and with . . . Rhia Grantham.'

Dominic smiled and ordered his drinks. Once they had them, they went back to where the two girls stood in one corner to avoid the crush. 'Look who I've found,' Farron said awkwardly.

Rhiannon put a smile on her face. 'Well, well,' she drawled. 'Fancy seeing you here.' Out of the corner of her eyes she saw the redhead move, and twisted her lips. No doubt she didn't dare let him out of her sight. Especially when there was an unattached female in sight.

'Darling,' the purr was worse than she had anticipated, and Rhiannon forced her bored look not to falter, even when the redhead pressed so close to his side a postage stamp couldn't have got between them.

'Moira Fletcher, this is Vienna Wright, Rhiannon Grantham, and you probably recognize Farron Manikuuna.' Dominic did the introductions with suave aplomb.

'Who wouldn't?' Moira flirted outrageously. Rhiannon shot Vienna a look and rolled her eyes. Vienna bit back her laughter and looked quickly away.

'I didn't know you had tickets for the concert,' Dominic probed.

Farron laughed. 'I didn't. Rhiannon rang us up out of the blue and invited us tonight. Needless to say we grabbed the chance.'

Rhiannon felt the redhead's hazel eyes sharpen on her, and kept her face as bland as milk and water.

'Lucky you,' Dominic said drily. 'You must have booked early,' he turned to her, but she had a smile waiting for him.

'Me?' she looked startled. 'Oh come on, don't be so modest. You know we're all here as your guests.' As all eyes turned to her in varying degrees of surprise she declared, 'Well, we are in your box, aren't we?'

Dominic felt his lips begin to twitch. The little stirrer! 'Yes, I had noticed that. Funny – I can't remember issuing the invitation.'

Rhiannon tut-tutted. 'You're getting forgetful in your old age, Dominic.'

'So it seems. Cheers,' he raised his glass, his glittering eyes fixed on her as he offered the salute to her utter gall and she nodded in acceptance as she sipped her own drink.

Moira didn't like it at all. Moving closer to him, pressing her arm against his ribs, she almost nestled against him like a damned ginger cat. 'I thought this was going to be a private party, Dom-Dom,' she said in a whisper loud enough to be heard by all.

Rhiannon turned abruptly away, her face pale in the overhead lighting. 'We'd better be getting back,' she said abruptly.

'So we should. Why don't you join us?' Dominic asked, ignoring the scarlet-tipped fingers on his arms that dug in briefly in anger, but Rhiannon was there before him.

'Oh, we wouldn't dream of interrupting – would we?' she asked of her two companions, who'd begun to smile as they caught on to exactly what she'd done.

'Oh no,' Vienna agreed quickly, siding with her immediately over the catty redhead. Farron, who hadn't yet made up his mind whether to be as mad as hell with her or kiss her for making Vienna's eyes sparkle so much, decided there was no reason Dominic's evening should be ruined as well. The redhead was lovely. No match for Rhiannon in looks of course, but then who was?

'No, we wouldn't want to intrude,' he agreed. 'Ladies,' he said, looking warningly at Rhiannon who gazed back at him, all innocence and light.

In the safety and privacy of the box, Vienna began to laugh. 'Rhia, you didn't. Did you?'

Rhiannon gurgled with happy and unrepentant laughter. 'I did!'

THE second half of the concert passed slowly after that, but when it was over they lingered in the box, waiting until the crush had eased. When they walked down the steps and into the evening air outside, the crowd was thin enough for them to spot the tall figure of Dominic and the fiery locks of his companion with relative ease.

'Hello again,' Rhiannon purred provocatively.

'How did you enjoy the show?' Moira asked, putting on her best smile but her eyes were sharp and cold.

'Magnificent,' Farron answered for them all.

'I do admire your bravery, Miss Grantham,' Moira said sweetly. 'Coming out without a date, and all that.'

'Not at all,' Rhiannon smiled just as sweetly. 'Nowadays no woman who's not a clinging vine is afraid to show that she's an independent person in her own right. Who needs a man to make her whole, or restrict her in what she can or cannot do, or say where she can or cannot go?'

Vienna silently applauded her. She too had taken an instant and female dislike to the redhead who now drew in a small breath, but made sure that her smiled never slipped.

'That's one way to look at it. Of course, it's also a good excuse for a woman to use if she can't get a date, isn't it?' she slipped in, stepping closer to Dominic and clinging round him like a snake.

Surprisingly it was Vienna who moved in to her defence. 'Hardly relevant in this case. Anyone with eyes could tell that Rhiannon has to fight men off with a stick.'

Moira looked about to put her down, recognizing at once that the small blonde was no match for her in the bitching stakes, but Farron came a little closer, looking ready to snap her head off if she dared. So she merely shrugged and said she was only speaking in the abstract, of course.

Yes, Rhiannon thought wrily, giving Vienna a knowing and thank-you smile. Very abstract! Dominic's soft laughter she ignored altogether.

'Are you planning on going on to a restaurant somewhere?' Dominic asked.

'I don't think so. Sweetheart?' Farron looked to Vienna, who shook her head. 'No, I think an early night is called for.'

'A lot of things are called for,' Dominic said archly, his look on Rhiannon making her grin widely.

Vienna took the moment to tug on Farron's arm and say quietly, 'You might as well ask him about getting some time off now.'

Farron nodded, but Dominic had already heard them.

'You need time off?'

'Please. But only when it's convenient. I know it's hard to get a replacement on short notice but well, Vienna and I decided to take a small vacation.' He could not mention the Swiss trip in front of everyone, but something in his eyes told Dominic that whatever was going on, it was more important than a mere break.

'Why not take it now?' he asked. 'I'll need you tomorrow — possibly the day after, but then you can have . . . a week? Two?'

'Oh, a week will do it I should think,' Farron said quickly. He didn't like taking advantage of their friendship in this way, but his first loyalty was, and always would be, to Vienna.

'Fine. I'll see to it tomorrow.'

Rhiannon nodded slowly. Yes, it was all there. The look of understanding that passed between father and son. Dominic's own bending over backwards to accommodate him. She was only mad at herself for not seeing it before. But surely Farron must realize Dominic felt more towards him than just friendship?

They said their goodbyes, leaving Dominic, Rhiannon and a very miffed Moira standing in an awkward silence before Rhiannon herself broke it. 'Well, I'd better be going.'

'Where's you car? I'll walk you. I shan't be a minute,' he told Moira, then slipped his hand around her waist and kissed her fully on the lips. Rhiannon turned away in disgust, but hadn't gone more than a few steps when she found him beside her. They walked in silence to her car, Dominic waving the chauffeur back in and opening the door for her himself. Leaning in the open window he shook his head. 'Your gall never ceases to amaze me. But leave Vienna out of your games. She's going through a bad time right now.'

'I know,' Rhiannon snapped, dismayed that he could think she'd do something to hurt the young girl.

'I mean it,' her warned. 'You can attack me as much as you like, but not her.'

'What makes you think I want to?' she asked, the hurt intensifying as Dominic smiled coldly.

'I know about your meeting with Richard Jago at the Hawaiian Hall a few months back. I don't know what you're up to, but . . .'

'I told Vienna about that,' Rhiannon snapped. 'In fact I went out of my way to warn her about that man. He gives me the creeps,' she shivered, then looked back at him in time to see his gaze flicker. 'Oh, ask her if you don't believe me,' she snapped, feeling absurdly upset that he didn't trust her. Which was truly ridiculous. He had every right not to trust her, didn't he?

He leaped back quickly as the car spurted away and he watched the limousine until it was out of sight. As he turned round he saw Moira waiting for him on the steps and just managed to keep a look of surprise from appearing on his face. He had forgotten her. But then, when he was with Rhiannon Grantham, he could forget anything and anybody.

And that was the crux of his whole problem.

Chapter 42

They were both in love with Switzerland. From their hotel they could see the dual lakes of the Thuner See and the Brienzer See, and beyond them the mountains that towered all around. They had arrived the day before, travelling on electric trains through lush meadows rife with campions, orchids and daisies. Cows with huge cowbells, circling buzzards and torrents of waterfalls had made the three-hour ride from Basle a pleasure neither would ever forget.

But now they stood outside the school, with its wooden-chalet charm and plethora of hanging baskets frothing with flowers, and for once Vienna was blind to the beauty of her surroundings. Farron looked across at her and squeezed her hand, and then, taking a deep breath, they pushed open the outer glass door and stepped inside. A young woman greeted them politely, speaking in perfect if accented English and promptly showed them to a door marked simply 'H. V. Swinbackher.'

Vienna could hardly believe the moment had arrived. The room they walked into was one of cozy, slightly shabby, old-world charm and graciousness. From behind a large oak desk a woman slowly rose to her feet, grey hair cut neatly into a becoming style. Gold-rimmed glasses sat over sharp blue eyes that looked at Vienna with a mixture of the politeness and determined civility that was called for in this very delicate situation.

'Miss Wright?' The woman smiled as she came from behind the desk and held out her hand, which was completely free of rings. 'Welcome to Switzerland.'

'Thank you. This is Mr Manikuuna.'

Farron shook the proffered hand, unsurprised to find its grip firm and reassuring. 'Mr Manikuuna. Please sit down.' She offered the chairs to both of them before resuming her place behind the table and bringing forward a beige folder at which Vienna stared for a long time, her mouth going as dry as sandpaper.

'I received your letter,' Hildegarde Swinbackher began, 'and immediately set my secretary to searching the records, as you know. I was not here when you attended, my dear. Frau Linquist, who was your principal, sadly died last year.'

'I see,' Vienna nodded, although her heart was pounding so loudly in her ears she could hardly hear what the woman said.

'As I told you in my letter, we did find a girl who so closely resembled your picture as to make identification almost positive.' Mrs Swinbackher never mentioned it, but she had accepted Vienna's invitation to check with the Honolulu hospital as to the truth of her amnesia claim, and had felt immediate pity for the girl – especially as she had read through her school file. She now tapped her finger on it and reaching inside, pulled out a photograph and handed it over. She was being overly cautious perhaps, but she had the school to protect and until she was certain that there was nothing in this extremely odd situation that could rebound on St Johan's, she was determined to satisfy herself on certain points.

Vienna's fingers trembled so badly that she was forced to rest the small passport-sized photo on her knee in order to look at it better. The picture was of a girl about eighteen years of age. Her face was free of make-up, her blonde hair straight and long but it was her face – younger, a little chubbier, but hers. The same eyes, the same expression. She let out her breath on a half-laugh, half-sob, and handed it to Farron who looked at it and nodded.

'It's you all right,' he said softly. 'No doubt about it.'

'Now that I have seen you in person, I too agree,' Mrs Swinbackher said cautiously, giving Vienna few minutes in which to recover some of her equilibrium.

'You can't understand how much this means to me,' Vienna said finally, her voice choked. 'I woke up in hospital, and there was . . . just nothing.' She held out her hands palm upwards in a wordless gesture of despair and Hildegarde Swinbackher felt her eyes mist over. Quickly she cleared her throat.

'I can understand that it must have been terrifying for you, my dear,' she admitted, her voice as composed and charming as ever. Women of breeding and class did not get maudlin in public. Nor did they ever, ever, make a scene. But Farron and Vienna could both sense the warm humanity that flowed from the woman, and Vienna particularly found herself relaxing now that the worst was over. She reached across for Farron's hand and squeezed his fingers. 'So,' she said, giving a deep breath. 'What can you tell me about myself?'

Again, Mrs Swinbackher hesitated. 'There was no ... forgive me, how shall I put it? The police could find no clue to your identity at all?'

Vienna shook her head. 'Nothing. Except this.' She held out her wrist and her gold bracelet glinted in the sunshine streaming in through the window. The Principal glanced at it and recognized it immediately for what it was, and smiled. It was not conclusive proof, of course, but it was enough.

She opened the folder and looked down. 'First of all, my dear, your name is not Vienna Wright but Pauline Clarke. With an "E".'

'Pauline?' Vienna echoed blankly. 'Are you sure?'

'Quite sure. Although I think your chosen name is much prettier.'

Vienna looked across at Farron, who smiled reassuringly. 'Pauline or Vienna,' he whispered softly, 'I love you both.'

'I don't think I can get used to Pauline,' she admitted to the older woman. 'I think I'll stick to Vienna. I chose it because of this,' she stroked the bracelet on her wrist almost lovingly.

'Ah yes,' Hildegarde nodded. 'I can understand how you came by that. The school regularly visits Vienna for the music festival. Those bracelets are often brought back by the girls as souvenirs. They're quite charming, aren't they?'

Vienna nodded. So simple – but she had never thought of it. 'Please, go on.'

Hildegarde nodded, but a small frown tugged her brows. 'I'm afraid that the information here is very slim but you may have all of it, of course. I'll get Gretchen to make you a photo-copy.'

'Thank you,' Vienna said, almost wilting in relief.

'Now, let's see. Yes – you were in many ways an unusual case. You came to us about a year after you'd left the orphanage.'

Orphanage! A terrible, empty word. No mother – no father, or brothers or sisters. 'I see,' Vienna managed to croak.

'The address is here,' Hildegarde said. 'In New York State – outside the city itself, I think.'

Vienna nodded, unable to speak. Farron felt only a blinding relief as all the suspicions of the last few months finally began to leave him. For a few seconds he felt utterly guilty at ever having thought she could be one of Gloria's prostitutes, but he knew, at last, that it didn't matter. He and Vienna loved one another, no matter what.

Farron asked the obvious question. 'How did Vienna come to be here?'

Hildegarde shuffled through some papers. 'It's all here . . .' she said absently as she searched. 'Ah yes. You came here on a bequest in your aunt's will.'

'Aunt? I thought I was an orphan.'

'You were. The woman in question was, I understand, very elderly – in her nineties at the time of her death. A Great-aunt, I should think. An old woman in her seventies, as she would have been when you were born, wouldn't have been permitted to look after a baby. The copy of the lawyer's letter is here and simply states that your aunt left the money in a trust fund for you to have a year's education at a Swiss finishing school. It was the lawyers and the late Principal who liaised to enrol you here.'

'I see. And my aunt didn't have any children?'

'I'm afraid not. No relatives of any kind. She was not well off, I gather. All her money was put into the trust fund for your year here.'

Farron thought it a strange thing for a maiden aunt to do. Perhaps she believed that the manners of a real 'lady' would be the best gift for a niece. It also explained a lot of things about Vienna – the ease with which she had become a *cordon bleu* cook, for instance. No doubt she'd learned the rudiments here.

'Well . . .' Vienna was at a loss for words, and Hildegarde again felt sympathy rush over her.

'I have asked around our teaching staff and there is one of your old teachers still here – Miss Schumacher, who teaches deportment and fashion. I told her about you, I hope you don't mind, and she's looking forward to meeting you again. Perhaps you'd like to see her now?' Hildegarde checked her watch. 'You have half an hour before her class.'

'I'd like that,' Vienna agreed immediately, cheering up just a little at the thought of actually meeting someone who knew her. Out in the office they waited for the secretary to copy the file, then followed her to Miss Schumacher's chalet. When the door opened it revealed a tall woman who bade them enter with cool ease. 'Ah yes – Pauline. Hello again. Thank you, Gretchen.' The voice was perfect – accentless and clear, and the secretary nodded and left.

'Come in, please. It gets chilly at this time of year.' It was cold in the shade and they walked gratefully into a room that was a mix between classroom, clothes' shop and home. On the walls were posters of chic Parisian models together with graphs indicating body positions when sitting, standing or lying. Miss Schumacher was not so much pretty as handsome. She had auburn hair that was carefully tinted to hide the grey patches, and cut into a smooth cap around her long, thin, sensitive face that was of the ageless variety. Wide tawny eyes looked out at the world with gracious superiority, and although there was nothing particularly warm about her there was nothing threatening either. In spite of himself, Farron was impressed. In a strange way she was over-whelmingly sexy, and he could understand how she would make an excellent teacher. What girl wouldn't envy her her poise? Even Vienna was feeling awkward. And as she walked forward a strange thing happened. Of their own accord, her shoulders came back an inch or so, her hands turned inwards and swung lightly and her head tilted back at a slight angle.

'I see your body has not forgotten the lessons drummed into it over six years ago, Pauline.'

Vienna jerked. It sounded strange to be called by that name, and even stranger to realize that the woman was right – she was walking differently. 'Thank you for seeing me, Miss Schumacher. I . . . it's very difficult, isn't it?'

'Please sit down.' The tall woman moved a mannequin dressed in culottes and put it against a wall. She paid Farron little or no attention. 'I take it you want me to tell you all I can remember of yourself, yes?'

'Please.'

Slowly, through this woman's eyes, she began to see herself as she was then. Given neither to sentiment nor embellishment, the deportment teacher told of how she had arrived looking pale and nervous, gravitating at first to the other American girls in the school but after a few months becoming more open to the cosmopolitan ambience of the school. She had apparently excelled in the cooking and secretarial classes, fluffed quite badly in the French lessons, and mainly kept to the school rules. 'You were not one of the hellraisers, unlike Cindy Fotherington, an English Right Honourable,' she referred to the daughter of a Lord or Lady with an unimpressed air, 'or Amelia Aston, one of our rich American imports. You were always rather quiet, very conscientious, but I had the impression that you were . . . how shall I put it? You seemed glad to be here – as if you had left something behind you in America that you did not like.'

'Can you tell me who I was particularly friendly with? Where they are now?'

'As I recall it your special friend, and it often amuses me that all you young women seem to require one, was Fiona Crowther, an Australian girl. But, I'm sorry to say, she was killed in a plane crash two years ago.'

Vienna shook her head. It was incredible – was everyone who had known her dead? Then she felt ashamed of herself. A friend of hers was dead. She might not remember her, but that didn't change the fact she had once been a good friend. Biting her lip, she silently apologized to Fiona Crowther, whoever she had been. 'I see. Can you tell me . . . when I was here, did I ever say that I wanted to go to Hawaii, or why?'

'No. I'm sure your plans were to return to New York when you left here.'

Vienna nodded. 'And there was no one else here that I was

close to? A . . .' she glanced at Farron briefly and shrugged helplessly, 'a boy, perhaps?'

Again the elegant woman shook her head. 'No. I'm sorry.'

Vienna felt a crushing sense of disappointment and frustration, but managed to smile. 'Well, thank you, Miss Schumacher. You've been very kind.'

They all stood up as one, the tall figure of the deportment teacher leading the way to the door. 'Perhaps you will have more luck in America,' the older woman said quietly as they stood on her doorstep in the noon sun. 'You lived there, grew up there, worked there. It is all in that file, so I understand. I'm sorry we couldn't have been of more help to you here.'

Vienna nodded. She'd been itching to read that folder through from cover to cover the moment she'd set eyes on it, and now she would have the opportunity. 'I understand. And thank you again.'

'Don't be too disappointed, love,' Farron said softly, draping his arm over her shoulders as they walked away. 'You know who you are – a mild and innocent little orphan from New York State. Not a Mata Hari from Chicago, or a . . .'

She laughed and punched him in the ribs. 'OK – you can say "I told you so".'

'I told you so.'

As they slowly walked away from the school and back into the village where the shops were open and fellow tourists meandered along the streets she said, 'I feel free and safe here.'

Her choice of words sparked a sense of foreboding in him, but he ignored it. She seemed so much better today – and last night she hadn't had the nightmare. Why rock the boat? They stopped to pet a cat that reminded them of their beloved Prof, currently queening it up with Farron's tutu, then spent a few minutes idly window-shopping. 'Why don't we stay on here for a few days and then go off to New York?' he asked casually, sensing her need for a little time.

'Oh, yes please! You're so good to me, you know. Now let's eat. I'm starving again.'

'Hmmm,' Farron closed his eyes in bliss as they sat at a discreet little corner table of a tiny café and ate their meal.

'Someone told me the Swiss make the best bread, cake and chocolate in the world.'

Vienna looked down at her own empty soup bowl and laughed. 'We'll get as fat as pigs.'

'Lovely. We Hawaiians like meat on our women.'

Taking him at his word she pulled her own dish of gâteau towards her and raised a spoonful of strawberry, cream, light sponge and jam into her mouth. In some ways she was glad she had learned only a little about herself today. She didn't think she could take in a lot of information all at once. Yet the folder lay on the table between them and it had to be faced. Slowly she read through it, but it told her only a few more facts —including the last known job she had had as a receptionist at a law firm in New York. She was twenty-four years old, her birthday falling on 9 January. Her parents were Francis and Glenda Clarke, deceased in a car accident when she was six months old. The information on them was sketchy, and this was something she was determined to rectify. In New York she'd start digging in earnest.

BACK at the hotel, Vienna lay on the bed and stared thoughtfully up at the ceiling. Knowing he'd need more money, Farron went through the operator to get Honolulu on the line, intending to ask Dominic if he could wire him some money to a bank in New York.

Suddenly Vienna shuddered and dragged her mind back from the precipice where it had wandered. No – she wouldn't think about that. Not now. But it was there, lurking, growing stronger with every minute. She knew Gary Lyons was only a thought away – a lapse in concentration and he'd be there, tormenting her, accusing her, driving her mad . . .

'*Aloha* – Farron?' Dominic's voice sounded far away on the other end of the line as Farron watched Vienna walk to the balcony and look out over the lakes.

'Yes, hi. How is everything?'

'Fine. More to the point – how is it with you?' Before he'd left, Farron had confided to Dominic the real reason for the trip, and also told him something of his worries concerning Vienna's deteriorating mental health. Without telling them,

Dominic had ordered a check to be run on Vince Drake. So far his medical credentials had proved to be excellent. Briefly, but leaving nothing out, Farron told Dominic all they'd learned.

'How's she taking it?'

Farron lowered his voice. 'OK, I think,' he lied, then admitted, 'No – not really. She seems to be coping but . . .'

'I understand. Just stick with her.'

'I intend to. Look, the reason I'm calling . . . Do you remember you said to phone if I needed anything?'

'Sure – shoot.'

'We want to spend some time in New York, covering the orphanage angle and the job. It'll take a while though and was something we didn't plan on.'

'You need more time off, then,' Dominic said crisply. 'And some cash.'

'I have my own money, it's just a question of transferring it to New York.'

'No problem. I'll book you into a hotel from here and have the money waiting for you at reception. Just let me know what time your plane lands and I'll have a car waiting for you.'

'Thanks. I thought we'd spend a couple of days here. It's a beautiful place and . . . Vienna didn't have the nightmare last night.'

'Sounds ideal to me,' Dominic agreed. 'Have a good rest – and go and visit Brienz. It's the wood-carving capital of the world.'

'We will. I'll ring up before we leave with the flight number. And thanks again.' He hung up and joined Vienna on the balcony. 'Everything's fixed.'

Vienna began to cry, slowly at first then, as Farron took her in his arms, her tears began to flow fast and furious, her breath sobbing out in gasps of pain. He longed to make love to her and comfort her that way but feared her rejection, so instead he rocked her in his arms, her small, pitifully thin shoulders shaking under the onslaught of her sobs. Two hours later she was sleeping on the bed where Farron had carried her. Every now and then she gave a sobbing sigh in her sleep. Farron paced, his mind going around in circles.

Towards ten that night she woke up, disorientated and bewildered, but mostly scared. She didn't want to go back to sleep – she knew the nightmare would come. What did it matter that she knew her real name? Pauline Clarke had killed Gary Lyons as surely as Vienna Wright had done, and she must still confess to it in order to gain some peace of mind.

THEY spent their last days in Switzerland exploring. In Brienz Farron ordered a wooden eagle to be made in time for Dominic's Christmas present and then they sailed back to their hotel across the lake, gorging themselves on delicious Swiss chocolate. They rode on trains that went up into small mountain villages like Wengen and on into the snowline, passing through the ski resort of Klein Scheideg and then down into Grindelwald, a sprawling town in the shadow of the Eiger, where they ate real apple strudel.

On their last afternoon they went to the Blue Lake. Expecting a huge lake, like the Thuner See, they found instead a tiny blue stretch of water no more than an acre square. The water itself was so clear it was of better quality than the water that came from the taps in the city. As they were rowed in a boat by a man dressed in traditional Austrian costume, they could see on the bottom where petrified tree trunks played host to the trout that swam there.

'Look – he's so close,' Vienna said quietly as a speckled trout rose to nudge her fingers with his snout, his cold wet body slipping between her fingers without fear. Around them woods stretched in all directions and mountains lazed in the afternoon light, their tops a brilliant white in the sun. But even here the terror lurked, and she kept checking the strange faces, expecting Gary Lyons to be grinning at her, his throat a red mask of blood.

In the restaurant she excused herself from a worried-looking Farron and escaped to the ladies room. She had to tell someone, soon, what she had done. She had to. Priests said confession was good for the soul, didn't they? Perhaps she was a Catholic anyway? Looking in the mirror she flinched. 'Are you Pauline Clarke?' she whispered, but received no answers. Perhaps New York could tell her. Then a shockwave jolted her.

Suddenly she knew that Gary Lyons would be waiting for her in New York. Gary Lyons would be waiting for his murderer in Hell itself . . .

Chapter 43

The Iolani Palace was the venue of a lavish party hosted by Janice Gould, the sixty-year-old matriach of Honolulu high society. Naturally, Rhiannon had been invited. Without exception, men wore tuxedos and their dates competed with each other for the title of best-dressed woman. Parisian originals vied with those from Rome and London, labels scribbled with names like Emmanuelle, De Florentino, and others. The palace itself was magnificent. Situated near the Governor's Mansion in Washington Place, it lay in the heart of town and even the famous statue of King Kamehameha seemed to point towards it. The entrance housed a sweeping porch and rows of Corinthian white pillars gave the Palace the air of Ancient Greece. Tall shuttered windows added to its elegance.

In the ballroom with its painted ceilings, huge crystal chandeliers and tapestries hung on every wall, a shining, multicoloured wooden floor began to fill with couples dancing to an orchestra so vast it stretched from one wall to the other. Waiters circulated in white coat and tails with trays filled with five of the best champagnes such as Moët & Chandon and the pink variety of Pommery and Grenda. Fine wines also flowed as if they were water – Chambertin, Obbstler, Soave, Pouilly Fuissé and Mouton Rothschild.

As she passed a group of men puffing happily on Havana cigars, Rhiannon caught the tail end of another piece of gossip. 'She's a wonderful sight I'll give her that, but Fairchild isn't one to be taken in by a pretty face.'

She smiled grimly. Where was Dominic, anyway? She knew he'd been invited. Suddenly her blood began to heat and her boredom fled. She could feel him near. And then she wondered why she'd come, unwilling to admit that she had simply needed to see him, to be near him, to hear his voice and . . . Rhiannon turned abruptly, intending to leave before she lost her sanity totally, but it was too late.

Dominic stood behind her, drinking in her appearance. Her dress was a rich amber silk, glowing luminously in the light from the chandeliers. The bodice, beaded with tiny crystals, clung in gently swelling circles over her breasts, showing the tops of them as creamy mounds. Her hair was swept up into a high arrangement of raven-black waves and in her hair sparkled yellow diamond flowers. A single chunk of deep amber, almost as big as a pigeon's egg, hung from a delicate platinum chain around her beck, the stone nestling between her magnificent breasts.

'Dominic,' she said by way of greeting, her voice melodic but deliberately penetrating. 'Remember this?' and she nodded to the conductor. The *It's Impossible* tune filled the room, and Dominic's mind winged back to the first night he'd seen her at the Princess Liliha Hotel at Waimea Bay. They'd danced to this same tune and he hadn't even known her name. It seemed a lifetime ago.

'I'll never forget it,' he said quietly and took her in his arms, their bodies fitting together perfectly. Whispers filled the room as her head rested against his shoulder, her eyes closing.

Rhiannon stirred, aware that under their amber silk, her breasts were hardening, her nipples beginning to tingle and ache. Dominic felt it too and knew she must feel the evidence of his own arousal pressed hard against her. Yet they kept their eyes closed until the music ended and then slowly pulled apart. But they both knew it was not over. Not nearly over . . .

Rhiannon knew now that her baby was a reality. Using a buying trip to the mainland for Gray-Gray raw silks as an excuse, she had visited an English gynaecologist and had her pregnancy confirmed. The news had both thrilled her and filled her with despair. During the restless nights she'd spent pondering her predicament, she'd managed to come to only one instinctive decision: she could not abort her baby. She simply could not. And more and more she was leaning towards the idea of keeping the baby and raising it herself. After all, many women did that, and managed it successfully. Why shouldn't she? But what would she tell her son or daughter when he or she asked about their father . . .

They dined at midnight. The food was a mixture of cordon bleu and traditional Hawaiian dishes. *Saimin*, a noodle soup, was followed by crab, and seafood salad consisting of sweet potatoes, prawns and seaweed, then grilled salmon. The main course was peacock — roasted and then served with the peacock feathers themselves artfully arranged to make a spectacular sight that drew gasps of amazement and approval as the waiters carried it in on trays held above their heads.

Throughout the meal, Rhiannon talked amiably and with obvious intelligence to those nearest her, but her every sense was tuned in on Dominic. Perhaps because she suspected this would be the last time she saw him before she let Jack Gunster approach the firm of Chicago lawyers who represented Dominic's distant relatives there. Jack was eager to have it over with and had even come up with a few more nails to hammer into Dominic's coffin. As she recalled this, Dominic glanced across the laden table and their eyes met. Rhiannon was the first to look away.

It was fast approaching three-thirty in the morning, and most of the guests had left. Rhiannon was in the hall, an attendant gone to fetch her wrap, when she felt a warm hand curl around her elbow. Her whole body flamed as a familiar deep voice said, 'I want to show you something.'

Curious, she followed Dominic across the great hall, past the grand staircase and down a gloomy corridor. Through the semi-darkness she saw him reach into his pocket for a key. 'My, my,' she whispered sardonically. 'You have keys to the Palace, no less.'

'I also have the key to the city, too. The Mayor gave it to me when I got back from Harvard.'

As she waited in stony silence she could hear him laughing quietly, and her lips began to twitch. Then she heard the metallic scrapings as he hunted for the keyhole and then the soft click as a large-sounding door opened. Walking into pitch blackness, her heartbeat picked up as she heard the door close behind her. She had no idea what surrounded her in the darkness, nor did she care. He was there and although she could no longer see him, her every other sense was attuned to

550

his presence. She could hear the rustle of his clothes as he moved – she could almost feel where he was just by letting her heart free to seek him out. Then a light clicked on and she blinked.

At once her vision cleared and she saw where she was – in the throne room. The floor beneath her consisted of black and white tiles; the ceiling was dome-shaped and hand-painted with fat cherubs. The walls were hung with portraits of past kings and queens in traditional costume, but the focus of the room was the huge throne that sat on a three-stepped raised dais against the middle of the far wall. It was wooden, with a heavily carved backrest, arms and clawed legs, the seat of red velvet and hung with gold braid. 'Some seat,' she said, keeping her voice level and nonchalant.

'You're a hard woman to impress, Rhiannon Grantham,' he said softly, then walked towards the imposing chair that was steeped in history, seemingly unaffected by its grandeur and the awesome power it represented. Turning, he looked at her and then sat down in it and despite herself she felt and heard a small gasp escape her. Suddenly he was Prince Dominic Hua Fairchild. It wasn't his fine clothes, nor the devil-may-care smile, nor even the relaxed, superior way he sat in that massive chair. As she walked across the floor towards him, she saw that his right to sit there was imprinted in his eyes – green, unafraid, strong undefeatable eyes. Her steps faltered, then ceased altogether as she stood with just one foot on the first step. Her skin went cold. Looking up at him suddenly she knew. *He was undefeatable.*

'It would look good in the lobby of the Blue Hawaiian, wouldn't it?' she said with forced breeziness, but her voice was nevertheless a little strained. 'I wonder if the government will sell it? I think, if they will, I'll have it put in the hotel – when it becomes mine, just to remind people of you.' She said the last almost lovingly, and Dominic felt his body's muscles clench in reaction to the soft, sensual tone of her voice that said such ugly, threatening words.

Before she quite knew how he'd done it, his hands were on her, dragging her forward and twisting her, and she felt herself turn and land squarely across his lap. Instinctively her hands curled around his neck to save herself, and she struggled to sit up. His arms were like steel. It incensed her, this physical superiority that men had over women.

'Does it make you feel big, Dominic?' she spat, but continued to struggle for several minutes while he looked down at her, his face tight and pitiless as she quickly became exhausted. Finally she lay back against his arm, panting slightly. Her dress had ridden even further down her breasts, and the rosy pink tips of her nipples were just beginning to peep over the top of the amber silk. Their eyes clashed and locked as the air around them hummed with pagan electricity. Then his lips swooped victoriously on to hers, forcing her clenched teeth apart to plunder the sweetness of her mouth. She moaned, her hands digging into his scalp and she levered herself upwards, her mouth as hungry as his now, as angry, and as needy. Passion roared in their ears like thunder whilst a sweeter song sang in their hearts.

But the chasm was still there. It forced them apart, removed clinging lips and her passionate body from his lap. Graham Grantham still reigned supreme from the grave. 'I have to go,' she said, her voice sounding small in that big throne room as she backed away from the man still sitting there, and retreated even more from the impulse that was growing in her to warn him, to tell him to watch out, to defend himself somehow.

'I know,' he said softly, and for a startled moment she wondered if he'd actually read her mind. Somehow she wouldn't have been surprised if he had.

She turned and walked to the door, only pausing to look back at him suspiciously as he said softly, and with seeming irrelevance, 'I've booked your old room back in the Blue Hawaiian. It's yours, whenever you want it.'

She couldn't think of a single thing to say. She had no witty comeback, or even a sarcastic insult to offer him, so she simply opened the door and left him, walking out through the Palace and to her car.

WHEN she got home she found that all her windows were boarded up and her doors padlocked. A letter attached to the door explained the eviction notice. There were certain

552

discrepancies, the lawyers for the previous owners informed her, in the purchasing of the property, and the matter had been placed in the hands of one of the top law firms in the city who had obtained an order from a judge to render the house, as far as she could gather, the property of the court until the matter was settled.

Suddenly she remembered Dominic's words in the throne room. 'I've booked your old rooms back at the Blue Hawaiian,' he'd said! 'You can have them whenever you want them,' he'd said! Slowly she leaned back against her car and began to laugh. But after she'd laughed herself sick she realized that it wasn't funny after all.

'The Pink Palace, please Sam,' she said, her voice hardly more than a whisper. Her belongings, the letter informed her, were all stored at a government building on King's Street and a ticket for them had been enclosed. She would, of course, have to pay rent for the period that they would be housed there.

'Dominic,' she whispered as the dawn began to colour the horizon.

Even at four o'clock in the morning, she was able to rent a room and she had barely drunk the coffee she'd ordered before a knock came at the door. Outside stood the bellboy with a large covered box. 'This arrived for you just a minute ago, Miss Grantham.'

Rhiannon tipped him then put the box on a table. It was heavy only in one part – whatever was inside was obviously a small thing and not in proportion to the box's actual size. Removing the cover, she was surprised to see the top layer of cardboard was littered with small holes, and even more surprised when she felt a slight movement from within. Frowning she quickly flipped open the top and looked inside, her mouth falling open at what she saw. Blinking up at her nervously was the prettiest little bantam hen she had ever seen. There was no message, but she didn't need one.

Dominic thought she was chicken!

For the third time in an hour, Rhiannon began to laugh helplessly, and from the box the chicken made an almost contented clucking sound.

'OK, Dominic,' she softly cooed to the chicken. 'OK.'
Carefully shutting the box again she left the room and handed
the key over to the receptionist, asking for a taxi and her bill.

If the taxi driver thought it odd to be collecting a woman
dressed in an amber silk ballgown at five forty-five in the
morning with a chicken tucked under her arm, he never said
so. At the Blue Hawaiian she entered the lobby and, carefully
putting the box and audibly clucking chicken on to the
reception desk, asked for her key. 'I believe you have the
Emerald Suite booked for me?'

The girl never even checked her list. 'Yes, Miss Grantham.'
She smiled as she handed over the key, but her eyes kept
straying to the box.

'I don't suppose you know anyone on the island who keeps
chickens, do you? For the eggs only I mean, and free range.
No batteries.'

The girl blinked. 'Er ... I believe Mr Manikuuna's
grandmother keeps chickens.'

'Marvellous. Have a messenger send her this from me, will
you – at a decent hour, of course.'

'Certainly,' the girl smiled and put the box carefully out of
sight below the reception desk, peeking inside and cooing
over the hen as she did so.

Rhiannon was grinning even as she got into the elevator
and she was still smirking when she reached her room.

DOMINIC wiped the last trace of shaving foam from his face
and walked naked through the penthouse to his bedroom.
Reaching for the phone he got reception.

'Has Miss Grantham checked in yet?'

'Yes, sir – about five o'clock this morning ... with a
chicken.'

'I see. Thank you.' If the lad who'd passed on this
information had expected a startled reply, he was left very
disappointed. Humming, Dominic pulled on a pair of black
cotton pants and was just doing up the buttons on his white
shirt when the bell went.

Frowning, for he had standing instructions that no one was
to be let up to the penthouse out of office hours save for

expected guests, he walked through the office and opened the door. Hua Lopan'ha leaned against the jamb, his face creased with lines of tiredness. '*Aloha*, Dom.'

'Hell, you look like death warmed up. Come in and have some coffee.'

The PI followed him into the large lounge where Dominic wordlessly poured the younger man a cup of coffee, noting his rumpled suit. 'What's so urgent?'

'The shrink you asked me to follow: last night he went to Frank Gillespie's place.'

Dominic's eyes narrowed. 'So he's a gambler.'

Hua shook his head. 'Worse. He'd been drinking in a bar just off Hotel Street before he went. When he arrived he was immediately met by Frank's hit squad and told he wasn't welcome until he'd paid off the rest of his debts. Note that I said "rest of his debts". It's important for later.'

'Go on.'

'The guy was drunk and shouting loud enough for anyone to hear. Said that the debts were being paid off, and his credit was good, so why not give him some leeway? The place was packed and he was causing a scene so they took him into Frank's office. I couldn't manage to get close enough to hear what was going on, but half an hour later Drake came back out again with a thousand dollars' worth of chips and Gillespie watching him like a satisfied hawk.'

Dominic waited whilst Hua thirstily guzzled his coffee before continuing, 'Gillespie left for a few minutes – to make a phone call, I'm sure, because an hour later, at about three, another guy arrived. One you've put me on to before.'

'One I've. . . ?' Dominic was lost for a moment and then it clicked. As Hua watched he straightened up on the sofa, his face taking on a look that meant trouble. Big trouble. 'Jago!' Dominic spat out the word like it was filth, and the PI nodded.

'Richard Jago,' he confirmed. 'He spoke to the shrink for a few minutes – his voice was low, but by the look on his face and the way the shrink reacted, I think he really gave him an earful. Then Gillespie and Jago disappeared into the office for ten minutes. When he came out, the shrink had lost all of the grand at the roulette table and was crying into his bourbon.

He was really cut up about something, but Gillespie's mafia were all around him and I couldn't get close enough to hear much, but he seemed to have a bad case of remorse over something or other.'

Dominic swore explicitly and walked to the window, looking out with thoughtful eyes. Hua helped himself to another cup of coffee. Hell, he was tired.

Jago and the shrink – the two ran around Dominic's brain. Jago and the shrink – they went together like rat-poison and rats. His blood ran cold as he thought back to what Farron had been telling him – about how Vienna had deteriorated badly since beginning the sessions. And to think he'd been paying the bastard! Rage grabbed him, but with it came cold calculation. He wanted them – he wanted them both, and Jago was a slippery bastard. Neither would get away with it, whatever 'it' was: of that he'd make damned sure. Turning he saw Hua half-dozing in the chair, and walking quickly to a rolltop bureau he removed ten one-hundred dollar bills from a wallet and handed the cash to Hua. 'You did a good job – this is just the bonus. Send me the bill when you've dug around a bit more. If you can I want proof, any kind at all, of a link between Jago, Drake and Gillespie.'

'I thought you might,' Hua said, taking the money and stuffing it carefully into his shirt-pocket. 'Do you mind if I go home and catch some sleep first?'

Dominic managed a smile – but it was a wintry one at best. His eyes were glittering with a hardness that made even Hua's blood freeze. Thank the gods that the look was not meant for him. He left quickly.

Striding to the reception desk a few minutes later, Dominic told them to inform his secretary that he wanted all his appointments for the day cancelled. He drove straight to Gloria's, and was frowning darkly when the door was opened to him by a wide-eyed oriental who picked up immediately on his black mood and fairly ran to Gloria's office.

'The Prince is here,' she hissed at a startled Gloria, who was still yawning and half-asleep. 'He's real mad.'

'Out,' Dominic said crisply to the girl whom he'd followed closely. He'd overheard her warning and wasn't pleased. 'Now!'

The girl disappeared.

'What's going on?' Gloria asked. Instinct told her it was bad. Very bad.

'I need your help,' Dominic began without preamble. 'Or rather, I need Frank Gillespie's help.'

Gloria sat down, and pointed to the chair. 'Coffee?'

'No time.' Briefly Dominic outlined the details about Jago's obsession with Vienna, his exile and return, and about Vienna's decision to see Drake, and as he spoke, Gloria felt herself going pale.

'You think there's some connection between Jago and Drake?' she asked, more to give herself time than anything. She already knew, of course, that Vienna was seeing Dr Vincent Drake, but she'd had no idea the psychiatrist was in with that bastard Jago and she thought furiously of a certain man with growing rage. 'I'll fire the incompetent bastard, damn him,' she told herself, but her face was expressionless. Apart from her pallor and the way she held herself so stiffly in the chair, she gave no other indication that she was, in actual fact, even more upset than Dominic.

'There has to be,' Dominic said, then told her of Farron's worries that Vienna's mental state was deteriorating, rather than improving.

I'll kill them, Gloria thought, thinking of Drake and Jago planning Vienna's destruction so coldbloodedly. I'll kill them, she promised herself, while her blue eyes stayed steadily on Dominic as he got to Frank's part in all this. And if he knew what was going on I'll kill him too, she vowed. I'll kill them all. *Pauline! Oh my darling baby, what have they done to you?*

'So you see, I need information – proof especially. And quickly, before they can do Vienna any more damage,' Dominic concluded, his voice grim.

'You'll have it,' Gloria said, her own voice like cracked ice.

Her quick agreement startled him. 'You'll talk to Gillespie?'

'Oh, I'll do more than talk to him,' Gloria said ominously. 'Within a few hours you'll know all that he does. It can't be done on the phone, but it'll get done. Believe me.'

'I'm going to get them, Glory.' He switched easily to her nickname, even as his eyes narrowed on her. 'I'm going to get both of them. And if you're mixed up in it, anywhere at all down the line, I'll get you too.' It seemed to Dominic more than obvious that Gloria Gaines knew a hell of a lot more than she was saying.

Gloria wasn't scared by the threat – she was too mad. 'Is there anything else you need?'

'No.' Dominic got up and walked to the door, then turned around and smiled weakly. 'I'm back in your debt again, it seems.'

Gloria looked at him steadily. 'If anything,' she said softly, 'it's the other way around.' If it hadn't been for his suspicions and his acting on them, Drake and Jago might have succeeded ... Oh God, what if they already had. According to that incompetent fool she'd hired, she and the boy were in Switzerland now, at the Finishing School. What if ...

'Glory?' Dominic said questioningly, and Gloria snapped out of it. She couldn't afford to panic now – she just couldn't. She had too much to do.

'I'm all right,' she assured him, but as soon as he'd gone she burst into tears.

THE weeping only lasted a minute. Like she'd said, she had too much to do. Calling up Frank she demanded he meet her on the *Hula Kai*, a boat that specialized in two-hour-long cruises, and once he'd found her there she immediately attacked him about what he knew of Drake.

'Hey,' Frank protested as they stood on the deck, the harbour slowly slipping away from them. 'What is this? I thought you just wanted to have lunch.'

'Tell me, Frank,' Gloria warned him, in no mood to play games.

'I know Jago came to the club last night – I know he and Drake are up to something.' Frank stared at her for a few minutes, a little taken aback by how quickly she got on to things. Hell, it was only a matter of eight or so hours, and already she'd heard. 'Look, Drake's been running up a debt for months. Eventually I told him no pay, no play. Then, about two months ago, he began paying me back. Last night he shows up demanding credit. I say no, but then he says he can guarantee I get paid – and tells me Richard Jago is his banker. So I'm curious. I gave the sap a thou and then called Jago. I was half-expecting him not to come; Drake was drunk – almost paralytic. But Jago did show, and personally guaranteed to pay the way.'

'You know who Jago is, don't you?'

'Sure, I knew he and the girl were once shacked up together, but . . .'

'I want you to lean on Drake. Hard.'

Frank straightened up, looking at her with a brooding expression. 'What the hell's going on?'

'Just do it, Frank – as a favour to an old friend, OK?' She let her voice soften as she realized belatedly just how nasty and aggressive she must have sounded.

'A favour?' Frank repeated. 'OK, Glory, I can do you a favour. But do you mind telling an old friend what's up?'

Gloria did so, deciding to appeal to Frank's sense of self-survival to spur him on. 'So if he *is* messing with the girl's mind, it's in our best interests to stop the son of a bitch.'

Frank swore. He himself had never liked or trusted shrinks – they scared him. And the thought of a man deliberately driving someone, but especially a sick young girl, insane, and doing it for money . . . that made him want to puke. Gloria watched the disgust on his face, and her heart filled with tender affection. She could, if she'd wanted to, immediately ensure all of Frank's cooperation, but that would require too great a sacrifice. No – best keep it like this. Best keep it strictly business, especially after all this time.

'Leave it to me. I'll have the lads pick up Drake and . . . persuade . . . him to confess,' Frank promised, his voice almost as grim as Dominic's had been.

'Good,' Gloria said, and although she knew just what form that 'persuasion' would take she didn't care.

In fact, she hoped Frank's 'lads' half-killed the bastard!

Chapter 44

They had flown in that morning, jetlagged but too excited to sleep the afternoon away in their hotel. Buying a guidebook in the lobby, they saw immediately that they were situated only four blocks away from Broadway to the south, and Central Park to the north. But while they explored, Vienna was dismayed to find that the famous city apparently sparked off no memories for her.

'Never mind, sweetheart, it's a big place,' Farron reassured her as they battled against the huge crowds on the sidewalks. 'I think we'd better find a café or something. If this is what it's like at four o'clock in the afternoon, I sure as hell don't want to be here come five.'

Vienna did manage a genuine smile at that. Besides, the crowds were frightening her. With so many faces, it seemed almost a certainty that one would be like his – Gary Lyons'.

They found a little café tucked away up one of the numerous side-streets, and she was glad to go inside. Although she'd said nothing to Farron, she was beginning to feel hemmed in by all those skyscrapers.

'Thanks.' She accepted the cup of coffee Farron brought her and took a tentative sip. It wasn't as good as Kona coffee. 'I hate New York,' she said, taking Farron by surprise as he squeezed in beside her in the two-seater booth.

'We haven't been here two hours yet,' he said softly. 'Give it a little time, hm?'

She nodded. He was being so patient with her – he was so kind and so good, and she was just a murdering bitch. Suddenly a thought crept into her brain that was so hideous it bathed her in a cold sweat: *what if she killed him, Farron?* What if the reason she couldn't stand him to make love to her was because she was beginning to hate him like she hated Gary Lyons? She stared at him, her eyes as round and as shattered as broken saucers, and beneath his tan Farron went white.

No, she thought, no. I love him. I do. But what if . . . Oh God. Abruptly she tried to get up but the seats were plastic and anchored to the floor, forcing her to scramble sideways in her desperate bid to escape grazing her ribs and banging her shins against the chair leg as she did so. Farron reached for her hand. 'No!' she almost screamed and ran towards the ladies' room.

Pushing open the spring door with one hand she held the other clamped over her mouth to stem the nausea. Following her, Farron ignored the sign on the door and was only seconds behind her as she ran into a cubicle, crouched down on her knees and was sick into the toilet.

'It's all right,' he whispered, crouching down beside her, putting one arm around her shoulders and holding his other palm across her forehead. 'It's OK. Sshh.' Her shoulders heaved as she retched again, but in truth she had been eating so little that her stomach was almost empty. She had made no move to stop him as he firmly held her up and half-walked, half-carried her to the washbasin where he ran some cold water in the bowl. He continued to hold her, whispering continuously to her in soothing Hawaiian. 'Come on,' he said softly. 'We'll go back to the hotel now.'

Vienna nodded numbly and leaned into him, closing her eyes as he led her out of the café and waved down a taxi. She didn't want to see them all looking at her – all those eyes, those accusing eyes. 'Those eyes,' she whispered as she slumped in the back of the taxi, her eyes still clenched tight.

'What eyes, sweetheart?'

'All those eyes – they know.'

Farron didn't ask; he already knew what she would reply. His face was etched in lines of worry as he stared at the dirty ceiling of the taxi. Dear God in heaven, he prayed, don't let this go on much longer.

Once in their room he pulled back the cover of the bed and sat her down, taking off her shoes and sliding her under the sheets. Realizing where she was, her eyes went round with panic. 'No! I don't want to go to sleep!' she cried out hysterically. Her hands came out to grasp his forearm, her fingers digging into him with the strength born of desperation.

'You don't have to go to sleep, sweetheart,' he whispered. 'Just lie still. I'll close the curtains.'

'No – don't! I don't want it to be dark! Can you open the window – so I can hear the cars?'

Farron nodded. 'OK. I'll be right back.'

Vienna watched him go and gave a deep, shaky sigh. She wanted to hear something normal, like traffic. She wanted the afternoon light bright in the room. She wanted to stay in the real world, and not the nightmare one that awaited her on the other side of sleep; one that was getting nearer and nearer every second, like a devil panting obscenely at her heels. 'Everything scares me,' she whispered forlornly.

Farron could feel himself stretching as taut as the strings of the guitar he played. How much longer could it go on? He stood looking down at her, wracked with helpless frustration. She had curled herself into the foetal position, her eyes wide open and staring across the room. Slowly he sat on the side of the bed and leaned forward, his head bowed as he stared between his feet at the beige carpet underneath. *Mental illness.* The phrase slipped into his mind when his guard was down, but instead of pushing it away, as he had done in the past, he began to consider it. He had to face it – for her sake. Things couldn't go on like this much longer.

IT was 7.45 when they went down to breakfast the next morning and sat across the table from each other, holding hands.

'Do you feel any better this morning?' Farron asked softly.

She thought about that, but it was strange. She could hardly remember yesterday afternoon at all. 'Yes, I do actually,' she said, and Farron smiled, relief and pessimism warring within him, for she'd had days like this before; brief, sparkling wonderful days when the black clouds would lift and he'd catch a glimpse of the old Vienna. But the clouds had always come back – worse than before. So while they ordered and ate breakfast, and while they talked and smiled and even joked, a gagging fear ate at his innards. What would tomorrow bring? What could be worse than yesterday?

At reception he asked about a car and was told one had already been booked for them and was waiting in the underground parking lot. By 9.30 they had left the vast metropolis behind and were heading towards Albany where they found that the orphanage was one of those almost depressingly large, government-funded types. Sleeping dorms lay like long white worms in the sun, whilst the classrooms for extra-curricular activities only were square, squat buildings of an unflattering mustard colour. The grounds were a mixture of concrete playing areas, complete with climbing frames and swings for the younger ones, whilst further out on the grass, track and fields sporting events had been marked out in white chalk. The place was surprisingly bankrupt of children, and they supposed that all but the tots were at school.

As they passed a small building they could hear singing – a childish song sung by the very young. She stopped to listen, her hand clinging more firmly to his as she felt a lump come to her throat. She had done that – she had probably sung that same song, in that same room. Quickly she looked away from the building with the dirty windows and cracking paintwork into the face of the man she loved – handsome, gentle, worried. He smiled and squeezed her hand and they slowly began to walk towards the office block – and her past. Before leaving Interlaken, Farron had phoned the orphanage director and told him only that Pauline Clarke and himself would be out to see him on a matter of great importance.

When they found his secretary, a smiling competent woman, she showed them straight in. The office was small but bright and clean. Flowering plants bloomed lushly and with positive health on every available space where natural light infiltrated the room. Awards and certificates in cheap gilt frames were hung in pride of place, smothering every wall, but it was the man who was standing in front of a desk at whom she stared with almost painful intensity. He was small – no more than five feet six, with a round belly and a round bald dome. Over his ears and circling the lower back of his head were curly tufts of almost carroty-red hair. His eyes were large and blue, but shortsighted, and over them he wore glasses with a thick black frame. He was – someone. She could feel the reaction in herself, a sort of warmness, a gladness seep into her bones. Yet nothing in her brain clicked in response. It was not a memory – just a feeling. But what a feeling! She knew him – she knew him and liked him!

'Pauline!' Michael Gray, Director of Sands Orphanage for the last thirty-five years, came towards her and only as he got closer did he notice her ravaged appearance. Immediately his beaming smile faltered. Michael Gray was what many people who knew him would call a saint. He had never married or had children of his own because he gave all his love, time and attention, to the hundreds of children who counted on him for their well-being. And none of them had ever been let down. Each dorm, of course, had a house-mother, and these women had his same dedication and love, but there was something a little extra in Michael Gray's soul. Nothing was too much trouble for his children – no hassle and no expense, most of which came from his own pockets.

In all his years he'd never forgotten one of his kids, and he remembered Pauline Clarke as well now as he had when she'd been growing up. So he saw at once the agony in her eyes. 'Pauline,' he said, his voice hushed. 'What is it, my love?'

For a moment he couldn't say any more. But Vienna knew. In her heart she knew, and she found herself walking towards him, her eyes filling with tears as the little man held out his arms to her and hugged her to him in a tight embrace. 'Come and sit down,' Michael whispered and led her to a sofa. His eyes sought out Farron over Vienna's head as she wept into his rounded chest as she had done many times before as a small girl. And it was Farron who told Michael the story.

By the time he'd finished Vienna had stopped crying and was sitting back against the settee, drying her eyes on the pristine white handkerchief Michael had given her. Throughout the recital of the facts, the orphanage director had listened in appalled silence, and now he turned on the seat to face her, his hand covering hers in a strengthening gesture of sympathy.

'I never dreamed that when you stopped writing it could have been because of anything like this,' he said softly, shaking his head.

'I used to write?'

'You always wrote once a week, ever since you left here. To both me and your house-mother,' he told her, struggling to grapple with the realities of amnesia.

'My house-mother?'

He shook his head helplessly. 'It's so hard to imagine how difficult it must be ... Carla Greenaway was your house-mother when you first arrived as a baby.'

'Oh. Can I see her?'

'Oh darling, I'm sorry. She's with her children at the moment in Albany – she's taken them to a museum there. She'll be back tonight, though.'

Vienna looked at Farron with a silent question in her eyes and saw him nod. 'We'll come back,' he said softly, then to Michael who was looking between them with knowing eyes, 'I'm Farron Manikunna, by the way.'

'He saved my life,' Vienna said and when he went to open his mouth, she shook her head at him. 'You did, Farron – and you still do. Every day.' Turning to the older man she said, 'What can you tell me of my parents, Michael?'

But Michael could tell her little more about her parents than the records from Switzerland had done. Instead, as the hours ticked on, he brought forth a steady stream of remembrances, sharing with them all that he could recall. Like her winning first prize in art class for a drawing of the orphanage dog – a mangy old labrador. He'd been called Flicks because he was so friendly his long tail constantly wagged and flicked everybody's legs.

It was a morning of tender pain and nostalgia – not for things remembered, but for things lost to her. She didn't actually recall any of the incidents he told her, but she knew they had happened just as he related them to her. It was a morning of learning that she had been a very normal little girl – with all of a little girl's foibles and charms. She had once pinched a least favourite boy's marbles and kicked up a fuss when she had been discovered, told off and forced to give them back. She had also been a little girl who shared half her Easter egg with a new arrival who had come on Easter Sunday. Because there had been a mix-up at records and no one had expected her, Michael and their house-mother had no egg to give her. Pauline Clarke had not been a particularly brilliant schoolgirl, but not a dunce either, Michael had told her. Her favourite lessons had been English, music and geography.

None of what Michael said surprised Farron. He'd always known she'd been wonderful.

'Of course, nearly all of you children had best friends – others of your own age that you were especially close to. Yours were Veronica Zachary, who lives now in Washington DC, and a boy called Gordon Whitmore.' Neither Farron nor Vienna missed the way Michael hesitated when he mentioned Gordon.

'I wish Veronica wasn't so far away,' Vienna said. 'What did she look like?' She was bursting with curiosity over a friend she felt she had never known.

Michael slapped his forehead with his palm. 'Oh, what a nerd I am. Wait here a second.' He surprised them by suddenly jumping to his feet and rushing out of the room, but he was gone only a few minutes, returning with several photo albums. 'This is your house.' Michael tapped the label on the first one. 'See? Gamma House, and all the years when the photos were taken are written underneath.' He pointed to the labels. 'It was my idea to keep a running visual record of all my kids,' he smiled as he turned the pages slowly, letting her see all the cheerful little faces, only stopping when her own little face was present, and then recalling the incident behind the picture. 'Yes – look. That's the drawing of Flicks.'

Vienna drew the photo album across her lap and looked down at a nine-year-old elfin face, grinning broadly and holding across her tummy a graphic picture of a ginger dog with uneven legs.

'A budding Michelangelo,' Farron teased, but he continued to listen with an eagerness that rivalled Vienna's as Michael chatted on, unstinting in his time although his secretary did interrupt once to remind him of an appointment and was told to cancel it. 'Of course, when you were sixteen you had to leave here, but by then we had a job lined up for you, and a place to live. And ... Gordon was there with you so you weren't too scared.'

It was the second time that hesitation had crept into his voice, and Vienna asked him to show her a picture of Gordon. There were photos of him as a little boy, first about six, then around eleven, and finally the last photos showed a handsome sixteen-year-old lad, already nearly six feet tall, with dark brown hair. None of the photographs meant anything to her, although they did arouse feelings – very mixed feelings. One photograph showed them making a cake; Gordon was holding a spoon filled with gunge in his hand, looking set to spray her with it, and she was holding up her hands in a protective gesture, laughing happily. The moment was one of fun and carefree playfulness, but there was something else . . .

Looking Michael straight in the eye she said, 'Is he living near here?'

Michael cleared his throat. 'Yes. I . . . have his address. If you want it.'

'Please,' she said, then looked at Farron. For the first time it occurred to her that Gordon might have been her first boyfriend – and that Farron might be feeling left out, even jealous. But he grinned and squeezed her hand, understanding written all over his face.

'Here's your dossier,' Michael said, slipping photo-copies he'd had his secretary prepare into a buff folder and securing them with a clip. 'And here's your last address. I don't know what will have happened to it. It was a rented flat as I recall. And here is where you work – or worked.'

Vienna took the papers in a daze. A flat of her own – with her own belongings! And a job – a job where people knew her. And Gordon. Yes, first she must see Gordon. 'Thank you, Michael,' Vienna said, fresh tears coming into her eyes.

'Oh, Pauline – any time. You know that. Now, you will come back tonight? I'll tell Carla all about you and I know she'll be on edge and unable to even think straight until she's seen you again.'

Vienna got to her feet, her legs feeling like jelly beneath her.

'We will come back – I promise. You don't understand how much I needed to see you.'

'Do you remember me, just a little, now?' Michael asked, his crinkled face so hopeful that she felt tears spurt in her eyes. Again she went to him to be hugged like a little girl. 'I feel you,' she said, her voice choked. 'That's more important.'

Michael nodded, his own eyes full. 'Yes, yes it is. All right, perhaps you'd better go now,' he laughed awkwardly, 'or we'll both start blubbering!'

They were halfway back to New York, where all three addresses were located, before she finally managed to get herself under control. 'He's a remarkable man,' she finally said.

Farron looked across at her and smiled. 'Yes, he is.'

'It was worth coming here, just to see him.'

'Yes. But we'll see the others too. Let's start with this Gordon fellow.'

She was looking fit to burst now, eager to learn more about herself. She now knew her life from babyhood to sixteen, but there was so much more. As they began to turn down streets that became more and more suburbanized, and where skyscrapers gave way to more modest apartment blocks, she began to tense up again. 'Farron – about Gordon . . .'

'It won't matter,' he said softly. 'Michael as good as said you two left together – and probably lived together for a few years at least. It doesn't matter, not to me,' he reassured her, and he wasn't lying. He still felt guilty about suspecting her of being in Gloria's stable of girls. He was not about to suspect or judge her ever again.

But when they pulled up in front of the unknown Gordon's apartment block Vienna was beginning to tremble. Gordon – he'd seemed nice from the photos. He'd been her best friend. She'd left the orphanage and lived with him. What was there to be scared of? And yet . . . she *was* scared.

In the lift Farron pressed the fifth button and once they'd got out they slowly walked down the corridor, checking numbers until they found the right one. 'He's probably at work at this time of day,' he murmured, but nevertheless knocked on the door. A moment later it opened to reveal a young man dressed in jeans and a plain white shirt. But not

Gordon. This boy was blond and no more than nineteen years old.

'Yes?' His brown eyes were friendly but wary, and Vienna blinked, trying to rearrange her thoughts.

'Er . . . is Gordon in?'

The young boy relaxed. 'No, he's at work at the moment. I'm Bob, can I do anything for you?'

Vienna looked helplessly at Farron, who took charge. 'I'm afraid not. It's really Gordon we came to see. The orphanage gave us his address.'

'Orphanage?' the young man repeated, and then, as if a light had just dawned, looked quickly at Vienna and said urgently, 'Are you Pauline Clarke?'

Vienna nodded. 'Yes.'

'Pheewww,' the young man stood aside as he let out his breath in a long slow sigh. 'Come in, please. Jeeze, Gordon's going to be real glad you came. He's been worried sick about you, ever since you went missing. He went to the place you worked but no one there knew where you were either.'

The apartment was small, but tidy. The chairs and sofa were of matching brown leather, the cushions, curtains and rug in front of a mock fireplace of the same deep amber orange. The walls were cream, the carpet underfoot beige. On the walls were hung reproductions of Andy Warhol. The apartment, Farron noticed at once, only had one bedroom. 'You live here too?' he asked casually, and Bob nodded.

'Yeah, I do. Please sit down, let me get you a drink. I must call Gordon – he'll be so relieved. He's been worried sick about you,' he repeated, and then hesitated, wondering which to do first. Farron looked at Vienna, wondering if she'd worked it out yet. She had. Not logically – but with that strange combination of feelings and intuition.

'Gordon's gay, isn't he?' she said simply, and Bob, who had been on his way to the kitchenette after having decided to make them a drink first, stopped and stared at her.

'Of course he is,' he said, patently surprised, then added more warily, 'But he said you knew.'

Vienna smiled a little sadly. 'There's a lot I don't know apparently.'

Mistaking her meaning, Bob came back into the room and slowly sank down on a chair in front of them, his face both earnest and a little embarrassed. 'Look, Pauline. When I met Gordon he told me all about you two – about you being engaged, about the orphanage. Everything. He said you knew.' The news of an engagement surprised both Farron and Vienna. They stared at him blankly, and then saw his youthful face begin to flush. 'I'm so sorry,' he mumbled. 'I'd never have opened my big mouth if I thought . . . but it's not like Gordon to lie.'

'He didn't lie,' Farron said, then seeing the puzzled look he received, briefly outlined the situation in a few sentences.

Bob leaned back in the chair, his hair shining silver in the sunlight as he shook his head. 'It's unbelievable,' he whispered, then promptly flushed again. 'I don't mean that I don't believe you,' he hastily backtracked. 'I mean it just seems . . . but it explains everything. I must call Gordon and tell him.' Vienna waited as the boy sprang from his chair and dashed into a side room – the bedroom probably. He was obviously very much in love with the man to whom she had once been engaged. In a way, it was touching.

'It makes sense now, doesn't it?' she said to Farron, who nodded.

'Yes, why you were so sad in Switzerland at first – and why Michael hesitated when talking about him.'

Yes, Vienna thought, Michael must have known. Perhaps he thought she needed an old friend to be with in those early days of being out and about in the big wide world without the institution to fall back on. They held hands on the sofa in a spirit of perfect understanding and when Bob returned they were both on their feet. 'He's coming right over,' Bob assured them, but Vienna shook her head.

'No – it doesn't matter. Tell Gordon when you see him that I said I'm sorry if he was scared. Tell him . . .' she looked at Farron and then reached for his hand, smiling as he stepped closer and looped his arm around her shoulders. 'Tell him I've found a man whom I love very much.' She looked at the younger man's uncertain face, and smiled softly. 'Even though I can't remember him, I know that he was very kind to me – a good friend. Will you do that?'

Bob rubbed his hands uncomfortably down his jeans. 'Sure I will, but he'll be here in half an hour.'

Vienna shook her head. 'No. Tell him it's all in the past and that I wish him luck – and know he wishes the same for me. OK?'

'OK.' The teenager showed them out, still looking uncertain. 'Bye now. And . . . good luck with the rest of your life.'

As it turned out, her own apartment building looked very much like the one they had just left, except that here a few straggling trees grew in tiny gardens no more than a few feet square. Looking up at the windows, Vienna felt vaguely depressed. Had she really lived here once? Her mind winged back to the bungalow on Oahu – the sweeping green lawns leading down to the sea. The frothing expanse of flowers everywhere, the panoramic views. It was like paradise compared to this.

'Not like home, is it?' Farron murmured with unerring understanding.

'No. Do you suppose the landlord is in?'

They found the office, but as the door opened were confronted by a diminutive woman no more than four feet in height. Her hair was salt-and-pepper and swept to the back of her head in an untidy bun. Her skin was swarthy and full of lines, but her eyes were like little black buttons – sharp and all-seeing. 'Yes, what you want?' she demanded, her voice thick with an Italian accent. She turned from Farron and looked at Vienna closely, her face falling into lines of astonishment and then anger.

'You!' She pointed a bony finger at Vienna accusingly. 'You! What a fine one you are . . .' she lapsed into a rapid and very angry Italian, backing into the office as she did so. Giving Vienna a wry look Farron closed the door behind them and waited until the little dynamo's tirade began to flag.

'Mrs . . .' Vienna began, and the little woman planted her hands on her hips, cocking her head to one side like a bird as she looked at her.

'Whaddya mean – Mrs?' She spread her hands in a graphic

gesture. 'For five-a years you live here. I'm-a Signora Loretti.'

'Mrs Loretti,' Vienna repeated. 'I don't remember you.'

Before she could explain herself, she was treated once more to a barrage of Italian, interspersed with English phrases such as, 'No man he ever forget Sophia Loretti,' and, 'Sophia Loretti may be small but she unforgettable!'

After a while, Vienna too began to wonder how she could have forgotten such a woman, and it took Farron, speaking slowly but firmly, to explain just what had happened, and then the change from harping accuser to mother-hen Italian *mama* was completed within a second, leaving Vienna momentarily bewildered.

'Oh, poor little *bambina*,' the tiny woman's arthritic hands were amazingly strong as she grabbed Vienna's arm and led her firmly to a rickety little chair. 'It eeze a terrible world. Even in such a place as Hawaii!' she threw up her hands. 'All the time I hear from my tenants, oh I want to go to Hawaii – as if it was heaven! Hah! There they hit the poor tourist over the head and steal their memories. Hah, some heaven,' she vigorously crossed herself then set about making coffee.

Bemused, Vienna looked up at Farron and saw that he had a hand over his mouth, smothering laughter. Of course, once he'd started, she did too, and the sight of Mrs Loretti, four feet high, hands on hips and a ferocious smile on her tiny crinkled face, only made it worse. 'Forgive me, Signora, but I'm just so happy to find out who I am,' Vienna tried to explain. 'Only this morning I went to the orphanage where I . . .'

'Orphanage?' The old woman said the word as if it was the worst thing imaginable and yet again the Italian spewed forth, only this time definitely sympathetic. Oh, for a child to be brought up in such a place! Mrs Loretti nearly cried over it. It took a while, but slowly they learned that Vienna had had a visitor in December. Their new friend could only tell them that it was an old woman, not a man. Her little tenant Pauline was a good girl – she never brought men back to her apartment. Farron smirked at this, looking so self-satisfied that Vienna surreptitiously nudged him in the ribs. Her landlady said that after the old woman had gone, apparently, Vienna had packed some things and had left within the week.

What had happened to make her leave so suddenly, she hadn't a clue, but Vienna had paid her last January's rent in advance and said she'd be back.

She'd kept the flat till April, Mrs Loretti assured her, profusely apologizing when she explained how she'd had to rent it out to new tenants, and all the while the poor little bambina had been lying at death's door, her memory gone. She herself had packed all Vienna's things and put them into storage – but it took the little woman half an hour to hunt around an unbelievably chaotic office before locating the storage company's ticket and address. They drank five cups of coffee and Farron was ruthlessly quizzed on his background and intentions towards Pauline. It wasn't until the Signora was satisfied that he loved her with all his heart and soul, and that he'd been brought up by a good Roman Catholic woman (which Farron knew would have made his *tutu* burst her sides with laughter) that they eventually escaped from the woman's office. With her demands to be happy and to have *molti molti bambini* still ringing in their ears, the pair collapsed into their car and burst into laughter.

'You sure do pick your landladies, Pauline Clark,' Farron teased her. 'And whaddya say we go back-a to the hotel-a for an afternoon-a tea, before going to the office-a?' he offered in a way-over-the-top Italian accent.

Vienna agreed. For once she was feeling really peckish, and the office where she worked wouldn't shut until five. It was now only three. Mrs Loretti was such a character that Vienna suddenly realized she'd almost forgotten about *him*. No – she mustn't think of him! But it was too late. In an unguarded moment she'd let him back into her mind. Farron sensed her change of mood immediately.

'Perhaps we should go to the office now,' he suggested, trying to get her former mood back. 'You can see all your old workmates.'

'No – let's go back to the hotel. I want to shower anyway.' But her voice was flat and Farron felt again the resurgence of fear biting deep in his gut.

But as they drove back to the hotel, Vienna's mind was on Richard Jago. Had living with Gordon, a man who didn't find her sexually attractive, made her insecure about herself and her desirability? Was that why she'd clung to Richard so fiercely at first? Because, even though she didn't remember why, she was still subconsciously scared of not being a real woman?

Farron easily understood why she'd felt a fresh burst of strength and confidence this morning after meeting Michael, and he just prayed this strength would hold out for the rest of the ordeal still to come.

BACK at the hotel, Farron left her briefly while he went to collect her things from storage. Maybe there would be a diary or other documents among them that might fill in some more missing pieces. Vienna picked up their key from the desk and then headed straight for their room, feeling suddenly alone and very vulnerable. What if he didn't come back? If he crashed the car or . . . No, stop that! she told herself firmly as she entered and slammed the door behind her. Walking determinedly to their bathroom, she turned on the shower taps, stripped and stepped beneath the spray. There was something soothing about the rain – something protective . . .

It was raining in the alley and it too was warm – like blood was warm. And when she looked up she saw that it *was* blood – dripping from the stabbed body of the blond man. She screamed and ran up the narrow street where the screaming of the other unseen woman grew louder, and in a doorway in front of her she saw a woman, framed against the light. 'Help me!' she cried out. 'Help me!'

She ran closer and could see the woman's face now – Gloria's face. It was Gloria Gaines. 'Gloria, help me,' she called out, but it was still raining, and when she looked up *he* was still there – he had followed her up the alley like a grisly cloud, raining his blood down upon her. Hearing a strange noise behind her she turned and saw a whirling black disk spinning through the air towards her, and suddenly she knew what it wanted: it wanted to behead her. She spun again and found Gloria coming towards her, a look of horror on her face. Her hands were outstretched, and Vienna began to run towards them, to outpace that spinning, scything disc. 'Help me!'

'Vienna! Vienna! Wake up!' Hands were shaking her and for a second she thought it was him – Lyons, descended from the sky, and she gave a strangled moan of terror. Then she opened her eyes and Farron was there, his white shirt soaked from the shower's spray.

'It's OK,' he shook her again, but gently. 'I'm here now – I'll never leave you again. Never.'

She crawled into his arms, naked and wet, and he turned off the spray and picked her up, walking with her into the bedroom. She was trembling, but not crying. She was beyond that now. Briskly rubbing her dry, he helped her into a terry robe, then set about drying her hair as she stood quiet and obedient, compliant as a child.

'Did you find it?' she asked, her voice so normal and calm that for a moment he didn't hear her actual words. Looking at her closely, he felt a chill run down his spine. She was too calm. Was she in shock?

'Yes. Yes, I did.' Leaving her he picked up the big blue leather-bound book he had dropped on to the bed the moment he'd heard her crying out for help, and returned it to her. She took it to the bed where she sat down wearily and drew her legs under her. Opening the first page of the diary, she began to read.

Just then the phone rang. For a while he ignored it as he watched her read intently, a frown of concentration forming on her face. Deciding it was safe to leave her for a moment he picked up the phone and walked with it into the bathroom. There the air was warm and moist and smelt of soap.

'Farron? It's Dominic.'

'Oh, hi,' Farron said absently, opening the door a crack to see if she was still all right. She was.

'Farron, I've chartered a private jet to bring you and Vienna back to Oahu immediately,' Dominic's voice began crisply but urgently. 'A car should call to pick you up in about . . .' there was a brief pause as, on the other end of line, he checked his watch, 'a quarter of an hour.'

For the first time it dawned on Farron that there was

something in Dominic's tone that he'd never heard there before. Something hard – something almost vicious, and he sank down on the edge of the bathtub, a feeling of terrible premonition driving all other thoughts away. 'Oh God, what's happened?' He heard his own voice, blank and harsh, but hadn't been aware of forming the words. Over the wire he could feel Dominic's presence as closely as if he'd been in the room with him.

'Vienna must see another doctor – another psychiatrist. Immediately.'

'I don't know,' he said doubtfully, thinking of Vienna's happiness this morning. 'Dom, she's learning about herself and I don't know that I should drag her away now.'

'Farron,' Dominic said, after a brief pause. 'Do you trust me?'

The question was more than it seemed, Farron knew that immediately. In the normal course of events, he trusted Dominic completely and the older man knew it. What he was really asking was, 'Do you trust me above all else?' Did he? Did he trust him with Vienna's life as much as he would with his own? The answer, when it came to him, was without a single doubt. 'Yes.'

'Then pack your things and catch that plane. There's no time to explain anything now.'

'Very well.' Once his mind was made up, the confusions and doubts were gone. 'I'll see you later.'

'Right. And son – it's nearly over.'

'Thank God,' Farron said with heartfelt relief and then hung up, no more words needed between them. He replaced the phone on the bedside table and only when he straightened and turned to look at her, did he notice that she was staring at the wall, a strange expression on her face. 'Vienna?' he spoke her name fearfully, as if expecting just the sound of it would crush her.

But when she looked at him it was with a clear straight gaze. 'Listen to this,' she said simply, and began to read from the diary. ' *"Matron Becker called on me today, just as I was going to work. I was surprised to see her – she'd retired from the orphanage years ago when I was only ten or eleven. But I* was glad to see her. Next to Carla and Michael, Matron was the nearest thing to a relative I had. But I saw at once she looked strange. I learned later that she was ill and she died within a week, so perhaps that was why she came to me when she did. What she had to tell me was . . . I can't find the words to put it down in this diary. I'm just too full, so full of hope and excitement and relief.

"Matron told me that my parents who'd been killed in the car crash were my adoptive parents, not my real parents at all. I couldn't believe it. But there was even more to come. She'd seen the original adoption papers, and knew that I'd been born in Oahu. My mother, apparently, worked in a gambling den, which was illegal of course, and had originally come from the Bronx in New York. I didn't know what to say. I just sat down in my big wicker chair, the one Michael gave me on leaving the orphanage, and stared at her.

"She looked uncomfortable for a moment when I asked her why my mother had given me up for adoption and then she told me that my mother was . . . and there's only one way to put it – a prostitute. I suppose I was shocked at first. But not nastily shocked. It didn't matter to me at all what my mother was or did – only that she was alive. I had a mother, and possibly a father too. It was like a miracle, a dream come true. I must go to Hawaii and find her – I must! It's every orphan's dream to find out that there's been a mistake, that she or he has a family after all. Who knows what might have happened in all these years? She might have married and I might have brothers and sisters somewhere. And Hawaii! Oh, today has got to be one of the happiest days of my life." '

Vienna finished reading, and let the book drop into her lap. Then she looked at Farron who was frowning, and she shook her head.

'Don't you see, Farron?' she said simply, looking at him with wide eyes. 'It's Gloria. Gloria Gaines is my mother.'

577

Chapter 45

The battered red Beetle pulled up in front of the Glorious Motel. The driver got out and knocked jauntily on the door which was opened by an old woman who looked at him with disgusted eyes. 'We don't open till seven.'

'I ain't here for no ass,' the driver said, his voice affronted. 'I don't have to pay for my pieces of tail. I wanna see the madam. She's expectin' me.' He put a hand on the door and pushed forward but surprisingly, it didn't move.

'Step one inch closer and you'll lose your toes,' the old woman told him and the driver instinctively withdrew his foot.

'Listen, you old . . .'

'Who's that?' a voice he recognized called from within and before the old battleaxe could open her mouth he yelled out, 'It's me, Miss Gaines.'

The voice called again. 'Let him in, Nancy.'

Inside, Gloria stood in her office doorway. 'Come in here,' she ordered, her voice like ice. Hell, where did Frank get them? As she took her seat behind her desk, the driver moved to sit in the facing chair and she said sharply: 'I didn't give you permission to sit.'

Ready to growl that he didn't need no brothel-keeper's permission to do anything, something in her steady gaze stopped him. 'You wanted to see me? Let's get down to it then, 'cause I ain't got all day.'

'On the contrary,' Gloria said, reaching for a small envelope that was lying ready on her desk. 'All day is precisely what you *have* got. You're fired.'

'*Fired*?' The man stared at her stupidly for a moment, and then his small greedy eyes fell to the envelope she was holding. 'That my money'?

'That's half the money we agreed,' Gloria corrected.

'Half — whaddya mean? What you trying to pull, you whoring son-of-'

'It's half,' Gloria interrupted totally unfazed, 'because you only did half of your job, which was if you remember, to watch – *watch*, mind – the girl and report on everyone who came into contact with her.'

'Yeah. I did that, didn't I?' he sneered.

She firmed her lips. 'You didn't. It's come to my attention that – never mind. The only thing that needs concern you is that you botched it. Now take your money and get out.'

'Botched hell,' he growled, leaning his knuckled fists on the desk and looming over her threateningly. 'You're just using this as an excuse to cheat me. You're all alike you women – all cheating bitches. And that little blonde ain't no different.'

'Take your money and get out.'

'Or what?' the man sneered, his piggy brown eyes smug and gloating, sure that no woman could ever get the better of him. Not even his wife – the cheating little whore. Yeah, his ex-wife ought to work in this dump.

'Or I shall call Frank and tell him I've got another little job I want him to do. Understand me? Good,' Gloria nodded, satisfied to see the man's unwashed skin grow pale. 'I can see that you do.'

'You women are all alike,' he whined. 'You were happy enough to see me when you wanted Lyons' body to disappear, weren't you?'

'But it didn't, did it?' Gloria snapped back. 'It reappeared and made life damned difficult for all of us.'

'Hey, that was a fluke,' the man protested. 'I do good work, I do.'

Gloria said something exceedingly graphic and even more unladylike. 'If you have any sense at all you'll take the money and go. And if,' she said warningly, as the man grabbed the envelope and turned on his heel, 'you have any ideas about making trouble, just remember – Frank doesn't owe you any loyalty. And you know Frank.'

The Beetle driver did know Frank. Muttering about nobody being honest any more, he left, slamming the door behind him. Wasting no time, she reached for the phone.

'Can I speak to Mr Fairchild, please,' she answered his

secretary's standard question quickly. 'Tell him it's Miss Gaines – he'll want to be interrupted.'

'Gloria?' Dom's voice was firm and without panic. But then, Gloria thought with a fond smile, when had she ever known Dominic to panic?

'I've just talked to Frank. He says the shrink is a weakling – he'll crack to order and spill his guts about anything we ask.'

'Good.' Dominic never wasted words either. 'I've just talked to Farron – he and Vienna will be just getting aboard the private jet about now, I should think. They'll be in tonight. It's quite a haul.'

'Right. Did he say how she was?' Gloria forced the question past stiff lips and prayed the query sounded casual.

'No – we didn't speak for very long. But I gather . . . I don't think she's doing too well. I've got Franz Jürgens flying in from Sweden at the moment. I'm putting him up in the guesthouse where they live. That way she can be in familiar surroundings.'

Gloria cleared her throat. 'That sounds fine. This Jürgens – he's good?'

'One of the best psychiatrists in the world. Do you know from Drake exactly what he did?'

'Not exactly,' Gloria said. 'Frank's got him stashed away in a place he knows near Diamond Head. We thought we might as well wait until your man gets here and then let the two shrinks discuss the problem together. Don't worry about Drake. He'll be as honest and truthful as a Boy Scout, you can be sure of that.'

It was a measure of his liking, respect and trust for Gloria that Dominic instinctively believed her. Yet he would be there – just to make sure for himself. 'OK. I'll let you know as soon as they fly in. I'll take them straight to the house in Waimea – Jürgens will be waiting for them there.'

'So will Drake,' Gloria promised grimly. 'What about Jago?'

'Don't worry about him,' Dominic said, his voice as hard as iron. 'We'll see to Jago.' Hanging up, he leaned back in his chair and rubbed his hand over his eyes. Time stretched like an instrument of torture when one felt eager for things to begin. But nothing could start until Farron and Vienna returned.

Dominic found the office was suddenly too quiet. Leaving his jacket draped over a chair, he walked to the elevator and got out at the lobby feeling restless. He was not very good at waiting. Leaving the hotel he drove aimlessly towards the Falling Pearls, but what was waiting for him there? Hell, he needed a drink.

He pulled in at the first bar he came to, which was little more than a small room, cramped with tables and chairs. An old Chinaman in one corner played chess with himself on a miniature board and nursed a beer that would no doubt last him hours. Sitting at the far end of the bar, slumped forward and snoring softly, was a grey-haired woman. One of her shoes had fallen off and lay underneath the bar stool.

'Scotch,' he ordered from a bored brunette with hard-boiled blue eyes.

There was a movement behind him as a man sat down beside him, looked at him absently, and then nodded. 'Mornin'.'

'Morning,' Dominic responded, his eyes briefly inspecting him and seeing only a personable young man. The woman slapped the drink down in front of him.

'Ten bucks.'

Dominic smiled. No doubt she'd had him pegged the moment he came in. 'I think you mean five, don't you?' he corrected her, and slapped a note on the bar, looking her in the eye until she backed down.

'Yeah,' she said. 'I meant five. Isn't that what I said?'

Dominic shook his head, but his smile wasn't hard. He caught the man by his side looking at him, a mixture of respect and amusement on his face.

'What'll you have?' the girl snapped, her voice like gravel.

Bryan blinked. 'Er . . . a ginger ale please,' he half-stuttered, looking a little taken aback by the fierceness of her question. He quickly pulled out a crumpled dollar bill from his jeans pocket to pay her. ' 'Scuse me,' the kid leaned across Dominic for some peanuts, his open palm directly over Dominic's half-full scotch as he leaned forward. His hand come back with a handful of nuts that he proceeded to eat one at a time. 'I love these things,' he confided with a sheepish grin, but Dominic hardly paid any attention.

He's distracted by something, Bryan Canon realized, allowing his eyes to fall naturally to the man's scotch, feeling a small pang of relief to see that the small pill he had just dropped in had already dissolved. It was the only thing in a job like this that could go wrong – the mark might see the pill fizzing.

Idly, as he waited for Dominic to drain the drink, he wondered what was on his mind. The guy looked keyed up for something. An experienced interpreter of body language, Bryan knew all the signs. If he hadn't been in this preoccupied mood, Bryan knew that Dominic might have suspected something; he knew a sharp man when he met one.

Now the second risk came. Dominic had finished the drink and if he tried to leave immediately Bryan was in trouble. He couldn't let a mark get into a car once he'd taken the drug – he could get killed that way. But Dominic ordered a beer and took it over to a table in the corner, swigging it straight from the bottle. Bryan watched him in surprise. Somehow, the man's title, his position and wealth had built up in Bryan's mind a very different picture from the man who could swig beer from a bottle and look natural doing it. For a moment he felt sorry that he'd never get the chance to peel away some of the Prince's layers to get a good look at what was inside. It would probably be . . . Bryan snapped to attention abruptly when he saw Dominic's eyelids begin to droop. Half-turning on his stool he sipped his ginger ale and kept watch.

Dominic yawned – hell, he was tired. He hadn't been sleeping too well lately. What with Rhiannon snapping at his heels and Jago and Drake giving him nothing but headaches into the bargain, his life hadn't been particularly restful of late. But hell – he shouldn't be this tired!

Slowly it dawned on him that something was wrong. For a while he couldn't tell what it was. The room slowly rocked from side to side as he looked up towards the bar. The kid was watching him. The barmaid . . . he couldn't quite focus on the barmaid, but she had her back to him. Blinking, trying to clear his vision, Dominic sat forward in his chair, his head spinning. He put the beer bottle on the table, but it missed and fell to the floor. His coordination was shot. His brain too, was sluggish. For a moment he had to struggle to think. What the hell was going on? He had to do something. What was it? Help? Did he need help? Pushing against the table, his arms felt weak and they shook alarmingly, but he managed to stand up, even though his legs felt like rubber. Call someone – where was a telephone? Dominic paused, surprised. He couldn't think how to use a telephone. He put a hand to his forehead and blinked rapidly but his vision, if anything, grew even more blurred. Fresh air – fresh air would help. Looking around for the door, the room began to swing as if he were on a fairground ride. He swallowed hard, his mouth and throat suddenly painfully dry. Strangely, he felt no fear and wasn't sure why. Staggering from the table, one hand on the wall beside him for both guidance and support he moved towards the door, feeling as if his legs belonged to someone else.

'I think you need a hand, sir, don't you?' The voice sounded very loud in his ears and he turned his head to look at the man who was looming near him, his face distorted and balloon-like. Then Dominic felt hands on him – surprisingly strong hands.

'I d-don't . . .' his voice came out hopelessly slurred.

The face in front of him smiled. 'Don't worry, you just had a little too much to drink. I'll take you home, OK?'

Dominic shook his head then wished he hadn't. What had he had to drink? He was damned if he could remember. He made a small sound of pain when the bright sunlight hit him, but he didn't remember walking out of the bar.

'Everything will be fine,' the voice reassured him. Once so loud, it now sounded far away, as if at the end of a long tunnel. He lurched towards his sports car.

'No, not that car,' Bryan said, his voice soothingly gentle. 'Over here.'

Half-carrying and half-dragging him, Bryan walked to a van and pulled Dominic into the interior, where a mattress was waiting. Bryan was stronger than he looked and needed to be. Dominic was now totally unconscious, a deadweight.

Once he had his mark positioned squarely on the mattress, Bryan reached for a plank of wood and positioned it next to the mattress, fitting both ends lengthwise in the van so that the sleeping man couldn't roll about during the drive. Before he clambered into the driver's seat Bryan professionally took the man's pulse and checked his pupils with a small torch. Everything was fine. The drive to Chinatown was completed well within the speed limit and with total care.

DOMINIC slowly became aware of an ache in his neck and moved cautiously, wincing as he opened his eyes. For a while he had no idea where he was, or how he had come to be there. Sitting up straighter he became aware of a dull headache pounding away, and slowly leaned his head against the seat backrest and unwound his window, breathing deeply of the evening air. Evening? He glanced at his watch, staring incredulously at the amount of time that had passed, then looked around him. He was in his car, in a parking lot. What the hell? He'd had a scotch – he remembered it distinctly. Then he'd taken a beer to a table . . . there'd been a man at the bar. Then what?

Suddenly he remembered that Farron and Vienna were due in in only a couple of hours, and he quickly started the engine and headed towards Falling Pearls. The private landing strip was near Ewa Beach on the west coast, but he needed a shower first; a cold one. His head still felt as if it had been stuffed with cottonwool.

In his bathroom he ran the water first hot then cold, then hot then cold again. It didn't do much for his headache but it made him feel more awake.

'Koana, fix me some aspirin, will you?' he asked of the butler who'd laid out a fresh set of clothes for him the moment he'd heard the shower going. The old man nodded, and quickly brought him a fizzing glass of water. Dominic tossed the drink back before walking to the mirror to check his reflection. He looked a little grey, but other than that he was fine. Nevertheless, something had happened that didn't make sense. And the more his head finally cleared, and the more he thought about it, the less he liked it.

'I'll be late tonight.' Dominic met the butler's eyes in the glass, and the old Hawaiian nodded and left quietly. Dominic walked to the phone. Hell, he'd been dialling this number more often in the past year than he had in the previous ten years put together. 'Hello, Hua? It's me again?'

'Dominic. I meant to call you. About Jago . . .'

'Not now; I have something else for you.' Briefly Dominic told him about the events of the day, and when he'd finished there was silence over the end of the line for a brief moment.

'Sounds to me like this young guy slipped you something. Think back – did he ever go near your drink?' Dominic didn't think so, then remembered the peanuts. 'Sounds like a real pro to me.' Hua commented grimly. 'I can't say for sure yet but it sounds as if you've been set up for something. Any idea by whom?'

Dominic had. Plenty. 'I want you to find the kid for me.'

'Can you remember the name of the bar?'

Dominic told him. 'The only people there were the barmaid and an old Chinaman playing chess. But the barmaid's the kind who sees nothing and hears even less, and the Chinese never looked up from the board – of that I'm sure.'

Hua laughed. 'You'd be surprised at the things old men see – especially Chinese men. And money talks.'

'I don't care how much you have to offer. I need results – and fast.'

'Don't worry. There aren't many young kids on this island as professional as this one sounds. Tell me all you can remember about him.'

Dominic did so, then glanced at his watch. 'Look – I've got to get going. Just find the kid and get proof as to who hired him. I must have proof, Hua,' Dominic stressed. 'I've no idea what actually happened between noon today and when I woke up over an hour ago, but I'm damned sure I'm not going to like it.'

'I understand. I'll get back to you the moment I have something.'

'OK. You might not be able to find me at the regular places. If not try my house up in Waimea Bay.'

'OK. Bye. And don't worry – he's as good as found.'

Dominic laughed without humour and hung up. Sprinting for his car he remembered Jürgens. Phoning his social secretary at her home, he got her on the fifth ring. 'Yvonne? It's me – what happened with Jürgens?'

Yvonne Blake had been his social secretary for years. A divorcee with three kids in college, she had the organizational skills of a diplomat's wife.

'Hi, where've you been?' she asked, but didn't wait for an answer. 'When I couldn't find you I met him at the airport and drove him up to the house. The domestic agency had already sent a couple over, so I told the housekeeper to go and unpack his stuff and I stayed with him for a few hours. I thought you'd show any minute.'

'Sorry about that. Is he settled in?'

'As cosy as a Swedish bug in a rug,' the voice was warm and humorous.

'Give him a call, will you, and tell him that his patient will be arriving within the next hour or so. Then call Gloria Gaines and tell her the same. She'll know what to do. Oh, and make my apologies to Jürgens, hm?'

'Gloria Gaines, eh?' Yvonne laughed. 'That sounds interesting.'

Dominic laughed. 'Get your mind out of the gutter. And thanks for holding the fort.'

'Any time. Bye, boss. Have fun!'

'Oh, I intend to,' Dominic said, his thoughts on Drake. 'I surely do.'

The airstrip was little more than a huge well-tended field, but as he arrived, the ground-hugging landing lights had already been lit. Within ten minutes the Lear jet had appeared in the dark sky and landed. Dominic watched the ground staff wheel the stairs to the jet's door.

Farron spotted him immediately but said nothing, simply taking Vienna's cold and shaking hand in his own. He'd had a hard time talking her into coming back with him. She'd wanted to see her house-mother so badly he'd resorted to bullying to get her to leave New York.

'There's a limo waiting,' Dominic said softly, appalled by Vienna's pallor as she walked into the glare of the waiting headlights and he could see properly the haggard and gaunt look of her face. Farron understood at once that Dominic was saying nothing in front of her and was grateful. She couldn't take much more. Already she was wilting with tiredness and his arm around her did more than comfort her – it very nearly supported all her weight.

The drive took only half an hour but it seemed longer. When they pulled up, Farron saw at once that the big house had lights spilling from almost every room. He also saw two cars parked in front – both unfamiliar to him. Dominic pulled in first, and as Farron helped Vienna out he saw Dominic walk to one car and talk briefly to whoever was inside. Then he straightened as they approached him, and nodded to the house where a woman stood in the doorway, her face wearing the incurious look of a servant.

'I have the master bedroom prepared, sir,' she said as all three of them walked into the hall.

'Thank you, Mrs Fairley. That will be all for tonight.'

Dominic met Farron's eyes. 'Let's get her to bed,' he said softly, and bending down to scoop Vienna's legs from under her Farron carried her unresistingly up the stairs. Halfway up he hesitated as he saw the man waiting at the top. He was tall but reed-slender with greying blonde hair and alert blue eyes that were, at the moment, firmly fixed on Vienna.

'Farron – this is Dr Jürgens.' Dominic performed the introductions quickly.

'Doctor,' Farron said, once they were all on the landing. 'I hope you can do something for her.'

'Yes. It is really a simple matter now that I know what has been done.'

Taken by surprise for a moment by the man's strong Scandinavian accent, Farron paled at the choice of words.

'What do you mean – what's she done?'

'Not the patient. I have spoken to Drake. I will not call him Doctor, for obvious reasons,' the Swede said with such venom that Farron glanced in bewilderment at Dominic, who nodded down at Vienna.

'She'll be safe with Dr Jürgens,' he promised and Farron took the hint, carrying Vienna into the bedroom and placing her gently on the bed. Dominic stayed in the doorway, not wanting to intrude.

'Farron?' Vienna said, her voice weak as she opened her eyes, which widened as she saw the tall Swede.

'This is Dr Jürgens, sweetheart,' Farron whispered, bending over and kissing her softly on the lips. 'He's going to take good care of you.'

'Where are you going?' she asked, her voice sharp and punctuated by fear.

'Ssh. We're home. I'll be right here – downstairs.'

'NO!' Vienna grabbed him. 'Don't leave me.'

At that point Dr Jürgens took over. Firmly disengaging her hand from Farron's arm, he kept hold of it, squeezing it tightly, waiting until she looked to him, before speaking. 'It will be all right now, Vienna,' he said, and to Farron he nodded towards the door.

For a moment Farron hesitated, torn apart by the pleading look in Vienna's eyes, and reluctant to leave her with a stranger. Then he remembered how helpless he was to do anything for her, and slowly straightened up. 'I'll only be downstairs, darling,' he promised.

Vienna began to cry and Farron felt the pain hit him firmly in the guts, almost making him double over. Then Dominic was there, his hand firm on his shoulder. 'The best thing you can do is leave her with Jürgens,' he said reassuringly, his hands strong as they guided Farron out of the room. They could hear the Swede's voice, quiet and soothing, then Vienna's sobs and a few answering words to his questions. Then they were on the landing and Dominic softly shut the door. 'Come on – you need a drink!'

Farron didn't argue. Once in the lounge Dominic poured him a large bourbon and handed it over. 'Who was in the car?' Farron asked, then took a long healthy swallow that burned his throat and made his eyes water.

'Frank Gillespie and Drake.'

'Dr Vincent Drake?'

'Yes – Drake,' Dominic repeated savagely.

Sinking into a leather armchair, Farron asked: 'What's going on?'

'Drake is behind Vienna's breakdown.' Breakdown was the only word that accurately fitted Vienna's pitiful state right now.

'You mean he was incompetent?' Farron asked, frowning.

'Not incompetent – corrupt. He was paid to plant ideas into her head under hypnosis. The nightmares, hallucinations, the desire to confess – all that was fed into her subconscious during their sessions together.'

Farron stared at him, unable to take in what he had just learned. '*Paid*? You mean he was paid to brainwash her, to drive her mad?' He felt ice creep into his blood and pressure in his brain threatened to burst his head wide open as a savage desire to kill gripped him. The emotion was alien to his usually placid and easygoing nature. 'Who?' he said at last. The word was spoken quietly, but Dominic was not fooled.

Holding Farron's eyes with his own, he told him. 'Jago.'

Jago – of course it was Jago. Who else? 'I'll kill him.'

'You won't,' Dominic contradicted as Farron leapt to his feet, his face contorted into a mask of hatred. 'What will Vienna do while you spend the next thirty years inside? Wait for you?'

In the doorway, Farron stopped but didn't turn around.

'If you want revenge on Jago,' Dominic said softly, 'the best thing you can do is to marry that girl, have children and live happily ever after.'

Farron grappled to overcome his rage and think clearly. He wanted to find Jago and rip his head off, but Dominic was right: the best revenge would be their own happiness. 'What if it's too late? What if Jürgens can't help her?'

'Listen to me, Farron,' Dominic said firmly. 'What Drake did was accomplished under hypnosis and can be undone in the same way. Before we arrived Drake told Jürgens everything – every detail, every method used and how long ago. And Jürgens is the best – you heard him say yourself that she'll recover, and she will. After all, it's not as if she really did kill Lyons, is it?'

Farron swallowed hard, feeling himself wilt with relief. 'It's been like a nightmare,' he whispered and Dominic too felt a lump in his throat. The hand that he laid on Farron's shoulder was infinitely gentle.

'I know. But it's over now. Drake's given us enough to get Jago as well. And I know a few judges – that pair will both be old men before they get out of jail.'

For a second the two men looked at each other with total understanding, then Dominic smiled. 'Come on – let's have another drink.'

Back in the lounge, Farron slumped into the armchair and watched Dominic refill his glass. 'How did you get on to all this in the first place?'

Dominic poured himself a bourbon then sat down heavily on the settee. 'After you said Vienna was getting worse, I had Drake checked out. He's a gambler – hence Gillespie's involvement. Jago was paying off the debts.'

'You're a suspicious son-of-a-bitch, aren't you?' Farron said affectionately, and saluted him with a glass. Dominic laughed.

'Sometimes, son – only sometimes,' he admitted drily, his mind on that morning. Hell, how could he have been so stupid as to let someone get the better of him like that? Who knew what had been done to him when he'd been out for the count?

'I don't know how I'm ever going to thank you, Dom,' Farron said now, all traces of laughter gone, and Dominic looked at him quickly, meeting head-on the steady brown eyes before looking away quickly. He wanted to see something else in those eyes besides gratitude, but he had no right. He'd signed away those rights thirty years ago when he'd handed the boy over to his grandmother.

'Forget it,' he said crisply, and stared down at his drink. Farron frowned, sensing some other mystery that had nothing to do with Vienna.

'Dom, is there anything else?'

Dominic stiffened as again that inner voice urged in his heart and brain: *'Now – tell him now!'* But he had kept silent for decades, and silence was a hard habit to break. Besides, the kid was exhausted. Just one look told him that. 'Anything else?' he repeated vaguely. 'I don't think so. Hey, you look shot. Why don't you get some sleep?'

'Yeah I might just do that,' Farron agreed wearily, wiping his hand across his bloodshot eyes. Suddenly he remembered

Vienna's diary. 'Hell, I almost forgot. We found a diary in New York – Vienna thinks Gloria Gaines is her mother.'

Dominic's mouth fell open. 'What? Why should . . .' he let the sentence trail away as sudden flashbacks speeded into his mind like rewound film. Gloria, pale and nervous. Gloria asking questions about Vienna. Gloria every bit as furious as he when he told her about Jago. Gloria, who'd moved so fast on Frank that Drake hadn't stood a chance. 'Of course,' he said, his voice a mere whisper, and Farron, who had watched the startled expression on his face change to one of total comprehension, found his own jaw dropping in surprise.

'You mean you think it's true?'

'I wouldn't be surprised now that I come to think of it. It makes sense.'

Just then, before Dominic could explain himself, a door opened upstairs and Franz Jürgens skipped lightly down to where both men waited for him. 'Well?' Farron and Dominic said the same word simultaneously, and the doctor's stern face managed a smile.

'It is just as the man Drake said,' he confirmed. 'I thought it best to make sure he hadn't been lying first.'

'Good idea,' Farron said bitterly, then, 'go on.'

'The damage is extensive, but the root core of it – that is, the hypnotic suggestions, can be removed. Possibly tomorrow, when she should be a little more stable. I've been calming her down now, preparing her for the first session in the morning. The sooner we start, the better. She is sleeping now.'

'But the damage – it isn't permanent, is it?' Farron asked, and could have kissed the stern-faced Swede when he shook his head.

'No. She will need extensive therapy for several months, but she can be made free of the lies told her by Drake. The amnesia, however, is a problem. I have tentatively explored with her the mental block she has, and it is the strongest I have ever come across. I really don't see her ever regaining her memory – at least not unless I can find out the cause of the trauma. I suspect that Drake told her that he *could* help her regain her memory just to ensure she kept visiting him for regular sessions.'

Farron nodded and told him of the progress they had made in Switzerland and New York. But as the three men went into the lounge to plan their strategy, upstairs Vienna was not sleeping.

Instead she lay looking at the ceiling, feeling blissfully calm – better than she'd felt in months. In fact, she was calm enough now to do what she knew had to be done. Getting out of bed she switched on the bedside lamp, and lifting the receiver of the phone on the bedside table, asked the operator to put her through to police headquarters.

PERRY Clements was in the interview room talking to a suspected arsonist responsible for the deaths of a family of five, when the call came through.

'Lieutenant.' It was Rolnalski who stuck his head around the door. 'Call for you. I think you'd better take it.' Perry nodded and walked quickly to his office. There he pressed the button flashing on line four and sat down.

'Lieutenant Clements,' he introduced himself into the silent receiver, and waited.

'Lieutenant, this is Vienna Wright. I'm not sure if you remember me, but . . .'

'Of course I remember you,' Perry said, frowning slightly. There was something wrong with her voice: it was . . . vacant. There was no life or emotion in it. 'What can I do for you, Vienna?'

There was a small silence and then, 'I wanted to tell you. I . . . remember now.'

'Remember what?' Perry probed softly, glancing across at a moribund African violet on his windowsill.

'I killed Gary Lyons. I murdered him.'

Perry closed his eyes then opened them again. 'I see. Where are you, Vienna?'

Like a little girl, Vienna recited the address and Perry wrote it down. 'What do I do now?' she asked, sounding even more like a little girl, and Perry felt the pencil in his hand snap. Looking down at it in some surprise he threw the two ends into the bin and said gently, 'You just stay right where you are. Don't move, all right? I'll come and see you.'

'All right, Lieutenant.' She hung up, then stared at the phone for a moment. Satisfied, she switched off the lamp and got back into bed. She was so tired . . .

IT was getting late and all three were still talking in the lounge when a car pulled up outside. Farron looked at Dominic. 'Expecting someone? Gillespie?'

'No. Gillespie left right after you came. He has Drake stashed safely away until . . .' The doorbell rang, and Dominic broke off the explanation to answer it. It was a very near thing as to which of the two men were the most surprised – Dominic to find Clements on his doorstep, or the Lieutenant to find Dominic in residence. 'Perry.' Dominic was marginally the first to recover. 'This is a surprise. Is something wrong?'

Perry looked him straight in the eye. 'I just got a call from Vienna Wright.'

Instinctively Dominic looked upwards and swore softly, then looked quickly back at the man waiting patiently but firmly in front of him. 'I think you'd better come in.'

Perry smiled sadly. 'I think I had,' he agreed.

Dominic took his coat. 'Through here. I don't think you've actually met my . . . Mr Manikuuna? This is Lieutenant Clements. Perry, this is Franz Jürgens – a psychiatrist from Sweden – Vienna's doctor.' Perry's eyes narrowed as he looked first at Dominic and then gave the doctor a more searching look. Obviously liking what he saw he nodded. 'How do you do, Doctor.'

'Doctor.' Dominic looked at the Swede meaningfully. 'Lieutenant Clements just received a call from Vienna.'

'Vienna!' It was Farron who looked most appalled. 'But she's sleeping.'

'Evidently not,' Perry said mildly, then added almost as an afterthought, 'she just confessed to the murder of Gary Lyons. Said she remembered killing him. Wouldn't happen to know anything about that, would you?'

For a long moment all four men looked at one another, and then Dominic said, 'You'd better sit down. This will probably take a while.'

Chapter 46

An ocean breeze swept invitingly across the café terrace, but Rhiannon opted instead for the discreet interior. Finding a corner table, shadowed by rattan screens covered in climbing vines, she sat down and ordered a piña colada. She was dressed in a light lilac suit with a cream blouse that matched her court shoes and her handbag, and the wide-brimmed hat that she wore. Silver and amethyst earrings glittered in her lobes, matched by the watch on her wrist. However, despite the cool and assured air that her apparel gave her, Rhia was very much aware that inside she was quivering like a leaf.

Her drink came and she took a deep sip as a shadow fell across the table. 'Hi,' Bryan said, almost cheerfully, and sat down without waiting to be asked.

'Hello,' Rhiannon responded, her voice subdued. Bryan ordered an orange juice with ice, and waited in silence until the drink was delivered. When they were alone he unzipped the simple plastic windcheater he was wearing and deposited on the table a large flat brown envelope. 'Did you have any trouble getting it?' she asked, making no move to touch it.

Bryan shifted his chair. 'None at all. He drank the drugged drink I slipped him and went out without a murmur.'

'He's all right, though?' She knew her voice was anxious but there wasn't a damned thing she could do about it.

'Perfectly.'

Rhiannon nodded. Reaching across she took the envelope, unfolded the flap, and pulled out the photographs. The first one showed him lying on his side, one hand on a redhead's hip, the other hand on her breast. The girl was naked, her make-up heavy.

Bryan watched her as she put the photographs away. She had looked at only one and he was pretty damned sure she wouldn't look at any more. Now that was unusual. This was the moment when his client would usually leer and sneer. He wished she'd do the same; it would have made him feel a hell of a lot better. But there was no gloating evident in her eyes or her words. As a matter of fact, she was looking rather green.

'You've done good work,' Rhiannon commented listlessly, and put the photos into her bag. Taking out the second instalment, she handed it over. 'Here's the money I promised.' Again he counted it out before carefully putting it away. 'I don't think,' she said, careful to keep her voice neutral, 'that we need meet again until after the court case has been won. How shall I contact you to pay the rest?'

'I'll contact you,' Bryan said easily then, for him, did something very unusual. 'Look – just because you've got the pictures doesn't mean you have to use them. No one's forcing you.' There was a tone in his voice that was very near to pleading, and she frowned slightly, sensing that something was not quite right. But what? When she looked up at him he looked as before. She shook her head. Now she was getting paranoid.

'You're wrong, you know,' she said wrily. 'Someone *is* forcing me to use them. Do you know what day it is?'

Bryan blinked, for a moment trying to come to terms with the idea of this woman being manipulated by someone. It didn't seem feasible somehow, but he hoped, oh how he hoped, that it was true. It might just save her neck. 'Er, no. It's not a national holiday, that's for sure.'

'No – not a holiday. It's my father's birthday.'

Bryan knew he was not going to get any more answers by the way she tossed her head back before reaching for her glass. Reluctantly he stood up, disinclined to leave her – but what could he do without jeopardising his own neck? Besides, he thought grimly, he'd done enough to her already. He hated letting down a client. It rankled him, but his first priority was his own welfare. Not hers. 'Bye Miss Grantham', he said, his voice soft and almost apologetic, and again Rhiannon looked up at him searchingly then watched in silence as he walked through the café and out on to the terrace. Shrugging, she picked up her bag and walked out, turning the corner and making for the limousine parked next to an exclusive restaurant.

Bryan Canon took a deep breath. That had been bad –

worse than he'd thought. In a cutthroat world your own survival came first, of course, but still . . . he'd hated to do it to her. He ran a hand through his hair and then slowly looked across to where an Hawaiian sat at one of the tables taking from his ear what looked like a hearing aid but wasn't. As he watched, the man put a small tape recorder down and switched it off, Bryan's cue to remove the small microphone he wore under the lapel of his shirt collar. Walking over to the table, Bryan dumped the piece of expensive equipment none-too-gently down on it.

Hua looked up and said absently, 'Thanks,' before he began taking a zoom lens off the camera resting beside him. Bryan nodded. Damn, how had the PI found him so quickly?

In the limousine Rhiannon stared out of the window before giving her instructions. 'The Blue Hawaiian, please Sam.'

THE drive was short and Rhiannon sighed deeply as she stepped out of the car and walked up the now-familiar path. With new eyes she looked at the hotel – the beautiful hotel that had been almost a lifetime's work. The same hotel he'd be forced to surrender to his vulture-like relatives. And of course it would be an easy matter to purchase the hotels from those money-hungry bastards. Others would want them of course, but she could do a deal before the trial. It was easy when expense no longer provided a stumbling block.

She went straight to the elevators and punched the penthouse button. She didn't dare hesitate. Already she felt as if she were being pulled apart, with her father's grip on one wrist pulling her one way, and Dominic's equally firm grip on her other wrist pulling her the opposite way. Why didn't they just break her apart and have done with it? His secretary looked up as she walked into the room, the woman's eyes widening slightly as she recognized the visitor. 'Hello, is Dominic in?' Rhiannon asked, her voice casual, almost cheerful. The secretary depressed the buzzer, and Dominic's voice came into the room, filtered and dehumanized by the machine, but it was still his voice, and Rhiannon felt her muscles weaken. The quivering intensified.

'Miss Grantham is here to see you, sir.'

The pause was brief. 'Send her in.'

Rhiannon nodded at the secretary and walked to his door, opening it and stepping inside without knocking. She looked slowly around the room, taking in its every detail before finally directing her gaze to the man sat behind the desk. Dominic's eyes were slowly returning from the cream shoes on her feet, taking in the pale silk stockings on her shapely calves. Then their eyes met with a green flash, and he smiled. She was dressed for business, and his survival instincts rushed to the fore, preventing him from letting on just how good it felt to be near her. Instead a cool, slightly bored look settled across his features as he ignored the gentle pressure of his love for her, and without preamble asked bluntly: 'What do you want, Rhia?'

Rhiannon felt a mule's kick to her stomach as he leaned back, his shirt stretching tightly over his chest, the startling whiteness of it highlighting the blackness of his hair and the deeply attractive dusky colour of his tanned skin. He looked lean and mean, and she felt a sudden, crazy desire to cave in. To just surrender, then and there, to walk across him, slip into his lap and kiss him until their brains curdled. She slowly slipped into the chair facing him. 'I was just passing by,' she began with deliberate sarcasm, 'and thought I'd drop in and say hello.'

'Did you now?' His wide mouth pulled into an ironic smile, but he noticed that she visibly flinched when the intercom sounded. She was nervous. For once her cool air and sophisticated clothes had failed to hide the fact that underneath it all she was jumpy. Intrigued, he ignored the buzzer: just why was she so skittish? But it was insistent and sighing impatiently, Dominic picked up the phone, listening as he was told the call he'd been expecting was on the line.

'OK. Put him on,' Dominic said, then looked at Rhiannon. 'I won't be a moment.'

'Take your time,' she drawled boredly. He gave her a mocking smile that for once failed to arouse her anger, and then transferred a good part of his attention to the man on the other end of the line. 'Hello, yes?'

Rhiannon watched him covertly, fascinated by the high

cheekbones that gave his face such a distinguished look, mesmerized by the movements of his lips when he talked, drawn by the fluid movements of his limbs when he reached forward to put down a pen. He was defeated –beaten. But he didn't know. She'd have the hotels and then – Farron. She felt the quivering suddenly speed without warning from her stomach to her limbs and she quickly looked at a painting as she saw his eyes swivel towards her. But he didn't fail to catch the telltale shudder that had wracked her body.

'Tell me,' Dominic said, listening with a blank face as Hua told him of the perfect recording he had of her and Bryan Canon, the man he had located and approached yesterday. 'I have pictures too,' Hua said. 'Of her handing over the money. There's no doubt that she paid him to commit amongst other things, kidnapping. You can also get her, if she uses the stuff, on blackmail, extortion and who the hell knows what else. With a good team of lawyers you could put her away for years.'

'I see. Thanks.'

If Hua was puzzled by his lack of enthusiasm he didn't push it. 'I'll drop the stuff over at your office this afternoon.'

'Fine. Bye.' Dominic hung up quickly and took a deep breath. Slowly he ran a hand through his hair and then swivelled the chair back to face her. 'I'll ask again just one more time: why are you here?'

Rhiannon sat up in her chair and crossed her legs. 'Actually I'm here on a mission of mercy to exercise my magnanimity.'

Dominic smiled coldly, a slow smile that revealed white teeth but little humour. 'Sounds interesting. But unlikely.'

Rhiannon flinched, unprepared to be hurt by so simple a thing. The words had been teasing enough, but she felt cold – as if his eyes had turned to ice and were slowly freezing her to death. Then she shrugged and got up, too restless to stay still, and slowly walked to the window, her gaze looking over the traffic-lined streets without really seeing them. Silently he watched her.

'I've come to tell you,' she began at last, her voice not as strong nor as gloating as she would have liked, 'that you have a few days to say goodbye to all this.' She turned as she talked, bravely fighting off the cowardly urge to keep her back to him, and found him unmoved. Lounging gracefully in his chair he still looked strong and invincible. But worse; he was still the man she loved.

'Oh?' He finally responded to her dramatic words with a raised brow and a sad smile. 'And why should I say goodbye to all this,' he repeated her words mockingly, 'when I'm not going anywhere?' His voice was soft, but there was something more within it. A threat? No, not quite a threat. More of . . . a warning? Rhiannon slowly walked towards him again, and resumed her seat. Then, still holding his eyes with her own, she opened her bag and took out the envelope, tossing it on to the desk where it laid between them like a loaded gun.

Dominic had heard from Hua yesterday about his missing hours, so he knew damned well what was in the envelope. But he was curious as to the actual specifics. Slowly, not taking his eyes off her, he dragged the envelope to him, surprised by the look of pain in her eyes that was quickly hidden as she dipped her head and the cream rim of the hat hid her eyes.

He took out the photos and paused at the sight of the first one. And only as he slowly looked through the rest did it dawn on him that the man she had chosen had been the best. 'Very artistically done,' he finally commented so mildly that her head snapped up and her green eyes widened in a disbelieving gaze as they noted his twitching lips. Dominic turned one photo upside down and smiled. 'Very nice girls, too – pity I wasn't aware of any of it.'

Stupidly Rhiannon felt jealousy surge and had to conquer it with a monumental effort of will. A moment later she was able to say with commendable aplomb, 'You always did have style, Dominic.'

Forcing a wry smile on to her lips, she watched in silence as he pushed the envelope away and leaned back in his chair once more, watching her with enigmatic eyes. 'So did you,' he returned the compliment.

He was bluffing, of course. But magnificently so, she thought. 'You can have those,' she said with sweet generosity. 'I have the originals.'

Dominic smiled. 'Naturally.'

She felt lost. Things were not going at all as she'd expected. She'd been prepared for anger, even a physical attack, but not this smiling acceptance. She got abruptly to her feet. She felt ill – quite literally ill. 'I'll give you three days,' she said, her voice harsh now, her manner so abrupt it took him by surprise. She almost ran across the room and her hand was on the door-handle before he said simply, 'Don't do it, Rhia.'

She froze at the softly spoken words and he could see her shoulderblades tense. He wanted to tell her that she couldn't win, to walk across that room, take her in his arms and kiss her, to strip her of those damned lovely clothes, to make love to her on the carpet, to never, ever let her go. But he couldn't. She wouldn't let him, and he wouldn't let himself do it. She had set him up and intended to destroy him. And unless she admitted to herself that they were in love, that they were meant to be together, then he could do nothing to help her – or himself. Nothing but stop her. And stop her good. 'Don't do it, sweetheart,' he said again, his voice so gentle that it hit her like bullets – four little bullets straight to her heart.

Rhiannon knew it must be her imagination, for her baby was too little to move, but she felt sure she could feel it stirring inside her, adding its own silent voice, urging her to stop the madness now, before it was too late. She leaned forward, almost sagging against the door. If only it wasn't her father's birthday today. If only it had been yesterday – or tomorrow. And here she was again, letting him down, not loving him enough actively to yearn for justice for him.

'It's Dad's birthday today,' she said blankly, her voice strangely disembodied and not at all like her own. As she slowly turned around, her face as pale as snow, Dominic closed his eyes. Of course it was – how could he have forgotten? Looking at her, desperate to save her from herself, he decided to play one last card, the final gamble.

'There's something about Graham I think you should know.'

Rhiannon shook her head. She'd been so hopeful because of his voice. If only he'd begged her not to do it – if only he'd pleaded, confessed, asked for forgiveness. She knew she would have given in. She'd forgive him anything – even that.

But not this. 'Not the blackmail story again, please,' she said tiredly.

'No – not that. Something else. Jessamine.'

Rhiannon sucked in her breath. NO! The word screamed in her brain. Don't tell me you loved her after all. Please don't – I'll die if you say that.

'Your mother was killed in a car accident.'

Rhiannon slumped against the door. 'I know that,' she said, her voice flat.

'What do you think you know about it?' Dominic asked quietly.

For the first time Rhiannon's mind snapped alert, sensing something dangerous in the air, something unexpected. 'I know she was driving home from shopping when she skidded on a wet road and crashed into a tree. It killed her instantly.'

Even before she'd finished speaking, Dominic was shaking his head. 'No – wrong on every count. It was night-time, and she was not driving. Graham and she had gone to a party, a friend's engagement bash. He'd had too much to drink and Jessamine said she'd drive. But your father couldn't have that – not in front of all those people who knew him. He insisted on driving. And drive he did but lost control of the car going too fast around a corner. He collided with another car, and in turning the wheel to try to avoid it, it was the passenger side that took the brunt of the impact. And she wasn't killed instantly – it took her three days in hospital before she finally died. Graham, needless to say, escaped with a few cuts and bruises.'

She stared at him, appalled. 'That's a dirty lie,' she spat. 'How could you?' She shook her head. 'You'd do anything to save your own neck, wouldn't you?'

'Your father was fined but not sent to jail. Arnold was a good lawyer, one of the best there was in those days, and he represented his son, giving a heart-wrenching speech to the judge about how he'd already paid by losing his wife. Graham took to the drink pretty hard for a few months after that, but something made him stop. You, I think,' he said, looking across at her, remembering the way Graham had always been holding her, clinging to her small baby's body like a life-raft.

'Oh yes?' Rhiannon sneered scornfully. 'And I suppose, for all your power and influence, and with this supposed blackmail going on, you couldn't pull the right strings to have him jailed? Oh, come on, Dominic! You forget, I've felt for myself the powerful influence you wield over all the mighty powers-that-be on this damned island.'

Dominic slowly shook his head. 'I could have done it,' he admitted, thinking back. 'I even wanted to do it for days after Jess died. But Graham . . .' he shook his head helplessly. 'I never could make up my mind whether I hated him more, or pitied him.' He still could not, would not, tell her the cause of Graham's blackmail hold over him. She'd lynch him with it.

'Save your pity for yourself, you lying bastard,' Rhiannon half-sobbed. 'You're going to need it.'

'You can check it up, Rhiannon. You know you can,' he said gently.

'And I'll bet you'll make sure that's just what the documentation will read, won't you?'

Dominic looked away from her, sick at heart. 'Get out, Rhiannon,' he said heavily. He couldn't remember ever feeling this defeated before – not even when he'd had to give up the adoption plans for Farron.

'With pleasure,' she spat, but her voice was shaking perilously, and her vision was becoming hopelessly blurred. 'I always knew you were rotten – deep inside. I just never knew how much until now.' She opened the door and walked out, slamming it hard behind her.

Dominic looked at the closed door with hurting eyes for several long seconds, a nightmare vision of her in prison grey flirting with his mind. Slowly he shook his head. 'Don't do it, kiddo,' he whispered softly, his eyes closing against the pain that rippled through him. 'For God's sake,' he whispered. 'Don't do it.'

ODESSA was on the patio by the pool, sighing blissfully under the massaging hands of the young Hawaiian girl, when the maid stepped out and told her there were two policemen at the door asking for her husband. Sitting up and refastening her bikini-top, she looked across to where Richard was sitting on a chair under the shade of the table's parasol, reading the morning's paper. Pulling on a matching beach robe she walked across to him and slipped her arms over his shoulders, running them over the white cotton of his shirt. 'Those two cops are back again. Do you know what they want?'

Richard slowly put the paper down and covered her hands briefly with his own. 'No idea,' he said truthfully. 'Where are they?'

'Maria showed them into the lounge, I expect.'

He got up slowly. He was tired, but then he hadn't been sleeping well lately. Yet it was more than that. All week he'd become conscious of a cancerous apathy overtaking him. He was not curious about why the two cops were back. Had she been arrested yet? Walking into the lounge, Odessa hot on his heels, Richard nodded at the two men waiting there for him. 'Gentlemen. What can I do for you?'

Perry had not forgotten how big the man was, but although the hulking size remained the same, he seemed smaller somehow and for a few seconds the older man was silent, trying to understand why. And then, as he looked into the doctor's grey eyes, he suddenly knew. 'Dr Richard Jago?' he said, his tone alerting Odessa at once that something was very wrong, and Rolnalski watched her carefully, sensing trouble. Richard, on the other hand, never even moved. Only his eyes flickered slightly, but not in anger. Not even in fear. Perry nodded to himself. So it was like that, was it? Somehow he could not feel sorry for him. 'I have a warrant for your arrest sir, on the charge of conspiracy to cause grievous bodily harm to Vienna Wright. There are also charges of fraud, conspiracy to pervert the cause of justice, conspiracy to . . .'

'What? Are you crazy?' It was Odessa who interrupted, her voice shrill and harsh, so unpleasant and grating that it sounded almost inhuman. 'Do you know who this is?' she screeched. 'Who *I* am?'

Richard did not take his eyes off Perry, but his words were for her, both mild and to the point. 'Odessa, shut up.' For a second or two there was a stunned silence as his wife stared at him, her eyes shocked and unblinking, like those of a hooked fish. Richard took advantage of the silence to walk towards the door, Rolnalski moving sideways like a crab in case he made a bolt for it. But Perry told him not to worry.

Richard reached for a grey jacket and looped it over his arm, half-turning to look back as Perry slowly walked forward and reached for the door. He didn't, Rolnalski noted, even look at his wife. 'Richard,' Odessa said pleadingly, her voice suddenly weak and vulnerable. She felt something shrivel and die inside her, but didn't know what it was.

Richard looked away from her – what did she matter? His eyes met those of the Lieutenant and found them strangely comprehending. Did *he* know? Did he understand? Somehow Richard believed that he did. Silently Perry opened the door and they stepped out into the bright sunshine, Rolnalski close behind them and efficiently reading him his rights. In the squad car at the bottom of the drive, Vince Drake looked at his partner in crime from the back seat, the brown eyes meeting his for only a moment before looking away again.

Perry saw the by-play and glanced at the man by his side. He stood still and blank-faced, obviously not taking the least bit of notice as Rolnalski finished his legal spiel.

'You might like to know that Vienna Wright is, at this moment, undergoing treatment with another hypnotherapist who's undoing all the damage Drake did,' Perry commented but could see no signs of remorse on the handsome face. 'Drake's been telling us that in his opinion you need to see a shrink yourself,' Perry tried again as they slowly ascended the steps and began to walk towards the second squad car.

Richard smiled drily. 'I shouldn't believe a word he says if I were you. The man's a liar.'

Perry almost smiled, but the bitter taste of last night was still with him; Dominic Fairchild and the Swedish doctor had explained what Jago and Drake had done to the girl, and it was still chilling his blood. 'In this case I'm inclined to believe him,' Perry said, his voice more vicious than he'd intended, and Richard looked around and down at him. Perry looked back without fear. 'Do you have any idea of the hell you put that young girl through?' he asked, his voice hard and puzzled. Such cruelty was more than even he could fully comprehend. 'Why did you do it?'

Richard smiled, a mere lift of his lips. Why?

'Don't tell me it was all done for love,' Perry warned him. 'You don't know the meaning of the word. If you'd had any love for that girl you'd have let her go free to find happiness with someone else. There are a lot of people out to make sure that justice is done, Dr Jago. If you have any hopes of a light sentence you can forget them.'

Richard laughed a soft but humorless laugh. 'Actually, Lieutenant, I wasn't thinking anything of the sort,' he said truthfully.

'You know that she hates you, don't you?' Perry asked, and Richard looked at him, his grey eyes searching. Did she? Yes, he supposed she must. Perhaps all was not lost, after all. 'I'll settle for that,' he said, his voice content.

Perry looked at him, finally comprehending the depths of this man's twisted obsession, and he slowly shook his head. Rolnalski, who was listening but not understanding a single word of their conversation, glanced at his superior with a worried expression as their suspect gave that cold, creepy smile of his and nodded. Then all three men turned their heads as a voice, loud and hysterical, shouted down at them.

'You won't keep him,' Odessa was yelling. 'I'll have a lawyer – the best damned lawyer you chicken-shit pigs have ever seen! I'll . . .' The words became obscene then, screamed in vitriolic anger until her voice was hoarse. Dressed in designer beachwear, her hair pampered by the best hairdressers, her hands and feet shining with the best manicure and pedicure the islands could offer, she was a broken woman. There was something fevered in her voice that belied the ugliness of her words, something so desperate in her eyes when they rested on her husband that it made Perry wince.

Richard turned away from the sight of her without a qualm and watched as a young cop fitted the handcuffs around his wrists. Perry watched him, fascinated in spite of himself. What was it about him that so attracted women? Was it just his size – his looks? 'She sounds very determined to get the best defence for you, Doctor,' Perry said. As Richard began to fold his large body into the back of the car, Perry carried on thoughtfully, 'It'll be interesting to see who wins. She has a lot of money and influence, that wife of yours.'

Richard sat down and moved across, Perry slipping in beside him. The slamming of the car door drowned out most of Odessa's wild curses and screaming threats but she had run down the steps, and through the sunshine Perry could see the glistening trace of tears on her cheeks. Behind her the servants were clustered in the doorway, whispering amongst themselves. He looked away, his kind heart pitifully sorry for her. 'Do you think she'll get you off?' Perry asked with genuine interest, although he himself would have bet his last penny that she wouldn't.

The policeman was surprised and even unnerved to find Jago's grey eyes fixed on him. The doctor's words were right to the point: 'Do you really think it matters?' Richard Jago asked.

THE big black limo sat outside on the quiet road for a long time before the door opened and the elegantly dressed woman finally stepped out. Rhiannon walked with dragging steps to the small bungalow and rang the bell. Farron opened the door in such clumsy haste that she was taken by surprise. He'd been banished to the bungalow that morning by Dr Jürgens, who'd insisted on peace and quiet to work with Vienna. When he'd heard the bell, Farron had thought it would be the doctor with some news.

In no mood to disguise his feelings, he said crisply, 'What do you want?'

Rhiannon felt a shiver of foreboding. 'What's wrong?' she demanded, and he remembered, belatedly, how good she'd been to Vienna, and felt ashamed.

'You'd better come in,' he said more gently, and she tensed.

'It's Vienna, isn't it?'

Farron nodded. 'Come on through. What will you have to drink?'

Another drink, Rhiannon thought grimly, and asked, 'What am I going to need?'

Farron looked at her for a second, then poured them both a double scotch. 'That bad, huh?' she muttered and took the drink. 'Well, no point taking bad news in dribs and drabs. Just sock it to me.'

He did. Quickly and concisely he told her what had happened, knowing that her expressions of shock, then anger and pity, were all genuine. When the words had all been said and the room was once more quiet, she shook her head. 'I had no idea.'

Farron rubbed a tired hand over his eyes. 'I know. And you did help – you made her laugh. You were a friend.'

Rhiannon slowly put her drink down and leaning forward she took a deep breath. 'I hope they burn, the bastards – both of them.'

'Oh, don't worry – they will. Dominic'll make sure of that.'

Rhiannon glanced up quickly at the mention of his name, and suddenly remembered why she had come. But she couldn't do it now. She was not that heartless. 'Yes, I imagine he will,' she agreed, her voice deadpan, but Farron had seen the sudden change in her eyes, and he too sat forward, his curiosity now roused beyond endurance.

'Why did you come?'

'I wanted to see Vienna.'

'Liar,' Farron contradicted without heat. 'You came here to tell me something, didn't you?' His voice was penetrating but not yet accusatory, and Rhiannon shook her head, unprepared for his instinctive shot in the dark.

But Farron was in no mood to let her wriggle out of it, though she did try to. 'It'll keep, Farron. You've had enough for one day without . . .' she brought herself up short, trailing off miserably.

'Without what?' Farron pounced on her hesitation immediately, and she shook her head, raising a shaking hand to her eyes, tears not far away.

'Please. Just forget I came.' She tried to get up, but Farron was quicker. Strong hands on her shoulders kept her in her seat, and she looked up into a face that suddenly reminded her so much of Dominic.

'You're not leaving until you've told me,' Farron warned her, his voice and hands firm, and it wasn't until she relaxed in a gesture of defeat that he went back to his own chair.

'Farron, don't . . .' she began, but he'd sensed for too long a mystery about Dominic, a mystery that somehow, in some way, deeply and personally affected him. And if Dominic wouldn't tell him, then she would. He was sick of lies and deceit. Heartily sick of mysteries.

'Start at the beginning. I want to hear it all,' he demanded, his voice cold.

'I don't know where to start,' she confessed, stalling for time.

'Start with those,' Farron suggested, looking curiously at the folders she was carrying, and Rhiannon, who'd forgotten about them, nodded.

'OK. Here – see for yourself. It's just proof that Dominic's done you more favours than you know. He paid for your schooling, your healthcare . . .' She handed over the papers, letting her words trail off. She couldn't remember when she'd felt less like talking in her life before.

Farron looked through the documents in ever-increasing bewilderment. His music scholarship had been non-existent – a sham created to cover the fact that his entire adult schooling had been paid for by his employer, who had then been unknown to him. He'd also, he read incredulously, paid only half the rent on his old flat. Vienna had said it seemed odd that the landlord had let him have the apartment so cheaply. 'But why?' he asked, utterly at sea.

'Because of this,' she said heavily, handing over a copy of the thirty-year-old will. Farron read it with growing incredulity but mercifully didn't ask how she had come by it. 'Some will, isn't it?' she said wryly.

'I'll say. But I still don't see what it's got to do with me – or this,' he gestured at the other documents, now lying scattered around his feet.

'Your mother was Akaki Manikuuna who worked for Gloria Gaines in the sixties.'

Farron frowned impatiently. 'I know that.'

'You were born in the same year as Frederick Fairchild died.'

Farron shook his head. He knew she was trying to tell him something but he was damned if he could follow her. Hell, he

608

was tired. More tired than he'd thought. 'I still don't see . . .'

'In there you'll see that Dominic bought your grand-mother's house. That he's paid her a . . . pension since you were born.' Farron shook his head. He hadn't read all the documents through, but he didn't disbelieve her.

'I know *Tutu* likes him – has always liked him, but Dominic helps lots of his people – in more ways than you know.'

By the tone of his voice she wonderd if Farron already loved the man, and just didn't know it. 'Do you know,' Rhiannon said, 'that the Fairchild men have always had a genetically inherited defect?'

'What?' Farron said blankly, for a moment having trouble following her line of thought. 'No, I didn't. But Dominic is perfectly all right, perfectly normal.' His voice began to rise in exasperation. 'Just what are you trying to pull, lady?'

Rhiannon sighed. 'I didn't say it was a hideous disfigure-ment. In fact it's a tiny feature, very easy to miss. It's simply that the little toe on one foot grows fractionally longer than its neighbour. Sound familiar?'

Farron stared at her, and then she saw the knowledge hit him. The papers fell from his limp fingers to the floor as his muscles drained in shock. 'Oh, my God,' he whispered.

She looked away. 'Yes,' her voice was emotionless. 'He's your father. He sired you with Akaki and then, when he read the will, he . . . abandoned you for the sake of his inheritance.' Her voice was without venom. She had no spirit left – no desire remained within her to poison his son against him, but she knew she must say the words. Farron heard her only vaguely. Shock kept other emotions at bay and only his brain ticked over as she carried on.

'I can hire the best lawyers, Farron,' she offered, but there was no pleasure in her voice. 'I can help you. If he were forced to legally acknowledge you, you'd be heir to all those millions. He . . .' Farron held up his hand, the gesture stopping her immediately. Walking around the back of his chair, he shook his head. *His father.* Whenever he'd thought of his father in the past, he'd imagined some dim and distant figure, a sailor perhaps, or a married man on holiday who'd never even been aware of his existence. But Dominic – his father. *Dominic – father.* The two words kept going around and around in his head in an ever-increasing shout of – of *what?* What did he feel? Angry, glad, relieved, disappointed?

'Farron. He . . .'

'I want you to leave – now.'

Rhiannon got to her feet and walked to the door. She turned to look at him, but he was staring at the floor, his forehead creased in concentration, and she didn't have either the heart, the will or the energy to push it. Without a word she opened the door and left.

Farron walked stiffly to the french windows and breathed deeply of the ocean air. He had a father after all. *Dominic.* He shook his head, still hardly able to take it all in. But now that he knew, he didn't doubt it. It all made perfect sense. All the pieces fitted. *Dominic. His father.*

But out of the entire jumble of his thoughts, only one question burned in his brain. 'Why didn't you tell me, Dad?' he asked softly. 'Why the hell didn't you tell me?'

And only one answer made sense. He was ashamed of him. Ashamed of his own son.

Chapter 47

James 'Jimmy' Dwight reached for the black wrought-iron bell-pull and straightened his tie before tugging it. He only wished that the news was better. Straight-talking didn't always suit a lawyer of Jimmy's calibre, and he didn't relish the upcoming interview.

'Hi, Koana. I'm not expected but I have to see His Highness. It's urgent.'

'Certainly, sir. Please, come this way.' He was shown into a small but attractive lounge where Chippendale furniture sat with ease on Savonnaire carpets and Venetian mirrors hung on walls of flocked peach velvet. Such dignified and harmonious displays of riches always made Little Jimmy Dwight's mouth water.

'James,' Dominic entered, giving the man a smiling nod. 'It's not often I see you here. What's up?'

Jimmy gulped. 'I've bad news, I'm afraid.'

Dominic nodded. He had a fair idea what it was, but kept silent – a trick he'd learned long ago: never let anyone know what *you* knew. Not even your lawyer. Especially not your lawyer. 'I see. Want a drink?' Jimmy shook his head. An abstemious lawyer was a hell of a lot more attractive than a drunken one. Dominic poured himself an innocuous red wine, and pointed to the settee. 'Sit yourself down. Now, James. What's up?'

Jimmy cleared his throat. 'It's about Miss Grantham, Your Highness.'

Dominic nodded. When had it *not* been her, he wondered. His life before Rhiannon seemed only a dim and distant shadow now – as if it had never been. His smile abruptly disappeared as he contemplated life without her. If she went ahead and tried to use those photos . . . if she did, he'd pounce. Hard and straight.

Jimmy coughed. 'She's called one of the trustees of your grandfather's will – one of the independents, and asked for a trustees' meeting. Naturally the Chicago connection has heard and sent a telegram saying . . .'

'Yes,' Dominic interrupted harshly. 'I can imagine what they're saying. When's the meeting?'

'Friday.' Three days. Dominic stood up and walked to the fireplace, placing his drink on the mantelshelf and leaning his arms wide across the expanse, looking down broodingly into the hearth. 'Your Highness?' Jimmy Dwight said nervously. 'What would you like me to do?'

Dominic straightened and turned around, his face only a little flushed from the heat of the flames. 'I want you present, of course.'

'Yes, of course, that goes without saying. Do you know what it's all about? It would help if we had a strategy planned.'

Dominic looked into the round and suddenly fierce face of his lawyer. He was very deceptive, this James Dwight. Physically, he resembled a cuddly little bear, with fluffy brown hair and big blue eyes. But he was a tiger. And he made so incongruous a tiger that many a prosecutor or rival attorney had been caught napping. But they only did it once. Little Jimmy Dwight had earned himself quite a reputation on the islands. 'I know what it's about,' he said finally, his voice grim. 'And it's nothing serious.' Clasping a friendly hand on his lawyer's shoulder he began to walk him through the big hall towards the door. 'Don't worry about the meeting. I'll give you the documentation that'll shoot them down in flames just before it convenes.'

'That's not long enough,' Jimmy stated nervously. He liked plenty of time. Time was a lawyer's best friend.

'It will be.'

Jimmy nodded. If Fairchild said so, he didn't doubt it and he drove out of the lush gardens of the Falling Pearls Palace a much happier man. He was so happy that he barely noticed the foreign sports car that whizzed past him.

On the threshold Dominic watched Farron's car pull to a halt in front of him, and a moment later Farron got out. '*Aloha*,' Dominic greeted him with a smile that suddenly faltered as a thought struck him. 'Is Vienna all right?'

Farron heard the anxiety in his voice and as he approached, the porch-light illuminated his father's face and showed the fear and concern in it. In that moment Farron wondered how the hell he could have missed all the signs before. 'She's fine,' he said quickly. 'Dr Jürgens banished me from the house for a few days, that's all.'

'It's probably for the best. You'd only get in the way and worry. Come on in.'

Farron walked ahead of him into the hall. He'd been to the Palace before quite a few times, but now he looked around it with new eyes. The chandeliers were seventeenth-century French crystal, imported from a château in the Bordeaux region. The portraits hung on the walls included one by Sir Joshua Reynolds and Gainsborough, and the grandfather clock in one corner had been made by a famous British clockmaker. Farron could even remember Dominic telling him that in their way the British were as good at that craft as the Swiss. Farron looked around at the wealth of this man who stood beside him and it took on a new significance. Re-reading the evidence Rhiannon Grantham had brought him, Farron had finally realized just how much his father had already given him. He'd followed his life, orchestrating it so that he had received only the best – everything he'd ever wanted. If he'd been Dominic's acknowledged son, if he had lived in this great palace, could he have had any more than he did now? A singing career and the love of the only woman in the world for him? No. But he was still angry. Angry that his father had never told him. Angry that he'd been kept in ignorance all these years. And angry that the princely Dominic Fairchild had so despised Akaki, that he would not acknowledge her son as his.

He knew that he already loved his father. Had loved him for some years, in fact. But how much more he could have loved him, if only he'd been given the chance!

'What would you like to drink?' Dominic asked, walking beside him into his private sitting room. 'Brandy?'

'Fine.' Farron was nervous. All afternoon he'd been anticipating this evening, going over and over all the possible conversations in his head until he was confident he was ready for anything. His main fear, though, had been that Dominic would deny it. That he'd say Rhiannon was lying. He didn't think he could take that.

Dominic appeared different somehow, and Farron knew why. For the first time he was looking at him not only as a friend and employer, but as a father as well.

'Want ice?'

Farron took a deep breath. 'No thanks . . . Father.'

The simple word seemed to echo, like the ricochet of a bullet, into Dominic's soul, his brain, his heart, his body. He reached for the brandy decanter, and picking it up with hands that shook, poured a small measure into the glasses. His movements had a slow, careful quality that belied the emotionally charged atmosphere.

Farron braced himself as his father picked up the glasses and turned around. Dominic's face was white beneath the tan, Farron saw at once, the sudden loss of healthy colour making his green eyes stand out like glittering glass. For a long moment they just looked at each other, each trying to read the other's face, each wondering what the other was thinking. Slowly Dominic walked forward and handed his son the glass. 'How did you find out?' he asked softly.

Farron relaxed visibly. 'I thought you were going to deny it.'

'No,' he said, his voice strangely thick and deeply unhappy. But then, what else could he have expected his son to think? Farron had every right to expect such a reaction from him.

Although Farron had known the truth the moment Rhiannon had told him, hearing it from Dominic's own lips was a different matter. It brought the reality of it crashing down around his ears, and raising the glass to his lips he took a heartening gulp of the fiery liquid. But the worst was over. 'Do you mind if I sit down?' he asked, feeling awkward for the first time in Dominic's presence.

'Of course not,' he said, then took the chair opposite him.

'Rhiannon came to see me this morning,' Farron began, and Dominic looked at him, the expression in his green eyes one of pain.

'I can imagine what she said.'

Farron shrugged. 'Actually she didn't say a lot. I got the feeling her heart wasn't quite in it.'

Dominic sighed. What the hell were they talking about Rhiannon for? He couldn't get his mind working – it was as if Farron's words had paralyzed him. 'I never thought I'd ever hear you call me . . . what you just did.'

'Father, you mean?' Farron said, determined to say the word. 'You know, it's funny you should say that because I never expected to use the word either. I always thought my father knew nothing of my existence. It never occurred to me he'd be too damned ashamed to acknowledge me. Or was it that you just didn't have the guts?' he asked, his voice cold as his anger warmed.

Dominic went white. 'You've every right to be accusing. There's probably something you don't know. About your grandfather . . .'

'She showed me the will,' Farron said quickly. He felt no vindictiveness, only a sense of disappointment tinged with faint contempt.

'You know everything, then?' Dominic said finally, his voice flat and hopeless.

'Not quite.'

Dominic, his face still white and strained but now perfectly calm, said: 'You can ask me anything you want and get the truth.'

'Tell me about it,' Farron demanded. 'I want to hear it all. From you.'

Dominic recognized the hurt and hostility lying just beneath the cool, abrupt tones, and felt a heavy weight settle on his heart. But he owed his son the truth now, so he nodded, looked down at his drink, and took a deep breath.

'I'd . . . known Akaki for several months – nearly a year before you were conceived, in fact. I'd come back from Oxford, in the spring of 1961, because Granddad was ill – dying, actually. After he'd . . . gone, I got a call from Akaki. It was more or less over between us by then. When I'd first met her I was only just seventeen. She represented – I don't know. Forbidden fruit, I suppose. Excitement, a dangerous woman, the kind your parents are always warning you about.'

'The kind you wanted, but were ashamed to admit wanting,' Farron clarified for him. He'd long since come to terms with the tragic figure that had been his mother. But, in all fairness, when he remembered back to his own teenage years he could easily see how Dominic's early fling had come about. He himself had had a wild affair with a schoolfriend's widowed mother. That had held a similar lure of forbidden excitement for them both. And it had been mindblowing, for the few brief months before it had burned itself out. Yes – Farron could understand and forgive how he'd come to be born. It was their relationship being kept anonymous afterwards that hurt him. Dominic had seen to his every need, in secret. He'd looked after him, in secret. Helped him, in secret. He was the biggest bloody secret in town, and he felt cheated because of it. It was as if his whole childhood had been one long lie.

'Anyway, at Oxford, with time and distance, and growing up quickly, I just . . . outgrew her.' Dominic frowned. 'It doesn't sound very good, does it?'

Farron twirled his glass, looking down into the liquid with thoughtful eyes. 'I understand it,' he said. 'It does twinge a little, I admit. After all, you are my parents, but I do understand it.'

Dominic nodded. He felt strangely relaxed now – able to tell him anything and everything. 'When she called I wasn't in a particularly good mood. She insisted I take her out, which I did, but only to tell her it was all over between us. Then she took me back to her place . . .'

'Your place you mean,' Farron corrected with a grim smile. 'Rhiannon was very thorough.'

Dominic laughed softly at that. 'I bet. Yes – I was paying for the bungalow, as it happens. Anyway, she showed me a baby in a crib.'

'Me?'

'Yes, you. At first I didn't believe you were mine, but when I lifted the blankets and saw your toes . . .' Dominic shook his head. 'I just can't describe it. It was wonderful. I felt so proud, so complete.'

'But you told her you couldn't marry her!' Farron said angrily.

'No! I told her we'd get married. I even bought her an engagement ring,' Dominic explained hastily, anxious that Farron should understand he hadn't given his son up without a fight. 'The will hadn't been read yet, you see. I intended to marry Akaki and would have done too, but your great-grandfather was a wily old bastard. Fred had heard the rumours, I guess, about me and your mother, and he was worried. He was an old man – a bigot. There's no other way to describe him. And things were different back then. Our native people never had the chance they have now to show that they could become doctors too, businessmen, artists. And my grandfather never even considered it wrong. If he'd had any other grandchild, a wholly white one, I wouldn't have got a look in. And we both knew it.'

Accurately reading behind the bitter words, Farron said softly: 'You loved him.'

'He brought me up – raised me,' Dominic said simply. 'He was the only close relative I had in the world. Like you and your grandmother.'

Farron nodded. 'So you decided to do what he wanted?'

'Hell, no!' Dominic laughed and shook his head. 'It was almost a habit with me to do exactly the opposite. As a kid, I was always in trouble with the old man for my defiance. Of course, Rhiannon never told you about the adoption plan. She wouldn't have known. It was her bloody father . . .' He trailed off and took a trembling breath. 'After the will I knew I couldn't marry Akaki and keep you as an illegitimate son. So I . . . gave her money. But she knew you were better off with me, so . . .'

Farron held up his hands. 'You don't have to defend her, Dad. I know what she was like. For all she loved her daughter, *Tutu* never kept the truth from me.'

Dominic nodded, but his head was reeling. 'I like the sound of that.'

Farron blinked. 'What?'

'Dad. You called me Dad.'

'Don't worry. I won't do it in public,' Farron said coldly, his feeling of love and well-being taking a distinct dive.

Dominic winced, but knowing he deserved it, made no

attempt to defend himself and continued the story. 'I knew this girl in Oxford – Amanda. Things had become pretty serious between us already, and I called her and asked her to marry me. She said yes, and flew over after the funeral. I think she knew, when I told her I planned to adopt a baby boy, that you were mine, although the official story was going to be that as Prince, the adoption of an Hawaiian baby from a poor, even deprived background, was to be an act of . . . I don't know. A declaration of my intentions now that I was the free and clear Fairchild heir.' Dominic swore softly. 'Hell, I'm not putting this right.'

Farron dragged in his breath harshly, ignoring the apology. The idea about the adoption was all news to him. 'Everyone would have guessed,' he said after thinking things through, accurately gauging how it must have been back then. 'You might have lost the hotels if the truth got out. I understand you had some relatives in the States . . .'

Dominic nodded his head. 'Yes, Fred's Chicago cousins. You see, the thing about the will was so complicated. You were born before my grandfather died, so he knew he couldn't legally force me to abandon you. But he knew that if the Cousins contested the will, I would be bound up in red tape for months, probably years. And I was in such a vulnerable position then. The company was poised to acquire more land and I was young and untested. If the company assets had been frozen, pending a legal battle over the inheritance, then even though I would have actually won, the company would have become practically worthless. The competition would have moved in, frozen me out and Fairchild's would be dead in the water. But even so, I was prepared to risk it. All I wanted back then was to inherit Fairchild's and raise you as my son. I was determined to have both you and the hotels. So much for the determination of youth, eh?'

Farron stared at him, impressed but not surprised by his determination. 'So, what went wrong?'

Dominic laughed, a single bitter laugh. 'What always seemed to go wrong.'

Farron continued to look at him in puzzled silence, and Dominic, catching the gaze, smiled wrily. 'Graham

Grantham, Farròn. Graham Grantham went wrong. He threatened to give the Chicago lawyers all the ammunition they needed to contest the will.'

'He knew about my mother? About Akaki?'

Dominic nodded. 'And it wouldn't have been hard for him to open his father's safe and read the will.'

'But why should he care? I mean, why should he cause trouble for you?'

Dominic sighed. 'He thought Rhiannon was my daughter. That I'd had an affair with his wife Jess. And forcing me to give you up was his way of getting even.'

Farron nodded. 'Yes. There was something about a mis-understanding between you and Graham in the folder Rhiannon gave me this afternoon. So who was her real father?'

'Arnold – Graham's father. He had green eyes, too. But at the time I had no idea. I thought Rhiannon was Graham's, whilst all the time he thought she was mine and blamed me for all his pain and problems. It was as if by hurting me he could ease his own misery. Hell, I nearly killed him. He even demanded money, as if goading me into finishing the job. I swear, Farron,' Dominic said, looking deeply into his son's eyes: 'I came this close . . .' he held out his fingers, a scant space between them, 'to killing the warped bastard when it finally dawned on me that I would lose you.' He shuddered.

Farron shook his head. 'And the money – you actually gave it to him?'

'Yes, I did. For you mainly, but also for me. I was in a precarious position then. I still had to go to Harvard when the company was in the hands of Smith Flanaghan. Not that that worried me, but the Chicago vultures were hovering . . . and you were only an infant, living with an old lady who was and is one of the finest people I know. I wasn't sure what a rash of publicity would have done to you. And I was determined not to lose the hotels. I still intended to work like mad, get my own companies founded and then adopt you come hell or high water.'

Farron was silent for a long moment, wondering why he hadn't done so. This was the question, the million-dollar question that had tormented the young man all afternoon. 'So why didn't you?' He finally took the bull by the horns. 'Why didn't you tell me when I was old enough, who you were? Or when I started to work at the hotel – why didn't you tell me then?'

Dominic looked at him, prepared for the question, his face an open book. 'Cowardice,' he said simply. 'Just that. I was scared I'd left it too late. Scared that once you knew what I'd done you'd . . . hate me. That you'd leave. That I'd never see you again. Having you so close, and yet, in many ways, so far away was like being tortured. You'll never know how often and how close I've come to telling you the truth during the past years. But no matter how second-hand my involvement was in your life, it was better than nothing. I just couldn't risk you leaving the hotel or even the island, in a mood of bitter anger towards me. I couldn't face the thought of you despising me. It was that simple. And the longer I left it, and the more we got to know and like each other, the more impossible it became for me to risk it. Your friendship meant too much to me to allow me to gamble with it. Besides, I knew that I would always be there for you – that I could help you, even if you didn't know it, whenever you got into trouble.'

Farron looked away. Yes, Dominic had done so much for him. But always in secret. Never once had he openly acknowledged him. Farron tried to shove the angry thought away and instead concentrate on getting to the end of the story. 'So how long did you pay blackmail money to Graham?'

'Too long. I had to wait until he got careless.'

'And when he did?'

Dominic looked away. 'When he did, I made my move. And he died.'

'Died?'

'A heart attack was what finally killed him, but he'd been drinking for years. When he went bankrupt it just about finished him off.'

'And his daughter blamed you?'

Dominic nodded. 'Yes, she blamed me.' He wasn't about to get into any details about that, not even with his son, but Farron had a good idea anyway.

'So, what do you do now?' he asked. 'I take it she doesn't know about the blackmail, that Graham was bleeding you for money because of me?'

'No.'

'But you can stop her, before she does any more damage?'

Dominic nodded but his voice was bleak as he said listlessly, 'Yes, I can stop her now.'

Farron sighed heavily. Dominic and Rhia. He'd long since suspected it, and now he knew it. What a mess!

'But let's talk about you now,' Dominic said, dragging his thoughts back from their painful pathways. 'How is Vienna?'

Farron was more than happy to follow his lead. They'd both laid their souls sufficiently bare for one day. 'I haven't seen her yet except for a few minutes this afternoon,' he admitted glumly. 'She's looking better, though. Oh, she's still pale and shaky, but her eyes are better. They don't look at me with that tortured, helpless expression any more, thank God!'

'Perry picked up Jago this afternoon. Went without a murmur, apparently.' Farron nodded. He didn't really care. 'Has she seen Gloria yet?'

Farron shook his head. 'No, not yet. I'll be going to see her soon, though, and let her know that we know. It's funny to think of Gloria in the role of mother. The first priority is getting Vienna straightened out about this Lyons thing. Dr Jürgens is going to hypnotically repress all thoughts of it. It's the only way, he's discovered, to give her peace of mind.'

'That's good.'

'Yes. I just can't thank you enough for what you've done for her.'

'You already did. On the phone that time in New York.'

Farron frowned, puzzled. 'I don't understand.'

'I asked if you trusted me, remember? And you said yes. You'll never know how much that meant to me.'

Farron smiled. 'It was easy. I've always trusted you.' Then his face fell suddenly. It was probably being unfair to Dominic, but half of him said that he had done nothing but lie to him for years. 'Don't worry, Dad. I won't embarrass you.' Farron could feel himself getting angry again, and he abruptly stood up and paced the room. Finally he stopped and looked his father in the eye. 'I understand why you had to give me up,' he said, and the turmoil was plain on his face. 'I really do, and I don't blame you. But all these years we've known each other, you *never* told me who you were! I can't forgive that so easily.'

'I know. I'm sorry. I wanted to but . . .'

'But you were scared I'd make a scene.' Suddenly Farron was unable to control his anger any longer. He'd bottled it up inside him all afternoon and now it burst forth. 'That's the real reason you never publicly acknowledged me, isn't it? Yes, I trust you, but you don't trust me. You knew if it got out that you had a son by a whore, you'd be the laughing stock of the islands.'

'No!' Dominic denied, appalled he could believe such a thing of him. 'Farron, no.'

'So you're trying to tell me you're not ashamed of me?' Farron asked, half of him believing that it was true, the other half sneeringly telling him that Dominic Fairchild was more interested in his precious good name than in his own flesh and blood.

Dominic looked at him, opened his mouth to say something, and then closed it again. Words were all well and good, but actions spoke louder. 'I love you, Farron,' he said softly. 'And I'm proud of you. I'll prove it to you somehow – that I promise you.'

Farron stared at him in silence for a moment, then wearily ran his hand through his hair. 'It doesn't matter,' he said flatly. 'And forget I said all that. I owe you so much already, I have no right to expect any more. Let's just forget it, hm? We're still friends, right?'

Dominic swallowed hard. 'You're my son too, Farron.'

'When it's convenient,' Farron added bluntly, then sighed tiredly. 'Look, I've got to get back. I'll see you around.'

Dominic watched him go, aching to call him back. Wanting to throw his arms around him and tell him how much he loved him. And he would, as soon as he could prove to his son that he was worthy of him. But how?

BEN sighed deeply as he walked across the lobby of the Blue

Hawaiian and looked down at the folder clasped tightly in his hands. What it contained was going to hurt her. His heart was heavy as he tapped on her door, and heavier still when, after opening it, her face lit up. 'Ben! I didn't know you were back on the islands.'

'My plane just landed,' he said, coming in and looking around the room which was stacked with boxes she'd just had delivered from the storage firm. 'You haven't been able to get your house back, then?'

Rhiannon's smile faded. 'No, but it doesn't matter. By Friday this hotel will be all mine.'

At her words Ben let out a slow breath. Three days! He had cut it close. Briefly he wondered if Fairchild was sweating, but somehow he doubted it. 'I see. Then I've arrived just in time.'

'You have,' Rhiannon agreed, but without enthusiasm. 'The show will start on Friday at a private meeting of . . .'

'I meant,' Ben interrupted, 'I arrived just in time to stop you making a terrible mistake.'

Rhiannon felt a cold shiver down her spine. 'What do you mean?' She forced the words past stiff lips, her eyes wide and wary. She looked, suddenly, very young and Ben silently cursed. He should have kept this agony from her somehow. But how? 'I've had some people checking out some things in London,' he said, by way of easing her into the shock. 'About your father. Several things you said didn't quite make sense at the time, and I thought . . .'

'You've been spying on Daddy?'

'Yes – just the way you had Dominic's every personal detail ferreted out,' he agreed, looking her straight in the eye, and Rhiannon flushed.

'I see.'

'No, I don't think you do. But you will once you've read this,' he waved the folder in the air between them and then put it deliberately down on to her bed. Rhiannon walked slowly to the window, hugging her arms with her hands, aware of gooseflesh pimpling her skin. 'Just be sure you read it before Friday, Rhia,' he said softly. 'For your own sake.'

Giving her a last, sad smile he said, 'I'll be in the Peacock Suite when you need me.' Then he turned and left.

She walked slowly to the edge of her bed and stood looking down at the innocuous folder for long minutes. Then, taking a deep breath, she perched cross-legged in the middle of her bed and snatched it up. Taking out the first page she began to read.

When she'd finished, unknown minutes later, her life lay in ruins about her. Only one thought pierced the numbness that had settled over her like a fog: Dominic had been telling the truth all along – about the blackmail, about the car crash that had killed her mother. About everything. Those cold, clear, unemotional documents gave her a view of her father she had never seen before.

For years he had taken money from a man who had once thought of him as a dear friend. At the very time of her birth her father had been plotting to deprive Farron of his father. And why? Because he had mistakenly thought Dominic had had an affair with Jess. As the harsh facts churned around and around in her head, Rhiannon swallowed, licking her dry lips and wiping her forehead with the back of her hand. She felt cold – cold all over. Her eyes were dry, but inside she could feel a flood of tears drowning her. Even the day he'd died, even at the very moment of death, he'd lied to her. His hatred of Dominic had been so immense that he'd sent her to destroy him.

But she could not place all the blame with Graham. Since she'd arrived, different people had been pointing out to her just what sort of man Dominic really was – honourable, fair, kind, strong. Clarice had tried to tell her, so had Vienna, Farron, even Ben. But would she listen? No – she'd let herself be blinded by her father's hatred.

Most of it was her own fault; *she had no one to blame but herself.*

As the night wore on, the darkness outside echoing the darkness she felt deep inside herself, Rhiannon finally began to stir. Listlessly she unfolded her legs and staggered from the bed to walk to the phone. Wallowing in self-pity was not good enough. Picking up the receiver she asked for Ben's room and stood listening to the single burring of the line before it was snatched up.

'Rhiannon. Are you . . . all right?'

At the sound of his concerned voice she only just managed to stop herself from collapsing into bitter, shameful laughter. All right? Hell no, she was *not* all right. Not even close. 'I want to talk to the lawyers, Ben,' she said dully. 'I have things I want them to get on to. Right away.'

As a stranger's voice came over the line, Rhiannon told it simply and succinctly what she wanted done, then hung up. She did not have the energy even to say goodbye to Ben. Walking to the window, gravitating to the bright lights that winked out from the great city surrounding her, she stood on the balcony for several minutes as the breeze blew softly in her hair.

She felt empty, and yet at the same time full – of guilt, and shame, and pain. Leaning on the railings she looked down the hundreds of feet to where the paved patio that surrounded the pool was lit by the garden lights. It was late and there was no one around, and everything was her own fault.

And she'd made the only man in the world she'd ever loved, hate her.

Chapter 48

Farron knocked on the door of the Glorious Motel, which opened to reveal a tall brunette, vaguely South American in looks. 'I've come to see Gloria,' he said quickly.

'Oh, I see. Wait here.' She looked disappointed.

When he'd returned from Dominic's he'd been delighted to find Vienna waiting for him in the bungalow. Dr Jürgens had been so satisfied with her progress he'd finally given in to her pleas to meet her mother. Telling her about Dominic had at first dumbfounded then delighted her, and made her even more determined that she see Gloria tonight. But it was out of the question that Vienna leave the house to come here – so . . .

'Gloria says to come right in,' the husky voice cut through his thoughts.

His palms itched as he knocked on the office door and walked in.

'Hello, Farron.' Gloria rose graciously from behind the desk. Looking at her with new eyes, taking in the short, neatly cut blonde hair and big blue eyes, he had a feeling of déjà vu. Just as he'd wondered before how he could have failed to realize that Dominic was his father, now he wondered how he'd never seen that this woman was Vienna's mother.

Gloria knew at once something was wrong. Farron was shuffling his feet uneasily, and his flickering gaze danced around the room.

'I wanted to talk to you about Frank Gillespie,' Farron blurted out. It was a lie, but he didn't feel able to come straight to the point. He was an ambassador for Vienna and the responsibility weighed heavily on him.

Gloria nodded, but remained puzzled. 'All right. Sit down, please. Coffee?'

Farron nodded and sat down, then left his cup untouched on the table top. Curiosity ate at Gloria like a worm, but nothing showed on her face. Raising her cup to her lips she took a small sip of the hot and strong liquid.

'Dominic told me that Frank had a lot to do with leaning on Drake.'

So he knew the whole story, Gloria thought. Yes – that made sense. Dominic wouldn't keep it from him. 'That's right.'

'Why?'

'Why?' Gloria repeated, for once at a loss. She blinked and grappled for an excuse. 'Well, Dominic came and asked me for a favour. He knew that I knew Frank, and that I had some influence with him, so instead of going to Frank direct he came to me. And, of course, I was happy to help.'

'Why?' he persisted softly.

Suddenly Gloria felt as if she'd wandered on to shaky ground and she didn't like it much. 'You look tired,' she dissembled, hoping to change the subject.

'I've had a hectic week. First we went to Switzerland, where Vienna went to school, then to New York.'

'New York?' Gloria repeated sharply.

'Hm,' Farron said, encouraged by her obvious desire to learn what he knew. 'There we learned Vienna's true name – Pauline Clarke.'

Gloria felt the cup shake in her hand but she kept a firm grip on it, even forcing herself to take a nonchalant sip though there was a lump in her throat so big it threatened to gag her. 'That's nice for her.'

'Yes. We found old friends, and . . . a diary.'

Gloria blanched. Farron hesitated, giving her every opportunity to come clean. But the fact that Gloria didn't wasn't because she was ashamed – she was just too stunned.

'In it,' Farron continued, 'we finally learned why Vienna was in Oahu. It turned out she was not an orphan at all. Her old matron told her that the parents killed in a car crash when she was still a baby were her adoptive parents. She had, in fact, got a mother in Oahu. Her natural mother, who'd left the Bronx for a better life and found one, in a way, but only after years of struggle and hardship.'

Still Gloria said nothing. She was incapable of speech. Mutely she stared at him with wounded blue eyes, making him shift uncomfortably in his chair. This was even worse than his recent soul-searching talk with his father! 'It seems her mother – her real one that is, had to give her up because she was . . . running a place like this.'

Gloria merely nodded. She could feel an almost calming sensation of relief. So Vienna knew. And she'd sent her man to tell her to keep the hell away from her in future. Didn't she know that she needed no such warning? Gloria would no more have jeopardized her daughter's rosy-looking future than she would have drowned her beloved cat. But, Gloria thought with a sudden harsh pang of misery, how could Pauline know that? Then another thought hit her so hard she almost rose from the chair. *Had she remembered about Lyons?*

'We know who you are, Gloria,' Farron finally dragged it out into the open. 'Vienna was sure in New York, but I wasn't. Not until I spoke to Dominic.'

Gloria licked her lips and swallowed hard, bringing herself under control. Watching her do so, Farron couldn't help but admire her. 'I see. And you've come to tell me that Pau- that Vienna wants me to stay away.' Gloria was white-faced now, and no amount of poise could disguise her agony.

'Actually,' he said softly, 'quite the opposite. She wants to see you, very badly. She asked me to come and fetch you. The doctor wouldn't permit her to leave the house, or she would have come here herself.'

Gloria reeled quite literally under the impact of his words. Prepared for the worst, as she had been all her life, Gloria Gaines wasn't sure how to cope with Fate when it was being kind.

Eventually the words came. 'How is she? Is she all right? I've been worried sick about her. Dominic told me Jürgens was the best, and I had him checked out myself, but is she OK? Really?' She was sitting forward on her seat, an anxious mother pleading for information about her beloved daughter. Farron smiled. Dominic and Gloria – what parents they were! And what better parents they'd make now that they were truly free to be so.

'She's fine,' he reassured her softly. 'She's still looking washed-out, but her spirit is back. You can see it in her eyes.'

Gloria felt tears slide down her cheeks. 'You can?'

Farron stood up. 'Come on – you can see for yourself.'

For a long moment Gloria stayed where she was, unable to move. Then she nodded and got blindly to her feet. 'OK.'

Never before had Gloria left the Motel at night, but tonight she did so, without even a backwards look. But while walking to his sports car which was parked down the alley, Gloria shuddered, unaware that Farron was looking around him with narrowed eyes.

'Tell me about it, Gloria,' Farron said quietly as soon as they'd left Chinatown behind them and were heading out of the city towards the quiet bay where Vienna waited. Gloria looked at his profile, saw that he already knew most of it and nodded. Why not? He had to know, if he was to keep Vienna safe.

'It started in early December,' she began quietly. 'I got a call from Frank who told me he'd had a visit from a girl, asking about a woman who . . . had worked for him once and who now owned a . . . motel.'

'Go on,' he encouraged softly.

'Well, I probed him about it, and he described my Pauline. I asked him if he'd told her about me and he said he had. For a moment I could have killed him.'

Farron laughed softly, overtook a trundling van, and said, 'I can imagine.'

'Anyway, later that day I got a call from my daughter. She said she needed to speak to me and I said OK. We arranged to meet . . . in a café.'

Farron stood on the accelerator just a little. 'No, you didn't,' he contradicted softly. 'You arranged to meet in an alley somewhere.'

'No!' Gloria denied hotly. 'Do you think I'd ask to meet my own daughter in some back alley?'

'No. You arranged for her to come to the motel, didn't you? To get it all over and done with in one go. To let her see, right from the start, who and what you were. Isn't that so, Gloria?' He turned to look at her briefly, and in the moonlight her face was chalk-white. For a while she didn't speak. The accuracy of his guess had taken her breath away. He was right, of course.

She'd agonized all that day about whether to tell her half-truths and live a beautiful sham. She'd even, at some frantic point in mid-afternoon, thought about renting a nice little bungalow in the middle of a nice little suburb and playing the widowed housewife. But when the call had come and she'd heard for the first time the clear and adult voice of her own daughter, the lies had seemed obscene. Quietly and simply she'd told Pauline where to find her. And then she'd waited.

'Yes,' Gloria said finally, her voice small. 'That's right. But she never arrived. I heard later she'd been mugged.'

Farron was shaking his head even before she'd finished. 'Gloria,' he said softly. 'Stop lying. I want to know the truth. I *need* to know it. Can't you see that?' he asked her, his voice both harsh and pleading. He pulled over on to the side of the road and parked under a grove of pandanus trees, switching off the engine to a night that was deathly quiet. Half-turning in his seat he faced her. 'What happened that night, Gloria?'

Playing for time she asked, 'Has she remembered? This Dr Jürgens, has he cured her?'

'Dr Jürgens has made sure, through hypnosis, that Vienna never remembers anything about Lyons or that night again. He's assured me privately that there will be no more memories, flashbacks or depressions. He's also told me that he doesn't think she'll ever get her true memory back either.'

Gloria felt a shaft of pain lance through her at that. 'I'm sorry,' she said, and meant it. Not the part about Lyons – that only filled her with sweet relief. But the thought of Pauline never remembering her past life . . . and all because of her. It was her fault. If only she hadn't asked her to come to the motel . . .

'What happened, Gloria?' Farron said again, and the urge to tell him was overpowering. If Pauline did reject her, she'd need someone who knew all the facts, like Farron, to look after her. 'I love her,' Farron said softly. 'Are you afraid to tell me because you think I might hurt her? Accuse her? If so, you don't know me very well.'

And so Gloria told him. Slowly at first, the words hard-found and almost whispered. 'I was expecting her. It was about eight-thirty, not too late. I'd told her to come to the back door – through the alley. To save her embarrassment.'

'I understand,' Farron said softly, waiting whilst Gloria reached into her bag for a handkerchief and wiped her eyes. 'There was trouble, suddenly, with one of the girls. She came running out, screaming, into the alley. I was there, watching for . . . Vienna. I tried to stop the girl, but she was screaming hysterically. I caught her arm and asked her what was wrong, but she looked over my shoulder and screamed again. Her eyes went wide . . . I'll never forget the look in them. As I turned around, this man – Gary Lyons, as it turned out, shoved me aside and went after her. I fell, and when I got up the first person I saw was this small blonde girl. My daughter.' Gloria's voice faltered as the memory came back with vivid detail. Farron listened, picturing it all, his heart aching for Vienna and what he suddenly knew, beyond a shadow of a doubt, that Gloria was going to tell him. 'She was standing at the end of the alley and a streetlight made her hair all silver – like a halo. I just knew she was my daughter.' Gloria shook her head. Reaching across for her cold hand, Farron squeezed it.

'Wanda, the one who'd run out first, was still screaming. I could see the man raise his hand to hit her. For a second I just froze. Then I heard running feet – the tapping of women's shoes on the ground. I looked up and Pauline was there, shouting at him to leave her alone. It made Lyons look around, and when he drew his hand back from Wanda's throat I saw he had a knife. It caught the light, making it glint silver. It was *awful*. Like a nightmare.'

Gloria shuddered, unable to go on, and Farron closed his eyes briefly. How many times, in the agonized night, had Vienna awoken in a cold sweat and told him she could see a knife, glinting in the light, coming towards her? Yet it hadn't been aimed at her, but at the other girl. 'Then what?' he prompted, a bitter taste in his mouth for the cruelties of life. But he had to hear it. Just once, then he'd never think of it again.

'Pauline grabbed his wrist – to try and stop him. Before I could reach them, Lyons shrugged her off and she fell backwards, staggering against some garbage cans that lined the wall behind her. I think I called out to her, but she didn't react. Instead she struggled to her feet and looked around for something to stop him. Wanda was terrified – that man meant to kill her, Farron,' Gloria said urgently. 'You must believe me – you must understand. It all happened so quickly. He had the knife, like this . . .' She demonstrated with her raised hand, 'and he was going to kill her.'

'I believe you, Gloria,' Farron said soothingly. 'I know it's the truth.'

Gloria nodded, and then took several calming breaths. When she spoke next her voice was flat. Defeated. 'Pauline picked up one of the big round lids from a garbage can. It was an old can – one of the tin ones. The lid was heavy, I could tell. She fell forward as she swung it and it wobbled, out of control. It hit Lyons squarely on the side of the head. There was this awful . . . *clang*. And then, well, you heard about the injury to his head.'

Farron squeezed her hand even tighter. 'Yes. Then what?'

'Lyons went down like a sack of potatoes. Wanda was still screaming her head off. But the momentum of the blow threw Pauline forward and she tripped over Lyons and fell against the wall, banging her head. She just . . . slowly fell down. I screamed then – I thought she was dead. I ran to her, and held her, sure she had been killed.' Gloria's voice was coming fast now, dry sobs wracking her, making her words slurred and uneven. 'By now some of my girls had heard the racket and came out. It was Nancy who felt her pulse and told me she wasn't dead. She had to shake me, to scream at me, to make me hear. I just fell apart. And it was Nancy who called Frank. She didn't know what else to do. The rest you know. He got rid of Lyons' body and took Vienna in his car to another alley. He kept her in his car until he heard the ambulance sirens and then he put her in the middle of the road, took her bag and money to make it look like the mugging he'd reported seeing, and then got out of there.' Gloria's voice trailed off into little more than a whisper. Lord, she felt tired. Drained.

Farron stared out into the night in silence for a long while. So that had been the big, round frisbee of her dreams – a garbage can lid. Slowly he leaned forward and restarted the engine. They did not speak again until he pulled up in front of the house.

'Ready?' Farron asked, turning to look at her.

Gloria smiled shakily. 'Hardly!'

In the hall Gloria watched a tall blond man approach, looking at her with farseeing eyes. 'This is the lady?' Dr Jürgens asked.

Farron nodded. 'Gloria Gaines, Dr Jürgens.'

Gloria held out her hand. 'Hello, Doctor. How is she?'

'Fine – fine. Anxious to see you, and a little scared too I think.'

Gloria licked her lips. 'I see. Is there anything I should do? Or not do? I don't want to upset her.'

'Just treat her kindly, Miss Gaines. That's all you have to do.'

Gloria nodded, her eyes flickering to a closed door where instinct told her her daughter waited. Dr Jürgens caught Farron's eye and smiled. Bowing over Gloria's hand he kissed it and then told Farron he'd be in the study, reading one of Dominic's excellent books, if he thought he was needed.

After he left an awkward silence stretched between them. 'Well?' Farron cleared his throat and said with forced cheerfulness, 'Vienna's waiting.'

'Yes. I know,' Gloria said, sudden guilt attacking her. What could she say to her to make her understand she'd only . . .

'Come on,' Farron took her arm gently, accurately reading her sudden panic. He wanted to tell her she had nothing to worry about, but he couldn't. Vienna deserved that privilege. Knocking on the door, Gloria waited, her mind going mercifully blank.

Vienna heard the knock and got up from the settee. 'Come in!' Her voice was barely a croak and she called more firmly, 'Come in.'

Farron was the first through the door and her gaze flew to his familiar face, loving his gentle smile. Then her eyes went quickly to the pale-looking woman who walked in slowly beside him, and two pairs of blue eyes met, and clung. 'Hello,' Vienna said, then felt stupid. A slow flush came up her cheeks, and Gloria smiled tremulously.

'Hello . . . how are you feeling?'

Vienna shrugged, her hands clinging together nervously in front of her. 'Much better, thanks.' Farron knew just how they felt and also that he had to leave them alone.

'I'll fix us some coffee,' he said, and was gone before either Gloria or Vienna could stop him. Slowly, her footsteps unsure, Gloria walked further into the room, her anxious eyes searching those of the young girl who stood watching her, yearning to say so many things, but not quite daring.

'Oh, Pauline . . .' Gloria felt the words rush out of her throat at the same time as her vision blurred with tears, and Vienna was filled with a great shaft of joy.

'Mother,' she said, the word almost incoherent, but Gloria heard, and understood. Holding out her arms, Gloria began to cry. With a sob of her own Vienna stumbled into her mother's arms, letting herself be wrapped in that loving embrace. Strong hands rubbed over her back and gently patted as both women began to weep the comforting tears of release.

'Oh, Pauline . . . Pauline,' Gloria said, her eyes screwed tightly shut as she clung to her daughter as if she never intended to let her go again. 'Let me look at you properly.' She pulled away just a little, so that they could look at each other. Suddenly they began to smile, then laugh, then cry again, and for long long minutes they just clung to each other, supporting and comforting one another as years of pain and months of tension and unease, slowly drained out of them.

'Come on – we'd better sit down.' It was Gloria who recovered first, mindful of the still-weakened state of her daughter. Vienna didn't protest as she was led to the couch, and their hands clung together as they sat side by side.

Reaching into her bag, Gloria retrieved her damp handkerchief and mopped her face, then handed another silk and lace square to Vienna, who did likewise, her nostrils twitching as they picked up the same floral scent that would, ever after, conjure up the picture of her mother. 'I was afraid you wouldn't come,' Vienna said after a silent minute had passed, and the time for words had finally come.

'I was afraid to,' Gloria admitted, then smiled with shame

as Vienna looked at her in surprise. 'I thought you wouldn't want me. Well, I'm not the kind of mother an orphan would dream of finding, am I?'

'Because of what you do for a living, you mean?' A wide smile pulled at Vienna's mouth. 'I don't know, it doesn't really mean anything to me. I don't feel disgusted!'

'Don't be scared to hurt my feelings. I know what I am, and came to terms with it a long time ago.'

Vienna nodded, looking down into her lap for a second, and then back at her. 'Tell me about yourself, Gloria,' she said, and the older woman laughed.

'Well, to begin with,' she smiled, 'Gloria Gaines isn't my real name . . .'

For half an hour, as Farron lurked nervously in the kitchen, and Dr Jürgens blissfully read a volume of poetry by William Blake, Gloria told her daughter the true story of her past – of her grinding life of poverty in the Bronx, the crime, the despair, the urgent need to escape. She told how Hawaii had sounded like paradise when her best friend and soon-to-be-lover Frank Gillespie had written and told her about it, asking her to come over and lending her the money to do so. Without exaggeration or shame, she told her how she'd worked for Frank, and how a run of bad luck had made him lose the casino and forced her to try and find other work – the kind of work that only a girl with no qualifications and no money could do. Gloria talked with genuine affection of Madame Bernice and the girls she worked with, but throughout it all she never once mentioned Vienna's father.

'I never wanted to give you up,' Gloria said now, her voice stretched tight with the pain of remembrance. 'At the motel I have a picture of you – you were such a beautiful baby, but I suppose all mothers say that.' Gloria laughed weakly. She'd been twisting the handkerchief in her lap all the time she'd been speaking and now she looked at Vienna with wise and sad eyes. 'But I knew I had to do it. I couldn't raise you in a place like that. Even if the authorities had let me, and I doubt they would. It tore me apart to do it. I know you have every right to doubt it but – '

Softly Vienna pressed her fingertip to her mother's lips. 'I know it did, Mother. I know.' Again silence reigned for several moments.

'When I heard that the good people who'd adopted you had been killed and that you were in an orphanage, there was nothing I could do.' Gloria shook her head. 'I ranted and raved, and cursed God. In a few years I had this place, and was doing well. I wanted to re-adopt you, but how could I? All prospective parents of adopted children are checked out by the Welfare people and you can imagine what they would have made of me. And by then I was too well-known to fake a new identity. It sounds as if I'm making excuses, but Pauline – no, Vienna,' Gloria corrected herself, 'I did want you back so much.'

'I understand and you mustn't get the wrong idea. I went back to the orphanage when I was in New York. There was a man there, the man who ran the place. I know I loved him like a father. Even though I couldn't remember,' Vienna stressed the word, 'I could feel it. And my house-mother. I'll have to go back to New York one day to see her.' Then, realizing this might have hurt her, she looked at Gloria anxiously. 'It's not that . . .'

'Hush,' this time it was Gloria's turn to silence her with a fingertip. 'I know. And I'm glad. I suppose I had a guilty idea that the orphanage was like one of those God-awful places out of a Dickens novel or something.'

Both women laughed at that, and Gloria listened anxiously as Vienna described the place to her, together with all the details that she and Farron had been able to discover about her life in New York. 'And Switzerland was lovely. I'm so glad my aunt . . .' Suddenly Vienna stopped, staring at Gloria who smiled quickly and looked away. 'But I didn't have an aunt, did I?' Understanding dawned in her blue eyes. 'That was you, wasn't it?'

Gloria nodded. 'I wanted you to have the best start in life that I could, under the circumstances, ever hope to give you.'

Vienna had never felt so wonderful before in her life. After the months of misery, suddenly everything was so perfect, so lovely, so *right*, that it left her feeling overwhelmed. Wordlessly she reached across and kissed her mother's cheek, managing to choke out afterwards, 'You did, Mother. You did.'

'After your accident, I wanted to see you, to tell you . . .' Gloria saw Vienna's face tense a little, and trailed off miserably.

'I did wonder why you never came to see me.' There was just a hint of reproach in her voice, and Gloria felt the guilty pain hit her once more.

'I know that you must have done,' she admitted miserably. 'And I knew that you must have felt so alone. But I . . .' Gloria paused, and bit back a soft moan of regret. 'Oh Vienna, I wanted to. But I began to think . . . We'd never actually met and I didn't know what you would have thought about me. I just decided that you didn't need this strange woman turning up in your life, saying she was your mother, and then seeing you hurt or disgusted because I was the infamous Gloria Gaines. I thought it was better for you if I didn't contaminate your life. But I did watch out for you, my darling. I had someone watching you, to make sure you were safe.'

Vienna smiled, a tremulous smile. 'Farron's told me all about what happened. I really owe you and Dominic a . . .'

'No,' Gloria shook her head firmly. 'You owe me nothing. I owe you . . .'

'It's all right — really,' Vienna interrupted quickly. 'I know now you only did what you thought was for the best. It was just that I was so lonely. I felt so alone that I yearned for someone to come forward and just say that they knew me. That I belonged to them. Can you understand that?' Vienna appealed, and as their eyes met, Gloria aburptly made up her mind.

'About your father.'

'You don't have to tell me. I have you now, and that's enough,' she assured her hastily, but Gloria shook her head.

'You have a father too. A good one, a good man. Here on the islands.'

Vienna stared at her, a look of happiness fleetingly settling on her face before she suddenly went as white as a ghost. Her eyes darkened to almost black as a purely horrific thought suddenly hit her. 'Oh God,' she said, her voice a whisper of mortal terror. 'It's not Dominic is it?'

Gloria stared at her for a second, too stunned to speak. 'Dominic? Why do you say that?'

Vienna shook her head, panic biting hard, threatening to eat her alive. Her hands dug into Gloria's, her fingernails unknowingly scoring deep painful grooves into her mother's palm. 'Tell me it isn't Dominic, Mother,' Vienna said, her voice a croaking whisper. 'It can't be. He's Farron's father and if he's mine as well . . .'

Suddenly Gloria understood. 'No. Oh, darling no!' she said urgently, her eyes earnest and gentle. 'Dominic's not your father. You and Farron aren't brother and sister!'

Vienna let out her breath in a whoosh of relief, then began to laugh as her colour flooded back. Great gales of laughter swept over her — she just couldn't help it. Laughing herself now, as much in relief as anything, Gloria cupped a hand around the back of Vienna's head and pulled her face to rest briefly against her breast as she lovingly ruffled her daughter's silky-smooth silver hair. When Vienna pulled back her face was shining.

'For one awful moment there,' she said, wagging a relieved finger in the air between them, and Gloria laughed.

'Dominic is a wonderful man, and one of the best friends I have. But your father — do you really want to know him? To meet him?' Too awed to speak, Vienna simply nodded. Gloria smiled. 'Then you shall. Actually, you've already met him once, but you wouldn't remember. It was before you were mugged,' Gloria told her, the word slipping without hesitation from her lips. Although Farron had said nothing about it, Gloria knew that neither of them would ever tell Vienna about Lyons. It would remain a secret between the two of them — a secret they'd both keep and take with them to their graves.

'I have?' Vienna said, both puzzled and intrigued. 'I've actually met him?'

'You have,' she confirmed softly. 'Your father is Frank Gillespie.'

Vienna's face went completely still as she digested this information. 'I've heard about him, from Farron,' she admitted softly. 'Isn't he some kind of gangster?'

Gloria began to gurgle with laughter – she couldn't stop herself. The thought of the look on Frank's face if someone had called him a gangster just cracked her up. Rocking on the settee, laughing so hard that even Farron heard her in the kitchen, Gloria shook her head helplessly, and after a startled second or two Vienna too began to laugh. Finally, when they were calm again, Gloria wiped away the tears from her eyes. 'Oh Vienna, you must think you have a real pair of desperados for parents.'

Vienna grinned, a little shamefaced.

'No, your father isn't a gangster,' Gloria reassured her. 'He had a childhood exactly like mine – he just managed to drag himself out of it in a slightly different way. He's a good man – a fair one. And he's going to be knocked for six when I tell him about you,' Gloria said, her eyes sparkling as she thought of it.

Vienna gaped. 'You mean he doesn't know?'

'No.' Gloria shook her head. 'No idea at all. We were friends, rather than lovers, by the time you were born. Since then, he's married and got two children of his own – both boys. His wife and I are great friends actually.'

Vienna hardly heard the last few words. Only two leapt out at her: *Two boys.* 'Brothers,' she breathed. 'I've got brothers?'

Gloria nodded, understanding suddenly what it must mean to her. 'Yes, you have. One's eleven and the other is nine.' Slowly the joy faded from her face. 'What is it, honey? What's wrong?'

Vienna shook her head. 'I don't suppose I'll be allowed to get to know them. I mean, I don't think my father's wife,' Vienna stumbled just a little over the word 'father', 'will be too pleased to learn about me, let alone allow me anywhere near her sons. Will she?' she added hopefully.

Gloria saw a picture of Frank's wife swim into focus in her head. Down-to-earth, friendly, wise Sheena. 'Oh darling,' Gloria clutched her hand again. 'You haven't got anything to worry about. After Frank's got over the shock and told Sheena, she'll have you and Farron around for dinner so fast your head'll spin. She'll be delighted, honey, believe me. Sheena and I are great friends – that ought to tell you what kind of woman she is.'

'Really?' A beatific smile of hope leapt to her face. 'You really think so?'

'I know so,' Gloria said firmly. And she would be proved right, only a week later. But now mother and daughter shared a moment of quiet peace, of burgeoning love, and when Farron softly opened the door and looked nervously in, the picture that faced him was of two blonde heads bent close together and two hands entwined. He sighed in happiness and Vienna heard the soft sound. Looking up, she abandoned Gloria and ran to him, throwing herself into his arms, laughing and crying at the same time.

'Oh, I love you,' she said in a firm growl, her arms looped tightly around his neck, her lips nuzzling the side of his neck. Looking up at him with soft, clear blue eyes, she said simply, 'I'm the luckiest girl alive.' She never thought about all that had gone before. The lost memory wasn't so important, not now that she knew what it contained, and she certainly never gave Richard Jago a second thought.

Farron never meant to blurt it out like he did. He had planned an intimate candlelit dinner, with a soft Hawaiian love song that he would sing just for her, followed by the finest champagne. But when she looked up and said the words that she did, the thought was so strong, the impulse so sudden, he couldn't resist it. 'Will you marry me now?' He heard the soft words spring from his lips, saw her eyes flicker and then burn with sheer delight, and thought his heart was going to burst with joy.

'Yes,' she said. 'Oh yes! Yes, yes, YES!'

Gloria looked away as they kissed, giving them privacy as she swallowed back yet more tears. Getting up to walk towards them she said, 'I'll call myself a cab.'

'There's no need. I'll drive you,' Farron said, but without real enthusiasm, and his hands never left Vienna's waist. Gloria's eyes sparkled knowingly.

'I'll take a cab,' she said firmly. 'And while I'm waiting, I'll keep that tall good-looking doctor company.'

Vienna smiled teasingly. 'What will Frank have to say about that?'

'Frank?' Farron queried, puzzled. What did Frank have to

do with anything? As mother and daughter laughed softly and secretly at his puzzled look, Gloria leaned forward and kissed first Vienna and then Farron, who blushed.

'I don't have to say, do I, how happy I am for you both? How pleased I am?'

'We'll save you the front pew in the church,' Farron said, just in case she had any silly ideas that they wouldn't want her at the wedding. By the happy and relieved smiled that flashed across her lips and the suspicious brightness that came into her eyes, Farron suspected she had done just that, and looking down into Vienna's shining face, he winked.

'You've got yourself a good one here, Paul ... Vienna,' Gloria corrected herself. 'Hold on to him.' Not waiting for a response, she opened the door and slipped out, at last feeling totally fulfilled and at perfect peace with herself and the world. Vienna watched her go, and then looked up at Farron with adoring eyes.

'Ask me again,' she demanded softly.

'Come here,' he whispered, taking her by the hand and leading her out through the french windows and on to the patio. There the moon shone brightly overhead, silver stars stood like gems against the midnight-blue velvet of the sky, and in a jacaranda tree a nightingale began to sing.

'This is better,' he whispered, as a small night-breeze gently wafted against their faces and brought with it the heady scent of the wild orchids that grew at the bottom of the garden. Reaching into his jeans pocket he withdrew a small flat box. He'd been carrying it around with him all day, just waiting. And now at long, long last, the waiting was over. Flicking the lid open, the moonlight sparkled on a china-blue Ceylon sapphire shaped into a perfect oval. Around it glimmered tiny diamonds, reflecting tiny prisms of light on her face as she looked down at it.

'The first time I saw it I knew it was the exact colour of your eyes,' Farron told her, feeling her small hand curl around his as those magnificent eyes of hers slowly lifted from the ring that he so reverently held. Holding out her left hand, Farron slipped the ring on to her finger.

Later, he would tell her that they would be married at

Christmas, in St Andrew's Cathedral. Later he would tell her he wanted the wedding to be whatever she wanted it to be – big and lavish, an affair to set the island rocking on its heels, or small and simple, with just close friends and both of their newfound parents in attendance. Later they would discuss all that and more. But tonight – tonight was theirs alone.

Slowly leaning forward, savouring every single second, their lips met and clung. And her lips were warm and sweet, firm and tender and her body moved eagerly, quickly to meet his, without restraint, without any hideous barriers between them. Dr Jürgens had done his work well, and as Vienna closed her eyes she felt passion, hot and sweet, uncoil deep inside her.

Softly, blissfully, Farron moaned.

Later was a long time in coming that night.

Chapter 49

Jimmy Dwight nearly danced into Dominic's office, his well-padded cheeks the colour of gleaming beetroot. His secretary leaned over and pressed the intercom buzzer. 'Mr Dwight is here to see you, sir.'

'Send him in,' he ordered busquely, waiting the scant seconds for his visitor to arrive with a relaxed air that would have fooled anyone but the keenly observant. What now? What the hell had she done this time?

Jimmy was still beaming and very nearly skipping when he entered the office. 'Your Highness,' he smiled. 'I don't suppose it's news to you but I thought I'd tell you I had word this morning from Miss Grantham's lawyers,' Jimmy's midwestern twang became more pronounced as the words tumbled in an excited torrent from his lips.

Dominic didn't move. 'Sit down, James,' he offered mildly and the smaller man quickly plonked himself down in a chair, hugging a very large black leather briefcase to his chest as if it contained the Crown jewels. 'You do know what's happened?' Jimmy asked, his effervescence finally fizzling out. 'I mean . . . it was all your doing, wasn't it?'

Dominic began to feel serious misgivings. 'I haven't heard anything yet. Tell me.'

Jimmy swallowed hard. 'Well, er, I was having breakfast when the doorbell rang, and there were six of Miss Grantham's legal team asking to come in. Naturally I was curious so I showed them into the study and they handed over these.' Jimmy decided to show instead of tell – it was less wearing on the nerves that way. Reaching into the well-hugged briefcase, he extracted a hefty bundle of papers. One look at his smug face gave Dominic his first clue, but it wasn't until he'd pulled the papers towards him and began to read, and continued to read with growing surprise, that the full importance of what had actually happened began to hit him. 'The boutiques. They've reverted to me?' he asked sharply with a raised brow as he looked at the laywer, merely needing confirmation that he'd read the legal jargon correctly.

Jimmy gave a quick and eager nod. 'Actually they've been given to you. She's signed everything over to you and this is really extraordinary . . .' Jimmy suffled the papers, his head half-craned so that he could read the page upside down, 'See, here? All the profits she's made in the boutiques since taking them over – they've all been made out in a personal cheque to you.'

'All the stocks that were mine before the New Year are now mine again?'

'Uh-huh,' Jimmy confirmed. 'The same goes for the Lanai Fruit Company stock. These are the papers, all you have to do is sign at the bottom. I'll witness them and . . .'

'And everything will be the same as it was before she came?'

'Precisely. She's even written out a resignation from both the Gray-Gray board and the Lanai Fruit board. Not strictly necessary of course,' Jimmy said with great satisfaction, 'since she now has no stock, but . . .'

'I get the picture,' Dominic cut in, his voice harsh. The papers spread out before him stared back at him but instead of feeling relief, or triumph or even satisfaction, he felt an ominous foreboding deep in the marrow of his bones. Quickly he leaned forward and pressed the intercom. 'Cynthia, get Phil for me, will you?'

'Yes, sir.' A moment later the third light lit up on the telephone and he picked it up. 'Mr Pearce, sir.' There was a click then Phil's voice.

'Hi.'

'I want you to get back here immediately.'

Philip reacted instantly to the tone. 'I'll catch the first plane out.'

Dominic hung up. Looking at the small and now thoroughly bewildered lawyer he told him to thrash out the details with his second-in-command when he arrived, and was up and leaving before Jimmy had even said, 'OK.'

'I'll be out all day,' Dominic told his secretary, still without stopping. In the lift he descended only one floor.

The corridor was deserted but he could hear vacuum

cleaners and maids humming. Her suite door was unlocked and he looked in – and froze. The maids had the room in a complete turmoil. Recognizing immediately that this was not the daily cleaning that was normally done, but the complete springclean that swung into operation whenever there was a change of guests in a room, he took a deep breath and turned on his heel. He could feel a fine trembling in every part of his body – like the numbing onset of shock, and he fought it back grimly. In the lobby he walked to the nearest free reception desk.

'Maria, why is the Emerald Suite being given the full cleaning treatment?'

The receptionist looked at him with an expression of surprise that she quickly repressed. It had been a matter of gossip amongst all the staff for months that Mr Fairchild knew everything that the English girl did.

'Maria!' Dominic all-but barked, making not only the girl herself jump, but all the other staff within hearing distance. Farron, who had come in to rehearse a new song with the band, also heard the sharply-raised voice and excusing himself from the rest of the guys, quickly walked out into the lobby. He was just in time to hear the receptionist's reply.

'Miss Grantham has checked out, Mr Fairchild.'

'When?'

'This morning. About seven-thirty, sir. Everything was in order, sir.'

'I see,' Dominic said, his voice once more calm and in control. 'Did she leave a forwarding address?'

Maria checked. 'No, sir. No address.'

Reaching across for the telephone, Dominic called the airport. 'Yes, this is Dominic Fairchild. Can you tell me if a passanger named Rhiannon Grantham – RHIANNON Grantham, is booked on any flight leaving today? Thanks, I'll wait.' Airports, of course, were not strictly supposed to give out that kind of information, but no one there was going to deny Dominic the answer.

Farron watched his father's shoulders sag slightly and heard his voice, totally dead and without any inflection whatsoever say, 'I see. Thank you.'

Rhiannon had left on a London-bound jet over half an hour ago. Half-turning from the desk, where all the staff were suddenly conspicuously busy, he smiled a little awkwardly when he saw Farron. '*Aloha*,' he said softly, walking towards him. 'How's the rehearsal going?'

'Great. Perfect, in fact.'

'Good. It's Tony's turn for the lunch-shift but perhaps you can sing the song as a "guest artiste"?'

'Sure,' Farron began, then, 'what's with the guest artiste stuff?'

Dominic laughed softly as they walked into the dining room, which was now beginning to fill with the early eat-and-let's-go element. 'Did I forget? You have a date with you-know-who at you-know-what recording studio.'

Farron stared at him in silence for a few uncomfortable seconds, then slowly smiled. 'Dad, I . . .' Suddenly he stopped and looked quickly around, but the barman was at the other end, serving one of their permanent guests. Relieved that he hadn't overheard, Farron silently cursed himself for being so stupid. Damn, he was going to have to be careful. Dominic saw it all and a secretive smile curved his lips. It was almost time he kept his promise. But the room wasn't quite full enough yet.

'Thanks, Dom.'

'Good luck with the try-out. To the future.' Clinking glasses, they both drank. Farron looked at him quickly, not missing his tension nor the pallor of his skin under the tan, and he wished, suddenly, that he'd talk about it. But while he longed to ask why Rhiannon Grantham was gone, he did not. Instead, needing to help ease the pain he decided to distract him. 'By the way, what are you doing on Christmas Eve?'

'Christman Eve?' Dominic repeated blankly, forcing his mind that far ahead. 'Nothing that I know of. Why?'

Farron grinned. 'Good. Then you won't mind going to St Andrew's with me and being my best man – will you?' There was just the slightest hint of a question in that statement, and Dominic felt a small pang hit him that even now Farron was not sure of him. But that would come – in time.

'So you finally got her to say yes?'

'I did.'

'Christmas Eve – good choice, that. But what'll the rest of us do, trying to find you a Christmas present to match the one that Vienna will be giving you?'

Farron roared with laughter, the sound bright and loud and uninhibited. It drew many eyes, but neither man noticed. 'You won't be able to,' he drawled. 'So forget it. Besides, having you as best man is all the present I want.'

'I'll be honoured,' Dominic assured him after he'd had time to draw a deep breath. 'Nothing will keep me away.'

'I'm glad.'

Looking around, Dominic saw Tony begin to walk on the stage, and turning to Farron he said softly: 'Want to tell the whole world?'

'I do, as a matter of fact.'

Dominic nodded his head at the stage. 'Go ahead, son.'

Smiling, Farron left his stool, unaware that Dominic had followed him until he began to mount the two steps that led up to the slightly raised dais and saw him there. But although he was surprised, he made no comment. His blood was flowing fast through his veins with sheer exhilaration, and in that second before he announced his love to all the world Farron thought he could never feel better in his life. As Ben Fielding walked slowly over to the bar, watching the men on stage with surprised interest, Farron took the microphone and a second later his melodious voice was coming over the speakers.

'Ladies and gentlemen, before Tony begins to serenade you, I hope you'll forgive me for making a quick announcement.' The room fell silent as all eyes went to the young musician. Young ladies watched Farron eagerly, but their attention wavered between the young man who sang songs to make their knees go weak, and the older, equally gorgeous man who stood behind him.

'I'd like to announce that on Christmas Eve, Vienna Wright and myself will be getting married.' It was simply said, but the depth of pride and happiness in his voice could not have been mistaken by anyone. At the bar Ben began to smile even as the crowd erupted in generous applause around them. Calls of congratulation flowed towards the stage as Farron smiled and began to move away, looking around in surprise as Dominic stopped him by firmly placing a detaining hand on his shoulder, at the same time holding up his other hand for silence.

'As those of you who spent the morning by the pool may have heard, Farron and the band have been rehearsing a new song, and I can see that all the band are still here, so with Tony's permission . . .' Dominic looked at the pianist waiting by the side of the stage, who was grinning widely and giving the go-ahead, 'I'd like to ask Farron and the band to play it.'

Enthusiastic applause broke out again, and Dominic waited until it had died down, a warmth and heady excitment rising in his own blood now as he faced the packed room. At last, after all these years, he was free to do what he'd always longed to. 'But before they do,' he continued, as the band began to gather around them, plugging in instruments and finding their places, 'I have an announcement of my own to make.'

He saw Farron look at him quickly, a questioning look on his face. Dominic's hand tightened on his shoulder, warming him through to the bone, but even so, his father's next words left him, as well as everyone else, totally stunned. 'I am especially pleased and proud of this young man,' Dominic told the out-of-town visitors, the newspaper editor and his latest female reporter sat in one corner, the senator and his wife sat directly in front of them, and the myriad number of business acquaintances, old friends and staff who had worked for him for years, meeting all their eyes without flinching as they looked at him, waiting and wondering. 'Because he is my son.' The words, in the deathly quiet room, seemed to drop like tiny bombs, and after the elongated second of shocked silence there came a hushed whisper, like a thousand tiny words being squeezed out of deflated lungs as the room seemed to let out its collective breath.

'Farron is my only son,' Dominic carried on, stating each word clearly, in case anyone had mistaken his meaning 'He is, in fact, my only child. And I shall be relying on him,' Dominic finished with a smile that was meant solely for Farron as he turned to look at him, 'to give me some grandchildren.'

648

All around them, pandemonium seemed to erupt. A flashlight from a camera illuminated them again and again as the female reporter began to earn her money, and a hundred shocked voices were finally freed to babble excitedly to each other about the best-kept secret the island had ever not-known! The two men who had caused it all stood side by side, touching, united, indestructible.

Farron felt his eyes begin to burn and he swallowed hard. 'Thanks, Dad.'

Dominic looked at him and smiled. 'Any time, son.' Then he slowly walked off the stage, moving without embarrass-ment through the tables of gawking onlookers, a tall, straight-backed, proud man — and a father.

Turning to his open-mouthed friends, Farron grinned. 'The song, guys. Remember the song?' Snapping out of it, the band pulled together, the first chords of Farron's latest number filling the room.

Intending to sit down at his table, Dominic saw Ben standing by the bar and abruptly changed course. As he approached he saw that the Englishman's eyes were suspiciously bright, and as Dominic slowly leaned back against the bar stool next to him the two men looked at one another in perfect understanding.

'You found some evidence,' Dominic guessed, more a statement than a question, and Ben nodded.

'I gave it to her last night.'

'I see.' He did not ask how she had taken it. He knew damned well how she would have taken it — and the knowledge of her pain made a small vein throb rapidly at his jaw.

'She's gone back to London,' Ben told him, discreetly looking away from the stiff-faced man who was battling hard with the twin demons of pride and pain.

'I know.' His voice was dead.

'She owes me quite a bit of money, actually,' Ben carried on, not giving a damn about the cost. 'Her magnanimity came dear.'

On the stage Farron was watching them and as he sang the last line of the song, Ben finally plucked up the courage to ask

Dominic the question that would either save or condemn the woman who had come to mean so much to him. 'Are you going after her?'

On stage, Farron practically read his lips, and as his brown eyes went to his father's face, seeing the tight, white profile, he saw his answer.

Dominic shook his head. 'No.'

The applause rang out, made even more enthusiatic because a mob thrown a fat and juicy bone were easy to please. They went into another song straight away, and Dominic looked around, surprised. But slowly, as the song unfolded, he began to smile. On the stage, Farron sang of a woman who made a man's life miserable. He sang of a woman who made him angry. He sang of a woman who made him live again. And when she went away, he sang of how that man had found his life was pointless.

After that had finished, just to make sure his father got the point, he sang '*Farewell Hawaii.*'

Across the crowded room Dominic looked at his son, green eyes and brown meeting in a moment of perfect accord. Then, laughing softly and shaking his head ruefully as he did so, Dominic slipped off the stool, turned and walked away, his footsteps quickening as he felt a nervous urgency attack him. In his penthouse he haphazardly packed an overnight bag, not saying a word to either his secretary or the still-waiting lawyer as he all but ran through both offices.

As he stepped into the underground carpark on the way to his car, a large black limousine drew level with him, gliding to a halt. About to move impatiently around the vehicle, Dominic paused as an electric window was lowered. Leaning out, Ben looked at him with a politely raised eyebrow. 'My Lear's waiting at the airport,' he commented mildly. 'I'm just off to London – need a lift?'

Epilogue

The sign read *Welcome to Heathrow*, but Rhiannon noticed nothing except the cold. Huddling into a coat that did little to keep her warm, she carried her single bag to the waiting taxi ranks and climbed into the nearest free one. 'The Savoy, please,' she directed the driver, leaning back into the taxi's softly sprung seat and sighing deeply. As they approached the great city's centre, she rubbed her eyes tiredly. Hell, she was done in.

'The Savoy, missus.' The driver's voice had her eyes snapping open, and reaching into her handbag she paid the man and walked into the hotel. Ben had phoned ahead as promised, and she was expected. A cheerful young boy, no more than fifteen, carried her bag to her room, chatting cheerfully about going to Hawaii himself one day. Tipping him generously, Rhiannon watched him leave with dull eyes and then looked around the room. How very English everything seemed suddenly. She was home – but she was not home. She could feel no lifting of her spirits to be standing on British soil again, no warm cosy gratitude to be back amidst the familiar things with which she had grown up – the cultured voices, the sight of red double-decker buses, the black umbrellas that lined the rain-sodden streets.

Shrugging off her coat, she walked through to the bedroom. After undressing, she hunted in her bag for a nightdress, settling for the long flowing silk négligé jacket that was the first thing she found. Slipping it over her totally naked body, she crawled on to the bed and curled up into a small tight ball like an injured cat, and fitfully dozed away a few miserable and lonely hours.

WHEN she woke up it was dark. For a second she lay still, blinking in the dim light, then she sat up and uncurled her legs, reaching across for the tiny jade table lamp to flick it on. Half-turning she suddenly froze as a figure uncurled itself from a chair and walked into the small circle of light coming from the muted lamp. 'Dominic!' his name came from her lips in a surprised gasp. No, she thought. I'm still dreaming. One, last, lovely dream . . .

'I can't say I'm all that impressed with you,' Dominic said softly and she shrank back against the satin-quilted headboard. Not a dream after all – that voice was very real. She could feel it shimmering over her skin, seeping inside it to make her go curiously weak. She flicked her tongue-tip over dry lips and swallowed hard, forcing her stunned brain into some sort of working order.

'I . . . don't suppose you are,' she said shakily.

Dominic slowly moved towards her and sat down on the side of her bed, his eyes never moving from her wan face. He'd just spent the last hour watching her sleep, listening to the soft rustling sounds she made, just waiting. He'd enjoyed watching her sleep. Now she looked away from him, out to where a street lamp cast an orange light on to the far wall of her bedroom.

'What are you doing here?' she finally managed to ask, the words emerging from a painfully constricted throat. 'Or didn't I do enough?' She smiled bleakly. 'Perhaps you don't feel you've had your pound of flesh yet, is that it? You want to gloat too?'

Dominic laughed softly, his big body relaxing as some asperity came back to her voice. Now that was more like the Rhiannon he knew and loved. 'Pound of flesh?' he repeated her words, his voice husky and deep, making her skin fairly erupt into sensitive gooseflesh from the tips of her ears to the tips of her toes. 'Now there's a spectacular thought.' She dragged in a breath and as she did so, felt his hand reach across the darkness and touch her calf, his fingers warm and cunning on her legs. She jumped like a nervous cat. 'Such nice flesh too,' he whispered, his hand rising to the bend of her knee. Helplessly she sighed, a soft moan coming from her lips. 'You might at least have said goodbye,' he chided softly. 'I know you like kicking me when I'm down, darling,' he carried on deeply sensuous, 'but you might try waiting until I've got up. You'll enjoy it more that way, I promise.'

His hand had migrated to the top of her thigh, his fingers easily pushing aside the silken garment that stayed in place only by a simple fastening of the belt at her waist. Rhiannon could feel her nipples harden against the silk as she breathed raggedly, biting back a moan as her womb began to contract and throb.

'Dominic,' she said, his name an aching plea. 'Please.'

'Please what, Rhiannon Grantham?' His hand stilled for a moment, hovering against her skin. 'What's the matter?' he tormented softly, leaning over her until his face shone in the small light from the lamp, illuminating the planes of his cheeks and the broad sweep of his forehead. Only his eyes glittered like green fire, burning her with their look. 'Feeling guilty?' he guessed, and she looked away, turning her head against the silken board with a small cry of distress. She deserved this, she knew. But it didn't make it any easier to take.

Quickly his finger came out to curl under her chin and force her head back to face him. 'Farron is getting married on Christmas Eve,' he said softly. 'Vienna will want you to be her bridesmaid. And I'm the best man,' he added softly. 'And you know what the chief bridesmaid and the best man get up to, don't you?' he asked archly, an almost evil smile on his face. She closed her eyes as a brief and tormenting picture flashed across her mind. Then her sluggish brain understood what his words meant. Brilliant green eyes snapped open to look at him as she searched his face for confirmation.

'Farron's forgiven you,' she said, her voice rich with relief and gratitude.

Dominic smiled. 'Disappointed?' he asked softly and knew he shouldn't torment her like this, but dammit he was only human. And he did deserve some revenge for all the damned inconvenience she'd caused.

Wordlessly she shook her head, her eyes mutely pleading before she managed to choke out, 'No, I'm glad. I really am. I know . . . what Daddy did. And I'm glad.'

'I made a big announcement today. I stood up in front of the whole hotel and told everyone that Farron was my son,' Dominic interrupted her.

Rhiannon eyes opened wide. 'You did? But what about the will?'

'Damn the will. If the Chicago vultures try and contest it, I'll fight. But I don't think they will. Nobody would be willing to back them now. Besides which, they're getting old. And if they try it, I'll counter-sue for the original hundred thousand dollars they were left.'

'Dominic?'

'Yes?'

She shook her head helplessly, and slowly he began to laugh. 'What's so damned funny?' she asked stiffly, and then gasped as his clever hands flicked open her belt and slid under the silk to encircle both her breasts. Arching her back instinctively she moaned deeply in her throat, her head falling back.

Dominic leaned over her, his eyes on fire. 'You can't say it, can you?' he said, his voice ragged and harsh now as his own body began to clamour for the sweet torture that it knew was coming. His face was so close to hers she could feel his clean, warm breath against her lips.

'Say what?' she whispered, then moaned again as his hands roughly pushed the silken jacket from her shoulders and the négligé fell from her body to lie around them, a shimmering pearl-pink in the soft lampglow.

Grasping her ankles he yanked her down to the middle of the bed, lying over her and curling his hands over hers, holding them still either side of her head. Her thick raven hair spread out like a halo around them, and Dominic felt his heart thundering in his chest as her flashing eyes clashed with his, spitting warning green fire. And then, lovingly, they softened as she stared up into his handsome, familiar face. She had thought she would never see him again. And if she hadn't it would surely have killed her.

'Say it,' he demanded.

Looking up into the green eyes above her she finally surrendered to the inevitable. 'I love you,' she admitted, her voice choked and full, and out of her eyes tears slowly spilled down her cheeks. Watching her waiting for him to stick in the final knife, Dominic smiled.

'And I love you.'

Rhiannon's eyes rounded wide in shock as, for a stunning, quivering second she could hardly believe what she'd heard. Then, with an inarticulate cry, she yanked her hands free and dragged his head down to hers, her lips opening beneath his with a heat that incinerated them both. Feverishly her hands went to his shirt-front, snapping it open and breaking off the buttons as she did so, sliding the garment off him to reveal smooth and strong broad shoulders, tanned a honey brown. Her lips went to his throat, his neck, his ears, their movements frantic now as Dominic freed himself from the rest of his clothes until bare skin clung to bare skin, lips to lips, hands to hands as her body arched upwards against his.

Opening her legs, she hooked her heels around his thighs, the pressure of them forcing his turgid swollen penis deep within the heart of her, its invasion stretching her body wide open to receive him. He felt her strength, the cocooning contraction of her body sucking him deeper and deeper into her velvet flesh, and cried out, her own cry of triumph echoing in his ears as she heard him. Again and again he plunged into her, all his strength, his great, leonine strength, spewing into her. Long, ragged, agonized, ecstatic minutes later, in total accord, they achieved mutual climax.

Scattered minds slowly recollected themselves and thunderously beating hearts slowed to a quieter, more sedate pace. He was still inside her, his head next to hers, his lips resting against her neck, breathing in her scent. Their sweat-soaked skin clung together, gluing them into one entity as her hand ran tenderly up and down his spine. He sighed and moved, reluctantly slipping out of her, but only to lie on his side close by, resting his head on one elbow as he looked down at her.

Rhiannon rolled her head to look up at him, and what was in her heart showed in her eyes.

'We'll go back to Oahu tomorrow,' he said, the words a statement.

'Oh yes?'

'And we'll be married in the New Year.'

'We will?'

'We will. After all, Grandfather's will says I have to marry a

Caucasian woman who's respectable and upstanding and all that. We may have to gloss over the last two, but at least you're white.'

Rhiannon thumped him. 'Such a romantic proposal. And what if I say no?'

Dominic smirked. 'I'll have you tossed into jail.'

Rhiannon's smile began to widen. 'You'll what?'

'I'll have you tossed into jail. Along with a certain young man called Bryan Canon.'

Rhiannon groaned laughingly, and closed her eyes. 'You found him, then?'

'I found him before you came to me with those very interesting photographs,' he said, his voice thick with laughter as she gaped at him.

'You mean you knew?' she said incredulously, her voice rising several octaves as she too scrambled on to her side, their eyes level now as she shrieked, 'All along, while I was in your office, *you knew*?'

Dominic was nodding his head smugly long before she'd finished talking. 'Then. . . ?' she let the question trail off as Dominic began to laugh.

'Uh-huh. You never stood a chance.'

Rhiannon felt angry for the briefest of moments – really angry, a red-mist-before-the-eyes anger, and then it disappeared. Anger stood no chance against love. Nothing stood a chance against love. 'You rotten little –' she began laughingly, but the words stopped dramatically as Dominic dipped his head to her breast, his teeth nibbling her delicate flesh. 'Dominic!' she moaned out his name, her head falling back helplessly against the bed as her body reacted to his touch.

His hand slipped slowly down to her stomach, caressing her gently before stopping abruptly. Leaning up on one elbow, a small frown appeared on his brows as he looked down at her, first into her eyes and then at his hand on her abdomen, where a small bulge he hadn't noticed before now quivered expectantly under his fingers.

'Rhiannon?' he said softly, questioningly. She smiled gently, and when his green eyes widened in sudden comprehension, a wonderful, brilliant light shining deep in his emerald irises, she nodded her head.

'Yes,' she said, confirming his unspoken words. 'A baby. For us. Your baby.'

Dominic felt his breath catch deep in his chest as his heart began to sing. He shook his head, but his hand pressed a little more possessively over her rounding curves. 'A baby?' he repeated, not sure he could believe it, not sure Fate could be so kind as to give him a second chance. Another child – his child. Moreover, one that he could actually help raise, one that he could love, nurture and watch grow. One that he could call his own, joyfully, proudly, to the whole world.

'Oh Rhiannon,' he breathed, his voice little more than a whisper. Taking her gently into his arms he laid his head on her breast, and a moment later her own heart twisted inside her as she felt his single warm tear slip over her skin.

'I would have told you,' she whispered. 'I came back to London, but I would have told you. I wouldn't have been able to keep away from you. And I would never have deprived you of your baby. Our baby. I swear it.'

Dominic closed his eyes, saying nothing but holding her tightly. There was no need for remonstrations or accusations. He was too damned happy. Too content. Too fulfilled.

Hours later, as he lay with his arms folded behind his head, she leaned across his inert satiated body, idly tracing one of his nipples with a gentle fingernail and said softly: 'Dominic?'

'Hm?'

'You wouldn't really have thrown me in jail if I'd refused to marry you, would you?'

Slowly Dominic opened his eyes and looked straight at her. 'Rhiannon!' He heaved a longsuffering sigh. 'You should know me well enough by now.'

He reached up and clicked off the light. 'Of course I would.'